JESSE FRESCO

First published by Seven Starfighters Publishing 2025
Copyright © 2025 by Jesse Fresco

This novel is entirely a work of fiction. The names, characters, and incidents portrayed in it are the work of the author's imagination. Any resemblance to actual persons, living or dead, events or localities is entirely coincidental.

"Fly For Your Life" and "Tech Noir" by Gunship © 2015 Horsie in the Hedge
Cover artwork by Ferenc Patkos www.drenusart.com
Interior artwork by Alison Wolfe www.alisonwolfe.art
Edited by Brian Paone

ISBN: 979-8-218-85422-5

For Derek Robinson, writer of the R.A.F. Quartet.
Without your work and your wit, this story
wouldn't exist.

And for Gunship.
To misquote Nietzsche, "Without (your) music, life
would be a mistake."

Special thanks to cosplayers GhostieMuffin
Cosplay
and Jenna Lynn Meowri for the use of their
likenesses in this story.

Special thanks as well to Brian Paone and Harry
Carpenter for assisting with editing.

And finally, for Lee Child, who once told me in
person, "Don't worry about what the audience
would want. Just write what you'd enjoy, and have
fun while you're doing it."
Thanks, Lee.

We own the sky
You and I
- "Fly For Your Life", Gunship

PROLOGUE

DO NOT MISS

When coffee had become nearly impossible to grow on planet Earth, humanity knew it was time to leave. Ocean temperatures had risen by four degrees Celsius, causing most sea life to slowly fade into extinction, and inhospitable weather made life on land extraordinarily harsh. There was no hiding or running from the impending apocalypse.

At the beginning of the twenty-second century, human life on planet Earth was reaching its end. Finger pointing to who was most responsible for the crisis plagued the United Nations political body for years, but in the end, it all came down to two factors: corporate greed and religious fanaticism. And with the impending extinction event on the horizon, large swaths of the population turned towards their religious systems for salvation.

While nations such as the United States, Russia, North Korea, and Saudi Arabia denied that human life had any negative influence upon the climate crisis, more scholarly nations knew better. Those nations turned starward as a means of escape. The planet was already well beyond the tipping point. The nations had declared Earth to be beyond repair, and Europe and Africa, with support from the United Nations, pooled their resources to develop a method of space travel that would lead them to a new home. China held firm on its own to develop its technologies outside of UN support and influence. Traditional chemical rocketry was a thing of the past. They needed new and faster methods to reach the Sol Systems closest stellar neighbor, Alpha

Centauri. This would be an extreme challenge, however, as resources became increasingly scarce, and human technological prowess hadn't even reached the Tier 1 phase on the Kardashev scale.

The triple-star system Alpha Centauri contained multiple planets primed for continuing human life. The United Nations considered one such candidate, Proxima Centauri B, to be the best option. However, the United States, seeing an opportunity for capitalist gain, attempted to file a declaration with the United Nations that American businesses would control Proxima Centauri B, should anyone send a manned flight here, to ensure the best possible development and terraforming outcome. Yet the United Nations laughed the declaration out of assembly. In retaliation for this humiliation, America—under control of egotist-empowered fascist leaders—attempted to instill massive tariffs and even threatened war upon all nations building more technologically advanced space programs. Following this gross overestimation of power, for the first and only time in the United Nations' history, they completely ejected an entire collective of people, the United States of America, from assembly and cast them from the planetary community. All trade and travel ceased with the United States. Within ten years, the country had fallen into complete disarray through civil war, and even after it had physically removed its egotistical leaders from power—either by trial or assassination—the UN never invited America to return. The left-wing movement to restore order and democracy had taken too long to act upon their stated intentions. Physicists, scientists, mathematicians, and the like collectively left the United States before the UN instituted the travel ban and headed for the European and African nations to continue their work. The United States became a completely isolated nation save for social media.

By consensus, the UN decided Proxima Centauri B would be humanity's next home. The key problem however was distance. At approximately 4.3 light years from Earth, it would take a spacecraft traveling at 60,000 kph, a total of 80,000 years to reach its destination. That would never work.

Development began on new forms of propulsion—specifically curvature propulsion. Despite how advanced it would be in terms of travel, it could not be fast enough to reach Proxima within a safe timeframe due to one simple issue: the human body was never meant for space travel. Zero-gravity environments would wreak havoc upon the human body, such as bone density loss, muscle atrophy, and biochemical changes within the DNA structure. It would be a cruel cosmic joke to travel such a distance to only find out that an astronaut's first steps on Proxima Centauri B would result in gravity breaking their bones almost immediately. On top of that, without Earth's protective atmosphere, cosmic radiation would ensure all space-faring individuals would, at some point during the exodus, develop some form of cancer. The odds were stacked against humanity. They needed something even faster than light without time dilation to reach Proxima in an extremely short time.

Resources dwindled as nearly all European and African countries placed their assets into the development of a new propulsion drive, one that had its feet firmly planted in the realm of science fiction: teleportation.

Through a combination of curvature propulsion and quantum tunneling, the very nature of teleportation slowly became a reality, allowing objects to transport instantaneously from one location to another. The first few experiments were without a doubt expected to be complete disasters. The amount of nuclear energy needed for transportation was extremely high, resulting in many engineers developing various forms of cancer. Many of these engineers did not survive. And then the first teleport of a physical object—which the scientists considered only half a success, as the object being transported twenty meters, a coffee cup—vanished forever.

The years passed, and the planet faltered, but scientists eventually made progress when the first successful teleport happened. A potted plant of sunflowers moved the distance of thirty meters from one end of a room to the other. The test was a success, so they green-lit animal trials. As the science-fiction concept of teleportation slowly became a reality, they named it.

During the potted-plant test, a high-speed camera recorded various angles of the event. Due to the quantum tunneling— disassembling the object into its base protons for teleportation—the object appeared to *leap* from its starting point to its end point. Scientists coined the oscillator used to travel through space as the acronym *FOIL*— focused oscillation and interspatial leaping—due to objects appearing to leap from point to point. Power supplies became smaller, and FOIL technology became a highly used mode of transportation for everyday life.

Scientists determined, with the right amount of power, a starship housing one thousand space-faring individuals could arrive at Proxima Centauri B within three months. These ships, though, would only have one chance to make the journey, due to food and fuel stores. Should calculations be incorrect, the fleet could be lost forever. In the dark forest of the galaxy, Earth was like a hunter searching for its target, armed with only a single bullet. With this in mind, all engineers, astronomers, and navigators adopted a singular phrase to boost their spirits and to maintain their determination: *When hunting with one bullet, do not miss.*

During the one-hundred-year development of the Earth exodus fleet, scientists still needed to solve a parallel issue. If Proxima Centauri B would be humanity's new home, agriculturists would need to make drastic changes to the planet for colonization. While the planet was 1.3 times larger than Earth—meaning gravity would be only slightly higher—the planet itself was tidal locked, without rotation and axis tilt. And while it technically resided in the Goldilocks Zone for life to form, the star it orbited emitted massive solar flares that raked the planet's surface. Any attempt at terraforming would prove futile, as the flares would decimate atmospheric build-up within an hour. The planet was also part of a trinary star system stricken with the three-body problem: three stars in awkward random orbits that could cause catastrophic damage to the planet if any of the stars neared the planet's orbit. Scientists determined they must move the planet.

An enormous engineering project would be priority upon reaching Proxima Centauri B—building skyscraper-sized booster engines into the planet's surface to relocate the world to a more habitable zone away from danger, while also allowing the planet to effectively replicate Earth's living conditions, such as the 23.4 degree axis tilt, twenty-four hour day/night cycles, and seasonal changes. They would transplant a small moon into the planet's orbit to create ocean tides and to reflect sunlight to Proxima during the night cycle. With the use of these *world engines*, they had developed a factory reset button for life, allowing any planet to relocate if necessary to create better terraforming conditions for colonization. Given enough time and money, humanity could accomplish anything.

As the twenty-second century ended, the exodus began. One hundred spacecraft, with one thousand individuals each, would be the first to begin the three-month trek. They would be the canary heading into the coal mine, seeking safe harbor for earthlings. Leaping across the velvety void of space was not without its challenges but, within three Earth months, the fleet had reached its destination. Of the one hundred ships that had left Earth, eighty-seven arrived. Six had suffered catastrophic engine failure and had relocated their crew and equipment to other ships within the fleet. Seven had completely disappeared, more than likely the result of miscalculation of FOIL coordinates. They were never found.

Scientists relocated Proxima Centauri B to a safer distance and terraformed it during eighty years to become humanity's new home. Life began anew, and Earth's conditions during its prime flourished. Yet something unexpected happened. An alien species established first contact.

A race known as the Luyten had been observing human progress on Proxima Centauri B and reached out to establish diplomatic relations. Humanity had adopted the moniker of *Terran*, for first contact. The first meeting took the Terran ambassador by surprise, as the Luyten ambassador looked extremely similar. The only differences were skin color, eye shape, and slightly elongated fingers. As a cultural exchange, benevolent Terran engineers provided Luyten ships with FOIL technology, allowing them to travel faster and farther than ever before. They had been using standard propulsion technology on colony ships for travel. Now, like the Terrans, life could be easier.

Over the next century, relations developed between other alien species, such as Skovians, Crecians, and Mukarian. Relations with the Terrans species jumpstarted their own progress, and they fast-forwarded into the space age. Coincidentally, all the alien species bore striking physical similarities to Terrans. Language-translation compendiums quickly solved the language barrier, thus allowing political and economic relations to begin. They finally solved the problem for the Fermi Paradox; why humanity had never found alien life before their exodus. In a bright spot of luck, Terrans were the most developed species within the known cosmos, and everyone else was playing catch-up. The justification for why Terrans provided technology to all other alien races was simple; they were running out of development resources on Proxima Centauri B. Travel to Earth for more supplies would take far too long, and without enough fuel to make the trip, any ships attempting to travel that distance would be lost forever. Desperation for support justified pushing everyone else forward.

In doing so, they determined this interdependence upon each other warranted a new form of government, a unified collective for the five known races of the cosmos. Thus, the Galactic Ekumen was born. However, total peace only lasted thirty-three years.

Like all collectives, conflict began. Capitalism reared its ugly head again, and wealthy corporate types overreached and settled into old ways. Simultaneously, more colony ships from Earth arrived with extremely wealthy and powerful individuals. The bad habits that the Terran colonizers were attempting to leave behind had apparently followed them like a cancer. War broke out between three of the five species: Terrans, Mukarians, and Crecians. This war, referred to as The Annexation War, became the first large-scale interstellar conflict. Land grabs, corporate interests, and a desire for more power led to the development of the Terran Navy—a military force capable of planetary combat. The development of smaller, more powerful aircraft and spacecraft became commonplace, and thus birthed one of the most dangerous professions in the known universe.

The starfighter.

CHAPTER 1

SHOOT YOUR SHOT

The engines screamed, and so did he. His A-7 Skyhawk starfighter pierced the clouds with samurai precision, its wings swept backward on its variable-sweep system for maximum velocity. The smaller type of starfighter boasted a golden yellow paint scheme, with a red stripe running down the wings' edges. The sparrow-beak-shaped fuselage came to a point just beyond the cockpit. The four-meter-high dual dorsal fins swept backward to connect with the fuselage on the back end atop the rectangular engine exhaust port. An elegant design suited a variety of purposes from combat to racing. And at that moment, every second counted; every slight jostle of turbulence became another loss of speed and stability. He had to make up as much time as possible. He yelled obscenities at himself as he dipped the sharp nose forward and dove hard for the deck below. The ship's engine screamed, the vertical descent made the world scream, and so did he along with them. His name was Cyril Eisner, callsign *Skyhawk*, and he was late for work.

A mix up at homebase had caused the delay, when they hadn't updated his ship's flight log to register for the day's operation. All starfighters needed to log and charter every flight in case of emergency and to register for radar and LADAR cover on the planet. A software update that morning had changed all that. A glitch had accidentally deleted his logs, as he had been brought on last minute, which required getting a proper update and confirmation from his employer. As he was from Proxima, they had to make a long-range transmission courier update to verify flight status. An hour had passed before they finally registered the log, and by then, the rest of the squadron was airborne for the operation. All Cyril could do on the landing pad was sit and wait for the log to go through. The moment it did, he jumped into his ship and punched the throttle as hard as possible toward the target's destination. The G-force was intense, slamming him into his seat, and a sonic boom blew out a building's windows as he flew by.

That day's mission was simple, and the pay would be decent, if they didn't deduct too much for tardiness.

MISSION: Security and air cover.

TARGET: Local mining haulers, six in total. Payload is highly volatile. Air transport is impossible due to explosive content. Transport will be moving at minimum possible speed. Air cover requested.

THREAT LEVEL: Local bandits and scavengers, possible hostile wildlife. Extreme caution advised.

Cyril hated being late. It was one of his pet peeves. Early was on time, on time was late, and beyond that, you're fired. At twenty-nine years old, his profession had turned him into a rough and tough pilot, but outside of work, he had a charming demeanor. It was difficult living a freelance life. Hustling for that next paycheck while losing sleep from excessive hours and stress meant he already had a slight receding hairline, and the gray was coming in early. It wasn't easy, but it was the life that suited him best. He never wanted anything more than to be a starfighter, but not under the thumb of any corporate hierarchy. If that meant the freelance world, then so be it.

Ten starfighters of a variety of designs for the day composed his squadron. The minimum requirement for a squadron was eight. As they were all freelancers, each pilot had their own personal ship or varied sizes and loadouts. However, if they met the minimum work requirements, such as at least four missiles and full ammunition on guns, employment was guaranteed. Due to the extreme nature of the payload, the client—Harbaso Mining Corp—had allocated funds for two additional pilots.

Cyril flew five hundred meters above the deck, racing to reach the squadron. The client had organized a ground path over the rough and rocky terrain a week beforehand for the haulers to follow, which would have the least amount of resistance. Any extreme jostle or bump could detonate the payload. Even though they had padded the haulers' interiors and had reduced the six massive wheels' suspensions to as low as possible, it was still a risk. The client had never made clear of the payload's contents, but that was of no concern to Cyril or to any of the other starfighters. They were there for protection. Nothing more as long as the check cleared. Despite their best efforts, the only path available was through raider territory, and whatever was inside the cargo would go for an extremely high price on the black market.

There would be a fight. No doubt about it for this one.

The ground was in no way inviting or hospitable for any civilian life. Tulson, the planet below, was not for the faint of heart. Of all the places to work in the Ekumen, this was one of the worst. The desert landscape of ancient rocks, dusty plains, sharp plateaus, and deep canyons made it basically a version of hell minus the fire, though once Cyril regrouped with the squadron, that would probably show up too. It was a gross color, as well. Orange and yellow, like vomit. Staring at it too long was enough to make a person nauseated. Rivers, streams, and even oceans had once filled Tulson. However, a meteorite impact over a millennium ago had turned it into a barren waste that was now good for nothing but mining. Such a shame.

He pulled up over the crest of a small mountain and finally saw his squadron in the distance. They were nothing but specks to the naked eye, but his HUD immediately registered his squadron's ID tags, highlighting them in green and marking all enemy craft in sharp red. Red squares and green diamonds zipped around on his HUD like old-age vector graphics. It was a mess. Reports of raider squadrons had been an understatement. It looked like a whole flight had prepared for this raid. But his group had experience, while most raiders usually learned through nothing but simulators or had barely any real flight time. Numbers meant nothing if they weren't properly trained.

Cyril switched on his radio and called out for his squadron leader. "Able Squadron, this is Skyhawk on station. Sorry I'm late. How much did I miss?"

Able Squadron's leader, a gruff old starfighter named Garrison, responded, "Condor to Skyhawk. Nice you could be bothered to join us, Eisner. Now shut up and get into the fight."

"Copy that, Condor. Arming up. It's okay, ladies and gentlemen, your savior is here."

"Eisner, shut the hell up and shoot something," responded Catherine, callsign *KitKat*.

Cyril flipped a couple switches and pulled up a lever next to his left leg which swept the wings of his starfighter forward, allowing for more maneuverability and for better attitude control. With a whirring and scraping sound, the wings swept forward and looked like the letter *W*, with the two wing tips extending slightly beyond the cockpit's nose. When swept backward, it resembled an upside-down *V*. A second seat, for the RIO (Radar Intercept Officer), sat behind the pilot for long-range radar, but he never used it, as Cyril always flew alone. The weapons bay was within the belly which opened to unfurl a twin set of air-to-air missiles on revolving spindles. As for guns, a pair of 20mm Vulcan gatling cannons with a four-hundred-round capacity were positioned directly beside the port and starboard of the ship's nose. He could also adjust the cannons' RPMs for precision targeting, if needed. Not an excessive amount of firepower, but in the right pilot's hands, anything could be deadly.

Wings swept, armed missiles, cannon safety off. He punched his throttle one more time, full power, straight ahead, toward the combat zone. A sonic boom erupted around the nose as he blazed through the sky. A day's work for a day's pay was within three thousand meters.

Cyril yanked on his flight stick and climbed to just over one thousand meters. A raider craft tailed one of his squadron mates. That starfighter, Allegra Cline, callsign *Honey Badger*, flew a BT-99 Diamondback—a ship designed for extreme payloads and for power at the expense of speed. But it could take a beating. From a glance, it resembled a large metal diamond if someone had flattened it into a pancake, then painted it a muted green. Essentially, a flying tank.

A raider outmaneuvered Honey Badger in his retrofitted stunt craft, with perpendicular orange wings and a massive pair of engines on the back end that spewed a thin trail of white smoke. Cyril flew in behind the raider to assist.

"Honey Badger, on your six. Help is on the way," Cyril calmly said.

"Anytime now, Skyhawk," she replied.

The raider didn't seem to notice, either due to pilot error or faulty equipment. Whichever the reason, this was an easy kill. Cyril's HUD locked on, *beep beep beep beeeeep*, then he pulled the trigger. The missile launched and shredded through the sky with a hot white smoke trail. It impacted the enemy's fuselage and exploded into bits and pieces. The pilot hadn't ejected in time. No survivors. Cyril punched his throttle, flew through the still floating black smoke of his kill, and formed up on Allegra's starboard wing. In unison, they pulled hard right and dove into the thick of the fight.

The raiders had downed two of the squadron starfighters by the time Cyril arrived—one by surprise attack, another through pilot error. In terms of enemy craft, his HUD registered twenty-two targets. Only eight ships remained in his squadron. Ground attackers in rugged worn-out trucks and dune buggies also attempted to hijack the transport trucks. They seemed willing to risk a ground assault, knowing how volatile the payload was. Cyril and Allegra took separate aerial targets side by side and opened fire. Two missiles flew in separate directions, but they found their targets. Two more down. Twenty left. The odds were slowly going in their favor.

On the ground, the transport team fought as well. Security personnel fended off attackers but quickly got overwhelmed.

The driver called out, "This is transport six. We're dry on ammo. Need immediate assistance."

The chatter on the ground became horrific. The attackers quickly extended a ladder bridge from a raider truck bed to the roof of transport six. The dust and grit of the brown chalky desert kicked up from the transports ahead of them and created a spew of clouds shrouding the ladder as three men scurried across from truck bed to rooftop.

The transport driver screamed again, "We're being boarded! Where are you, Able Squadron?"

Cyril broke formation, then dipped and dove straight at the deck. He flew over eight hundred meters away and descended to fifty meters from the ground, then flew toward the rear of the convoy. He couldn't open fire on the transports for obvious reasons. No time to think, just act. He swept his wings again, making them perpendicular to his cockpit. Then he dipped a little more. Forty meters above ground. Thirty. Twenty. Ten. His emergency alarm repeated, "Altitude! Altitude! Pull up! Pull up!"

He was headed toward a near collision, which was the intended purpose. At close to a hundred fifty knots, he buzzed over the convoy and, with it, used his ship's wings like a butcher's knife to slice off the boarding party from transport six. Blood, guts, and entrails covered his starboard wing, and the impact had barely registered even in his flight controls. The three boarding men didn't even feel it when the wing chopped them in half.

Cyril pulled up hard to seventy meters, cut his engines, and switched to his V/TOL center turbine. Now in hover mode, he spun one hundred eighty degrees, took aim at the attacking raiders' trucks, switched to guns, and burst-fired his Vulcan cannon. Rounds punched through the trucks' and buggies' metal frames, eviscerating body after body. Nothing could stop Cyril. He rained fire upon them as round after round burst forth from his gun barrels. Four trucks went up in flames. The rest stopped their pursuit and turned to run, brown dust clouds trailing in their wake. He flipped to his afterburners, swept his wings backward, and punched it into the dogfight five hundred meters above.

KitKat and Honey Badger were formed up with one other starfighter tracking a small pair of raiders. They were handling it just fine, so Cyril formed up on Garrison's port side on the opposite end of the combat area. The battle had become a circular field of combat, with both sides encircling the convoy below to establish control of the situation.

Garrison growled, "Eisner, what the fuck was that?"

"A moment of inspiration," Cyril snarked.

Garrison just shook his head and got a hard tone on another raider six hundred meters away. Another scrap pile fell from the sky. The pilot ejected at just the last second and descended into the grim desert below.

Garrison switched his radio to an open channel. "To all enemy craft, this is your final chance to vacate the area. Your ground attack has failed. You'll only make things worse for yourselves. Last chance to bug out."

Of the seventeen ships remaining, fourteen bugged out. For some reason, three stayed behind, either from pride or pure stupidity, but they stayed in the fight and formed a V-pattern. Able Squadron still had its eight remaining starfighters, so this was hardly a fair fight. All eight formed a larger V-formation, with Cyril taking a middle position on the starboard side. Condor led the charge as the two groups flew directly at each other, like a pair of opposing armies charging on a battlefield.

Garrison switched to the closed channel of Able Squadron. "Torch these fuckin' idiots."

All eight ships unloaded their cannons, and a hail of gunfire razed the air with tracer rounds and sliced up the three remaining raiders like an aerial blender. The three ships fell from the sky and slammed into the ground, their smoldering corpses of charred metal burned red and black in the dusty, dead desert.

The squadron had neutralized all its targets. If all went well, it would be clear sailing to the mining depot, two hundred kilometers south. Before they continued, Garrison marked, on his world map, the crash sites of the two squadron members who had gone down. There was no way to retrieve their bodies or ID tags while still on mission. Homebase would have to dispatch a medical transport, then send an insurance payout to the pilots' families, along with general condolences. If they couldn't find any family, they would transfer the funds to the company coffers.

The next five hours were relatively uneventful. All ships pulled general flybys or switched to V/TOL and simply coasted over the convoy. The upfront combat had brought everyone to an adrenaline high, but once it wore off, the crash hit hard. Yawning became an annoyance and was contagious. Cyril flipped on his personal radio to play some music—synthwave, something simple with the volume low enough to still hear radio chatter. There wasn't much small talk. The raiders were still out there, and the squadron needed to stay alert. Once the depot was in sight, spirits went high again. The day was almost over.

The depot was a large walled-off compound, featuring a shielded dome and a metal pyramid structure, with lattice work between the two of them. The enormous chunky metal gates unlocked and slowly swung open. A flurry of sand fell from the outcroppings on the gate as it moved. Security trucks rolled out to greet the convoy and to escort them inside. Once the final transport was in, the gates swung shut and locked. Mission accomplished.

The eight starfighters formed up and gained altitude to five thousand meters. The ground from that height looked somewhat gorgeous, but only somewhat. The rolling dunes looked smooth from high above, and the orange sunlight cast sharp shadows across the distant mountains. The flight home would be a solid ninety minutes at top speed, but spirits were high. This had been a dangerous mission but with only two casualties. And no payload was lost. Overall, a win.

Nineteen kilometers from home, the control tower squawked, "Able Squadron, we have a solid signal on you. Nineteen kilometers out at one-zero-eight. Welcome home."

"Roger that, Ignition Tower. Good to be back. Clear landing pads," Garrison responded.

The eight ships descended from the sky at a thirty-five-degree angle as they approached. Ignition Control Station was like an oasis of civilization in the middle of nowhere. The desert surrounded what was essentially a small city, albeit a heavily guarded one, with sniper towers, gun turrets, and automated flak cannons. The landing pad was just over the combined size of three football fields. Ten other starfighters were still stationed on site for city personnel. The remaining space was always allocated to freelance ships and a FOIL pad for small off-world transport craft. Once they filed their paperwork and the company analyzed their gun camera footage, all eight of them would head home.

They switched into V/TOL mode and, one by one, descended to their respective landing pads. As Cyril descended, his radio called out his elevation. Forty meters, thirty meters, twenty, ten, contact. He magnetically locked his landing struts to the pad, disarmed his weapon bays, and killed the engine. After being inside his ship for so long, with his engines blazing, the quiet felt amazing.

The pilots dismounted their ships and grouped up before heading into the administration building. Finishing the mission wasn't enough. After action reports, paperwork, logging gun cam footage for insurance purposes, and, of course, retrieving the bodies of the two downed pilots meant everyone would more than likely be staying for the remainder of the day. It was the grueling, miserable part of the job.

Everyone despised it. After checking in with security, each starfighter would sit down, with a pencil and paper, to notate what they could recall of the operation: direction of flight, time in the sky, who fired the first shot, number of kills, number of losses—all the minutiae that just had to be done for the company.

Everyone felt beat, but security wouldn't let them leave until everyone completed their narratives.

The boardroom had no windows and felt claustrophobic. The walls were flat white, and a long row of square LED lighting fixtures hung from the ceiling, giving the room an artificial glow that could nauseate a person if they stayed in there too long. Cyril sat with his legs on the fake hardwood table, writing his perspective, alongside everyone else. The silence was only broken by the light scritch-scratch of pencils to paper.

Cyril took this opportunity to formally state how he was infuriated with Harbaso's lackadaisical approach to software updates, which had made him late for his launch time. He hoped they wouldn't dock part of his pay for being tardy. There were plenty of reasons to justify his absenteeism, but corporations rarely gave a shit about the little guys' excuses.

After about thirty minutes, everyone had finished. Garrison collected the reports to send them to their employers. Garrison looked ancient, like a man long past his prime. His gray hair had long since whitened, but he was still in decent enough shape to be a starfighter. He'd been doing this for a long time, and his face was a canyon-riddled mess, with hardened eyes. Not even a smile could break his grim demeanor. He resembled the kind of man who had made every wrong choice in life, and yet, he was still there. Cyril always thought Garrison looked like a broken man who just covered it up with anger. But Garrison was a good leader and an excellent pilot; however, Cyril and Garrison fucking hated each other. Just because they worked together didn't make them friends.

KitKat was another story. The sweetest bean, dark-skinned and adorable, she got along perfectly with everyone. She had a thin but muscular frame and very salacious eyes. She also had the filthiest mouth ever, which added to her charm. A solid pilot too, even though she'd been doing it only for a few years. KitKat had started in the Terran Navy but quickly retired and had moved into private work, then eventually had gone freelance. Being her own boss and working at her own pace felt like a relief to her, even if the money was inconsistent. She and Cyril had become fast friends, even if they only ever saw each other at work. She lived on the planet Olympus, whereas Cyril was based on Proxima Centauri B. Because of this, aligning schedules to meet up outside of work was an enormous hassle.

Allegra was the strong, quiet one. Light-skinned, short-cropped dark hair and dark eyes. Cyril never asked her anything about her personal life or if she even had one. She was also extraordinarily buff, probably a bodybuilder in a past life, and stood at a solid six feet. She'd landed being an ace pilot extremely quickly, but it was also odd how killing never seemed to phase her. Something always seemed a little … off about her. Whether it was a level of sociopathy, no one knew, but she was great in a fight and an ace in the sky. She and Cyril got along just fine, but they never really had anything to talk about. Anytime the crew would celebrate mission completion, she'd wander off on her own or sit in a corner by herself and never speak. Whenever Cyril would try to approach her, the conversation would be short. If it didn't involve work, then there was nothing much to say. Cyril thought she was a murderer and hid it very well.

The others in the group on the sortie were new faces. No one Cyril knew. Freelancers would come and go as different companies hired them, or they'd be put under a full-time contract if someone liked them well enough and would never be seen in the freelance world again. Cyril preferred to be a lone gun for hire. He could adjust his work rate as necessary and could demand different compensation depending on the mission circumstances. In the atmosphere was at a decent rate. Just above the atmosphere, a little bit higher. But deep space, that was the big money. High risk equaled high reward. The only drawback was that all expenses landed on him. Taxes, resupply, repairs, etc. all came out of his pocket. It could be rough, and there'd been times of rationing munitions and maybe a little stealing here and there, but it was the life he wanted. The Tulson mission was his first one back after the slow winter seasonal drought.

Garrison reentered the boardroom with a bag of blank flash drives, ordered all pilots to download their gun camera footage from their ships, then return them to the security office for inspection. AI bot programs would analyze the gun camera footage to match what each pilot had written in their after action report. This way, if any inconsistencies existed or if a pilot had tampered with their camera footage, the bots could file a red flag against the pilot until the employer resolved the matter. If a pilot had changed their story or had tampered with footage or had left their camera off, the employer would immediately blacklist the pilot. Getting off the blacklist was nearly impossible. It was a death sentence for a pilot's career.

Cyril headed outside into the hot, dusty air and hopped into his ship. The wind had kicked up a bit and spun a large tan tornado through the landing pad area. The dust stuck to his already sweating skin and changed his face from tan to dark brown. Even though the sun was setting, and the sky was many shades of pink and purple, it still felt almost hellish outside with the heat. He couldn't wait to go home.

He inserted the flash drive into his cockpit's control panel and flipped through his files. He downloaded the most recent camera footage, unplugged the drive, and hopped out. Before he returned to the security station, he checked his ship's starboard wing. A large gash of now dried brown blood covered the wing, and it was caked in dust, dirt, and grime but only had a small dent which he could easily fix. Before he headed home, he would need to wash it thoroughly. It wasn't really the best look to fly through a populated cityscape, with human entrails all over the wings. Gave the wrong impression.

He headed inside, dropped off his drive, and asked the staff for a bucket of water and a few sponges. After the janitor brought them to him, he headed out just as KitKat entered. They bumped into each other as she walked through the door. A big sploosh of water drenched the floor.

"Oh shit, I'm sorry, Cyril," she yelled.

"No, it's fine." Cyril nodded to the janitor. "Hey, um, I spilled water over here."

The janitor returned with a mop and silently soaked it up.

"So, what's with the water?" KitKat asked.

"Oh, you know, cleaning up a murder. You're welcome to join me," he slickly responded.

"Oh, blood and guts. My favorite! One sec," she said, almost giggling, and quietly clapped her hands together.

She dropped her drive on the security officers' desk and followed Cyril to his ship. The sun was extremely low, and the heat was finally dissipating. It felt quite nice, with the breeze, and the stars were making themselves known to the world. As they traversed the dust-caked landing strip, the sunlight hit every ship just right, making them look majestic and powerful—even the cheap ones. Usually this always just felt like a job, but sometimes it felt like a privilege. They approached the Skyhawk's starboard wing to inspect the sprayed blood from three separate impact points, creating three big splotches extending into a forked pattern, like someone had chucked brown paint onto the edge of the wing.

"How the hell did that happen?" she asked.

"Cut a bunch of guys in half."

KitKat went bug-eyed and faced him, her smile turned upside down.

"What, you didn't see that? That was amazing!"

She kept staring, and he giggled. "You know, when you said you were cleaning up a murder, I thought it was a joke."

"Are you disappointed? Come on. Afterward, I'll buy you a beer."

KitKat helped Cyril pull over the stepladder from the edge of the landing pad, and they climbed onto the wing. They got on their hands and knees and sponged away. The blood and dust washed off easily, and the heat quickly sizzled away the water. It was too quiet, so Cyril flipped on some music from his cockpit controls and blared it through his external speakers. A little synthwave as dusk settled felt just right. It was a good vibe, even if it was slightly macabre. He and KitKat chitchatted, told filthy jokes, and discussed what work they had lined up next. Cyril had nothing booked, but she was set up on a small security escort job for a VIP. Nothing too fancy, and the chances of combat were next to zero, so it wasn't a big paycheck, but it was something. Beggars couldn't be choosers.

After about thirty minutes, they'd finished washing the last of the blood off the wing. It looked brand new, sans the small dent, and cleaner than the rest of the ship, as the planet's fine dust coated everything it touched. When he returned home, he'd need to give the whole thing a proper cleaning and tune-up. His engine filters were probably caked in the planet's muck.

They dumped the bucket of bloody water over the edge of the wing and stepped onto the landing pad. Cyril had promised her a beer, so they headed to the local brewery to grab some tall boys.

While they could have stayed inside the bar to enjoy the air conditioning, KitKat said, "It's just too perfect outside to be in here."

Thus, the pair returned to Cyril's ship, climbed onto the wing to sit next to the central fuselage, then leaned back to stargaze. They cracked open their beers and clacked them together. The last few rays of sunshine finally melted away, and the stars filled the sky. The benefit of being in an unpopulated area was no light pollution. Only lights on the base and the landing pad lights below were on, plus a few red security lights pulsing above the control tower. Above was a gorgeous collection of pin spots everywhere as the universe drifted slowly. The temperature cooled, the music was smooth, and he and KitKat sat there, drinking their celebratory beers, watching the world turn.

Cyril broke the silence with, "It's too bad you live on Olympus. We could actually see each other outside of work."

KitKat sighed. "I know. It sucks. But Olympus is cheap, and all my clients are there. Hard to just pick up and start over and shit."

"Especially in our line of work." He took a long swig of his beer. "You still seeing what's-his-nuts? Ed something?"

"Jeff," she corrected, laughing. "You totally fucking missed that one. No, we split. He just couldn't handle that I would have to take work whenever it arrived. Really drove a big wedge between us. Eventually found out he was fucking around on me while I was gone for long stretches." She drank again and went quiet.

"Fuck, I'm sorry. You okay?"

"Yeah, it's fine. I'm fine. It was for the best. Honestly, I don't even know why I try to date. Like, who can keep up with it in this fuckin' business? We're never around for our partners."

"That's why every time I've gotten close to something that would become a deeper relationship, I just cut it off or say, 'Hey, this isn't gonna work.' Better to break hearts with honesty rather than cruelty."

The music switched songs and played "Nightcall" by Kavinsky.

"I just realized something," KitKat said. "Your ship is a Skyhawk, and your callsign is also Skyhawk?"

"It was a good name. Why ruin a good thing?" Cyril sent her a sly smile.

KitKat shook her head, rolled her eyes, and took another gulp while chuckling. A pilot typically inherited a callsign by virtue of habits or from making a mistake. Someone vomits on their first flight, good luck losing the name *Chunks*. They crash during a simple landing because of a dumb error, they're officially nicknamed *Crashdown*. Cyril had broken the mold and, from sheer ego, had given himself his own callsign—*Skyhawk*. Like he had stated, it was too good to pass up. KitKat had inherited hers because of her love of a specific chocolate candy.

"You're really gonna do this shit forever?" she asked.

He shrugged. "Don't know what else I'd do. Nowhere else to go. I'm not really good at anything else. Only thing I really look forward to is the next job. It's all day by day."

"Look up, Cyril. There's a whole lot out there."

"So much and so far away."

They went silent again and cracked another set of beers. The sun was now completely gone, and the air finally got colder. Also, the alcohol finally kicked in.

Cyril then asked, "Wanna hook up?"

KitKat turned, slid into his lap, and kissed him deeply. Cyril knew this was clearly just a drunken hook-up. There wasn't really any deep love, but they were both drunk and lonely and horny. To fuck on the wing of his ship, under a starry night sky, wasn't something that happened often. They decided to enjoy the moment and have a little fun before the reality of the universe set back in tomorrow. It was a good night for both of them.

Morning came eventually, and the sun had resumed its rightful place overhead. The AI bots hadn't finished scanning all the gun camera footage till midnight, so everyone had shacked up in the barracks. They were nothing special. Long rows of single beds with generic sheeting, a wall-mounted TV with an outdated gaming console attached to it, a small library of well-worn paperbacks, old couches and loveseats, dusty fans overhead. Clearly this place was meant to be used only every now and again. It had served its purpose for the night, so everyone crawled out of bed at 8:30 a.m., tidied up, grabbed their personals, and headed to the security office.

Cyril and KitKat shared coy smiles as they exited the barracks. Those smiles quickly disappeared as they hit the outside air. It was absolutely brutal, worse than the previous day. No cloud cover meant no awnings for shade. Just wide-open space. The brisk walk turned into light jogging toward the administration building. Even though it only took twenty seconds, everyone was already drenched in a coat of sweat when they ducked inside.

Garrison stepped to the front, sweat running down his brow. He wiped it away, rubbed it on the sleeve of his flight suit, and approached the desk manager. A new guy had stepped in for the morning shift and had been updated on yesterday's mission. He passed a clipboard to Garrison, which he read through slowly. He released a long sigh, signed the top page, flipped through the rest of the packet, removed one page, and handed the clipboard to everyone else for them to sign their pages. Everyone found their names and signed off, except for Cyril. His page was missing.

"Eisner, come with me," Garrison said as he walked toward the boardroom.

Cyril followed, shrugging as he passed KitKat and Allegra. He entered the boardroom and saw two men, who wore suits and sat at the opposite end of a long table. Garrison stood beside a whiteboard.

One of the suits said, "Have a seat."

Cyril obeyed. He folded his hands and twiddled his fingers while the two suits perused the paper that Garrison had passed to them. The gruff old starfighter stared down Cyril with utter contempt, as Cyril thought Garrison had a very punchable face.

The suits whispered to each other, though Cyril couldn't hear them. Finally, one of the suits spoke up. "Mister Eisner, you're a hell of a pilot, I see."

"I have my moments," Cyril responded flatly.

"Do you think this is one of those?"

"It's certainly something. Did I do something wrong? Because the only thing I'm guilty of is being late yesterday from your company's screw up. I booked it fast as—"

"This isn't about you being late. We know about that. That's forgiven. What we question is the … tactics used yesterday during the convoy run."

Garrison retorted, "Flying your ship so close to the convoy could have destroyed the cargo. And turning your starboard wing into a giant butcher knife was well beyond the safety protocols."

"Not to mention the vibration of your ship's engines so close overhead to the cargo could have set it off. You and your crew are lucky to be here right now," the second suit said.

Cyril named them *Blue* and *Brown* after the color of their sweat-stained shirts. They were trying to pin something on him, not for any real reason. Safety meetings like this happened all the time. Sure, Cyril's blade from the sky had been unorthodox, but it had gotten the job done. Deep down, he hated bullies, and he hated being talked down to. They wanted to humiliate him? They'd need to try harder.

"Okay, I see what you're trying to get at. You think that because my approach was risky that I, therefore, shouldn't be paid the full amount of what's owed to me. My tardiness aside—and thanks for forgiving that—I pulled your asses out of the fire. The convoy was being boarded, and I did what was necessary to secure the payload. You can hate it all you want, but there wasn't really much time to think in that scenario. So I turned my wing into a samurai sword and made chop suey. Who gives a fuck? Would you prefer I fired directly at the convoy instead?"

"That's not what we're—"

"Let me demonstrate." Cyril approached the whiteboard and grabbed a marker.

Garrison glared at him as Cyril drew on the board. Small boxes at the bottom represented the convoy trucks, and a big *W* up top represented his ship. He put little stick figure men atop the convoy and faced the suits and Garrison.

"Let's go through this. The convoy down below is screaming, 'Help! Help!' I hear the call, break formation, and within the span of maybe … three seconds, I gotta think up a plan." He drew a line showing his descent toward the convoy and a new *W*. "I dive down, knowing I can't shoot them. Targets on the roof are too small, and they're boarding the final truck. My ship fires 20mm rounds which can prolapse the asshole on anything. I shoot; I risk hitting everything in front of them. So, what do I do?" He drew another line to show his flight path slicing the three stick figures in half. "I swoop my wings forward, turn 'em into paste, and secure the cargo, without putting anyone else in danger. Was it risky? Yeah. But this was a high-risk assignment, right? Sometimes you just pull a plan outta your ass. Plan A fails, you go to plan B; plan B fails, you go to plan C, plan C fails, fucking figure it out." Cyril chucked the marker at the white board. "I just saved your cargo and the rest of the flight. You should be thanking me. I did my job to the best of my ability, and you're holding me accountable for a doomsday scenario that didn't even happen. Call it reckless if you want, but the job got done. And it was the only risky maneuver in the whole flight. So go ahead"—Cyril sat down and folded his hands—"yell at me and get it over with."

Silence filled the room, and the suits looked slightly embarrassed. Cyril had pushed back so hard that they'd metaphorically ended up in a corner. Garrison maintained his gruff expression, but Cyril ignored him.

Finally, Blue relinquished. "Okay, you've made your point. We still have to declare it a risky maneuver and inform the home office of your actions, but we'll underwrite it with *extenuating circumstances*. No docking of pay, though consider this an extreme warning."

Brown interjected, "You used up your nine lives in one go. More than likely you'll be on a month-long probationary period. Harbaso will not file any further contracts for you at this time."

"Good enough," Cyril said flatly but with a hint of contempt. He had literally done everything right, and they were still passing punishment on him. *I should have just let 'em take the trucks.*

They annotated his paperwork, passed him the page, and he signed it. He said nothing else and walked out without them formally dismissing him. Outside, the rest of the starfighters were waiting, looking utterly bored. Cyril sat next to Allegra on a threadbare couch, as it was the only seat available.

"Get your ass chewed out?" she asked.

Cyril turned his head; his eyes half closed in mild annoyance.

After a few moments, Garrison and the suits exited, and he collected a packet of blue credit cards from the security office. Any pilot who wasn't a full-timer on the planet would receive credit cards with preloaded payment. Cash didn't always transfer via currency exchange, and direct deposit was technologically impossible. Credit would always be for off-worlders. Garrison flipped through the cards and distributed them to each pilot. They had been engraved with each person's name. Garrison refused to look at Cyril when he passed him the card. Two cards remained. The two downed pilots. Garrison returned those to the security attendant and asked about the progress of retrieving the pilots. Apparently, the ship was arriving right now.

A quadcopter and two of the base's starfighters landed on the main strip. A pair of medics and several construction workers disembarked and pulled down two body bags. Another pair of quadcopters flew toward the other end of the base. Beneath them, suspended from cables, were the shredded hulks of the dead pilots' ships. The medics carried the bodies into the med station morgue in preparation for their return to their respective planets. The eight starfighters in the security office watched silently. This was the risk of the job. Anyone could go at any time. They were all expendable, and they had accepted that a long time ago.

Another hour passed. The sun crushed down on the base, and the tarmac emitted heat waves that obscured the view from one end of the landing strip to the other. The medics finally had prepared the two bodies for return, collected their personals, and determined their planets of origin. They loaded the cadavers into an exoplanetary med ship and told the pilot to wait for the other starfighters to get set for flight to the FOIL station.

While waiting for everyone to prep for liftoff, Cyril calculated his expenses. His full payment had been forty-five thousand. He had fired two air-to-air missiles, 212 20mm rounds of ammunition, and the dent on his wing would need to have a panel removed and replaced. Power core cells were still in the seventy-percentile range, so no need for a replacement. More than likely repairs and resupply would run a good ten thousand. After taxes and insurance costs, Cyril would pocket a solid twenty-two thousand. Overall, not too shabby and fairly conservative. It could have been much worse. The best jobs were obviously the ones without any combat. Those were rare but cherished when they occurred.

He stuffed the handwritten note with his payment credit card into a pocket on his flight suit and spooled his ship's power cells for flight. The engine hummed, and the V/TOL turbine spun.

Garrison said on comms, "Ignition Tower, this is Able Squadron. We're ready to go home. Call clear path please."

"Roger, Able Squadron, path is clear. You are good for takeoff. Have a nice day."

Slowly, one by one, each starfighter rose straight up, then switched to flight mode and circled the base in a flight pattern till everyone was ready to go. The last ship to rise was the exoplanetary med ship. The FOIL station was north by ten kilometers. It would be a relatively short flight. Nobody really spoke. Nothing to say. They were all beat and ready to go home. The sun was still crushing down on everyone, so each starfighter had switched their polarizers to 80 percent opacity during flight.

The large rectangular FOIL landing strip was about one kilometer in length and in width. It was essentially a mobile runway, with a bridge for flight control. All it could do was go up and down and FOIL from the planet's surface into space. The squadron circled the pad while each ship would break away, claim a landing space, and mag lock their landing struts to the metal surface. The med ship landed dead center for weight distribution.

Once landed, the bridge commander of the landing pad squawked on the radio, "All struts mag locked. Prepare for ascension."

The massive turbines below the pad came to life and slowly lifted it, like the ascent of a rollercoaster.

The bridge commander continued, "FOIL in five … four … three … two … one. Leap!"

Space and time flowed in reverse directions. Everyone's stomachs fell away, and, in a blink, they'd gone from the charred orange landscape of Tulson to the vacuum of space just outside the planet's atmosphere. The feeling of zero gravity kicked in immediately. Rookie pilots always upchucked the first few times doing a FOIL. Thankfully, no amateurs were on this go around.

The ships adjusted to zero gravity mode, shutting down their V/TOL engines and switching to thrusters. The vacuum of space was different from planetary flight. Ships move in whatever direction they're commanded, and inertia takes over. It was a completely different discipline and was much harder to master. It was especially dangerous during deep-space missions where no direct sunlight was available. Black shapes in the void. Cyril had only done a small number of deep-space assignments.

Every starfighter flipped on their caution lights and their LED wing displays. In the dark, all the lighting helped identify who was who. Cyril's Skyhawk had built-in LED strips on the edges of his wings which illuminated them into a V-shaped design from wing tip to stern. One small section was busted on his starboard wing from turning it into a piledriver—another thing he'd have to replace once home. Every ship disengaged their mag locks and thrusted slowly upward and floated away from the FOIL pad.

Once they'd reached safe distance, Garrison called out, "Able Squadron clear, thanks Tulson. Enjoy the sunshine down there."

No response came from the bridge commander, just the sudden zero sound, blink-out-of-existence, FOIL leap as the pad disappeared. The ships floated free, then created a vertical diamond formation, the med ship taking up space behind them. Two kilometers away, an Ekumen freighter waited for them—their taxi home. The crew knew each pilot's home planets and would leap to each one for drop-off.

The starfighters slowly moved forward. The frigate doors silently slid open to reveal a totally empty cargo bay. It was an enormous, clunky box-shaped ship that had no elegance whatsoever. One by one, each ship claimed a spot, and once full, the doors slid closed again. They mag-locked their landing struts and gave the signal that they were ready to go. Getting to and from planets around the Ekumen was a tedious task, no doubt, but it was the safest and most cost-efficient method. The old method of travel to and from planets would take years, and getting to and from planetary surfaces was extremely energy inefficient due to escape velocity and reentry issues. FOIL leaping had solved innumerable problems. The inverse of time and space happened again. One moment, they were there above Tulson, and then suddenly, they were directly over Olympus.

KitKat and several others disengaged their mag locks as the doors opened. "Bye, Skyhawk," KitKat said as she passed by overhead.

Cyril watched her fly by and said goodbye as well. He smooched his lips together and blew her a kiss. He heard her on the radio do the same. She and three other ships began their flight path to the planetary FOIL pad, two kilometers away. The doors closed again. Time and space inverted once more, and they were above Proxima. The remaining four starfighters floated free from the frigate and headed to the FOIL pad. The med ship stayed locked, as it was headed elsewhere. As they flew, the frigate disappeared. They went through the same rigamarole of landing and locking. Twenty seconds later, and with a thunderclap, they were a thousand meters above the surface of Proxima.

The most startling part of leaping from zero-G to atmosphere was the "gum drop." Gravity would "catch" the FOIL pad when it leaped into the atmosphere, creating a short drop that would always startle everyone. It became labeled the *gum drop* when the first attempt at zero-G-to-atmosphere leaping involved a pilot who was chewing gum, and the sudden fall "made me drop my gum," as he had said. The name stuck, and the pilot had to live out that embarrassment till he was caught in a cross FOIL four years later. They never recovered his body.

The FOIL pad slowly descended toward an enormous field of eight other pads all aligned in a neat row. Once the pad was five hundred meters above the surface, it hovered to allow the starfighters to disengage their mag locks. Cyril spun up his turbine and ascended, then punched the throttle forward to blast right past everyone else. Not a safe maneuver at all, but it was mainly meant as a giant *fuck you* to Garrison. He hoped he didn't have to see him again for a while.

Allegra also ascended and flew in the opposite direction of everyone else. The sunset on Proxima painted the sky nice and pink as the planet turned on its manmade axis. About ten kilometers away, the bright lights from Balamb shimmered. Balamb was the capital city of the western continent of Proxima and the home of corporate industry on the planet. Cyril had grown up in the suburbs just outside of town. He rarely ever visited his childhood home, where his father still lived. Because of that, he always took the long route around the suburbs instead of flying over them.

McClelland and Magellan Inc., the airfield where he housed his ship, was on the eastern side of town. He cruised east and approached the mostly empty landing strip. He radioed down, "M&M tower, this is Skyhawk, requesting permission to land."

"Roger, Skyhawk. You are cleared to land. Welcome home," the tower responded.

Cyril went through the motions, dropped his landing struts, vertically descended, and mag-locked once landed. He killed the engine and switched off the power. The canopy opened upward from back to front, and the interior step ladder on the port side next to his cockpit dropped down. He climbed out, removed his flight helmet, and went to the main hangar. The sunlight was almost gone now. Having endured Tulson's desert heat for a few days, it felt almost chilly outside, like autumn was just around the corner even though it was still July.

The main hangar had a couple starfighters under repair. One looked to be a total loss and was ready for a scrap pile. Probably a crash that had been brought there for recycling. The main office was beside the hangar, and the lights were still on, so someone was working late. He knocked on the office door and waited, his helmet resting in the crook of his right arm.

A short blonde woman opened the door, with a cute face, like a chipmunk. Short, sandy-haired, and green-eyed, Stacy Magellan was the daughter of Douglas Magellan who had built the M&M landing strip fifty years prior. After his passing, she'd inherited it. Growing up on the airfield, she loved everything with wings. Though sometimes she disliked the things piloting those wings. Cyril could never quite pin her down. When they'd talk, he could never quite tell if she was being direct, flirty, or just not into him.

When she opened the door, she looked dead exhausted and not in the mood for games. "Hey, Cyril, you don't have any cocaine, do you?" she asked through cloudy sunken eyes.

"Ahh, no. Sorry."

"Ugh, caffeine just isn't cutting it anymore." She walked to her desk which was covered in papers and files. The fluorescent lights overhead were harsh. Family photos and designs for an expansion of the landing strip adorned the walls, alongside a series of medals her father had earned being in the Terran Navy. Stacy sat and resumed writing something.

Cyril entered and accidentally kicked a piece of trash—an empty energy drink can. The waste basket was overflowing with them. Everyone had a vice.

"Working late, as always, I see." Cyril eyed a photo of a young Stacy and her father sitting in the pilot seat of an old quadcopter, both smiling. "I was gonna ask you about something, but it can wait."

"No, just say it now, because all this shit's gonna be here tomorrow too." She rubbed her exhausted-looking eyes.

"Well, I just need some repairs. A panel on my starboard wing and a patch of LED strip lighting. Easy stuff. No rush on it. I'm not booked for anything else right now. And I can pay my monthly landing space fee now if you need it." Cyril sat in an extremely uncomfortable chair on the opposite side of her desk.

"Well, you know the direct deposit account. Just send it now."

Cyril reached into his pocket, then remembered he didn't have his phone. Not needing it off world, he'd left it in his locker. "Be right back." He went around the corner to the locker area and entered his combination. He snatched his phone from the top shelf and direct-paid his landing space fee, then returned to the office. "Done. Anything else I can help with?"

"Unless you know anything about accounting, not really, Cyril."

"Ah, no. Again, sorry."

"It's fine. Fuck it. I'll do it tomorrow. Let's go look at your ship." She got up from her chair and rubbed her eyes again as she walked around the desk.

Night was almost upon them, so Stacy grabbed a red landing torch as they left the hangar toward his ship. It was quiet outside as he followed her, nothing but the *clack clack clack* of their boots. They rounded the nose of his ship toward the starboard wing.

Stacy aimed the torch at the dented panel and furrowed her brows. "How the hell did that happen?"

"Umm, I hit a bird," he said sheepishly.

She regarded him blankly.

Cyril shrugged. "It was a big bird."

She shook her head and pulled a step ladder to the wing. She stepped onto the wing and crouched. It was almost totally night now, and only the red of her torch illuminated her face. She slid her hand along the groove of the impact site. Cyril didn't really want to say how that was the final resting place of three separate guys' torsos, so he let that one lie. She walked along the length of the wing and traced out the LED strip lights, tracking down where the circuit was broken.

"Cyril, flip on your exterior lights, please," Stacy said.

He climbed the ladder into the cockpit, leaned inside, and flipped on the LED exterior lights. All fired up except the damaged section.

Stacy aimed her wristwatch at the unlit section and took a photo. She descended the ladder and took a photo from the front and below. "All right, kill the lights."

Cyril flipped them off, and they dimmed into darkness. He stepped down the ladder and stood beside her. She was running up numbers on her wristwatch. He wasn't a tall man, but she was certainly a short woman. She had to look up at him when she spoke. "We'll need to remove three separate panels and splice in new strip lights."

"Why three panels? The damage was only on two."

"The buckling of two caused stress and pressure on the surrounding panels. The force of impact from the … big bird looks like an outward flow. Three panels plus the LED lights and labor gonna run you about four thousand."

"Reasonable. I'll try to avoid big birds from now on. Think my insurance would cover part of it?"

"I don't know. Were you aiming at the bird?"

Cyril stayed quiet for a moment. "I'll just pay for it myself."

"I thought so."

"How long will it take to fix it?"

"Gimme a day. Easy fix. I've got the stuff in storage."

"Good, good. Well, now that we're done here, you wanna go get drunk and make bad decisions?"

Stacy couldn't help but chuckle at how awful that pickup line sounded.

"Hey, I just got in from Tulson and woke up only a couple hours ago. It's still early for me."

"And it's late for me, not that I'm not charmed," Stacy slyly said as she walked away.

"Oh, so I am charming sometimes," Cyril said as he matched her pace alongside her.

"You're adorable, but I'm a little busy and fucking exhausted. You'll just need to wet your whistle and your cock elsewhere tonight, or morning, or whatever time of day it is for you right now."

They reentered her office and winced again at the overhead fluorescent lighting.

Stacy sat to write an invoice for his ship's repairs and handed it to him. "Get it back to me before your next flight."

Cyril took the invoice, folded it, and put it into his left breast pocket. "Yes, ma'am," he said with a smile. "Last chance for that drink. I'm headed out now."

"Some other time," Stacy said, a smirk on her lips.

"All right." Cyril turned and left. A moment later, he spun around and leaned his head through the opened door. "Seriously, last chance."

"Leave," Stacy yelled as she threw a pencil at him. She missed, but the point was made. She chuckled to herself as he disappeared.

He traipsed to the locker area, where he stored all his personals when on assignment. He entered the combination and took the rest of his stuff. A small duffle bag was in the locker, with a spare set of clothes. He changed into a black T-shirt adorned with a videogame logo, jeans, black sneakers, and a black sweatshirt. He took the blue credit card from his spacesuit and slid it into his wallet. He hung his flight suit in the locker, retrieved Stacy's repair invoice, and stuffed it into his pocket. Lastly, he placed his helmet on the top shelf, facemask outward. With all his belongings recovered, he stepped out the front entrance of the hangar. It was finally dark, and the stars were out. If he looked hard enough, he could see the very star Tulson orbited. So far away and he had just been there about an hour ago.

Cyril called an autocab to pick him up, and within ten minutes, it arrived. He didn't own a car because he spent enough money keeping his ship in the air. He hopped into the cab and announced his destination—Mallory's Heroes, his favorite eastside dive. Only a fifteen-minute ride from M&M. The car quietly merged onto the eastbound highway. During the drive, Cyril checked his phone notifications. He'd been away for three days, so messages had piled up. Lots of junk emails, some text messages from friends, and one request for work the following week from a company he'd worked with before, Thundershot Inc. It was on the planet Gacrux. Another security job, this time from local wildlife. High risk, for sure, but it was also for on-foot protection as well as flight security, so it meant double pay. He replied quickly and apologized for having taken so long to respond. All that done, he messaged his friends Jess and Jace to see if they were up for drinks. Both said yes and that they'd meet him at Mallory's.

He flipped to his social media and saw a news article discussing Arcturus Allied Inc. which was making a deal with the various governing bodies to distribute widespread immunizations to all alien races across the Ekumen. That had been a problem for a while, species carrying diseases and creating pandemics. Full immunization was a massive undertaking. Arcturus was attempting to solve the problem.

Cyril was always skeptical of larger companies like that. One had requested him, a long time ago, to assist with on-foot security for an Arcturus competitor. He had declined because the rate had been too low, but if the money was right in the future, he might consider it.

He browsed a little more, then stopped. He leaned against the door and peered out the autocab window. The streetlamps flew by as he gazed skyward. The orange LED lampposts blocked out the starlight, so it looked like nothing but a black void above. He turned on some music and felt the car hum as it drove. The ride was smooth, with no potholes and with almost no traffic. He'd forgotten it was a Sunday. Not many people would be out that night.

The cab took an off ramp and rounded a bend onto a long strip of various restaurants, shops, and dive bars. The cab stopped gracefully in front of Mallory's Heroes, its overhead neon sign pink and blue. He exited the autocab and meandered through the bar's front door.

The bouncer was about to ask for Cyril's ID before noticing it was a regular patron, who knew each other by name. Vincent the bouncer had earned the nickname *Gumby* from having a condition called Ehler-Danlos Syndrome. His skin could stretch like rubber, and being a big guy, he turned it into an act, occasionally pocketing some extra cash for a weird trick or movement. Typically, people with that condition would feel extreme pain from the disease, but Gumby had gotten lucky with no pain, and his skin just stretched like a superhero character. He let Cyril in with no issues.

As Cyril entered, a camera drone buzzed by over the street, keeping neighborhood watch. He hated them, finding them annoying and creepy. It was also some of the only law enforcement that ventured that far outside the city. Inside, music blared, TVs featured the sports or the news channels, the arcade at the rear bustled with the regulars trying to win some extra beer money, and the smell of fresh fried food permeated the air. That night, a live band who Cyril had never heard of before played some kind of blues music. The wood floors were scuffed from dancing, spilled drinks, and the occasional fight. Dart boards covered the righthand wall, with more holes in it than the boards themselves. And a second-floor dining level canopied the designated dancing area. Pin spotlights lit the floor for dancing and karaoke. The place also had a very distinct smell of beer, sweat, and fried food.

He approached Mallory, the owner, who was fixing cocktails behind the bar. She had blond hair and thick glasses, was tall, wore a green tank top and jeans, and had piercing blue eyes that could laser a person in half. Unlike Stacy, Cyril never tried his luck with her.

"Mal, a Guinness when you get a chance," Cyril said as he sat on a barstool.

"Ahh, Cyril, back in town, I see. Was it eventful out on Tulson?" she responded, passing her drinks to the couple in front of her.

"Lost two pilots, but no one I knew. We got through it okay. Hey, did you know the wing of a starfighter can chop three human bodies in half?"

"Why would I know that?"

Cyril smiled.

"Wow. I don't even wanna know the context."

"But that's the best part, and you're really missing juicy details."

"I'm good. I'll pass. You back in town for a while?"

"Till next week, then I'm headed to Gacrux. Big job, can't turn it down."

"Good to hear. Well, for now, welcome back." She poured a Guinness and let the head cascade over the side before she filled a full pint. She passed it to Cyril and took his credit card for a tab.

Holding his pint, Cyril surveyed the bar. He tapped his foot along to the music. He always loved coming here after a mission. Good days or bad, it healed him somehow—the atmosphere, the vibes, the good yet not-watered-down drinks. It was the local watering hole for starfighters on that side of town. He lived only thirty minutes away, so it was no inconvenience to get there. He chilled out, listened to the music, sipped his beer, and half-watched people in the rear play at the billiards tables. Twenty minutes passed, and his friend Jess entered.

Jess was a tiny little thing, cute as a button but hard as fuck. The stereotypical "I'm sweet but I listen to death metal in the shower" type. Long brown hair, brown eyes, and her defining feature: a forked tongue. Her girlfriends really enjoyed that part. In a way, she resembled a demonic toy doll. Cyril couldn't really remember where they'd first become friends. It was probably during a drunken stupor. But they kept showing up in each other's lives and never ever left. She was a starfighter as well but still a rookie. He'd tried bringing her onto higher-end assignments, but her skill level wasn't at a point where anyone was willing to fully insure her. She accepted smaller jobs in the meantime. She'd get there eventually. Everyone did, if they lived long enough.

Jess ran up to him and attack-hugged him. Their schedules were tough to line up, as she also was in a metal band during off hours. They'd finally found a night when they were both free. When she pounced on him, nearly a quarter of his beer sloshed onto the floor.

"Oh, hello there," Cyril said, espying his beer and lamenting that which was lost.

"Oh, it's so good to see you! How was Tulson? Tell me everything!"

"Well, first, sit down and let me get a refill."

Mallory topped off his Guinness, having seen the accident, then came around to clean the mess. Jess apologized, but Mallory shrugged it off. Cyril and Jess chatted about Tulson—the heat, the punishing sun, the dogfights, the heat, the three guys who had been turned into hamburgers, the heat, Garrison being a dick, hooking up with someone (he didn't mention who), and, of course, the heat. Jess had been off world only a handful of times so to hear about other planets felt so alien to her. There was still so much she wanted to see.

She talked about how she and her band were putting together their second album and invited Cyril to come to the next show. Unfortunately, that show fell right in line with when he'd be off world on Gacrux. He apologized but said he'd still love to see them play sometime. He always found Jess cute, but she was a wild one. Out of his league. A total metalhead, with quite an eclectic group of friends. Not really his scene, but he really liked her a lot as a person. And appropriately, her starfighter callsign, upon Cyril's suggestion, was *Metalhead*. She ordered a vodka gimlet and toasted with Cyril as Jace entered.

Jace was a Skovian from the planet Cygnus. He had darker skin but very light eyes, almost amber. Dark hair as well. Cygnus was slightly closer to its star than Proxima was to its own, so his skin color was on the darker side. Skovians and Terrans were nearly indistinguishable. Jace had learned English a while back, and Cyril was sloppily working on his Skovian just in case someone on Cygnus requested him for a job. Most people knew multiple languages, but Cyril was just too lazy for that.

"Good to see you've returned from the void once again," Jace said as he shook Cyril's hand. Jace still had a thick accent, feeling proper and airy.

"Well, it wasn't a void, but yes, it's good to be back. Heading back out soon though. Gacrux next week. Have you ever been there?" Cyril sipped his beer.

"Two things. One, bring bug spray. And two, watch out for, what you would call, giant centipedes. This big." He outstretched his hands to shoulder width, then ordered a drink from Mallory—a whiskey, straight up.

Cyril shook at the thought of having to deal with giant centipedes. With Jace's drink in hand, the three of them toasted. Cyril offered to put their drinks on his tab. He had the money for it tonight. No one protested.

They chilled, drank, and talked throughout the evening. Jess got tipsy and danced along to the music. Cyril joined and danced beside her. They eventually ended up at the billiards tables around midnight. Jace and Cyril played a round; Jace won. Jace and Jess played a round; Jess won. Jess and Cyril played a round; Jess won again. As usual, small but fierce.

After losing, Cyril noticed a gorgeous redhead sitting with a friend at a table on the opposite end of the room. She had nearly white skin, very small eyes, was very gifted in her chest and wore a low-cut shirt to prove it. Cyril noticed her watching him. He took the final sip of his fourth Guinness and went to Mallory to ask for a fifth.

"Mal, another please. Hey, who's the redhead?" he asked, leaning in toward Mallory.

"Been in here a few times, seems to be new to the area. I think she's from Luyten. That light skin gives it away." She handed him his drink.

Cyril took it without breaking eye contact with the gorgeous woman. "Mm …"

"My dude, if you're gonna shoot your shot, go already. She's practically eye-fucking you. I've been seeing it all night."

He killed half his drink in one gulp and decided, *Fuck it, shoot your shot*. He approached Jace and Jess and leaned in. "So that redhead over there has been staring at me for the better part of an hour. I'm gonna go for it."

He removed his sweatshirt to reveal his muscular arms and shoulders. Starfighters were required to stay in peak physical shape to handle the G-forces of flight. It had other benefits as well. With that, he departed their company.

Jess got a little jealous, but upon seeing who he was going after, she was quite proud of him. She smirked and racked up a new game of pool for her and Jace.

Cyril reached the redhead's table, while she and her brown-haired friend eyed him and sipped on cocktails. Cyril flashed a smirk. "You know, I couldn't help but notice you were staring at me over there. Did you see something you liked?"

"I don't know yet." A flirty smile crossed her face. She sucked on the straw of her cocktail. She had a very quiet but flirtatious demeanor about her.

"Well, watching me for that long meant one of three things. One, you're admiring the scenery. Two, you wanted to ask me a question. Or three, you want me to buy you another drink. I'm leaning toward it maybe being three."

"Maybe." She bit the end of her straw.

She was completely out of Cyril's league, but again, alcohol knew what was best. And at that moment, he could pull anyone.

"I'll be right back," Cyril said and ventured to the bar. "Hey, Mal. What are they drinking?"

"Manhattans."

"Gimme two, please." With that, he returned to the table with two Manhattans, his half-finished Guinness still sitting on the table edge. He handed them their fresh drinks and gestured to the seat between the two ladies. "This seat taken?"

"It is now." She pushed aside her finished drink and accepted the next. Her extremely bright green eyes, that would catch anyone's attention, burned right through Cyril's head. He was as entranced as she was. Whether it was real or just the alcohol talking, it didn't matter. They were about to have a great night.

"What's your name?" Cyril asked, then sipped his beer.

"Jenna."

"Hey, Jenna. I'm Cyril. Cyril Eisner. I'm a starfighter."

" I don't know yet. "

Chapter 2

In a Pinch

A ceiling-sized mirror hung above him. His head pounded, and he lay in a bed that he didn't remember getting into. Dawn had already broken, and he could hear car traffic outside the window. He pushed himself upright and saw the rose-red bed sheets. Were it not for the splitting hangover, he might otherwise be comfortable. A makeup stand, dressers, a standing mirror opposite the foot of the bed, a shoe rack, some generic artwork, photos, and a couple potted plants on the windowsill decorated the room. He didn't quite remember what had happened after a certain point the night before, but given that he threw the sheets off himself to see he had nothing on, Cyril assumed he'd probably had a good time.

Someone was in the shower. Must be Jenna, the woman from the night before. At least he could remember her name. He contemplated joining her, but his headache was overwhelming, so he laid back down and rested the crook of his left arm over his eyes, trying to block out the sunlight. The shower stopped, and he heard the curtain roll back. He still couldn't be bothered to get up. The bed was just far too comfortable.

The door opened, and she came out. She had dried off and wasn't wearing a towel around herself; she was still working on her hair. Jenna was stunning, and her milky-white skin glowed in the sunlight. She didn't even mind that the window curtains were drawn open. How Cyril had been able to pull that, he would probably never know.

He dropped his arm from his eyes. "Good morning."

She faced him while drying her hair. "Morning."

"Well, I feel fresh and rested," he lied.

"Glad to hear it," she said, smiling. She pulled out a hair dryer and turned it on.

"You look really amazing," he yelled over the scream of the hair dryer.

She switched it off and turned around. "What?"

"I said you look really amazing." He swung his legs over the edge of the bed and planted his feet on the hardwood floor.

"And you look extremely hung over."

Cyril chuckled because she wasn't wrong. He felt terrible, so he probably looked like it too.

She faced the mirror to resume drying her hair.

He forced himself from bed, walked into the bathroom, and shut the door. The hot air from the shower still floated about the room. As he relieved himself, he noticed a photo resting on a shelf above the toilet of Jenna with another guy. That was when he got it. He was just a fling. Something to have fun with while her partner was away. He finished, washed his hands, and stepped back out.

Jenna was finishing getting dressed. She wore a gray business suit, which meant she was someone important.

Getting a fresh glance around the room, Cyril saw her apartment was very expensive. Now he knew how he had pulled her. He was cheap.

"Going to work?" he asked, already knowing the answer.

She finished applying eyeliner. "Yeah, I gotta be in at nine. Think you could get dressed now, please?"

"Sure." He collected his clothes scattered across the room. *Must've been a wild night.* It was a shame he couldn't really remember it. Then Cyril asked the dumbest question ever. "Did you have a good time?"

She turned around with a devil-may-care smile, walked over, and wrapped her arms around him. He hugged back, and she kissed him on the lips. His hangover disappeared as he got hard again.

"You were amazing. I haven't cum like that in a while, but I need you to go." She noticed him rising to the occasion.

Cyril shrugged. "I mean, do I have to go immediately?"

Jenna looked deep into his eyes and kissed him as she reached down and stroked him. He couldn't believe he'd managed to score such a gorgeous woman, but it was best to live in the moment.

The apartment door in the living room unlocked and opened. The moment shattered, and both of their blood streams turned to ice as they snapped their heads toward the door. Her partner had come home. Whether he worked nights or had been away on business, Cyril didn't know.

She whispered to Cyril, "Go out the window!"

He mouthed back, *What the fuck?*

She pushed Cyril toward the window as he put on his underwear. She opened the window and shoved him onto the ledge. He sidled over a couple feet between the two-bedroom windows to keep hidden. The ledge was about three feet deep and a good fifty meters off the ground. His erection was long since gone.

Even though he had no fear of heights, he never liked being that high without a set of wings around him. He peered over the edge at the traffic below. Inside the apartment, he heard Jenna and her partner chatting, playing along that she had been there alone and had missed him so much. *At least she's a decent liar.* Cyril got dressed as silently as he could. His shirt was no problem, but with the pants, he had to take his time. The zipper was loud in the warm morning air. He saw someone across the street watching him from their balcony. He smiled and waved. It felt stupid, but he didn't know what else to do.

Inside the room, it seemed Jenna and her partner had gone from chatting to kissing. Cyril hated the predicament that it wasn't him in there. The only thing left to do was escape without her boyfriend catching him. Going back into the room was a bad idea. Obviously, he couldn't jump down. Maybe someone around the building also had an open window and would let him pass through out of the kindness of their heart.

Then the perfect opportunity happened. He heard the bathroom door close, and Jenna popped out from the open window. She hurriedly waved him inside. He followed and saw the bathroom door was shut and heard the shower running. His one chance to escape. As they crossed the room, the door opened, and her partner, naked, stepped out. Everything, including time itself, froze.

"Oh, fuck," Cyril said and bolted through the living room.

Jenna's partner followed, sprinting totally naked after him. Cyril unlocked the door in a flash and jetted down the hallway, unsure if that direction led to stairs or an elevator. It was a fifty/fifty shot, and he just hoped luck was on his side. Thankfully, it led to a stairwell. He rammed open the door and rushed down the stairs.

Jenna's naked boyfriend stopped at the railing of the stairwell. "You motherfucker! I'll cut your fucking dick off if you ever come back!"

"Well, I don't know where I am, so that probably won't happen! Thank Jenna for a great night!" Cyril laughed as he reached the ground floor and dashed out the emergency exit.

He ended up in an alleyway and hooked right. As he reached the end, he peeked out from the corner and looked left and right. Nobody was coming after him, and it looked like it was at the backside of the building. Cyril used his phone to request an autocab, with a pickup point two blocks away. He wanted a little distance between himself and the apartment building just in case that guy was watching. He had about fifteen minutes until the cab arrived.

On the way, he stopped into a random coffee shop for a large coffee with hazelnut cream, his favorite flavor. Now that the adrenaline was wearing off, the hangover returned. He hoped the coffee would cure it. It felt like two jackhammers were pounding into the sides of his skull.

He reached the pickup point, and just when he sat on a nearby bench, his phone pinged, and the cab pulled up. The ride was smooth and easy, but he hadn't realized how far he actually was from home. He'd ended up all the way on the north end of town, the upper-class district. He wondered why Jenna would have gone to all the trouble just to be at Mallory's that night, with a friend, if she was high class enough to pull anyone from the more upscale end of town. Then he realized why. He was from the section of town she didn't often visit, and he was the same for her end of town. No chance of ever crossing paths again. She was just lonely and horny and needed a night of fun. There was no possibility of anyone ever noticing them together. Even the friend she had been with the previous night was in on it and would never mention it. She had used him.

It was a little disappointing and slightly depressing to think that was all it had been, but, deep down, Cyril knew better. He was by no means ugly or unattractive but not the model material Jenna probably frequented. In fact, the glance Cyril had gotten of her partner made him realize how much more physically attractive her partner was compared to him. Though, Cyril had glimpsed the boyfriend's cock as he had exited the bathroom, and it was enough to disappoint even a person with low standards. In that department, Cyril had been gifted by whatever gods existed. Cyril Eisner could sum up the things he was good at with the three Fs: flying, fighting, and fucking. Yeah, she had used him the night before. Sure, he would probably never see her again, but at least she'd had a good time. In a twisted way, he'd provided a good service to a lonely woman. Or at least that was how he rationalized a woman cheating on her significant other simply because the sex was dogshit bad.

The autocab arrived at his apartment building just as he finished his coffee. He stepped out, chucked his cup into a waste bin, and approached his building. A downgrade from Jenna's apartment but he did well enough for himself. A simple brownstone apartment building with a key fob security system. Very standard in the middle-class section of town. He'd worked his way up from near poverty to end up smack dab in the middle of the economic classes, making just enough as a freelancer to keep himself going, with a decent portion left over but not enough to elevate beyond his status. Thus, he had plateaued at being right in the middle, but it was comfortable, for sure.

As Cyril was about to swipe his key fob, his phone rang—his Uncle Gino. He sighed and answered. "Hey, Uncle Gino."

"Cyril, how are things? You in town or out on business?"

"I mean, I'm answering my phone, so clearly, I'm in town. I just got in, so I'm exhausted."

"Well, be sure to get some rest 'cause it's your father's birthday today, and we're having a get together at the house. He'd like you to be there."

"Really? If he wants me there, why isn't he calling me himself?" Cyril asked, a slight hint of fire in his question.

"Cyril, please just come, okay? The family misses you, and we'd like to try to mend some fences. You've been out of your dad's life for a decade now."

"Yeah, and it's been phenomenal, because I don't have to take his shit anymore."

"Just do this as a favor. For me, please."

Cyril said nothing.

"You won't have to stay long. Just come by, bring a gift maybe, say hi to everyone, and then you can leave, okay?"

Cyril sighed loudly. "Fine, I'll be there."

"Good. I'll make sure everyone knows you're coming," Gino said, his voice rising from the gutter.

"Great," Cyril flatly responded. He hung up and leaned against the railing leading up the steps to his apartment. He'd worked as hard as possible to get as far from his family as he could. While he made a good living, and he could easily transfer to another world, Proxima felt like home. And all his friends were there.

His headache was coming back.

He pushed himself off the railing and swiped his key fob. The door buzzed, and he entered. The door had a nasty habit of springing shut too fast, so he had to push it all the way open to get inside. He didn't feel like checking his mail, so he passed the mailboxes lining the wall and climbed two flights of stairs. He reached the second floor, turned left, and went to the second door on the left. Apartment 202. Home.

He keyed the lock, it clicked, and as soon as he was inside, he kicked off his shoes. Never wearing shoes in his apartment made it easier to clean. "Lights on," he called out. All around the apartment, LED lighting in various shifting color patterns fired up. The living room was beside the kitchen, separated by a moderately sized cooking island in the middle. Movie and game posters hung along the walls, alongside photos of friends, group photos after finished assignments, and various random pieces of artwork.

He retrieved an ice pack from the top freezer side of his refrigerator. His headache only worsened as he considered being in his father's presence that night. He trudged to the couch, fell forward, spun midair, and crashed into the soft cushions. His bed felt like a million kilometers away.

With the ice pack covering his whole face, he yelled, "Radio. Synthwave. Easy listening."

A smooth, synthy jazz number played from his puck radio on the coffee table—the kind of musical number ideal for flying down the coastal highway at sunset. That and the ice pack helped to distract from the thought of the bullshit he'd endure later.

His father, Lawrence Eisner, was an awful man. If anything, he was a punk, a bully, a wretched old crone who was long past his prime. He was a retired police officer who had also served in the Terran Navy during the Annexation War. Ground infantry who had worked his way up and had retired at the rank of captain. After his Naval retirement, Lawrence had entered law enforcement. His service had gained him a high standing in their home community. He had wanted Cyril to follow in his footsteps, but Cyril had a severe problem with authority, so that didn't really work out.

To say Lawrence was downright abusive was an understatement. He'd harassed, berated, humiliated, and damn near tortured Cyril for years after his mother had left. His mother had been his rock, his shield, and, when necessary, his hammer. But she had just disappeared one night and left a note that she'd had enough. Cyril never understood why she hadn't taken him with her. Without his mother, Lawrence had thrown every imaginable insult his way. No physical assaults could be traced back to him and involve the police, but words left scars just as deep as fists. Any time Cyril could spend away from home, he would. Once he had graduated from high school, he had only one direction: as far from his father as possible. He had applied to various flight academies, and while his grades had been good enough, it just hadn't been financially possible. Ducking his father at every chance he could, crashing with friends and other family members, he had worked as a mechanic and eventually as a technician on starfighters at a shop. During that time, he had begun basic flight training with some of the local freelancers. Turned out, he was a natural, and their recommendations over time had landed him his first few jobs. He had saved up what he could to purchase his ship for cheap at an auction. From there, the sky literally was the limit, and it was as far as he could get from his abusive father. It felt good to grind his way up from nothing into something that mattered, at least to him.

He dreaded being in the same room as his father again. This would simply be a favor to his uncle for having taken him in and protecting him for a while during his youth. He wouldn't be bringing a present. A birthday gift was a bit much for a scumbag like Lawrence Eisner.

And his morning had started out so well.

He ended up falling asleep for a good three hours, ice pack still on his face. When he awoke, his face felt numb. But the headache was gone finally. The stereo still played smooth, synthy vaporwave tracks. He checked his phone and saw a couple missed messages. One was from Jess asking how the previous night had gone. He swiped that aside to answer an email. Thundershot had replied to confirm his booking for the following week. The email read:

> MISSION: In-air escort and ground security

> TARGET: High profile VIPs. Anniversary safari to Gacrux. Two days, one night expedition.

> THREATS: Local wildlife can be extremely hostile. Provide support and defense in case of emergency. VIPS are associated with Arcturus Allied Inc. Safety is the highest priority.

The payment would be substantially higher than Tulson. Eighty thousand dollars. Thirty for air cover, fifty for ground support and escort. Ground security meant Cyril would need to brush up on his firearms skills. He was a bit out of practice. Ground security was usually handled privately, but this must have been a special request due to Gacrux's distance from Proxima or due to scheduling conflicts. Either way, money was money, and this was a solid contract.

That reminded him that he needed to submit his credit card payment from Tulson. He pulled the card from his wallet and launched the bank app on his phone. He entered the transfer code and his account number, screenshot the card face, and waited as his bank confirmed it. And with a ding, he was forty-five thousand dollars richer.

He pushed himself off the couch, chucking aside the ice pack aside, and went into his bedroom. It was out of sorts—laundry piled up, dusty as well. He hadn't had time to take care of it all before he had rolled out for Tulson. Now with a week free, he'd eventually get to it. He retrieved a large plastic case from his closet and snapped open the latches to reveal the disassembled parts of his GX-5 Eruptor 9-round bolt-action rifle, with explosive-tipped rounds. Wildlife on Gacrux could be rough—large lizards, insects, enormous mammalian life. Best to bring the heavy artillery.

He pulled out a second box containing his modified M9 Beretta, based off the classic Beretta design but with a weighted grip and elongated barrel for stability, accuracy, and the flanges of the barrel-absorbed recoil. With a fifteen-round magazine, it was a good back-up in a pinch. A little voice inside his head told him to bring it to his father's party that night. That would go over well when the fighting inevitably started. He smashed down that voice and brought both weapons to the living room.

He set them on the coffee table, then returned to his bedroom closet for a cleaning kit. Over the next thirty minutes, he cleaned and aligned both weapons. Even a small bit of rust or build-up could block a chamber or throw off accuracy. They needed to be tiptop before going into the field. He would need to find time before traveling to hit the shooting range just to get his skills in check. With the firearms cleaned, he secured them in their respective boxes, placed both cases in the corner of the living room, and flopped onto the couch. He opened his phone to message Jess.

> CYRIL: Hey, last night was great … though I don't really remember LOL!
>
> JESS: OHHH, it must've been really good. I'm jealous. She was fucking hot.
>
> CYRIL: God, yeah. Doubt I'll ever see her again, but it was fun. You get home okay?
>
> JESS: Yeah. At my buddy Dave's, working on some tracks now. Stuff is rendering.
>
> CYRIL: Cool cool. I have to go see my dad tonight.
>
> JESS: Oh god why?!
>
> CYRIL: It's his birthday, and my uncle asked me to go as a favor. I really don't wanna go. I hate him so much.
>
> JESS: Damn, I'm sorry. Hey, we're almost done here. Want me to go with you?
>
> CYRIL: I mean, if you want to, but I have a feeling it's gonna turn into a shouting match.
>
> JESS: It's okay, my guy, I'll protect you. I shout louder than anyone else. You know that.

> CYRIL: Then please protect me, goddess of metal LOL. I'll
> send you the address. It's out in the suburbs.
> JESS: That's a bit of a hike, but I'll be there. I can drive you
> if you need a ride.
> CYRIL: I'll grab an autocab there, but I'll take a ride home.
> I'll be there around 3:30. :-)
> JESS: See you then.

He closed his phone and stared at the ceiling, not really thinking of anything as he got lost in the music. Part of him just wanted to fall asleep again and to pretend he had missed the party by accident, but now Jess was invested. He knew he was delaying the inevitable. Cleaning weapons and chatting on the phone would just stave off his father's bile for so long. He owed his uncle this favor, and it would be a dick move to not live up to it.

With a heavy sigh, he went to the bedroom to change. Fresh blue jeans and a plain gray T-shirt again. Nothing complicated. He grabbed the ice pack from the living room, chucked it into the freezer, then downed a whole bottle of water. Something told him that more alcohol would be involved with getting through the night. That voice in the back of his brain once again told him to bring a gun. Just in case.

He returned to the bedroom and removed another small plastic case from the closet that housed a small six-shooter snubnosed revolver—an emergency weapon made for concealment during private security assignments. He'd never fired it. The revolver was in a small black leather holster, with an ankle strap. He contemplated bringing it along but decided against it. Probably wouldn't leave a good impression, drawing a firearm on his father, no matter how much he may deserve it.

***

Cyril arrived ten minutes late. As his autocab pulled up, he saw Jess's car parked a bit up the street. He approached her car, but she didn't look up, as she was deep into a game on her phone. He tapped on the car window, and her head snapped up in surprise. She smiled, then got out and hugged him.

"Sorry I'm late. Didn't really wanna be here," Cyril said, half joking.

"No, I get it."

They turned and looked down the street at the house. The afternoon sun was still high, casting golden rays across the neighborhood, and the temperature was a bit crisp. Birds squawked, and trees rustled in the gentle breeze. It would be gorgeous under any other circumstances. Not many good memories came from that place. A kind of gloom enveloped it for him, one he was happy to have escaped from so long ago. And now he was back for the first time in ten years. He breathed deep, then exhaled. At least it was nice out.

"You good, babe?" she asked with concern in her voice.

"Yeah, let's get this over with. We won't stay long," he said as he started walking.

Every step felt heavy, like his feet had cinder blocks strapped to them or like his shoes were trapped in thick mud. *One foot in front of the other. Just get it done, stay calm, stay cool. And let him know you're not afraid.* As they walked, a car rounded a corner and headed down their street. They stopped to let it pass, then eventually walked up the driveway filled with cars; Lawrence's friends probably owned them, as not much family was left, as far as Cyril knew.

Blue siding and a solar-panel rooftop adorned the two-story modern-style house, with a hardwood-floored porch area. The well-kept grass was clearly a landscaping job. Two flags hung above the porch steps—one for the Terran Navy, which had the symbol of a triangular starship over Proxima, and another for the local police union, which showed two rifles in an *X* over a law enforcement badge. To say he and his father weren't politically aligned in any way was an understatement.

Cyril and Jess stopped a few feet from the front door, and she half-jokingly asked, "Want me to hold your hand?"

Cyril chuckled. "Nah, I'm good."

He stepped forward and knocked. They waited. He turned to survey the neighborhood; another gentle breeze tossed around some leaves in the yard. An animal howled in the distance. Then the door opened. Cyril turned to see his Uncle Gino, a tall lanky man with deep-brown eyes and a shaved head.

"Hey, there he is," Gino said, smiling.

"Hey, Uncle Gino," Cyril responded quietly.

"Glad you could make it." Gino gestured to Jess. "This your girlfriend?"

Jess chuckled.

"No, just friends. Jess, this is my Uncle Gino. I stayed with him for a year after I moved outta here."

Jess shook Gino's hand. "Hi."

Gino's eyes widened for a moment in bewilderment. "Sorry, what's up with your tongue?"

"Oh, I split it." She stuck out her tongue and moved both sides individually, mimicking a snake or a lizard.

Gino was flabbergasted and speechless.

"It's weird for some people, I know."

"I see that," he finally said. "Well, come on in. Everyone's out back. Your Aunt Rochelle is back there too."

Jess and Cyril stepped inside. His father had remodeled it from the last time he'd been there. The polished hardwood floors looked brand new, and the furniture was fresh and clean. A more than one-hundred-inch wall screen television had been installed on the wall next to the front door. His father's police retirement and military pension had done well for him. He was set for the remainder of his life. No need to work a single day ever again. Photos hung on the walls of his father's military and police service mixed with photos of his mother. He studied one of his father, mother, and him, but the edge that he was on had been folded over, so it was just his father and mother placed into a smaller frame.

Gino stepped beside Cyril to looked at the photo too. "Thanks for coming, Cyril. I know it may not seem like it, but he does miss you."

"If that's true, why am I missing from all these photos? I'm just here as a favor because I owe you, Uncle Gino. We're only staying for an hour, then we're gone. I have things to do."

"All right. Want anything to drink?" Gino asked.

"Something alcoholic," Cyril replied flatly.

"Sparkling water, if you've got it," Jess said.

"As a matter of fact, we do."

They followed Gino into the kitchen area, which was wide open to the living room. The house seemed so much larger on the inside since its remodeling. Gino drew fresh water from the fridge and dropped in a carbonation cube. It fizzled and filled the drink with bubbles as he handed it to Jess. He retrieved an unfamiliar brand of beer from the fridge and handed it to Cyril, who popped the top, took a sip, and frowned when he realized it was an IPA. Not his favorite type but he would endure.

*" Sorry, what's up
with your tongue ? "*

The countertops were clean black marble, and the cabinets were freshly painted glossy white. Either it had been a recent renovation project or his father had done it long ago and since almost no one visited, everything just seemed fresh. Either way, he couldn't help but feel jealous of the lush life of excess his father was living.

"So, are you still flying?" Gino asked Cyril as he reached for another beer from the fridge.

"Yeah, I just got back from Tulson yesterday. Escort mission."

"Nice. Same ship?"

"Yeah, A-7 Skyhawk. Hasn't let me down yet."

"Glad to hear it. And what do you do, young lady?" Gino asked Jess.

"I fly too, but I'm still considered a rookie in the field. Still working my way up. Cyril keeps trying to bring me on assignments, but I keep getting rejected for higher contracts. Skill level and insurance."

Cyril nodded at her. "Eh, you'll get there. Just takes time and"— Cyril's father entered through the back door—"effort."

Lawrence was slightly taller than his son, and while lanky, he was fit and in peak shape for someone in his late fifties. They looked very similar otherwise—same hair color, eye color, jaw line. His father even had a deeply receding hairline, which Cyril knew would be him one day.

"What are you doin' here?" his father asked, gruffly.

"Happy birthday, Dad," Cyril said, slightly smirking.

Lawrence walked past everyone and went into the bathroom. They could feel the awkwardness in the air.

Cyril turned to Gino and sighed. "Yeah, he really missed me."

"Cyril, please, give him a chance. Can you please just try to be patient?"

Cyril took a long swig of his awful beer just to ensure his brain was properly buzzed for the impending fight, then groaned. "All right, fine."

Lawrence left the bathroom, passed everyone, grabbed a beer from the fridge, and slammed the door shut. He strode outside without another word.

Gino eyed Cyril. "You didn't bring a gift, did you?"

Cyril shrugged. "I guess I'm the gift."

They all went outside. Grass covered the flat back yard, with no trees for shade. A few family members were present—people he had seen maybe once or twice in his lifetime, so there was no real connection there—but most of the attendees were clearly old veterans or officers who his father had served with, making him and Jess feel very out of place.

His Aunt Rochelle was talking to someone before spotting him and rushed over to say hello. Ultimately, she was just trying to escape a dull conversation. She hugged Cyril. Awkward though it was, he committed to the hug. "You got so big, Cyril. You still flying?"

"Yup, still flying."

Aunt Rochelle was sweet but seemed a bit oblivious and even airheaded at times—the kind of person always looking on the bright side, no matter how rough things could become. She had her graying hair in a ponytail down her back and wore jeans and a T-shirt adorned with some company's logo. She was keeping it casual too. Then she noticed Jess and her weird tongue. They introduced themselves to each other while Cyril zoned out and watched his father grill food from afar.

His father turned to regard him, said nothing, and resumed grilling.

Cyril decided it would be best to just keep his distance for the next hour.

He and Jess found a pair of seats on the lawn and tried to feel as relaxed as they could be surrounded by cops and military who clearly leaned right-wing. Cyril never agreed with his father's politics; Jess wasn't particularly political.

Some of his father's friends approached to strike up a conversation. "You must be the long-lost son," a very rotund man said.

"Yep, that's me." Cyril took another sip of his drink.

The big man sat next to Cyril, and his much thinner friend sat next to Jess. The big man proffered his hand. "Harvey Reese. I served with your father during the Annexation War. You probably don't remember me, do you?"

Cyril shook his hand. "No. Most people here feel like fresh faces." He really didn't wanna talk to the guy, but there was nowhere to run. He gritted his teeth and smiled. "I just figured I'd stop by and see how Dad was doing," Cyril lied.

"I mean, you could go ask him. He's right there."

"Nah, he's busy. I'll talk to him later," he lied again. He noticed the other guy was interested in seeing Jess's tongue.

She was clearly a bit uncomfortable but indulged him anyway and did her trick. It was always wild to Cyril how she managed to withstand the pain of doing that.

"Uncle Gino asked me to come," Cyril added, "because he wants to try to mend fences or something, so here I am."

"I remember you and your dad not really getting along awhile back. That still the case?"

"It's always been the case," Lawrence interjected as he passed them with a plate of hot dogs and hamburgers. He stopped between Reese and Cyril to scrutinize them.

"Dad, I don't wanna fight, all right?" Cyril said, barely looking at his father.

"Why don't you look at me when you talk, boy?" Lawrence asked, anger swelling in the back of his voice.

Cyril slowly looked up, anger building in his chest. "There, now I'm lookin' at you," Cyril responded with as much confidence as he could muster.

Lawrence shook his head and walked toward the dinner table. He set the plates on the table without another word.

Jess went from a bit uncomfortable to very uncomfortable in a nanosecond. She needed something a little stronger than seltzer water. "Something else to drink?" she asked as she stood up.

"Yeah, bring me anything else but this," Cyril said.

Jess went into the house, leaving Cyril alone with the pair of veterans who weirded her out.

The sun was setting, and the temperature cooled. People chatted among each other and carried on about everything from work to family life. Cyril told stories about being a starfighter, and, in return, he got war stories from various people. Time dripped by, minute by minute. Then his Uncle Gino called everyone to the table for dinner. Now would be the awkward part.

Cyril and Jess sat together in the center of a bench on the house-facing side. The sun behind them highlighted the house, reflecting the blue paneling at them. The feast was extensive: hamburgers, hot dogs, racks of ribs, bread rolls, mixed veggies, and potatoes. The conversations continued, but Cyril and Jess kept to themselves. If there was one thing Jess was the best at it, it was killing a rack of ribs. Her face was plastered with sauce before Cyril even finished building his plate. She smiled at him without showing her teeth. Her face, caked with barbecue sauce, resembled a vampire feasting for the first time. Cyril grinned at how adorable she looked.

Across the table, another veteran friend of Lawrence's said, "I heard you were a starfighter, Cyril. Did you serve?"

"Uh, no. I'm full freelance. Learned everything on my own."

"Oh wow. Got your own ship? An LLC too?"

"Own ship, yes. Not an LLC. Just working for myself. I go where I'm asked."

"You really should establish yourself as an LLC. It's a better payout, and the insurance benefits are much higher."

"That's what I've heard, but I'm okay for now. I'm already booked for next week. Going to Gacrux for two days. On-foot security, as well as air cover."

"Yeah, my kid could have been an ace for the Terran Navy, but instead he's bottom feeding for pennies," Lawrence cut in.

Jess thought, *Oh great, here we go.*

"Actually, it's eighty thousand for two days and one night. And it's gonna be easy. And I happen to like my job," Cyril said, doing his best to withhold his annoyance.

"Oh, that's nice. You found something you love after you ditch outta here. I don't see or hear from you for a decade, and you think 'cause Gino has a liking to you that you can just come back in like it's nothing?"

Jess slowly picked at her ribs and said nothing.

"I came here as a favor to him. And in about"—Cyril checked his phone—"twelve minutes, that favor will be paid, and you can go back to pretending I don't exist."

"You never were grateful for anything I did for you," Lawrence said, full of scorn.

"And what did you do for me?"

"A roof over your head, food in your stomach, and I gave you an in for the service, and you ran from all of it."

"You gave me anger problems and commitment issues. I don't owe you anything."

"Such a fucking pussy. I can't believe you came from me."

Everyone paused. Silence. Hair could be heard growing from a hundred meters away.

Cyril muttered, "You know, maybe that's why Mom ran. She was sick of dealing with your abusive ass."

"Oh, really? Then why'd she leave you too, you little shit?"

"That's enough," Gino interrupted. "We're not here to fight."

"Oh, we're fighting," Lawrence said. "All this kid was ever good at was fighting. No discipline, no decency, never did what he was told. That's how he ended up a bum."

Cyril wanted to sock him right in his square jaw, teach him to never mess with him again. He clenched his fists, ready to fight.

"Look at you. You came here with this little bitch as, what, your protection? You scared of me? Do I rattle you? Is that it?"

Fuck it. Cyril strode rigid and tough toward his father at the end of the table. Lawrence rose from his seat and met Cyril's gaze. They stared each other down, ready to pounce. Lawrence smiled. Cyril gritted his teeth.

"Well, looks like your balls finally dropped after all. Go ahead, take a shot. Get it outta your system," Lawrence said, unflinching.

Cyril regretted not bringing that snubnosed pistol with him. All his problems could be solved in a single shot. "Don't think I won't do it, you old fuck," Cyril growled.

No one moved.

Jess walked around the table and got between them. "Babe, stop. It's okay, we'll leave," she whispered.

"Go on. Do it. You know you want to," Lawrence said, enjoying tormenting Cyril again, like he had so many times before.

Cyril did nothing.

"Yeah, that's what I thought. Weak. You were always weak. Get outta my house, and if you ever come back, I'll have you arrested for trespassing, you ungrateful parasite."

They turned and walked away into the house. No one said anything as they left, not even Gino, who realized this had all been a huge mistake. As they walked through the living room, Cyril stopped at a photo on the wall, the one that was supposed to be the full family photo. He punched the picture, shattering the glass frame. His knuckles bled, but he didn't even feel it. Jess said nothing. She knew what was happening in his head. Cyril had mentioned his father so many times, but to see it in person made it all click for her.

As they got into the car, neither of them spoke. They sat for a minute in total silence. Cyril looked out the window, while Jess watched him and could feel his thoughts floating over to her. It was a lot to take in.

She started the engine. It hummed to life, and they drove off. Cyril didn't turn to look at the house as they passed. They rode in silence toward the highway. Cyril's phone pinged. He reached down to check, expecting it to be Uncle Gino. It was Stacy at M&M airfield. She had fully repaired, rearmed, and cleaned his ship. He was ready to fly again.

"Can you drop me at M&M?" Cyril asked quietly.

"Sure," she replied. She considered turning on some music but decided against it.

The car hummed along on the road. Traffic was light, and the sky had become twilight.

"Autodrive," Jess said. "McClelland & Magellan Airfield."

Her GPS beeped as the car's autodrive took over. She removed her hands from the wheel to hold Cyril's hand. It was still bleeding. She reached behind her seat for an old band shirt she had tucked away. She wrapped it around his hand and held it to stop the bleeding.

Cyril didn't respond, just kept looking out the window.

"You okay?" she asked.

"I'm fine."

"It's okay to not be okay."

"I said, I'm fine!" He sighed and let his shoulders droop. "I'm sorry."

"For what?"

"Everything."

She held his hand the whole way to the airfield.

When they arrived, the car pulled alongside the chain link front gate and slowed to a stop. The GPS beeped again.

Cyril unwrapped his hand. "Thanks for the ride," he said as he opened the door and stepped out.

"Hey," Jess shouted.

Cyril leaned down to look through the open door.

"Message me later."

"Okay," he said, then shut the door. He walked toward the gate.

Jess sat there to watch him go, then drove off.

Cyril flashed his ID at the security reader next to the gate and went through. The security camera above identified him through facial recognition. The chain link gate opened, and he entered.

The field still bustled with people wrapping up the day's work. Cars passed, heading toward the exit. He entered the main hangar and saw the engineers and mechanics fixing a damaged ship, while a second crew cleaned the floors where the wrecked starfighter had been yesterday. They had disassembled it for scrap and had piled its guts on the floor. The lights were on in Stacy's office, as usual. He walked up to the door and knocked.

She answered the door, looking not much more rested. "You're late. I said five." She noticed Cyril's glum face. "Hey, are you okay?"

"I'm fine. My ship good to go?"

"Yeah, just need you to pay and sign." She stepped outside her office and rounded the corner to a massive wall near the main hangar door of data pads for all ships under maintenance. She reached for the third row just above her head and pulled down the pad for his Skyhawk.

He signed off without even reading what it said. Stacy handed him a code reader. Cyril pulled out his phone, swiped it over the face of the reader, and the payment processed immediately.

"I'm gonna go up for a while. Can you run up my charter?" Cyril asked.

"All right, where are you going?"

Cyril turned toward the tarmac outside. "Out."

"Out? When are you gonna be back?"

"Later!"

Cyril passed the break room, stopped, took a few steps backward to enter, then came out a second later with a six pack of beer. "Hey, guys, I'm stealing your beer! I'll pay you back," he shouted as he left.

"Hey, what the fuck, man?" a mechanic shouted.

Stacy approached the mechanic. "Just let him go. He's having a bad day." She rested her hands on her hips. "He won't do anything too stupid, I hope."

The tarmac lights switched on as Cyril walked down the strip. Night settled over the city. No ships were coming or going. It was quiet. He rounded the Skyhawk's nose to inspect the starboard wing. It looked like nothing had happened. Brand new. The paneling didn't look as weathered as the rest, so it stood out a little, but if it flew, that was good enough. He climbed the stepladder beside his ship and slid open the cockpit smoothly. He stepped inside, buckled in with no flight suit, and stuffed the six pack under his seat. It was extremely dangerous going up without a suit due to temperature and oxygen supply, but he just wanted to be off the ground for a while.

He fired up the center turbine, engaged his engines, and flipped on his radio. "M&M tower, this is Skyhawk, requesting permission for takeoff. Over," Cyril spoke into his radio. Since he wasn't wearing his helmet, he resorted to his back-up headset.

"Roger, Skyhawk, you're cleared for flight," the radio squawked back.

He throttled up and slowly rose. Once he was fifty meters up, he pulled in his landing struts and throttled his main engines forward as he disengaged the center turbine. He shot into the sky.

Stacy watched him go till he was out of sight.

***

Cyril hovered in the clouds at over three thousand meters off the ground. He was just high enough to maintain cabin heat and oxygen flow. For the better part of half an hour, he had been blasting music on his radio to drown out the white noise of the engine. He cracked open beer number four and chugged. Once he had killed it, he chucked the can to the floorboard. His stomach was full, and he'd need to piss soon, so he called it quits. Being up there, in the dark sky, everything felt peaceful. The only place he seemed to find peace was among the wispy clouds. The radio played some Phil Collins music. Somehow that mixed with his random synth playlist. It felt appropriate though.

He recalled that afternoon, ready to slug his father, and how he hadn't done it. Cyril realized that the whole evening following the incident, Uncle Gino hadn't messaged or called. He assumed they had totally burned that bridge. He should have stayed home. He should have walked away before things escalated. He should've, he should've, he should've. But he hadn't. Had he slugged his dad, he would have gone to jail, sure, but a small part of him echoed what his father had said. *"Go on, do it. You know you want to."* And he had wanted to. He absolutely had.

Cyril considered that fifth beer yet decided against it again. He needed to be sober enough to fly to the airfield. The one decent thing that came out of the day was that his favor for his uncle was paid. He never had to interact with anyone in the family ever again. Cyril was better off finding his own way through life. He could never extend an olive branch regarding his father though. His mother had made the right choice with running. It still hurt that she had left him to face his father alone though. He would never forgive her for leaving, and he would never forgive his father for abusing. Some people were beyond redemption. Cyril sometimes felt he was too.

The music kicked up and snapped Cyril from his thoughts. Enough sulking. He was burning up his power cell and needed to piss like a horse.

He flipped on the engines and shut down the center turbine. He slowed forward, then began his descent. The city of Balamb glowed bright neon colors in the distance, and he saw the landing lights of M&M airfield. He would place the two leftover beers in the fridge, then direct pay an extra fifty to the airfield for beer money. He owed them that much. *Buy yourselves another twelve pack, guys. It's on me.* He went through the routine of landing, and as he landed, Phil Collins finished his ballad.

CHAPTER 3

THE LITTLE THINGS

Cyril fired another shot from his Eruptor at the target's face, and the blank round face exploded into a mass of ceramic chunks. The last week had been a repetitive routine to keep his mind busy. He was brushing up on his small arms accuracy in prep for the following day's assignment. Day after day he visited the firing range for two hours of training on his rifle and sidearm. His shoulder was bruised, and his hands were numb and shaking. After expending his last magazine for the day, he packed up his weapons, restocked his ammo at the shop front, and headed home.

His routine: wake up, train in the gym, practice at the firing range, eat, relax, then sleep. Six days in a row, that was all he had done. The falling out with everyone after his father's birthday last week had set his mind on a brutal path of needing to stay disciplined to not lose control. Jess checked on him during the first few days after the incident but eventually stopped. He would handle his failure like an adult and deal with it in his own way. To him, that meant stress relief at the gym and fantasy relief at the firing range. It helped.

When he got home, he received an email update with a full crew roster for the assignment. The list stated a full squadron of eight starfighters as per insurance requirements. The squadron's name was Trumpet Squadron. Listed in the groups was:

CYRIL "SKYHAWK" EISNER

ALLEGRA "HONEY BADGER" CLINE

Jace "Astaroth" Rinkson

Richard "Jester" Galantine

David "Blasto" Bosk

Kyra "Twister" Hadley

Whitney "Roku" Quinn

Flight Lead: Stephen "Condor" Garrison

Cyril learned Jace had jumped on board at the last minute due to a cancellation, but seeing Garrison's name made him audibly groan. At some point, Cyril figured they would come to blows, but for this assignment, he would be as professional as possible. Unlike last time, this assignment didn't need any heroics or theatrics. They were glorified, overpaid security guards for a rich couple on an anniversary safari. This would be damn near a vacation.

The rest of the email stated the various pieces of wildlife that might pose threats. Large birds that could cause bird strikes, poisonous snakes and enormous insects, and some larger carnivorous mammal life. However, the landing site for the assignment was well within a safe zone. They would provide an aerial tour of the surrounding area, land, and begin a short expedition along a planned route.

The VIPs were Brentwood Forester and Layla Forester nee Mullarkey. Husband and wife. Layla Forester was the sister of Daniel Mullarkey, head of Arcturus Allied. They had the money for such a grand expedition as an anniversary gift to themselves. What they were spending was more than Cyril made in a year, and they wouldn't even notice the funds had left their bank accounts. *Good for them.*

He confirmed the email and booked his charter with M&M airfield for tomorrow morning. Everyone on Proxima was to meet at 0800hrs at the FOIL pad outside Balamb. Cyril packed his bags and set them by the door. With his tasks finished, he sat on the couch to browse his social media and messages, then messaged Jess.

> CYRIL: Hey, it's me. Sorry about this whole week. I've been dealing with a lot in my head. Last week I was totally out of line, and it was definitely not cool. I'm sorry.

JESS: Yeah, it wasn't cool, but I get it. You've got a lot going on between you and your dad. He's an abusive creep. Still, that was out of hand. Thank fuck you didn't hit him.

CYRIL: I just wanted to scare him. I wasn't gonna do anything else.

JESS: I know, but it did scare me a bit, dude. Maybe you should see someone about this stuff.

CYRIL: I never seem to have time. Jace and I are leaving for Gacrux tomorrow.

JESS: When you get back, will you please see someone? I'm really worried about you.

CYRIL: Okay.

JESS: Promise?

CYRIL: Promise.

JESS: Okay. I'm about to go on stage. We're playing tonight at the Whiskey if you want to come by.

CYRIL: I'd love to, but I have to get to bed early for my flight tomorrow. Gotta be at the field by 8.

JESS: Okay, babe. Please take care of yourself and look for some therapists. You really do need to get that straightened out.

CYRIL: I will.

JESS: Okay. Love ya, babe.

CYRIL: Love you too. Have a good show.

He closed his phone and laid on the couch. As he stared at the ceiling, he wandered around in his brain. Maybe he should see someone. He considered searching for therapists that night, but he figured it could wait till after he returned. Besides, if some cosmic event or bad luck blew him away on Gacrux, what would be the point? He'd cross that bridge when he returned in a few days.

"Radio. Synthwave. Smooth," he called out.

His radio puck played a slick number with a poppy tone. He grabbed his game controller from the coffee table. With nothing else to do, he'd waste the rest of the day on the couch, shooting bad guys on a screen.

The next day, he arrived at the airfield at 0730hrs. As per his philosophy, early was on time. He changed into his flight suit and stuffed his plain clothes and phone into his locker. Stacy hadn't gotten in yet. A couple mechanics were there early, setting up for the day. He went to the tarmac as the golden sun was still low. It wasn't too hot outside, but that would change as the day wore on. He inspected every nook and cranny on his ship, checking flaps, running lights, radio, weapon bays, mag lock system, and navigation. Everything was in working order. He hopped down and shoved his gear into the underside cargo hold, just big enough to fit his bag and his weapons cases. Right as he closed the hatch, he noticed Jace approaching him.

As they clapped hands, Jace asked, "Ready to go?"

"Dude, I've been waiting on you," Cyril said, chuckling.

They mounted up and took off.

Jace's ship was a jet-black F-55 Corsair, with two red stripes running down the top and sides. It had a slicked back, needle-shaped design in the front leading to a set of delta wings on the tail. It resembled a large dart that had great speed and attitude control. It wasn't heavily armored, but it was fast and agile. Its weapon assortment was similar to that of Cyril's Skyhawk—a 20mm Vulcan gatling cannon under the nose and a standard complement of air-to-air and air-to-surface missiles. According to Jace, he had inherited the ship from his father. It was absolutely an older design, for sure. Not many flew Corsairs anymore. The story made sense to Cyril, but considering the number of times Jace had upgraded, repaired, and replaced its parts, it may as well be a whole new ship. It was solid for sure, but Cyril still preferred his Skyhawk.

They flew side by side, with Cyril on Jace's port side wing. The sun was higher now. He turned on his polarizer to 60 percent opacity. The entire cockpit shaded dark, filtering the sunlight till it was just a large orange orb floating in the sky. They saw the FOIL pad in the distance still grounded, and two other ships belonging to Allegra and Garrison were already mag-locked and ready to go. The rest of the squadron would arrive from separate locations around the planet. They approached, went V/TOL, and landed side by side. They engaged their mag locks and killed their engines. Jace was on his right; Allegra and her Diamondback were to his left. He could never get over her ship's size. It seemed like such an excessive waste to have a ship that large and cumbersome as a freelancer. The maintenance and power supply costs alone would cut into her profit margin. Like Jace's ship, it probably held sentimental value. *To each their own.*

The four massive engines surrounding the pad, one at each corner, roared to life, and the pad rose. He'd FOILed so many times that Cyril could practically sleep through the tedious process of going from location to location. One second, they were staring at the sun, then the next, the stars. He disengaged his polarizer, and his stomach slowly gave way to zero gravity. The granola bar Cyril had eaten floated around in his stomach. One by one, the ships departed, moving from one FOIL pad to another. Then that pad leaped again, and they floated upside down near Gacrux. They flew a few kilometers toward the planet and landed again on the planetary FOIL pad.

Gacrux was a lush, green planet—almost too green. Building-size trees, amazing clear water rivers and lakes, and beautiful white sand beaches made it a damn near paradise. It was also home to extremely hostile lifeforms and dreadful heat. Large bugs and birds would attack without provocation, which made it popular for thrill-seeking rich folk. It was also the reason for the lack of urban development. It would cost too much to clear the terrain and eliminate hostile wildlife. Also, the remains of ancient civilizations dotted the topography. Because of the lack of urban development, it was also a popular location for the hunting community, which had become a problem. Poaching had brought several species to near extinction. In response, the Ekumen planetary governing body had built several settlements, with their own wildlife enforcers, to ward off poachers and game hunters. The only way to visit Gacrux was as a tourist and to go through an extensive vetting process, with exorbitant fees, for travel and safety. Thus, Gacrux had become, by default, a wildlife preserve and vacation destination for only the most elite.

The four ships sat on the pad, facing the planet. A second FOIL pad materialized a few kilometers away. Four more starfighters detached from that pad and maneuvered toward the one bound for Gacrux. They landed and mag-locked onto the surface. The next moment, they were in Gacrux's atmosphere. The food in Cyril's stomach dropped again as they leaped in. The sound kicked up in an instant as well. Going from total silence to the roar of the turbines was always a shock.

Everyone fired up their center turbines, released their mag locks one by one, and ascended off the pad. They formed a diamond pattern and navigated southwest. The cloud cover was patchy and hazy. A thunderstorm had rolled through a few hours beforehand. They dove beneath the clouds for a clear view of the landscape. Thick green everywhere. A rushing river with harsh rapids flowed right below them. Garrison ordered everyone to follow the river. It would lead them to their landing zone, Fort Clearspring.

They flew for another ten minutes, until they saw a large open muddy field that had been leveled as a natural landing area west of a circular grouping of buildings—solid stone structures with radio antennae and a fire watch tower. The eight ships broke formation and landed in random patterns. No lines or barriers denoted landing zones, so it was a free-for-all. Cyril touched down, with Jace on his left. He shut down the power, and when he opened his canopy, his facemask fogged up. The humidity was brutal. Hot, gross, and muggy. The recent storm had begun to evaporate from the heat. They could practically swim in the syrupy mixture of wet air.

Cyril hopped down from the cockpit and felt the thick, dense mud beneath his feet. He removed his helmet and could finally see clearly again. He could smell the moist mixture of wet grassy and pungent mud. Everyone unpacked their ships and headed toward the settlement.

A tall, wiry Skovian man, with a long ponytail, greeted them. His skin was brown, and his sharp face had a chin that came almost to a point. He wore a proper olive-green one-piece work suit, as was the standard uniform for the compound workers. "Welcome, everyone," he said with very enunciated vowels. It was clear that he spent more time speaking to animals than people. "Was your flight smooth?"

"No problems. I see it rained recently," Garrison said, sweating just as hard as everyone else.

"Yes, a downpour just came through. We're expecting another one later today. Let's get inside. I can tell you're all boiling in your suits. I'm Jerrod Ictithan. I'll be your … I suppose assignment manager here for the next few days. Though I doubt you'll be around here very much."

"We shall see, Mr. Ictithan. Glad to be here," Garrison said.

They followed Jerrod through the double doors of the largest building on the south side. The interior felt cooler but not by much. At least it was dry. Skovian skin texture was better acclimated to hotter temperatures, so they had designed their living conditions for their environment in the main building. Three-fourths of the workers were Skovian.

The group set down their gear and inhaled the dry air. The open and spacious room featured a staircase next to the righthand entrance that wrapped upward to a second-floor observation lounge. Overlapping muddy footprints graffitied the floor. The building's rustic, natural feel was an attempt to blend in with the world outside. The help desk sat to the left of the entrance. A few couches and chairs were spread throughout the room. It felt almost like a hotel, only hotter.

Each pilot signed in on the main desk's login tablet. Due to the humidity, paper wasn't an option, so everything was electronic.

Once the last pilot had signed in, Jerrod said, "Everyone signed in? Only the eight of you?"

Some nodded. Most were silent.

"Follow me," Jerrod said, turning around.

They followed Jerrod into the soupy air outside and crossed the courtyard to a pair of bungalows—four people per. Cyril hated the idea of shacking up with other people because of the high chance of someone being a snorer.

Garrison turned to face them. "All right, split up. Four and four. Cline, you, Eisner, Rinkson, and Hadley. Everyone else, with me."

Cyril was relieved the bungalows weren't preassigned. If he had to stay with Garrison, he might suffocate him in his sleep.

Cyril, Allegra, Jace, and Kyra entered the well-maintained left-side bungalow. It had clearly been used but the upkeep was recent. The tan squat house featured aluminum side paneling and yellow LED strips along the roof for nighttime. A large barrel around the back had a water filtration system attached to it. Plumbing was kept to a minimum to not disturb the environment too much. Solar panels and batteries powered the house. Four meters by five meters of panels lined both sides of the slanted rooftop. Were it not for the climate, Cyril would absolutely love to own a home like that. Pick up that building and plop it on a nice beach or on a grass field somewhere and call it retirement.

The four starfighters climbed the steps on a quaint wooden porch area and opened the door. It was sparse inside but would be acceptable for their two-day residency.

Once everyone was inside, Cyril closed the door and looked out the window. "All right, he's gone. Crank the fucking AC now," he yelled.

Kyra was already looking for the thermostat. Everything was as simple and as downgraded as possible to keep power usage at a minimum. She finally found it next to the kitchen doorway. She dropped the temperature to seventy degrees and flipped it to high. A loud pop came from behind the house as the AC unit surged to life.

Cyril stood below one of the ducts, waiting for the rush of air. When it finally came, he sighed and smiled. "Thank fuck."

"It feels completely acceptable to me," Jace said, reclining on the couch.

"That's 'cause you're a fucking weirdo."

Jace flipped an obscene gesture only Skovian's used. He held his index and pinky fingers with his thumb and extended his ring and middle fingers into a V-shape. Cyril gave him the middle finger in return as he plopped onto the couch.

Allegra found the bedroom and saw two bunk beds. She chucked her bags onto the lower bunk to the right of the doorway and headed to the kitchen to see what was in the fridge. She opened it and saw nothing, then closed the door in bitter disappointment.

Kyra took her bags into the bedroom, followed by Jace. Cyril brought up the rear as he pried himself from the couch. It was extremely comfortable, and he really didn't want to move, but he needed to pick a bed for the night.

As he entered the doorway, he bumped into Kyra. "Oh, sorry. Cyril Eisner," he said as he proffered his hand.

Kyra shook his hand. "Kyra Hadley. I've heard of you, Eisner."

"All good, I hope."

"No, not even close. But you're still alive and getting work, so I guess that counts for something." She pursed her lips and returned to the living room.

Cyril sighed and whispered to himself, "Well, that's off to a great start."

The only remaining bunk was on the bottom left. With a sigh, he slid his bag and weapon case under the bed. Then he laid on the mattress to feel its comfort level. It was just average. Enough for a couple nights but nothing to really appreciate. He retrieved his weapons case from underneath the bed and opened it to assemble his Eruptor. Once finished, he leaned it against the wall, closed the case, and slid it under the bed.

In the living room, everyone was chilling—Jace and Kyra on the couch, Allegra in the kitchen drinking a glass of water.

A knock sounded at the door. Without invitation, Garrison entered. "Team meeting." He turned and headed down the porch steps.

Everyone followed. They reentered the gross humidity and immediately sweated again, except for Jace, who seemed to be enjoying himself. Once everyone was gathered, Garrison told them to wait. A few moments later, Jerrod walked outside with two facility staff carrying a large six-foot-wide coffin case. They set the case in front of the eight pilots and stepped backward.

"The two VIPs will be here within the hour. We've brought you our finest local weaponry to assist you in your assignment for the next two days," Jerrod said.

"We brought our own firearms. The service notes said to be prepared," Allegra said.

"I'm afraid that was a mistake. You see, we don't permit standard firearms on Gacrux. The sound can disrupt habitats, and the spent bullet casings are trash that we do not want in our establishment. We prefer to use completely clean, waste-free weapons if necessary."

The two facility workers kneeled and opened the coffin. Inside was an assortment of various odd-looking firearms. Cyril had never seen anything like them before.

Jerrod extracted a large rifle, with a triangular barrel and a square stock. "These are LS-22s. We call them *Nullguns*. Non-lethal solar-powered energy weapons designed to stave off any living creature you may encounter. One shot ..." Jerrod aimed the weapon at a rock, five meters away. The weapon fired an energy pulse in a consecutive rhythm. The rock shifted and rolled away but remained undamaged. "And it will force away anything that may be approaching. Completely safe, no waste, powered by solar cells. Short recharge time too. This knob on top adjusts your energy output. Obviously, higher settings will be stronger pulses. We recommend keeping them at the medium setting to not burn out your charges too quickly. Any questions?"

"Yeah, just one." Cyril raised his hand. "Are you serious?"

"Eisner," Garrison growled in annoyance.

"I understand and appreciate your desire to keep things clean and efficient," Cyril continued. "I get it. But in an emergency, we need to be prepared for anything."

Several others nodded in agreement.

"Which is why we are also issuing these." Jerrod produced a small handgun that resembled a miniature version of the Nullgun. "These are LS-10s. We call them *Pincers*. These have a lethal setting but only a handful of shots and no recharge functionality. In an emergency, you will have these as a backup." He turned and fired at the same rock on the ground.

A thin, almost invisible, laser emanated from the barrel, and the rock exploded, sending small chunks into the mud. The group was impressed.

"I stand corrected. Thank you," Cyril said.

Everyone stepped forward to collect one of each. Once the coffin was empty, the two facility workers replaced the cover and took it away. As they walked toward the main building, a distant jet engine's roar became louder. Everyone turned westward to see a large transport craft, the kind only those with large bank accounts could afford. It was smooth and white, with round-tipped wings. No sharp edges anywhere. It passed overhead and kicked up some dirt and gravel. The ship landed in the open field as close to the buildings as possible. A dangerous maneuver.

Jerrod and Garrison lead the group to the ship. Its side door opened and rotated toward the ground. The inside of the door was flat, until an attendant inside flipped a switch, and the once flat door sprouted carpeted stairs. The group stood waiting in a semi-circle. Finally, a young man with a well-coiffed head of blond hair and wearing expensive clothes exited, followed by a brunette woman with a sleek face and kind eyes. She wore outdoor rain gear and carried a large pack, with what appeared to be camping supplies.

Cyril whispered at Jace, "Um, are we going camping or something?"

Jerrod approached the man. "You must be Brentwood and Layla Forester. I'm Jerrod Ictithan. Welcome to Gacrux. A safe flight, I hope." Jerrod extended both hands, palms up, to shake, as was the traditional customary Skovian greeting.

Brentwood didn't reach out to shake his hands.

"You're Skovian, Mr. Ictithan.," Brentwood said.

"Yes, sir."

"Well, that doesn't matter. We'll be on our own for this trip. Is this our security detail?"

Jerrod dropped his arms with no comment. "That it is, sir."

Garrison slung his rifle and approached Brentwood, proffering his hand. Brentwood shook it. "Stephen Garrison, flight lead. We'll be your security for the next two days."

"Two days? You didn't get the update in time, did you?" Brentwood said.

Oh no, Cyril thought.

"We added an extra day, since we are traveling into the mountains. Will that be a problem?"

Garrison eyed the group, then faced Brentwood. "It shouldn't be an issue. We can figure it out if our accommodations are still available." He addressed the group: "Does anyone have an issue staying an extra day?"

Galantine and Bosk raised their hands.

"I have to be back on Cygnus for another detail," Galantine said.

"All right, and you?" Garrison said, pointing to Bosk.

"Family time. Haven't been home in a couple weeks."

"All right, our squadron on the last day will be a little light, but we can make it work," Garrison said to Jerrod.

This was against insurance policies, for sure. All flights needed to be eight starfighters at the minimum, or the company would scrap the operation. This was an odd circumstance, however. As an error in scheduling had occurred, and the operation was already underway, the current flight would have to make do with their undermanned last day. The upside would be that all the remaining pilots would receive an extra forty thousand on top of their previous payment.

"Also, I see you have a Skovian working in your group." Brentwood pointed to Jace.

"Yes. Will that be a problem?" Garrison asked

"No. No problem," Brentwood said, glaring at Jace.

If it isn't a problem, why'd you bring it up? Cyril though.

"It's beautiful out here! I haven't been out of the city in months," Layla said, surveying the lush green jungle in the distance. She was also sweating but didn't seem to notice. A nature-loving socialite felt like an oxymoron. She approached the group of starfighters to politely introduce herself with a handshake.

Everyone was confused. That kind of courtesy never happened. It felt alien. Brentwood spoke with Garrison the entire time, ignoring the group. He was clearly the money and was mainly there just to be alongside his wife. He obviously would have preferred anywhere else for an anniversary vacation. Gacrux must have been a personal request from Layla.

"I'll show you to your rooms," Jerrod said and escorted Brentwood and Layla to the buildings

Garrison faced the group. "Get your gear ready. We'll be heading out soon."

The group trotted to their bungalows. Cyril was a bit disappointed he'd put so much effort into cleaning and practicing with his rifle, only for Jerrod to tell them that the Skovians would provide specialized weapons just for this job. And then there was adding an extra day, which on the one hand, Cyril liked, because it meant more money, but on the other, it disrupted his routine, and he liked nice, organized things. Tulson a week prior was a spontaneous job opportunity he had taken to pay off some repairs from the job prior to that one. Every mission, in a way, paid for the next one. He could have declined to stay and fly out with Bosk and Galantine, but he had no real excuse. It would look bad. But what also looked bad was the planning. It seemed like a very scattershot operation. He wondered what other surprises this job would spring on them.

In the bungalow, Cyril disassembled his rifle and placed it in the case.

"Like, are they serious with these?" Kyra said in the next room, fumbling with the Nullgun and Pincer. "These are toys. If a bug wants to eat your face, this isn't gonna stop them."

"As long as it eats that scumbag Brentwood first, I don't mind," Jace said.

Cyril and Allegra chuckled.

"You see the way he looked at me?"

"Yeah, I saw," Cyril said. "Rich and racist? How cliché."

"I wonder what would happen if you used this on a person." Jace ran his fingers along the barrel of his Nullgun.

"Well, we apparently have three days now, so you might just find out," Cyril said, cracking a smile.

Everyone grabbed their helmets, weapons, and rain gear, then headed to the landing area. They huddled and waited. Twenty minutes later, Layla and Brentwood, now both clad in rain gear, returned to the landing area of their ship.

Garrison pulled out a data pad and turned to the group. It displayed a map of the local area, with all their travel itinerary. "Our first destination will be the beachline, thirty kilometers east. We're there for a few hours, then we're off on an aerial tour of the northern region. Let's keep it light and quiet today, everyone. Watch out for wildlife. Lots of chances for bird strike." He turned to see Jerrod speaking with the two VIPs.

Brentwood seemed slightly uncomfortable speaking to Jerrod. Garrison went to join them. As the crew waited, sweat pooled up in their flight suits. After a few seconds, Garrison turned around, put his hand in the air, with his index finger pointing up, and swirled it in a circle—the sign for lift off.

Everyone rushed to their ships, stowed their gear and weapons, and climbed into their cockpits. Cyril strapped in, flipped on the power, and immediately blasted the AC. The cockpit went ice cold quickly, a brief respite from the steamy exterior. The canopy fogged up, so he kicked on the cabin heater too to dissipate the fog. He fired up the center turbine, checked his flaps and rudders again, then waited. Garrison called out radio checks. Everyone signed off with their callsigns. Garrison was the first one up, and the rest of the crew quickly followed. The VIP ship was the last to ascend. Once everyone was airborne, the starfighters formed a large line abreast flanking both sides of the VIP ship, four to port, four to starboard. They headed eastward. As they flew, the patchy clouds drifted into the distance and gave way to the sunshine above.

There was no turbulence and no chop. Smooth as could be hoped for. Then Kyra flipped her ship, inverting herself, as she flew in formation.

Garrison squawked on the radio, "Condor to Twister, what are you doing?"

"Below us. Look at the birds," she said, her voice filled with wonderment.

Garrison inverted his ship too, followed by Allegra, then Galantine. Cyril followed suit. Everyone saw what Kyra saw—a massive migration of large blue-and-yellow-feathered birds. The eerie rising and falling of their wings mimicked westbound river rapids. Their beauty even entranced Cyril.

After a few moments, Garrison righted himself. "All right, that's enough, Trumpet Squadron. Back on assignment."

Everyone righted their ships and stayed on course.

Then the radio squawked again. "Trumpet Squadron, this is VIP One, we have an … unusual request for you."

"Condor to VIP One, go ahead," Garrison said. "What's the request?"

"Apparently, Mrs. Forester saw your flight invert your ships and has now requested an impromptu airshow while enroute. Do you think that's possible?"

"Stand by, VIP One." Garrison flipped his radio signal to Trumpet Squadron only. When he got back on the radio, he let out a long sigh. "Anyone up for some stunt flying? I need the fastest of you to come forward." Garrison accelerated ahead of the pack and ascended another hundred meters.

Of the eight ships in the flight, four could stunt fly: Condor, Roku, Twister, and Skyhawk. The four of them formed a diamond formation, while the remaining four spaced out to surround the VIP ship, two on each side.

"All right, let's keep this simple. Nothing too wild, nothing too crazy. Stay portside of VIP One. Two and two. Roku with me. Twister with Skyhawk. First up, Quadruple Aileron rolls, then break off into ascending loops remaining inverted. Copy, Trumpet?"

Everyone copied.

Garrison flipped over and flew westward. Twister, Roku, and Skyhawk followed. Once they were five hundred meters away, the four of them flipped again. The show began with the four of them in a parallel line. They easily executed the aileron roll. With no wind shear, all four ships easily spun in a circular pattern as they flew past VIP 1. It wasn't as exciting without smoke trails flowing behind their wingtips, but it was the best they could do. Once they had passed VIP 1's cockpit, they leveled out, pulled up hard, inverted, and flew past VIP 1 again.

"Good work, everyone. Let's keep it up. Next move, stall turn into a floating leaf. Space out and go one by one. Twister, you start."

Twister thrusted forward ahead of the pack. She pulled a hard ascent, reduced power, flipped her ship end-over-end to the right, then floated down like a leaf falling from a tree. After four seconds, she punched hard on her afterburners and surged forward ahead of VIP 1. The rest of the pack did the same maneuver—thrust into ascent, flip end-over-end, fall toward the deck, then kick up the engines before impact. They navigated behind VIP 1 and lined up again.

"All right, one more time. Tail slide past VIP One into sharp ascent. Let's give them a flyby but stay within a safe distance. Watch your wingspans. We move forward together. Two on the left, two on the right," Garrison said.

"Copy, Condor," they all replied.

There was no room for chatter of any kind. One wrong move would be instant death. Everyone stayed sharp and focused. Twister and Skyhawk flanked right; Condor and Roku flanked left. They punched their engines forward, racing past VIP 1. Once they were four hundred meters ahead, they cut hard on their flaps and spun the tails of their ships around a hundred eighty degrees. This was a rough maneuver on the stress and integrity of a ship's hull. Cyril's wings lurched as he spun. All four ships turned and saw VIP 1 and the four other starfighters in the distance. They pushed their engines hard and thrusted ahead, doing a flyby over the tops of all five ships.

"All right, great work, everyone. Back in formation," Garrison said.

They banked around and headed toward VIP 1 again. They leveled out and rejoined the rest of the squadron.

"VIP One, I hope that was everything they wanted."

The pilot of VIP 1 responded, "As far as an impromptu air show, not too bad, Trumpet Squadron. We'll be coming up on the beachhead any moment now. Mrs. Forester thanks you for the show."

The radio went quiet, and everyone relaxed again. Minutes later, they flew over a large archipelago of islands, with white sand beaches—a harsh contrast to the jungle terrain of the morning. The rainstorm had missed the beach area, so the sand was soft, clean, and dry. The water was also an icy blue, with waves crashing against the shoreline that spewed up milky ocean spray. VIP 1 descended toward a large open area of the beach. It kicked up the sand, creating a circular swirl in its landing spot. The beach was long and narrow yet wide enough to fit all the starfighter ships in a straight line. One by one they set down along the beachline, forming a makeshift convoy of aircraft. Once everyone was down, all the pilots dismounted, retrieved their Nullguns and Pincers from their cargo holds, and headed toward VIP 1.

It was still humid, but the air coming off the ocean water cooled them. Cyril could see returning there for his own vacation one day, if he could afford it. The sand slipped and slid beneath their flight boots as they walked. In the trees, large birds with long necks and colorful bills squawked and screamed, insects screeched their mating calls everywhere, and the trees rustled and swayed as small animals climbed all over.

As the starfighters reached VIP 1, Brentwood and Layla stepped out, still wearing rain gear. Two servants carrying bags of equipment followed them. After a few moments of surveying the beach, Brentwood and Layla stripped off their rain gear to reveal swimsuits. Layla ran into the ocean and dove into a crashing wave, while Brentwood followed. The two servants, both wearing white shorts and gray polo shirts, opened one bag filled with stakes, poles, and a waterproof fabric. They took their time and built a four meter by six meter tent and set up a pair of cushioned reclining chairs inside. They retrieved a bottle of expensive champagne on ice, with two glasses, and a small table, with a charcuterie board, from VIP 1.

"Must be nice to have money," Kyra whispered to no one.

Cyril guffawed at that, but no one else commented.

Brentwood and Layla swam in the ocean while everyone watched from the shore, at a loss about what to do next.

Garrison faced the group. "Grab some shade and relax. We're gonna be here awhile, and keep your comments to yourself from now on, Twister."

"Yes, sir," she said sheepishly.

The only available shade was under the wings of starfighters or in the jungle trees. As no one wanted to hang out with the bugs and birds, the eight pilots took up residence under the wings of Garrison's U-8 Sabre ship—very standard and mass produced for efficiency. In any other circumstance, one could very easily confuse it for a standard aircraft. The only truly defining feature was the bulbous fuselage designed to have a larger munitions capacity. But it was a decent ship, very useful in any situation and cheap to power and repair.

Jace was already on his back in the sand, his head propped on his flight helmet, watching the crashing waves. Everyone else found their comfort spot and relaxed.

"Hey, Cline," Kyra yelled out. "Got a question. Is it true you once lost your entire squadron on Kepler Quintana?"

"It wasn't my squadron. I was just part of it."

"So, you did?"

"Yeah."

"Can I ask how?"

"Why do you care?"

"Curiosity, I guess."

She sighed. "Fine. Fourteen of us were assigned to escort two ships filled with the incoming political cabinet on the main continent of Quintana. I don't remember why they didn't use military support. Had something to do with the shortfall, I think. The civil war was dying down, but they were still paranoid of insurrectionists and bombings. The plan was to leapfrog a FOIL pad across the continent from one end to the other. Then the pad broke down, and we couldn't leap again. So we had to fly through hostile territory owned by the opposing faction.

"We tried to weave our way around, go low to avoid radar, but our luck ran out, and we got swarmed. Any ship you could think of—Darts, Junkers, Boas, everything—coming right at us. We still had another hundred kilometers to go till we made it to safe territory, and then the first transport got hit kamikaze style. Just popped like a balloon. I could swear I saw people screaming and burning as they fell to the ground.

"Flight leader went down quick. He was in over his head, so I took command. Lost two more right after. Goddamn Junkers just wouldn't stop coming. I ordered everyone to move into a protection pattern around the last transport and gun it for the capital. Twenty kilometers out, I took three ships with me and turned back to cover our asses. Numbers must've been at around twenty at that point. We were just trying to draw them off a little longer till backup could arrive. And when it did, the backup took out the transport and the rest of the squadron."

"What the fuck," Kyra exclaimed.

Everyone's jaws fell open.

"Insurrectionists had taken the airbase near the capital overnight and cut off communications. They were waiting until we arrived to get us all at once. They hadn't counted on us taking the long route. They thought we were still using the FOIL pad. Taking us out along the way just made it a little harder. After the transport went down, it was just me and the other three. Mission was a total failure at that point. We dove as low as possible and headed for the canyons. There was literally nowhere to run, so we would have to hide and wait out their search. We got some distance and disappeared. Duffy bought it when he shredded the tree line. The three of us who were left took cover in an old salt mine. It was inside a hollowed-out mountain, just big enough to fit all our ships in. Figured it could hide us from their radar. We sat there and waited for a whole day.

"The only option was to hightail it back to the other side of the continent, and that meant going back the way we came. We kept low and slow, taking our time, trying to not kick the hornet's nest, but our luck was already gone. They swarmed us sixty kilometers out. We called for backup, but they were too far away. We just had to punch it and hope for the best. Travis went down, then Lucille. If it wasn't for my ship's armor plating, I'd have joined them. Thing fucking saved my life. Backup finally got there and scared off the insurrectionists. I didn't work for a month after that, and I never took another job on Quintana ever again."

Everyone remained quiet. The only sound was the crashing waves on the shore.

"I don't think they ever recovered the bodies," Allegra whispered slowly, then went quiet and stared into the horizon.

"I'm sorry," Kyra said.

"It's fine." Allegra picked some imaginary lint off her arm and threw it away. "I'm fine."

The two servants approached the group of pilots with eight wine glasses and a bottle of champagne. One of them, a very gaunt-looking man, said, "The Forester's would like to offer you some champagne if you were so inclined."

"Yeah, we need it," Cyril said. "And leave the bottle."

Garrison didn't protest. He took the first glass and filled it to the top.

***

A couple hours ticked by. Everyone was relaxing. A few pilots had taken naps under the wing. Galantine had returned to his ship to do some small maintenance and cleaning; most chatted and enjoyed the shade. The sun began to set, and a new storm approached from the ocean.

The Foresters called it quits for the day, which meant back to base. They packed their gear, collected any trash, and settled into their ships. The return flight was smooth and quiet. No one talked. Allegra's story had hit a nerve. That was the harsh reality they all faced daily. As freelancers, they were expendable. Replaceable. The only time they had value was if they accomplished their objective. Otherwise, another person would fill their slot. No one was special. Camaraderie among the working class was what held them together, and their employers held little to no interest in their freelance employees' futures or safety. They were useful until they weren't.

The ships landed at base half an hour before the storm pounded on them. Everyone took shelter and called it a day. Despite doing next to nothing, everyone felt beat. The sunshine and humidity had drained them. Kyra and Allegra hit the sack early. Jace and Cyril relaxed in the living room. Jace splayed out on the couch, while Cyril relaxed in the recliner. A wall-mounted television had some preselected films already loaded onto the drive. They tossed on a dumb comedy and wished some alcohol was available.

A knock sounded at the door. Cyril got up and opened it to reveal a facility staff worker, soaked to the bone from the downpour, carrying a large plastic tote. Cyril took the bag and thanked the staff worker. He saw Quinn standing in the rain in the center of the courtyard not doing anything, just standing and looking skyward, with her arms outstretched at her sides.

The facility worker left just as Cyril said, "Jace, come here."

Jace peered through the window next to Cyril and was just as equally confused by Quinn's actions.

"What the hell's she doin'?" Cyril asked.

"No idea, brother," Jace replied.

It was raining in sheets but without lightning, blanketing the land with row after row of fat drops. Tropical rainstorms were always a sight to behold. Nothing could compare. They closed the door without an answer. Cyril set the tote bag on the kitchen table and opened one of the boxes from inside—a warm meal of boar's meat, with fresh vegetables and wild rice. A decent meal for the night. They had provided a set of four bottles of fresh water too. Jace went to the bedroom and whispered that dinner was ready. Only Kyra came out. Allegra stayed in her bunk. The three of them sat at the table and quietly ate. Cyril would occasionally peek through the window blinds at Quinn. She was still standing there, the rain battering her.

"What do you keep looking at?" Kyra asked.

"Quinn's standing out there in the rain," Cyril said.

Kyra got up to see for herself. "Oh, I get it. You don't know where she came from. She's been on deep-space assignments for four months." She returned to her chair to continue eating.

"Ahh, she hasn't seen or felt rain in a while." Cyril sat down as well.

"Yup, it's the little things that you miss," she said, shoveling a spoonful of rice into her mouth.

"Yeah, I guess so."

They resumed eating and left Quinn to her solitude.

***

The next day, the humidity was sweltering again. The sunrays beat onto the land, evaporating yesterday's rainfall. The goopy air would make the day a trial of patience. Garrison shared the plan for the day on his data pad. No flying. Everything was a hiking expedition into the deep reaches of the northern jungle.

The Foresters—or more specifically, Layla—wanted to explore the ancient ruins that were part of a preservation effort. She was dragging Brentwood along, clearly against his will. The crew had seen them fighting in the morning before breakfast. Garrison ignored their quarrel while explaining there might be hostile insects or animal life on their path.

The crew retrieved their weapons from their ships and changed into proper hiking attire for the walk. Jerrod gave facility worker clothing to those who had no proper attire. Galantine, Quinn, and Jace brought no such clothing and were relegated to looking like basic employees—olive-green jumpsuits, gray hiking boots, and rain gear in case of another surprise shower. They looked like they belonged to a mechanic shop, not handling firearms in the jungle.

Three facility workers would accompany the crew, with packs of food, water, first aid, and tents for camping that night. Facility workers would drive them to the hiking path in large trucks. Once on the path, they would be on their own for the next two days. The final day would be the return hike to base. Galantine and Bosk would return to base before the current day ended to head home early. As no satellites orbited Gacrux and with minimal amounts of radio towers, they would have no way to communicate with homebase should something go wrong. They would be completely disconnected from society.

The crew loaded into two vehicles and headed north toward the trail at 0830 hrs. Cyril sat in a truck with his bunkmates, a facility worker, and Layla. Were it not so humid, the rushing air at the back of the trucks would feel amazing. As it was, it felt gross and damp the whole way. The wet mud and grass also smelled of rotting animal excrement, like compost that had been set outside in the sun for far too long.

The Forester's morning fight had split Brentwood and Layla. Brentwood had taken the other truck, while Layla had hopped in with Cyril's company. A set of two benches, one on each side of the truck, had been installed for comfort. Cyril watched Layla. Her eyes were bloodshot. She'd been crying. He offered his canteen to her. She accepted it. Right as she raised it to her mouth, the truck hit a massive bump ,and water gushed from the open lid and sprayed her in the face. He couldn't help but chuckle. Layla saw him chuckling and did the same. The most perfect timing for bad luck. She eventually got a sip, snapped the lid shut, and handed it to Cyril. She wiped her face with the sleeve of her shirt and looked at Cyril again.

"You okay?" he asked loudly over the roar of the engine.

"Yeah, I'm fine. Thank you," she answered just as loud.

They smiled at each other. Jace noticed but said nothing. He simply shot Cyril a hard glance that said, *My man, don't try to hit that.* Cyril said nothing and shrugged.

They came to a rolling stop near a forty-degree upward slope of the base of a mountain covered in trees with drooping limbs and webs of vines. Everyone hopped from the trucks and tossed on their packs. The facility worker distributed tubes of spray-on sunblock for the day. Everyone layered up and smelled like oil. They formed up on Garrison for the mission briefing.

Garrison retrieved his data pad which displayed a map of the mountain. "Single file line. I'm on point. Quinn, you'll be right behind me. Everyone else, spread out down the line and give the clients their space. Watch your steps, keep drinking water, stay sharp for anything moving out there. Everyone good to go?"

Everyone nodded.

"Good. Let's go to work."

They started their walk. The Foresters took up the center of the line, while the facility workers trailed the rear. Cyril was in line behind Brentwood and Layla. He caught shades and bits of their conversations. Brentwood, it seemed, was only there to satisfy Layla. He thought it would be mostly beach time. He hated the jungle. He hated bugs. He hated the heat. And he was beginning to hate Layla.

The next couple days should be fun, Cyril thought, wiping a waterfall of sweat from his brow.

The trail weaved up the mountain like a snake, the dirt having been packed down by previous hikers. Birds and bugs chirped, whistled, and squeaked everywhere. The treetops were dense but still letting shafts of light pass through to the ground below. The ruins they were headed to were built into caves on the opposite side of the mountain they were hiking up. The trees eventually gave way to a rocky, slate chip hiking path. A steep drop on the left and hard slabs of slate to the right. Overhead, black birds so large that they could lift an adult human circled. All the starfighters kept one eye on the trail, and the other skyward.

Brentwood made the comment, "Why couldn't we just fly to this place? Why walk all the way?"

"Not enough landing space where we're going," Garrison said.

"Still, could have figured something out," Brentwood grunted.

Garrison ignored him. Though he was a company man, even Brentwood was beginning to get on his nerves.

While they walked, small critters with rock shells scurried away, covering the ground. A species of insect had adapted to the mountainous area and used rocks as shells for protection and camouflage. Brentwood kicked some away that tried to crawl up his pants. They rounded a bend and saw a flock of birds with elongated necks, sharp beaks, and huge wings tearing away at an animal corpse.

Garrison and Quinn rushed forward and blasted them with their Nullguns. The guns pulsated a whirring sound as they aimed at the pack. The birds backed up and squealed. The Nullguns angered them more than terrified them. They eventually flew off, leaving the shredded corpse behind. The slaughter was so horrific that they couldn't identify the animal. Garrison and Quinn kicked the carcass over the edge of the mountain, and as it rolled down the slate chips, its guts spewed out, leaving a red skid mark along the mountainside, like an incision slowly being drawn open by a knife.

They rounded the bend and came upon a large triangular cavern. The crew took a rest outside the entrance on a wide-open landing that previous archaeologists, explorers, and tourists had packed down. Everyone felt beat. The facility staff brought them cold water and fresh fruit. Spirits brightened. The elevation up the mountain had stripped much of the humidity, but the sun beating down on them took them from sweating to just straight burning. Even with the sunblock, the UV rays scorched through the oils. They applied a second layer while they rested.

"Oh, that fucking sun. Why can't we just go back to the beach?" Brentwood groaned.

Everyone ignored him. Once their strength returned, they got back in line and marched into the cave. Two people stayed behind, Bosk and Galantine, to guard the entrance in case the birds got curious and returned. As they entered, they felt relief at the darkness. The sun was no longer assaulting them. The facility workers turned a corner and flipped a breaker box. Lights illuminated the cavern system. Glow sticks, LED strips, and floating light drones lit a massive network of centuries-old statues and rock houses. Everyone was in awe, even Brentwood. The houses comprised the very same slate rock that lined the outside of the mountain, with a brown sod mixture filling in the cracks between the pieces to form the walls. None of the houses had roofs. Layla smiled wide and traversed a flattened path packed into the floor.

"Mrs. Forester, please wait for us! Do not get too far ahead!" Garrison's booming voice echoed in the cave, like three Garrisons spoke simultaneously. "All right, spread out, groups of two," Garrison said to the group. "Full pattern search. Secure the area. You see anything weird, blast it. Let's go."

They split into groups and wove through the network of open pathways and houses. Garrison and Quinn kept Brentwood with them as they caught up with Layla. The facility workers stayed together and moved with Allegra and Jace. Cyril teamed up with Kyra. They headed to the righthand side of the cave, following a long line of glow sticks hanging from a seemingly never-ending wire. A circular light drone buzzed overhead as it rounded the room. Shadows rose and fell as it passed. They kept their Nullguns at the high ready. They heard small chirping and squeaks in every nook and cranny. Due to the cave's echoes though, it was impossible to tell where they came from.

The cave felt like a nice reprieve from the brutal heat. It was warm but dry, so no one sweated waterfalls anymore. Cyril and Kyra relaxed and rounded the room, beholding the architecture. Strange alien stalactites and stalagmites hung from the ceiling and rose from the floor. Some kind of scripture, in a language lost to time, graffitied the walls. Whoever had occupied the caves was long since gone. Only the caves of their civilization were a monument to their existence. It felt like a museum where it was not forbidden to touch something. Kyra ran her fingers around a stalagmite and felt the ridges of time pass over her fingerprints.

"Careful, it might get horny," Cyril said, pointing out the obvious phallic appearance.

Kyra scoffed. "You have the best timing, Eisner, you know that?"

"Once a month, I'm on point with my comedic timing. That was it."

"So, you're tapped out now?"

"I'm all tapped out now. Let's keep—" Cyril saw the ground ahead of them move.

It shuffled for a moment, then went still. He slowly raised his Nullgun and released a quick pulse. The dirt on the floor blasted up in a huge dust cloud, and a massive scaly centipede scurried up the wall and crawled into a small crack. They still heard the *tic-tic-tic* of its legs after it had disappeared.

Cyril shuddered and scraped away imaginary insects that seemed to be crawling all on him. "*Eagghh*! I hate bugs so much. Jace, I found your fucking centipedes!"

"Was it everything you hoped for?" Jace yelled from somewhere.

"Big baby," Kyra said.

They rounded the cave and met up with the rest of the crew. Layla inspected a large table sitting on a flat surface and up a sharp incline of steps. No one could identify it, but they assumed it was an altar. Young cultures leaned toward religion until science eventually stole all the miracles. Brentwood was curious but not excited. Cyril noticed how he kept checking his watch. *How the fuck are these two still together?*

From there, the afternoon was relatively uneventful. They moved deeper inside the caves and found more ancient houses, more scripture, more statues, more bugs. It had become boring. Brentwood was there to placate his wife but yawned several times. At 1800 hrs, the facility workers stated the caves would be closing. Larger bugs would be coming out, and they still needed to build the camp. They returned to the entrance and emerged into the heat as the staff shut off the lights

The group descended the mountain path and branched to the right toward clear level ground—a tourist camping area. The facility workers erected pop-up tents and stoves for cooking. They also placed small sonic nodes around the camp site to drive away any curious animals or insects. The first tent built was the Forester's. Jace and Allegra assisted a facility worker with building that tent while Cyril and Kyra helped with the kitchen area. The Foresters stood at the edge of the camp, having what seemed to be a tense conversation. Garrison, Quinn, Bosk, and Galantine constructed the crew tents around the edges of camp.

Once they had built everything, Bosk and Galantine reminded Garrison that they had to head to base for their flight home. One facility worker was tasked to follow them as a guide, and they headed out with a ration of food and water. No one seemed to notice or to care.

Even as the sun set across the treetops, the heat had zapped most of the energy from the crew.

Cyril laid out a foam bedroll, with a small inflatable pillow, in his tent. He closed his eyes and began to doze off. Jace entered the tent, unfurled his own bedroll, two meters away from Cyril, and laid down as well.

"Tell me again, Jace, why do I do this job," Cyril asked with an exasperated tone.

"You like money, not good at anything else, you hate yourself," Jace said. "Take your pick."

"All the above," Cyril said, falling asleep. Not every job was exciting or adventurous. Some were just that: a job. Show up, do what was asked, get paid, leave.

The Forester's conversation grew a bit louder. Cyril only caught a word here, a phrase there, but it was enough to stir him from bed. He stepped outside, slinging his Nullgun over his shoulder. They were a bit deeper into the woods, just outside camp. Allegra had stepped out to check as well. Garrison was in the kitchen area, filling his canteen with water. No one else stirred.

As Cyril approached the warring couple, Brentwood slapped Layla across the face. She fell to the ground, crying. Cyril raised his Nullgun and sprinted toward Brentwood. Cyril dialed it up to full power and pulled the trigger. Brentwood collapsed, cupping his ears. Crawling on the ground, Brentwood tried to push himself away with his feet, but Cyril got closer till he stood over Brentwood and blasted the Nullgun directly into the man's face. Cyril yelled in anger as he fired. He released the trigger and kicked Brentwood in the stomach. The man yelped as Cyril kicked all the air out of him.

The crew were up now. Everyone rushed to see what was happening.

As Garrison approached, he aimed his gun at Cyril, burning with anger. "What the hell are you doing?"

"He hit her, so I hit him," Cyril said. He examined Layla's face. Her nose was bleeding, and her right cheek was red and swollen.

"That does not mean you get to *hit the fucking client, Eisner*," Garrison yelled.

"I'm doing my job, Garrison. Maybe you should do the same. Kyra!"

She stepped forward.

"Get me a med kit for Mrs. Forester. Jace, you and Quinn check the perimeter for any wildlife that might have gotten curious about the noise. Allegra, see if we have anything we can use for bindings for Mr. Forester here. You!" He pointed at Garrison. "Continue to shut the fuck up. And you"—he glared at Brentwood—"you stay down there till you cool off." He kicked Brentwood again, knocking the air from his lungs once more.

Garrison had finally had enough. "Eisner, do not hit him again! You've overstepped your authority on this one. Give me your guns."

Cyril stared at Garrison. "Come take them."

Garrison placed his finger on the trigger of his Nullgun and raised it. No one knew what to do. Everyone stayed back. "Last chance, Eisner. Drop your weapons now, and maybe, just maybe, I won't have you blacklisted."

"You'd rather protect your paycheck than defend a woman being assaulted. You're a scumbag, Garrison. Blacklist me if you want, but I'll be right here watching out for her. Like I said, you want my guns? Come take them." Cyril rested his finger on the trigger of his gun.

Brentwood still writhed on the ground, his left ear bleeding. One of his eardrums had burst. Allegra shouldered her gun as well. Everyone else did the same. The sounds of nature had gone quiet. The world was eager to know who would flinch first.

Layla got to her feet as she wiped blood from her nose. She stepped between the two men and approached Garrison.

Garrison lowered his weapon.

"Mr. Garrison, I'll make sure you're still fully compensated for your time and efforts, but as of now, I would like Mr. Eisner to be my personal escort for the remainder of our time here."

"But I—"

"That's nonnegotiable. I'll have a separate set of sleeping arrangements for him to remain close to me. You'll all eat well tonight. As for him"—she sneered at her husband on the ground—"just do whatever you want. I have some climbing rope in my pack which will work. If you attempt to have Mr. Eisner blacklisted, I'll make sure you never fly again."

The world breathed a sigh of relief. The crew relaxed, and Garrison was flabbergasted, unsure of what to do.

Cyril stepped beside Layla just as Kyra had returned with a med kit. She handed it to him and stepped backward.

As Cyril and Layla walked toward the Forester tent, he brushed past Garrison and said, "The fuck are you lookin' at?"

Everyone went to their tasks, as Cyril had ordered. While he hated the idea of ever being in command, when called upon to do it, he could lead. He had the spirit but never the drive. Seeing Layla get hit sparked him into action though.

The pair entered the Forester's tent. She dug through her pack for a forty-meter length of rope. She went outside to hand the rope to Quinn, then stepped back inside and wiped away more blood. Cyril pulled a wad of gauze from the med kit as she sat in a folding chair. He dabbed her bleeding nose as she stared forward.

"You gonna ask why he hit me?" she said.

"No. Doesn't matter. No reason to ever do that."

She said nothing. He wiped the blood from her face. Her cheek was swelling like a grapefruit. He got an ice pad from the kit and cracked it. It softened and swelled, then cooled to feel as cold as ice. He placed it on her cheek, then put her hand on it. He removed a fresh piece of gauze from the kit and resumed cleaning her face.

"Thank you, Mr. Eisner."

"Just doing my job. And *Cyril* is fine. *Mr. Eisner* makes me sound like I'm fifty. Though at this rate, I doubt I'll ever make it to that age."

"You don't have to worry about your job. I'll make sure you're employed after today. You know, my brother's company, Arcturus, could use someone like you."

"He-he, no thanks. I'm full freelance."

"You could still be freelance. You'd just be contracted if needed. I'll give you my contact info when we get back. You'll never have to worry about work."

"I'll keep it in mind, then."

They both went quiet as Cyril finished. Three patches of gauze later and the bleeding had stopped. She stuffed one last piece up her nose just in case.

Cyril cleaned up and said, "I'm gonna go have a talk with your husband."

She said nothing. He walked out and handed the med kit to Quinn. They had tied Brentwood's wrists and ankles at the edge of the camp. The sun was quickly setting, and the jungle was more alive than ever.

Brentwood was nestled against a tree under Allegra's guard.

Cyril cradled his rifle and walked over. "I got it from here, Allie."

She stepped away. Cyril knelt in front of Brentwood.

"You are so fucked," Brentwood growled.

"How original," Cyril responded flatly.

"You got involved in shit that doesn't concern you. You're no one. No one even knows your name."

"Your wife does."

"Fuck you." Brentwood spit at Cyril but missed.

"Mmhmm. Now, the way I see it, there's a few ways we can go about this. One, we leave you tied up and toss you into the jungle for the bugs to eat your eyeballs right out of their sockets. Two, you cool your head, learn your place, and we untie you. Or three"—Cyril unholstered his Pincer and aimed it at Brentwood's head —"I slow roast your brain till your head explodes. It's up to you. I'm sure your wife would like that right now."

Brentwood sidled up farther into the tree trunk as Cyril got closer with his Pincer, as if he were trying to melt into the tree to hide. "All right, you made your point."

"Good. Now, where do you think your place is?"

Layla exited her tent, and Brentwood eyed her. She walked away.

Brentwood sighed. "Away from her."

"That's right. Good boy. We'll give you another half hour till we untie you. Enjoy the view. It is your anniversary, after all." Cyril stood, holstered his weapon, and walked to the mess tent.

As everyone kept busy with various tasks, the staff prepared a decent dinner. Everyone branched off into their little cliques to chat while eating. Garrison constantly eyed Cyril. Seeing his command be subverted drove him mad.

The sun set, and the stars emerged. It was a clear night, no clouds. The camp was right in the middle of a flat spot where the trees opened up, giving whoever was there a full view of the night sky. It was calm and quiet except for insects buzzing around. Brentwood had taken up residence in a small tent on the opposite side of the camp site. Cyril was relaxing outside his tent with Jace.

"You fucked up, you know that," Jace said.

"Someone had to do something, Jace," Cyril said.

"Sometimes doing the right thing is not always the right thing. Better to just mind your own business."

"So, I should have just let it go?"

"No, but you could have filed a complaint or let Garrison handle it. Now you'll have him up your ass if you ever try to fly again."

"I didn't like seeing her get hit. I couldn't sit on this one. Sorry if that disappoints you."

"It's not disappointing. It's just … frustrating. You react before you think. You need to learn to slow down. Not everything has to happen at light speed."

"Maybe. Maybe not. Too late now."

Layla sat by herself at the camp edge, facing the mountain. She hadn't said a word to anyone since the afternoon.

Cyril stood and joined her. "Are you okay?"

"I'm fine," she said flatly, not looking at him.

He sat beside her. They listened to the squeaking and chirping of distant bugs and animals. Cyril faced her and saw she'd been crying again.

"Has he ever hit you before?"

She said nothing.

"We can go to the police when we get back."

"No. They won't help. You don't understand. The Forester family owns more than you know."

"They own the cops in Balamb?"

"I mean, not exactly. But they have a lot of influence."

"So do you. You carry the Mullarkey name, right? That side of your family is powerful too."

"I suppose. I thought Brentwood was different. He was so good in the beginning, but after we were married, something changed. He got distant, cold. He only agreed to come here because it's our fifth anniversary, and I thought we needed to spend more time together. It was like pulling teeth, but he finally agreed. I told him there was a beach, but I left out the rest."

"He thought this was some resort colony and never bothered to check into it because it was the last thing on his mind?"

"Yeah," she said, her voice full of resignation. She realized how much of a mistake the whole trip had been.

"You never did answer my question. Has he ever hit you before today?"

She remained quiet but started crying again. Cyril wasn't sure what to do. Put his arm around her? Console her? She was the client, and he was now her personal bodyguard for the remainder of the trip. Not wanting to make a mess of things again, he sat silently while she cried. A glint in the sky caught his eye. Then another, and another. Then a whole swarm of lights streaked through the sky. Not just shooting stars. The planet was passing through a debris cloud. A rainbow of lights scraped through the atmosphere and lit the world.

"Hey, look up," he said to Layla.

She did, and the crying stopped.

They stood to watch the glorious beauty of the cosmos pass through the atmosphere. Red, blue, yellow, even green streaks traced through the upper atmosphere. The night was aglow with wonder. The rest of the crew, even Brentwood, watched. A silent fireworks show. It went on for another hour. Nobody spoke. They lay on the ground to watch the glory of the universe pour into Gacrux.

Cyril side-eyed Layla. "The little things, ya know?"

She smiled at him.

***

The next day, the heat returned with a vengeance. Muggy and moist, the crew roused from their beds early. The facility workers put on the kettle and made fresh coffee, tea, and a full breakfast. Brentwood sat alone; Cyril sat next to Layla, with his weapon draped over his lap. Garrison was with the rest of the crew but looked glum. Once they finished breakfast, they broke down camp and began the long hike home.

They moved in a single file line, following the exact path toward the facility. As they walked, they saw their previous tracks, as well as Galantine's and Bosk's tracks. After two hours, they rounded a large tree filled with hanging water vines. They noticed the two starfighters' tracks stopped moving forward and turned into a jumble of steps left, right, and backward.

Garrison ordered everyone to stop. A smell of pungent rot permeated the air, like something nearby had died recently. He walked forward over a small berm and looked down. "Cline, get up here."

She stepped beside him. The crew spread out and formed a perimeter. They could tell something was wrong.

"Jace, watch Layla. I'll be back," Cyril said.

Jace stood beside Layla. Cyril joined Garrison and Allegra down the path and spotted a pile of chewed-up bodies: Bosk, Galantine, and their guide back home. Intestines and bones were strewn around, a horror film on display. Some large animal or insect had eaten them.

"Why didn't we hear them scream?" Cyril asked.

"It's the moisture and the trees. Cuts down the soundwaves. They could've been screaming for hours, and we wouldn't hear them. Ugh, that smell," Garrison said. "We keep moving. We'll send back a retrieval team once we're home."

"I'd suggest we try a different path too," Cyril said.

Garrison stared at Cyril, still angry.

"But, hey, you're the boss."

Garrison passed Cyril to climb the berm and approach a facility worker. "Is there another path we can take?"

"No, this is the only way. We try to disrupt the wildlife as little as possible," the worker said.

"At this point, I'd say that's pretty much done. All right, everyone, be on your toes, stay alert. Things might get hairy." Garrison shouldered his Nullgun and went to the front of the pack.

Everyone followed suit.

Cyril stepped back beside Layla. She eyed the mangled bodies as they passed.

"Don't look," he said.

She couldn't help but look again.

"I'll get you home. Promise," he whispered to her.

They snaked down the bloody path and kept their guns at the ready. It felt like a million eyes watched from all directions. They pushed forward.

"Hey, you hear that?" Kyra asked.

"No, what?" Quinn replied.

"Nothing. Where's all the bugs? The birds?" she asked.

Everyone finally noticed. It was silent. Dead silent. Only their footsteps upon the ground were audible.

Suddenly, an oversized slimy termite crawled from a burrow in a massive tree trunk and pattered toward the crew. It was followed by another, then five, then ten. A swarm rushed them, ready for a feast.

"Contact," Kyra yelled out.

They fired their Nullguns at the swarm. The bugs scattered away and encircled the crew. Above, a set of birds, camouflaged into the tree branches, made themselves known and dive-bombed, snatching up several termites and piercing their hides with razor-sharp talons. The dismembered insects dripped horrid black bug juice all over the crew, including Cyril. It had a grotesque, corpse smell. The remnants of Bosk and Galantine were in the slime, as well. An eyeball plopped to the ground, and Brentwood vomited.

"We can't get surrounded," Garrison yelled. "Keep moving forward and hold them back till we get to the clearing!"

They pushed forward in a circle down the path, with the Foresters in the center. The walk turned into a brisk jog. More bugs crawled out. The facility workers pulled the ultrasonic nodes from their packs. Before they could turn them on, another pair of birds, boasting two-meter wingspans, dive-bombed the workers, snatched them up with their talons, and flew off. Both workers screamed in terror as they disappeared into the treetops above. The nodes fell into the jungle, lost forever.

"Fuck it. Run," Garrison yelled.

They sprinted down the path, bobbing and weaving around the bugs and keeping their gazes on the trees above. As they rounded another large tree, they saw the open clearing toward Fort Clearspring a couple kilometers away. Jace and Cyril switched their Nullguns to full strength and dropped back to the rear of the group. They fired a massive double-whammy blast that shunned the termites into the ground. With their weapon's batteries drained, Jace and Cyril switched to their sidearms.

Catching up with the crew, they spotted the carnivorous birds reengaging for another attack. Brentwood panicked and ran off. He ditched the crew, even as they screamed for him to come back. His ruptured eardrum threw off his equilibrium, making him bob and weave as he ran. A massive bird, the leader of the flock, extended its talons in front as it dove toward Brentwood. Cyril and Jace aimed and fired together. The bird's wings exploded into a gush of blood and bone. It bellowed a deathly scream as it plummeted to the ground. Right as Brentwood looked back, the bird's torso crashed into him and crushed his body.

"Well, I guess that solves one of your problems," Jace said.

"Thank fuck for small miracles," Cyril said, smiling. He couldn't help but find it funny.

The crew pushed forward and reached the clearing. The birds circled overhead, but the bugs refused to leave the shade of the jungle. The sunlight became a sort of shield. The crew could now relax and move as a unit toward the facility. Several more birds joined the attack and dive-bombed every few minutes. One dove toward Cyril. He ducked, but a talon sliced him across his left shoulder. A deep cut erupted blood as he got to his feet, took aim, and fired. The bird exploded overhead and sprayed the crew with gore. Quinn grabbed the med kit to bandage Cyril as best she could while they moved. It was sloppy, but the bleeding stopped.

The next half hour was a grind. The birds would dive; the crew would duck. Over and over, dive and duck, till they finally reached Clearspring. The ultrasonic nodes surrounding the home base warded off the birds, and everyone could finally relax. Jerrod came outside and was shocked to see blood, guts, dirt, and gore covering the crew.

"My gods, let me get you all assistance," he gasped.

They collapsed in the courtyard, completely beaten. Outside of huffing and puffing, no one spoke. A med team arrived to bring fresh water and bandages. They cleaned and dressed Cyril's shoulder, then filled the wound with medi-foam, which felt like a balloon inflating inside his shoulder. Garrison explained the situation, what had happened, and how many they had lost. Within minutes, they formed a retrieval team and rolled out in trucks to collect the bodies in the jungle.

Cyril sat next to Layla. She was in a daze. Half joking, he said, "Hey, best anniversary ever?"

Layla snapped out of it and chuckled, then hugged him. "Thank you," she whispered into his ear.

He hugged her back. "We'll get you home, Layla."

"And don't worry about anything. You won't lose your job. I'll make sure of it."

"I'll hold you to that," he said.

One by one, the crew laid back and roasted under the brutal sun, too exhausted to get up.

Then Cyril said, "I need a drink."

Chapter 4

Down the Drain

The return trip to Proxima had been an undertaking for the ages. They had filed report after report, the facility added extra security for Layla's safety, and Garrison once again attempted to file a claim to have Cyril blacklisted. However, as Layla had promised, due to the extenuating circumstances of what had happened in the jungle, and with no camera evidence to document every detail, Cyril was let off the hook. She had his back and had even given him her personal number in case things got out of hand. She had to write it out for him, as he had no phone on his person. Before leaving Gacrux, they had again discussed him working freelance for Arcturus Allied. He politely declined once more but said he would hang onto the number just in case. He gave her his, and she added it to her contacts list.

Before getting in their ships to head to the FOIL pad, Jace said to Cyril, "Somehow you keep flirting with disaster and always scrape your way out. How is it possible?"

Cyril smiled back. "I'm charming."

Everyone manned their ships, thankful to be leaving the boiling jungle behind, and lifted off. Jerrod was especially thankful to see everyone go. The expedition was a PR disaster and would take weeks to sort out. Two starfighters, multiple facility workers, and one of the VIPs dead, plus whatever waste they left in the jungle. He would be busy cleaning it up for close to a week. The company would ship the two starfighters to their respective planets, while Brentwood would return to Proxima, and thus, his bagged body was put into VIP 1's cargo storage. They never found the facility workers who the ravenous birds carried away.

Upon reentering Proxima's atmosphere, everyone went their separate ways. It was midday. Cloudy and gloomy.

Garrison got on a private channel and radioed Cyril. "This isn't over, Eisner. You cross me again—"

"Shut up, company man. You're a fucking punk. Get lost," Cyril responded and blocked his transmission.

Cyril lifted off from the FOIL pad and buzzed over Garrison's cockpit. Best of enemies, one might say. Cyril and Jace landed at M&M airfield and checked in with Stacy, who was under the fuselage of a quad wing stunt ship in the main hangar.

"You miss us while we were gone?" Cyril asked, leaning down under the right wing.

"I missed Jace so much," Stacy answered. "How are you, gorgeous?"

"Still alive despite being Eisner's wingman," Jace said.

Cyril and Jace shared a goofy stare as Stacy came from under the fuselage and stood in front of them. "How was the jungle?"

"Adventurous," Cyril said. "I'll need a new fuel cell soon. Do you have any in stock?"

"Not right now, but I can get one on order."

"Appreciate it. You got a first-aid kit?"

"It's in the bathroom." She pointed her thumb over her shoulder.

"Thanks. I'll try not to get blood everywhere." Cyril rubbed his shoulder and winced.

"I don't wanna know. Just do your thing," she said, waving him off.

Cyril walked away, while Jace and Stacy kept talking, very clearly flirting. He removed his flight gear, stowed it in his locker, and headed into the bathroom. His shoulder had been pulsing and throbbing all day. Something felt wrong. He shut the bathroom door and pulled off his shirt. Dirt, grime, and grease covered the bathroom, and the toilet seat had stains on it. It was disgusting, but at least it didn't smell. He pulled the first-aid kit from under the sink, then inspected the bandage. The gauze looked messy, with seeping blood. The bird's claw had dug deep, possibly nicking a vein. He unwrapped his shoulder and saw the issue. The gel had become dislodged from the cut, and the wound wasn't fully closing. The talon had slashed away too much skin and muscle. He collected all the gauze from the kit and rewrapped his shoulder. He put on his shirt and walked to his locker. His weapons would stay stashed there till after a doctor could check his shoulder. He grabbed his pack and passed Jace as he was leaving.

"You okay? You look really pale," Jace said, concerned.

"Oh, you know, just slowly bleeding to death. I'm going to the hospital to get my shoulder looked at. I'll see you."

"Be safe, brother."

Cyril called for an autocab to drive him to the closest hospital. As he rode in the cab, he felt queasy and dizzy, then passed out.

***

Layla stayed quiet the entire flight home to Balamb. She kept feeling like he was in the room with her, and even though his mangled corpse was in the cargo hold, his presence still loomed large. The Forester family was powerful and would seek compensation for losing their son. The Mullarkey's would fight back. Legal battles were on the horizon. She was not looking forward to it, but a small part of her was happy he was finally gone. The abuse and neglect were over, but it still hurt.

When the ships jumped into Proxima's atmosphere, she watched the squadron of starfighters lift off from their FOIL pad and zip away in various directions. She watched Cyril Eisner's ship disappear into the distance, followed by his wingman Jace. She smiled. It felt good knowing someone in the universe cared without the need for compensation.

She went to the bathroom, locked the door, leaned on the edge of the sink, and stared at her reflection in the mirror. The bruise on her face had blackened, and her nose had swelled. She kept feeling like he was behind her or just outside the door, waiting and ready to strike. He was a phantom, haunting her.

"Fuck you, you motherfucker," she whispered to the mirror. She soaked a hand towel in cold water and sat in her seat again as she pressed the cold towel to her bruised face.

The two servants silently watched her.

The ship landed thirty minutes later at an Arcturus Allied private airfield. They disembarked, loaded a limousine with Layla and Brentwood's luggage, and drove to the city. The servants rode in a separate vehicle from her. Layla wanted privacy. A first call vehicle would arrive shortly after she left to retrieve Brentwood's body.

On the way home, Layla's cellphone buzzed. It was her brother. "Daniel," she said.

"I heard about Brentwood. Are you okay?"

"I'm fine. How did you find out so fast?"

"Courier service delivered paperwork from Gacrux a few hours ago. I saw the photos of the body. Sorry for your loss."

"Thanks," she said listlessly.

"Obviously, I know this isn't really the time, but we will need to think about the legal element of his death. The Foresters can be ruthless and may try to repossess all of Brentwood's assets. I can get my best—"

"Dan, I don't have the patience for this right now. I just want to be left alone."

"I understand that, but that's not how this works. Things are already in motion whether you like it or not. The cremation will be tomorrow. After that, we will have to settle ownership rights. The Foresters are one of our top donors. His father sits on my board of directors, for fuck's sake."

She expelled a long sigh. "Why can't you just stop thinking about business for five minutes? My husband just died on our wedding anniversary, and you're worried about your shareholders."

There was silence for a moment.

Daniel's voice changed. He dropped all the pretense and said, "I know Brentwood was a bastard. And I know he was a terrible husband—you don't have to pretend about that—but your marriage merged assets to give us leverage on the capital we needed to keep going. Without you, without him, we would still be beneath five other companies. You know Dad would be disappointed in both of us if we let this opportunity go to waste. I built this up for us. There are big plans ahead, and you're to thank for that. So, if Brentwood being a little confrontational at times with you was somehow damaging, then I need you to hear this: shrug it off and suck it up. You're a big girl, you're a Mullarkey, and you're my sister. You're better than your pain.

And I will not let five years' worth of work on our upcoming project go down the drain just because you need a good cry. Get it out of your system and show up tomorrow for the cremation at noon. I'll send the details to your email. Hope you feel better. Get some rest." Daniel ended the call.

The soft hum of the road grew louder in Layla's ears. She felt like crying. She felt like screaming. She felt like she needed something to punch or to kick or to choke or to shoot—no matter who or what it was. Brentwood's ghost felt like it was leaning on her, suffocating her. Daniel was always about business. Personal attachments only extended as far as there was something to gain. She inhaled and exhaled, over and over, till they finally reached home, a high-rise penthouse for only the most privileged. It ascended thirty stories and had a flat rooftop, with an infinity pool extending over the edge. Each apartment below had its own outcropped balcony. The servants unloaded the car and followed Layla to the top floor.

Maids had recently cleaned the apartment, and the fresh scent of pine permeated the air. The servants followed her and dropped the suitcases to the side of a massive circular room, with a small two-step staircase down to a circular couch. Glass windows adorned the western wall, a one-hundred-inch flat screen hung on the northern wall, and an all-white cabinet kitchen with marble flooring lay at the end of a short hallway to the south. Gorgeous bedrooms faced the east.

"Thank you. I'd like to be alone," she said to them.

They quietly left.

Layla stood at the balcony window. The gray sky hid the sun, but shafts of golden light pierced through the clouds from time to time. She wandered around, looking at various photos on the walls and on shelves. Brentwood still loomed large over her. He was in almost every photo with her. She flipped down every photo and deleted all digital photos from any wall screen. His eyes still seemed to be watching. She locked the apartment door and switched her phone to Airplane Mode. Anything she could do to be disconnected and to get eyes off her. She got into bed and tried to think of nothing. A few minutes passed, then she slid from under the sheets and crawled underneath the bed. She lay there, gripping the carpet, till she fell asleep. The bruise on her face throbbed the whole time.

***

Cyril didn't know where he was. Rows of spherical LED lights glowed brightly overhead. His shoulder throbbed, and his skull was pounding too. Cyril looked left at a beeping EKG machine, and to his right was an IV drip running into his arm.

"Fuck, this is gonna be expensive," were the first words he groaned to himself. He looked around, found a call button, and pressed hard.

A few moments later, a black-haired nurse entered, wearing blue scrubs.

"Did I pass out?" he asked.

"Your cab arrived with you unconscious. It wouldn't leave until you got out, so it sat out front for a few minutes. We hauled you in and got you into emergency surgery."

"Surgery?"

She took a data pad off the wall and handed it to him. It showed a digital version of his body, with his wound highlighted in red. There wasn't just a slash. Small dots peppered around the wound.

"Whatever caused that laceration also infected it with necro mites," she said.

"The hell is that?" he said, still disoriented.

"It's a parasite that feeds off flesh, causing necrotizing fasciitis. Basically, your skin and muscle tissue were rotting away. Also, I need to get a full history from you now that you're up."

Cyril handed back the data pad. She typed his answers as they reviewed his basic history: birth date, home address, allergies, family relations, work history, et cetera.

"What caused the laceration, Mr. Eisner?"

"A bird."

"A bird?" she asked, with a raised eyebrow.

"A very big bird. I was on Gacrux for the last three days. Private security. We got swarmed by birds and bugs on the way back to our homebase. One of them dive-bombed me and got a good swipe in. Just lucky, I guess."

"Well, it seems what slashed you was carrying parasites on its talons. Parasites like that transfer from host to host. If you had made it here an hour later, you'd have been DOA. The surgeons washed out the parasites and closed your wound. Another day in here and you should be good to go."

"Well, that's good news."

"Anything I can get you, Mr. Eisner?"

"Yeah, my phone and my jacket. Also, I had a suitcase in the cab."

She retrieved his personals from the closet opposite his bed. He located his blue credit card payment from Gacrux and used his phone to upload full payment to his account. Whatever the bill would be for his hospital stay, he'd at least have something in savings. He handed his jacket to the nurse, and she returned it to the closet.

"Anything else?" she asked.

"Water, please. With ice." Just thinking about Gacrux made him sweat.

"I'll be right back."

"Thanks."

He checked his phone again. His shoulder felt tight and throbbed when he tried to lift his left arm, so he had to use his right hand to type. His notifications were off the charts. Multiple messages from Jace, an inquiry from Arcturus Allied about the incident on Gacrux—so much that he cleared everything else and answered personal messages. He let Jace know he was in the hospital. He also messaged Jess the same info. The nurse returned with a large cup of ice water, and Cyril sucked it down within seconds. She went to the restroom, refilled the cup, and placed it on the bedside tray table. He thanked her as she left the room.

With nothing else to do, he stared off into space. *No more jobs for rich bastards. This shit isn't worth it.*

***

Layla awoke at midnight. The apartment was pitch black and silent. She crawled from under the bed and sat on its edge. The moment of misery and depression had mostly passed. She used the bathroom, then washed off her makeup. Her eyes were still red from crying, and the bruise was purple. Everyone would see the bruise in the morning during the cremation, her family as well as her in-laws, and would probably ask, *What do you think she did to deserve it?* But that was her brain thinking too far ahead. Still twelve hours were left till she had to see Brentwood one last time before he was a pile of ash.

She lay on the circular couch and scrolled through her messages, email, social media, internet videos, everything to waste time, since she wasn't tired enough to go back to bed. Then she scrolled through her contacts and saw a new name: Cyril Eisner. She was wondering how he was after his injury. Late or not, it would be worth at least one message, so she texted.

> LAYLA: Hello, Mr. Eisner. It's Layla Forester. I was just messaging to check in on you after your injury. I hope you're doing well. I can see if Arcturus can help cover medical bills if necessary.

She set down her phone, then got an immediate reply. She grabbed her phone, its screen now the only light in the apartment.

> CYRIL: Hey there. I'm in the hospital right now. Had to have surgery. Almost died.
> LAYLA: Died?! Oh no, I'm so sorry for all this.
> CYRIL: It's fine. I was doing my job. You don't have to apologize for anything.
> LAYLA: Still, I feel responsible. This is my fault.
> CYRIL: It's not. It's really not. Just bad luck. Wanna hear something gross?
> LAYLA: I guess. Why not?
> CYRIL: Apparently, the bird that slashed me, its talons were carrying parasites called necro mites which cause necrotizing fasciitis. Basically, for about twelve hours, my flesh was being eaten and rotting. Gross, huh?
> LAYLA: That's horrific.
> CYRIL: You bet it is.
> LAYLA: I thought you might be asleep right now. Why are you up?
> CYRIL: Pain. Shoulder hurts. I gotta be here another day. Just watching funny videos online.
> LAYLA: Send me some. I could use a laugh.
> CYRIL: Sure. Coming right up.

They exchanged funny internet videos for the next twenty minutes—animals falling over, people doing dumb shit. They both laughed so much they'd forgotten their pain, both physical and mental.

LAYLA: I really should try to sleep. Brentwood's cremation is
    tomorrow.
CYRIL: Fuck that guy. You're better than him.
LAYLA: LOL I don't know about that. But thank you.
CYRIL: Hey, do me a solid tomorrow?
LAYLA: What?
CYRIL: Shit in the urn.
LAYLA: OMG no! LOLOLOL
CYRIL: Good night, Layla.
LAYLA: Goodnight, Mr. Eisner.
CYRIL: Please call me Cyril.
LAYLA: Right. Good night, Cyril.

She set down her phone, curled up on the couch, and fell asleep again. She slept without dreams.

The next morning, the sun blasted through the windows, making everything orange. She roused from her sleep, hair a mess. Her phone battery had died overnight. She plugged it into the bedroom's outlet, then showered. She let the lava-temperature water pelt her skin and thought about nothing. Her feelings from yesterday would melt away under that heat. After fifteen minutes, she dried off and opened her phone again.

The details of Brentwood's cremation were in her email, as Daniel said they would be. Noon at the Kilbury Funeral Home. Daniel would be present, as would Douglas and Ilana Forester, Brentwood's parents. It would be a small service, to avoid extensive press coverage. She turned off her phone, put it on the charger to get it to 100 percent, then continued getting ready in the bathroom.

She covered the bruise on her face with concealer, then did up her hair, eyeliner, lipstick. The works. She chose whatever dark clothing from her closet that would be best suited—a black dress suit and white blouse with black heels. Simple and not much effort. She checked the clock—0930 hrs. She quickly ate a fruit breakfast and drank two cups of coffee in the kitchen. Afterward she brushed her teeth and grabbed her purse to leave. At 1015 hrs, she called her driver, Miles, to pick her up out front of the building.

As she left the apartment, she stood at the door and realized how quiet it was—no chatting on the phone, no blaring television, just silence. With that, she left and rode the elevator downstairs to her town car.

Miles opened the door. "Good morning, Mrs. Forester. I'm sorry for your loss."

"Thank you," she said flatly without looking at him.

She got in and texted Daniel that she was on the way. He didn't reply, but he read the message. The whole ride there, she stared out the window. She recalled all the times when Brentwood had been loving in the beginning, then how he had turned cruel. She had gone from his lover to his possession. He wasn't the only one in the past who had done that to her. Their anniversary had been a longshot to rekindle some joy between them—a longshot that didn't pay off. At that moment, hate replaced every ounce of love. Hate for his control. Hate for his abuse. Hate for his hate.

She opened her phone and reread her chat with Cyril Eisner from the previous night. Something he had written repulsed her the night before, but now it didn't seem like such a bad idea—*Shit in the urn*. It was disgusting, repulsive, and juvenile. It was better than Brentwood deserved. It made her chuckle. She wouldn't do that, but some kind of last-minute revenge was in order. What it would be, though, still eluded her.

I'll cross that bridge later, she thought and rode on in silence.

***

Cyril had been in and out of sleep all night. His shoulder throbbed. At 0300 hrs, he finally relented and asked the doctor to give him a sedative. He awoke at 1230 hrs, having had no dreams. His phone's notifications showed repeated messages from Jace and Jess, asking if he was okay and which hospital he was in. He replied and called the nurse.

"Hey, how much longer do I have to stay in here," Cyril asked as he forced himself to sit upright in bed.

"You'll be discharged later today once the doctor goes over a few things with you. I'll bring him in," the nurse said.

"Thanks." Cyril laid back down. His phone pinged. It was Jess saying she was on the way. His shoulder still hurt but nowhere nearly as bad as the previous day. Still, he groaned and grunted with a bandaged shoulder and destroyed pride. *A goddamn bird. For fuck's sake.*

The doctor, a middle-aged man with hair that was a little too perfect and with teeth a little too white, entered the room carrying a manila envelope, all smiles, and far too happy in the profession he had chosen. "Good morning, Mr. Eisner. I'm Doctor Heighline. How are you feeling this morning?"

"Like a can of smashed assholes, Doc," Cyril answered.

"You're lucky to be alive, Mr. Eisner. You were bleeding out in your cab yesterday."

"Ugh. A goddamn bird," Cyril whispered.

"I'm sure it was a big bird."

Cyril furrowed his brow and rolled his eyes. "When can I leave?"

"This afternoon. We need to run a few more tests, clean your wound again, and provide you some antibiotics in case of infection." He opened the envelope and placed a set of x-rays on a light board opposite the bed. The x-rays showed closeups of his shoulder, with black blobs surrounding the large slice. "You see, right here, in this area is where necro mites were feeding upon your muscle tissue. They eat the living tissue and redeposit it as waste in the wound to claim their territory. After a while, it turns gangrenes and smells. We caught it just in time and removed the parasites."

"Yeah, the nurse mentioned that last night. This just gonna leave a scar, or will there be anything permanent?"

"No long-term damage other than a scar. You're lucky. Though you will need a few weeks of physical therapy. And with your occupation, I would not recommend flying anywhere for a while."

"I gotta work, Doc."

"Not with that arm. Six weeks of bed rest plus physical therapy. You'll need to find something else to keep yourself going in the meantime."

"You're just a fortune cookie of advice, Doctor. You know that?"

"It's why I'm paid a hundred thousand a year, Mr. Eisner. The nurse will help get your medication in order. Enjoy your day." He repacked the x-rays into the envelope and left. Heighline never stopped smiling, which annoyed Cyril.

Cyril's phone pinged again. Jess had just parked and was on the way up. He laid back down and closed his eyes. With no way to fly, he had to find something to keep going during his six weeks off. With only one arm, it would need to be something simple. Desk work, retail, something to keep himself from dipping into savings. He started dozing off again just as Jess walked in.

"You could have died, and you don't call me right away?" she yelled. She was carrying a plastic bag filled with snacks and water.

"Good morning to you too," Cyril said.

She dropped the bag beside the bed, then slapped Cyril across the face. Not hard but enough to grab his attention. He recoiled, then she hugged him hard.

"You asshole. Don't ever do that again," she yelled as she squeezed him.

He winced in pain but hugged back. "I missed you too." He patted her back.

She finally let go and picked up the bag, then set out the contents on the table—some chips, fruit, and bottles of water.

"I'm getting out later today, but I'll take them anyway."

"So, what was it got you?"

"Got slashed by a bird on Gacrux, and apparently, its talons were carrying a flesh-eating parasite. Wanna see the scar?"

"Fuck yeah," she yelled with a huge smile.

Cyril peeled down his shoulder bandage to reveal a stitched slice, eight inches long from the back of his shoulder to his clavicle. He was lucky it had missed the bone.

"Oh, that's so wicked."

"God, you're fucking weird."

She smiled and stuck out her forked tongue.

He rolled the bandage into place and laid back. "Jace coming too?"

"He should be here soon."

"I'm already here," Jace said, walking in. He still looked exhausted from the day before.

"Wow, that's perfect timing," Cyril said.

"I would have driven you yesterday. You could have just asked if it was that bad."

Cyril shrugged. "Eh, sorry."

Jess smacked his bandaged shoulder. He yelped. "Sorry? What is wrong with you?"

"Stop hitting me!"

"You kinda deserved that one." Jace laughed.

"I'm the one in the bed. Why am I the whipping boy?"

"Because you could have died, Cyril," Jess said, highly annoyed.

He shrugged again and rolled his eyes. Jace snatched a banana off Cyril's tray and sat by the window. Jess opened one of the bottles of water and took a sip.

Cyril said, "So, I'll be out of work for the next six weeks. No flying. And I'll need physical therapy. If either of you have any leads on something part time, I'll take it."

"I can talk to the manager at the Guggenheim where I usually play. See if they need someone for ticket sales," Jess said. "Super easy, you're in a chair all day, boring, but it's something."

"I get to be lazy. Fantastic," Cyril said.

Jess chuckled and sat beside Cyril.

"You could probably go work at M&M too. I'm sure Stacy needs some help with her back log of paperwork," Jace said as he peeled the banana.

"That's not a bad idea. Also gives me a chance to flirt with her a bit more," Cyril said, smiling.

"Wh-Why do you do that?" Jace asked as he bit into his banana.

"Do what?"

"Take every chance to flirt with or hit on anything that walks past you. Seriously, what was the longest relationship you've ever had?"

Cyril rolled his eyes upward and thought about it. "Probably eleven months," he said sheepishly.

"And since then, you jump from person to person, fling after fling. You really need to stop that," Jace mumbled with a mouthful of fruit.

"I don't have time for relationships. I'm freelance, and so are you."

"But I make it work," Jace said, having finally swallowed. "I intentionally take time off. And Jess knows this too. She does what we do, and she writes music, and she performs, but she still finds time for a real life."

"I mean, I'm still single as fuck right now, but he's right, Cyril. You really do look at women as just objects. You gotta stop that. We gave you a pass on that redhead because goddamn. But that was the last free pass."

"I do not look at them as objects. And I'm-I'm bi, just like the rest of you. I—" Cyril stopped mid-sentence, realizing it was a losing battle. "Okay, I'll … work on it."

"Good," Jess said. "Did you call that therapist, like I told you to?"

Cyril sighed. "No."

Jess raised her hand.

"Stop it!"

"Why didn't you call? You need to get some help for that issue with your dad."

Cyril was quiet for a moment. "Well, if you want the morbid answer, I didn't know if I'd come back from Gacrux. If I died out there, what would have been the point of making an appointment?"

Jess and Jace were silent and dumbfounded. Finally, Jace flatly said, "You are a fucking moron."

"I can't win today, can I?"

"Yeah, because you refuse to play the game correctly," Jess said.

"What does that mean? This isn't a game; this is my life."

"Brother, we care about you, but we can't help you if you don't help yourself," Jace said, leaning forward in his chair.

The air felt like it had gone stale, or like it had been sucked out of the room. Cyril looked at Jace, then at Jess, then back to Jace. The silence was deafening.

Finally, Cyril sighed. "All right, I'll call him."

"And I'm gonna drive you to your first appointment," Jess said assertively.

"Okay, fine. I'll call him now. Gimme the number," Cyril said as he grabbed his phone, but it pinged in his hand—Layla. Cyril scrunched his face, then opened his messages to read the single sentence.

LAYLA: I'm not gonna shit in the urn, but I have an idea that's pretty good.

Cyril scoffed, then chuckled.

Jess and Jace looked at him, confused. Jace asked, "What's so funny?"

"Heh, nothing," Cyril said, then dialed the therapist's number Jess had recommended.

***

The town car slowed to a stop outside the funeral home roundabout. A small assembly of press and drone cameras floated around the doorway, ready to press for statements. The funeral home was a very traditional building—two stories, classic brick and mason, white roof, pillars out front flanking the doorway. Miles opened the passenger side door. Layla stepped into the crisp midday air and donned her sunglasses. The press immediately hounded her, waving handheld mics, and drone cameras flew a little too close, getting right in her face, like a pack of flies. She swatted away the cameras, pushed through the crowd, and went inside. The questions asked were all the same. "How do you feel about your husband's passing?" "What are your plans now?" "Could you tell us what happened?" All the same talking points scraping for a headline.

As she entered, the air went cold and dry.

The receptionist, a young, handsome Skovian, greeted her. "Mrs. Forester, your family is just down the hallway, waiting for you."

She proceeded down the hallway, turned left, and saw the members of her immediate family waiting outside the morgue entrance. As she approached, she removed her sunglasses.

Daniel was the first to notice the concealer-covered bruise on her face. He cupped her chin and turned her face side to side. "Eh, it's not that bad." His hand, like the rest of his body, was enormous. He towered over her. He was more than six feet tall and round like a barrel but all muscle. The opposite of the stereotype businessman.

"Thanks," she said.

To her left were Brentwood's father and mother, Douglas and Ilana. Douglas was tall and lanky, with thin gray hair and glasses. He wore a blue suit and tie. Ilana looked like a woman desperate to hold on to her youth, with enough plastic surgery to float in the ocean. Brown hair, green eyes, facelift followed by Botox injections. She wore a suit like Layla and carried an oversized purse. Neither she nor Douglas particularly liked Layla. She was more tolerated than liked by them. They believed Brentwood could have done better and felt the marriage may have been some kind of ploy to bring the two families, the Mullarkeys and the Foresters, together for financial reasons. Despite their grievances, they greeted Layla.

"We're glad you could be here with us," Douglas lied.

"He was my husband. I'll miss him," she fibbed. *He was an asshole.* Layla was surprised only the four of them were there. "Is it just the four of us? Where's everyone else?"

"We're keeping this as low profile as possible," Daniel said, "The press is already enjoying the fact that Brentwood died in such an embarrassing manner."

"How did that get out to the press?" she asked anxiously.

"Apparently, one of the people retrieving the body yesterday took photos of the coroner's report from Gacrux. It got leaked online when the body returned. You haven't been keeping up?"

"I haven't really felt the need to relive the last few days."

"My son was a brave man. It was an accident," Douglas said.

No, he was a coward, Layla thought.

"Well, let's go see Brentwood, then. He can tell us all about it," Daniel said.

Douglas and Ilana scowled as he passed to enter through a set of double doors which led to the back area. The rest followed his lead. The mortician was just beyond the double doors, filing paperwork. She led them to the crematorium through a winding set of hallways. The smell of the building went from zero to one hundred in a single door swing. The pungent odor of chemicals was a stench no one would ever forget once it entered their nostrils. It was too clean, with no feeling of life.

They rounded a curved hallway and saw Brentwood's body lying on a mesh metal grating in front of a stainless-steel oven. He wore a suit and tie, but his body was still clearly mangled. His torso, having been crushed, was misshapen, and his skull had an obvious fracture in it. A mortician had inserted an implant into his skull to reform it to look somewhat normal. Layla didn't know what the point of all that effort was.

The mortician handed Douglas a clipboard with paperwork to clear the final disposal of Brentwood's body. He signed it, as did Ilana and Layla. Daniel stood to the side behind them. Ilana kissed her son's forehead one last time and whispered something in his left ear. Douglas said nothing. No emotion on his face. Layla stood there, waiting her turn to say something. Ilana stepped away.

Layla stepped forward to stand above Brentwood's head. She pondered what she should say—something hateful, something filled with pity, or nothing at all. Finally, she leaned down and whispered into his right ear, "This is better than you deserve." Then she stepped backward.

With words spoken, the mortician stepped in front of the grating and grabbed the handles. She slid the grating into the oven, then shut and locked the door. She opened the ventilators and turned a valve, filling the oven with gas, which then became flames. The snap-crackle-pop of the fire charring Brentwood's body made Ilana wretch and cry.

As Douglas escorted Ilana toward the main hallway, Daniel spoke without turning. "I hope this doesn't ruin our business partnership in the future. There's a lot of plans moving forward that I would hate to see flushed down the drain."

Douglas said nothing and moved on with Ilana.

Layla watched every moment of Brentwood burning in front of her. She wished it had a window so she could see his broken body finally disintegrate into ash.

The mortician said, "Ma'am, this will take about an hour. We'll bring you the ashes once it's finished."

"I know. I want to watch this," Layla said softly.

The mortician shrugged and left the room. Nothing but the sound of the oven burning filled the space.

"Sorry for your loss," Daniel said, then walked out.

"No, you're not," she said to no one. She found a rolling chair at the side of the room, pulled it over, and sat to enjoy the show.

Sometime later, the mortician returned. Layla still sat there, transfixed on the metal door, ready to see the results. The mortician closed the valve, unlocked the door, donned a set of gloves, and opened the oven. Only a pile of gray ashes rested beneath the metal grating.

She picked up a silver urn, with a large vacuum tube connected to the top. She flipped the switch and vacuumed the ashes. Two minutes later, she had collected Brentwood into the urn.

The mortician popped off the tube, added a twist-on lid, and handed the urn to Layla. "Sorry for your loss."

"Why does everyone keep saying that? *I'm* not sorry," she said sternly.

The mortician noticed the concealed bruise on Layla's face and understood what Layla meant.

Layla began to leave but stopped. She turned to face the mortician. "Is there a bathroom nearby?"

"Follow me."

They traversed a new set of hallways farther into the building to a spacious employee restroom. The walls were flat white, and the linoleum floor was extra clean. Layla closed and locked the door. A large countertop sink stood beside a tropical potted plant surrounded by sand instead of soil, and a freshly cleaned toilet rested to the left. She placed the urn on the countertop and opened her phone messages to text Cyril: *I'm not gonna shit in the urn, but I have an idea that's pretty good.*

She sent the message and picked up the urn. She unscrewed the lid and stepped in front of the toilet. She turned the urn sideways, and all of Brentwood's ashes fell into the bowl. They floated on top, slowly absorbing the water. As the bowl turned milky gray, she set the urn on the countertop. Right before she was about to flush, she had another idea. She dropped her pants and sat. The morning coffee went right through her.

Once finished, she stood, buttoned up, and reached for the handle. Through gritted teeth, she growled, "Farewell, you sonofabitch," and flushed. He swirled in the bowl, round and round, till he finally went down. And thus ended the pathetic existence of Brentwood Forester, abuser and well-known corporate shill.

With a sense of relief, she grabbed the urn and began to walk out, then realized a slight issue. Nothing remained inside. What if someone looked out of curiosity? She would be the first person they would ask. Then she smiled at the potted plant. She snatched handfuls of sand and filled the urn to about halfway. To the uninformed, no one could tell the difference. Problem solved. She cleaned the countertop of any residual sand and washed her hands, then walked into the hallway.

The mortician was waiting. They smiled at each other and returned the way they had entered. The family still waited outside. Daniel and Douglas discussed business, while Ilana sat in a chair next to the righthand wall. Ilana had stopped crying but looked exhausted and defeated.

Layla presented the urn to Ilana. "Sorry for your loss." She struggled to stifle a laugh.

Daniel and Douglas eyed Layla, but she said nothing and left the building.

The press was still outside, waiting to pounce on whoever left first. Camera drones flew high above the building and filled the air with the sound of buzzing bees. She pushed through the crowd. They were still asking the same questions.

As Miles opened the passenger door, one person asked, "Do you have any thoughts at all about how this will affect your family business going forward?"

Like a rubber band twisted around too many times, something inside her snapped. She turned to face the reporter and removed her glasses. Using her jacket's left sleeve, she wiped away the concealer covering her bruise. "You see this? He did this! My husband was an abusive piece of shit, and I don't give a fuck how this affects my family's business. I don't care! I'm glad he's gone, and I'm not sorry for saying that." She turned to her driver. "Miles, get me the fuck out of here."

In a rush, they got into the car and locked the doors. The window was crowded with people yelling and asking for further comments. She stared forward and kept quiet.

As the car pulled away, the camera drones followed. They pursued for a short time before finally trailing off. As they drove, she texted Cyril. A two-word sentence. *Mission accomplished.* He responded with a poop emoji. She chuckled and replied with the closest image she could find that represented urine: a glass of lemonade, with an umbrella on the rim.

Chapter 5

Time to Heal

"Oh God, fuck my fucking ass," Cyril groaned.

It was week two of physical therapy. Three days a week, a therapist would stretch, pull, massage, and exercise Cyril's shoulder in weird ways to rebuild the nerve endings and muscle tissue. On the off days, he would wear his arm in a sling. Being injured was dreadfully boring and, at that moment, painful. His shoulder would feel like a throbbing tennis ball each morning, and a good night's sleep still eluded him. But he attended every required session. If he wanted to fly again, he would suffer for it. A shot of fire surged through his shoulder blade and across his chest as his physical therapist lifted and stretched his arm to his side and rotated it.

Various pieces of exercise equipment and therapy devices, like Bose balls, treadmills, free weights, parallel bars, etc., filled the sterile white and extremely cold room. The space had no smell, unlike a standard gym drenched in sweat, heat, and body odor. They required him to lift a certain amount of weight and to stretch himself properly before he was finished for the day. Begrudgingly, he let the therapist do her job, despite the torturous levels of pain. Later that afternoon, he'd deal with another form of pain—the other mandated therapy. Jess would hound him about it if he didn't attend that one.

The day after the hospital had discharged Cyril, Jess had driven him to his first mental health therapy session. Doctor Minese came highly recommended, and Jess had forced him to go. During the session, she sat in the waiting room, listening to music, while Cyril had recounted his full personal history.

*****

Doctor Minese was bald, a bit lanky, but had a kind face, glasses, and a goatee. Session one was all small talk, a simple means of getting to know him, understanding him as a person, before the heavy stuff later.

Minese finally asked a big question. "Do you understand why you're here, Cyril?"

"Because I'm fucked up, I guess."

"Well, there's all kinds of ways to be fucked up, but it's about figuring out what kind and how much."

"I'm gonna guess a lot if I'm being forced to be here."

"No one's forcing you to be here. Your friend in the waiting room cares about you and wants to see you get well. You didn't fight coming here, did you?"

"No."

"Then I think that's a good first step."

On the drive home, Cyril was silent while Jess drove. When they reached Cyril's apartment, he said, "Thanks for putting up with my bullshit."

She rubbed his cheek. "You're an asshole, but we'll work on it. Now get outta my car."

They smiled at each other, and he got out.

Two weeks later, as they wrapped and twisted Cyril's arm, because it was for his own good, he hated life. The room contained mostly elderly people, except for one olive-skinned woman who wore a hospital gown, had long reddish-brown hair and a sharp yet inviting face, and sported a wrap on her left foot as she used the parallel bars with assistance. Cyril had seen her there a few times but hadn't said anything, as there was never a moment. The setting was not exactly appropriate for chitchat. She was beyond cute. She was gorgeous. Even with a disheveled appearance from staying in the hospital, she was a knockout

Watching her relearn how to walk kept him occupied while the therapist worked on his arm. He was curious how she had broken her foot—bad fall, crushed in an accident, attacked by someone? If nothing else, it might be worth saying hello. Jess and Jace had called him out a few weeks ago for his mistreatment of women. Here was his chance to avoid that and actually get to know someone. Not a fling, a real thing. Even his therapist had drawn attention to it during his most recent session.

Minese had stated, *"You feel drawn to simple flings because you are afraid of commitment. You're afraid of being hurt or of being abandoned if they leave, so you jump from person to person for simple fun. And there's also the issue with your parents. You haven't settled your childhood trauma, so you find solace in immediate gratification."* The truth was like an ice pick through the heart. But it *was* the truth.

"All right, two o'clock. That's our time, Mr. Eisner." The physical therapist released his arm.

Cyril slipped his arm into his sling, used his other arm to point across the room, and whispered, "Hey, who's she?"

"I don't know. Another patient. Why?"

"No reason. Just curious." Cyril collected his jacket and personal items from the wall locker.

The red-haired woman was still working at the bars. She had reached one end, had turned around, and was returning to the opposite side.

Cyril watched her for a moment before he realized he was staring. He broke his gaze, slung his jacket over his shoulder, and headed for the door. As he passed the bars, he snuck one final glance, and she looked up to see him leaving. Her deep green eyes locked on his gaze for half a second before he broke away.

As he left the building, he called for an autocab. It pulled up to the roundabout within minutes of his request and started to drive him across town to his next appointment. The traffic was heavy in the afternoon as everyone filtered out of work. He stared out the window at a pair of unfamiliar starfighters flying by overhead. He sighed, then stopped looking out the window. It killed him to be unable to fly. An agonizing penalty for a dumb mistake. *Fucking bird*, he thought.

The cab arrived at his therapist's office. He exited and bumped into one of the many pedestrians on the crowded sidewalk rushing to get home as the sun set. He pushed through the crowd toward the block-shaped three-story office building set between a department store and a coffee shop, which somehow felt like a wicked cliché. He pressed the elevator call button and went to the third floor. He turned left and walked a few paces to enter the simple wooden office door adorned with a centered translucent window. He used a data pad to sign into the receptionist-less waiting room. Soft music played, along with the sound of a flowing stream, to sooth the patients before the therapists tackled the crazed personal problems. He imagined Jess in the waiting room two weeks earlier, listening to death metal, while browsing her social media. It gave him a slight chuckle as he sat and waited.

He texted a photo of himself in the waiting room, giving the middle finger, to Jess and Jace to confirm he was there, otherwise he wouldn't hear the end of it. After they replied quickly, he put away his phone and waited. The stream sound was quite calming. He imagined himself sitting next to a rushing river on a warm seventy-degree cloudless day—maybe even sitting next to someone he liked. Maybe that woman he had seen at physical therapy. Her face was forever burned into his memory. *Who was she?*

Minese opened his office door to allow Cyril to sit on his usual spot at the end of the gray leather couch next to the wall. Sitting in the middle felt weird. Wall-hanging paintings, journals and textbooks on floating shelves, and a small clock secured on the wall opposite the door furnished the office. Minese sat in a brown leather chair, with a high back and padded headrest, across from Cyril. A data pad rested in his lap for notes.

Minese opened Cyril's file. "So, how's life treating you?"

Cyril raised his slung arm as much as he could. "Well, still grounded obviously."

"But the physical therapy is going okay?"

"So far, yeah. Still not sleeping well."

"I can tell. You've got circles around your eyes." Minese waved his pointer finger around his eyes.

"I've always had circles," Cyril said flatly.

"They're much more pronounced this week."

"If I keep it up, I'll pass for a raccoon."

They both chuckled.

"But seriously, how are you feeling this week?" Minese asked again yet much more direct.

"I mean, being grounded, not working, not doing much. It's depressing. But I'm doing okay, I suppose." Cyril looked out the window at another passing starfighter and sighed.

"You know, Cyril, it's okay to do nothing. You don't have to constantly be on the go, go, go. You can just stop and enjoy things."

"What I enjoy is work."

"I disagree. I think what you enjoy is distraction."

"How so?"

"Well, when you're not working, what are you doing?"

"At the bar, playing games, maybe doing some reading."

"And trying to hook up with random people. So, nothing necessarily constructive."

After a long pause, Cyril replied, "I suppose not. But I'm not exactly the creative type."

"I didn't mean you had to create something but maybe put in some time to do things that disconnect from the electronic world. There's a whole galaxy out there, and you tend to stay at home."

"It's a simple life. Away from bullshit."

"Life is bullshit, Cyril."

Cyril raised an eyebrow. "That's not exactly the kind of statement I expected to hear."

Minese made a note. "Life is ultimately a series of small great moments surrounded by a mountain of bullshit. It's how you find those events that change your perspective on bullshit. If all you do is keep wading through the bullshit, you'll never find the small moments."

They both fell quiet. Cyril scanned the room. He hated making eye contact when someone was right about his life choices. The clock's hands ticked by. Ten minutes had passed. Fifty more to go.

"Tell me, what was the last great small moment you experienced? And you can't mention anything work related."

Cyril thought long and hard. It had been so long since one of those small moments actually happened. Random hookups were fun, but they happened so often that they didn't mean much. Outside of work, life was generally boring. Despite his career choice, his personal life was generally a drag. Not much to speak of. Except for—

"Anything at all, Cyril. Pick a moment. Any moment." Minese spread his arms high and wide, speaking louder with his hands than his voice.

"Well… there is one thing. I don't know if you'd call it a moment, but it's something."

"Okay, that's a start. Let's hear it."

"It was today actually. I was at physical therapy, and there was this woman there. I'd seen her before but have never said anything. We still haven't said anything. But she's drop-dead gorgeous. Red hair, green eyes, cute face. Totally out of my league. But as I was walking out, we locked eyes for a split second, and I could swear she smiled at me. I don't know for certain, maybe I'm misremembering, but that moment felt good. I don't really know why, but it felt good."

"*Hmm.* Could I venture a guess?"

"I mean, that's what I'm paying you for, so why not?"

"I think you are falling into your old pattern and nothing more. You're looking at this woman, whose name you don't even know, and thinking if this is another chance at a fling, a hookup, a one-night stand, or whatever, and once you've satisfied that urge, you'll forget she exists."

Cyril stayed quiet for a moment. "I pay you too much."

"Am I wrong though?"

"I mean…" The room went silent again. Cyril heard the distant sounds of the stream from the waiting room and wished he was anywhere but there. He sighed. "Maybe. I don't know."

"Then you need to really ask yourself if this is the same old Cyril, or are you really going to try to do something different? Because, I'm sorry, you can't do both."

Cyril fiddled with his fingers and scratched an imaginary itch on his left cheek. He was at a loss. The woman was nameless and for all he knew a complete bitch, but she was gorgeous and had caught his attention. He had invented a scenario where he would approach her, they would flirt and grab a drink, and who knew where it would go from there. But, in that office, his therapist had used Cyril's past behavior to back him into a corner.

"You asked me for a small great moment. To me, that was one," Cyril finally answered bluntly.

"Then I think you need to find a way to build on that moment and not to create a mountain of bullshit surrounding it."

Cyril hated that Minese was right. He checked the clock again. Only another five minutes had passed. The session was beginning to feel like an eternity.

***

The sun was setting. Rain clouds were rolling in. The humidity was up as well. Cyril left the office just as the first few drizzles came down and feeling worse than when he'd arrived, and his arm throbbed again. *I thought therapy was supposed to make me feel better.* He stopped in the coffee shop next door to buy a drink—always a large cup to fuel his caffeine addiction. He sat next to a window and watched the passersby. That part of town at that time of day had streets bustled with life, even as the rain began to fall. A pair of Skovians conversed across the street, a young man and a Crecian walked arm-in-arm past the window, and a Mukarian waited for a cab. Cyril always marveled at the bulky and large humanoid size of Mukarian arms. Crecians were the opposite, standing usually barely over five feet, with large eyes yet small bodies. The world rolled on as Cyril sat in the shop.

He tapped his fingers on the table and sipped his drink. His brain was still processing the session, like a part of his body was stuck in there, still being put through the ringer. He shrugged it off and retrieved his phone. Beads of rain battered the window like gunfire. He opened his email and saw a job offer. He declined it with a statement that he was on medical leave. He perused a few messages from Jess and Jace of funny videos and pictures. Jess had sent him a reminder to be at the Guggenheim in ninety minutes for his shift. He had accepted a cashier job. It wasn't much, but it brought in grocery money and got him out of the house. He sent a simple reply, put down the phone, then resumed staring out the window.

Maybe there was validity to what Minese had said about burying himself in work, sex, and entertainment to distract from his problems. Escaping his father and building himself from nothing had been a long, hard road. Why shouldn't he enjoy the freedom to do as he pleased? He was still young; life was far ahead of him. Therapy felt like a waste, but he did it for Jess and Jace. Losing their friendship would be devastating. So, every week, he'd grit his teeth and go for his hour and see what came out of his system, if anything. At some point, they would address issues with his father. He knew a catastrophic explosion would happen when that discussion began. There weren't enough swear words in the human language to fully encapsulate his feelings.

Contemplating mental breakdowns, he texted Layla. She was in hiding, as her public meltdown from two weeks prior had gone viral across the system. He sent a simple *Hi* and put down the phone. The streets cleared as the rain blitzed the streets. Several people rushed into the coffee shop from desperation, soaked to the bone, then his phone pinged.

> LAYLA: Hey.
> CYRIL: You doing okay? Just checking on you.
> LAYLA: Yeah, I'm okay. I haven't really gone out much or anything.
> CYRIL: I understand.
> LAYLA: Daniel and everyone at Arcturus are a little pissed at me.
> CYRIL: You don't owe them anything. You were right to call out your husband as a creep. Fuck him.
> LAYLA: Yeah.
> CYRIL: It'll blow over. Also, I haven't forgotten your offer for work. I'm currently on medical leave. Arm is in a sling. I can't fly for another month.
> LAYLA: If you'd like to meet with someone at Arcturus, I can send a message. That will at least get you on the freelance call list.
> CYRIL: Sure. The hospital kind of ate through my funds, and I'm just doing something simple to keep busy. I'll take anything.
> LAYLA: I'll see what I can do.
> CYRIL: Appreciate it. I gotta go now. I have work in a little over an hour. Helping a friend at a club tonight.
> LAYLA: Stay safe.
> CYRIL: You too.

He downed the remainder of his coffee in one gulp and called for an autocab. When it pulled up outside, he dashed through the downpour and jumped into the back seat. The cab pulled away and U-turned. On a normal day, the drive across town was a solid forty-five minutes. Due to the rain and traffic, he arrived twenty minutes ahead of his shift.

The Guggenheim was a dive, no doubt. Rundown, rusty steel, black walls and ceiling, and a bartender who didn't measure drinks and always overcharged, but ticket prices were low, and the bands were local. It was perfect for the young crowd looking to unload some anger. Not his kind of scene, but he admired it from afar behind the ticket counter.

He removed his jacket and went backstage. Jess and her band, Unwavered, were still setting up for the show. She was screaming into a mirror to prep her voice. Makeup caked her face, and her hair was in two pigtails. She wore a black tank top, with black pants that had straps and chains around the waistline. She spotted him in the mirror, turned around, and ran to hug him. She once again squeezed too hard. Cyril winced.

"Sorry," she said as she released.

Cyril shrugged.

"So how was your thing today?" she asked.

"Fine, I guess."

She raised an eyebrow, which meant he needed to keep talking.

"All right, we talked about how I don't really commit enough to things. I gotta work on that."

"I'm just fucking with you. I know it's private."

"Oh. I thought you were gonna interrogate me or something."

"No, you're fine. I'm just glad you're finally going."

"Me too, I suppose. Oh, I got a lead on some work once I'm healed up. You know Arcturus Allied?"

"Who doesn't?"

"Well, I'm hopefully meeting with someone at the company to bring me on as a contractor soon. I'm burning through money for this hospital shit. I thought insurance was supposed to help you."

"They're all scams. You know that," she said, fixing her bangs.

Her bandmates yelled for her as they left the room.

"Time for soundcheck. See you later, babe." She sprinted from the room and onto the stage.

Cyril returned to the front counter and saw a line extended outside. He quickly took up his post to scan in attendees, take their credit information, and check IDs. It was tedious, monotonous, and overall boring, but it was work.

The lights dimmed, and the show began. Jess's band was second. First up was another local group called Toxify. Cyril was unimpressed. Nothing but screaming with no rhythm and no showmanship whatsoever. Even their attire was bland. Presenting oneself to a crowd was just as important as the music they played. In a word: shit. They performed three songs, then left the stage. The lively crowd only gave them mild applause, though probably from basic generosity. Unwavered was up next.

"Welcome to the Guggenheim, you fuckers," Jess screamed.

The crowd went wild and cheered.

Jess growled in a demonic voice, "Who's ready for pain?"

They cheered again, even louder.

Metal thrashed on the guitars, the drums hammered, and music echoed through the room. Cyril checked in people while half-watching. Definitely not his crowd, definitely not his music, but seeing Jess perform was a hell of a show. She pounded the stage, a performer at heart. Her small but muscular frame had a hell of a presence. Midway through the set, she raised a bag of fake blood, sliced it open, and doused herself for everyone to watch. Then she spit the blood all over the front row. Cyril recoiled in horror even though he knew it was fake. She screamed into the mic, looking like a murder victim, and the crowd ate it up.

The set ended, and they walked off stage. Afterward, two more bands took to the stage and played their sets. The fake blood made the stage slippery, and the singer of the next band ended up falling flat on his ass in the middle of his first song. He rolled with it as much as possible despite being clearly embarrassed. The last band played their set, then the crowd filtered out.

Cyril grabbed his jacket and went backstage again. Jess was freshly showered and chatted while enjoying some drinks with her band on a couch.

"Well, I'm out," Cyril said.

Jess stood and hugged him. "Get home safe. Text me when you're there."

"I will. Hell of a show. Where did you get the idea for the fake blood?"

Jess pointed to the stitches on his shoulder. "Right there. That was a wicked scar. I figured we could use some blood in our act."

"Glad my pain could be of service," he said sarcastically.

She hugged him again, and he left into the tapering rain. Once home, he plopped onto his couch, with a glass of water, and watched the rain. After such a loud evening, he needed a quiet night of easy music, dim lighting, and soft rain. The pitter patter on the window felt somewhat comforting. He sent Jess a text that he was home. She did not reply, which he expected at that time of night. He laid on the couch and let the rainfall carry him to sleep.

***

Daniel Mullarkey was not a nice man, but he was powerful, which, to him, meant he was not required to be nice. A burly beast ready to fight anyone who wanted to throw down, he had an aggression problem and held grudges. As a child, he would regularly get into fights, which lead to an esteemed boxing career for which he still maintained his physical size. He had fought twenty-six matches, and of those, only two were losses. But he still held a grudge for those two. He'd aspired to using his power to hunt down and eviscerate the two men who had beat him. He hated losing. He hated failing. It always added another grudge to his ever-growing list. And inside the glass penthouse suite atop Arcturus Tower, Daniel Mullarkey had a grudge against his sister Layla, who had humiliated him with her outburst and was creating fervor with his key investors.

He leaned against the high-ceiling window, his right palm pressed flat to the glass, his left hand holding a bourbon hi-ball. Raindrops streaked the window. The sound reverberated through the enormous office. Bits of furniture were strewn throughout. A massage chair, several couches and loveseats, and pieces of abstract art and marble sculptures added some much-needed variety. A rare and expensive dining set, comprised a four-meter-long black table and a single chair, composed of rare wood from Cygnus—commonly referred to as *Steelwood*, for its light weight but density that matched case-hardened steel—rested against the west side for the nights when Daniel would sleep at the office. He owned a second set at his home. Tall windows surrounded the black marble-floored room, which matched the dimensions of the building's foundation, with two glass elevators on the southside wall. A few meters from Daniel's desk hung a row of ten flat screens, with various bits of information regarding Arcturus's finances, stock reports, future projects, and open emails. One such screen included an email from Douglas Forester stating his intention to file a lawsuit for defamation of character should Daniel's sister not present a formal apology and retract her statement. Daniel had been attempting to reach Layla all day. She had refused his calls and texts. The drinking began soon after the fifth unanswered call.

He shot back the last bits of his drink and snarled at the sharp flavor. He approached his desk, composed of two stone marble columns at the edges of a glass top, with black backing. A touch pad was built into the desk. He typed in a set of numbers, and a video call began with his chief of security, Bentley.

Bentley was a portly man yet tall, though he was also a bit sketchy in appearance. He always appeared out of breath, red in the face, and like he had just masturbated in the public restroom. But he was solid at maintaining security throughout Arcturus Allied and its subsidiary companies on Proxima. As a family man, with a wife and a teenage son, he had taken the job at Arcturus purely for monetary reasons, not knowing anything about them. He was ex-law enforcement and had worked his way to lieutenant. Despite that, his subordinates felt he had a weird vibe and hated him. Years of grinding for a minuscule paycheck had finally broken him, and he had entered the private sector, applying for security jobs around Balamb. Every company had turned him away for an interview except for Arcturus Allied. His luck had finally turned when he met Daniel Mullarkey.

Daniel poured another glass of liquor. "Bentley, I know this is outside your jurisdiction, but I want you to go to my sister's apartment building and drag her broken ass right here, right now. Got it?"

"It's ten o'clock, though. She's probably asleep."

"Then wake her ass up! I gotta talk to her."

"You got it, boss."

The call ended, and Daniel took a seat as he waited for Layla to arrive.

An hour later, the elevator doors opened. Bentley stepped out, dragging Layla by the arm. She wasn't resisting, but Bentley felt the need to assert his power. No escape, no matter what. Daniel had removed his suit jacket and tie, and he had almost finished the bottle of bourbon, which had been full that afternoon.

Layla finally broke free from Bentley and stepped away from him. "What the fuck do you want, Dan? What's so goddamn important?"

Given his size, Daniel was adept at holding his liquor, though he was beginning to stumble. He leaned on the edge of his desk and pointed at the screen that displayed the open email. "Read that," he said and killed another glass. He went to pour what would be the final glass for the night while she read the email regarding defamation.

She turned around. "Yeah, I read this. I get the company emails too."

"Any thoughts?" Daniel nodded drunkenly.

"I am not apologizing for what I said," she whispered.

"Layla, this is not a debate. The future of Arcturus is dependent on what happens by tomorrow morning. They want you to recant everything you said. Say you were distraught or something, I don't care."

"We can weather this. This isn't the first time something like this has happened within any company."

"Not between the people at the top, though. Forester is threatening to pull out of our deal."

"Then find another!"

Daniel said nothing as he stared at her.

"Wait. He doesn't have something on you, does he?"

Daniel ran his finger around the rim of the glass as he turned to watch the rain.

"Oh, this is about saving your reputation while throwing me into the mud. I get it."

"A big investment is happening soon. I need Forester and the rest of the board on my side. He pulls out and says anything, we're all going tits-up. So just do the right thing and retract what you said."

"What does he have that's so important?"

"Need to know, and you don't need to know."

"This is my time to get what I want. And I just want to be alone. I'm not saying anything, and I will not apologize."

Rage burst from Daniel as he chucked his full glass across the room. It slammed into the window and shattered. Even Bentley was surprised and jumped. "*Yes, you fucking will*!" Daniel screamed in her face.

Layla froze; her legs turned to lead, and her feet were welded to the floor. She trembled and looked away. This wasn't the first time he'd done this, and it was just as terrifying as all the others.

He glared at her for a moment, then approached the window. The rain was still coming down. "You… will put together… a formal apology… and publicly state it live for everyone to see. Do you understand?"

She remained silent.

He spun around to face her. "*Do you understand?*"

"No, I won't!"

Daniel drunkenly marched toward her and grabbed her neck to strangle her. She grabbed his wrist with both hands and dug in her fingernails. Unfazed, he squeezed tighter. Bentley pulled Daniel away and dragged him toward the window.

Layla fell to the floor, hacking and coughing, straining to catch her breath, then raised her head. "He hit me. He hurt me. I'll never forgive him. And I'll never forgive you."

"You don't have to. You just have to do as you're told," Daniel said, breaking free from Bentley's grip.

He stumbled to the liquor cabinet to search for anything to drink. There was a half-finished bottle of vodka, but nothing to mix it with. He drank from the bottle anyway. "Do you think I didn't know he was awful to you? Of course I did. Everybody did. But bringing our two families together meant we were partners finally. The perfect merger, absolute control. And you just had to fuck all of that up because your feelings got hurt. What a waste. How the fuck are we related?" He took another swig of vodka and wiped his lips. "So, here's what's gonna happen. You're gonna go home, sleep it off, and tomorrow morning, you will show up here with a formal apology, and we will make all this go away, and everything will be right as rain. How does that sound? I'm the brains of this company, but you're the pretty face. So put on a smile and show it to the world. Everyone loves a good redemption story."

Layla felt stuck to the floor, as if she had become one with it. She looked at Bentley like he might save her, but that was wishful thinking. She sat there, time refusing to move. Daniel killed the remainder of the vodka and hurled the bottle in her direction. It exploded to her right. She recoiled and looked up at him. His eyes were bloodshot, and his face was red with anger.

Finally, she whispered, "Okay. I'll do it."

"Good. Now get the fuck outta here," he growled, then leaned on the window with both palms.

Bentley picked up Layla and dragged her toward the elevator even as she tried to walk.

"This is how business works, Layla," Daniel said. "You know this. Everyone must learn their place."

As the elevator doors closed, Layla collapsed to the floor and dry heaved. Bentley was at a loss, unsure what to do and hoping the elevator would move faster. When the doors opened, he waited for her to get to her feet. She rose and moved lethargically, step by step, toward the front entrance of the building. The lobby looked larger than normal. The tower's hollowed-out interior seemed to climb up and up forever. She felt so small in that enormous place. But she pushed through it, her legs feeling like bricks.

The autocab dropped her off at home, and when she entered her apartment, she crawled under the bed and cried.

***

Two weeks passed. The day was humid and muggy and miserable, but the heat felt good on Cyril's shoulder. While the physical therapist was required to work with Cyril a couple days a week, the doctor had requested he work out in the rehab center every day on his own time to rebuild muscle tissue and to maintain flexibility. Cyril was lifting light weights in the physical therapy gym when the red-haired woman came in wearing her boot. She looked just as gorgeous as the last time he had seen her. She removed her boot next to the parallel bars and walked slowly. Cyril occasionally snuck a glance.

She took it slow to not put too much pressure on her broken foot. She winced a little, but she pushed forward and reached the end of the bars. She turned and walked in the opposite direction. Cyril swapped his weights for resistance bands. He lifted outward to his side in a repetitive motion as he watched the red-haired woman repeat her trajectory along the bars.

"Achilles tendon?" he asked.

She eyed him. "What gave you that idea?"

"Intuition."

"Well, aren't you smart?"

"I have my moments."

She reached the end of the bars. "And what happened to you?"

"Got attacked by a bird."

She stopped walking and regarded him with furrowed brows.

"It was a big bird," he sheepishly said.

"That must've been exciting. For the bird, I mean."

"You have no idea. What about you?"

"I… fell."

Cyril made a note of her hesitation and pocketed it away for another day. "*Mm.* But you're back on your feet now. Kind of."

"Getting there. Still have a couple weeks left to heal." She reached the starting point again, then sat in a chair to take a break. She grabbed a bottle of water and snapped open the top.

"Same. I'm totally out of work till my arm is healed up." Cyril switched to a medicine ball and stood in place, his arms directly in front of him to hold the weight to rebuild his core strength.

She took a sip of water. "What do you do for a living?"

"Starfighter."

"So, you're a pilot?"

"No, a starfighter. A pilot just works on one planet. I travel for work from system to system. Also, I work in zero G."

"So, you're a long-range pilot?"

Cyril went crestfallen, then flatly said, "Sure."

She chuckled as she sipped from her bottle.

He put down the medicine ball and sat in the chair next to the free weights. "I'm Cyril."

"Marie." The light coming through the window hit her hair at just the right angle to make it glow fire red.

Cyril sipped from his bottle. "Nice to meet you."

She approached the wall, placed her palms flat, and did lunges, slightly stretching her Achilles.

"So, what do you do?" Cyril asked.

"I work in a lab. Sample testing on infectious diseases, tracing flow between species."

"That's… boring."

"Yeah, I know. It's nothing special. I'm trying to get something better."

"What's the 'something better'?"

"Mortician."

Cyril said nothing, but his eyes widened.

"What?" she said, bewildered.

"Seems like you skipped from the infection part to the dead part."

"I don't mind being around dead bodies. It's quiet. Peaceful."

"Huh, never thought of dead bodies as being peaceful, but I guess I can see it. Seen my fair share."

"I'd imagine your line of work gets dangerous."

Cyril exposed the stitched-up scar on his shoulder. "Yeah, you never see it coming, either."

Marie turned to see it. "Oh God. That's cool."

Cyril chuckled. "You'd love my friend Jess. You'd get along perfectly with her."

"I like her already."

They both laughed.

"Hey, how much longer you got here?" Cyril asked.

"A couple more rounds on the bars, then some stretches."

"Wanna go get a coffee?"

"I don't drink coffee."

"Tea?"

"I try to avoid caffeine."

"A glass of water?"

"You're really trying here, aren't you?"

"Fortune favors the bold."

"Heh. Sure, I'll join you for a drink of water. Let me finish up first."

"I'll wait for you in the lobby." Cyril donned his sling, grabbed his water bottle, and headed to the bathroom. He changed clothes, cleaned himself, and went to the lobby to wait for Marie.

***

The humidity had finally dissipated, and the sun shone. It was hot but dry. Everything was right in the world. As coffee was out of the question, they'd found a small surf and turf restaurant not far from the physical therapy center. Cyril and Marie sat outside, him drinking regular water, her drinking seltzer water. The way the light caught her reddish-brown hair mesmerized him. Her green eyes seemed to be wells of emerald, and her lips, even without lipstick, were still bright red. Cyril never believed in fate but always appreciated it when the universe threw him a bone.

They'd ordered their meals and chitchatted while they waited. He had ordered a chicken parmesan sandwich; she had ordered a fresh calamari salad. As with most starter conversations, their jobs were the topic.

"Okay, what was the worst job you ever did?" Marie asked.

"Ooffff, worst job? That's a loaded question," he said, taking a sip of his drink.

"How so?"

"Well, there's all kinds of ways to say *worst*. Like, *bad*, as in it was a horrible experience, or *bad*, as in I almost died?"

"*Hmmm*, you pick. Dealer's choice."

"Well… if I had to really think about it, gauging everything, asteroid mining in deep space near Gliese 5."

"Why that one?"

"Deep space operations are always the most dangerous. There's nothing to support you. No ground to put your feet on. No gravity to help you fall. It's cold, dark death everywhere. One thing goes wrong, you're as fucked as a life sentence prisoner in Callico Bay. Plus, it was my first deep-space job."

"Fuck."

"Yeah. So, I think this was, I wanna say, four or five years ago. It's all a blur at this point. It was a full squadron, me and seven others. We're out there, defending a mining ship, as it sends out drones for cutting and collecting. It's just one big rock, not big enough to be a moon, so it falls into the asteroid category. What should have been easy turned shitty when the magistrate of a nearby planet shows up and tries to lay claim to the rock we're cutting up. Our ship captain says it's maritime out in space, but the magistrate says it falls under Gliesian supply lines, so it's theirs. So, they're going back and forth, drones have just stopped in place, and we're all just sitting there, waiting for someone to make a decision. You've never known boredom till you've dealt with people from Gliese, I swear to God."

"Crecians colonized that planet, right? I've never been there."

"Yup, that they did. God, I'm getting annoyed thinking about it."

"What's wrong with them?"

"It's nothing personal, but for God's sake, they're so slow. Their whole society is built upon being a bureaucratic floodgate. Everything is checked and rechecked and then checked again. It's like being in a DMV from hell. So, all of us are just sitting around for hours and hours, waiting for someone to finally decide what to do."

"I thought this was a story about the worst job ever."

"Oh, I'm getting to the shitty stuff. So, we're all chilling out in the ship's rec room. I'm reading a book. My buddy Jace is playing cards with someone, I don't remember who, and then we finally get the call."

"Which was?"

"Mission was canceled. They had full stake on the rock."

"Well, shit."

"Yeah. So, we had to transfer all our payload to one of their haulers that still showed up late. And then we headed home."

"So, what's the bad part?"

Cyril took a long sip of his water. "They didn't pay us."

"*What?*"

"Nope." He slowly shook his head. "Because of the territorial stake on that asteroid and its location near Gliese 5, that contract was technically void, and no one could legally provide financial compensation to anyone involved. Somebody fucked up somewhere. No contract, no pay out. We all wasted our time and energy for a dud contract. And I turned down other work to take a deep-space operation because they pay the best. Ended up flying home emptyhanded." He finished his drink, waved the waiter over, and asked for another.

The waiter filled his glass, and Cyril took another sip. "What a waste of my time. So yeah, that's the worst one, because it was a bore and totally wasteful."

"I would have thought a job with lots of death and destruction would be the worst."

"Heh. Here's how I look at it. I'm expendable; I know that. Just how my business goes. We all know that going in. And to be honest, most missions don't even involve any kind of combat. Maybe 30 percent of what I do I ever get involved in something really dangerous. So... I'd say my odds are still looking pretty good."

"Until they aren't," Marie said, with a grim cartoon voice.

They both laughed.

"All right, it's your turn. Worst job you ever had?"

"Oh God, where do I start? *Hmm*. I worked as waitress for a little while. I hated it because people suck."

"No argument."

"*Umm*, I was a go-go dancer for a little while. Rest in peace to my knees."

"Where'd you dance?"

"Tech Noir over on Clackton Street."

"Oh, no shit. I've been there before. Maybe I was in there one night when you were dancing."

"Maybe you were." She smiled.

"Small universe, huh?"

"Oh, so small. *Umm*, I'd honestly say that the night shift as an ER nurse was probably the worst. Long nights, no sleep, hence the circles around my eyes."

"You have very pretty eyes."

She smiled. "*Aww*, thanks. You're not half bad yourself. And you have rings, too."

The waiter arrived with their food, and they dove right in.

With a mouth full of calamari, she continued. "So, one night, it's the Mukarian New Year, so guaranteed to be crazy. We had this triple hit of partiers roll in, and you know how big they are. They were drunk, high, and everything in between. They barreled through the ER; one punched right through a wall. We finally just said fuck it and just called animal control to tranq 'em, because even our security couldn't stop them. One of them blasted music through their phone, and they danced like they were in another club or something."

Cyril couldn't help but laugh. Marie just sat there and smiled while slowly shaking her head. The story to her always sounded too wild to be true.

"Oh God, Mukarians. If nothing else, you can always count on them for entertainment," Cyril said.

They chitchatted about common topics while they ate their meal: favorite films, tastiest foods, places they'd traveled, where they saw themselves in ten years. Neither of them had an answer for that last one.

Cyril decided ask what had been curdling in the back of his mind. "So, can I ask you a personal question?"

"Depends on how personal." She sipped her drink as she finished her meal.

"What really happened to your leg?"

She froze. The air immediately went cold, and the sky appeared to blacken. She said nothing.

"Too personal?" Cyril asked.

She downed the rest of her drink and smacked her lips. "No, it's fine." She looked as if she was working up the courage to expose some dark secret. In the back of Cyril's mind, he knew what she was going to say before she even said it. "Boyfriend and I had a fight. And he… threw me. Hit my ankle wrong on a table. It's complicated."

"Didn't know you had a boyfriend."

"You didn't ask. Anyway, it's fine. It's over."

"No, it's not. He hit you. He's gotta pay for it."

"No, Cyril, it's fine. We just had an argument, and it got outta hand. It's already taken care of. Cops took him away."

"But will he stay away, is the question."

She didn't answer. It felt like a canyon of dead space had apparated between them.

He hated hearing about women getting hit. If he was armed, he would hunt down Marie's ex-boyfriend and handle business in the most painful ways he could ever imagine. Instead, he retrieved his phone. "What's your cell number? If he comes back and tries to do anything, you text or call me. Okay?"

"Is this just your way of trying to get my number?"

"I'm serious. He ever hurts you again, I'll make sure it's taken care of."

"I don't need a hero to rescue me. I can handle it."

"All the same, in an emergency, do you have anyone else nearby that would come to help in a situation like that?"

She shrugged, then pulled out her phone, and they exchanged numbers.

"Heh. Got your number. That worked."

Marie smiled and chucked a cloth napkin at him. The waiter arrived with the bill, but Cyril snatched the tablet before Marie had a chance to pay her share. It annoyed her, but she smiled anyway.

As they walked down the street, the sky darkened—another rainstorm. Marie called for an autocab, and they waited for it to arrive.

"So, when can I see you again?" Cyril asked.

"I'm at therapy in a couple days, around two o'clock."

"I'll see if they can move my time to then."

"Well, I guess I'll see you there."

The cab arrived, and Marie struggled to put her crutches in the back seat. As she closed the door, Cyril waved goodbye and began to walk away.

Marie lowered the window and stuck out her head. "Hey, got a question!"

Cyril walked back over. "Yeah, what's up?"

"What's your flying name?"

"Flying name?"

"You know, don't pilots get another name when they're in the sky?"

"Oh, my callsign! Yeah, yeah. Skyhawk."

"Skyhawk. *Hmmm.*"

"*Hmmm?*"

"Seems like it fits."

"How do you figure?"

"Bold but a little pretentious," she said and laughed.

Cyril smiled and shook his head. "Okay, I'll give you that one."

"Goodbye, Cyril."

"Bye, Marie."

The cab pulled away, and he watched her go westward for a block before it turned left out of sight. He could have called a cab for himself, but the sky hadn't dunked on him yet, so he decided to enjoy a long walk home. He paced himself, step by step. He'd known Marie for all of three hours and couldn't stop thinking about her. She had a face as sweet as candy, and that hair was straight fire.

Jess's and Jace's voices popped into his brain. *Don't look at her like she's just a hookup. Respect. You know that.*

He crawled back inside himself and attempted to silence the voices but to no avail. He had a habit, a bad habit. And habits were hard to break.

He stopped at a coffee shop for his daily caffeine fix and sat in the back. He cleared notifications and saw an email requesting him for a job a week from now. He replied he would be available and asked for details. He jumped into the text thread between Jess, Jace, and himself.

> CYRIL: So, get this. I met this gorgeous woman at therapy today.
> JESS: I thought you had therapy tomorrow.
> CYRIL: No, the other therapy is today. This woman, Marie, she's really sweet.
> JACE: You didn't just hit it and quit it, did you? That's what the other therapy is trying to fix.
> CYRIL: Fuck, no. Guys, we just had lunch and talked, okay? Nothing else happened.
> JESS: HEY! PROGRESS!
> CYRIL: See? I can be mature, I swear.
> JACE: Ehhhhh…
> CYRIL: Oh, shut up.
> JACE: Glad you actually put in real effort. You seeing her again?
> CYRIL: She has physical therapy again in two days. She broke her Achilles. I'm gonna try to move my time to then.
> JESS: Just don't stalk her, dude.
> CYRIL: I'm not stalking her. I even said to her I'd move my time. She knows I'll be there. It's not stalking. I'd just like to see her again.
> JACE: Take it slow, my friend. You just met her.
> CYRIL: Going as slow as I can.

Cyril flipped through his socials as he drank his coffee. He spotted an article about the Mullarkey family and their company, Arcturus Allied, holding a charity event for impoverished youth on Proxima in a few days. He realized he hadn't heard from Layla in a while, and with his arm healing and with his funds running dry, it might be time to bend the knee and get in with a company like Arcturus. Beggars couldn't be choosers. He messaged Layla, not expecting a reply. A few minutes later, his phone pinged.

> CYRIL: Hey there.
> LAYLA: Hey.
> CYRIL: Hadn't heard from you in a bit. Was just checking in. Also, that offer for work with Arcturus. Was wondering if that was still available? I haven't heard from anyone yet.
> LAYLA: I'm okay. Just busy. Things kind of fell apart recently. Yeah, I can put you in touch with our recruitment office. There's just been a lot happening recently.
> CYRIL: Appreciate it. Saw there's some kind of charity event in a few days. Is it open to the public?
> LAYLA: Yeah. But it's usually just the people I associate with that go.
> CYRIL: Maybe I'll stop by. I'm almost healed up.
> LAYLA: Okay.
> CYRIL: Seriously, are you okay?
> LAYLA: I'm fine. Please stop asking. If you go to the event, I'll say hi.

The last statement felt so brusque that Cyril knew something was off. It felt too harsh for her. He knew about her breakdown at her husband's funeral and about the formal apology she had made a few weeks later. So, what was with the anger? He needed answers. Two days from that moment, it would be a very busy day.

***

"So, how are you feeling lately?" Doctor Minese asked, his leather chair creaking as he settled into it.

"I'm doing okay. Much better, actually," Cyril answered, full of positivity.

"Something good finally happened?"

"Yeah. Met someone yesterday. Name's Marie." In the back of his mind, this therapy session felt like a waste of time. He was feeling good.

"I'm hoping this was a real connection and not your standard hookup habits."

"No. We just had lunch. She was at physical therapy, just like I was."

"Is this the woman you mentioned a few weeks back?"

"Yeah. Same one. She has a broken Achilles."

"That's a shame. Those are tough to heal. How did she break it?"

"Apparently she got into a fight with her boyfriend. They've split, according to her. Or I hope so, at least."

"For her sake or for yours?"

"Oh, for God's sake, gimme a little bit of credit."

Minese made a note on his tablet.

"What was that?"

"I'm noticing a pattern here."

"Which is?"

"You tend to get involved with women who are in some form of relationship. Whether it be infidelity or close to breakups. You've mentioned at least eight separate individuals in the past three years who have been hookups or short-term partners. Though I'm guessing there's some you either aren't mentioning or don't remember."

"And what are you getting at?"

"Several things. You lack commitment skills when it comes to your personal life. And you also seem to be attracted to women who are in some form of danger. Should I bring up the Layla Forester event?"

"Layla Mullarkey now. And no, you don't. I was just texting her yesterday, actually."

"Interesting."

"Why is that interesting?"

"She's extremely upper class. I'm surprised she still communicates with you. You're a freelance pilot who sits toward the middle class, and just barely holding on to it at that."

"Thanks for the encouragement."

"If I was encouraging you, I wouldn't say what I'm about to say. I think you need to cut ties with this Layla. That's a world that doesn't involve someone like you."

"So, just stay in my lane? What does this have to do with me and who I fuck?"

"Are you trying to fuck her?"

Cyril paused to consider it. He remembered being in the truck on Gacrux when he had passed his water to Layla. Jace had shaken his head at Cyril and had given him a knowing glance. *Don't punch above your weight.* In the moment, Cyril had felt he had that shot, but now, knowing what she was enduring, knowing about the abuse and the hate, he wanted something else.

"That was a cheap shot, and you know it," Cyril said. "No. I don't want to fuck her. I want to protect her."

Minese made another note. "Do you feel the same about Marie? Did learning that her boyfriend, ex or not, attacking her set you off?"

Cyril ran his fingers down his pant legs—his nervous tic. "Yeah. It did. I told her I would handle it if he ever came back. She said it wasn't worth it."

"It's not, Cyril. Violence won't stop trauma. It makes the pain go deeper, and it finds other ways to manifest. Ways more damaging to surrounding parties."

"I can't just let him hurt her. Same goes for Layla."

"Is she in danger too?"

"I don't know. But it's on my to-do list."

Minese made another note.

Cyril stayed quiet for a moment, then continued. "But Marie is great though, and she has amazing hair. Much better than mine, I can tell you that."

"May I propose a scenario?" Minese turned over his data pad.

"Go for it."

"Let's say you and Marie become a thing. The boyfriend disappears, and it's just you two. What happens then? Could you put in the effort to commit?"

"For her, yeah. I'd give it a shot."

"Now, I'd like to ask you another question. Do you think you've had enough time to heal?"

"Yeah, my arm is pretty much fine now."

"I don't mean your arm. I mean your mind. You've been to every session here for a month, which means progress, but do you think a month is enough time to shake off bad habits and reshape an entire lifestyle?"

"I don't know, man. You're the one with the college degree. You tell me."

"Trauma-healing and habit-breaking takes months, sometimes years, to correct. It involves absolute commitment. And this Marie seems like, from what little I know, she's also dealing with an extreme form of trauma. Do you think this is something that's a worthwhile pursuit while you're still in the middle of your healing?"

"I'm not gonna just live like a hermit in a shack in the woods."

"That's not what I'm saying. My point is you need to understand your limits. I can tell you right now that commitment is your biggest flaw, and it will be an even bigger problem if you try to go into it without your whole heart."

"I guess that's a good point. In that case, do you think asking her to have lunch with me again would be off limits?"

"Pace yourself, know your limits, and I think you can work around your issues."

"Sometimes you do actually have decent advice."

"That's what you pay me for, Cyril. Higher the price, the better the advice."

Chapter 6

Know Your Place

Marie recommended Skovian noodles for lunch. They ordered two large bowls of noodles, with freshly chopped vegetables and pork meat, along with glasses of wine. The bright, colorful, and extremely sleek family-owned restaurant was only half packed but was lively enough for a weekday. The freshly waxed floors shone; local artwork and photographs covered the walls. While it wasn't exactly a date, they seemed to treat it as one.

Cyril added hot sauce to his noodles. "How much longer till you're out of your boot?" He was finally free of his arm sling and felt the need to ask when Marie would follow suit.

"Another week. I bet my foot is nice and crusty." She chuckled.

"Oh, yummy. I can't wait to see that."

"I'll send you photos. A hot bath sounds so good right now."

"Do you have one of those long scratching sticks to get those itches down there?"

"Oh, you know it." She slurped down a mouthful of noodles. "I had one last night that I just kept scratching for like five minutes. Oh my God, it felt so good."

"I can only imagine."

"Nice to see you're out of your sling. Back to work soon?"

"Yeah, I have a small job lined up next week."

"Something dangerous?"

"*Eh*, we'll see. So far, it seems simple enough. Drawing out raiders for the local police to go after them. We'll probably end up doing most of the work though."

"Are you always just a hired hand, or do you ever give the orders?"

Cyril sipped his wine. "I don't really like to be in charge. I hate the responsibility."

"That's fair, but doesn't it pay better?"

"Oh yeah, of course. But… let's just say I have a problem with authority. I don't like being told what to do, and it would be hypocritical if I started giving orders."

"May I flatter you for a moment?"

Cyril scoffed. "By all means, go right ahead."

"I think you would make a great leader."

"Ha-ha, oh God. Captain Cyril 'Skyhawk' Eisner. I don't know how I'd sleep at night."

"Well, I don't really know anything about flying, so I'm just making a bold guess, but from where I'm sitting, I could see you doing just fine."

"I'll take the compliment."

"You fuckin' better."

The server delivered the check, and Cyril tried to pay the tab again, but Marie snatched it before he could get his hands on it.

"My turn," she said. She paid in full while smiling.

They left the restaurant and began walking. Not necessarily anywhere. Just walking. They discussed politics, movies, games they'd played, Cyril's childhood, and they eventually landed on family matters.

Marie asked, "What about your mom and dad?"

"Not much to say. My mom took off, and my dad is an asshole."

"I'm sorry to hear that."

"It's fine. What about you?"

"Mom is still around. She lives way outside of town in the suburbs. Dad passed away a couple years back. Hit and run. We never found out who did it."

"I'm sorry."

"Yeah, just one of those things, you know?"

"What things?"

"Lack of closure. Catharsis and closure aren't always possible. Just gotta live with it."

"I hear that. Sounds like something a therapist would say to a patient."

Marie laughed. "Am I that transparent?"

"*Eh*, more like translucent."

They sauntered to a park bench and sat in the shade of a willow tree. The sun beamed from directly above, so the shade became a nice respite from the heat.

"Looking forward to being in the air again?" Marie asked.

"Oh God, yeah. You don't know how much you miss it till you can't do it."

"I wouldn't know, so I can't relate."

Cyril paused and faced her. "Wait. Are you saying you've never even been in a normal airplane before?"

Marie shook her head. "Nope, never even been on a roller coaster. Closest I've gotten is a train."

"Wow, you're such a whittle baby." Cyril pinched her left cheek.

She swiped away his hand and laughed. "I never really had a reason to get my feet off the ground. I prefer to be somewhere I can actually stand up."

"You've never even left Balamb?"

She shook her head. "No. Once I moved here from home, this felt like it. Doesn't seem like there's much out there for me. Besides, I like where I am."

"And you're the one telling me that I should take charge and become the strong leader?"

"Do as I say, not as I do," she said in a forceful but playful tone.

"*Heh*. Hypocrite!"

They chuckled as they sat to enjoy the quiet. The park was mostly vacant at midday—a few passersby with dogs, some joggers, but most people were still in the middle of their workday.

Cyril, from sheer curiosity, asked, "Any news on the ex?"

"House arrest for a month," she said sullenly. "No contact with me."

"He does anything, you call me. Okay?"

"Cyril, I don't need a hero. I can handle it myself. Besides, we just met a few days ago. Know your place, you know?"

"Just because we just met doesn't mean I shouldn't care."

"I appreciate it, but I'm okay, really."

"Okay." Cyril's phone buzzed with an unknown number. "Sorry, gimme a sec." He stood, walked a few paces, and answered. "Hello?"

"Is this Cyril Eisner?" a deep male voice on the other end asked.

"Speaking."

"This is Detective Mandrake of the Balamb City Police. Your father is Lawrence Eisner, correct?"

Cyril sighed. "What happened?"

"Your father was arrested for assault and battery. We need someone to post bail."

"Call my uncle. He's a better option."

"We've already tried Gino Eisner. He's currently off planet. You were the only one we could get ahold of. Are you available to come by this afternoon?"

"Fuck's sake," he whispered to himself. "Sure. I'm on my way. Which precinct?"

"Ninth Precinct on Sickle Avenue."

"Thanks." Cyril hung up and rubbed his temples.

"What wrong?" Marie asked.

Cyril turned to face her. "Dad got arrested. He needs to be bailed out."

"Thought you hated him. Leave him."

"I can't. I gotta go."

Marie approached him. "Seriously, Cyril. You don't have to go. He can just wait till his court date."

"I can't. It's complicated. Text me later?"

Marie paused, then sighed. "What if I go with you?"

"I don't think that's a good idea."

"No, it's fine. I want to go with you."

He looked into her eyes. They were genuine in their intent. "*Heh*, all right. Let's go see my dad."

They began walking.

"This isn't exactly what I was expecting for a second date."

"Slow down, man. We aren't quite there yet. We haven't even had a real first date."

"Well then, what would you call this?"

"An unfortunate side quest."

"*Heh*, fair enough."

***

The police department was on the opposite side of Balamb, so Cyril called an autocab. They rode silently. No one felt like speaking. He hated her tagging along to see his old man. It felt embarrassing, and he knew his father would lay into him just for the fun of it. Traffic thickened as they neared the department, so they walked the remaining kilometer. Not two minutes into their trek, they were sweating from the sun. They stopped in a coffee shop so Cyril could fuel up for the upcoming fight before entering the station. Marie bought a bottle of water and gulped it down. They crossed the street to the precinct, and Cyril held the door for Marie as they entered.

It was overly cold inside, with the AC pushed to the max. Cyril took a long swig of his coffee to heat himself, then chucked the empty cup into the garbage. A large section of chairs sat to the left, a few people sprinkled among them. Various pieces of police memorabilia and photos hung from the walls, including the police union flag. They approached a glass-encased service desk to the right of the entrance which had a heavy glass door just past it. Cyril tapped on the glass above the desk.

A woman officer looked up from her paperwork and pressed a button for the speaker installed in the glass. "May I help you?"

"I'm here to sign out my father. He's in lock up."

"Name?"

"Lawrence Eisner."

"One second." She switched off the speaker and pressed a separate button. She spoke into a table mic, but Cyril could only see her lips move. After a moment, the glass door buzzed. "Go on through and turn left at the first intersection."

Cyril and Marie traipsed down the hallway, turned left, and entered the lockup area. Two separate rows of metal cells, with plastic windows, lined each side of the room. Most were vacant save for two. One had a drunken man sleeping off a hangover; the other housed his father, laying down napping. A stench of drying vomit filled the air, more than likely from within the drunken man's cell.

Cyril eyed Marie. "Marie, this is my wonderful father, Lawrence."

"You spoiled little shit, can't even be nice," Lawrence muttered.

"I'm just here to sign you out, then I'm gone."

Lawrence sat upright, set his feet on the disgusting stained floor, then noticed Marie. "And who the fuck is this?"

"A friend of mine. Marie."

"Well, ain't you cute," Lawrence said in a creepy tone.

Marie recoiled in repulsion. The stories of Cyril's father being a wretched person were beginning to make sense to her.

"Don't listen to him," Cyril whispered to Marie.

Cyril went to the officer's desk and asked to sign out his father. Bail came to ten thousand dollars. Cyril groaned but paid the fee. Even though he would get the money back after his father's trial, it was still a hefty expense.

The officer approached the cell door. "All right, Larry, time to go. Your boy posted your bail."

"Well, wasn't that sweet of him."

"It sure was," the officer said.

Lawrence exited the cell and proffered his hand to the officer as they smiled at each other.

"You two know each other?" Cyril asked.

"Of course I know Deacon. I worked with him for three years in the major crimes division. Sad to see they stuck him down here in the pits, but it was nice to have company all night," Lawrence said.

"We'll get that drink soon, Larry," Deacon shook Lawrence's hand.

"Are we done?" Cyril asked gruffly.

Lawrence glared at Cyril. "Yeah… we're done."

"Good. Let's go, Marie."

As they turned to leave, Lawrence said, "You could have left me in here till I go to trial, but you didn't. And you know why?"

"No, why?" Cyril asked without turning around.

"Cyril, let's just go," Marie whispered.

Lawrence walked around in front of Cyril and Marie. "Because you're weak. And pathetic. And you're a loser who just does what he's told. And you're scared of me."

Cyril remained silent while he stared at his father.

"How can you be so cruel?" Marie asked resentfully.

"Easy. Who's gonna stop me? Him? You really are cute. He knows his place. And so should you."

"Come on, babe, let's go." Marie grabbed Cyril's arm and pulled him around Lawrence.

They traversed the hallway and left the building. They sat on a bench to the left of the front doors under a tree. Cyril leaned forward and rested his elbows on his knees with his head in his hands.

Marie sidled closer. "I'm sorry."

"For what?"

"I didn't know he was that bad."

"Now you do," he murmured.

He felt angry, embarrassed, and depressed all at the same time. And it was because he knew his father was right. There was no reason he couldn't have hung up the phone and left his father to rot in his cell. No reason to bend the knee to him. But he did. Deep down, he was weak, and he hated it.

Cyril chuckled. "On the bright side, I guess I have something to discuss with my therapist."

Marie scoffed. "Guess so."

Cyril checked his phone and stood. "Shit, I gotta go. I have an event tonight."

"What event?"

"Some charity event that Arcturus Allied is hosting. Basically, a bunch of rich fucks blowing smoke up each other's asses."

"That sounds awful. Why are you going to that?"

"Trying to make connections for work. I just spent ten grand getting my dad out of jail. I'm gonna need a bunch of work soon."

"I guess I understand. Just try to not get too much smoke blown up your own ass."

"I'm only going for an hour. I'll swipe some expensive shit on my way out too."

"Good. Take 'em for everything they have."

"*Heh*, I intend to."

They said their goodbyes, then Marie called an autocab home. Cyril called his own cab, headed home, showered, and found the most expensive thing he owned as his attire for the night—a dark blue button-up shirt with a gray vest and dark blue pants. He only owned the outfit in case of major events, which rarely ever happened. It felt a little snug as he had gotten slightly bigger since he had bought it three years prior, but it would work for the evening.

He was still angry and really didn't feel like going out, but he had made a promise to attend. He had to know what was going on with Layla, even just out of sheer morbid curiosity. To hell with his therapist's advice. Something felt wrong, and he needed to know what it was.

***

It was stuffy, like all charity events. The wealthiest and most powerful on the western seaboard wined and dined, flaunted their wealth, praised each other's efforts, and offered kind words and prayers. The irony was not lost on Cyril as he stayed at the back of the dim room, an outsider among them. He was the only person of his social status to attend, sticking out like a clown who had shown up to the wrong party. He had already downed two glasses of champagne and was working on his third. There were occasional glances or odd looks, but most people paid him no attention. They were too busy metaphorically blowing each other.

He had arrived an hour earlier, which was an hour after the event's start. Close to three hundred people attended, which made tracking down Layla difficult. Better to just sit in one spot and keep a lookout. Maybe the crowd thought he was security, perhaps they thought he was part of the dining staff, slacking off, or just a simpleton who had wandered in and refused to leave. In any case, he sat alone at a small parlor table toward the back, working on his third glass and keeping watch. While on the one hand he was there to secure employment, he was more concerned with Layla.

They were holding the event in a high-class auditorium, with a neoclassical style, which felt posh but professional—an almost forty-meter-high ceiling, marble columns, and freshly renovated floors. Some patterns of lights and shapes danced around on the walls and ceiling, adding some life to the dull evening. The amount of money it had cost to build the place was probably more than they were offering to charity at the event itself. Once again, the irony and the hypocrisy was not lost on Cyril.

He finished his third glass and approached the bar for a refill. He needed something stronger. The opulent atmosphere reminded him how much he missed Mallory's Heroes. The bar had dual lines, both moving quickly. Cyril was third in line. He stood behind a short and petite woman, with flat red hair and thick glasses. She dressed in a very prim and proper manner, perhaps a bit too much for any kind of social setting. She ordered a gin and tonic, and Cyril followed suit by asking for a martini. The price was outrageous, but he hid his cringe and paid without revealing he was "one of the poors" among them. The red-haired woman had stepped aside the bar and drank alone while texting.

"Excuse me," Cyril asked her, "I'm looking for Layla Mullarkey. She mentioned she would be here tonight. Do you have any idea where I can find her?"

The red-haired woman stared at him with enough contempt to damn an entire generation of the human race. With a seething anger that could rip apart the world, she spat, "I don't think someone of your… status… needs to be involved with a woman such as Layla. Now fuck off, pig." The woman slammed back her drink and stormed off.

Cyril returned to his table to consider various ways to commit murder and where to hide a body. Ten minutes flowed by as he sipped his drink. Even with music blasting, he was absolutely bored, so he texted Marie.

> CYRIL: Well, I've been told to fuck off by a rich bitch, so I guess I'm doing something right.
> MARIE: You're a real go-getter. Nailed it.
> CYRIL: I try my best. I'm so bored.
> MARIE: Did you find the person you were looking for?
> CYRIL: Not yet. Too many people milling around. We'd probably go in circles if I got up and looked.

He sent her a picture of himself with his drink.

> CYRIL: So, instead, I'm doing the next best thing.
> MARIE: HA! Love it.
> CYRIL: I'm sorry about today. My dad is a piece of shit.
> MARIE: Why are you apologizing? You didn't do anything wrong.

CYRIL: No, but it was embarrassing. I should have gone
    alone.
MARIE: It's okay. You don't have to say you're sorry.
CYRIL: Thanks. Maybe I will get up and try looking around. I
    don't think I can stand to be around these people much
    longer. I've already considered six ways to dispose of a
    body.
MARIE: I can give you way more than six. ,-)
CYRIL: Heh, I bet you could. All right, I'm gonna go. TTYL.
MARIE: TTYL :-)

He finished his drink and stood. He lost his footing for a brief second. The vodka was extra strong, but he regained his balance and set off to find Layla.

At least thirty round tables filled the middle of the room for dinner. By the time he had arrived, the main course had ended, and the dessert and excessive drinking had begun. The crowds were disparate, and everyone had found their own clique and pockets of conversation, none of which interested Cyril. He pushed through a group of a few women and promptly bumped into a man a foot taller than him.

The big man turned and looked down at Cyril.

"Excuse me. I've had a little bit to drink," Cyril said.

"I'm sure you have," the big man said.

"*Um*, I'm looking for someone. Layla Mullarkey."

"And who are you?"

"Eisner. Cyril Eisner. Freelance starfighter." He proffered his right hand.

"*Hmm*. Mullarkey. Daniel Mullarkey. Layla is my sister." He grasped Cyril's hand and clamped down hard. "How exactly do you of all people know my sister?" Daniel released Cyril's hand from his viselike grip.

Cyril did his best to shake it off without anyone noticing. "I helped her get off Gacrux. I was part of her security detail."

"*Ahh*, so you're the one."

"One what?"

"Who took a shot at my brother-in-law."

Oh shit. "Well, it's not exactly like that. It's complicated."

"No, it's not. You took a swing and blasted him with a, what is it called? A null gun? I saw the report."

Cyril was almost frozen but continued. "Like I said, it's complicated."

"And how would you like to uncomplicate it?"

A small crowd formed behind Mullarkey, all looking as vampiric and blood thirsty as him. The cabal was ready to strike the moment Mullarkey said the word. Cyril was sweating and doing a poor job of hiding it. He was tough, but he knew when he was outmatched, outnumbered, and outgunned. There would be no winning this fight. And Daniel Mullarkey was fucking huge compared to him.

Mullarkey burst out laughing, and the rest of them followed his lead. Everyone laughed right in Cyril's face. A bunch of bullies enjoying their triumph, whatever triumph it was. "I'm just fucking with you, Eisner!" Mullarkey threw his bear arm around Cyril's shoulders and guided him through the crowd.

It had been a while since Cyril had felt so small.

"Yeah, Layla's here. She's up front. I appreciate you helping to get her off Gacrux, by the way. It was her idea to go there for her anniversary. I don't know why. And don't worry about Brentwood." He leaned closer to Cyril. "Honestly, the guy was a fucking asshole and deserved it. I wish I could have done it myself. The report said that a bird landed on him. That true?"

"Yeah, it's true. Just lucky, I guess."

"Ha! Just lucky. I love this guy. Come on, I'll take you to Layla."

They weaved through the crowd till they reached the front of the room near the stage. Layla sat at the table with three empty martini glasses in front of her. The red-haired woman sat next to a large man with a red face. They regarded Eisner with utter disdain.

Mullarkey took a seat and asked Cyril to sit beside him. "Drink of choice? I'll have it brought over to you."

"Just a beer, I think."

"A simple man. I like that." Mullarkey ordered him the cheapest beer possible, perhaps as an insult. Once it arrived, Mullarkey raised a glass for a toast. The others around the table, except for the red-haired woman and Layla, did the same. "To Mr. Cyril Eisner, freelance starfighter and the savior of my sister. You're a goddamn hero, Cyril. To you."

The others at the table raised their glasses and sang their praise. They were obviously drunk. Cyril could feel their contempt down to the core of his being. If he was armed, he'd be ready for mass murder. Layla smirked at him but didn't drink. Something was off.

Mullarkey set down his glass. "So, Mr. Eisner, what brings you to these parts? Not exactly the kind of crowd you run with, I assume."

"You could say that."

"*Heh*, yeah. So, what brings you here?"

"I'm looking for employment. Layla mentioned last month that a company such as yours might need pilots for off-world assignments."

"We could always use another hand. I'm sure we could find a spot on our freelance call list. Can't we, Bentley?"

"I'm sure we could," Bentley replied.

"See? Simple as that. We'll forward you some paperwork and get you all set up. You don't mind doing some dirty work every now and then, do you?"

"What qualifies as dirty work?"

"We sometimes have shipments going through hostile areas—raiders, bandits, undesirables, all the like. You've seen your fair share of those, I'd assume."

"That's what I usually do, so I don't have a problem with that."

"Of course. Mx. Moriarty over there can handle getting you onto our call list, can't you?"

"I don't like him," Moriarty said. Were they a snake, they'd spit venom.

"Now, Ellen. That's just poor manners. He's a new hire. A fresh face. And from what I've read, an ace in the sky. Or did I hear wrong?"

That was the last straw. The level of contempt, disrespect, and disdain spewing from Mullarkey's mouth was enough to make a monk become a mass shooter. Cyril turned himself completely toward Mullarkey. "Yes, I'm an ace, with an accumulated total of seventy airborne kills and twenty-nine ground kills. I've been to over thirteen separate planets and have seen wildlife that would turn a Mukarian into a Crecian. I absolutely never back down from a fight, and I don't like seeing women get hit. How's that for a fucking resume?" It took fifteen airborne kills to register as an ace. Cyril was well beyond that and proud of it.

The alcohol evaporated from Mullarkey's system in a nanosecond as he leaned back in his chair. "You'll go far, Mr. Eisner. I think we could use you, for sure. Moriarty, copy Mr. Eisner's contact information and send him some paperwork. Mx. Moriarty handles our new hires as well as public relations."

"*She* handles public relations," Cyril asked.

"I am not a *she*," Moriarty snapped. "I'm nonbinary and would appreciate it if you would address me as such."

"Okay, sorry. I didn't know. What should I call you?"

"You seriously don't know?"

"No. Should I?"

"The fact I need to tell you means it's not worth telling you. You're too closeminded for me to bother."

Cyril surveyed everyone at the table, thinking it must be an elaborate prank, but, in fact, Moriarty was just that confrontational and narcissistic. He regarded Mullarkey, unsure of what to say.

"Just ignore that," Mullarkey said.

Cyril spied Layla, who had said as many words as a corpse.

Mullarkey asked a waiter for a pad of paper and a pen. He returned a moment later and handed them to Mullarkey, who then passed them to Cyril. He wrote his contact information, handed it to Mullarkey, who then offered it to Moriarty, who accepted it with absolute condescension. The merry-go-round of information transfer was incredibly annoying.

Bitch, Cyril thought.

An old man's voice came from a loudspeaker. "Ladies and gentlemen, before we wrap out the night, we'd like to have the sponsor of tonight's event, Mr. Daniel Mullarkey, come on stage to say a few words."

"Well, if you'll excuse me," Mullarkey said. He rose from his chair and circled the table to a set of stairs at the back of a carpeted stage. A massive LED screen behind him showed the Arcturus Allied logo, an image of a bear in mid-roar, with the sun glowing behind it. A stagehand to the side handed Mullarkey a microphone. Once he was on stage, the screen turned into an enlarged image of Mullarkey's face. "Well, it's been quite a night, hasn't it?"

The crowd applauded. Cyril's gaze met Layla's, and he cocked his head—the telepathic signal of *We should go*. But she sat still. A server brought her another drink, and she took a huge gulp. Cyril refocused on Mullarkey, whose ego was on full display.

"I cannot thank you enough for all your hard work, your donations, to the staff, your alcohol."

The crowd laughed.

"But seriously, thank you. This has been a difficult time for my family, but that does not mean we stop progress. It doesn't mean we stop striving for perfection, for sanctity, for unity. We bury our feelings, and we push forward. Humanity's progress, as well as all the other species out there, requires that we put our personal feelings aside and reach for the farthest star possible. Reaching into your wallets is also appreciated, of course."

The crowd laughed again. Cyril groaned under his breath, knowing everything Mullarkey said was bullshit.

"A month ago, my family suffered a tragedy. My brother-in-law, Brentwood Forester, was taken from us in an unfortunate accident. My sister, right down there, felt that loss the most. But we pushed past it. We've worked tirelessly to end the extreme poverty and homelessness that still exists on the streets of Balamb. But it's not just people like us who can make a difference. It's also the common man, the simple man. And a man like that is here with us tonight. The man who rescued my sister from suffering the same fate as my brother-in-law. Stand up, please, Mr. Cyril Eisner."

Oh, fuck me. What the fuck? Shit no! Cyril thought.

The crowd applauded, not sure exactly who they applauded for. Cyril watched Layla say nothing. He stood, and a spotlight illuminated him. Mullarkey waved at him to come on stage. Cyril was sweating again, horribly embarrassed, but obliged. He walked on the stage and stood beside Mullarkey. The spotlight blazed upon him, blinding him from seeing the audience, which was slightly comforting.

Mullarkey threw his big gorilla arm over Cyril's shoulder. "This man got my sister home. And he did everything he could to save my sister's husband. I cannot thank you enough for what you did, Mr. Eisner. If you could, please give us some words." He passed the mic to Cyril and stepped backward.

More than likely, Mullarkey was using this as a perfect opportunity to embarrass Cyril again—another bullying tactic. Pretend to be a friend, then take him down at his worst possible moment. But a fire burned inside Cyril, a seething rage and hate for Mullarkey that knew only the same level as his father. In some ways, Mullarkey reminded Cyril of his father—just another punk. If Cyril was to say anything to the crowd of jackals before him, they'd better be worth his spit.

He stood there for a few moments in awkward silence, then the words finally came. "I came here tonight uninvited. I was simply checking on Mrs. Mullarkey. I'm no one special, and that's okay. The charity here tonight for all the underprivileged and underappreciated people across our city should be celebrated, though. Yet, at the same time, I feel more could be done. I clawed my way up from nothing to where I am now. I'm a pilot, a starfighter, and I don't have any aspirations of being anything more than that. Yes, I'm simple, but I would have appreciated a little help along the way and to have those in power"—he faced Mullarkey with a glare—"not look down upon me." He refocused on the audience. "In my life, I've killed ninety-nine people in armed combat. Most of them at long range in my ship. My service is simple: work for hire, pay me to go there, I go there. And there's no shame in that. I know my place. But people, like me, who do the dirty work deserve a special kind of respect. The ones who actually put their feet in the shit deserve your gratitude. Because, let's be honest, how many of you would ever associate with someone like me if I didn't crash your party tonight?"

The crowd was dead silent. Grass growing made more noise.

To recover quickly, Cyril seized his chance. "But, on behalf of Arcturus Allied, and as a new hire for Mr. Mullarkey's company, I thank you for all your donations tonight."

The crowd slowly worked up to applause, a few cheers sprinkled in. Cyril handed the mic to Mullarkey.

"Wow. That was a hell of a speech. Thank you everyone, and get home safely," Mullarkey yelled out.

The crowd stood and applauded even louder.

Mullarkey wrapped his arm around Cyril again, almost too tight. He turned off the mic and leaned into Cyril's ear. "You've got some big balls on you, Eisner."

"Funny, all my exes said the same thing."

Layla stood and walked away. Cyril freed himself from the bear hug and strode off the stage to follow Layla toward an elevator at the back. He just missed the doors but saw the elevator was headed up toward a balcony level. A flight of stairs ascended to the right. He followed them up two floors and found the landing level for the balcony. Past the elevator was a set of double doors that led to an exterior balcony overlooking the main entrance.

The night was dark, and the light pollution hid the stars. Layla stood on the balcony, overlooking the city. No tall buildings nor landmarks were nearby. It was mostly roadways surrounding a small park below. Cyril pushed open the door and stepped into the crisp night. Layla didn't turn around but knew he was there. A car honked below. Beyond that, it was quiet.

"Why are you here, Cyril?" she bitterly asked.

"I needed to know you were okay," he said, slightly embarrassed.

She turned around. "I'm fine. You can leave now."

Cyril stood alongside Layla next to the balcony's edge, where they stayed silent for a moment.

Then she said, "Good speech, though."

"Thanks. Thought it up on the spot myself."

She giggled, and so did he. The giggling diminished into awkward silence. They stared down at the people leaving and waiting for the valets to deliver their vehicles.

"I guess I'll be getting some work with your company soon."

"I guess you will. Congrats."

"I don't like any of those people down there, though."

"You know, I don't either."

"May I ask you a question?"

"Are you gonna leave if I don't answer?"

"*Eh*, you can't get rid of me that easy."

"Then ask away."

"How are you so different from the rest of them?"

"What do you mean?"

"You don't have a stick up your ass. You don't really fit in with the rest of them. Same blood but it seems like something didn't take. I thought all rich people were selfish pricks."

"We're not all like that."

"Yeah, I suppose not."

"Why are you really here, Cyril?" Anger was finding its way out of her, a bitterness that Cyril didn't know existed.

"Like I said, I just wanted to make sure you were okay. That last message you sent me felt… off."

"It's none of your business what me or my family does. You understand?" She turned and headed for the door.

"It doesn't mean I can't be worried about you."

"Who are *you*? Who do *you* think you are? What are *you* to me?" Cyril said nothing.

"You got me home from Gacrux. We parted ways. And that's it. It didn't mean anything. I'm grateful for you getting me home, but there wasn't anything more."

"I wasn't implying there was more. It doesn't mean I can't care."

The cars below were the only sound as Cyril and Layla stared each other down.

"Do you wanna fuck me?" Layla asked.

"What?" Cyril asked, aghast.

"Do you… want… to fuck me?"

"Are you serious right now?" Cyril whispered.

Layla approached Cyril and got close. Too close. "Well, do you? That's what you want, isn't it? That's all it ever was really about. I'll let you do it right here. Right here, right now. If it'll get you to leave me alone, I'll let you fuck me."

Cyril was taken aback. He hadn't expected this kind of behavior or attitude. Then he leaned in to smell her breath. "You're drunk, Layla. You don't know what you're saying."

She broke down crying. Cyril wrapped his arms around her, and she cried onto his chest. Despite having been there all night and seeing the people she associated with and experiencing the world she inhabited, he was nowhere closer to understanding what was happening with her. At that moment, it didn't matter.

The balcony doors opened, and Mullarkey walked outside, with Bentley and Moriarty trailing him. He furrowed his brow and pursed his lips as he saw Cyril holding Layla. "Something happening up here, Mr. Eisner?"

"She's had a little too much to drink," Cyril said.

Layla slowly pulled from Cyril and wiped away her tears. She composed herself as best as she could and headed toward the door. As she passed the trio, Bentley and Moriarty followed her, leaving

Mullarkey and Cyril alone on the balcony. Cyril faced the ledge and looked across the city. Mullarkey stepped alongside him.

"Well, just the two of us," Cyril said.

"Let's cut the shit, Eisner. I'm grateful to you for bringing my sister home, but you need to learn where you stand when compared to my family. Like you said in that ballsy speech down there, know your place. As a basic courtesy, I'm giving you an opportunity for a job. The press down there knows about you now. I *have* to hire you just on principle. It'll look good. Consider it a pity favor. Nothing more."

"I do know my place. Opposite you." Cyril had to look up at Mullarkey as he said that.

"You're just a starfighter, Eisner. I'd suggest you stay away from my sister. She has no business associating with the likes of you. That said, I could absolutely use you in my workforce."

"Well, then send me some dates, and I'll be happy to work for you." Cyril finally could spit the contempt back in Mullarkey's face.

Mullarkey ignored the contempt yet followed up with, "I'll have Moriarty get in touch with you, and we'll get you flying under our company name in no time. There's a lot of work coming up throughout the next year. We'd be happy to have you."

"I have no doubt."

"But remember… know your place, Eisner."

"Yes, sir."

"Good. Glad we had this conversation. Consider this a job interview, and you passed. Get home safe, Mr. Eisner." Mullarkey turned and headed through the door.

Cyril looked down at the street and saw Layla enter a black limousine, followed by Bentley. Moriarty was nowhere to be seen.

He leaned against the ledge and recalled Layla's words. She was clearly distraught over something—something deeper than being a widow. He knew that wasn't what was troubling her. Daniel Mullarkey was more than likely the issue. He seemed controlling, forceful, and contemptuous, as well as untouchable. Mullarkey was right, though. Cyril's place was in no way where Mullarkey was, nor Layla's. They were so far above him that no starfighter could ever hope to fly that high. It was a lost cause. No chance in hell of figuring out what was going on.

"Fuck it," Cyril muttered and texted Marie.

CYRIL: Well, got some work coming up, so that's a plus. Haven't murdered anyone yet, but the night is young.

There was no reply. More than likely, she was asleep. He let out a long, resigned sigh and headed downstairs, each step feeling heavier than the last.

CHAPTER 7

MAKE 'EM COUNT

The cloud cover was thick, puffy, and gray. A thunderstorm had just rolled through. The remnants were petering off and giving way to the sun above. Tau Ceti f was just inside the habitable zone of its solar system and had a star similar to Earth's yellow sun. The Linel Corporation-headed Crecian colonization program had terraformed the planet during the last hundred years into a generally favored planet for rest and relaxation. Tau Ceti f was also 11 percent larger than any Terran-colonized world, which meant gravity was slightly higher, and therefore time was dilated compared to the rest of the Ekumen, but the conditions were still considered within reason for colonization.

As of late, raiders posed a serious problem. A criminal enterprise from an off-world gang had taken residency on Tau Ceti f and wreaked havoc on trade routes, and robberies were rising. The local police force sent a request through Polar Mass Incorporated for freelancers to escort a large delivery of perishable food to a neighboring city. However, this was all just a feint. It was, in fact, a ploy to draw out any criminal forces who might attempt to impede delivery of said food resources. As the government was unwilling to offer any of its own police force as targets, the local law enforcement requested for freelancers and mercenaries to go planet side and become targets for an exorbitant fee. They were, in effect, bait.

Fast forward a week later, Cyril Eisner was back airborne, alongside eleven other pilots, escorting three cargo ships out in the open, waiting to be attacked. The payment for being bait was substantial. Police headquarters had leaked a basic travel itinerary to trick enemy attack squadrons on the route to the intended destination. As the enemy forces, the Rijellian Raiders, made themselves known, the trap would be sprung. At least that was the plan, but plans rarely go off without a hitch.

> MISSION: Draw out enemy forces and eliminate with extreme prejudice
>
> TARGET: Rijellian Raiders
>
> THREAT LEVEL: Extreme (Be fully armed and prepared for combat)

The one caveat to accept the assignment was that two members of the local police force must be alongside the freelancers for general security measures and observation. Four of the starfighter's ships had back seats for a RIO. Cyril's Skyhawk was one of them, and through bad luck, he'd been saddled with a security officer named Wezlen. Though a Crecian, he was slightly taller than normal, standing at just over a meter and a half tall, but still came across like a worm. Cyril rolled his eyes at the officer's buzzcut and wide jaw that looked as though it was made of glass, assuming this was what passed for law enforcement on Tau Ceti f. Allegra's Diamondback was also fitted with an RIO, and she was just as unlucky him. Cyril had expressed his disdain for having a passenger, but the squadron leader overruled him. He would cope somehow. The squadron name was designated Halo Squadron.

Most of the faces in the squadron were familiar to Cyril. They were:

> CYRIL "SKYHAWK" EISNER
>
> ALLEGRA "HONEY BADGER" CLINE
>
> JESS "METALHEAD" TOWNLEY
>
> CATHERINE "KITKAT" YOUNG
>
> MORGAN "PIPER" SEXTON
>
> HASTER "KARAOKE" JENTOW
>
> CALLISTO "AUGER" JONES

Seth "Gameboy" Decker

Hope "Terrifier" Wyatt

Sam "Punisher" Samuels

Flight Lead: Mikhail "Rex" Reston

This was Jess's fifth off-world contract. Seeing Tau Ceti f felt so unique, with its rich colors and bright sun. Though still fresh to the field, she handled her own, and her ship, the FV-12 Firestar, was squat yet tough. A stubby fuselage with a pointed cockpit made the ship resemble a flying wing, and was built it with power and acceleration in mind. What it lacked in armaments it made up for in speed. Nimble and slick, it could blaze through the sky faster than all the other fighters. Jess had flown it several times in races and came out first three out of four times. The one loss was due to mechanical failure. As this was a highly dangerous contract, there had been many rejections on call lists. Due to the high rejection volume, they had accepted her without question. Her reasons for saying yes were money and because she saw that Cyril would be in the squadron. She knew he would have her back no matter what.

The only new faces were Piper and Punisher. Piper was an older starfighter who had been full freelance for close to a decade. A well-read man with a bushy beard, he'd gained his callsign as he smoked a pipe during his off hours and was generally a well-liked man. A solid pilot to have at one's wing.

Punisher was another story. New to the field but a natural. Also a hothead who could snap at any time. There had been reports of a quick temper and impulsive behavior. Not someone who could ever lead a squadron. He was extremely skilled in the cockpit, but he also took unnecessary risks, such as breaking away from his wing to chase a target or flying dangerously close to other squadron members. A cowboy, for sure. Rex had warned Punisher before takeoff that any dangerous maneuvers would mean immediate cancellation of his contract. It was no surprise to anyone why he had accepted the job. He wanted to hunt.

Rex was someone Cyril hadn't seen in a while. He had been on the opposite side of the galaxy for a long-term assignment. A well-kempt man, with a thin mustache and the face of a classical actor, he had a solid rep in the freelance world. Didn't ride his crew too hard but could inspire when necessary. That didn't mean he never cracked the whip from time to time. He'd been a squadron leader for over three years with no failed operations. Like most of the other pilots, he did not have a wife nor any children. His passion was flight, and he had established himself with a solid rep in a quick time. Cyril was happy to be flying under someone other than Garrison.

With the cloud cover still on their side, the squadron of twelve split into two groups of six and six. Flight A was composed of Skyhawk, Metalhead, Punisher, Terrifier, and Rex. Flight B was Honey Badger, Piper, KitKat, Karaoke, Auger, and Gameboy. Rex led Flight A; Honey Badger led Flight B. Cyril always believed Allegra was destined for command. This was a small taste of it. They flew in two V-pattern formations above the clouds, with each ship fifty meters apart. The transport ships were waiting below for raiders to attack them. Rex had designated the three transports as Zebra One, Two, and Three. The moment the attack would start, the fighters would dive in and pounce on the enemy. Their destination was eleven hundred kilometers away in Nickel City, which the Crecian government had named after the massive nickel deposit they had excavate to flatten the terrain years prior. They'd been in the air for thirty minutes, waiting for the first attack. None came.

"This is quite unfortunate," Wezlen said from the RIO seat.

"Maybe they knew you were coming and decided to stay home," Cyril said teasingly.

"Three transports. Who wouldn't jump at this opportunity?"

"Smart people. The radar back there is operational, if you want to keep busy and not annoy me. Metalhead, how are you doing over there, babe?"

"Green, green, Skyhawk."

"Glad to hear it. Happy you could join us."

"All fighters, cut the chatter. Keep this channel clear," Rex said in a casual tone.

"Copy that, Rex," Cyril said.

They flew in silence again. The cloud cover ahead was dissipating, so they made a course correction. All ships banked right thirty degrees to remain in decent cover. The worst part was always the waiting. They knew the enemy was watching them, but they had no idea where those eyes were. Somewhere below was a full squadron ready to pounce. The question was, when would they finally make up their minds?

"So exactly how do I work this?" Wezlen asked.

"You don't know how to read a radar?" Cyril asked.

"Not all of us were born with wings, sir. Give me the crash course, please?"

Maybe I should just crash. That'll teach you, Cyril thought, shaking his head. He found Wezlen to be annoying and a pest. Cyril's cockpit was sacred. He did not allow just anyone in its seats. This felt like a violation.

"Excuse me, sir. I asked—"

"I heard you. There's a small switch to your left that says Radar Cooling. Flip it."

Wezlen flipped the switch. "Done. What next?"

"Now, there's another set of switches called WCS and LED. Hit those."

Wezlen scanned the cockpit for a moment, then found them near his right leg. He flipped them. The screen in the seat in front of him displayed all tactical data and telemetry for the surrounding area.

Cyril continued. "Now, there's a small dial to your left that says MAGVAR. That's your magnetic variance. You spin that to scan the area in a circle for any pings. And that's all you need to know. Got it?"

"Sir, I'm getting pings all around us!"

"That's just our squadron. You need to extend the range with another dial next to the MAGVAR, called the CAP wheel. Set it to maximum, and you'll get more beyond our squadron."

"Oh. How do you operate this if you're the only one in your ship?"

"I had a separate system installed up front. I never use that one."

"I see," Wezlen said, befuddled. He spun the wheel to max and saw the view screen in front of him extend to three thousand meters. "*Ah*, it really is that easy."

"Used to be a complicated system. It was redesigned for idiots," Cyril said. Wezlen didn't notice the jab.

"All fighters, thunderstorms ahead. Watch for lightning strikes," Rex said.

All fighters replied with a green light signal on their HUDs. It was easier than every person chiming in and cluttering the radio. In the distance, a lightning bolt arced across the cloud cover. The fighters had to keep their eyes peeled for more arcs in case one decided they needed a quick jolt.

They waited as they inched closer to their destination. Someone yawned as Cyril's radar pinged.

Wezlen noticed as well and said, "Sir, I think I found something."

"Good for you. You get a cookie later. Skyhawk to Rex, we have income bogeys bearing three-zero-zero, elevation one thousand meters. Gotta be that party we were waiting for."

"Copy that, Skyhawk. Wait for signal confirmation. No radio chatter to the transports. Wait for the signal."

Everyone went silent again. The engines seemed louder as the anticipation of combat danced on the edge of everyone's fingertips. Punisher got twitchy and looked down outside his canopy yet saw nothing but clouds. He was on the verge of saying *to hell with it* and diving into the thick of it. A red blinking icon popped up on everyone's HUD—the signal of attack.

"That's our cue," Rex said. "All fighters, dive, dive, dive."

The twelve fighters dipped their noses forward, punched their throttles, and flew toward the cloud cover.

"Halo Squadron, line abreast. Be ready to break," Rex said.

All the fighters formed into a single line of twelve as they descended. Cyril swept his wings to their backward position as they descended for maximum speed. The G-forces slammed them into their seats as the ships screamed toward the silvery clouds.

Someone had left their radio on vox and breathed heavily into their headset. Cyril chimed in and said, "To the person breathing like they're jacking off, turn off your radio already."

The radio turned off, and the breathing stopped. Training had taught specific breathing exercises to all pilots during flights with extreme G-maneuvers to handle the stress of flight. A single G felt like pulling a tight turn in a car, but seven Gs felt like an elephant sitting on the pilot's chest. Muscles locked up, blood flow became harder to pump, vision blurred, dizziness, and the chance of G-LOC (G-induced loss of consciousness) became not just probable but highly likely. Every pilot during the dive breathed quickly to keep the blood flowing.

In many ways, the breathing exercises were akin to a woman in labor—sharp breaths in and out to keep the brain and muscles active.

As they entered the clouds, water pellets streaked across Cyril's canopy. The maneuver slammed Wezlen into his seat, making him nauseated, and he groaned and wheezed.

"Wezlen, if you puke in my ship, I'll eject you in a heartbeat."

Wezlen couldn't hold back and vomited. His breakfast filled his helmet to his nostrils. He unbuckled his helmet, drained the vomit onto his lap, then buckled it again. The puke slid backward into the seat and coated the rear end of the cockpit.

"Motherfucker," Cyril whispered angrily.

The clouds finally cleared to reveal the world below. A scenic view of tree-covered mountains, with rivers running between the peaks. The small trees were packed together so densely that it almost resembled a green carpet from above. Above the thick forest, the three transports were under siege by a swarm of low-grade Banshees— junker fighters cobbled together from scraps yet deadly in large numbers. And the numbers were definitely on the Banshee's side. Forty-six of them to be exact. They circled the three ships, attempting to force them to land. Cyril's eyes widened. Rex remained cool and collected despite the odds.

"My God," a stunned Jess whispered over the radio.

The raiders hadn't spotted them from above, which gave them a slight advantage.

"Tally forty-six low. Pick your targets, train your shots. Don't shoot unless you're gonna hit. Make 'em count. Good luck, Halo Squadron," Rex said.

As they descended, Punisher and Honey Badger homed on two fighters and fired. Their targets didn't even know what hit them. The rest of the enemy squadron wised up to what was happening. The pilots had sprung the trap, and the raiders scattered like ants.

Halo Squadron split into pairs. Metalhead stayed on Skyhawk's wing in pursuit of a trio of Banshees pulling around a mountainside. Cyril swept his wings forward and stayed close to Jess. They followed a rapid river around the mountainside as they chased the raiders. Cyril noted the Banshees' color scheme matched the forest below, implying their hideout must be nearby.

"Wezlen, need you to do me a favor," Cyril said.

"*Uh*, what?" Wezlen groaned, feeling nauseous again.

"Keep looking out behind us. You see smoke, you tell me. I think they're hiding in the trees. Got it?"

"Look for smoke. Okay."

"Metalhead, watch your targeting. They might be camouflaged."

"Copy that, Skyhawk."

They powered around the mountain, their vapor cones slicing across their wings and cockpits. When they reached the other side, the fighters were gone. Vanished. Not even on the horizon.

"What the fuck?"

A tone locked on Cyril, and his heart skipped three beats. "Wezlen, there's a tone on us! *Where are they?*"

Wezlen looked back and saw three fighters ascend from the deck toward them. They had rounded the mountain, pulled a hard stop, then went V/TOL in a small clearing in the trees to wait for them to pass. Their colors and small size camouflaged them perfectly.

"They're behind us! They were waiting," Wezlen yelled.

"Metalhead, tight turn! Break right," Cyril yelled.

As Jess split to the right and Cyril banked left, all three raiders fired. Two missiles went after Cyril, one after Jess. He gained altitude by punching straight skyward. As he rocketed up, he popped a set of flares that released a drum beat cacophony as they ejected from the fuselage. The two tracking missiles took the bait and exploded. He cut the throttle, yawed left, and fired the throttle again.

"Metalhead, how you doin'?"

"I'm good. Missile hit the deck. Dove low, popped flares," she said, almost out of breath.

"Copy that. I got two on me. Keep rounding the mountain. I'm gonna draw them to you. When you get your shot, take it, even if I'm in the way."

"Cyril, what—"

"Just do it. I know what I'm doing."

"I don't really like this plan," Wezlen said with dismay.

"Well, then get out and walk," Cyril retorted.

Metalhead rounded the mountain on the west side, while Cyril dove to round the east side. He took a few pot shots at a random passing fighter but missed. He kicked himself for getting greedy. With the number of raiders after them compared to the amount of ammunition between the twelve starfighters, they'd be lucky to win the fight.

As he rounded the mountain, he saw Jess approaching him, a single fighter on her tail. Cyril grabbed tone on the enemy fighter, but he didn't fire. He rolled sideways, and Jess followed. She snagged tone on one of the fighters behind Cyril and yelled, "Ready!"

"Break and fire," Cyril yelled.

They fired simultaneously, their missiles streaking past each other. Cyril's and Jess's cockpits came so close they could almost reach out and high five. Both missiles found their targets and exploded into balls of flame. One fighter remained on Cyril's tail.

He watched the chaos above them, featuring too many fighters to keep count of, buzzing around like insects in the summer months. Tone landed on Cyril again. "Hang on. We're goin' weightless!" He pulled up, killed his throttle, pulled his airbrakes, and pitched down. The missile just barely sailed past the nose of his ship and into the distance.

Wezlen wailed as gravity disappeared. Chunks of his vomit splashed into the canopy, then fell into his lap and onto his helmet. The enemy fighter flew by below them and broke right. Cyril punched the throttle, pulled right, switched the guns, and let out a mean spray. The engine burst wide open, and the ship fell from the sky. The pilot ejected as it began to tumble and twist.

"That's three down. Metalhead, form on me," Cyril said.

Jess came around and formed up.

"That sit-and-wait trick. Gonna have to remember that one."

"That was nuts. Let's get back up top," Jess said.

They pulled up and found a set of raiders trailing Rex and Terrifier. Skyhawk and Metalhead got tone and fired. Cyril's target went down; Jess's pulled away and launched flares.

"Fuck," she screamed.

"It's okay. Plenty more to go around," Cyril said.

On and on, the battle raged. The worst part of aerial dogfights was how they were very unlike films or videogames. It was more like a game of long-range chess. Wait for the opponent to make a move, then countermove. Rinse and repeat until one side made a mistake. Someone would get greedy, they would get loose, they would get impatient. Then one side would seize the opportunity and exploit it.

For thirty minutes, missiles and gunfire and wreckage riddled the sky. Honey Badger took a gunfire swipe across her left wing but nothing too devastating. Jess took missile shrapnel into her fuselage after a flare countermeasure. She had problems with power distribution to her engines and switched to the auxiliary line. She could still fly but needed to take it easy and could only reach 70 percent of her maximum thrust.

Another ten minutes passed. Of the original forty-six enemy fighters, missiles had destroyed seventeen, gunfire had disabled three, and four had bugged out. Halo let them go. That left twenty-six active fighters. Between the twelve starfighters, armaments ran low.

"Halo Squadron, we are approaching our target destination. Will radio for reinforcements," the transport captain said.

"Copy that, Zebra One. Reinforcements urgent. Repeat, reinforcements urgent," Rex yelled.

A swipe of gunfire crossed Punisher's bow, and a single shot disabled his HUD. His canopy polarizer flickered on and off. "Fuck, I can't see!"

"Punisher, what's the problem?" KitKat asked as she flew alongside.

"I can't see a goddamn thing!"

"Dump it. It's toast. Eject already."

He punched his HUD and control panel. "Come on, you sonofabitch. Fly or die!" With one solid punch, the polarizer stopped flickering, and his HUD flipped on again, though without displaying any telemetry data. "Oh, there we go. All good now."

"What was the problem?" KitKat craned her head to survey the damage.

"Eh, my polarizer is all fucked up."

"Goddamn idiot." KitKat shook her head.

"Man, that was really weird."

With Punisher's HUD disabled, it didn't register an incoming projectile, and a missile punched through the undercarriage of the ship without warning, and he exploded. KitKat watched him pop like a balloon, then knifed hard left, and dove toward the deck. Halo Squadron's first loss.

"Halo Squadron, Punisher is down. Check your visuals and watch your six. No more screw ups," Rex commanded.

All fighters sent a visual copy. The radio was, for the most part, quiet. Each fighter did their job, hunting and destroying. Too much chatter would be distracting and block up incoming radio traffic from outside the combat zone. Allegra dropped another raider with gunfire. Twenty-five remaining.

Cyril circled around and ascended seven hundred meters. He inverted and looked down at the action. With so much happening, he needed a full visual of the action below. Two raiders chased KitKat. He pulled back hard on his flight stick and dove, while Wezlen offered up wails and groans, then vomited in his helmet again. The wind whistled across the wings of the Skyhawk as Cyril nosedived. His HUD picked up the two raiders, their red diamonds enlarging in his view as he blazed toward them. KitKat had taken a peppering of gunfire across her left wing and was struggling to compensate.

"Skyhawk to KitKat, inbound on your tangos. Hang tight, girl."

"Copy, Skyhawk. Losing attitude control. Gonna have to ditch soon."

"Almost there…" He locked onto one raider and fired his final missile. It hit dead in the raider's engines and erupted into flames. The second pulled away and tried to make a run for it. Cyril kept his hand on the throttle and steadily followed behind, dropping his throttle to increase his turn radius. Then he punched the throttle to gain distance. With only guns left, he had to be in close range. He finally closed in at six hundred meters, but that was too much of a gamble to blow ammunition. He maintained the cat-and-mouse game, slowing and accelerating. Once he was within four hundred meters, he tapped his trigger, releasing short spurts. A few rounds hit, and the raider spewed black smoke. Cyril took the initiative, punched the throttle, closed to two hundred meters, and opened fire. The engines spewed flames, and the raider plummeted to the forest below. The pilot ejected as it nosedived.

Cyril pulled up on KitKat's port side. Several panels hung on for dear life, and the left-wing flaps were completely gone. She was done in the fight.

"Skyhawk to KitKat, your left wing is toast. Head to the rendezvous. Punch your throttle and get outta here. You did good."

"Thanks for the assist, Skyhawk. See you back home." She pulled off to the right and dove toward the deck. No raiders followed.

Cyril rejoined Jess and Allegra. The trio stayed together as they combed the combat area for more targets. Another three raiders had bugged out, either due to mechanical failure or they had burned through all their ammunition. Halo Squadron was gaining the upper hand. One by one, raider after raider dropped. Halo was much more capable than a ragtag raider group.

A single raider with a yellow stripe running up its dorsal wing took a shot perpendicular to Rex and sliced a mean streak across the center of his fuselage. The engines sputtered, and everything on his instrument panel flashed red.

"Halo Squadron, lost attitude control. Losing power. I'm in the dirt. Honey Badger, you're in command. Get them—" Then the power cut out.

From a distance, Cyril, Jess, and Allegra watched Rex punch out of his cockpit and dart straight up. His ship slowly dipped and finally crashed, shredding the treetops below. Allegra was now squadron leader.

"Halo Squadron, Rex is down. Honey Badger is now in command," Allegra said. She looked out her canopy and saw Rex's chute deploy as he drifted into the trees. "Rex is on the ground. Zebra One, will need medivac soon. How copy, over?"

"Copy, Halo Squadron. Command insignia transferred to Honey Badger. Medivac standing by."

The fight continued. Cyril was down to his last seventy-five rounds of ammunition. A raider chased Terrifier below. He descended and pursued. The raider caught on quickly though and pulled away. It engaged its V/TOL engine and 'bunny-hopped.' Cyril flew right past.

"I didn't know they could do that," Wezlen yelled, astonished.

"That's a new one on me too," Cyril replied. Now he was the one being hunted. He dove lower, barely staying above the terrain. Then missile lock.

"*Smoke*," Wezlen yelled.

Cyril pulled back hard and popped his last set of flares. The missile veered off and exploded. He kept pulling back. The G-force strained his vision, blood left his brain, and he began to gray out. All color disappeared from the sky. At the last second, he pushed forward hard and regained control. He felt like he was floating and shook himself from his trance. Wezlen passed out from G-LOC. He knifed to the right and looked up. The raider was still on him and had one missile on its right-wing mount.

"Halo Squadron, need assistance. Tango on my—"

The raider exploded. A missile had hit the top of its fuselage. Jess was the shooter.

"Thank you, Metalhead," Cyril said, relieved.

"Anytime, Skyhawk."

They rejoined and saw Halo Squadron had downed another six raiders.

Allegra got on the vox radio channel and said, "To all raiders, this is your final warning. Retreat now, or you will be *decimated*!"

Two fighters got the message and retreated. The rest stayed to fight. Six raiders remained.

"Halo Squadron, pick your targets and engage. Tear them to pieces."

Terrifier and Metalhead scored hits but no kills. Both their targets retreated, badly damaged, and limped home. Piper and Karaoke worked together to bait one fighter into the other's gun range. Another one down. Then two raiders chased Cyril. They zipped in behind him and popped off shots. Two rounds hit one of the dorsal fins but without extensive damage. With no flares left, Cyril looked to the horizon. Lightning arced across the sky. He gunned the throttle forward and swept his wings back.

"Sir, aren't we supposed to stay out of the storm?" Wezlen asked nervously. He had just woken up.

"Yep."

"Then, shouldn't you turn around?"

"Nope." He slammed his throttle forward as hard as possible as he retracted his wings. As he gunned it, he juked back and forth, baiting them to follow.

They did, desperate for the kill. Rain raked Cyril's canopy as he rushed into the storm. Streaks of lightning snapped every few seconds, like electric tree branches materializing into existence. It was a rough one. The turbulence was so choppy he felt like he might break his wrist just keeping the ship level. But he did, and forward he pushed. Soon, nothing surrounded him but dark gray clouds and white lightning. If a mountain was in front of him, he wouldn't know until he was properly embedded into its side. Once he had gained enough distance inside, he pulled back his throttle, knifed right, and retreated.

Lightning was actually not a significant threat to aircraft, as they were all properly insulated from electrical charge, but the loss of navigation would confuse the raiders, and they'd be lost forever. He kept himself steady as the clouds dissipated, and he finally left the storm behind. The raiders had lost sight of him and did not follow. They were long gone. He rejoined with the rest of Halo Squadron. No one else had been downed.

"Skyhawk to Halo Squadron, I think we can count those two tangos as out."

"Copy, Skyhawk. We'll call that a win. RTB," Honey Badger said.

Of the twelve original ships, Rex's ship had been destroyed, but he had ejected. KitKat had suffered catastrophic equipment failure but reached the rendezvous. And the only human loss to the group had been Punisher, due to equipment failure and complete stupidity. The remaining fighters formed up and headed for the rendezvous with Zebra One, Two, and Three in Nickel City.

***

The hydraulics on the canopy flipped on. It opened and let in the cool damp air. Cyril unbuckled and removed his helmet. He stood, set it on the seat, and pressed a button to release the foot ladder on the left side of the fuselage. He had arrived at base in line with the rest of Halo Squadron but was eager to get out of his ship as soon as possible. Once the fighting had ended, he notated how much vomit had been flung around the interior of the cockpit. Wezlen was more than ashamed of himself but still in a daze by the time they'd landed.

"What were you thinking, having a big breakfast before going airborne?" Cyril yelled as he descended his ladder. "Get outta my ship!"

"I'm sorry, Mr. Eisner. It was an accident," Wezlen replied in shame, drying vomit covering his face. He climbed slowly from the RIO seat to the ground.

"No, an accident is 'I rear ended someone because I'm texting.' You intentionally had your eggs and oatmeal this morning, knowing you were going up. Get the fuck outta my ship! Now!"

"I apologize, Mr. Eisner. Do not yell at me. Remember who you work for."

"Yeah. Not you. You're a desk rider. Go back to it."

Wezlen said nothing more and walked away. He tripped and stumbled. Feeling the earth beneath his feet was like stepping off a roller coaster for the first time.

Cyril shook his head and walked around the back of his ship to inspect the damage. The right dorsal fin had taken two gunshot rounds straight through; however, he could easily patch that up. Some G-force stress showed on both wings. Several bolts and rivets had come loose, and one panel was slightly cracked open. Again, nothing too difficult to fix. He had known the risks going into the assignment, but he also knew his ship's capabilities. The A-7 had been with him through thick and thin—a dependable machine to get him home. This was nowhere near the worst thing that had happened to her. More than likely, she would see worse in the future. Cyril would always get her home though.

He climbed into his cockpit and flipped on his HUD to check his armaments. He had fired all four missiles, had deployed all the flares, and only seventy-five rounds of his 20mm ammunition remained. Rearming would cost more than the repairs. His power cell was also depleted to just under 40 percent. That could wait, but it would be best to have a spare on standby back home. He turned his HUD off and investigated the back seat. Splattering of Wezlen's vomit caked the seat, the radar panel, the breakers, even the interior of the canopy. It would take at least an hour to clean.

As Cyril sighed, KitKat approached his ship. "Hey, Eisner," KitKat said playfully.

"Hey, there she is. How you doin', babe?"

"I'm good. Thanks for the assist."

"Heh. Anything for you. How's your ship?"

"Basically, scrap at this point. Gonna be outta commission for a while. Might have to hitch a ride back home."

"I can take you, if you need a ride."

"Well, I'd suggest cleaning that up first, 'cause I'm not getting in that vomitron there."

Cyril eyed the RIO seat and sighed. "Yeah, I'll get right on that," he said, with a fake smile.

"Good. They're bringing Rex in now. Debrief in an hour."

As she began walking away, Cyril called after her. "Hey, you think you can give me a hand?"

She turned around and walked backward while she shouted, "I think I've cleaned up enough excrement from your ship to last three lifetimes. That one's all you."

"Thanks. I love you too," he shouted as she turned around and kept walking.

She chuckled to herself as she went into the mess hall.

He leaned on the edge of his headrest. "*Ahh*, fuck my ass."

For the next thirty minutes, Cyril painstakingly scrubbed and washed the back seat. It smelled wretched, and there was no quick way of going about it. Just scrub, scrub, scrub. It was monotonous and mind-numbing.

As he scrubbed, he heard someone climb the ladder behind him. "I don't envy you at all, Cyril," Jess said. She handed him a blank flash drive for his gun camera footage.

He took it and pocketed it. "What are you talking about? I'm livin' the dream."

She smiled.

"So, how do you like it here on Tau Ceti?

"Feels weird. Time and gravity feel… wrong."

"It's the size of the planet. Time for us is a little slower because the gravity is slightly heavier. What is a couple days for us is probably a week on Proxima."

She slapped her forehead and sighed. "Oh fuck. I missed my show."

"You forgot about the time dilation, didn't you?"

"Yeah."

"You get used to it. This is one of only two Ekumen planets that have this problem. Everywhere else is normal time." He finished wiping off the radar view screen and chucked the disgusting rag over the edge of the cockpit. It landed on the gray landing pad with a wet slap. He was finally finished with the seat and the radar. The canopy was next.

"Hey, thanks for carrying me today," Jess said sincerely.

"*Hmm?*"

"I didn't do very well. I was impatient. And I wasted too much ammo and took hits."

Cyril stood and pointed at the damaged dorsal fin on this ship. "Jess, I took hits too." Then he pointed at the left wing. "I have stress fractures from G-force overturns, and I burned through almost all my ammo. I didn't carry you. You did just fine. Relax. If anything, I owe you the thanks for the save up there."

"You're welcome. I feel exhausted."

"You're coming down off the adrenaline, and the gravity is messing with you. You're gonna sleep great tonight."

"I hope so," she said while yawning.

A bulky oval-shaped medivac transport descended to the tarmac. Once it landed, Rex stepped out, carrying his helmet bag. A pair of EMTs deboarded next, carrying a gurney with a body bag—Punisher's body. Jess and Cyril watched them pass.

"Damn," Jess whispered.

"Not everyone goes home, Jess. That's the name of the game," Cyril said. "Somewhere out there is a bullet with all our names on it. The trick is to die before it finds you."

Jess said nothing. The thought was morbid but probably true.

"Well, hey, I gotta finish up here. I'll see you at debrief."

"Yeah, see you then," she said sullenly. She had never been part of a squadron that had taken a hit like that, never lost a flight mate. The realization that anyone could go at any time scared her. She stepped off the ladder and walked with hunched shoulders to the administration building.

Cyril closed the canopy, dipped a fresh rag into the slop bucket between his feet, and resumed cleaning off Wezlen's upchuck.

Half an hour later, he was finally finished. He downloaded his ship's camera files and headed to administration. When he reached the boardroom for debrief, he saw they had started early.

"Nice of you to join us, Mr. Eisner," Rex said, still in his flight suit. A large gash marred his forehead, probably from a tree during his parachute descent.

"Sorry, lost track of time. Had to clean up a bit of a mess."

"Please keep track from now on. Anyway, we've received word that the raiding party was found on the outskirts sixty kilometers from here. They'd been using a cave system for their base of operations. Allegra, you said reinforcements never arrived, correct?"

"That's right. After you were out, we were on our own."

"That means somewhere down the chain that order didn't make it to the support fighters. Which means an insider. Which means a leak."

"Someone's working with them?" Piper asked.

The crew murmured to each other.

"That's right. But that's a law enforcement issue now. We're done. Hand in your gun cam footage and write your reports. After that, you're all off duty till tomorrow at seven-hundred hours. Excellent work today, everyone. And Allegra, I'll be putting in a good word for you. You've got command chops. I'll be recommending you for flight lead."

"Thank you, sir. I appreciate it, but I was just doing my job."

"But you do it too well to just be another jockey. Expect calls when you get back to Proxima. Dismissed."

Everyone filed out the room, handing their flash drives to Rex as they passed. Each pilot grabbed a clipboard from the security desk and went into the room to notate their flight reports. When they finished, they left them on the table in the center of the room and headed for the mess hall.

Dinner was pasta with meat sauce, freshly cut chicken breast, and bread rolls. Nothing fancy, but every pilot devoured their meal like they'd been starved for days. The action had burned all their energy. When they finished, they returned to the barracks, and everyone collapsed into their beds. Some went to sleep right away, some just laid there and chatted. Cyril and Jess both passed out immediately.

He awoke in the middle of the night to use the bathroom. Once he had finished, he didn't feel tired anymore. He walked outside and looked up into the night sky. It was crystal-clear, and the glimmer of the Milky Way was in perfect view. With no moon around Tau Ceti f, the darkness on the ground was nearly pitch black. Small blue emergency lights surrounded the rooftops of every building and every walkway. He smelled burning tobacco.

"It's strange being on a planet with no moon," Piper said from a small bench to the right of the barracks entrance. "Always seems like something's missing." He wore small glasses, a brown beret, and smoked his trademark pipe of freshly cut tobacco. The sweet smell was the only scent in the air.

"And I bet a trip to the beach sucks too without tides," Cyril said, chuckling.

"An absolute waste. Please, join me."

Cyril sat next to Piper.

"A hell of a day, wasn't it?" Piper asked.

"Yes, it was. Overall, a resounding success."

"Too bad about Punisher, though."

"Yeah, well, what can you do?"

"You know, my second off-planet flight, we lost all but two fighters. Myself and one other. Massive error in judgment on the part of intelligence. Totally outgunned. They got everything wrong. Mission was a failure before it even started. It was enough to make me question my life choices." He inhaled a long drag of tobacco.

"And what conclusion did you come to?"

"I didn't die because it wasn't my time. Not everything is chance. There's gotta be some kind of a plan to the universe."

"I'm not exactly what you'd call the religious type."

"Did I mention God? Or religion? Or faith? I said, *the universe.* Thirteen point eight billion years ago, nothing. Just big black. And now this. Everything and everyone right here, right now. Can't just be chance."

"And what if it is?" Cyril queried.

"If it is just chance, then every decision you make, make 'em count."

KitKat stepped outside, careful not to slam the barracks door, wearing shorts and a tank top. Her dark skin seemed to glow in the blue emergency lighting.

"Hey," Cyril said to her.

"Hey, why are you guys up?" she asked.

"Waxing philosophical, my dear, but I think I'm done for the night." Piper tapped his pipe on the edge of the bench and placed it in his breast pocket. "I'll see you both in the morning." He went inside, also careful to close the door gently behind him.

KitKat took Piper's seat next to Cyril. The smell of sweet tobacco lingered in the air. "Get your ship cleaned up?"

"As good as it can be. If I could dip the whole thing in bleach, I would," Cyril said.

"Well, I'm sure you'll have plenty of time when you get back. You're still good to give me a ride home?"

"Yeah, I can drop you off on Olympus. They're gonna haul your ship back, right?"

"Yup, it's gonna get loaded onto a freighter tomorrow morning."

"That's good."

Then KitKat sidled closer to Cyril, ran her hand between his legs, and kissed his neck. Her breathing was heavy in his ear. "Wanna hook up?" she whispered.

"Cat…"

"No one's around. We can do it right here." She reached into his pants.

"Cat," he said, just a notch beneath sternly.

"What? What's wrong?"

"I just… I can't, ya know."

"Why?"

"I kinda… met someone. And I'm… you know how it is."

She pulled her hand from his pants and slid away. "Yeah, I know how it is."

"I'm really sorry, Cat."

"Why are you sorry? We live on two totally different planets. It was bound to happen at some point."

"You're not mad?"

"No. A little disappointed, because I'm damn near feral horny right now, but it's okay. I get it."

"Sorry to disappoint you."

They both went quiet and awkwardness set in.

"So, what's her name?" Cat asked, doing her best to break the nervous tension.

"Marie."

"Marie. That's a beautiful name. She's lucky."

"Well, we're not like dating-dating, but I'm just… It's complicated."

"Cyril, you don't have to explain, man. I get it. It's all good."

"Thanks, babe."

They smiled at each other.

"You're sure?"

"If you ask that again, I'm gonna punch you in the dick."

They laughed.

She stood and said, "Well, I'm gonna go rub one out in the bathroom because, holy fuck, I need to."

Cyril chortled. "Have fun."

"I'll try to." Then she whispered in Cyril's ear, "It's a shame you're not joining me. Goodnight, Cyril." She gave him a peck on the cheek.

"Goodnight, Cat. See you in the morning."

She walked inside and gently closed the door.

Cyril sat in the quiet. No birds or insects were around. He looked up to see if he could find Proxima—even though it was impossible without proper navigation charts—and thought about Marie. Maybe she was stargazing at that exact same time, though that was also an impossibility, given the time dilation of Tau Ceti f.

He felt bad for turning down Cat. Their last hook up on Tulson had been a good one. And then he thought about Marie again and how he felt something else was there—something more than just a one-off every now and then hookup. Piper had said it best, the perfect way to sum up the last five minutes:

If it is just chance, then every decision you make, make 'em count.

He intended to do just that when he returns to Proxima.

Make 'em count.

CHAPTER 8

SMELLED LIKE CHERRIES

For Cyril, it had only been two days on Tau Ceti f; however, on Proxima, it had been two weeks. He was past due on his rent, and all the food in his fridge had gone bad. He'd forgotten to empty it out before he left, and a massive pile of notifications had stacked up in his phone—multiple job postings, requests for his services, an email from Minese stating he had missed therapy the previous week, and one email from Arcturus. It stated they required a physical exam for full employment. He replied that he would be available the following week and would respond with full details. It took a full half hour to reply to every message and notification. Apparently, while he had been away, his speech at the Arcturus fundraiser had gone viral. Many in the press referred to him as the "Freelancer for the free world," and he had become a minor internet celebrity across the continent. He chuckled at that thought, shook his head, and closed his internet browser.

Back at M&M airfield, another ship had commandeered his landing spot, as he hadn't paid the monthly fee. He took the next spot over and sent payment to Stacy. Jess had arrived home before him, as he had to make a pit stop on Olympus to drop off KitKat. They had said their goodbyes without awkwardness, then he headed home. He still felt a tinge of guilt for turning her down on Tau Ceti f, but if he was gonna turn over a new leaf, he had to truly commit. *Grow up already.*

Marie had sent him multiple messages. *Hey there … You okay? … Where R U?*

He sent a detailed reply to explain his tardiness. She responded immediately.

> MARIE: Oh, thank God, I was like, is he dead?
> CYRIL: Nope, just away for work.
> MARIE: How was it?
> CYRIL: Scenic, for sure.
> MARIE: You'll have to tell me all about it sometime.
> CYRIL: I will. Speaking of which, wanna get drinks with me?
> MARIE: Hell yeah, let's do it!
> CYRIL: Awesome. There's a bar I go to called Mallory's Heroes. It's where a lot of the local starfighters get together, since it's close to the airfield. We can go somewhere else if it's better though.
> MARIE: No, that sounds great. If you're gonna tell me some fun stories, may as well be in the right place.
> CYRIL: Then, it's a date.
> MARIE: Yes, it is. When exactly?
> CYRIL: I literally just landed half an hour ago, so how about tomorrow night? When do you get off work?
> MARIE: I finish around five, but I can roll out a little early. I just checked the location of the bar. It's not too far from where I work. Meet there at around six so I can go home and change?
> CYRIL: Perfect.
> MARIE: See you tomorrow, then?
> CYRIL: See you tomorrow night.

As he was texting, Jess walked toward him. She'd been conversing with Stacy regarding ship repairs since arriving home. "What are you smiling about?"

"Marie and I are going out tomorrow night."

"Oh, that's great! I'm proud of you, babe. Where are you going?"

"Well, she wants to hear starfighter stories, so I figured Mallory's."

Jess removed her flight suit and stashed it in her locker. Underneath her suit, she wore shorts and a sports bra, and tattoos of various shapes and designs covered her. She pulled a pair of jeans and a tank top from her locker. As she put them on, she said, "I mean, Mallory's isn't exactly the classiest place. Is this a classy lady?"

"Well, she works in infectious diseases and wants to be a mortician."

"Oh, never mind. Mallory's is perfect."

"*Mm-hmm.*" Cyril stashed his own suit and placed his helmet on the top shelf, then they went to Stacey's office. She still looked dead exhausted. "Hey, Stace, I need to rearm and repair."

She handed Cyril a pad of paper and a pen. "Write it out, and I'll get to it. How bad is the damage?"

Cyril wrote his list and handed it back. "Full rearm and one panel on my right dorsal fin needs to be replaced. I'm sure you've got that in stock. Also, throw in a new power supply."

"Full rearm and repairs for both of you. That's gonna be a lot. You both good for it?" Stacy asked.

"After what we did? Yeah, we're good," Cyril said with a smile.

"All right, I'll put in the order for the rearm. Dorsal plating, I definitely have in stock. That I can have done by tomorrow."

"Also, there's some G-force strain on both my wings. If you can have the mechanics take a look, I'd appreciate it," Cyril said.

"I'll add it to the list. Why do you look so chipper?"

"Eh, no reason." He smiled.

"*Mm-hmm*, I'm sure there's no reason with you. Get outta here."

They grabbed their personals and hopped in Jess's car. On the drive to Cyril's apartment, he calculated the full pricing for rearm and repair. The full fee for their services on Tau Ceti f was two hundred fifty thousand, and after taxes, two hundred thousand. Repairs came to fifteen thousand, new power supply was thirty thousand, and a full rearm was fifty thousand. That left one hundred five thousand in profit. Not the best, but not the worst. He wouldn't starve anytime soon, but the weight of the finances showed how costly it was to keep up in the freelance market. No free rides anywhere. Everything had a price.

Jess fared worse. Repairs to her ship's fuselage would put it out of commission for a few weeks, and the price tag was rough. In total, she only pocketed around sixty thousand. He broke the news to her as they rode in the car.

She sighed. "At least we're not dead."

His phone buzzed with a call from Arcturus Allied.

"Hello?"

"Is this Cyril Eisner?" a shrill woman's voice asked.

"Yes, it is."

"This is Ellen Moriarty with Arcturus Allied."

Cyril put his phone on Speaker and tapped Jess's shoulder. "Yeah, sorry for the late reply. I was off world on Tau Ceti f. Time dilation screwed up my schedule, Mx. Moriarty."

"I am not a *Ms*. I am nonbinary," they said with extreme fervor.

"That's what I said. I used the proper language. You might have just misheard. My signal isn't very good right now. I'm on the east side."

"Whatever. I just got your return email. Be at our main office in Balamb next Monday at seven in the morning. Do not be late. You'll need to go through a physical examination and a flight coordination test before we can add you to our freelance listing. We also need a full resume and work history for the past five years."

"That's a lot of work history to organize."

"Do it or don't come in. And, off the record, despite what Mr. Mullarkey thought of your speech a few weeks back, I still think you're a chauvinist pig."

"You met me for a total of two minutes."

"I'm a good judge of character. I've met hundreds of men like you, and they're all the same."

Jess's mouth dropped open in shock, but she stayed quiet.

Cyril did his best to keep from laughing. "Well, Mx. Moriarty, I will do my best to correct my behavior to gain your approval, and I hope to be of service to the company. I suspected it would be an uphill battle to gain your appreciation and approval, so I prepared myself to be disappointed by your disappointment, and I was not let down in my disappointment."

Cyril and Jess strained to not giggle as the other end of the line was silent.

"Just be here at seven on Monday. Goodbye, pig." The call ended.

Cyril and Jess burst out laughing.

"What the fuck? Who acts like that?" Jess asked.

"You got me."

"Oh, my God, there is sand in that woman's vagina."

"Well, they're nonbinary, like they said, but I'm sure they still have a vagina. And I think it's a cactus, not sand."

"Dear lord, don't tell me you're going to work for them."

"Jess, I need the money. How much did we both lose in our paychecks on Tau Ceti f?"

Jess sighed. "Fair."

"I'll put your name in if I get the job. Jace too."

"We'll see. If that's the caliber of people who work there, I'll pass."

"They're a big name. They probably offer benefits as well. I'm at a point where I need to start moving upward. Grinding like this is… well, just that, a grind."

"No, I get it. Just be careful."

"When am I not careful?"

Jess faced him with a deadpan stare.

"Don't fuckin' answer that."

They rode on. The traffic became congested as people headed home from work. She pulled up to his apartment, hugged him, he stepped out, and she drove off.

His apartment was the same as when he had left, though mail had piled up in his box; a past due rent bill was stuffed in the middle, and he paid it upon seeing the sum. He went through the rigorous task of cleaning out the rotten food in his fridge. Old meat had gone bad. He chucked it into the garbage and gave the fridge a decent one over.

Once he had finished, he set about doing all the menial tasks of the day—laundry, cleaning, entering his work schedule into his calendar. Then he sat on the couch with a cup of coffee, turned on some music, and relaxed. Returning home from an assignment so dangerous felt rewarding, like a gift. He'd cheated death again. Lived to fight another day. Piper's statement of making every decision count still rang in his ears. Putting a good foot forward was the only way to gain ground.

He thought about Jess, Jace, and Marie. And Layla. He pulled out his phone to text her.

> CYRIL: Hey. Got an appointment set up for Monday to join Arcturus. Hope you're doing well.

No reply. He considered writing another message but decided against it. Best to let sleeping dogs lie. That niggling thing remained in the back of his brain. Something was off, didn't feel right. But he was small, nothing he could do. It wasn't his business. Just look forward and never go back.

***

The meeting wasn't just boring; it was aggressively boring. Daniel had tasked Layla as a liaison to negotiate a distribution deal with the chief ambassador of Kepler-186F. Ambassador Winnik Koy was a Mukarian and towered over Layla and the rest of the staff in the meeting. Big, burly arms, a long face, a deep voice. In any other setting, he would be perceived as some type of fantastical creature, yet he spoke eloquently, with gravitas becoming of a politician. The one request for the meeting was that they conducted it on Kepler and not Proxima. Arcturus obliged. As Daniel hated traveling off world, he sent Layla in his stead. She hated it, being his parrot, but complied.

Vertical shades surrounded the soundproofed meeting room. A small recording device sat in the center of a square wooden table—the only official record maintained for the meeting. No copies would return with Layla to Proxima. This was a delicate issue that would determine if Arcturus would begin trial runs of an immunization program on Kepler-186F or if they would have to pack up shop and search elsewhere. It was the best and the cheapest place to start.

Since Brentwood's death, she had been *volun-told* to step into a marketing role for the company. Several high-ranking employees within Arcturus resented, and some even protested the nepotism on full display, but it wasn't so much nepotism as it was necessity. Layla's meltdown in front of the press had sent a message that not all was well within the company—infighting, power grabs, and the like. It was best to consolidate power to maintain control. Layla's recent loss also factored into her recent promotion to marketing. It would play well for an emotional crutch, let the press see things were getting back on track, and given that she was already a well-spoken young woman with a degree in marketing, meant she was well ahead of the game. She hated it, and Daniel knew it. It was manipulative on his part.

A security officer named Locke—a thin, bald man, with a hard yet slender face, who looked like he'd been chiseled from marble— escorted her to Kepler-186F. Despite the circumstances, Layla found him comforting. She reminded him a bit of Cyril, willing to do anything to protect her. But only a bit.

Arcturus had designed their vaccine to immunize against cross-species contamination, due to reports of various diseases transferring between races. Outbreaks required deportation of colonies and mass quarantine of indigenous populations to protect against further infection. Government bureaucracy was only so effective in stemming the spread. Arcturus seized the opportunity to step in and begin full trial studies of the infections. Diseases such as TCLI (Tau Ceti Lymph Node Infection), NLN (Noctis Linguistic Necrosis), and Yummel's Syndrome created serious problems for any off-world travel and trade. Various companies had been working to develop vaccinations, but none of those companies were as powerful or as wealthy as Arcturus. They'd gained full support through the Ekumen governing body to begin vaccine trials. Though the Ekumen governance approved, planet-to-planet approval was still a touchy issue. The prejudices of the Annexation War were still very raw.

Now, Layla Mullarkey had to convince the local government to move forward with distribution of a trial run of a vaccine. The main issue was how they would disperse it. It did not sit well with the indigenous people on Kepler-186F. Single injections were considered too expensive and too slow. Arcturus's plan involved an aerosol dispersion over a control group in a localized area. They then would distribute the aerosol in an airborne fashion through large ships performing flybys, not unlike aerial water tankers extinguishing forest fires. Winnik Koy, as to be expected, claimed it seemed *oppressive* and *despotic*.

He wasn't wrong.

"While our situation is certainly a risk, it is by no means the complete disaster that your company has made it out to be, Ms. Mullarkey," Winnik Koy said. "We've contained our outbreaks and restricted our travel for the time being. Arcturus has blown everything out of proportion."

Layla sat forward and folded her hands. "I don't doubt that you are handling your disease control with the utmost priority, but how often can this happen while everything is maintained at this level? That's a road to financial ruin. I've seen it before." She hated to admit it, but she was very good at the job.

Koy shook his head. "Money is money. Throw a rock, you'll find a donor—or a lobbyist. If you were to ask me if I think Arcturus's system of delivery would be effective, I would say most definitely, yet it's the visual of it all. Ships dispersing gas over my people. It would not play well for various individuals' political image, and certainly not well for cultural pride, needing another species to come in and rescue us from our own problems. Especially Terrans."

He wasn't taking the bait, playing at the angle of solving the problem quickly. Another tactic—patriotism—would have to do. She thought quickly on her feet. "The Ekumen was established for exactly that reason, a cultural collective of assistance. Your own research has fallen behind as you've diverted funds from medical research into disaster relief and now into biological containment. The people look up to you, to your governance, to your sense of honor and heritage. Mukarians have always been considered the salt of the system, the grunts diving into the shit to do the work no one else is willing to take on. To bring both our species together, that's why we're here in the first place. We're just trying to help."

Winnik paused. It was quiet. A chair creaked. He studied Layla and her hard-as-stone eyes and stared right back. No matter what, he couldn't quite figure her out. Was she toying with him, playing him for a fool, or was she genuine? She'd become impenetrable. He was beginning to like this human woman. She was a challenge.

"You may be right, Ms. Mullarkey, but we also recognize the can is always being kicked down the road. There's always the next time, and the next. And yet, I still have a reservation."

"What reservation would that be, Ambassador?"

"You are Terran. Humanity has had a… questionable history with interspecies relations. Trust is elusive with you. Prejudice can be high here on Kepler. What gives you the right to be here to solve our issues for us rather than us finding our own way?"

"I don't see it as a right. I see it as an opportunity for growth and change and for the betterment of the Ekumen. What we solve here can be solved on all other planets. Outbreaks will be a thing of the past. Humanity may be an insolent child from time to time, but that doesn't mean our conversation cannot be informative if some of us are well versed. I know you're implying the human race's sordid history of war, conflict, and fanaticism. If we were all still like that, we wouldn't be here right now. We'd still be the inbred cannibals left behind on Earth. A thing of the past. We are only looking forward now."

Winnik studied her again. She was right, but so was he. Humanity *had* earned its seat, and yet it was still worth being cautious. Humans had a wretched history, and the rest of the Ekumen knew it. Maneuvering into a seat of power among the collective body had been no easy task, but they had proved their worth. Only one hundred and twenty years had passed since the Ekumen was first established, and just over thirty had passed since the Annexation War had ended. Yet it was stronger than ever. Humanity had improved travel methods by introducing FOIL technology. They were owed a debt of gratitude. It was getting harder to say no to human assistance.

"Let me put it to you another way, Ambassador Koy," Layla posited as she stood and approached the window blinds. "My husband was taken from me a little over a month ago. Killed on our anniversary. We had our problems, fighting between the two of us, but we always found common ground." She swiped aside one of the blades to see out the window at the rain and the distant orange sky due to the red sun. "We still found the best in each other, even while at each other's throats. I admit my meltdown after his death was due to stress and an overload of emotion, but he was a good man and wanted what was best for the Ekumen. Were I not here, he would be, saying the exact same thing. Humanity is here for the growth of the Ekumen. We're here to help. And if all else fails, we can arrange financial compensation for you and your people. But it is, of course, up to you, sir."

It worked. Winnick relented. Layla would be an amazing politician. Or lawyer.

"I see what you're saying, Ms. Mullarkey, and my sympathies for your loss. Brentwood Forester was a great man, and he is dearly missed. I'll recommend that the Kepler state representatives review your efforts and go ahead with a controlled dispersion."

"Thank you, Ambassador Koy. You're a good man."

"Well, I'm a Mukarian, not a man, but I understand your analogy. Good day, Ms. Mullarkey."

The Mukarian ambassadors party filtered out one by one. A scribe entered the room and removed a small data chip from the recorder in the middle of the table, which he would transcribe, translate, and file for archiving. Layla and Locke exited last. They were scheduled to depart the following day but decided to leave immediately. The embassy was ten kilometers from the landing strip. Their car inched through the rain, weaving around traffic. A car accident to the side of the freeway slowed them for a short time, but after that, it was clear all the way to the ship.

They entered the sleek landing craft and sat. After takeoff, Locke pulled a pen from his breast pocket and twisted it from top to bottom, one hundred eighty degrees. A green light shone from both ends. He scoured every nook and cranny of the cabin. While the meeting had gone well, they were paranoid of tracking devices or wiretaps feeding information to the Mukarian government. Locke found no bugs anywhere.

He retrieved a small syringe from the rear of the cabin. It was empty. He nodded to Layla; she nodded back. Then he stuck it into her neck, pressed a button on the side, and pulled the plunger. The syringe filled with gray fluid containing sensory nanites capable of recording whatever an individual saw or heard—a backup record in case the Mukarian government tried to withhold the official record of the meeting and imply Arcturus was being pushy. In other words, blackmail material. Again, Layla would be an exceptional politician.

Locke capped the syringe and placed it into a small black padded case. It would archived in the black box servers in Arcturus's database. Every landing craft had a set of onboard sensory nanites in case of last-minute assignments. Locke sat across from Layla as she silently bandaged her neck with a band aid.

Locke cracked a smile. "You did it."

"Did what?"

"Popped your cherry. Won 'em over on the first try. Good job."

She didn't laugh.

***

It was a Friday night, and Mallory's was popping. All the locals were getting ready for the weekend, the regulars were double-dipping their drink orders to stay ahead of the bartenders, and Cyril was sitting at the bar, enjoying his beer while waiting for Marie to arrive. He was dressed nice but casual with a black T-shirt and jeans—freshly purchased as well. It was just drinks and dinner. A woman like her would appreciate a place like Mallory's. Not exactly a dive, but it had character. The jukebox played a nice oldie, and a few patrons grooved on the dance floor. Cyril's phone pinged.

JESS: Turn around.

He turned to see Jess and Jace standing behind him. She stuck out her forked tongue and smiled. Jace smiled wide with pearly white teeth.

"What the fuck are you guys doing here?" Cyril asked slightly vexed.

"We've never seen this girl, so we came to see the action," Jess said.

"Plus, we're here to make sure you don't fuck it all up," Jace added.

"I've been on a date before. I'm good." Cyril sipped his beer.

"Be that as it may… we wanna watch the show," Jace professed, grinning wide.

"I'm so glad I can provide you with some entertainment for the evening."

"You better, boy. I haven't even seen a photo of her yet," Jess said. Cyril's phone pinged again.

MARIE: Coming in.

"Well, here's your first look," Cyril said.

The trio faced the door. It opened, and the world screeched to a halt. Her red hair now had black highlights, and it was blown out. She wore a black top, with a short skirt and black leggings. Short heels too that clacked when she walked. The boot on her foot was gone. Her earrings were a pair of snakes that ran up the back of her ears. She sported dark eyeshadow and blood red lips to match her hair. She looked stunning. A boxer could be knocked out without a punch ever being thrown. Dryve and Fatherdude's classic song "Red Cherry" played on the jukebox. She saw Cyril and smiled.

She was perfect.

The door slowly whooshed closed as she approached the trio. Jess's mouth hung open, Jace was dead quiet, even holding his breath, and Cyril grinned as Marie stopped in front of them.

"Hi," Cyril said.

"Hi," Marie replied. "Who's this?"

"Uh, these are my friends Jess and Jace. They're also starfighters, so they're in here a bunch. They just happened to be here when I arrived. Isn't that right, guys?" Cyril miffed, his eyes wide.

"Yeah, we were just in the area. Figured we'd stop by for a drink," Jess lied. She bit her lip, clearly jealous of Cyril's good fortune.

Jace was silent.

"Yo, Jace, you awake?" Cyril shouted as he snapped his fingers.

"Huh? Yeah. I'm good. We'll be over at the end of the bar." Jace slapped Cyril's shoulder, leaned in, and whispered, "You fuck this up, I'm swooping in."

He and Jess walked around Marie and toward the opposite end of the bar near the windows, then turned around. Jess waved toward her face to imply "What a hottie," while Jace raised both hands, spread his fingers, and mouthed, "She's a ten."

Cyril shot an annoyed smile at them, then refocused on Marie. "Sorry about that. Hi again."

"Hi again," she said.

They smiled.

"You are drop-dead gorgeous."

"You ain't half bad yourself, handsome. Now, don't be rude, and buy me a drink. I've had a very long day."

He chuckled, called Mallory over, and declared, "Anything the lady wants, put it on my tab."

"Ms. I-Don't-Know-What-Your-Name-Is, order the most expensive thing possible," Mallory suggested. "Put this motherfucker in debt to me."

"*Aww*, he seems like such a nice guy," Marie said.

Mallory scoffed. "What can I get you?"

"Tequila, straight up with a chaser."

"Wow, that kinda day, huh?" Cyril asked.

"Yeah, that kinda day."

Mallory returned with the tequila and chaser. Marie chatted about her day, mix ups on sample orders, and backed up calls for pathogen studies. Cyril just sat and smiled, captivated by her, and floated in the ocean of her eyes as she spoke. Mallory's Heroes had been his spot for finding hookups and one-night stands for the past four years. While he hadn't always been successful, he had a decent average. For four years, he had maintained the bachelor lifestyle. Tell his date everything they wanted to hear, and he'd be in their bed by midnight. But this time, it felt different. He didn't say much. Just listened and hung on her every word.

At the end of her long-winded rant about her day, she exhaled heavily. "So, how was your day?"

Cyril chuckled. "It was okay. I took care of some stuff around the house. Just another day, really."

"Must be nice to be a freelancer. Set your own hours, work at your own pace."

"Ha! Everyone says that until they actually do it. I pay my own taxes, my own insurance, my own repairs, and the rearms for my ship. It adds up, so I take everything as it comes."

"But still, you're not beholden to anyone. You're your own person."

"I suppose you could say that."

Cyril's phone rang. It was Stacy at M&M Airfield. "Eh, sorry, one sec." He answered. "Yeah?"

"Cyril, your ship is ready, fully rearmed and repaired. Need you to come in to sign off for everything," Stacy said.

"Oh, excellent." He smiled at Marie. "Hey, can I come in tonight to take care of that?"

"Be here in the next half hour or reschedule for Monday."

"I think I can make tonight work. Be there in a few minutes." He hung up. "So, question, would you be cool if we went to the airfield really quick? I gotta sign off on my ship's repairs. It's literally fifteen minutes away. We'll come right back."

"Yeah, let's go. I've never seen a ship up close, so this is exciting," she said cheerfully, the tequila already making her tipsy.

Cyril paid the tab, then they went to Jess and Jace's table.

"So, I'm taking Marie with me to sign off on my ship's repairs at the airfield. She's never seen a starfighter before. You two still gonna be here when we get back?"

"We'll be here, babe," Jess said.

"Have fun," Jace followed up.

Cyril and Marie hopped in an autocab and made the fifteen-minute trip to the airfield. The sky glowed pink and purple, and the temperature was just right. The main hangar doors were open, exposing the museum-like interior. Stacy had been disassembling another decommissioned starfighter for scrap inside.

Marie's mouth dropped open. "Holy shit, that thing is huge."

"I could make a crass joke, but I'll abstain," Cyril quipped.

She swiped him playfully across the shoulder and laughed.

"You gave that to me; I had to take it."

"*Yeeeeaaahhhh*, I did, didn't I?"

They entered into Stacy's office, but she wasn't there. They checked the break room. Also, not there. They found her sitting in a folding chair on the tarmac, watching the sunset and drinking a beer.

"Stacy, this is Marie. Marie, this is Stacy Magellan. She owns the airfield you now stand upon."

Stacy lifted her beer. "Nice to meet you. I will probably forget your name in ten minutes."

"No offense taken. I'm terrible with names too," Marie said.

"Anyway, you need me to sign off?" Cyril asked.

"Yeah, let's go. Then I can catch the last bit of sunset."

Stacy went to the workbench next to the hangar doors for the data pad that contained his work order and handed it to him. Cyril reviewed the full repair, the rearm list, and the final bill, which was slightly higher than expected, as the stress warping on the wings was pricey. Stacy had to manipulate them into place and reinforce them with interior braces, but Cyril would need a full dismantle and rebuild in the future. Cyril signed on the bottom line.

"Thank you. Happy doing business, as always," Stacy said.

While Cyril and Marie headed toward his ship, Cyril turned toward Stacy. "Hey, you made it through another week. It's Friday night. Go enjoy it!"

Marie's mouth hung open in awe as they approached the ship. To a pilot, a ship was a ship. Some were better than others, but at the end of the day, they all performed the same function: flying and fighting. To the uninitiated, seeing a ship up close felt like crossing into forbidden territory. She'd never even been off the ground before. It seemed ethereal to be near such a machine.

"Well, here it is. My ship. The A-7 Skyhawk."

"Wow. This is so cool."

"One sec." He climbed the ladder next to the cockpit and walked along the edge and down toward the left wing. "It's got a variable wing system so the wings can swipe forward and backward in flight."

"What does that do?" Marie shouted.

"One direction gives you more speed, the other gives you more maneuverability."

"*Ahh*, I see. Very cool."

Cyril walked along the wingspan and checked the paneling. It looked brand new. He knew all the work was mainly interior, but he checked anyway. He also inspected the dorsal fin that the missile had hit. That also looked brand new, fresh as the day he'd bought it.

Marie walked under the fuselage and reached to touch it. The hull felt smooth, slick, and cool. Rivets peppered the paneling and slid across her fingers. "Wow. Hey, where are the guns?"

Cyril stepped off the wing to the floor and crouched to absorb his drop. "Inside the hull." He walked to the center fuselage and wrapped his knuckles on the portside weapons bay. "Everything is interior for aerodynamics. Missiles are in here; guns are next to the cockpit."

"Wow. Never thought I'd be this close to one of these. You must be really proud of it."

"Yup, she's my girl." He ran his hand lovingly across a panel.

"Why do guys always ascribe female gender to their things?"

"What do you mean?"

"Like, guys owning a fancy car or motorcycle, they always say 'it's their girl' or something. Is there a reason, or is it just a weird thing?"

He stared off into space, considering it, but came up with nothing. "You know, I can't think of anything right now, but by the time we get back to the bar, I'll have thought up a reason. Deal?"

"Deal."

They beamed at each other.

And then, he had a wild idea. "Hey, you wanna go for a ride?"

"What, in this?"

"No, on my magic carpet. Yes, this."

"That allowed?"

"I don't see why not. Got two seats."

She got close to him, gazed into his eyes, and whispered, "You trying to sweep me off my feet, Cyril Eisner, ace starfighter pilot?" She was close enough for him to smell her cherry-scented perfume.

"Something like that, I suppose," he whispered, smirking at her.

"Well then, sweep me off my feet." She got closer and nuzzled his nose with hers.

"I'll be right back." He walked toward Stacy as she finished her last beer.

Five empty bottles rested beside her chair. She saw him approaching and rolled her eyes.

"*Heeeyyyy*," Cyril said sheepishly.

"What do you want?" Stacy sighed, slightly peeved, her lips barely opening.

"So, I was just curious. Could I maybe take it up for a test flight tonight? I gotta have it ready for Monday."

"You could come by tomorrow for the test flight. No reason to do it tonight."

"Yeah, but..." Cyril craned his head toward Marie. "You know..."

"You're trying to impress her, aren't you?"

"Basically," Cyril said quickly.

Stacy groaned and a sighed simultaneously. "You've got one hour of flight time. I'll log you out. One hour, no more. Go."

"Thank you. I won't push it too hard." Cyril clasped his hands together, then returned to Marie. "You ready?"

She smiled as she leaned against the fuselage.

***

The sun was just barely cresting over the horizon, and the purple twilight blanketed the city of Balamb. Neon-yellow LED strips, embedded into the asphalt, illuminated the West Coast highway. Friday night traffic lazily twisted and turned down the road, everyone heading home for the weekend. And above, the A-7 Skyhawk rounded the highest peak and buzzed past the opposite direction of the traffic. Its shadow fell upon the ridge line next to the highway as the last bits of light faded. The ship cruised at a steady 440 knots—the slowest speed possible for a ship of that size. A few scattered clouds drifted above, and there was no wind shear.

Marie had borrowed one of Stacy's flight suits and rode in the RIO seat. The first time she had been off the ground was everything she'd hoped for.

Cyril checked all his flight controls. The pitch, yaw, stabilizers, rudders, and the variable wings. The wings were currently swept forward for testing. He knifed forty-five degrees left as they rounded the highway, four hundred fifty meters above the deck. Marie looked out the window at the cars passing below and the milky-white waves crashing silently on the shoreline. It was a thrill.

"Wanna do something really cool?" Cyril asked.

"Absolutely!"

"Hang on. Here we go." He rolled the ship so the cockpit faced the ocean.

Her hair fell toward the canopy. Blood rushed to her head, but she didn't care. It was the most amazing thing she'd ever seen. Nothing could compare.

Cyril righted the ship and wrapped around the highway below.

"*Oh, yes*! *This is amazing*," Marie yelled.

"Yes, it is," Cyril said, smiling.

The sun was now totally gone, and night was setting in. They would need to head back soon, but there was still time for a little more fun.

"Faster, Cyril!"

"You got it." He swept back the wings, punched the throttle forward, and pulled back hard on the stick. They ascended, up and up, until a sonic boom burst as they hit Mach one and broke the sound barrier.

***

Jess, Jace, Cyril, and Marie sat around a circular high table. Mallory's Heroes had gotten packed while they were gone. All walks of life, including several other local starfighters, had dropped by. Allegra had even come in for a few drinks, as she was in the area. She said hello to the crew, then sat by herself in the corner to drink alone. This confused

Cyril, as she lived on the opposite side of town. He didn't pursue the thought much further and resumed talking with his people.

The four of them were on the road to getting blitzed. Upon returning to the bar, Marie ordered a tequila sunrise. She was on a high and didn't want to come down. "Bang a Gong (Get It On)" by T-Rex fired up on the jukebox, and patrons filled the dance floor. Cyril set down his empty pint of Guinness and asked the waiter for another.

"Look at me. I'm still shaking." Marie vibrated, and her hands struggled to hold her drink.

"It's the adrenaline. It'll wear off soon, then you'll get sleepy," Jess said, repeating what Cyril had said to her on Tau Ceti f. "We all eventually got used to it. Only on extreme missions do we ever really feel it now."

"I don't know how you guys do that so much. And as your job, too. I admit I'm kind of envious, Mr. Eisner. You're, like, really talented, you know that?"

Cyril's new beer arrived. He took a sip. "Oh, I love it when you kiss my ass. Keep it going." Alcohol brought out the best sarcasm and quick wit.

"That's all you get for now. Let me get a few more drinks in me, and then I'll see about more compliments."

Cyril snapped his fingers. "I just figured it out."

"What?" Marie asked.

"Why do guys ascribe female gender to their things? It's because every man loves being inside a beautiful woman."

Marie laughed with a mouthful of tequila. She couldn't hold it and spat it into her glass. "*Heh.* That's pretty good."

"Thank you. I'll be here all night."

They clinked their glasses together and kept drinking.

The chatting continued. Marie finished her cocktail and switched to beer. What had started as a date between just the two of them had become a full-on group hangout. Cyril didn't mind. He was happy to be around her, and she was happy to be around them. She interrogated them about missions they'd been on, maneuvers they had pulled off, and other random questions. Jess had more stories about her music than flying, but the duo got along perfectly, just as Cyril had predicted. They had the same goth vibes and matched almost exactly.

"So, tell me a funny story that happened. Something really funny had to happen at some point while on an assignment," Marie asked.

"Oh boy, a funny story. I gotta think about that." Cyril went through the catalogue of missions in his brain, trying to think of anything that might be considered funny.

Then Jace suggested, "Cotton Eye Joe."

Cyril burst out laughing.

"Oh God, the Cotton Eye Joe thing. You tell this story. It was your idea."

"All right, so one of the flight leads we end up with from time to time is this guy named Garrison. Real hard ass."

"I second that," Cyril said.

"I third that," Jess added.

"So, one mission, I think this was about three years ago, we broke into his ship one night and rewired everything to only link back to his radio. Every button he would push would just operate the radio. Totally inoperable for flight. And we put only one song on the radio control. And what was that song, Cyril?"

"I'm pulling it up right now." Cyril played "Cotton Eye Joe" from his phone.

Marie recoiled like she had just swallowed something sour. "Oh God, that's awful!"

"Oh, I know, right? You should have been there. It was hilarious."

Jace struggled to breathe as he spoke. "He kept pushing more and more buttons, and the song kept resetting."

"He got so pissed off that he chucked his fucking helmet out of the ship and got out," Cyril said, falling into the crook of his arm and laughing. "What was the other song we put in there? We put something else in. I could swear we did."

"Oh, it was the Nazi marching theme," Jace said.

"Oh, that's right! How appropriate. Every button plays 'Cotton Eye Joe' except one. I think that's when he chucked his helmet."

"Probably. God, that was three years ago."

"Man, time flies. God, we got railed for that one," Cyril said, then faced Marie. "You feeling better, babe?"

"I'm much better now. Thank you," she expressed with a warm grin.

They stared at each other and smiled.

Jess shot a quick jest. "Absolutely disgusting, you two."

Cyril and Marie stuck out their tongues at Jess.

Cyril finished his beer and accidentally let out a massive belch. "Excuse me."

Marie took a long chug of her own beer and released a bigger belch.

Everyone laughed.

"That was so hot," Cyril remarked.

She smooched her lips at him and took another sip.

Cyril looked over his shoulder at Allegra still drinking alone in the corner and intermittently watching people, while browsing her phone and appearing depressed.

"Should we invite Allie over? She doesn't look good," Cyril said.

"Yeah, she looks worse than usual. Hope she's okay," Jess uttered.

"What's up with her?" Marie asked.

"It's a really long and really depressing story," Cyril said. "Trust me, you don't wanna know."

Jess approached Allegra's table and kneeled in front of her. Allegra stood and hugged Jess. When Jess returned, and she said, "Her cat died, so she doesn't want to be home right now. She just wants to be by herself. She was driving around for an hour and ended up here. But she appreciates the offer."

"Damn," Cyril whispered.

The four of them raised their glasses to Allegra. She raised hers and smiled.

Their conversation eventually moved into playing a game of billiards. Two versus two. Cyril and Marie against Jace and Jess. Allegra watched from a distance but said nothing. They racked the balls. Cyril broke. A solid went into a corner pocket. He took another shot, but nothing was available. His hit just scattered a few more balls. No pockets. Jess took a shot and pocketed a stripe. She took another hit and sunk another stripe. Then another hit, but a miss that time.

Marie stepped up, leaned forward, and aimed. Cyril swung his arm around and spanked Marie's right ass cheek. She recoiled and moaned. "*Mm...* do it again." He spanked again, and she moaned again. She pocketed a solid, faced Cyril, and got on her tiptoes. "Thanks for that." She nuzzled his nose like back on the airstrip, then circled the table for another shot.

Eventually Jess and Jace took the win. They were all pretty hammered, so there were no hard feelings. Jess racked up a second game, and once again, Jess and Jace won. Best two out of three meant they were done for the night. Marie excused herself to the bathroom and Jess followed.

Once they had gone, Cyril said to Jace, "She's great, isn't she?"

"You snagged a good one. Try not to fuck this up."

"I won't."

In the bathroom, after Jess and Marie relieved themselves, they fixed the highlights around their eyes, and Marie applied a fresh layer of lipstick.

"So, what do you think of Cyril?" Jess asked.

"Oh, he's fantastic. He's super sweet; he listens really well, handsome as a devil. No complaints so far."

"I'm glad you two are hitting it off. But I just wanted to warn you about some things."

"What things?"

"He's got a bad history. His dad was really awful to him, so he's got some issues that—"

"I know about his dad. I actually went with Cyril when he bailed his dad outta jail."

"He was in jail, and Cyril bailed him out? Why?"

"He said he just had to. I saw how terrible his father was. I get it. Everyone has their problems."

"What are yours?"

"Evil ex-boyfriend."

"Girl, we all got that one. Try again."

They laughed and walked out. In the main room, Cyril and Jace were arguing with a large burly guy, slightly taller than Cyril but about the same height as Jace, yet much more muscular. Jess and Marie stopped.

"Speaking of evil ex-boyfriends," Marie muttered.

"Leave! Now," Cyril yelled.

"I'm just here to—Marie! Come here! I need to talk to you!" The burly man headed toward her, but Cyril and Jace blocked his way as "Not Dead Yet" by The Bad Examples played on the jukebox.

"Guys, this is my ex-boyfriend. What do you want, Ben?"

"I wanna talk to you."

"Well, she doesn't wanna talk to you," Jess shouted.

"How did you even find me?" Marie asked.

Ben stumbled over his words and eventually landed on, "I pinged your phone. It was the only way I could find you."

"You *pinged my phone*? Do you know how *creepy that is*?"

"All right, that's it. You're leaving," Cyril declared.

Ben looked down at Cyril. "Who *the fuck* are you?"

"The new boyfriend."

A rocket of a punch rammed right into Cyril's stomach. He crumpled forward and landed on his knees. It hurt, but he had braced for it at just the last second. Faking being seriously hurt gave him, at minimum, a two-second opening. "Okay, let's do this," Cyril growled.

He leaped up and speared himself into Ben, knocking the burly ex backward into a set of high tables. One was empty, the other had empty beer glasses covering it—theirs from earlier. The crowd turned to watch. Gumby ran in from outside and unholstered his taser. Ben rose and knocked it from Gumby's hands. He shoved Gumby backward and faced Cyril.

With all his strength, Cyril landed a one-two punch on Ben's face, then followed with an uppercut. Being smaller, he was faster. But Ben was big and built tough. He retaliated with a hard jab to Cyril's face. Cyril stumbled backward and saw colorful stars.

Then, from nowhere, Allegra jumped in, wielding one of the billiard balls in her left hand. She dashed forward and unleashed hell on Ben's face. He stumbled backward. Every swing had an added clunk sound. A fire roared inside her, and this was the perfect place to unleash it. Ben dropped to his knees and fell backward. She got atop him and threw punch after punch, until finally Cyril, Jace, and Jess dragged her away, kicking and screaming. The ball fell from her hand and clattered to the floor. Mallory was already phoning the cops. Ben spit up a small geyser of blood, then rolled onto his right side. More blood spilled from his mouth, and three teeth were shattered.

They calmed Allegra while waiting for the cops to arrive. It took a solid thirty minutes. Gumby tied Ben's arms behind his back and administered first aid. Ben didn't speak to Marie, not because his jaw was broken but because there was nothing to say. Jace, Jess, Cyril, Marie, and Allegra sat at the back of the room and quietly waited for the police to take Ben away. Cyril's lip was bleeding. Marie put an ice pack on it and held it there for him.

"This place is usually much calmer, I promise," Cyril groaned through a swollen lip.

"I'm so embarrassed. I am so sorry," Marie mumbled, shaking her head.

"You don't have to apologize for anything. Shitty people do shitty things," Jace said.

"It's been taken care of. Don't worry about it. I'm more worried about you." Jess pointed to Allegra, who said nothing. "Yo, Allie, I'm talking to you."

"I'm fine. Please don't talk to me."

Everyone went quiet as Allegra cocooned herself. The cops finally hauled Ben out the front door. He gave one final look toward Marie. Cyril held up a middle finger as a goodbye gesture, then Ben was gone.

A pair of officers questioned them about the incident. They gave short statements and cleared themselves of any wrongdoing. Mallory gave the police a flash drive copy of the security camera feed from the incident as evidence. They filed it and left. Mallory sent a round of complimentary beers to the crew's table. Cyril took a long swig and winced through the pain.

"Was he the one who hurt you?" Cyril asked Marie.

"Yes."

"If he does it again, I'll kill him."

"Stop that. It's done, Cyril."

"I hope so."

They all sat quietly, drinking beers and enjoying each other's company. Allegra finally called it a night and rolled out.

As they watched her go, Jess whispered, "What a sad, broken woman."

"Yeah," Cyril agreed.

The vibe sunk and felt glum. Cyril set down the ice pack and went to the jukebox—a rarity in a bar. Most people wanted only live music or the standard canned radio music. Mallory had gone out of her way for nostalgia's sake. The usual crowd appreciated it. It was too late for anything heavy, and sad music would only worsen it. Something slow, something sweet, something lovely. And there it was, plain as day. "Open Arms" by Journey. A slow dance to end the night. He punched the numbers and pressed Play. By that time, the bar was mostly empty. The fight had scared most people out. No one to say no.

As the song started, he returned to the table and proffered his hand. "Come on, dance with me."

"Oh my God, Cyril. No," Marie replied, embarrassed.

"Yes, come on. It'll make you feel better."

She relented, took his hand, and went onto the dance floor with him. She giggled and muttered, "This is so corny."

"Oh, I know," Cyril said, fighting to suppress the pain in his lip. "But is it working?"

"Eh, a little bit," she agreed but rolled her eyes.

They swayed to the music and stared into each other's eyes. His left hand wrapped around her waist, and his right hand was at shoulder level, clasped with her left hand. Jace and Jess watched from their table to the side. Mallory joined them, having just closed last call.

"Did you think the night was gonna go like this?" Cyril asked.

"Not what I was expecting."

They swayed and rocked, holding each other close. She smelled like cherries. The moment felt just right for them both. And then something in Cyril deep down said, *Just do it*. He put his right hand on the back of her head, pulled her close, and kissed her. Even though it hurt like hell, it was worth it. She locked her lips with his, and they gripped each other. They twisted their heads back and forth, their tongues crossing, their lips locked. Time stood still. The world could end, and they wouldn't know it. The sky could fall, the stars explode, civilization could be destroyed in an instant, and it wouldn't matter, because that one moment made it all worth it.

They released, and Cyril went in for one more quick peck.

Marie bit her lower lip and whispered, "You're a really good kisser."

"Well, that's not the only thing I'm really good at."

"Shut up." She giggled as she slapped his chest. "This is a good moment. Don't ruin it."

"It could be a better moment later on, you know."

"I'm not gonna fuck you on the first date, Eisner. I'm still getting to know you."

"Well, what do you think so far?" Cyril leaned back, his hands wrapping around her waist.

"Well… you're strong."

"*Mmhmm*." He nodded.

"You're extremely good at your job."

"Yeah." He smiled.

"A little brash. Have a bit of an ego"

"*Eww*." He winced.

"But I think you're a good person. It's been a while since I met someone who was just decent to me."

"Well, I'm glad I made the cut," he said sincerely.

She smiled at him, wrapped her arms around him, and nuzzled into his chest. "Oh, your chest is like a bear."

"You wanna snuggle into it?"

"*Mmhmm*."

"Then, snuggle away," he whispered in her ear. He leaned his head on hers and ran his fingers through her hair. The cherry scent was even stronger. She smelled so good that he could eat her up. The world fell away. All the anger, the money issues, his father, everything. All gone. The world was finally quiet, except for the music and her breathing into his chest.

Jace turned to Jess. "You think he's finally growing up?"

"*Hmph*. Good for him," Jess said, smiling. "Good for him."

"Never thought I'd see the day," Mallory disclosed, then knocked back a shot of bourbon.

The song hit its crescendo and fell into its closing notes.

"Song is ending," Cyril said.

She pulled away from his chest.

"One more time?"

"Yes," she whispered.

They leaned in and kissed again.

CHAPTER 9

WANNA LIVE FOREVER?

Cyril sat in the lobby of Arcturus Allied for an hour. A manila folder, filled with pages of work history and recommendations from the previous five years, had taken him an entire day to organize. The full-marble lobby was big, bold, and brutalist—something built to last. The only soft surfaces were the chairs scattered to the side of the entrance near the front desk. Ayn Rand would be proud.

They had told him to arrive at seven in the morning, yet he was still forced to wait. Corporate bureaucracy was always slow, but something told him that this was just an insult lobbed at him by Moriarty. They'd said seven just to force him to be up by five so he would arrive cranky. Cyril hated early morning calls. Just because he was used to it didn't mean he liked it.

He read emails, answered old messages, and accepted a last-minute job three days from then. Simple support work off world. An easy paycheck with a company he had been working with for several years—Nester Inc. The pay wouldn't be huge, but there would be no combat. It was basically free money. He also sent a message to Marie.

CYRIL: Hey, miss you. I'm up early for work. Airdrop coffee to me.

As he finished his message, a tall and lanky twentysomething intern, with barely any facial hair, approached him. Seeing him reminded Cyril that he'd forgotten to shave that morning. He didn't look disheveled, but he was not as professional as one should look for a job interview.

"Cyril Eisner?" the intern asked.

"Yup, that's me."

"Mx. Moriarty will see you now."

"Great. They were supposed to see me an hour ago."

"They had another meeting."

"At seven a.m. on a Monday? I have no doubt."

The intern led Cyril to a set of elevators comprised of circular glass, with a waist-high railing, at the other end of the building. As they ascended, he watched the opposite elevator descending. He turned to see the golden sun rising over the city. Buildings cast harsh shadows on the streets below. No other building in the city was larger than Arcturus tower. It stood over the city like a monument, or a sentinel of humanities progress on Proxima.

They stopped at the thirty-third floor and exited the elevator. It looked like any other office building. Simple tan carpet, white walls, ceiling tiles that broke too easily if tapped. They turned right to enter a set of black double doors. A long pool of halfway-filled cubicles greeted them, as the morning shift was still filing in. Monitors glowed overhead of each cubicle with stock prices, company updates, and other jargon Cyril had no understanding of. Each cubicle also featured a pair of VR goggles.

"What's up with the VR headsets?" Cyril asked.

"We do everything digitally," the intern answered. "Rarely does anything find its way to paper. It just makes things easier and faster."

"What if your system goes down?"

"Not possible. We have a backup."

"And if that goes down?"

"We have a backup for the backup."

Cyril rolled his eyes. "Wow. You guys really thought of everything."

They rounded a corner and walked down a short hallway toward an office. The title on the door read, MX. MORIARTY. The intern knocked. "Mx. Moriarty, a Mr. Cyril Eisner is here to see you."

"Fine. Let him in," Moriarty said.

The intern opened the door, and the office was just as drab and colorless as the cubicle area. However, potted plants rested along the windowsill. As it was a corner office, the sunlight was plentiful and punched up the warmth in the office. A squirt bottle sat next to the far end of the row of plants. A carnivorous one, with a strange green beak dangling over the edge, hung from the ceiling and draped down. Some photos of Moriarty with famous dignitaries, politicians, and corporate types hung on the walls, but nothing deeply personal. No family photos, pets, lovers. Nothing. He thought of asking why but decided against it. They already hated Cyril's guts and were only doing this job interview as a favor. Had it been up to Moriarty, he would have been out the door the moment he had entered.

The intern left and closed the door. Moriarty was deeply involved in some work on their data pad. Awkwardness set in immediately. They barely acknowledged him. A pair of hardback chairs sat in front of Moriarty's desk. Cyril began to sit in one of them when they said, "Did I say you could sit down?"

"Well, I assumed we're having a meeting. I think better while sitting," Cyril joked.

"You think you're funny, *huh*?"

"Once a month, I have a bit of wit. I'm all tapped out now."

They looked up from their data pad. "Shut up. Stop talking."

Cyril said nothing.

"Give me your file."

He passed his manila folder to Moriarty, who opened it with little interest. Neither of them wanted to be there, but the bureaucracy from above had said it was necessary. A small part of him wanted to strangle Moriarty for being such a massive cunt, but he needed the job, as his bank account needed consistent pay. Still, the thought made him chuckle. Moriarty didn't seem to notice.

They pawed through the papers with all the enthusiasm of a dead fly in a desk drawer. Cyril looked around and tried to keep himself occupied to resist pulling out his phone. He found it fascinating that the plant that dropped from its hanging pot was carnivorous. The concept of a plant devouring a creature was so weird and alien. He had no idea how it worked. Did it crush its prey, dissolve them, swallow them bit by bit? The random thought kept him occupied for a solid twenty seconds.

By then, Moriarty had lost interest in Cyril's file and chucked it onto their desk. "What do you think you can offer to this company, Mr. Eisner?"

He considered saying something remotely witty but decided against it. Instead, he landed on, "Well, if I'm to be completely honest, you're in need of reliable security services for off-world assignments. My record speaks for itself."

"Yes, it does. Ninety-nine confirmed kills—"

Cyril raised a finger. "That number has since gone up. Sorry, I forgot to update that on the resume."

"*Over* ninety-nine confirmed kills. Over seven years of flight experience, four spent in the freelance business. High marks from various employers."

"That's what my file says."

"I also did some digging and found that you have a problem with authority and can be brash and aggressive. Care to explain why I should ever approve of you for contract employment with Arcturus?"

"In combat, who do you want? Someone who tries to settle a fight with conversation or with live ammunition? And my issues with authority are leveled more at specific individuals, not companies in general." That was a bold-faced lie. Cyril resented large corporations, as they tended to crush lower-income individuals, such as himself. But income was income. Take their money and still call them pricks.

Moriarty harrumphed. Silence. They really hated him. He could see it in their eyes. The feeling was mutual. The sun burned his eyes, and he was tired, cranky, and not up for anyone's bullshit. Every fiber of his being said, *Fuck it*. Cyril decided to be bold and say what was on his mind. "May I be completely honest?"

"Go right ahead."

"I know you hate me. And I can't even really tell why. I think you're a sad, empty person who hates their own existence. But let's be totally honest here. I'm getting this job, not because of your approval. It's because I guaranteed my employment a few weeks ago when I gave that speech at the charity event. You guys weren't expecting me to say all that, were you? To be totally honest and to win over the crowd? Well, I did, and the press was there recording all of it. If you don't hire me, I can just post online how I was denied fulltime employment with Arcturus because of one person's grudge—yours—

which is based purely upon prejudice. Not only is that bad for Arcturus, but it would also be bad for you. I'm not sure how you developed such hate, and quite frankly, I don't even care. But, at this point, hiring me isn't a choice. It's an obligation. You wouldn't want to make Arcturus look bad for denying work to a simple, lowly starfighter like myself, would you? That would just be so, so bad for your company's image, wouldn't it?"

Moriarty said nothing. Cyril could see a nuclear bomb detonate in their head. Because deep down, they knew he was right. This was all just a formality. He had the job before he even walked through the door. The press loved what he had said. His speech had been reposted on the internet for weeks following the charity event's live stream. If they didn't hire him, it would reflect poorly on the hiring practices of Arcturus. He may have been just a lowly starfighter, but right then, he had the ace in the hole.

Moriarty wasn't always as cold and as sharp as an ice pick. They had been beaten into that shape, molded by the trials and failures of life. In their youth, they had been cast aside for promotions or for better working conditions. Ascending the corporate ladder was a cutthroat game. Be ready to stab the next person should the chance of promotion be offered. Time and time again, life had proven that being nice and courteous would get someone nowhere higher than a secretary or a scribe. Being nice got no one anywhere. Moriarty had embraced the feeling of power, control, and manipulation long ago, and, slowly but surely, they made their way to the very top. Reaching the peak meant standing on the dead bodies of their enemies.

From what Cyril had just said, he had done the same and was willing to go the distance to stab Moriarty in the back to attain fulltime employment. In a small way, Moriarty admired that level of audacity. It didn't change their personal feelings toward him, but professionally, he had earned the smallest amount of respect. But only the smallest.

"Fine. You've got the job, Mr. Eisner. You'll need to undergo a physical examination and a performance test. Follow me." They both rose to leave, when they followed up with, "But you're right, I do hate you. I hate your very existence and that you're breathing the same air as me. You disgust me. You're a wretched misogynist. All men are only after one thing. I'm better than you, Cyril Eisner. Never forget that."

"Sure," Cyril said blankly.

Moriarty rounded their desk to leave. Cyril followed them down three floors to an in-house gymnasium and a recreation center. Employees could come to the thirtieth floor to relax, exercise, or enjoy a massage or sauna; the company provided anything they wanted. And yet, the floor was mostly vacant. A layer of dust covered every exercise machine in the big wide-open room. It was all an empty gesture, one made to peacock to the press. No one had the time to even consider getting in R&R, exercise, or anything to reduce stress in the work environment. If any staff had a meltdown, the company would send them home to recover and would tell them to return after three days. If they didn't, the company would replace them. Arcturus, for all its financial prowess and political power, was a meat grinder, chewing people up and spitting them out as nothing more than chunky salsa. At no point did Cyril ever regret not having a desk job. He was fine paying the higher taxes as a freelancer.

Inside a small medical office at the far end of the gymnasium, a man wearing brown pants, a dress shirt, and blue tie gathered tools and paperwork. Cyril and Moriarty entered and greeted Doctor Cameron.

"Cameron, here's our new hire. Give him the full rundown, and then send the results to me this afternoon," Moriarty said, then left without saying goodbye.

Cameron proffered his hand. "Mr. Eisner, please have a seat. How are you doing this morning?"

Cyril shook his hand. "Much better now that they're gone."

Cameron chuckled in agreement.

The next hour was a full rundown of Cyril's physical health, past medical history, reflexes, mobility, flexibility, stamina, and endurance. He hated being poked and prodded, as it made him uncomfortable, like he was a specimen in a petri dish. He undressed to his underwear and showed Cameron his scars from previous missions. Throughout his flight career, he had suffered the slash on his shoulder, a broken ankle and tibia, two concussions, and one superficial gunshot wound through his left forearm which had left only a small scar. The doctor drew two vials of blood and ran them through a centrifuge to test the quality of oxygenation, platelet count, and plasma.

While it ran its cycle, Cameron inquired about Cyril's average alcohol consumption.

"Whenever I'm in the mood."

Cameron didn't laugh.

Cyril followed up with, "Maybe two or three beers a week." It was a lie, but the truth would have raised more questions.

The machine finished its cycle, and Cameron checked the two vials for their quality. He sampled them out and examined them under a microscope. A large screen displayed the images next to Cyril's head.

Cameron said, "Given your history, you're in very good shape."

"Thanks. Must be the sarcasm."

Cameron chuckled and gave Cyril a basic pair of gray sweatpants and a sweatshirt adorned with the Arcturus logo. He changed in the office and headed into the gymnasium for physical training. First was mobility tests—high jumps, stretches, arm and leg span. Next was a twenty-minute run on the treadmill, using an oxygen deprivation mask. Cyril hated running. He made the run at 75 percent oxygen capacity and was drenched in sweat by the end. Next was pullup and pushup tests. Minimum requirement for pullups was ten in a row. He did twelve. Minimum requirement for pushups was fifteen. He just barely made the fifteen in a row, as he was gassed by that point.

They conducted various tests for reflexes. A machine at the far end of the room fired five small tennis balls at Cyril—his objective to catch at least two—and he caught three. He completed the tests above company standards. They performed another simple reflex test consisting of a metal rod falling from three feet above Cyril, where he must catch it in front of him, without crouching, before it hit the floor. He barely caught it at the last second.

The final set of tests was simple muscle strength. One max rep for him to hold for twenty seconds. As they went through each muscular group, the elevator door opened. Daniel Mullarkey stepped out. Cyril rolled his eyes and felt his stomach churn with hate.

"Cameron, how's our new hire doing?" Mullarkey asked as he crossed the room.

"Exceeding in almost every test, sir. Well above average."

"Excellent. I expected no less." He circled Cyril as Cyril was about to perform a bicep test by holding two forty-pound dumbbells perpendicular to his body for twenty seconds. "Good to see you,

Eisner. I recently found out that your pilot callsign is Skyhawk. Interesting name. I'm sure you'll be a great addition to our team."

"Oh, I'm looking forward to it, Mr. Mullarkey. I've got butterflies in my stomach just thinking about it." He lifted the two dumbbells and began his twenty-second hold.

Cameron started his timer, and the waiting began. The first five seconds were easy enough, but any weight under tension always quickly exhausted muscles. Mullarkey then reached out and pressed his hands ever so gently atop the dumbbells and stared Cyril down, smiling.

Cyril stared right back. *You're not gonna beat me, motherfucker.*

Mullarkey pushed harder.

Ten seconds passed, and they kept staring at each other. Cyril's arms shook, but he didn't let go. He wouldn't drop; he wouldn't lose.

Fifteen seconds. Mullarkey pushed harder. "Come on, Skyhawk. Show me what you got. Cameron, how long does he have to hold for?"

"Three, two, one. Time," Cameron said.

"No, keep going. Show me how tough you are. Stop when I say so."

Cyril kept holding. Sweat ran off his forehead, and his biceps burned. His legs shook as blood rushed to his arms. He refused to drop.

Twenty-five seconds. Mullarkey pushed harder.

Cyril gritted his teeth and winced but held in place. *Fuck you, Mullarkey. I won't break. Not for you.*

"All right, that's enough," Cameron said sternly.

"No, he's still got more in him. Don't you, Skyhawk? Come on, keep going!"

Thirty seconds. His muscles were pumping battery acid, and he felt light on his feet. Every neuron in his brain told him to relinquish, but he kept holding. Mullarkey was nearly putting half his body weight on the dumbbells. As a significantly larger man than Cyril, it was an incredible amount of weight. Cyril couldn't just hold anymore, so he lifted to compensate for the extra weight.

Forty seconds. Mullarkey released his hands and stepped backward. Cyril stumbled and fell flat on his back. The impact punched the wind from his chest, and the dumbbells flew behind him.

One tumbled, end-over-end, toward another machine; one rolled in a circle on the mats before stopping.

Mullarkey chuckled. "Impressive, Skyhawk. With that kind of attitude, you might just live forever. You'll make a great addition to our off-world crew. Welcome aboard. Thanks, Doc. Make sure he gets a T-shirt on the way out." Mullarkey headed to the elevator, called it, and entered.

Cyril watched the doors close and saw Mullarkey's stupid fucking grin disappear as the elevator ascended out of sight.

"That fucking guy," Cyril whispered. He dropped flat on the mat and stared up at the ceiling. His arms felt like they didn't exist anymore. There was no pain, just emptiness, as the blood left his arms and wormed through the rest of his body. He felt like he was floating.

Cameron stepped closer and looked down at him. "Are you okay, Mr. Eisner?"

"Yeah, Doc. Never better," Cyril wheezed. "I'm just gonna lay here for a minute, if you don't mind."

"Take your time." Cameron stepped away and returned to the office to finish paperwork.

While Cyril was slightly embarrassed about falling on his ass, he took solace in one thing. *I didn't break, you asshole. I didn't break.*

Twenty minutes later, testing finished, and Cameron gave his final assessment. Cyril had performed well above average, though his reflexes could use some work, but Cameron recommended that Cyril reduce alcohol intake. Cyril listened, nodded, then internally disregarded his recommendations. *How dare you try to interrupt my Friday nights?* He changed into his clothes and asked what was next. Cameron led him upstairs one floor to a flight-training room. Cyril was under the impression that he would use his ship for flight testing. It turned out that the flight test was simulator based.

He went through basic flight maneuvers, takeoff and landing, then had to run the test based upon average-sized starfighters, as well as large dropships and megaliners. He passed each test with a perfect score. Cameron gave him the stamp of approval and cleared him for active service with Arcturus. Before leaving the simulator room, Cameron ensured Cyril got a free T-shirt, with the Arcturus logo. Cyril accepted it with annoyance.

***

Locke exited the limousine first for security. Once he saw it was clear, he opened the opposite door. Layla stepped out and put on her sunglasses. Workers came and went all around them in the crisp morning air. She carried the black plastic case, with the sensory nanite syringe. As they approached the front entrance of Arcturus, the front door guards greeted her and opened the doors. The cool air conditioning immediately hit her—maybe a few degrees too cold—but she endured.

As she and Locke passed the front desk, the elevator descended, with Cyril Eisner riding it. Her heart skipped a beat. They hadn't spoken since that night on the balcony. She swallowed hard and strode toward the elevator. It slowly stopped on the ground floor.

Cyril gave a little wave as the doors opened. "Layla. Good to see you."

"You too, Eisner. Why are you here?"

"Physical exam. Just got the green light to work with you guys. I even got a T-shirt." He held up the shirt and smiled.

She smirked. "Good for you, Cyril."

"How are you doing?"

"Sir, I'm gonna need you to move on now," Locke said gruffly.

"It's okay, Locke. We're just talking. I'm fine. Go grab us some coffee."

"I'll take one too, if you're buying," Cyril said.

Locke ignored him and walked away.

"But yeah, how are you doing?"

"I'm fine."

"That's good. Better than bad."

"Cyril, I want to apologize for that night. I wasn't really—"

"You were drunk. It's okay."

"Still, I'm sorry for what I said."

"Layla, seriously, it's okay. Don't worry about it. Now that I kinda sort of work here, it's not gonna be that easy to get rid of me."

"Looking forward to seeing you in action again."

"Can't wait." He pointed to the black case. "What's that?"

She looked down at the case in her hand. "It's above your pay grade, Cyril."

"I suppose so. I haven't even been paid once by you guys yet."

Locke returned with two cups of coffee and handed one to Layla. Locke took a sip, as did Layla. Cyril looked around, saw no third cup, then made a cup-holding motion with his hand and took an imaginary sip. Layla chuckled.

Cyril winked at Locke. "I have a vivid imagination."

"Then imagine yourself walking out the door, sir." Locke took another long, slurpy sip.

"Well, I'll see you around, Layla," Cyril said.

"Same, Eisner. Good luck."

Cyril passed them to exit the front door. Layla watched him go and still felt a tinge of guilt for their balcony conversation. The fact they kept crossing paths was somewhat comforting though.

Locke and Layla rode the elevator to the penthouse. They exited to see Daniel on a video conference call spanning three large screens. Daniel had installed two new ones while she had been on Kepler, bringing the number of office screens to twelve, which constantly fed information to him. The flooding sunlight illuminated everything. Harsh shadows fell from the furniture. Bentley was to the side on a separate call.

Daniel noticed the pair enter. "Ladies and gentlemen, if you'll excuse me, I need to have a discussion with my sister. I'll give you a call back in twenty minutes." The call ended, and the screens blackened. "Good news, I hope?"

"Ambassador Koy will recommend a control test to the Kepler council. They'll send a courier when they've settled on details." Layla set the plastic case on Daniel's desk. "The nanites got the entire conversation."

"Good. I'll watch in a second."

"Sir, a Mr. Cyril Eisner passed us as we entered the building downstairs," Locke said. "He engaged in conversation with your sister."

"Oh. Eisner," Daniel whispered.

"We just said hello to each other. Nothing else," Layla said.

"Really?"

"Really," Layla said steely.

Daniel stepped closer and towered above Layla. "Well, I'm glad you two got to catch up." He returned to his desk and opened the case.

"In fact, I might put him on the Kepler dispersal assignment when we get the go-ahead for it. Lord knows I'll need some good pilots for our first drop."

"Why are you so mean to him?"

"*Heh*, I'm not mean. He's beneath us, Layla. Don't interact with the wildlife more than you must. He's useful, and he'll do as he's told." He pulled the silver vial from its case and inserted it into a circular drive on the edge of his desk. The nanites emptied into the desk and displayed a visual recording on the monitors of everything Layla had done between the injection and their removal. He sat in his chair to watch. "You can go now, Layla. You did a good job. Bentley, drive her home, please."

"Yes, sir," Bentley said.

Locke, Layla, and Bentley headed to the elevator. Locke and Bentley flanked her on each side. Bentley pressed the Down button. Daniel was still sitting behind the desk, watching her conversation with Winnick Koy, as the elevator lowered, and he left her sight.

***

"I was beginning to think you weren't coming back," Minese said.

"Life got busy. And time dilation can really ruin a schedule," Cyril said.

"I would venture to guess that life has improved."

"I just walked in the door. How can you tell?"

"You're standing up straighter. Your posture has improved. You look happier overall."

"I mean, I am."

"So, what has changed?"

He swore that Marie's cherry-flavored scent was still on his clothes. "That woman, Marie. She's something else."

"Not a one-night stand?" Minese inquired.

"No. We've gone out a few times. Had a real date last Friday. Had a bit of an epiphany recently. I was out on Tau Ceti—"

"What's that?"

"It's a planet, a long way from here. Anyway, it was a tough assignment. We were outnumbered and outgunned. Even the weather was against us. Made it through with only one loss. That night, I stepped outside for some air and talked with one of the other guys in the squadron. He told me about how he almost got taken down a while back. Only he and one other guy made it out alive. Anyway, that's not the point. He made the point that if you're gonna do anything, make it count, because you could go at any time. I've been doing this for seven years now. Luck runs out eventually. So, I made a deal with myself that when I got back, I'd finally make it count."

"Because you wanna see Marie again…"

"Yeah." That cherry smell was definitely all over him.

Minese made a note. "She give you that busted lip too?"

"Actually, it was her abusive ex-boyfriend. He followed her to the bar we were at Friday night. Me and my crew took care of him." Cyril gently rubbed is still swollen lip.

"When you say, 'took care of him', you don't mean…" He pointed a finger gun at Cyril.

"No! He got knocked around a bit, then the cops dragged his ass away. I told Marie that if he ever comes near her again, I'd do that."

"That's a mistake." Minese tapped on his pad.

"How is that a mistake?"

"You leaned back toward aggression. You need to learn to let things go, Eisner. It's unhealthy to hole up so much anger. Besides, if you kill her ex, you go to jail forever. Then you never get to see her again."

Cyril said nothing and looked out the window at the afternoon's wispy clouds drifting in. His arms still hurt. "Maybe I'm just an angry person, Doc. It's just the hand I was dealt."

Minese made another note.

"What did you just write?"

"My session, my notes. You'll find out what the note says when you figure out what was wrong about what you just said."

He thought about it. What could he have said that was so wrong? His life was the way it was because that was the path the universe had put him on. His father had driven him in this direction. Someone couldn't just change the direction of an avalanche while it snowballed down a mountain.

Crestfallen, he said, "I honestly don't know."

"Then you'll have to think about it and try to figure it out for next time."

"Fine."

They both went quiet, and Minese made another note. "While I am happy for you, and I do think you mean well with regards to changing your lifestyle, I would also advise caution."

"*Heh*, for what?"

"Do you believe Marie has given you a new purpose?"

"Yeah." Cyril wasn't sure what his therapist was getting at, but he realized the river sound from the lobby was louder that afternoon.

"You believe that without her entering your life, you would still be trying to find your way and figuring out what direction to take?"

"Probably."

"Then, here's the issue. I know people who have been in your position. I have one other person like that on my schedule. What you're developing is called an unhealthy dependency."

"What's that?"

"Alcoholics need alcohol. Drug addicts need drugs. Lonely people need to not feel alone, so they'll attach themselves to a person they believe can help them fill that void in their life. They need constant validation, and they become overly reliant on that as their way to happiness. It makes them feel good. Essentially, you're getting high on someone else's love. Coupled with the Superman complex you have, and how you essentially rescued her on Friday night, then it could be a bad mixture. It starts as a circle, but it eventually becomes a downward spiral if you're not careful. I'm willing to guess Marie also has mental health issues?"

"I've never asked."

"Probably worth bringing up at some point. I'm not saying it can't work, but it's difficult."

"I mean, life's difficult."

"Yes, but it's only as difficult as you make it."

"Okay."

The rest of the session revolved around how he felt about his job, but the Marie thing kept creeping into his mind. What if he *was* getting ahead of himself? What if this all failed? What if he hurt her?

He needed to talk to her. Soon.

***

He spun his cup of half-finished coffee on the table and stared into the blackness within. That weird thought kept creeping up his spine—*unhealthy dependency*. He had been dependent on only himself for a long time, not even trying to engage in deep relationships. Flings here and there, but anything deeper than the most basic engagement had been outside his comfort zone. But something about this one just fit well. Really well. But Minese had brought up a disconcerting point. Maybe he *was* getting ahead of himself.

People flowed into the coffee shop for their end-of-the-day caffeine fix. He wasn't the only addict in town; that was for sure. The rich smell of griding beans permeated the air. The line of customers wrapped around on itself, but service was on point that night. A couple on the other side of the shop chatted and giggled. He finished his cup in a single gulp, then retrieved his phone to text Marie.

CYRIL: Hey.
MARIE: Hey! I was just thinking about you!
CYRIL: I'm psychic. That's how I nailed the perfect timing.
MARIE: Makes total sense. What's up, babe?
CYRIL: I just finished my therapy session. Could we talk?

Marie typed nothing. After a beat, Cyril continued.

CYRIL: Nothing bad. Just wanted to get some stuff off my chest.
MARIE: Sure. I'm finishing up here at work. Get dinner?
CYRIL: Yeah. What are you feeling?
MARIE: Pizza?
CYRIL: I'll slap a child for a pizza right now.
MARIE: Spoken like a true gentleman. I'll send you the address of this awesome place. One hour?
CYRIL: One hour. See you there.

She texted the address of a place across town called Days of Old, a classical pizzeria. As Cyril stood to leave, he realized the pain in his arms were gone and that he was unconsciously smiling. Then Minese's voice crept back in. Whether Minese was a devil or an angel on Cyril's shoulder at that point, he wasn't quite sure. *"Advise caution,"* Minese had said.

He took an autocab to the north side of Balamb. Traffic was rough. He'd make it just in time. As the autocab pulled up, he messaged Marie.

CYRIL: Here.

She saw the message.

He hopped out and smelled baking dough, marinara sauce, cheese, everything. He could kill a whole pizza by himself if he put his mind to it. He entered the classy little place, and the hostess greeted him, asking how many.

"I'm meeting someone," Cyril said loudly.

It was a busy night and filled with patrons, but he spotted Marie in a booth next to a window. As he approached her, Cyril watched brick ovens fire up in the back through a three-foot-wide hole in the wall divider. Photographs of various celebrities who had visited and a large painted portrait of the owners hung on the walls. The wooden-slatted floor creaked as he walked across it. The resin-stained wooden walls emitted a very retro feel, something everyone could enjoy. A few flat TVs on Mute hung from the ceiling and played sports and news while classic rock music played overhead.

He reached the table and sat opposite from her. She had clearly arrived early, as she was already on her second beer. A pitcher of light beer sat next to the window; there were no plans to get sloshed that night, as she had work in the morning.

He removed his coat and set his hands on the table. "Hi."

"Hi," she said, smiling. Her hands were under her chin. "Get here okay?"

"Traffic was awful, but I'm here."

"That's good."

"How was work?"

"*Eh*. Nothing to talk about. Boring."

"Hey, boring is better than bad."

"Very true," she said, nodding.

The mid-forties waitress, with a bump on her very long nose's bridge, approached the table. "Nice to see he arrived."

"He finally got here," Marie agreed.

"How long have you been waiting for me?" Cyril asked.

"A long time for you, babe. Now, what can I get for you?" The waitress removed a pocket-sized data pad.

"I was thinking just normal sausage and pepperoni. You cool with that?" Marie asked.

"Sounds good to me," he answered.

The waitress made a note. "All right, it should be about fifteen minutes. Need another pitcher?"

"We're good for now. Just another glass," Marie said.

"Be right back." She returned with a fresh glass, silverware, and a small stack of napkins.

Cyril poured himself a glass of beer and took a sip.

"I'm sorry it's not Guinness," Marie said.

He chuckled. "I won't hold it against you."

They stared at each other for a moment. Finally, Marie giggled. "What?"

"Nothin'. Just lookin' at you," he said as took another sip.

She harrumphed. "So, you said you wanted to talk about something."

Reality set back in, and his smile faded. He took a long gulp and suppressed a burp. "Yeah. *Umm…* goddammit, I don't even know where to start."

"Beginning is always a good place."

"Right. Well, um, you know I'm in therapy, because if I wasn't, I wouldn't hear the end of it from Jess and Jace."

"Jess is the sweetest, by the way."

"She *is* adorable. *Uh*, but basically, I was in my session today, and you came up. Nothing bad, just, you know, you talk about your life and all—"

"Cyril, I'm in therapy too. I get it."

"Oh. Why didn't you tell me?"

"You never asked."

"Fair." He cleared his throat. The pizzeria was so loud now that he could barely hear "Survive" by Lovers Lake playing overhead. "Well, what came up was… us."

Advise caution.

"Okay."

"I'm not great… with relationships. I'm–I'm a total fuck-up."

Marie said nothing.

"Before you, the longest relationship I ever had was less than a year. I… have issues with committing to people."

"Because of what you went through with your father, you're now insecure with yourself, and you need validation from others to feel fulfilled."

Cyril's arms dropped to the table with a thud. "I think you should be my therapist."

"Cyril, I'm just as fucked up. You saw how Ben was. I didn't think I could get out of that. And thank you for the other night, by the way."

"You're welcome."

"But I get it. You don't know who to trust or if you can even trust yourself."

The waitress set down a massive twelve-slice pepperoni and sausage pizza. It was still bubbling, right out of the oven. "Can I get you anything else?"

"Nope. All good," Marie said.

The waitress smiled and walked away.

"Anyway, I…" Cyril trailed off. He was stumbling around like a blind man in the woods. No direction, bumping into trees, tripping over himself. What was he trying to say? Was he trying to warn her? To scare her off? Was he better off alone? "I don't… I really—"

"Hang on, it's so loud in here that I can barely hear you." She slid from her bench and sat next to him. He slid closer to the window to make room for her. "Okay, I'm here."

That was it. That phrase. *I'm here.* He had a feeling she would leave, that he would wake up one morning to find her not there. Someone would get hurt.

Advise caution.

He carefully chose his words. Cyril and Marie sat so close together that her cherry smell again permeated the air. He whispered, "I know I look like I have it together, Marie, but I don't. I'm a mess."

She chuckled. "I'm a mess too. You'll have to do better than that."

"I've hurt people. I know it seems like I'm good at this, but I get to a certain point, and I don't know what to do. I'm like a dog chasing a car. I don't know what to do once I've caught it. I just don't want to hurt you. I wanna do the right—"

She snapped forward and kissed him hard on the lips. Her tongue slipped into his mouth, and she put her hand on his cheek. Again, time seemed to stop. The kiss ended, and they gazed into each other's eyes.

"How do you feel now?" she whispered.

After a long pause, he said, "Sorry, what was I saying?"

They laughed.

Advise caution? Fuck that.

They ate, drank, laughed, and kissed some more, throwing caution to the wind. It was a good night. They stayed until closing time—10:30 pm. They walked into the night air and shivered in the early fall weather. Nighttime grew colder. Marie called an autocab. As she shuddered, Cyril wrapped his arms around her and held her like a bear. She smiled and enjoyed the warmth of his embrace. He kissed her neck and nibbled on her left ear. She giggled, then broke from the hug, spun around, and kissed him hard on the lips. Then the autocab arrived.

"This is my ride," she said, slightly disappointed.

"So it is."

"Hey, it's okay to be a mess. You'll figure it out. It's a day-to-day thing."

His hands rubbed up and down the middle of her back. She felt so soft and warm. How had he landed something so good? He hoped that whatever cosmic coincidence had brought them together was admiring its work.

"Let's be messes together," he teased.

She guffawed. "Deal. Hey, are you busy Friday night?"

"*Uh*, I am off tomorrow, but I go off planet Wednesday for work, come back Thursday, and then, yes, I'll be free Friday."

"Well, I can get us into Tech Noir for free. My favorite band is playing. Wanna go?"

"Let me think about it." He considered it for one point five seconds. "Yes, I'd love to go."

She giggled. "Okay. It's a date." She kissed him again, left his warm embrace, entered the cab, then lowered the window. "Goodnight, Skyhawk."

"Goodnight, Marie."

The cab pulled away. Cyril watched it travel two blocks, then turn right. He felt so good that he didn't even call a cab for himself. It was too nice outside to not walk home. He smiled, and all the pain in his arms was gone.

***

Two days passed. He was off planet on a deep space operation. While deep space was always the most dangerous environment, the mission was a piece of cake. Nester, Inc. had hired a minimum regiment of eight starfighters as a precaution, but the chances of any threats were near zero. Cyril knew two of them—Kyra and Jace. Kyra was flight lead for this mission, as she was working her way up the ranks for more command positions. They were flying under the name *Enigma Squadron*.

The list of starfighters were:

> Cyril "Skyhawk" Eisner
>
> Jace "Astaroth" Rinkson
>
> Ullon "Paperboy" Traynor
>
> Hughie "Tracer" Homes
>
> Alex "Frogger" Jameson
>
> Sarah "Livewire" Dipaccio
>
> Kai "Mixer" Moore
>
> Flight Lead: Kyra "Twister" Hadley
>
> MISSION: Security and support.
>
> TARGET: Asteroid harvesting. 1181 Kelium. Water reclamation.
>
> THREAT LEVEL: Minimal. Possible natural threats, i.e. micro meteorites. No enemy threat perceived.

They had designed the big gray box-shaped mining ship, named the *Adeline*, to hold massive amounts of cargo. Armor plating covered each flat side. The ship doubled as a FOIL pad and carried a full crew of twenty-two shipmates of various species. They would sell the water they collected during the expedition to small villages on the Ekumen outskirts for farming purposes and terraforming. A full supply of forty mining drones complimented the onboard crew, twenty of which they had deployed to the surface of an icy asteroid—1181 Kelium—and were cutting into the outcropped sections for retrieval. Once cut, they would dispatch a hideously looking, H-shaped ship called a Platypus, with dents all along the thick undercarriage, to capture the pieces in a massive claw on the underbelly and return them to the *Adeline*. It was built to be tough, but tough was also ugly.

The eight starfighters formed a pair of diamonds flanking the sides of the *Adeline*. Four to port, four to starboard. Each ship had a total flight time of two and half hours due to air supply restrictions. When empty, they would have to dock inside the *Adeline*'s cargo hold, where engineers would refill the tanks. Then they'd return to their designated stations. It was a tedious routine and one of the many drawbacks of deep space operations, but at least oxygen refills were free. They had refilled twice already.

Everyone was bored. The worst thing that had happened was Jace's radio had a small glitch receiving years-old deep-space transmissions. He recorded it and stored the audio file to transmit for investigation. Besides that, the crew kept themselves occupied with music and chitchat. One pilot, Paperboy, dozed off. They heard soft snores over the comms, as he had left his radio on Vox mode. Kyra flew to the snoring pilot's ship and bumped his left wing. He heard a chunky thud in his cockpit, and the jolt shocked him awake.

Kyra said, "Sleep on your own time." She flew back to her position, and the day continued.

Paperboy never dozed off again.

The third shift dragged on. The drones sliced off pieces of the asteroid and used the Platypus to return them to the *Adeline*. Cyril lowered his chin to the left inside his helmet to take a small sip of water. During space operations, all suits had an extra slot installed in the left breast pocket for a water bottle. A tube would run up the length of the chest area and into the helmet next to the pilot's mouth. It was irritating around the neck, but no one complained. He turned on some quiet music, which was broadcast to the whole crew. It helped lighten the tedium.

"*Kill the Messenger*," Jace said.

"What?" Cyril asked.

"It's a game. You mention a movie title, then another person chimes in with another film that starts with the last letter of what the first person said. So, the next letter is *R*. What do you got next?"

"*Hmmm… Raiders of the Lost Ark*," Cyril said confidently.

"Good choice," Kyra agreed. "But the full title is *Indiana Jones and the Raiders of the Lost Ark*. But I'll give you a pass. Only this one time." She giggled. "That puts you back at *K* though."

"*King Kong*," Mixer blurted out.

"A classic. *Gone in 60 Seconds*," Tracer said.

"*Star Wars*," Livewire said.

"Oh, fuck you. That's too easy, given our occupation," Cyril shouted, chuckling.

"Fine. *Solaris*," Livewire replied.

"Never seen it," Cyril muttered.

"You're missing out," she responded.

"So, back to *S*," Tracer said.

"It's not your turn, Tracer," Kyra yelped.

"Like there's an order to any of this," he stated. "*Hmmm… Sugarland Express*. No, that puts us back at *S* again. Damn, this is hard. Give me a sec."

Frogger interjected, "Well, while you're thinking about it— *Sorcerer*."

"Damn, that is a good one," Tracer concurred.

The radio crackled to life. "Enigma Squadron, this is *Adeline*. We're at full capacity. Begin docking for FOIL drive."

"Twister to *Adeline*, copy that," Kyra said. "Beginning docking procedures now. All right, Enigma, let's go home." After a beat, she said, "*Ragini*."

"Fuck, solid choice," Tracer said, full of enthusiasm.

The eight ships spun around and slowly drifted toward the *Adeline*'s hull. They deployed their landing struts and controlled their descent with their thrusters. Each ship landed at various flat contact points and engaged their mag locks.

"I got one. *In the Heat of the Night*," Tracer finally said.

"*Taste of Cherry*," Paperboy said.

Hmph. Cherries, Cyril thought and smirked. Gravity shifted, reality warped, time slowed, and, right as they jumped, he said one last title. "*The Year of Living Dangerously*."

***

The pay was fantastic. Over ninety thousand, with zero expenses. No resupply, no repairs, no new power cell. After taxes, he netted a solid profit. As Nester Inc. was based directly out of Balamb, they would make payment via direct deposit. Cyril opened his locker at M&M airfield to a transfer confirmation request on his phone. He texted YES, and within three seconds, he was ninety grand richer. Well, technically, seventy-two grand richer after taxes, but still, that was nothing to scoff at. Jobs like that were sparse, so he would savor every dollar he'd earned.

Jace closed his locker a few feet away. "Mallory's?"

"Hell yeah," Cyril agreed.

He cleared some messages and emails but no new job requests, yet a few messages from Marie that started with the simple, *Hi*, which then became, *Oh, right you're working. My bad.* Then one more message she had sent recently.

> MARIE: I know we've known each other only a little while, but I really like you a lot, and I can't wait for Friday. Miss you, babe. Hope you're safe out there across the stars.
> CYRIL: Hey, you. I'm back. Easy job. Nothing but profit. Looking forward to tomorrow night too. I'm headed to Mallory's right now with Jace for a beer if you'd like to join.

He pressed Send, then headed to Mallory's in Jace's high-quality sportscar—slick and sleek, comfy heated seats, rounded on all sides, with a quality crash rating, and though it had autodrive capability, Jace preferred to keep his hands on the wheel. When they had returned to Proxima, it was midday and crisp. The sun was high in a cloudless sky. Traffic was light, and they arrived at Mallory's faster than normal, as Jace had refused to take his foot off the accelerator. They parked outside the pub, and Cyril realized he had been gripping the armrest and passenger door rail so hard that his hands had left small imprints from Jace's love of speeding.

They exited the car as Cyril checked his phone. No response from Marie yet. *Probably working.* They entered and saw the day manager, a plucky middle-aged guy named Frank, working at the half-filled bar, with people on their lunch breaks.

"Hey, Frank," Jace said.

"Jace, my man, just get back?" Frank asked.

"Literally just got in. I want something with some kick. You know how to make a fireball?"

"You mean the shot?"

"No, it's a mixed drink. A Terran drink that's meant to perk you up. One ounce of bourbon, three ounces of cinnamon schnapps, and a touch of tabasco sauce."

"That sounds like acid," Cyril said.

"I would hope so."

"I think I can manage that," Frank said. "And you, Cyril?"

"Same old Guinness because I'm sane."

"You got it."

As Frank prepped Jace's acid drink, they took up a pair of stools at the bar and perused the lunch menu. Cyril decided he wanted a club sandwich, Jace wanted pasta—seafood ravioli specifically. The drinks arrived; they toasted to another mission accomplished. Cyril was curious and asked for a sip of Jace's fireball. He took a cocktail straw from behind the bar, stabbed it into the drink, and sipped. He recoiled, as his mouth felt like it was overflowing with lava. He coughed hard, but it cleared his nasal cavity like nothing else before it.

Jace chuckled. "Good shit, *huh*?"

Cyril chased it with his Guinness to extinguish the fire.

"So, how's things with Marie?"

Cyril coughed once more. "Really well, actually. We're going out tomorrow night."

"Oh, really? Where?"

"Tech Noir. She used to dance there, so she's getting us in for free."

"Oh, nice. Congrats, man. I'm glad things are going well. She's a good one."

"Yes, she is." He checked his phone again. Still nothing.

"You know, I'm proud of you, man."

"For what?"

"For gettin' your shit together. You were just sorta coasting, doing the same thing over and over, but I'm happy you put in the effort. That thing on Gacrux was when I saw something that didn't seem right about you, so I'm glad you're putting in the work."

"Gacrux was a one-time thing. Someone had to step up for Layla. And that dick Brentwood deserved what he got. Plus, if I didn't get my shit together, I wouldn't hear the end of it from Jess. I'm more scared of her than I am of you."

"Oh, she would fuck you up. I'd just shake my head and walk away."

Cyril scoffed and took a sip of his beer.

"Still, though, you look better."

"Yeah, I guess I am. Love you, man." Cyril held up his beer.

"Love you too, brother." Jace raised his glass for another toast. Then Cyril's phone pinged.

MARIE: Hey! Welcome back! Glad it went well. Can't really come out for a drink because I'm at work. It's still the middle of the day. Your sleep schedule must be totally fucked. Plus, I'm gonna be stuck late at work tonight. But I'll see you tomorrow. In the meantime, here's something to keep you occupied. ;-)

Beneath the text was a photo of Marie in what looked like her office bathroom. She had lifted her shirt and had pulled down her bra. She was sticking out her tongue and smiling. Her nipples were pierced, and she was pinching the left one. Cyril smirked, replied with a bunch of hearts, then closed his phone.

"What the hell are you laughing at?" Jace asked.

"Heh, wouldn't you like to know?" Cyril downed the rest of his beer in one gulp.

***

Friday finally came. It was drizzling and humid. In the distance, the sun was turning sapphire red as it crossed the horizon. It was six at night, and the traffic was congested, but she didn't care. Marie stepped out of the shower and blow-dried her hair. She was trying to decide between two outfits. Simple jeans and a tank top with string straps over the shoulders or something a little fancier—a black-and-white-striped pencil dress from her go-go dancing days. She obviously wanted to look good, but comfort was more important that night. She finished drying her hair, then stood at the edge of her bed and thought hard.

Fuck it, I don't wanna wear the heels. Jeans and a tank top it was.

She applied her favorite lipstick, added some eyeshadow and mascara, then shaded her cheeks a bit. It was all guaranteed to come off at Tech Noir. It would get blazing hot, even with the AC at full blast. But for the first hour, she wanted to look her best. For herself and for him. She smiled at herself in the mirror and stowed her makeup.

Her phone buzzed.

CYRIL: Hey, babe, I'm ready to go. Should I come by to pick you up or meet at the club?
MARIE: I'm finishing up now. I'll meet you there.

She sent a photo of herself. Cyril replied in kind. He was wearing jeans and a plain gray T-shirt. She smiled and closed her phone.

It had all happened so fast that she couldn't believe she was jumping into another relationship so quickly. She had taken so much damage from Ben that she'd sworn off anything for a long while. But something about Cyril intrigued her, made her change her mind. He literally had taken a beating for her. And he was kind, funny, charming, and attractive. And such a great kisser. Tonight, though, would be the night, for sure. She was ready.

She called a cab and headed to Tech Noir. The rain had stopped, but the streets were still slick and reflecting the streetlamps. Crowds jammed outside, looking to decompress after the work week. A mixture of all species stood in line to get in. Two Mukarians guarded the door. They carried extendable batons and mace. Marie knew them both—Kellen and Hog. They were big and rough looking, but they were always sweet to her. On more than one occasion, they'd torn away handsy patrons inside the club and chucked them onto the street.

She approached Hog. "Hey, how's the floor looking tonight?"

"Oh, it's Friday, Ms. Masters. Packed as always. You dancing again?"

"Pleasure not business. Waiting for someone. Think you can slip us inside ahead of the line?"

He smirked. "What line?"

An autocab arrived, and Cyril exited. She noticed he'd gotten a well-kempt haircut and had shaved. He looked hot.

He saw her standing by Kellen and Hog and walked over. "Hey, you."

She smirked. "Hey, yourself."

"Friends?" Cyril gestured to the two Mukarians.

"Kellen, Hog, this is Cyril, my plus one tonight."

"Use the service entrance. We'll radio that you're coming in," Kellen said.

"Thanks, love. You're the best." Then to Cyril, "Ready?"

"Absolutely."

Hog placed his right hand on Cyril's shoulder, leaned down, and growled, "You break her heart, I'll break your bones."

"Which ones?"

"All of them."

"I'll keep that in mind. Watch the door, big guy." Cyril gave him a little smack on the shoulder and walked away.

Hog watched him go.

Marie said, "We're good, Hog. He's a good guy."

Hog scoffed and resumed watching the outside line grow even longer.

Marie led Cyril around the side of the building and into the alley. The service entrance was up a short flight of black stairs, with rust-marked rails. Tech Noir was a decent club, but some parts needed updating and repair. An eye-in-the-sky camera looked down at them. She waved at it, and the door buzzed. She pulled it open, and that club smell of smoke, ozone, alcohol, and sweat hit them as they entered. Thumping music echoed through the hallway and reverberated through the walls. She loved it.

They traversed a dim hallway and rounded a corner. The dressing rooms were on the right, and the stage entrance was to the left. They rounded another corner, and Marie squealed as a group people approached them from the end of corridor.

She stopped in her tracks and whispered to Cyril, "That's Gunmetal. My favorite band."

"Go say hi."

"I can't just go say hi. They're touring here. That's rude."

"If you don't, I will," he said with a shit-eating grin.

"You wouldn't dare." She shot him a steely look.

Cyril walked ahead of her and waved. "Hey, guys! You're Gunmetal, right?"

The lead singer, a thin guy wearing a black button-up shirt and black jeans, said, "Yup, that's us."

"Well, I'm gonna start out by saying I'm a fan myself, but your biggest fan is right down the hallway, and she is very shy." Cyril pointed over his shoulder at Marie, who had a slightly embarrassed expression.

She raised her hand, smiled, and waved.

"Oh, jeez," the lead singer said. "You can come closer. We don't bite… much."

Everyone chuckled. Marie joined the group and gave a quick wave.

"Hi, I'm Dan. I play bass." He proffered his hand.

She shook it. The two other bandmembers, both named Alex, introduced themselves, as well. She shook their hands too.

"I love your guy's music so much. *Syphon Filter* is probably the best album I've heard in the last five years. You're my favorite group," Marie said, keeping her head down.

"We appreciate that. We do what we do for you."

"Your music got me through some tough times, so thank you for that." She grinned from ear to ear.

"You're welcome. And thank you for being here tonight," Dan said. "Hey, what song do you want to hear the most?"

She sighed. "Oh, boy, I… don't know. They're all good."

"Well, we came here to dance tonight, right?" Cyril interjected. "What's the best one for dancing?"

"Oh, we got the perfect one. We can adjust the lineup a bit, I think," the first Alex said.

"We'll give you a good time. We gotta go in for soundcheck. Have fun tonight," Dan said.

They walked around Cyril and Marie in the cramped hallway, then rounded the corner.

Marie's eyes were wide, and a smile stretched from ear to ear, while she bounced on her tiptoes in joy. "That was so bizarre. This club never gets anyone of that caliber."

"See? Wasn't so bad," he said wrapping his arms around her waist.

"Gotta say, I was kinda scared, but they're so normal. You have no idea how many times I would listen to their music after fights with Ben. I'd just go somewhere quiet and play the same song over and over. Don't know if you've ever done that. But meeting the people who helped you get through rough times… that was kind of a trip."

"You did fine, babe."

"I'm still highly annoyed at you," she said, as if faking anger.

"*Eh*, you'll get over it." He gave her the biggest smirk possible.

She laughed. "Come on, let's hit the floor. Hopefully we can still grab drinks before the bar line is too long."

They proceeded down the hallway again and passed through a set of black curtains. They finally entered the club area from stage right. The place was packed. A Crecian DJ was on stage, playing mixed tracks. The dance floor was crowded, so the bar line was relatively short. It was dark and smoky, and lasers blazed across the ceiling. Neon soaked the room into a blue and purple color palette, and an LED screen backlit the extra-short DJ. They had to stand on a small box to be tall enough to operate the board.

Tech Noir was one of the higher-class venues on that side of town. Not exactly upscale, but not a dive either. It was a place all its own. High ceilings, a circular balcony, a wide pit, with a thirty-foot runway jutting from center stage. The soundproofed walls allowed them to blast the music as loud as possible without noise violations. Men, women, and nonbinary people danced in the cages to the music, one person per cage. In total, ten cages filled the room, some on the ground, some on stage, and some hung from the ceiling. Ladders descended from a catwalk, which acted as their entrance and exit.

Marie leaned toward Cyril's right ear and yelled, "I used to dance in that one." She pointed across the room to a cage on stage left that a bald nonbinary person occupied, dancing in a mesh shirt and short skirt. She took his hand, and they went to the bar. They squeezed between two people, and she flagged down the bartender, Howser.

"Marie! Haven't seen you in a minute," Howser shouted.

"Life got complicated," she also shouted. The music was definitely on volume eleven.

"When is it not complicated?" Howser retorted. "Usual?"

"Yep!"

"Make that two," Cyril yelled as he passed his card to Howser.

The bartender took it and mixed a pair of drinks.

"So, what is your usual anyway?"

She smirked. "You'll find out."

Howser returned with a pair of oversized glasses filled with a layered liquid that went from blue to green to orange, from top to bottom. White smoke flowed over the rim of the glass from the dry ice. They grabbed their drinks and toasted. Marie took a long swig, no problem. Cyril immediately recoiled and coughed. She laughed.

"Holy shit, is that lighter fluid?" he coughed out.

"*Heh*, you wish."

"Man, what is that?"

"Curaçao, spicy green tea vodka, and Campari. A little bit of everything."

"This is 80 percent alcohol."

"Oh, come on. Don't be a pussy." She leaned in and gave him a quick peck on the lips, then took another sip.

He manned up and took another long sip. He stifled a cough for a moment but finally relinquished. He doubled over and coughed into his hand.

"*Pfft*. Pussy. It's a far cry from Guinness, isn't it?"

"Not even in the same dimension."

They drank and chatted. Once they finished, they hit the floor. The DJ was still going hard, pumping techno beats and heavy synthwave. Jumping and swaying and pounding to the beat, and the crowd had a static charge of energy pulsing through them. It was intense and palpable. Cyril and Marie danced side by side, grinding on each other, as the DJ went from track to track. The alcohol kicked in quickly, and they felt like they were floating. It would be a hell of a hangover the following day, but that night would be worth it. The DJ wrapped up his set and exited stage left.

They took a break and returned to the bar for another drink. Marie ordered another of her lighter fluid cocktails, while Cyril went basic with a Jack and Coke. He was sweating profusely, and his shirt had gone from light gray to dark gray.

"God, I thought I was in decent shape. I can't stop sweating," he said, huffing and puffing.

"You *are* in decent shape. It's just hot in here."

"Oh, that's what that was. Got it."

Gunmetal came out on stage. The crowd cheered, and the band waved, then began setting up their instruments and getting prepped.

Marie gave a whooping cheer. "God, I can't believe I got to meet them."

"Man, I wonder who managed to make that happen," Cyril said.

She slapped his arm, grabbed his shirt, pulled him close, and kissed him hard on the lips.

"Hello, out there, Tech Noir! You guys ready for the good vibes tonight?" Dan yelled from the stage. The crowd cheered in agreement. "Then, let's fly!"

The band started with a heavy guitar solo and a synth beat, which led into the first song.

Marie perked up and said, "Oh my God, it's my favorite song! Dance with me!"

"Gimme a sec. I need a breather."

"Nope, no way. I danced with you; you dance with me." She got close to Cyril and lip-synched the lyrics. *What's the matter? You wanna live forever?* She stepped backward and whipped her head around, her long red hair, blue under the lights, seemed to flow in slow motion.

Re-energized, Cyril chugged the remainder of his drink and joined her on the floor. They danced and bounced to the beat. The crowd surrounded the runway as the lead vocalist walked down it. The energy in Tech Noir was so intense that it could blow the roof off. Marie knew all the lyrics by heart and sang along. Cyril wrapped his hands around her waist and ground against her back. She pressed herself into him. They were sweating profusely, damn near overheating. Then Cyril spun her around and kissed her hard on the lips right in the middle of the crowd. She embraced him and kissed him back.

The song settled into a slow, thumping beat. Their lips parted, and they stared into each other's eyes. She smiled and kept rocking her shoulders. She eyed his pants, bit her lip, and looked up at him. *Give me more! Give me more!* She spun around again and ground against his crotch. *Give me more! Give me more!* Cyril moved his hand from her waist to her belly, slipped it into the front of her pants, and slid two fingers inside her. She moaned and felt him sliding in and out, in and out. She was so hot that she could barely contain herself from taking him right there on the club floor for everyone to watch. She craned her head backward and to the left and looked up at him. *Give me more! Give me more!* He kissed her from behind as she became wetter and wetter. She was so close and needed him inside of her.

The singer screamed as the song hit its crescendo. Thundering beats, lights blasting everywhere, guitar riffs on full force. A nuclear explosion of power pulsed through the speakers. Dan strutted down the runway again to high-five and shake hands with the crowd as he sang. He saw Cyril and Marie kissing in the crowd. They broke their kiss and looked up at Dan. He pointed to them in a congratulatory way, like he was saying, *"Told you that you were gonna have a good night."*

The dancing kept going, and the beat kept pumping. And as the song ended, Marie climaxed all over Cyril's fingers. She shuddered and shook. Her eyes rolled back. Time melted, and her legs weakened. Cyril held her up so she wouldn't fall. She regained her footing and turned around. As she stared into his eyes, he held up his soaked fingers, still covered in her juices, and slipped them into her mouth. She took them all the way in and cleaned them off. The flavor of her cum and the saltiness of her sweat mixed, and she savored every bit of it. Then she leaned in again and kissed him hard. She slid her hand down and felt his throbbing cock in his pants. He was big too.

She stopped kissing him for a moment. "Life is good." Then she went in for another round.

***

They reached Cyril's apartment just after midnight. Marie was well past drunk; Cyril was buzzed but not quite hammered. They walked in giggling. Cyril had cracked a joke in the elevator, and they couldn't stop laughing. The alcohol was doing its work. They were also soaked, as it had downpoured when they left Tech Noir.

As the door shut, Cyril said, "Synth vibes on."

The apartment flooded with purple and pink lighting, and smooth synth music played. Marie grabbed his sweat-soaked shirt and shoved him against the wall. She was like an animal as she kissed him hard, nearly biting his tongue. She slid her hand up and down his crotch, stroking him, feeling him grow.

He grabbed her ass, picked her up, spun around, and pinned her to the wall. She laughed and wrapped her arms around him and went back to kissing. There was no separating them. They were ready to tear each other apart and love every second of it.

Cyril stopped for a moment. "Bedroom?"

She shook her head. "No. Fuck me right here."

He smiled, spun around again, and chucked her onto the island in the kitchen. She landed with a thump and slid down the countertop on her back. He unzipped his pants and climbed atop her. They kissed again as he slid his hand under her tank top and squeezed her soft breasts, playing with her pierced nipples.

She moaned, "Oh, yes," and rolled her head back.

He yanked off her tank top, leaned down, and bit her nipple—soft at first, then harder and harder.

"Oh my God, that feels so good."

"Remember when I said kissing wasn't the only thing I'm good at?"

"Shut up and fuck me. Please. I need it." She grabbed his shirt again and pulled him to her face. "I want you inside me, now. Please."

He hopped off the island, slid off her pants, then did the same himself. He removed his shirt, then climbed onto the island and kissed her a little more along her neck, then felt her lips with the tip of his cock. He slowly slipped the first inch of himself inside her.

"Oh, wow, that's thick. Okay, go slow. It's been a while." She exhaled.

He moved slowly, staring into her eyes. One inch, two, three, four, five, six, seven, till all eight were inside her.

She pulsed around him as he kissed her again. "Oh my God, you're fucking huge."

"You okay?"

"Yeah, yeah. I'm good. Now… fuck me hard."

He slid in and out, over and over, feeling her tighten with each thrust. Her eyes rolled back, and she couldn't speak. It felt so good. It had been months since she'd had anyone inside her and never anyone as big as him. They had only just started, but she was already so close to orgasming.

"Keep going. I'm gonna cum. Don't stop!"

He moved faster and faster, thrusting harder and harder. She tightened and finally climaxed all over him. She shuddered and convulsed and felt the world stop in place once again. Her body quaked and quivered. He held her as she shook, still deep inside her and rock hard.

"Oh my God, that was amazing. I'm sorry I was so quick," she said through staggered breaths.

"Well, I'm not done yet. I didn't finish. We're gonna be going for a while. You ready?"

She smiled, and they went for round two.

***

The bright morning sun bled through the drapes of the bedroom. The rain was all gone, and the streets had dried. Marie and Cyril lay in his bed, his arm draped over her. His bed was against the wall. He slept on the wall side, while Marie slept on the floor side.

She slowly rose from her slumber. A wicked hangover punched at her skull from the inside. She forced herself up and went to the bathroom. As she rounded the corner, she raised the slider for the sink light. She noticed the pink and purple lighting from the night before still glowed in the living room, as the bathroom was adjacent to it. The music still played softly as well. She relieved herself, then dunked her head under the faucet for some water. She hadn't drunk enough the night before. Surveying her reflection in the mirror, she saw her makeup was all kinds of messed up. Her eyeshadow was smeared, lipstick was effectively gone, and her cheek blush looked like it was patchy, as if she had either been crying or it had been a good night. Considering how she was still in Cyril's apartment and had awoken in his bed, and she was quite sore, it had definitely been a good night.

She washed up and returned to the bedroom. Cyril was still dead asleep. She decided to look around. It was a well-kept bedroom, though a thin layer of dust covered the dresser. She assumed it was due to Cyril's work schedule. Posters for movies, comic book characters, and an entire bookshelf, consisting of more than twenty Lee Child novels in each row, furnished the room. Most people didn't read paperbacks anymore, which made these collectors' items. He was well read at least, though mostly pulp. Some framed photos hung on the wall. One showed Jess, Jace, and Cyril huddled together at a firing range. Jess had the biggest gun of the group. Another photo atop his bookshelf revealed a woman holding a baby. She assumed that this was Cyril's mother holding him when he had been young. She picked it up and looked at it.

"*Hmph*, baby Cyril," she whispered. "Hard to believe you were ever a baby."

She eyed him still asleep. He looked handsome even while sleeping. She moved to the closet. She was being nosy but couldn't help herself. Clothes hung on the rack, a pair of boots lay on the floor, and a large olive-green case leaned against the wall. She quietly pulled it out and opened it to expose pieces of a large rifle—the same one from the photo on the wall. She knew next to nothing about firearms. In fact, they terrified her. She closed the lid and stowed it in the closet. Cyril rolled over in bed and repositioned, still asleep.

Marie's phone buzzed. She sprinted to pick it up to stop the buzzing on the nightstand. It was her mother. She sat on the edge of the bed and answered. "Hey, Mom."

"Bunny, I'm just checking on you. I just heard that Ben got arrested again and wanted to see if you were okay."

"Yeah, I'm okay. I had some friends take care of that whole thing."

"Glad that they did. A shame how things turned out."

"Yeah, well, that's just how things turned out."

"But you're okay?"

"Yeah. I'm doing okay. Really good, actually."

"That's good. I'm glad to hear that. You're taking care of yourself, right?"

"Best I can, Mom. I'll try to visit next month. I'll look into train tickets."

"Okay, sweetie. Oh, I didn't wake you, did I?"

"No, I was already awake. Went to the bathroom."

"Good. Again, I'm sorry about Ben."

"Mom, it's okay. I'm kind of seeing someone else now. Someone better."

"Someone better? Well, color me curious."

"You'll meet him one day… I think."

"I hope so."

"Yeah. Love you, Mom."

"Love you too, bunny." She hung up.

Marie put the phone on the nightstand, crawled under the covers, and draped her arm over Cyril's shoulder. She played with his hair, then quietly whispered in his ear, "I love you, Cyril."

He didn't hear her. He was still asleep.

Chapter 10

Pain Is Weakness

"I wake up in the morning, and I piss excellence," Daniel Mullarkey said to himself in the mirror after he finished shaving and trimming his goatee. He admired himself—his size, his power. He could build a new world or crush the current one. And either way, everyone would thank him for it. He buttoned his white dress shirt and slipped on a blue tie, then donned a set of blue slacks and a blue blazer. Work awaited him at Arcturus. It was a big day ahead. The deal for Project Samson was moving forward.

As a dedicated bachelor, he lived a simple lifestyle. No other person could completely match his dedication to physical and mental prowess. Awake at 0530, a ninety-minute gym session, then off to work, arriving at 0900. A full workday till 2100, then home by 2145. A second quick workout and preparation for the following day. Then in bed by 2300. He never achieved a full eight-hour REM sleep. Sleep was for the weak. Early to rise, late to rest. One of his adages was *Force yourself up and get the most out of your day; you only live once, so squeeze out every second possible.* Because of the lack of proper rest, his hair was graying at only thirty-five years old.

Exhaustion is for the uncommitted. Full commitment requires pain, and pain is weakness leaving the body. Take what you want, when you want it. He recited this to himself each morning. His mantra. His code. No crying, no complaining. Work harder or not at all.

He parked his luxury car in the underground garage of Arcturus, then went to the lobby. People were arriving like rows of ducks. Even for a weekend, the work never ended. The galaxy never stopped turning, so why should they? What was a weekend there, was a weekday elsewhere.

Bentley and Locke met Mullarkey in the lobby and followed him side by side. Employees backed off and parted like the tides of the ocean as their boss passed by. Mullarkey's size intimidated everyone. He was a giant compared to the rest. Most CEOs were old and crusty or young and waifish. Not Mullarkey. He refused to be reduced to a cliché.

As they entered his office, the sun beamed in. Bentley flipped on the window polarizer and dimmed the sunlight to nothing but an orange orb in the sky. Mullarkey walked around his desk, his footsteps clack-clack-clacking on the marble floor.

"Bentley, get the board on a video call. The final documents should be coming through via data courier any second now," Mullarkey said.

"Yes, sir."

"Locke, where's Layla?"

"I'd assume at home, sir."

"Get her in here. I want her here for the call."

"Yes, sir."

Bentley called the Arcturus board offices, while Locke called the front desk of Layla's apartment building. Daniel sat behind his desk and turned on the lefthand monitors. The stock reports were starting up as the market opened. Even the markets of Balamb never took time off. With Arcturus on the ascent, he watched the numbers like a hawk. He opened emails, clearing out old messages and answering new ones. He shuffled those that didn't require his immediate attention into a folder group for his assistants on the lower levels to answer. Menial questions were beneath him.

He opened the file for Project Samson and reviewed the specs one more time before the investment meeting.

Project Samson: An immunization program dedicated to the eradication of cross-species pathogens to be delivered via aerial dispersion.

Arcturus's security teams were Proxima-based and could not deliver full payloads off world on schedule, which meant he would need outside contractors. The budget was gargantuan, well above anything the company had ever attempted before. But the Ekumen governance had agreed that cross-species contamination was a growing issue. After rigorous debate, Arcturus had claimed the contract and began trials.

"Sir, Layla is on her way in," Locke said.

"Thank you," Daniel said and continued reading.

"The board is ready for the call, sir," Bentley said.

"Put them through." Daniel swiveled in his chair toward the large monitors and stood.

Ten of the twelve screens flipped from stock and news reports to camera feeds of the ten board members. Douglas Forester was in the top right of the monitors. The board was composed of seven men and three women—all Caucasian Terrans.

"Good morning, ladies and gentlemen. Today is the day when we finally close the deal—the final signing of the agreement for phase one of Project Samson. The contract should be arriving any moment now. My sister should be arriving soon as well."

"I just want to clarify that this first test is in a colony town of only thirty thousand. Is that correct?" Forester asked.

"That's correct," Mullarkey confirmed as he paced. "This is more than anything just for a demonstration. There were some gross statements about aerial dispersion. We need to save face and gain the full trust and support of populus on Kepler. After that, we move on to larger colonies, cities, and planets."

"Daniel, have you looked at the figures for this? We're already approaching our budget, and we haven't even begun the first widespread test. How is your security force supposed to cover payroll?" asked Greegs, another board member.

"That's the thing, sir. We'll be hiring freelancers at a lower rate. Saves us a bit here and there. That will put us just within margin. We may be pinching pennies, but we at least will have pennies."

"*Hmm*. I still feel as if there's something we've missed. Perhaps we're rushing this," inquired Hines, another board member, in the center of the bottom row of screens.

"Ma'am, let me make this clear. We have waited years for this moment, and it is finally within our grasp—the complete inoculation of the Ekumen. Not only will it be for the greater good, but all of us will be hailed as heroes. The lives we save with this will reshape our status in the Body Politic. We'll be at the top, and whatever we move forward with afterward will be a blank check. Humanity shouldn't have to constantly reassert itself over and over. We were the best right from the start."

Layla exited the elevator. Locke stepped to her right and followed behind her.

Mullarkey continued. "Besides, the deal is done. We're committed now. All in, no stops. And we have this woman to thank for it."

Layla stopped alongside Daniel. He wrapped his right arm around her shoulders and squeezed tight. She looked uncomfortable but said nothing.

"My sister negotiated the deal with Winnick Koy on Kepler to secure our contract. Without her, we would be dead in the water."

"Layla, you've done a great service for all of us and for the Ekumen. We won't forget your contributions to Project Samson," Greegs said.

"She's a true patriot, just like all of us," Daniel said.

Layla squirmed her way from Daniel's grasp and stepped a few feet away.

"Layla, how are you holding up since your husband's passing?" Hines asked.

"I'm fine, I suppose. I apologize again for my outburst at the funeral home, Mr. Forester,"

"It's quite all right. You were in distress and manic. It happens to the best of us, I suppose."

"Yeah." She looked away from the screens.

"Well, anyway, this is a great leap forward for Arcturus. The carrier drone should arrive any minute to deliver the files," Daniel said.

Above the atmosphere of Proxima Centauri B, a FOIL-equipped probe, carrying nothing more than a data packet, leaped into range of the closest satellite. It uploaded all encrypted data to the transmission network, which was then delivered to the Arturus Allied database. Once fully delivered, the probe spooled up its FOIL drive again and leaped away. This happened all in the span of ten seconds.

An email blip appeared on the top left monitor in the office. Daniel returned to his desk and opened the folder—the final signed paperwork for test dispersion on the colony town Elek on Kepler-186F. "And there it is! We have what we need. We can begin the first step toward a better galaxy. Thanks to all of you." He faced Layla. "And you, of course."

She said nothing.

"Daniel, you've been a spearhead for Project Samson from day one. Your father would be proud," Forester said.

"I'm sure he would. Thank you for your time, ladies and gentlemen. Enjoy the rest of your day."

As the board members began signing off, Douglas said, "Daniel, I'd like to discuss a personal matter with you, if you're available after this."

"Of course, Douglas. Thank you, everyone." All monitors except Forester's went blank. Forester's face expanded to fill all ten monitors into one image. "Douglas, what do you need?"

"I may have kept a straight face for the board, but I just wanted to express my disdain for having your sister be the one negotiating the deal on Kepler."

"If this has to do with the situation involving your son's death, let me just say that it had nothing to do with that," Daniel said curtly.

"She referred to my son as an abuser. I'm disgusted that she's still working with us. You're lucky I withdrew my lawsuit," Douglas said, nearly growling like an animal.

"I will stand by my sister's side, no matter what, Mr. Forester. I don't travel off world, and the thought of having to make deals with the Mukkers makes my skin crawl. Plus, sending a woman who is adept at negotiations and marketing instead of a man guarantees a certain level of... sympathy, especially when one has lost a loving husband so recently."

"You spun my son's death to gain a sympathy vote?" he snarled.

"It worked, didn't it? We got the contract. She did as she was told, didn't you?"

Layla kept quiet and bit her fingernails.

"You truly are something else, Daniel. I swear—"

"I would be very careful with what you say next, Forester! You and I both know what Project Samson really is. You crack, lose your cool, or simply come after me for bitter revenge, I'll drag you down too. Know your fucking place, old man."

Douglas began to speak, then caught his tongue. He did know what Project Samson was, and if it got out to the public, it would devastate not just Arcturus but the entire Terran side of the Ekumen. "Fine. You win. But I don't want to see that woman's face in these meetings ever again. Understood?"

"Of course. Glad we've come to an agreement. Have a nice day… Doug." Daniel ended the call, and the screens reverted to their normal displays.

"Do you need me for anything else?" Layla asked.

Daniel walked behind his desk again. "After we finish the Kepler test, I'll need you to go to Creece. We'll need to get the Crecians on board and move forward from there. They're always the hardest to bargain with. Too much bureaucracy."

"You don't really need me. You could send anyone. Send Moriarty."

"Moriarty is an unhinged twat—good at their job but terrible at negotiations. Bentley and Locke, they're just security. Everyone else on the board isn't adept enough to handle negotiations. You're the best person we have. Showing up with lawyers and lobbyists would give the wrong impression. You're fully qualified with your background, and you're the sister of the most well-known CEO in Balamb, so it gives you prestige points. Locke will be right there with you the whole time during every meeting, should things get out of hand."

"Fuck you, Daniel," Layla whispered.

"Fuck me?"

"Yeah, fuck you."

"Locke, Bentley. Leave please."

Locke and Bentley entered the elevator and rode it down to the security floor, leaving Layla and Daniel alone.

Daniel rose from behind his desk and approached Layla. "I've given you so much and have carried on Dad's legacy. And yet, you still spit it back in my face. Fuck me, huh?" He grabbed her arm and threw her against the marble desk.

She landed bent over against the edge.

Daniel throttled the back of her neck and forced her down. "Is this what Brentwood used to do to make his point? Was it exactly like this? You'll do as you're told, or I'm gonna hurt you. It's difficult to make a person disappear but not impossible. I wake up in the morning, and

I piss excellence. You need to learn to do the same. Do you understand?"

"Yes," Layla whimpered.

"Louder!"

"Yes!"

"Good. Now get the fuck outta here." He released her neck and moved behind his desk.

Layla slowly pushed herself upright from the desk as she wiped away tears.

"No crying. Not in my office," Daniel declared, while typing on his keyboard and without looking at her.

She suppressed more tears and went to the elevator, which felt like it took an eternity to arrive. She entered it and disappeared as the glass lift dropped out of sight. Daniel pressed the call button on his desk and pulled up Moriarty.

"Moriarty, begin calls for freelancers in the city. Phase one of Samson is a go. We'll need pilots to head to Kepler in a few weeks. Good ones too."

"I'll start going through the call lists," she said.

The call ended, then Daniel made a cup of coffee at his wet bar. He marveled at the orange orb of Alpha Centauri in the sky through his window. It was glorious, and all of it was his. He repeated his mantra. *Exhaustion is for the uncommitted. Full commitment requires pain, and pain is weakness leaving the body. Take what you want, when you want it.*

***

They spent the weekend together—stayed in, watched shitty TV, ate pizza, fucked a hell of a lot more, showered, then did it all over again. Two days straight. It was the happiest either of them had been in a long time. Cyril held her close after they had gone for their fifth round Sunday morning. She was warm in his arms, and Marie's hair was soft against his neck. He would nibble at her ears as she giggled. Then he would tickle her, and she would laugh and go, "No, no, no!" They tussled, threw around for a few minutes, and wound up with him atop her, her arms pinned above her head on the mattress. He looked into her eyes. She looked right back.

"What are you thinking about?"

"*Hmmm…* you want more pizza, or should we get sushi?"

"You fucking asshole," she yelled, laughing. "If my arms weren't pinned down, I'd slap you right now."

"Oh, yeah? Go ahead and try. Go on."

She tried as hard as she could to free herself, but he was too big, too strong. He had her trapped. She struggled and struggled but to no avail.

Cyril laughed the whole time. "Oh, come on. I thought you were strong."

"*Argh*, goddammit. You motherfucker."

"Not so tough now, are you?"

"I fucking hate you."

"No, you don't."

She was quiet for a moment, then whispered, "No, I don't." Another pause lapsed as she looked into his eyes, then said, "Kiss me."

He leaned in and kissed her softly on the lips. He let his guard down by pulling one hand away to touch her cheek. She wrapped her left arm around him and pull him to the other side of the bed and tickled his stomach. It was his weak spot, and she knew it very well.

"No, no, no, no, no!" He laughed and yelled as she tickled him. "You bitch! You fucking tricked me!"

"Yeah, who's the weak one now, asshole?" she yelled.

He flailed around and managed to grab her arms to stop the tickling. They wrestled again. Cyril gained the upper hand, flung her onto her back, and pinned her again. "You know what? Maybe this'll shut you up." He rammed himself, rock hard, all the way inside her in one thrust.

"Holy shit. Wow," she gasped loudly.

"You like that? Still think it's funny?"

She giggled. "I think it's fucking hilarious."

He fucked her so hard for the next thirty minutes that when they finished, she stumbled bow-legged to the bathroom. She kept saying he had finally broken her with that last round.

As she left his sight, he proudly said, "My work here is done."

His phone pinged with a work request for the following day. Last minute call. Recovery and rescue assignment on an outer-rim planet called Sela. High-orbit crash of a capital ship. Settlements were minimal. Possible raiders hiding in the caves that littered the snowy mountains. It would be tough, but the pay was extremely high. He was about to press Yes, then he noticed the bathroom light shining into the hallway and the running faucet as Marie cleaned up and brushed her teeth.

" Kiss me. "

His mind went through possible scenarios. What if he didn't come back? What if that was the one where he bought it? What if he was trapped in that snowy desert forever, and she eventually forgot about him? Everyone's luck ran out eventually. He knew he should press

Yes, but he also wanted to press No. Money was good, but he wasn't starving. Another job would come along. Like the planet that they were asking him to go to, he was frozen.

Marie returned completely naked and still slightly stumbling. She saw his expression as he focused on his phone. "Babe, what's wrong?"

"I just got asked to work tomorrow," he said, still staring at the message on his phone.

She plopped onto the bed next to him. "That's great. Take it."

"It's a dangerous one. Off world. Somewhere called Sela. It's barely on the edge of the Ekumen. I think it's part of the Crecian territory."

"So, what's so dangerous?"

"There's no back up. Minimal settlements. Raiding parties. It's a recovery and rescue operation, so we'll need to land and operate on foot. If I crash, I'll freeze. The maximum temperature is minus seven Celsius. It's a giant snowball in space. If I bite it there, no one will ever find me."

"Oh, babe, come here." She wrapped her arms around him.

"Woah. I just got really scared. That never happens to me."

She put her hand on his cheek. "I think I know why you're scared, babe."

He turned his head to her. "Yeah. Yeah, I guess I do know why."

"You're not gonna die. You're gonna go do your job, make your money, and come back to me. Say it. Say, 'I'll come back to you.'"

"I'll come back to you. I promise."

"You fuckin' better."

***

Cold temperatures actually improve flight capability. It cools the engines, and the dense air allows for greater lift. Unfortunately, the snowy landscape of Sela was tough on the eyes. Every starfighter's canopy was at full polarization. The sky was bright, not a cloud anywhere. The sunlight reflected off the snowy surface back into the sky like a freshly cleaned mirror. Staring at it too long without polarizers would lead to snow blindness, the corneas of their eyes becoming sunburned, rendering them completely blind. With the polarizers at maximum, the sky went from blue to a dull gray, and the ground morphed from a bright white to a flat white.

Depth perception was another issue. Forest, deserts, grassland all registered the changes in their elevation visibly. With snow, everything looked flat. Fifty meters or five hundred meters, it all looked like the same distance—a nightmare for pilots. Instrument navigation was critical.

Sela had no satellites in orbit. It was a small waystation planet for individuals attempting to set up shop on the edge of Ekumen territory. As it had no prosperous natural resources of its own, and was too cold for large-scale settlements, the Ekumen had decided to leave it be. What they did there was their own business. What was critical on the planet, though, was the crashed frigate, the *Monroe*. Part of a convoy run of high-value artwork and museum artifacts, it had accidentally FOILed to the wrong coordinates, jumping directly into Sela's atmosphere. It was rare to jump directly into a planetary body, but it was not impossible. For all pilots, it was better to not think about it.

A small town called Tull had heard a distress beacon on standard radio broadcasts. Shortwave radio was still the best means of communication between settlements on the planet. Relay posts peppered mountain ranges and valleys. Once they heard the call, they dispatched a scout team to trace the beacon before raiding parties had driven them off. They then sent a data courier to Proxima to seek aid.

That was two days ago.

It was still unknown if anyone survived the crash. Chances of survival by that point were near zero. But the artifacts inside the ship were still considered valuable, and thus they organized a retrieval squadron and dispatched a recon ship to orbit Sela and trace the beacon's location—seventy-two kilometers west of Tull in a flat snowfield surrounded by a mountain range.

The squadron was composed of twelve starfighters and two dropships codenamed Alpha and Bravo. They carried ten personnel each—two engineers, six scout troops, and two medical techs. The squadron codename was Tiger.

CYRIL "SKYHAWK" EISNER

FIGS "TRIGGER" MILLS

KYRA "TWISTER" HADLEY

CATHERINE "KITKAT" YOUNG

MORGAN "PIPER" SEXTON

HASTER "KARAOKE" JENTOW

CALLISTO "AUGER" JONES

SETH "GAMEBOY" DECKER

HOPE "TERRIFIER" WYATT

JAY "DAZER" HAYES

RACHAEL "LOKI" NORRIS

FLIGHT LEAD: STEPHEN "CONDOR" GARRISON

MISSION: RESCUE AND RECOVERY; CREW AND HIGH-VALUE ARTWORK. ESCORT ENGINEERING AND MEDICAL DROPSHIPS TO DESTINATION.

TARGET: CAPITAL FRIGATE MONROE, CRASH LANDING FROM ORBIT.

THREAT LEVEL: MODERATE TO HIGH, POSSIBLE RAIDING PARTIES HIDING IN LOCAL CAVES AND IN ICE SHELF SYSTEMS. USE EXTREME CAUTION. PREPARE FOR A HARSH COLD WEATHER CLIMATE. ON FOOT SUPPORT MAY BE NECESSARY. SMALL ARMS REQUIRED FOR SUPPORT AND DEFENSE.

Garrison was flight lead again, continuing his grudge against Cyril. During the mission briefing, Garrison would cast glances at Cyril so sharp that they could cut through diamonds.

Before boarding their ships to head out, Garrison pulled Cyril aside. "Are we going to have a problem this time, Eisner?"

"Not unless you make one. Sir."

They glared at each other for a moment, then Garrison brushed past him on the landing pad. The crew wore specialized flight suits that their client, The Hubbard Art Institute, had provided. They were insulated and lined with thermal padding, which packed on an four kilograms per person. Fitting into their pilot's seats was snug, maybe a bit too snug. The client also provided facemasks and sunglasses, in case anyone needed to exit their ship. Everyone looked ridiculous, but they were warm, and the cold weather was truly brutal. Without proper attire, frostbite occurred within fifteen minutes, and movement through the deep snow proved difficult. Snowcats would have to clear the landing pads daily for all incoming craft.

They were twenty kilometers out, flying at fifteen hundred meters. "Stay frosty, Tiger Squadron. This is where raider activity was last reported," Garrison stated.

"I don't think it'll be a problem staying frosty on this planet," KitKat quipped.

"You wanna build a snowman after this, KitKat?" Cyril asked.

She laughed.

"Quiet. Keep the channel clear, Skyhawk."

Cyril flipped off his radio. "Asshole."

They flew on. Fifteen kilometers from the target.

The radio squawked. "Piper to Condor. Recommend weapons test. This cold might affect our gun belts and barrels."

"Condor to Piper, copy that. Weapons free. Everyone fire off a squirt."

All ships fired a short burst of gunfire, between thirty and fifty rounds. All but one fighter fired. Twister. "Fuck," she screamed. "Twister to Condor, my belts are frozen. I can't get a shot off. All I have is my missiles if we get in a jam."

"Shit," Garrison whispered. "Condor to Twister, your call. Stay or go?"

She sighed. "Returning to base. I'll need a wingman to fly support."

"Auger to Twister, I got you. Joining on your wing. Will rejoin squadron once Twister is home." Auger pulled out of formation and knifed left. He formed up on Twister's starboard side, and they trekked back toward Tull. The flight was reduced to ten operational fighters and the two dropships.

Ten kilometers from the target but still no sign of raiders or the *Monroe*.

The distress beacon beeped repeatedly on the comms, broken up by static. "Capital ship *Monroe* … requi … tance in … Under att … sending on all ra … captain cap … send resc … Cap … *Monroe* needs imm … set to repeat …" The message repeated the same canned statement.

"Not ominous at all," Dazer said. "Your call, boss."

Garrison checked his LADAR scopes. Nothing in the sky nor on the ground ahead. The barren waste of Sela lay before them like a white bed sheet with ripples everywhere. He spun his radar dial to check all three hundred sixty degrees around the squadron. Still nothing. Any threat seemed to have long since passed.

"Tiger Squadron, maintain course and altitude. Stay alert."

Five kilometers out, they finally saw the wreckage of the *Monroe* behind a mountain range peak. A diagonal black pillar on metal in the distance grew larger as they approached. It had landed nose first into the ice and jutted upward like a skyscraper on the verge of toppling over. They made a circular pass overhead to survey the wreckage. Westward snowfall caked the ship's dull black and gray metal.

"Yup, that's a crashed ship, all right," Loki said. "Loki to Condor, should we begin landing procedures?"

Condor said nothing. Something felt wrong. "Tiger Squadron, descend to one thousand meters. Continue circular pattern."

The squadron descended. No life signs, no enemy raiders.

They circled till Garrison made the call. "All right, I'm satisfied. Dropships Alpha and Bravo, begin landing procedures."

The dropships descended. Swaths of fresh powder sprayed up around them as they touched down on the frozen landscape. The doors opened, and the scout troopers, dressed head to toe in white combat attire and white assault rifles, marched out and scanned the area. Behind them, the engineers and med techs followed.

In the sky, Tiger Squadron continued its circular flight to guard the *Monroe*'s perimeter. Nothing in the sky but them. The world seemed unequivocally dead.

"Tiger Squadron, descend to three hundred meters and switch to V/TOL. Circular phalanx perimeter formation. Two hundred meters apart. Stay alert for contacts."

All ten ships formed a ring around the *Monroe*, facing out toward the frozen waste. They hovered in place and waited. On the ground, the engineers cut into the hull, while assault troopers formed a defensive perimeter around them. The hull was composed of six-inch-thick titanium, with carbon nanofiber lining, designed to withstand enemy attacks or emergency landings. The cutting took twenty minutes to open a two-by-two square space to fit inside.

Garrison still felt something was off. If the scout party had reported raiders at the crash site four days prior, where were they now? Why had it been so easy to approach?

Then Loki said what everyone felt. "Anyone else got that tingle in their spine?"

"Yeah, something's not right here," Cyril agreed.

Garrison extended his radar to the maximum distance of three hundred seventy-five kilometers to scan. Still nothing. A creeping feeling ran through his body. All ten ships were essentially floating targets for a ground attack. But the ground was clear as well.

"Ground team, report," Garrison said.

"We're inside," Commanding Officer Haggerty said. "Having to climb toward the bridge, but we're not picking up any survivors on our thermals. This is probably just a recovery operation at this point."

"Copy that, ground team. Keep us updated. Assault teams Alpha, Bravo, stay alert and check your long-range scanning." Garrison, feeling like someone was watching him, rotated his LADAR dial again. Nothing. Then he switched on his IRST (Infrared Search and Tracking). The world outside turned dark gray, and the distant horizon turned black.

And there they were. Extremely small white dots peppered the mountainsides surrounding the crash site. He zoomed in his external camera and realized why they had appeared so small. White wool covered them to simulate snow cover. From that angle, they appeared to be inside small snow caves dug into the mountainside to maintain overwatch on the crashed ship. Only the smallest part of the cave exit was exposed to allow whoever hid inside a view of the ship and of the surrounding squadron. The exit window of the cave through the wool was extremely narrow, but it was just enough to register a heat signature on infrared.

They were waiting. And they were everywhere.

Oh shit, Garrison thought. The reasoning was so obvious that he kicked himself for not catching it on approach. The raiders had no way of getting inside the ship, so they had waited for the recovery team to arrive and cut their way in, then begin the assault during the retrieval of the cargo. More than likely, the raiders had surface-to-air launchers and sniper rifles aimed at Tiger Squadron. Enemy starfighters were probably camouflaged in the valleys surrounding the crash, just waiting for the signal to attack. Tiger was in the middle of a trap waiting to be sprung.

At a certain point, the shooting would start, but before that, he would have to inform the rest of the squadron. What was most terrifying was the possibility of the raiders tracking their radio communications and hearing everything. Should he alert the squadron, the game would be up. He decided to consult his second-in-command, which would have been Twister, then he remembered she had headed back due to iced-up gun belts. Next in line was his least favorite person in the universe—Cyril Eisner.

He groaned and switched to direct communication. "Condor to Skyhawk, switch to auxiliary channel Charlie Tango."

Cyril flipped channels. "What did I do now, Garrison?"

"Shut up. They're out there in the snowfield. On the mountainside. Switch on your IRST. See them?"

Cyril flipped on his IRST, then craned his head around to see what Garrison saw. "Oh, shit."

"Yeah. Trap. They were waiting for us to cut into the ship. I don't know if they're monitoring communications, but we need to move as fast as possible. With Twister out, you're second-in-command. If I go down, it's up to you to get them home."

"How do we inform the rest of the crew?"

"Morse code. I doubt the raiders know that, but it'll only buy us time. They'll eventually catch on."

"I can take two others and strafe that mountainside. That should get a bunch of them off us."

"Sounds good."

"Well, if this is where you go down, Garrison, I just want you to know that the displeasure is all mine, and I fucking hate your guts."

"The feeling is mutual, you insubordinate bastard. Now, get ready. Switching back to standard comms."

Garrison sent the morse code translation for TRAP to Tiger Squadron, the dropship pilots, and the assault team. It beeped and beeped, going letter by letter. Once fully received, all of Tiger Squadron responded with a green light acknowledgment.

The dropship pilots and Haggerty responded with a single word—COPY. The only way to escape the trap was to spring it. Haggerty ordered all his men inside the ship. They climbed in one by one till they were out of sight.

Garrison gave the order. "Tiger Squadron… dash forward now! Engage!"

All fighters broke the circular defense pattern and dashed forward as fast as possible, switching from V/TOL to afterburners.

Two surface-to-air missiles fired and blazed through the sky. They tracked onto Terrifier and Dazer. Both launched countermeasures, and the missiles exploded without causing damage. The defense was totally broken. Some starfighters headed off on their own to pick off a dot here or there, while Cyril swung his ship's wings forward and formed up with two others for a strafing run. Garrison and Gameboy formed up and circled low and fast to hunt for targets.

Skyhawk, Loki, and Dazer circled back and switched to guns. Small white dots—snipers and rocket launchers—now littered the mountain. They got within five hundred meters and fired a three-second squirt on the mountainside. The chainsaw *BRRRT* was loud in the cold air. A sniper round pinged off Cyril's starboard wing. Only minimal damage. They ascended and broke left. Another two rockets fired. They deployed flares, and the missiles exploded far behind them.

"Condor to assault team. Alpha, Bravo, status update," Garrison yelled.

"We're holed up inside the *Monroe*," Haggerty said. "Tech crews are ready to haul the cargo out now. No crew survived. We'll retrieve the bodies though."

"Copy that, Alpha. Here's the plan. Reorient the dropship's back end to face the opening. That'll give you as much cover as possible for retrieval." He checked his radar. Ten pings had popped up and were closing fast. "Tiger Squadron, incoming. Ten tangos on approach. Get that cargo out ASAP, Haggerty. We can only hold them for so long."

Both dropships lifted off and turned their rears toward the *Monroe*. A rocket launched from the mountainside and pierced Bravo's portside. It exploded and dropped into the powder below like a charred skeleton. No one survived.

"Fuck," Garrison screamed. "Piper, Karaoke, on my flanks. We gotta cover the remaining ship."

"Copy that, Condor. Let's plow the road," Piper said.

Condor, Piper, and Karaoke formed a three-ship line, one hundred meters in front of the Alpha dropship. They strafed left to right in unison, firing guns and pairs of missiles at the mountainside, like a razorblade of tracer rounds raking across the snowy terrain. A random missile fired into the air, not headed toward anyone, and disappeared into the distance. Right as Garrison reveled in their success, his smile faded, and ten enemy fighters breeched the crest of the ridgeline.

"Here they come," Piper announced.

"Condor to Alpha, it's now or never. Status," Garrison yelled.

"Almost done. We're having to pack in like sardines here," Haggerty said.

"Better than being dead. Can the ship handle the weight?"

"We'll find out."

"Tiger Squadron, pick your targets and go. Alpha, begin your ascent now. We'll guide you home."

The dropship punched the throttle and lifted off. It was extremely overweight, but with only one ship remaining, there was no choice. The pilots strained to pull up and activated the afterburners to ascend. Tiger Squadron notated the incoming ships headed for the dropship.

"Fire everything! Get them to split up," Garrison yelled.

All ten starfighters fired missiles and guns; a hail of death headed straight for the raiders. One missile connected and blasted an enemy fighter out of the sky. They deflected the rest with countermeasures or quick maneuvers.

Cyril squinted and used his HUD to zoom in on two fighters. "Sonofabitch, they also have Skyhawks."

"So what?" Loki asked.

"This is my thing. You saw that movie. There can be only one. So those two are mine," he growled. He broke formation from Loki and Dazer and made a run at one of the two enemy Skyhawks. He swung around and got behind the group and selected the closest one. It was gunmetal gray while the other was velvet red.

As he knifed around to get on its six, another enemy fighter cut their throttle and dropped behind Cyril. It got tone and fired a missile. Cyril popped flares, ascended, looped around, killed his throttle, and got tone on his attacker. He launched a missile, which blasted his would-be killer to pieces. He punched the throttle again and continued the chase.

Two down, eight to go.

Tiger Squadron began a circular pattern around the dropship for protection. Enemy fighters would rush in, take a shot, and dip out before taking hits. Cyril chased the gunmetal-gray Skyhawk. He knifed left, sweeping around to get on its tail. They were evenly matched; it would come down to pilot skill, and this one was good. Really good. He lowered his speed for a tighter turn, but his computer screeched, "STALL STALL STALL." He punched the throttle again, dove to gain speed, then ascended into the group.

KitKat and Karaoke nailed two more kills. One with a missile, the other with guns.

Four down, six to go.

As KitKat looped back around, she took a stream of gunfire through her hull and through the cockpit. The rounds blew off both her legs, and blood sprayed all over the cockpit. Her flight controls, weapon systems, everything, failed. Alarms blared, and stats flashed red. Then the engine died. "Oh God, somebody help me," she screamed.

"KitKat, pull up. You're nosediving," Cyril screamed.

"I–I… can't…" She passed out.

"*Cat!*"

Her ship whined and screamed as it nosedived toward the snow.

"*Caaatttt!*"

She crashed nose first into the snowfield and exploded. A fireball erupted from the hull and charred her body to cinders. Cyril pulled around to view the crash as he flew overhead. He lamented for a moment, then pulled up to rejoin the fight.

They still had the numbers on their side, but the dropship struggled with the excess weight. The pilots could barely keep it airborne. Then another three fighters appeared on their scopes—backup hiding in the mountains.

"Tiger Squadron, we have more incoming. Three tangos on approach. Get ready," Garrison yelled. "Alpha, you need to move faster."

"Moving as fast as we can, Tiger. We're overweight."

"Dump everything you don't need. Tear the insides apart and chuck everything you don't need out the back. Weapons, med kits, chairs, doesn't matter. Just get the weight down!"

The dropship crew ripped chairs from the floors, cut out the walls' armor lining, and piled anything they didn't immediately need that wasn't the *Monroe*'s cargo toward the back. They lowered the rear door and chucked out pieces of the ship. The cold felt like needles on their skin as the door opened. Pieces of the ship fell out and crashed into the snowy mountains below, like a trail of breadcrumbs following them home. They had significantly reduced the weight, and Alpha gained an extra eighty knots of flight speed.

Cyril got tone on an incoming fighter and fired. Another kill. He'd lost sight of the two enemy Skyhawks.

"Tiger, taking fire. Need assistance," Loki yelled.

Cyril pulled right and spotted two enemy fighters chasing her in the distance; one was the red Skyhawk. Cyril only had one missile remaining, so he switched to guns. He punched the throttle and swooped in behind the enemy ships. They didn't notice, as they were taking shots at Loki. He fired a two-second burst, ripping apart the red Skyhawk. The engines exploded, and it fell from the sky. When the other enemy craft noticed its wingman had been blown away, it pulled a hard left and disengaged.

"Loki, status," Cyril said.

"Engine failure. I'm dead in the water."

"Can you land?"

"I can guide it in and land on the belly."

"I'll stay on your wing." Cyril followed behind Loki and watched as she pulled her flaps and airbrakes.

Her ship was a T-77 Mockingbird, a punchy but stout ship, with a sleek fuselage and sharp wings that cut back toward the tail at a thirty-five-degree angle. It was also painted acid green, which made it stand out among the white backdrop of the snowfield below. She glided down and settled into the snowfield below. The belly of her ship scraped across the ground for fifty meters before slamming into a large rock buried under the snow, which jolted her forward like a car collision on a highway. Finally, it stopped.

Cyril switched to V/TOL and landed next to her now-dead ship. "Loki, get in! I have a RIO seat! *Loki*?"

"I think I broke my ribs," she groaned.

"Goddammit! I'm coming!" Cyril opened his canopy and hopped into the snow. He trudged through the thick powder toward Loki's cockpit and pulled it open. "Come on, grab onto me!" He pulled her from the cockpit and helped her to the ground.

As they slogged toward Cyril's ship, he noticed enemy fighters approaching to finish the job.

"Fuck, this hurts," she screamed.

"Come on. Pain is weakness leaving the body. It lets you know you're still alive."

A strafe of gunfire raked across the ground and destroyed the remains of Loki's ship.

"*Noooo*," she screamed.

"I'll buy you a new one! Come on, we gotta go! Get in!" He helped Loki ascend the foot holds and climb into the RIO seat. He took his position up front, closed the canopy, and fired up the center turbine. As he ascended, another stream of gunfire strafed where he had landed a few seconds before. He punched the throttle forward, narrowly missing their shots, and rejoined Tiger Squadron above.

They were still fifty-eight kilometers from Tull. The squadron radio squawked. "Auger to Tiger Squadron, back on station. Joining the fight."

Garrison cracked a smirk. "Condor to Auger, copy that. Perfect timing. Pick your targets and engage."

They destroyed two more enemy ships, then Karaoke took a hail of gunfire across their right wing. They spun into a barrel roll, making it impossible to eject, and crashed into a mountainside. Cyril pulled around on the enemy fighter, let off another quick shot of gunfire, missed, and pulled away.

"Why the hell are they fighting so hard just to steal artwork?" Loki asked.

"They didn't know what was in the *Monroe*," Cyril said. "For all they know, we hauled out cash or food or some kind of weapon. And now I doubt they would give up after we've taken down a whole bunch of their squadron."

"*Argh*, fuck," Loki groaned.

"You okay back there?"

"In agonizing pain, so I guess I'm fine, all things considered."

Forty kilometers from Tull. Garrison fired his final missile, but it zinged wide and flew into the distance. He cursed himself, then took a cascade of gunfire though the center fuselage. His engine died. He switched to backup batteries, which kept his HUD and radio operational, but no power flowed to the engines. He slowly dipped toward the deck. "Tiger Squadron, engine failure. Punching out."

He pulled the red ejection handle to his right. No response. He pulled again. Nothing. He reached behind him and pulled the emergency release ropes. They were jammed. He was stuck, headed straight for the snowy hell below. "Tiger Squadron, I'm stuck. Can't punch out. Skyhawk, you're in command now. Get them home!"

His ship landed belly first into a rocky snow patch. He skipped and skidded, the jagged earth shredding the underbelly. Ahead of him loomed a large sharp outcropping of a mountain, like a sideways guillotine. His ship darted toward it, unable to stop. As his last act, he screamed, *"I always hated you, Eisnerrrr!"*

His ship slammed nose first into the mountain wall. The outcropping took off the top half of the ship first, then sliced Garrison's body in half. He bellowed a horrifying yelp as he was torn asunder. The ship exploded, and the fires billowed black smoke, surrounding the knifelike outcropping.

"Fuck," Cyril whispered. "Tiger Squadron, watch your targets. Trigger, Piper, and Auger, go high above. Ascend to twelve hundred meters. Gameboy, Terrifier, and Dazer, go low. Five hundred meters. I'll stay in the center with the dropship. When they take a shot at me or at the dropship, dive in and blow them away."

"Woah, wait. We're bait now," Loki blurted out.

"It's our only option. We're gettin' smashed. They're not gonna blow up the dropship and destroy the cargo, but we can tempt them into taking a shot at us."

"Fine then. If I see smoke, I'll let you know."

"Sounds good. Tiger Squadron, get to your positions. Skyhawk to Alpha, Condor is down. Skyhawk is now in command." It felt weird to Cyril, to say he now had command. He had never yearned for a command position, and now he was stuck with it.

"Copy that, Skyhawk. Command insignia transferred," Alpha said. "We're moving as fast as we can. Thirty kilometers from home."

Tiger Squadron took their positions and kept watch over the dropship. Cyril matched their speed and yawed left and right, trying to bait enemy fighters into attacking. One finally moved in. Piper dove and ripped apart the enemy fighter with gunfire. Another fighter shot at Piper but missed. He gained elevation and returned to twelve hundred meters.

Twenty kilometers from Tull. Only three enemy fighters remained. One was the gunmetal-gray Skyhawk. Cyril still had his eyes on that one. It circled, level with the dropship, but wasn't taking any shots.

"What are you doing?" Cyril whispered to himself. He switched to his thermal view and saw that the next mountain ahead of them had five white dots on it. The enemy was baiting them into another ground attack. "Alpha, change course! Hard right! Incoming!"

A set of five rockets fired upward toward Tiger Squadron. Two flew off without hitting, while countermeasures deflected another two—the last countermeasures available from Gameboy and Terrifier. Cyril throttled forward ahead of Alpha, dove, and launched his final set of flares. The last missile exploded harmlessly, saving Alpha. Gameboy, Terrifier, and Dazer strafed the mountainside, and the white powder erupted blood red as the shooters exploded.

"Loki, where's that other Skyhawk? It disappeared from my scopes," Cyril observed.

"I don't—ten o'clock high," she screamed.

The enemy Skyhawk had ascended, went into an intentional stall, then flipped around and made a diving attack. It let out a stream of gunfire that shredded the top of Cyril's left dorsal fin

"We're hit! We're hit!"

"Fuck," he screamed. His attitude control became sluggish but manageable. The enemy pulled in behind him. He pulled away and got fast and low toward the deck. "Tiger Squadron, I'm gonna lead this guy away from the dropship. Need assistance."

"Copy that, Skyhawk. Dazer in pursuit." Dazer pulled away from the group and settled in behind the gunmetal-gray Skyhawk.

A narrow valley weaved through a set of mountains below. The three dove and chased each other. Dazer was out of missiles. They switched to guns and let out burst after burst. The tracers hit more rocks and mountain walls than ships. Soon, they were out of ammunition.

"Dazer to Skyhawk, I'm bingo on ammo. Not sure how much help I can be anymore."

"Copy that, Dazer. Get back with the squadron. I can handle this from here."

"Sorry. Good luck, flight lead."

Flight lead. So weird to hear that, Cyril thought. They bobbed and weaved through the valley. Skyhawk versus Skyhawk. It was all about skill now. The enemy took another shot as the valley bent left. The enemy fired again, and three rounds pinged off the top of Cyril's fuselage.

"We're hit again, Eisner," Loki yelled.

"Goddammit!"

"If you're really an ace, now's the time to prove it!"

The valley became narrower. Cyril pulled up hard into a steep climb.

"Oh shit," Loki screamed.

Cyril recalled the fight on Tau Ceti f and figured he would try one of those enemy tactics. He switched the center turbine to full power during the ascent, giving his ship a slight bounce upward. He cut the throttle and engaged his air brakes, and the enemy ship flew underneath him. He fired up his engines again, nosed down, disengaged the turbine and air brakes, got tone, and fired his final missile. It zipped toward the enemy Skyhawk, which launched a set of flares as it accelerated away. The missile exploded, and the enemy banked right.

"Goddammit!" Cyril switched to guns and continued the chase.

They got low and fast again across an ice shelf. The sun was setting, and the ice below glowed blue. He needed to close the distance, so he swept his wings back to add more speed at the cost of maneuverability, but it was worth it. He closed in to two hundred meters. No escape anymore.

"I got this one for you, Cat." Cyril squeezed the trigger and fired the last of his 20mm rounds. They sliced the enemy ship in half. It exploded, and Cyril knifed sideways and flew through the smoky remains. The two halves of the enemy ship crashed onto the ice shelf, and a belt of snow quickly covered them.

"Got you, you sonofabitch!" Cyril swept his wings forward again, did a tight turn, and headed toward the dropship. "Skyhawk to Tiger Squadron. Sitrep."

"Piper to Skyhawk, all enemy fighters down. Clear all the way home. How are you holding up, flight lead?"

"Got shredded a bit, but I can make it back to Tull. Good job, everyone. Let's go home."

He pulled his ship in behind Alpha. The sun was almost gone, and the twilight barely peeked over the horizon. It would have been beautiful had the day not been so tragic.

***

Upon returning to Tull, they discovered a mole, hiding in town, had been feeding information to the raiding parties. They were summarily arrested upon Tiger Squadron's return. The following day, a salvage ship recovered the remains of KitKat, Karaoke, and Condor, as well as Loki's ship to sell for scrap to purchase a new one. Cyril's ship was beaten to hell. Multiple gunshots and stress damage weakened the hull, and one of the dorsal fins hung on by only a few bolts. He would be grounded for a solid two weeks.

Cyril and Loki stood at the barracks entrance as the medical ship landed with the bodies of the three crashed starfighters. A team of med techs exited, wearing the oversized thermal suits, and removed three black body bags. They loaded them onto stretchers and rolled them to the morgue in the medical station. Loki's injuries weren't as bad as she had originally thought when she was out on the field—only two broken ribs—thus she was still mobile, albeit in pain.

"You knew her well, didn't you?" Loki asked Cyril.

Cyril silently wiped away some tears and walked across the tarmac toward the medical station, ignoring the cold.

The company would ship the bodies of KitKat, Karaoke, and Condor to their respective planets. Cyril went to the morgue to view Cat's body. Her corpse was charred and black, and her face was contorted into a constant state of pain, as if she had crashed while unconscious and like the fire had woken her up again, just so she could be burned alive. He did his best to stifle more tears. He eventually broke. They had never been a couple, but he could've seen a future with her. This life, the freelance life, was never fair.

He didn't know Karaoke outside of work. No idea where they would ship him to. The top and bottom halves of Garrison were packed into a body bag to return to Proxima. Cyril shed no tears for him.

The Hubbard Art Institute paid extra to Cyril, as he had assumed command of the mission and had led the rest of the squadron home safely. They had returned the art collection with only minor damage. Upon filing their reports, the remainder of the squadron praised Cyril's quick thinking and flight capability, and thus, the company awarded him with a commendation and a recommendation for future flight lead positions. He accepted, though he didn't want them. People had died on assignment before but no one who he was close to. He guessed this was how Allegra felt.

He returned to M&M Airfield on a sunny Wednesday afternoon. He exited his ship and shambled to his locker with the enthusiasm of a zombie dragging its feet. Even though it was warm outside, he still felt the coldness of Sela.

Stacy asked him if he needed anything.

Cyril said flatly, "Just fix it. I don't care how much it costs."

She said nothing, and he walked away.

As he emptied his personals out of his locker, he opened his messages to Jace and Jess.

CYRIL: Garrison's dead. Crashed.
JESS: Damn. Never thought that would ever happen. Finally.

Jace sent a GIF of a ship crashing. He thought it was funny.

CYRIL: KitKat's dead too. She crashed and burned alive.
JESS: OMG NO
CYRIL: Yeah. They shipped her back to Olympus. I'm gonna go see Marie. Gonna be quiet for a few days.
JACE: Okay, mate. Message if you need anything. We're always around.

Cyril switched to his chat with Marie.

CYRIL: I'm home. Can I come see you please?
MARIE: Yeah. I get off work soon. Everything okay?

CYRIL: No. Can I come see you?
MARIE: I'll leave now.

She texted her address. He got into an autocab and went to Marie's brownstone apartment building, which emanated a warm texture and elegance, though he barely noticed it as he climbed the stairs to her third-floor apartment. He quietly knocked.

She opened the door, horrified by his ghostlike appearance—disheveled hair, pale skin, and on the verge of bursting into tears. He entered and collapsed into her arms. Finally, he cracked and crumpled to his knees. She held him as he fell.

"That was a nightmare," he said, crying.

She whispered, "It's over now."

CHAPTER 11

THE ULTIMATE CURE

Cyril stayed in bed for a whole day. Marie had helped him to the bedroom on the day before, but he barely moved all night. As she slept beside him, she heard him crying off and on. She would hold him, and the crying would eventually stop. Marie called out of work for the remainder of the week, citing family matters—an obvious lie but no one protested. She would bring Cyril food that he wouldn't eat and water that he wouldn't drink. When he finally got out of bed, after the second day, he sat by the window to watch the world pass by. It rained that Friday. He watched it for a full hour.

"Babe, do you need anything?" Marie asked as she leaned through the bedroom doorway.

"*Mm-mmm,*" Cyril mumbled.

She closed the door and went into the kitchen. It killed her that she couldn't say or do anything that could ease his misery. He hadn't even said exactly what had happened. She would ask, but he would deflect with, *"You don't want to know."* She eventually had dropped the subject.

She kept herself busy all day by working remotely, filing reports, and creating spreadsheets—minutia she could have easily done at her office. Then she cleaned the kitchen and the bathroom—anything to keep her mind occupied. She could only say or do so much. Once she exhausted housekeeping tasks, she sat on the couch to watch the downpour, tapping the window like a cacophony of pebbles.

She returned to the bedroom to see Cyril had moved from the window to the bed. He lay atop the covers, staring up at the ceiling.

She curled up beside him. "I just wanna know what happened," she whispered.

He said nothing.

"Babe, please speak to me."

"I don't wanna talk about it."

"Say anything."

"Anything."

It was pointless. She squeezed in closer, draped her arm over his chest, and ran her thumb over his five-day-old facial stubble. "I'll be right here when you're ready to talk."

He said nothing.

She kissed his cheek, closed her eyes, and pretended to nap.

***

In her penthouse high above the streets, Layla Mullarkey was getting drunk. The liquor cabinet was half empty, and she had nowhere to go for another two days. She had finished her fourth glass of whiskey and just poured her fifth. She leaned against her apartment balcony railing. A large overhanging roof covered the patio outside. Sheets of rainwater spilled over the edge to the streets below. She drank alone and thanked Brentwood for locking her away from people. Daniel had done the same. *They always want nothing but power and control.* She sipped her drink and watched the layers of rain fall across Balamb.

On Sunday morning, she would leave for Creece to discuss the next distribution deal. At the very least, she would be far from Daniel, but the dread of returning always crept back in. She couldn't hide. He would find her. She couldn't run. He would chase her. She drank again to scrub out the thoughts of what he'd done, was doing, and would do.

She felt empty. Hollow. A void of a person. She yearned for someone to talk to, to be nearby. The closest she had to real friends were Bentley and Locke, which felt sad and pathetic. Locke had recently joined Arcturus as a new hire, specifically to watch Layla after her meltdown, as per Daniel's orders. And Bentley was a disgusting sex pervert. She had walked in on him at the office while he masturbated to security camera footage of women around the building.

When she had addressed it to Daniel, he had simply said, *"He's disgusting, but he does good work. Leave it at that."* Thinking about him made her skin crawl.

Layla finished glass number five and stumbled in for another. Who would say she was going too far? Another wouldn't hurt. Why not?

On her way back out, she tripped on a dining room chair and fell face first onto the carpet. In anger, she punched the floor and screamed. The punching eventually slowed, and the crying began. She sat upright, leaned against the wall, and stared out into space. The world felt so dark and lonely.

She opened her phone to scroll through her contacts. Most were work related, not people she could confide in. Family? They weren't interested in her problems. They would just tell her to suck it up and cope. She scrolled through again and landed on one name—Cyril Eisner. Was he the type of person who would listen? He had helped her before. Would he do it again?

She pressed Call, and the phone rang. And rang. No answer. A voice mail started. "This is Cyril Eisner, freelance starfighter. Can't get to the phone right now, but I'll get back when I can. You know what to do."

Beep.

She froze, trying to think of what to say, then the words came. "Hey, Cyril. It's Layla. I was hoping to catch you, but I guess you're busy. I just, *uh*… I guess I just needed someone to talk to. I haven't really been feeling so great lately. Daniel is…" She sighed. "I don't know. I don't know what I'm doing anymore. I don't know why I'm here. I just really need someone to talk to. You know how I said I was grateful to you for getting me off Gacrux? Part of me wishes you had let me die." She started crying again. "I'm sorry. I–I'm drunk. I'll leave you alone. I don't even know why I'm calling you. We're in totally different worlds. I guess I just need more friends, right? All right, I'll–I'll go now. Bye."

She hung up and dropped the phone into her lap. A wisp of rain sputtered through the door and soaked the carpet. It would be so easy to walk to the railing, step up, and jump. So easy. Too easy. But she couldn't bring herself to do it, not just because of the excessive alcohol but due to pure cowardice. Life was terrifying, but death scared her even more—not knowing if anything else came afterward. What if she jumped, got to the other side, and there was just … nothing? A life wasted. Nothing lived for, nothing died for.

As she rose, her phone dropped onto the carpet. On shaky legs, she shambled to the bedroom, crawled underneath the bed, and hid from the world again. The patio door remained open, and the rain fell harder, sounding like the clamor of gunfire.

***

"She burned alive," Cyril spoke.

"What?" Marie responded.

"Cat. One of the other pilots. We were sent to recover cargo and the crew of a ship that crashed. We lost three starfighters. One guy called Karaoke, the flight lead Garrison, and Cat. Her callsign was KitKat. She crashed and burned alive in her cockpit."

"Oh my God."

"I saw her body. Her face…"

"Babe, I'm sorry. I guess you knew her well."

"We had a… thing. Every time we were on assignment, we would get together. She lived on Olympus. Work was the only time we would ever cross paths."

"You mean you would hook up?"

"Yeah. Yeah, we would hook up."

Marie said nothing.

"We were together on Tau Ceti f awhile back. You know, the one with the time dilation problem. We were outside at night, and she started getting all over me. I told her to stop."

"Why?"

He looked at her. "Because you and I had just started seeing each other. I was trying to do better."

"I wouldn't have minded if you had just hooked up. That's not that big a deal. Sex is sex. I'm open with it. You were off planet. Probably a stressful day. I would have understood."

He returned to staring upwards. "Well, damn."

"Did you love her?"

"In a way, I guess." He rolled toward Marie. "But not like with you."

She smiled and kissed him.

"People die all the time in my business, but I've never lost someone that close."

"I can't even pretend to know what you're going through, but I'm here."

"Thank you."

She kissed him again.

"That guy, Garrison, he got shot down too. Nobody really cared though. He was an asshole."

"I remember you saying that. It would have been funny if right before he had gotten taken out, you had somehow piped 'Cotton Eye Joe' into his cockpit."

Cyril burst out laughing; Marie did the same.

"Yeah, missed opportunity. I ended up leading the squadron home."

"Have you ever done that before?"

"Nope. First time. But they gave me a bonus for it and said they'd put in a recommendation for me to get more command positions."

"Hey, there you go. You probably don't feel it now, but, like I said, you could be a great leader."

Cyril scoffed. "People keep saying that. But I don't want it."

"Why?"

"I don't know. I just don't."

"Want and need are two different things, babe. You might not want it, but maybe you need it."

"I don't know. Maybe."

"Did it at least feel good when you were commanding your pilots?"

He pondered it. "Yeah. I guess I did kinda like it."

"Then don't turn it down next time they ask. Did Cat die while you were in command?"

"No."

"Did anyone else die while you were in command?"

"No."

"Then there's your answer. You got everyone you could home."

Cyril fell silent. Had he been in command and not Garrison, maybe Cat would still be alive. He could have saved her, saved everyone. That was all he wanted. He missed Cat more than ever now and wept again.

Marie pulled him close and wrapped her arms around him.

"I didn't save her," Cyril said through his tears.

"It's okay, babe. It's okay to cry. I'm right here. I'm right here."

***

The rain slowed to a quiet *tap-tap-tap* as night rolled in. Marie and Cyril fell asleep in each other's arms. He awoke first and quietly unwound himself from her arms. She stayed asleep as he got out of bed to use the bathroom. He showered and stood in the hot water, letting it almost burn him. It felt good and shocked him from his stupor.

After drying off, he went into the living room to find his jacket and sat on the couch with his phone. Various bookshelves around the apartment held textbooks or anime action figures. Marie had never revealed that she was a lover of anime, but that proved it. A large statue of a mech sat atop the manga bookshelf, donning sharp features while carrying a massive gun in one hand and a sword in the other. The shelves below contained small figurines, though none were as impressive as the one above. He cleared some text messages, answered some emails, and declined various work requests, partially because his ship was out of commission but mostly because he just didn't feel like it. Sela was one of the worst assignments he had ever accepted. He needed time off to collect himself.

A grumpy-faced fluffy orange cat jumped into his lap and curled into a ball. Its collar read, BENNY. He chuckled and petted Benny while answering messages. Jess and Jace both replied.

> JESS: Hey, how are you doing?
> JACE: Checking in on you, brother.
> CYRIL: I'm alive. Spending time with Marie. We'll get together soon. Just need some quiet time. I'm grounded for a while. My ship is fucked.
> JESS: We love you, man. Stay in touch.
> CYRIL: I will.

He noticed a missed call and a voicemail—Layla. He listened to the message as he looked out the window. She was clearly drunk and upset, in a deep depression. He saved the message and considered calling, but it was past midnight. Not the best time for a phone call. Text would be better.

CYRIL: Hey, got your message. I'm sorry you're not doing well. I didn't really expect to hear from you again. I just lost a friend during an off-world assignment, so I've been torn up too. I wish I could do more, but, like you said, we're in totally different worlds. What happened on Gacrux was rough, but you deserve to be alive. You're one of the few rich people who I think might be a decent person. If that makes you an outcast to them, then fine. And, to be honest, your brother is an asshole. I'd love to beat him up sometime. I'll be in touch soon. Hoping to get my first assignment with Arcturus soon. Message me later.

He closed his phone and sat in silence, then he eyed Benny. "Everyone is a mess, aren't they?"

Benny purred as Cyril stroked his soft fur.

"*Heh*. What the fuck do you know? You're a cat."

The next morning, Cyril was awake before Marie and cooked breakfast—eggs, with butter-covered toast. She didn't have coffee or tea, so he poured a glass of pineapple juice to start his day. Her fridge was stocked with enough food for only one person, so he made do with what she had. There was no bacon, which was a crime against humanity. He also filled Benny's water and food bowl. It was the least he could do, given how much Marie had been there for him during the last couple days. Benny loudly slurped the water loudly as Cyril cooked.

"You know, if I didn't have to work so much, I could see myself as a cat person," he said to Benny.

The cat looked up and meowed. Cyril chuckled.

Marie walked in, her hair a mess, and yawned. "Hey."

"Hey, good morning, gorgeous. Got some eggs and toast for you." He poured the scrambled eggs onto a plate and set the buttered toast beside them.

"Um, I actually like my eggs over-easy."

Cyril's smile dropped away.

"I'm fucking with you."

Cyril sighed and chuckled. "You know what? Fuck you, bitch." He turned to clean the stove.

"Cocksucker."

"I've only done that a couple times. Don't hold that against me."

They both laughed. He sipped his pineapple juice and glanced at the floor.

"There's the Cyril I know."

Cyril gave her a half smile.

"How you doin', babe?"

"I'm okay. It's getting better."

"Time does that."

"The ultimate cure."

"Yup."

"Yup."

He stared at her and his smile grew.

She snickered. "What?"

"Nothing." He walked around the table, coiled her into a bear hug from behind, and whispered in her ear, "Thank you for putting up with me."

She craned her head back to look up at him. "*Eh*, you're worth it."

He scoffed, and she kissed him, then shoveled a spoonful of eggs into her mouth. He walked to the edge of the kitchen and leaned against the half wall dividing the kitchen and the living room.

"What do you wanna do today?" she asked.

"*Uh*, well, I gotta stop by the airfield. I sorta just… walked off."

"You gotta fix your ship?"

"Yeah, I'm grounded for a while, so I gotta see Stacy. Then… I don't know. Kinda wanna just stay in."

"That's fine. We can just chill here."

"Okay. Maybe Mallory's tonight?"

"Sure. I actually really like that place."

"I'll let Jess and Jace know we're going tonight."

"Okay, babe." She finished her eggs and toast, then put the dish in the sink. She wrapped her arms around his waist and got on her tiptoes to nuzzle his nose.

They got dressed and headed out. The streets were still wet, but the sun was shining. They stopped at a local coffee shop for drinks, then got on the road. The autocab dropped them off at half past noon. The pair went through the security gate and headed for Stacy's office. She wasn't there. Then a large bang behind them startled them.

Stacy was under the belly of a clunky cornflower-blue ship called a Chopper, with big flat wings that draped down on the tips at a ninety-degree angle. Twin orange-striped dorsal fins on the tail peaked into sharp points. It resembled a big blue brick with wings—nothing elegant or sexy about it. Why anyone would want to fly it was anyone's guess. Stacy had removed a damaged fuselage panel and had dropped it by accident.

When she saw Cyril and Marie, she approached them, removing her gloves. "Welcome back. I saw your ship. Looks like you got hit pretty hard."

"Yeah. Lost three pilots and four ships on Sela," Cyril stated.

"Sorry to hear that. I'll get your bill." She went into her office to get her data pad. She typed in his name and handed him the pad. "Sorry for more bad news."

The invoice shocked Cyril. The cost was nearly the amount he had made on Sela, which, after factoring in taxes, meant he lost money on that assignment. The pit in his stomach widened when he saw it would take three weeks, not two, for a total repair and a rearm, as ammunition was on backorder.

"Goddammit," he whispered.

"Sorry. Best I can do. I even called other airfields to see if they had anything in stock. Try not to get shot next time."

Cyril shook his head and said nothing.

"It's okay, babe. You'll get it back." Marie rubbed his back. "It's not a big deal."

"It *is* a big deal. How am I supposed to go to work? Even if it could fly, I've got nothing to shoot with." That statement had come out harsher than he had intended, and he immediately regretted it. "I just need to walk away for a second." He signed on the pad's bottom line, handed Stacy the data pad, and walked onto the steaming tarmac, trying to think of nothing.

The sun was high, evaporating the vapor waves of last night's rainfall from the concrete.

***

"He seems grumpier than usual," Stacy noted.

"He lost a friend out there," Marie said, watching Cyril walk to the middle of the runway.

"That's the sad part about the business we're in."

Marie faced Stacy. "What?"

"The only way to not lose friends is not to have any."

Marie refocused on Cyril, now a speck in the distance, feeling nothing but sorrow for him.

***

Cyril examined his ship's damages. In the bright light, it looked even worse than it had on Sela—bullet holes everywhere, the left dorsal fin shredded to ribbons, the right wing had taken a beating, and all ammunition had been expended. He was lucky to have reached Tull under those conditions. He climbed into the cockpit and switched on his systems. The power cell was also at less than 30 percent. He would need to replace that also. He leaned back against the headrest and closed his eyes.

Marie climbed up and leaned over the edge of the cockpit. "Hey."

"Hey," he responded flatly.

"Whatcha doin'?"

"Going through the ship's systems to see if there's any more surprises." He flipped through all the onboard systems—weapons, navigation, cabin heater, oxygen supply, targeting. The navigation system was having issues getting proper range beyond fifty kilometers, which meant the onboard radar had also taken damage. "And, of course, my fucking NAV system is screwed too." He punched the front panel and leaned on the side of the cockpit.

Marie recoiled from the cockpit. "Babe, you're scaring me."

Cyril eyed her, and she looked terrified. "I'm sorry."

She said nothing.

"I didn't mean to. I'm sorry." He reached to touch her face, but she flinched. He put his hand on her left cheek and pulled her close. "I'm sorry," he said with all the sincerity he could muster.

"I know you're upset, but please don't do that again."

"I won't. I'm just… you know."

"Yeah, I know."

He sighed. After a beat, she nuzzled his nose again.

He chuckled. "All right, I think I've had enough misery for one day. Let's go."

Marie climbed down as Cyril shut off his ship's systems. He stepped onto the footholds and closed the canopy. They headed toward the main hangar, and Cyril's phone pinged with a text confirming a ten-thousand-dollar direct deposit refund from the Balamb bail office for his father's bail money.

"*Heh*. Thanks, Dad. You asshole."

They went to Cyril's apartment, ordered noodles, and drank wine while watching movies. He showed her some action classics he loved, like *Indiana Jones and the Raiders of the Lost Ark* and *Die Hard*. She loved *Raiders of the Lost Ark* but thought *Die Hard* was very unrealistic. Her response appalled Cyril. They switched to a cooking show and cuddled. She felt warm in his arms.

She looked up at him at one point and said, "I'm sorry."

"Sorry? Sorry for what?"

She whispered, "I farted."

"What? What do—oh God, no!"

A putrid smell that could kill an animal permeated the room. Cyril immediately ripped himself from her embrace and dashed to the window, shoved it upward, and waved the awful fumes into the city. Let the rest of Balamb deal with it.

Marie laughed. "You love me! You love me!"

He turned to see her smug as a goddamn bank robber who had just made the perfect getaway.

"You love me," she said again.

He scooped her into his arms. "Yeah, and I'm gonna show that to you right now." He carried her to the bedroom and left the window in the living room open.

***

Jess and Jace arrived at 8 pm. Jess wore jeans and a blue tank top adorned with her band's logo. Claw rings decorated every finger. She had just come from band practice. Jace wore black pants and a brown shirt. A religious necklace, depicting a humanoid with outstretched arms and legs in front of a sun, hung around his neck, honoring his cultural heritage that life grew from the sun's willpower. He knew it was all nonsense, but to have some kind of faith brought him a level of connection to home that he never got in Balamb. Plus, he thought it looked cool.

They entered together and saw Cyril and Marie already against the left-hand wall opposite the bar. He had a beer, while she sipped a margarita. Everyone hugged; they had accepted Marie into their clique despite her lack of connection to their occupation. Jess and Jace ordered mixed drinks and joined the table.

They chatted about Jess's band, then Marie discussed music with Jess as Jace and Cyril complained about work and how screwed his ship was. After twenty minutes, they ran out of things to discuss and sat in silence. Weirdly, there wasn't much dancing that night, like a cloud hung over the whole bar. They people-watched for a short time. A pair of unfamiliar pilots racked a game of pool. A barfly ordered another beer, drowning his sorrows about where his life had taken him. A couple were on a date which was not going particularly well. In other words, despite the gloom, a normal night at Mallory's Heroes.

To lighten the mood, Cyril flipped through the charts inside the jukebox for the perfect song. Then it hit him—"Time After Time" by Cyndi Lauper. Multiple versions were available, but he picked the synthwave cover. The tune started, and his spirits lifted.

Cyril bought four shots of tequila from the bar and delivered them to the table. "She loved this song. To Cat."

They toasted and knocked the shots back. The liquor burned so good all the way down.

Cyril leaned on his left hand, lost in thought. Marie leaned over and wrapped herself around his right arm. He appreciated that Marie had no jealousy, no bitterness. She got it. Cyril and Cat had been workmates who had occasional flings. It was nothing new, and it made everything that much easier.

"Someone tell me a story about her," Marie kindly requested.

Cyril, Jace, and Jess regarded each other in thought. What would be a good story? A funny one? An intense one? Or something trivial?

Jace finally spoke up. "One time, we were on a job near some moon. Can't even remember its name. It was probably two years ago. These jobs blend together at a certain point. Anyway, full squadron. We're out there for a defense operation. Mining crew is gathering some kind of rare ore. A local crime family wanted to claim it for themselves, but the company who hired us told them to fuck off. So yeah, that didn't sit well with them. It was first come, first serve. All maritime, so no law enforcement would step in. We were hired as defenders. Mining drones would go in, get as much ore as possible, and buzz out before the mob showed up. Someone at the company leaked the info to the mob, and we all arrived at the same time."

"*Heh*. Same thing happened on Sela. Someone sold us out," Cyril said.

"Weird how that's been happening a lot. Anyway, it was brutal. We lose one immediately. I don't even remember her name. And this is zero-G, so we're flipping and tossing and tumbling all over the place. G-forces have me slammed in the seat. I almost passed out twice from G-LOC. I get two bandits on me, and they're chasing me across the surface of the moon. I'm dipping as low as possible to avoid gunfire and trying to throw off their aim with the terrain. They lock on; I pop flares. I'm screaming for help. Cat flies in from above and nails them both with a rocket pod strike. Just *blam*! Gone. Hitting moving targets with unguided rockets is an expert shot."

"I should probably add rockets to my ship, just in case," Cyril noted.

"Definitely recommended. We form up to rejoin the group, and another two start tailing us. She does this wild pinwheel move where she fires her starboard thrusters at full, lays on the trigger, and just sprays and prays. Got one and scared the other one away. We only lost one other ship after that. Some Mukarian guy named Poil. I don't remember his callsign."

"God, she was a good pilot," Cyril uttered.

"Yeah, she was," Jace agreed.

They went quiet again.

"I could never do what you guys do. Did she have any family?" Marie asked.

"I think she had a brother. Parents are on Olympus too," Jess said.

"I just realized something," Cyril said. "Does anyone have a photo of her?"

They eyed each other, puzzled, then said nothing. Cyril's head dropped in disappointment. Without a photo, she would be forgotten. Her face would fade away, her voice would go silent, and the memory would eventually be long gone. Just another pilot. Another piece of meat that went through the grinder.

"Hey, let's all take a photo together," Marie declared.

"What?" Cyril asked, shaking himself from his stupor.

"You're afraid she'll be forgotten. If we all have a photo together, we'll be safe from that ever happening to us."

"That's a good point. I mean, the three of us have some photos together but not here."

"Then, we'll do one now." Marie retrieved her phone and scrunched toward Cyril.

Jace and Jess walked around and got behind them.

"All right. One… two… three."

The camera snapped, capturing all four of them together. Jess stuck out her forked tongue and gave a peace sign. Jace smiled and showed off his nearly perfect white teeth. Cyril smirked and leaned on Marie's shoulder. With their memories preserved, Jace and Jess returned to their seats.

"I can get a physical copy made for each of you if you want," Marie offered.

"Oh, hell yeah," Jess said. "Speaking of photos, did you notice the wall over there?" She pointed to the wall next to the end of the bar filled with photos of young and old pilots. A sign above the wall read, THE LONG GONE.

Marie approached the wall. None of the photos had names underneath them. There was no order to the photos either, just randomly pinned wherever they could fit. Some overlapped and blocked others beneath them. She assumed many were either retired or were long dead.

Cyril walked up behind her and pointed to a Crecian, with a head of long blond hair and small eyes. "I knew that guy. His name was Remmy."

"What happened to him?"

"What do you think?"

She nodded at him but said nothing.

"It sucks in this business sometimes. The only way not to lose friends—"

"Is not to have any," Marie finished. "Stacy said that earlier today at the airfield. I guess that sentiment gets around."

"Yeah. I'm wondering when I'm gonna bite it too."

"Don't say that. Please."

"I've had some close calls recently."

"Then, take time off. Do something else." She wrapped her hands around his waist.

He stared at the wall of fallen starfighters and whispered, "You should run away from me."

"What?"

"I'm just gonna disappoint you or hurt you, or I'm gonna die and leave you alone."

"Babe…"

He looked down at her. "No, I mean it. Last chance. You can walk away now, and I won't feel bad about you going. I'll understand."

"I'm not goin' anywhere. You don't get off that easy," she professed, with tears in her eyes. "And we're never having this conversation again."

He met her gaze and hugged her.

She whispered, "I love you."

He whispered in her ear, "Same."

When they let go, Marie asked, "Hey, stupid question, just popped into my head. Did you ever try hooking up with Stacy? Because she always has this kind of, I don't know, attitude with you."

He chortled. "Yeah, I've tried."

"No dice?"

"No dice."

"A shame. She's cute."

"Yeah, she is." He nuzzled her nose. "But you're cuter."

Marie scrunched her face and smiled.

Cyril grinned. "Hey, wanna get drunk and make bad decisions?"

"Absolutely."

They ordered more alcohol, danced, played pool, and chatted with Mallory. Jess and Marie even had a short make-out session in their inebriated state. Cyril and Jace just watched and felt nothing but envy.

At 2 am, they closed the place down and literally stumbled into the foggy and muggy night. The streetlamps illuminated the wet concrete, and the lines on the road glowed from below with the LED lighting. Cyril and Marie leaned against each other, while Jace carried a sleeping Jess, who looked tiny in his huge arms.

Cyril stepped into the empty street and screamed into the darkness above, "I'll miss you, Cat!"

Jace yelled too and howled like an animal.

Cyril fell to his knees. "Sorry I couldn't save you."

Marie stumbled to him and tried to lift him. She fell to the ground next to him and started laughing, as did Cyril. Jace sat on a nearby bench to text for an autocab. Cyril and Marie dragged each other from the street and sat on the curb. An autocab pulled up five minutes later.

"Your ride is here, my dude," Cyril announced to Jace.

"I called that one for you two. I'll get Jess home," Jace said.

"Well, okay, man. We're out. Goodnight."

"Goodnight, brother."

Cyril and Marie crawled into the back seat and closed the door. As the cab began moving, they leaned on each other and fell asleep. They awoke as the autocab parked outside Cyril's apartment and repeated, "Please exit the vehicle. Please exit the vehicle," till it annoyed them enough to leave.

They were not black-out drunk but inebriated enough that anywhere would be a comfortable enough bed. They trudged up the steps to Cyril's apartment and stumbled inside, Marie tripping over her own feet. Cyril picked her up and carried her to the bedroom. Once she was on the soft sheets, he went to the bathroom, relieved himself, then wobbled to the bedroom. The spins had set in, which meant sleep wasn't far off. He fell next to Marie and curled around her, holding her like a big drunken bear. She was already lightly snoring. He kissed her left cheek, closed his eyes, and passed out.

That night he dreamt about Cat.

CHAPTER 12

THE BUSY SEASON

They cruised through Kepler-186F's sky at 350 knots—a gorgeous planet, a near copy of Terran Earth before the fall, yet its red sun made the sky a tangerine orange. But it was cloudy that day, with big puffy marshmallow-like clumps drifting leisurely through the sky. A squadron of ten megaliner carrier ships flew in a line abreast formation five thousand meters above the surface. Tractors and drones cleared fields in the flat farmland below and picked fruit for the harvest season. Spring had arrived in that area of Kepler-186F. And so had Arcturus Allied.

Cyril eagerly accepted his first freelance job with Arcturus, a copilot position on one of the big, bulbous, and slow megaliners. Enormous wings outstretched like they were trying to wrap around the planet itself. The dual jet engines underneath the wingspans could reach a maximum speed of 550 knots, but the simple principles of flight still applied. As Cyril's ship was out of commission, he filled in his schedule with basic pilot duty. Yet despite his enthusiasm, it was incredibly boring.

Wide windows encased the spacious cockpit, and his seat was so comfy that he had nearly fallen asleep during flight. Buttons, knobs, dials, and instrument readouts littered every surface, which was the downside of larger ships. The bigger they were, the more complicated they would be. Most of the instrument panels went untouched though. Still, to the uninitiated, it could be overwhelming.

> **MISSION:** TRANSPORT AND PAYLOAD DELIVERY. DISPERSAL OF INOCULATION AGENT.
>
> **TARGET:** ELEK. FARMING COMMUNITY. POPULATION **32,556**.
>
> **THREAT LEVEL:** ZERO.

The pay wasn't high by any standard, but it was something while he waited for Stacy to fix the Skyhawk. The worst thing that had happened so far was that the cockpit heater had failed. It was chilly. He wrapped himself in a bomber jacket supplied by the local airfield and sat back in his copilot seat. The lead pilot, a nonbinary Luyten named Filly Hutten, kept one hand on the flight stick but was lounging as well. Like all Luytens, they had extremely pale skin, small hazel eyes, and sharp features. Cyril recalled his hook up a while back with Jenna. He wished he could remember that night.

"Oh, it's times like this when I miss my ship," Cyril said, yawning.

"What equipment are you flying?" Filly asked in a perky feminine voice.

"A-7 Skyhawk. It's out of commission."

"Skyhawk, huh? Haven't seen one of those recently."

"It's an older model, but I like it. Got beat up on Sela, so here I am. What are you flying?"

"M-22 Tempest."

"Never seen one of those."

"It's a smaller ship—a stunt ship, mainly. It's got a short center fuselage, with a quad wing design. Great acceleration and low speed turning."

"Sounds familiar. A friend of mine flies a Firestar. Those things are beasts."

"Oh, a Firestar. Man, those are tough to come by these days."

"I think she inherited it. But yeah, I can't wait to be back in my own ship. This thing is like flying a turtle through a car wash."

"What's a turtle?"

"It's a Terran animal. A reptile."

"*Huh.* Never heard of those. I'll have to look them up. What's your callsign, anyway? I forgot to ask."

"Skyhawk."

"Skyhawk? But that's also your ship's name."

"Yeah."

"You used your ship's name as your callsign?"

"Goddamn, why does everyone find that so weird?"

"It's not weird. It's just… dumb."

"Thank you," he said flatly. "What's yours?"

"Sunfire."

"Why that one?"

"Because it sounded good. And someone made a comment that my white skin burned like fire in the sunlight. Then they yelled, 'The beacons of Gondor are lit!' I didn't know what that meant till I looked it up."

"Did it turn you into a Tolkien fan?"

"No comment."

The ship hit a bit of turbulence and rocked.

"Fair enough," Cyril said. "Anyway, how'd you land this job?"

"Friend of a friend said Arcturus was looking for pilots. Had a gap in my work schedule, so here I am. You?"

"The CEO's sister actually put in my name."

"No shit? Wow, high recommendation."

"I was one of her bodyguards on Gacrux a while back. She wanted to show her appreciation."

"Hey, there's worse ways to land a job."

A hundred kilometers out, the megaliners descended to two thousand meters. Once over the target destination of Elek, each ship would disperse an aerosol spray to fill the atmosphere above the town. It would slowly float down and coat the town with a milky mist. Cyril didn't really know how the inoculation worked, and the specifics weren't interesting to him. Like all freelance operations, it didn't matter what the job was for or who was involved. Political allegiances and cultural definitions were of no concern to him. All that mattered was the mission and the moment.

Elek rolled into view. It was a quaint little place. Tiny buildings, a watchtower, a small airstrip, scattered trees. Just a normal quiet village in the middle of nowhere, minding its own business. And above, ten megaliners soared through the sky. Cyril imagined how terrifying it must look from the ground. *Have no fear, Arcturus is here,* he thought.

He pressed a switch on the console. "Opening pod bay doors."

The doors in the belly splayed open, exposing the chemical vats inside. Once the ships were a thousand meters out, they slowed their air speed.

"Releasing… now." He pressed another button, and the vats sprayed their fluid into the atmosphere.

All ten ships pumped liter after liter of mist, filling the sky till it was milky white. It drifted and twirled through their jetwash and descended slowly toward Elek. Once again, Cyril thought it must look terrifying to the uninformed. The ships banked left and circled back toward the direction they'd approached from.

"And we're dry. Closing bay doors." Cyril pressed the first button again, and the bay doors closed.

The ten megaliners formed up to return to base.

"Alright, that was easy. Join me for a beer when we get back?" Cyril asked Filly.

"Yeah, why not?"

As they headed home, the inoculation agent continued its slow and lethargic descent, coating the town of Elek in a dense fog, till it disappeared among the countryside.

At base, the motley crew of pilots traversed the tarmac two by two. A high slanted wall, with wire running along the top edge, surrounded the base, and a control tower stood like an enormous sentinel over the airfield, its bulbous saucer top casting its shadow below. The sunset had turned the sky from orange to a beautiful peach color. And it was warmer too, as the sunlight had cooked the concrete all day, like a baking sheet. The other eighteen pilots were an assorted lot, all ages and races. Luyten, Crecian, Skovian, Terran, and Mukarian, though Cyril did wonder how a Mukarian had managed to squeeze into the megaliner. The cockpits were spacious but not by that much.

They checked in at command and logged their flight data. As this was a corporate assignment, the standard individual reports were unnecessary—no combat, no report. Everyone had the rest of the day off. Some chose to leave Kepler-186F to head home. Some chose to stay for the day to enjoy the town. Cyril and Filly changed out of their flight suits and met near the airfield's front gate. Filly looked gorgeous, with their light skin, and now that their flight helmet was off, Cyril noticed they had bright orange hair that billowed in the wind.

"Ready to go?" Cyril asked.

"Go go. Where's the nearest flat?"

"Flat?" Cyril furrowed his brows.

"Where food and drinks are served."

"Oh, you mean bar or pub. That's what Terrans call them."

"Bar or pub? *Huh*. Why call them that?"

"*Bar* because in those places, literally only a wooden or metal bar separates the patron from the alcohol. *Pub*, I think, is meant to stand for *public*, as in, this is where the public meets up for a get-together."

"Interesting. I'll add those to my vocabulary. I'm still working my way through Terran language customs. So where is the nearest, *err*, pub?"

"No idea. Never been here."

"I guess we're off for an adventure," Filly stated.

Cyril considered using a quote from *The Hobbit* as a joke, but Filly's disdain for Tolkien told him he'd best keep his mouth shut.

They walked the streets, looking for anywhere that served alcohol. The industrial city was extremely different from life in Balamb—not quite the calm gentrified world Proxima had become. Kepler was right at the beginning of its technological revolution, when Terrans had established first contact with the Mukarians. Were it not for the Terrans, the residents would still be behind everyone else's advancements, scraping their way upward. The mixture of high and low tech was jarring to say the least. One part of town contained brick and mortar buildings, and then suddenly, camera sentry drones would fly by on patrol. It made Cyril feel weird, like it was a city out of time.

They rounded a corner and found what looked like a pub. The door was made of worn brown wood. A dive, for sure. Odd music played inside the dim pub—not a traditional bar by any means, as there was no bartender. A line of taps was built into the wall opposite the entrance, each hosting its own brand of alcohol. Whether it was spirits or beer, Cyril couldn't tell. He didn't recognize any of the names. A card reader hung above each tap. Cyril pulled out his blue credit card, his payment for the day, and tapped it on a brand called Locash. He grabbed a metal tankard from a tray nearby and filled it.

He took one sip. Not the best, but not the worst. Definitely watered down.

Filly tapped a brand called Orange Yuke. They took a sip, spit it out into the overflow tray under the taps, and poured out the rest after it.

"That good, *huh*?" Cyril joked.

They washed out their tankard and filled it with the Locash brand.

People sparsely populated a few wooden tables—some couples but mostly single patrons. Cyril and Filly grabbed a table near the window.

Cyril raised his tankard. "To an easy paycheck."

They toasted and sipped their watery beers.

"Man, it's like a funeral happened in here or something."

"Mukarian culture isn't known for its extensive musical taste," Filly said.

Cyril chuckled. "Fair. And yet, they know how to party when the time is right." Cyril couldn't tell what kind of music was playing, whether it was blues or jizz music. Either way, it sounded terrible.

"Working-class people," Filly said as they took another sip.

"At least it's something. A Terran philosopher once said, 'Without music, life would be a mistake.'"

"Sounds like my kinda guy. What was his name?"

"Can't remember."

"Damn. Another thing I need to look up. What's lined up for you after this?" Filly asked and took a big gulp.

"No idea. We're about to enter the busy season on Proxima though. Hoping I get my ship fixed before it starts."

"Yeah, I've heard it's gonna be slammed this year. With the Arcturus contracts kicking up too, we'll be going at this for a long time."

"When's the next spray supposed to be?"

"I think next week."

A large Mukarian approached their table and towered over them. He was one of the working class—filthy hands and dirt-covered face. Mukarians resembled the mythical creatures Tolkien wrote about. Probably just out of work for the day. Seeing two Terrans in his bar was an annoyance to the local ambiance. "Are you the ones spraying that shit on my home?" the giant asked with a deep voice.

Cyril and Filly froze. They looked at each other, then at the hulk above them. Filly finally spoke up. "We're pilots. Just finished for the day."

"Just because our magistrates said you could spew that poison on our planet doesn't mean *we* said you could. Leave. Now."

"My dude, we got no beef with you," Cyril posited. As he lifted his cup to take a sip, the Mukarian slapped it from his hand. It skittered across the floor and stopped at the feet of another bar patron. The music continued through the speakers, but all the bar chatter stopped.

"You're not welcome here! Leave," the angry giant yelled.

Cyril stood. The Mukarian was a solid foot taller than Cyril, but he was also a bully, which pressed Cyril's nuclear detonation button. Cyril's head stopped at the Mukarian's chest level. "What is your fucking problem, asshole?" Cyril asked, anger seething deep in his voice.

"Terran… trash. All of you."

Filly stood and grabbed Cyril's arm. "Come on, Cyril. It's not worth it. Let's go."

Cyril glared at the Mukarian for another moment before turning away. "We'll find another bar. One where the beer isn't watered-down *runna*." (*Runna* was the Luyten word for *urine*.) They both headed for the door.

"Get the fuck off our planet, parasites," the Mukarian yelled.

The pair pushed open the door and walked outside. Night was descending. As they walked down the street, Cyril yelled back, "Your beer fucking sucks!" They walked a few more paces. He turned to Filly. "Doesn't he get that this is supposed to help everyone?"

"Who cares? Come one, I'll get the next round."

They walked a few more blocks as residents shot them odd glances, like they were in hostile territory. The atmosphere felt oppressive after twenty minutes on the street. They finally found another pub—a much classier place—with a bartender and a fully stocked alcohol selection. Once again, they were the shortest people in the packed place. They grabbed the last two free stools and ordered the best beers on tap. Brusque music played on the stereo system, but it was better than the last place. The pair of pilots drank quietly to not patronize anyone else.

"Continuing our conversation, do you know exactly what day next week the next spray is?" Cyril asked Filly.

"Not totally sure. I'd have to check my calendar."

"Gotcha." Cyril took a sip of his beer, then paused. "Oh shit."

"That good, *huh*?" they asked, repeating what Cyril had said at the previous establishment and expecting the same result.

"I just realized something."

"What?"

"Today's my birthday."

"Oh, no way!"

"Yeah. I'm thirty. I totally forgot. Maybe I have been working too much."

"Well, this round and the next one are on me." They raised their glass. "Happy birthday, Skyhawk."

"See? When you say it like that, it doesn't sound dumb." He clinked his glass with theirs.

"No, it's still dumb. I was just being nice."

"You bitch."

They smiled and drank their beer. This time, it wasn't watered down.

***

Traveling between planets on mass transit annoyed Cyril. He was crammed into a horde of passengers heading to Proxima. He held onto a metal rung above his head as the ship rocked, preparing to leap into the atmosphere. Without his starfighter, he would have to ride the exo-jitneys—automated carriages that could hold up to sixty people per jump. The process of FOILing to and from locations was generally the same as any other ship, but the cramped conditions, combined with risk of spreading disease, made it as appealing as a proctology exam.

Kepler-186F had been a piece of cake, so he couldn't complain too much. A paycheck without much work and with no expenses wasn't something to shrug off. Some lower-end pilots could make a solid living by running basic cargo missions, but it would also be an incredibly boring lifestyle. Not really his scene.

The exo-jitney entered the gum drop as gravity suddenly took hold. Everyone quickly braced themselves, then relaxed. They descended toward the local transit station and landed softly, then the doors whooshed opened. The crowd flooded out. Cyril waited till everyone else had gone and left last. As he exited, he checked his phone messages, now that signal had returned. The standard emails for work had piled up. Busy season was about to begin.

Busy season was always hellish. Jumping from job to job, only returning to refuel and rearm, then head back out. Sleep was a luxury. It was also, however, the most lucrative time of the year. After one month of work, the rest of the season could disappear. No one would ever be left wanting more. The season occurred as all the major companies attempted to meet their quotas of shipping, receiving, and mining before the end of the fiscal galactic year based upon the Terran calendar. It was a rush to the finish that everyone jumped at the chance to get in on. He accepted three separate back-to-back jobs, which meant he would be away from Proxima for a two-week stretch once Stacy repaired his ship.

A message from Marie showed up too.

MARIE: Hey, babe, I know you'll see this when you return, so just saying I miss you. Message me when you're back. I love you.
CYRIL: Hey you. I'm back. Easy money.
MARIE: Welcome back. Hey, could I ask a favor?
CYRIL: No, I will not murder anyone for you.
MARIE: When then I guess we're done. LOL No, would you meet me at the airfield?
CYRIL: The airfield? Why?
MARIE: I just wanna go to the airfield.
CYRIL: Ooookkkkaaaayyyy. I'll see you there. It'll probably take about thirty to get there.
MARIE: See you in thirty.

He put his phone in his pocket. *What's at the airfield? Ship isn't done yet.* He ordered an autocab and got on the road. The afternoon traffic was light. He hopped out of the cab and walked through the security gate. The field still had some workers repairing a ship in the hangar. A new ship had replaced the bulky blue one that previously occupied the main hangar space. As he entered, he saw Marie and Stacy chatting.

Marie ran to him, jumped into his arms, and kissed him over and over again.

"Well, hello, you little hellion." Cyril laughed.

"Hey, you." Marie leaned into his ear and whispered, "Happy birthday."

"What? How did you—"

"I asked her a week ago." Marie craned her head back toward Stacy.

Stacy waved as she leaned against a workbench.

"*Heh*, okay. Well, we're here at the airfield. There's nothing here."

Marie hopped down and grabbed his hand. She pulled him along toward outside the main hangar doors. Stacy followed. They turned left, and Marie took him to his ship, fully repaired and rearmed ahead of schedule.

"Oh shit, it's done? It wasn't supposed to be done till next week," he said.

"You have a good girlfriend, Cyril. She convinced me to work overtime on it," Stacy said.

"And I bought you a little present for it." Marie handed him something that resembled a circular watch with a leather strap, but it didn't tell time. Three small holes were at the bottom of the screen. "Tell the engine to turn on. Start with the ship's name."

He raised an eyebrow at her, then held the band to his mouth. "*Skyhawk*, engine start." The engine revved up and roared to life. Cyril went wide eyed, shocked as to what Marie had bought him. "No way!"

Marie chuckled. "It's an aerial drone system. You tell your ship what you want it to do, and it does it. I know how much you love your ship, so I looked around for something you might need. If you're ever working on the ground and need something up high, you can have it ready to go. I was trying to think like you would if you're ever in a fight"

"Babe, this is too expensive. It's too much. I don't deserve this."

"Nah, it wasn't that much. It's basically just wireless comms for your ship. Plus, Jace and Jess chipped in."

"Well, damn, where are they?"

"Off world, right now. Just you and me for a few days, babe."

"Oh no, whatever will I do?"

"I can think of a few things." She nuzzled close to him and reached under his shirt to feel his stomach.

"*Heh. Skyhawk*, lift off. Ascend to one hundred meters."

The ship's center turbine spun, and the ship ascended rapidly to one hundred meters, where it hovered.

"*Skyhawk*, forward one hundred meters and rotate right one hundred eighty degrees."

It moved forward one hundred meters, then made a flat rotation one hundred eighty degrees. It worked perfectly. Cyril thought of several instances in the past where this would have come in handy. Gacrux, probably. Sela, definitely.

"*Skyhawk*, return to the first location and land."

The ship quickly descended, rotated to its original position, and softly landed.

"*Skyhawk*, engine off."

The engine's roar slowly faded, and the airfield went quiet.

Cyril grinned at Marie and whispered, "I love it."

"I knew you would." Marie smiled and stood on her tiptoes to kiss his cheek.

"I can't thank you enough for this."

"Yeah, you can." She craned her head toward his ship and raised her eyebrows.

He smiled. "Hey, Stacy—"

"Yeah, I'll chart you out. Have fun," she said as she turned back toward the hangar.

"You ready?"

"Definitely."

***

When they got to Marie's apartment, they ate a massive plate of sushi and watched one of her favorite movies, *The Goodbye Girl*. Cyril thought it was cute. Then they kissed and cuddled on the couch. Benny hopped up a couple times to demand pets. Marie eventually gave him a fresh chew toy stuffed with catnip to occupy him. Then they resumed kissing, knowing it would lead to more later.

"Hey, I have a surprise for you," Marie whispered.

"Oh, really? Another one?"

"*Mmhmm.* Go to the bedroom. I'll be there in a minute."

Marie headed to the bathroom as Cyril went to the bedroom, undressed, and slipped underneath the silky sheets. He heard her moving around in the bathroom. Something fell and banged on the floor. "You good in there?"

"Yep, one second."

He crossed his hands behind his head and reclined on the soft pillows. He realized the one thing that had eluded him for so long—happiness. Genuine happiness. It wasn't a fluke. It wasn't a one-night stand. He actually felt happy. He closed his eyes and savored the moment.

Soft music started outside the bedroom. Then the bathroom door opened.

He opened his eyes to see Marie standing in the doorway. "Woah."

She donned a leather strap bustier, with leather panties and a ringed collar, and wore heavy eyeshadow, blush, and black lipstick. She looked stunning as she sashayed to the bottom edge of the bed and crawled toward him. She mounted him, pinned his arms, and kissed him. "Happy birthday," she whispered.

"Best birthday ever."

"You deserve it." She kissed him again.

"One question…"

"*Mmhmm?*"

"Is anal on the table tonight?'

Marie chuckled. "For me or for you?"

"*Heh,* we'll see."

Marie giggled and kissed him again.

***

They fucked for over an hour. Three rounds. They were both exhausted and laid next to each other, sweaty and completely out of breath. Marie's makeup was smeared, and her lipstick graffitied Cyril's face. She forced herself out of bed to clean up. Cyril dozed for a bit before she returned and chucked a damp towel at him.

"Clean up first before you go to sleep," she said, chuckling.

"Oh, I figured I would go for coffee tomorrow morning looking like this. You know, scare the patrons," he joked as he wiped lipstick off his face.

"They would either be very confused or be very jealous." She plopped into bed, face down, and yelled into the pillow, "Holy shit, that was amazing!"

"I'm glad to be of service."

She faced him. "No, I mean it. You're amazing."

"*Eh*, get to know me a little better. You'll get over that."

"Why do you always do that?"

"Do what?"

"Degrade yourself. I gave you a compliment. Probably the highest compliment a guy could ever achieve, and you brush it off like it doesn't mean anything."

"I was just making a joke."

Marie got onto her elbow and pulled the covers over them. "I'm serious, Cyril. You're really good in bed. And I do think you're amazing."

Cyril stared at her with a blank face.

"Just…" She waved her hand in front of her face, pointing out his flat expression. "…nothing, *huh*?"

He looked away. "I have a hard time taking genuine compliments."

"Because of you father?"

Cyril said nothing.

"Babe, it's okay. I get it." She cuddled up, wrapped him in her arms, and kissed him. "I get it."

"Thank you."

Her smile reached her ears. "No, thank you."

They cuddled for the next few minutes, then she dozed off. Cyril stared up at the ceiling. The *tap-tap-tap* from the rain on the window soothed him. He loved the sound. When she lightly snored, he looked down at her and whispered, "I don't deserve you." Then he closed his eyes and joined her in dreamland.

***

The busy season finally arrived. It was a brutal onslaught of day-in, day-out operations. Cyril would leave Proxima, head off for a two-day assignment, return to refuel and rearm, then head back out again. He would only stop at M&M airfield for half an hour to answer phone messages. More assignments would pop up as he returned, meaning the busy season would go on even longer than four weeks. Marie expressed her anxiety about him being overworked. Cyril would always answer, "That's just the way the business is this time of year."

One day, he was on Tulson; two days later, he was on Aspho, the next week on Creece—employed by a mixture of companies he had worked for many times, some first-time offers, and some corporate, like Acturus. His time on Creece was a nice respite from the onslaught of brutal scheduling. He could relax, being nothing more than a cargo pilot hauling more of the inoculation spray over large swaths of Creece's eastern continent. Autopilot meant he could nap between drops. Loki turned up as his copilot on one drop. He hadn't gotten a good look at her last time he had seen her on Sela. She had tan skin, deep brown eyes, luscious brown hair, and full lips, with a baby-fat face. Were he his old self, he would have jumped at the chance with her. They didn't talk much, as they were both extremely worn down and exhausted. Autopilot ended up doing most of the work.

While he was away, his therapy sessions had taken a back seat. Upon one return to Proxima, an email stated he was a week delinquent on a scheduled session and had been docked forty-five dollars for noncancellation. He messaged that he would be available again within the following two weeks.

Those two weeks passed, and he was still out on assignment, on Gacrux again. This time, they dispatched him for another ground assignment. A band of poachers were illegally hunting endangered species, and the local authorities needed outside assistance to handle the situation. The GWP (Global Wildlife Protection) sent Cyril and a squadron of seven other starfighters to track the hunters and detain if possible or to eliminate if necessary. Snipers had one starfighter, a Crecian with the callsign *Gopher*, pinned down from a distance through a tree line. What rescued Gopher was Cyril's new present from Marie. He used his ship as a drone to scope out the area and commit a high-altitude strike against the poachers' last location. An air-to-surface missile took them out. Mission accomplished.

Using drones was always a risky move. Before starfighter was a common profession, drones handled most exoplanetary assignments. It was cheap, with no loss of life. What changed that method was one simple fault in the system: hacking. One assignment on Tau Ceti f had been a disaster, where a rival company hacked a total of thirty-five drones during a routine security escort. The drones turned against their original control team and destroyed the very target they were protecting. From that point on, it was back to manned aerial missions, and analog technology began to work its way back into daily life. The busy season was a biproduct of this lack of drone usage. It would be easier to handle with them involved, but the risk was far too high. No drone would ever best a pilot's intuition, quick thinking, and unpredictable flight skills.

After the Gacrux assignment, Cyril landed at M&M airfield and fell asleep in his cockpit. He was absolutely toast from the brutal schedule. He hadn't showered in a week, and he smelled awful. One of the mechanics on the field shook him awake and asked if he was okay. Cyril had forgotten where he was for a moment, before remembering he had to be on assignment at Kepler-186F for Arcturus that night. He swapped his power cell again, gritted his teeth at the cost, and headed back out.

The first run of Kepler focused on a small town. The company had extended the contract though, and the new goal was half of the western seaboard of Howl's main continent.

Filly was Cyril's copilot again. They recoiled at the sight of him. "Okay, until you get a fucking shower, we don't take off."

Cyril slumped away, showered, shaved, made himself presentable, then hopped into his pilot's seat for another inoculation run. They coated the land in the milky mist. It took half a day to get it all finished. He set the ship to autopilot and napped during most of it. Another mission completed, another paycheck gained, and he was homeward bound. After that, he finally got a break in his schedule.

He spent his first day sleeping. Over twelve hours in bed, he didn't move once. The second day, he spent time with Marie. They went to a steakhouse for dinner, where he was still recovering from the lack of sleep. He was quiet. She caught him staring at the floor in a daze, seemingly sleeping with his eyes open.

She shook him. "Hey, where are you right now?"

"I'm right here," he said through hazy thoughts.

"No, you're not. You're exhausted. You need a break, babe."

"I'm fine."

"You really don't look like it. Your eyes are bloodshot, and you're moving really slowly."

"I said, I'm fine." He didn't mean for that to sound harsh, but he truly was exhausted.

They both went quiet. Their food arrived. Marie got herself a filet mignon with a baked potato and Brussel sprouts. Cyril ordered a ribeye with fries. He rubbed his eyes, ready for bed again, dreading the following day. He had to return to Tau Ceti f, which meant time would shift again. Two weeks would pass on Proxima.

He should have said no, but it was Arcturus, which was consistent and easy. After that one, he could finally relax.

"Cyril, if you took on more command roles, you'd be paid more, right?" Marie asked.

"Yeah, a command position gets more income."

"Then, I think you should try for those. You told me that you lead your squadron home on Sela and got high marks for it. You shouldn't have to work so much. You could relax. You don't have to grind anymore, babe. You're too good for being at the bottom."

"I'm not at the bottom." He shoved a big wad of steak into his mouth.

"I didn't mean it like that."

"Then what did you mean? That I'm slumming it? I like what I do."

"You're exhausted."

"I like what I do. I don't wanna talk about it."

"Okay."

The rest of dinner was quiet. The busy season was driving a rift between them. In the span of a month, they had only seen each other twice. The gap was widening, with no sign of stopping. But the season was almost over, then repairs to their relationship could begin. Just one more job.

They went to Cyril's apartment and laid in bed together. It was a quiet night. He was too tired for sex, and she wasn't in the mood. Dinner had been uncomfortable, to say the least.

He lay there, looking into the darkness of the room. "Okay, I'll try to go into command. I'll do it for you."

"You're sure?"

"Yeah. You're right. I *am* exhausted."

"Thank you, babe. I love you."

He kissed her. "I'll do it for you, babe."

The next day, he was in another megaliner on Tau Ceti f for another Arcturus inoculation spray job, with Loki as his copilot again. Cyril mentioned he was going to try for more command positions.

As they flew on autopilot toward their target destination, she said, "You'd be a great flight lead. Back on Sela, you got most of us home. I owe you my life. I never did tell you that, so thank you."

"You're welcome. Nothing to it."

"So, do you have any plans for tonight, when we get back?"

"I'll head home right away. This planet fucks with time something fierce."

"True. Too bad you're not sticking around. I could use a drinking buddy."

The offer was tempting. Very tempting. She was gorgeous and definitely his type and had clearly shown an interest. He mulled it over. The devil and angel popped up on his shoulders. One said, *"Hey, you already have someone back home. Don't fuck this up."* The other said, *"My guy, how would she know, and Loki definitely wants you."* A part of him, with how harsh the busy season was, had really been yearning for the occasional stress-relief hook-up. Marie had even mentioned that when Cat had tried to hook up with him the last time he had been on Tau Ceti f, she wouldn't have been upset, because sex was just sex. There was no emotional investment. But things were rocky between him and Marie. To do that now, even if she never knew, would bear down on his conscience.

He mentally flicked away the devil. "I'm flattered, but I'm seeing someone."

"Of course you are. Anyone would be lucky to have you."

Cyril smirked. The rest of the operation was quiet and a piece of cake all the way to mission completion.

When he arrived home, a flurry of messages popped up in his inbox. Only one was for a job, thankfully. The rest were either spam or follow-up messages on performance. Most, he disregarded. One specifically requested him for a future lead position. It felt good to be on someone's radar like that. He stowed the phone in his pocket and headed to Mallory's for a celebratory beer. Jace, Jess, and Marie all joined him.

The bar was slammed that night. It was getting colder outside, and everyone was drinking to stay warm. The busy season was finally ending. He had survived once again. His profit-to-expense ratio was around three to one. Overall, he could take a decent amount of time off or accept simple work to keep busy.

As they played a game of pool, two versus two—Cyril and Marie versus Jace and Jess—he pulled Marie aside. "Apparently, I was requested to be a flight lead in the future. If something comes up, I'll take the job. Then I can have more time off."

"I'm proud of you, babe," she said affectionately.

"I'm sorry I haven't been here. I've done this so long that I'm just used to the grind."

"It's what you know. And habits are hard to break. But the only grinding I want at this point involves you inside me." She reached down and felt the growing bulge in his pants.

Cyril laughed. "That reminds me, I got propositioned by my copilot on Kepler. She said she just wanted drinks, but I could tell she wanted more."

"Did you?"

"No."

"Why?"

"Because I'm with you and… we've… been growing apart recently. I didn't want to screw that up."

She put her hand on his cheek, leaned up, and kissed him. "Was she cute, at least?"

"Drop-dead gorgeous."

"I'm jealous. I would have totally said yes."

"You fuckin' bitch."

She giggled, leaned forward, and hit a striped ball into a corner pocket.

As they headed out for the night, they passed the wall of photos. Their group photo from just over a month earlier hung on the left-hand side over the bar.

"When did that get added" Cyril asked.

"I brought that in," Marie answered.

Jess leaned on Cyril, totally buzzed, and slurred, "You got a real good girl, my guy. I'd wife her up if she were mine."

Marie walked toward Jess and kissed her on the lips.

Jace said, "You two are a pair of ungodly whores."

"And we're proud of that," they both yelled.

The four of them called it a night and left. Cyril and Marie took an autocab to her place. They had sex, but he was still exhausted. It felt more performative than pleasurable. They both still achieved orgasm, but it was nowhere near as exciting as it usually was. They cuddled in bed, listening to music.

"Sorry I wasn't as good tonight," he said.

"Don't let it happen again, or I'll scold you in public for it."

He smiled and kissed her, and they fell asleep in each other's arms.

CHAPTER 13

A DEAL BREAKER

Another planet secured. Daniel Mullarkey slid a white magnetic chess piece of a bear onto the planet Luyten. He had added the vertical board, comprised of transparent magnetic glass—three meters across, two meters high, resting on two thick arched legs and displaying the entirety of the Galactic Ekumen—into his office a few weeks prior. He stepped backward from pushing the piece onto the board and admired his work. The Ekumen was in the grasp of Arcturus, the guardian bear high above it all.

It was a glorious Monday morning. The sun shone and baked the inside of his office, helping to offset the cold air outside. Winter would be especially harsh that year. Snow had yet to arrive, but it wasn't far off. And even though it was only 11 in the morning, he poured himself a glass of scotch. It wasn't morning everywhere.

Moriarty and Bentley arrived in the glass elevator. Moriarty held a manila folder; Bentley carried a flash drive. Their shoes clicked and clacked in the grand space of Mullarkey's office as they approached and set their items on his desk.

"Weekly schedule for you. I get why you want this stuff on paper and not the servers, but I am still going to express my irritation," Moriarty said with disdain.

"Noted. You're irritated," Daniel responded, looking out the window.

"Also, I have something you might want to see, sir," Bentley added.

"What is it?" Mullarkey turned around.

Bentley plugged the flash drive into the desk's USB port and opened a video file onto one of the twelve screens containing security camera footage from a high isometric angle of Douglas Forester, in a public park, speaking with an unidentifiable person whose blue hoodie covered their face. Bentley raised the volume, and the trio watched. Bentley had cleaned up the audio as much as possible, but it was still messy and popped with static.

"What they're planning to do with Samson, I can't go along with it anymore. Just because I'm old doesn't mean I'm crazy," Douglas said on the screen.

"Can you get me data files on it? Anything at all?" the hooded man asked.

"Mullarkey has compartmentalized everything. He's hiding what it actually is. He's put as much as possible on paper to stop it from being leaked to the public. All I know is the general details he's let slip."

"What about testifying in court?"

"Not enough to take down the company. They have it all hidden away."

"We'll need to get someone on the inside to get the files."

"Whatever happens, I just want Daniel Mullarkey to go down. He used my son to get Samson off the ground. He's a conniver, a manipulator. His sister probably, as well. They have an... odd relationship. I need justice for my son."

"We'll get someone inside. Wait five minutes, then leave in the opposite direction of me."

The video file ended. Daniel squeezed the glass in his hand so hard that it shattered. He didn't react as the bloody shards crinkled to the floor. Then he said with seething rage, "Get Douglas Forester in here. Now."

***

Locke and Bentley escorted Douglas to the penthouse office at 1500 hours and stood side-by-side at the back of the elevator as they ascended. The doors opened, and everyone exited. Douglas had no idea why Daniel had called him to the office. There was no board meeting for the next two weeks. A company car had shown up at his home, and the driver had asked him to get in.

Daniel poured himself and Douglas drinks. He had bandaged his injured hand, but a small bit of blood had seeped through. As they approached the desk, Daniel said, "Bentley, Locke, you can go. Douglas, join me for a drink."

The two security men left in the elevator. Daniel used his bandaged hand to pass the glass to Douglas. They toasted and drank. It burned Douglas's throat. He hated scotch. He was more of a gin lover.

Daniel poured a refill. "I was going through my daily routine this morning, and I realized that we hadn't seen each other in person since your son's funeral. I figured it was time to get together again. We're still technically family, after all."

Daniel went to the window on the opposite side of the room and looked at the sun. The polarizer on the window was at 30 percent. He raised it to 60. The glowing orb became a large circle in the distance. It was setting earlier, as winter tightened its grasp on that hemisphere of Proxima. Daniel set his glass on the steelwood table and watched the sunset.

"We have our annual board meetings, Dan. I figured that was enough for the both of us," Douglas said. He took another sip. It was sharper scotch than he had ever had before. He winced and set the glass on Daniel's desk.

"I don't think those count as family time. I know you don't like me very much, but you must admit that we do need each other. Absolute trust. Last time, you accused me of using your son's death as a pity play to move Samson forward." His voice echoed and boomed through the colossal space of the penthouse.

"You admitted as much."

"I was half truthful. It wasn't a pity play. Brentwood was supposed to be the one closing our deals for Samson. I wanted to keep him in the deal in some way. So, through the proxy of my sister, your son has been instrumental in getting Project Samson as far as it has gone. You should be proud."

"What do you want, Daniel? Don't bullshit me. I know you hate me. The marriage between your sister and my son was just for business reasons."

"*Eh*, they had something for a while, but that quickly fell away. Trust was broken between them at some point. Trust." Daniel faced Douglas. "It's a hard thing to come by these days."

Oh, no. He knows, Douglas thought but hid his panic. "If we have nothing to talk about that could have been discussed on a phone call, then I'll excuse myself. Goodbye, Daniel."

As Douglas turned to walk away, Daniel shouted, "So, when were you going to rat us out to the authorities?"

Oh, shit.

Daniel circled a frozen Douglas, seemingly growing twice as large. Anger boiled in his veins as he restrained himself from throttling Douglas right then and there. "In this city, you thought you could sell us out and shut us down?"

"What the hell are you talking about?" Douglas replied. *Just play along. Get out of the room!*

Daniel pulled out a small remote, pressed a button, and the audio of Douglas speaking to the man in the park played.

Douglas had to force himself to breathe. The taste of scotch still burned his tongue.

Daniel glared at him and smiled. "We tracked down your informant friend. Really wasn't that hard. He's been taken care of. As have you."

"What are you—" A drop of blood fell from Douglas's nose. Then another. And another. Droplets became a stream. *The scotch!* He vomited a geyser of blood.

Daniel leaped out of the way as Douglas crumpled to the floor, shaking and convulsing. Blood pumped from his tear ducts, and his ear spewed gushes of fluid.

Daniel, proud of his triumph, stood over Douglas. "I wake up in the morning, and I piss excellence. I know my place in the universe. I know the Terran's place in the universe. At the very top. Samson will make sure of that. Terran above all."

Douglas regarded Daniel through blood-soaked eyes.

"And, by the way, your son was a fucking moron!" Daniel smiled, then crushed Douglas's face with the heel of his shoe.

***

Cyril lay on the couch in his therapist's office. Minese had taken him at the last minute to make up for the lost time of the busy season. He would be the last appointment for the day. The sun set over the horizon as Cyril let it all out, what he was really feeling.

"I don't know if this is gonna work with me and her," he said, resigned.

"Why do you say that? Has that much happened in the last month?" Minese responded as he scribbled a note.

"That's the thing. I've been working so much that it seems like nothing has happened. No progress because I've been gone. It was great at the start, but now? I come back, and she almost feels like a stranger."

"Relationships require sacrifice, Cyril. Maybe it's time to find something more consistent here. There's plenty of work that keeps you on a regular nine-to-five. Much safer too, I bet."

"I like what I do, though."

"You've almost been killed how many times in the last six months?"

"I've lost count."

Minese made another note.

Cyril got up and walked to the window. He watched the sun dip below the horizon as night took over. "I like going fast. I like the danger, I guess. It feels good. I don't know if I could ever settle into a normal lifestyle. Be like everyone else."

"Have you tried it?" Minese asked after a beat.

"Well… no. Not really."

"Cyril, shot in the dark here. Do you enjoy killing people?"

"What?" Cyril asked, as if he had been personally insulted.

A car horn outside honked loudly.

"In your profession, you must take people's lives, whether in the air or on the ground. Do you enjoy it?"

Cyril quietly pondered it as the clock on the wall ticked loudly. "I don't know. Maybe. Maybe not. It's usually long distance. Just… blips on a radar."

"Your history with your father, your rough childhood, your lack of close personal relationships points to, at the very least, a minimal level of sociopathy."

Cyril was taken aback. "Excuse me? You think I'm a sociopath?"

"Not at all. You clearly feel guilt, shame, anger. Sociopaths disregard all social norms. Everything feels alien to them. You're still a part of the human race, but you exhibit minimal traits—impulsivity, aggression, you used to engage in one-night stands through superficial charm. And the killing of other pilots, you seem to feel disconnected from it."

"It's part of my job. I don't feel anything for them because I don't have the time. I can't have a bleeding heart for everyone I take down."

"Bleeding heart is extreme. But empathy, that's something you need to work on."

Cyril said nothing and sat down. "Empathy. I do have empathy. You've said before that I have a superman complex."

"But you do that for you. You feel good about yourself from that. Empathy is love and respect for everyone else, regardless of yourself. This situation with Marie, you say she feels like a stranger now."

"Yeah."

"Then the empathetic response is to fix that for *her*, not for yourself. Make her feel welcome in your life again. Do something nice for her, be kind, bring her gifts, and do it for her and her alone."

"Just be nice, *huh*?"

"If you wanna learn how to swim, you just have to jump in the water."

"I hate swimming, and I hate deep water."

"Just an analogy, but you, forgive the pun, get my drift."

"Yeah. I get it."

Cyril's phone pinged with an emergency email requesting pilots for a rescue and recovery operation for the following day. They had requested him as flight lead. *Jump in the water*, he thought. He pressed the Yes tab and closed his phone.

"Something important?" Minese asked.

"Yeah. Jumping in with both feet," Cyril finally said.

***

Marie slipped a test culture of dead tissue cells on a slide under her microscope. She was working late, dressed in a full bio suit, to examine the effects of a new strain of SARS on Crecian tissue. The disease had little to no effect on Crecians, but it easily spread to humans, which meant Crecians could be considered carriers. It was unclear if it had to do with the distinction between Terran DNA and Crecian DNA. The hope was to develop a full antigen to wipe out the new strain before it spread across Proxima. Viral infection rates had been on the rise, which meant she worked overtime nearly every week.

When she finished examining her final slide, she made notes on her data pad and headed to the decontamination chamber. She raised her arms, and a nozzle sprayed her with chlorine dioxide gas. Once the gas cleared, the outer door opened, and she headed to her locker. She stripped off her suit to her waistline and sat. Sitting reminded her how exhausted she really was. Every day was exactly the same. Wake up, go to work, leave. Rinse, lather, repeat. She was approaching burnout and needed a drink.

She changed into her clothes and headed to the main research area. She logged her findings at her desk and clocked out for the night. As she exited the building, she noticed Cyril sitting on a bench outside the main entrance, holding a bouquet of deep-purple Hyacinths. He stood as she went to hug him. "Hey," she said sleepily.

"Hey."

They remained quiet for a moment. It felt like they were back to square one.

"I got these for you." He handed the flowers to her.

She breathed deep, smelling the sharp yet beautiful fragrance.

"I'm sorry," he said.

"Why?"

"Because we've grown apart. And I want to grow back together again."

She said nothing.

"I really want to fix this. I'll do what it takes."

She said nothing.

"I wanna be with you. I really do."

"I wanna be with you also. I've been working too much myself."

"I guess we both kinda fucked up, *huh*?"

"You more than me, but yeah. We fucked up."

"How about we unfuck this fuck up?"

She chuckled. "Okay. And thank you for the flowers."

"I realized as I was coming over that I'd never bought you flowers before, so I didn't really know what your favorite kind was. I just kind of guessed."

She smelled them again. "They're not my favorite kind, but I love them."

"What's your favorite?"

"Sunflowers."

"That'll be for next time."

"Okay, then." She finally smiled.

Cyril gave her a kiss. "Hey, you hungry? Wanna get something to eat?"

"I'm… dead exhausted." Marie rubbed her eyes. "I just wanna go home."

"Okay, we'll go home."

They took an autocab to Marie's place. Cyril put the flowers in a jug of water on the kitchen counter while Marie showered, then he slipped into the bathroom to join her. They bathed each other, washed each other's hair, kissed, hugged, and basked in the lava water that Marie loved so much.

Afterward, they lay in bed, Benny curled into a ball at Marie's feet. She lay face down while Cyril straddled her back to massage her. Her shoulders were knotted up like baseballs, and her back was rippled like a field of rocks. He pushed and pulled, poked and prodded, relieving the tension she carried inside her.

"Hey. I think I'm gonna quit soon," he said.

"What?" she asked as she yawned.

"Starfighting. I'm gonna retire. I'm gonna look for something simple and consistent so I can be here for you more often. Maybe I'll be a flight instructor or something."

"That's good," she whispered.

"I had my therapy session today. Doctor said I need to start making sacrifices not for myself but for everyone else. I've spent so long with my routine that I need to force myself to break it. If we're gonna make this work, I gotta be here. I'm only booked for one more job tomorrow, then I'm done."

Marie said nothing.

"Babe?"

She was completely zonked out, quietly snoring.

Cyril climbed off as gently as possible and lay next to her. Her face was turned toward him. He touched her hair. It was still damp but soft. He ran his fingers down her face, leaned in, and nuzzled her nose. He whispered, "You're the best thing that's happened to me. I'm a terrible person, and you deserve better. So, I'll be better for you."

She didn't hear him. She was totally asleep.

***

Marie snapped awake at quarter after 7 in the morning. Work started at 8:30 AM. She forced herself up, slapped herself from her daze, and began her morning routine. As she brushed her teeth, she smelled food cooking in the kitchen. Marie walked out to see Cyril making breakfast—eggs and toast with juice. He had moved the flowers into a proper vase and had set them on the coffee table.

He noticed her as he poured the eggs onto the plate. "Morning."

"Morning," she said, mumbling through her toothbrush.

"I'd ask how you slept, but you didn't move at all last night. You were tired."

She returned to the bathroom, spit into the sink, cleaned her toothbrush, and walked back out. "Yeah, and I'm still tired," she muttered groggily.

"Welcome to my life."

"*Heh*. Thanks for making breakfast. I'm gonna be late if I don't go soon."

"Same, actually." He circled the table, draped his arms over her shoulders, and looked into her eyes. "You fell asleep last night and missed what I said."

"What did you say?"

"Last job is today. I'm quitting."

Her eyes widened with surprise. "Really?"

"Yeah. I can be here more often if I quit."

"Babe, I didn't mean for you to quit. Just slow down."

"No, I need to. I'll do it."

She craned her head back and kissed him. "You're not gonna sell your ship or something, right? Because that's a dealbreaker for me."

"Oh, *that's* the dealbreaker?"

"*Mmhmm*. You better take me up every now and then."

"Deal. Now eat your eggs before they're cold."

She sat down to eat and realized Cyril only had a glass of juice. "You're not eating?" she asked through a mouthful of toast.

"No, the mission today is a deep-space assignment. Zero gravity. Can't have a stomach full of food. It'll just come right back up."

"*Oooohhhh*. You know this from experience?" she asked as she scooped her eggs.

"I learned the hard way."

"Disgusting."

"Yup. But it should be easy. Jess is going up with me. I'm flight lead."

"Congrats, babe. Tell her I said hi."

"I will." He checked his phone. "Shit, I gotta head out. I'll be back tonight." He leaned down, kissed her once, twice, three times, then grabbed his jacket and bag to head out. He opened the door and said, "Have a good day at work. Love ya."

She smiled as the door closed. *He finally said it. Love you.*

***

MISSION: RECOVERY OPERATION.

TARGET: CRASHED FREIGHTER IN NEED OF ASSISTANCE.

THREAT LEVEL: MINIMAL TO MODERATE. LESS THAN 30 PERCENT CHANCE OF COMBAT. LOCAL CRIME GROUPS HAVE BEEN DETECTED SPORADICALLY. USE CAUTION.

The FOIL pad leaped into the vacuum of space. Its rectangular metal body carried eight starfighters, all magnetically attached. As flight lead, Cyril had picked the squadron codename *Rat Pack Squadron*, because it was a mixture of a little bit of everything. Everyone felt unique and added their own flavor to the group, ranging from their late twenties to their early fifties. As it was his final mission, who would complain? The crew consisted of:

JESS "METALHEAD" TOWNLEY

MORGAN "PIPER" SEXTON

Callisto "Auger" Jones

Jay "Dazer" Hayes

Ilya "Jumper" Biln

Frank "Dragon" Tolwin

Laura "Spiker" McCallister

Flight Lead: Cyril "Skyhawk" Eisner

"Rat Pack Squadron, detach," Cyril said.

One by one, the ships disengaged their maglock landing struts, thrusted upward, and slowly moved fifty meters away. The ships turned about-face, formed a line, and waited. The rescue vessel hadn't arrived yet. The FOIL pad spun up its drive and leaped away. The eight fighters floated in the void.

In the distance, Brevan—an ugly brown planet with a thin atmosphere—floated lifelessly. Full terraforming effects were still years away. Freighters had transported all mined resources from the atmosphere.

One freighter, the *Juniper*, had experienced engine failure and FOIL drive malfunction. It had taken far too long to reestablish communications to call for rescue. By the time they had reestablished communication, the ship was on a collision course. It had impacted into the local moon, where it sat lifelessly. When it had crashed, the bow suffered extensive damage, but the crew had enough food, water, and oxygen for three days. Trinity Mining Corp had hired a contracting company called Watchtower Inc. to quickly assemble the Rat Pack, then dispatched them to escort the recovery ship and its crew to safety.

Rat Pack waited for ten minutes. Finally, the recovery ship, the *Hugo*, leaped into the area. From Rat Packs' point of view, the ship was tilted on its side and facing away from the moon. Its odd silver-gray trapezoidal shape featured a slender but sharp edge body, with the elongated edges on the lower decks. Multiple sets of flak cannons spun from the sides when the ship entered the area.

The radio hissed to life. "Rat Pack One, this is *Hugo*. How are things today?"

"Rat Pack One to *Hugo*, can't complain. Another day at the office. Ready on station. And Rat Pack One's official callsign designation is Skyhawk."

"Copy that, Skyhawk. Coming about for recovery. Contacting the *Juniper* now. Over and out."

"All right, let's go to work and sit around for the next two hours," Cyril said to the Rat Pack.

The squadron thrusted forward and formed up on the *Hugo*'s port and starboard sides, four and four. Flight in zero gravity was extremely different from flight in the atmosphere. The laws of inertia bound each ship, keeping them moving in one direction, until something changed its course. Flying was twitchy and jittery, and G forces could become extreme, almost to the point of snapping bones. Moving about felt less like flight and more like slipping and sliding across oil. Combat, if it was part of the assignment, also proved extremely different. With no gravity or atmosphere to impede flight controls, ships could flip end over end, move in any direction when commanded, and the backblast of missiles firing could disrupt flight controls for a split second. It was the kind of work that required only the best of the best.

The flight to the moon took twenty minutes from the leap point.

Jess chimed in on the radio. "Skyhawk, switch to auxiliary radio channel Echo Tango."

"Copy that, Metalhead. Switching." He switched channels. "What's up, Jess?"

"Just wanted to chat without anyone else hearing."

"Well, I can't stay here too long. I need to stay in contact with *Hugo*."

"I was just wondering how things were with Marie."

"They're okay, I guess. Busy season kind of did some damage, but we're gonna fix it."

"That's good. I'm really happy that you're happy. You seem like a totally different person now."

"I'll let you know when I completely feel that. Let's get back on station."

"Copy. Love you."

"Love you too." He flipped back to standard comms.

They flew forward another thirty seconds before *Hugo* squawked in on the radio. "*Hugo* to Skyhawk, we're not receiving any communication from the *Juniper*. Not even emergency channels."

"Copy that, *Hugo*. Could it be a radio malfunction on either end?"

"Negative, Skyhawk. Signal is getting through. Just… no response."

"Shit," Cyril whispered. "Copy that, *Hugo*. I'll send two fighters forward to recon. Will relay back once we get an assessment."

"Copy that, Skyhawk. Stay safe. Good hunting."

"Skyhawk to Rat Pack, I need two volunteers for recon."

"Auger to Skyhawk, I'll go check it out."

"Jumper to Skyhawk, I'll fly support."

"All right, both of you are up. Go on ahead, recon the area, and head back."

"Copy that. See you in a few," Auger said.

The two starfighters dashed toward the pockmarked gray moon. Their ships shrunk till they were nothing but specks in the distance. Cyril's HUD identified them as green diamonds as they ascended and circumnavigated the moon's surface. Once they were over the edge, their icons disappeared, and their comms went dark. With no satellites nearby, all radio communication required line of sight. The Rat Pack sat and waited in the cold vacuum of space.

Five minutes passed. Then ten. No response, and no sign of Auger and Jumper.

"Something's wrong," Cyril muttered. "Skyhawk to *Hugo*, my fighters should have reported back by now. Go for alert status. The Rat Pack is moving in."

"Copy that, Skyhawk. Will stay on station. Readying up our flak cannons."

"Copy that, *Hugo*. Over and out. Rat Pack Squadron, ready missiles and prep for combat situation. We're going in."

The fighters gave green confirmation signals.

Cyril armed his missiles and rechecked all his systems. Once completed, he said, "All fighters, forward."

The six ships moved as one large unit in a line abreast formation fifty meters apart from each other. As they approached, Cyril ordered them into a vertical line formation, one following the other. The moon enlarged, the pock marks growing into enormous craters, remnants of cataclysmic events billions of years prior, now silent in the vacuum of space. The silence was always something that made him uneasy. In the atmosphere, engines roared, guns blazed like chainsaws, and the wind would sonic-boom. In space, all of that was absent, like a phantom limb.

The squadron approached a steep mountain at the edge of a crater and hugged the surface of the incline. The comfort of approaching as precariously as possible and peeking over a mountainside fared better than the alternative of going in with guns blazing. With Auger's and Jumper's disappearance, the squadron was at 75 percent strength. Still decent odds but not great.

Cyril impelled forward slowly and floated over the ridge line to see more craters on the other side. The rest of the Rat Pack followed him over the limb of the ridge. He felt like a hiking instructor leading a group through a weekend expedition, dipping into craters and sidling through mountain ranges. They traversed through to a long winding canyon and cautiously maneuvered from point to point. He checked his LADAR. No contacts.

"Stay sharp. Check your visual scanning," he said quietly.

LADAR was critical in space flight, as it rendered a full three-dimensional map of everything surrounding the ship. In space, all directions surrounding the ships became points of opportunity for a surprise attack.

The canyon mouth opened, and they found themselves in a flat, powdery field so white that it nearly glowed. The lunar limb of the sunlight was visible from five hundred meters away, looking like a harsh black void slicing off the rest of the moon. They pressed forward, staying close to the deck. Spurts of powder kicked up from their engines and ejected into the nothingness.

"All fighters, switch to infrared." Cyril flipped on his infrared scanning, and his cockpit darkened as the canopy polarized.

All surrounding ships rendered white, and the moon surface showed a dull gray. Deep in the distance, just past the edge of the lunar limb, the very edge of the *Juniper* sat flat and motionless, a hulking mass accentuated in the darkness. Debris from the ship floated around and danced in the vacuum.

"Watch the debris, it could—" A body impacted into his canopy. Or rather, half a body. The dead emitted no heat signature. "All stop," Cyril yelled.

Everyone halted. He spun his ship about, flipped on his forward running lights, and saw a torso tumbling and spinning slowly—Auger, blown in half from the waist down, spewing red droplets into space.

"Fuck. Check your LADAR now!" Cyril flipped upside down and barrel-rolled upright. His LADAR illuminated with a horde of contacts coming straight at them from behind the *Juniper*. "All fighters, break now! Pick your targets and engage. Metalhead, get high and signal for *Hugo* to move in for assistance."

"Copy that, Skyhawk." Jess elevated her ship's nose and rocketed straight up and away from the moon.

Two wide and hideously looking green-and-orange-plated enemy fighters, shaped like two-pronged forks with circular wings that stretched from the center to the tail, gave chase. Cyril thrusted up and tailed them. As he dashed forward, he yawed left and punched hard on the engines. The force slammed him into his seat as he aligned with the two enemy fighters. He got tone and let one missile fly. It impacted on the enemy's engine, igniting a one-second-long fireball before quickly burning out, then the debris floated unconstrained into space. The second fighter peeled away and flipped end over end to fire its guns at him. Cyril darted left and spun three times. He pitched back to the right, fired a squirt of his own guns, and missed. The enemy dashed away and rejoined its group below.

Jess finally reached radio altitude and yelled, "Metalhead to *Hugo*, under attack. Need assistance immediately."

"Copy that, Metalhead. On approach. Be there in ten," *Hugo* responded.

Jess spun around and formed on Cyril's starboard wing. "Who the fuck are these guys?" she asked out of breath.

"Doesn't matter. Figure it out later," Cyril said. "Stay on my wing and let's get back down there."

They punched downward toward the powdery moon. On approach, Jess got tone on a fighter trailing Piper. She locked on, fired, and bagged a kill, but twelve enemy fighters appeared. The squadron flipped and dove, breaking away, and reformed as the enemy ships continued their assault.

"Where the fuck are they coming from?" Dazer asked, huffing and puffing, as they fought the G-forces. "There must be a ship or a FOIL pad somewhere."

"They've gotta be hiding near the *Juniper*," Piper said.

"Just keep fighting. *Hugo* will be here soon," Cyril responded.

"Already here, Rat Pack. On station," *Hugo* said, floating three thousand meters away. Its flak cannons aimed downward at the moon's surface. "Clear out. Orbital barrage incoming."

"All fighters, clear the area," Cyril ordered. "*Go, go, go!*"

The six starfighters formed up in a messy pack and dashed upward and away from the surface. The *Hugo*'s 65mm flak cannons pelted the moon's surface. Massive shells erupted in the powder and ejected geysers of dust and flame into space. The gigantic guns fired silently, spewing fireballs as each round blasted from the barrels. The six starfighters approached five Gs as they escaped the combat zone, their bodies slamming into their seats.

On the surface, the debris and shell impacts pelted ship after ship, knocking out two with direct hits and another two with debris disrupting engine flow. They lost control and crashed into the sea of chalky moonrock beneath them.

The Rat Pack slowed and spun about to survey the devastation. The moon's surface underwent a permanent facelift from the number of hammering shells.

"That's right, burn, you fuckers," Cyril sneered. Part of him really enjoyed watching the enemy fighters get annihilated. The fun was short-lived, however.

"Rat Pack Squadron, guns are dry. Reloading. Hope that helps you out a bit," *Hugo* said.

"Copy that, *Hugo*. Thanks for the assist."

The eight remaining enemy ships retreated into the darkness beyond the lunar limb.

"Rat Pack, report in. Full assessment," Cyril said.

"All good here. No damage. Down to two missiles," Jess said.

"Took a swipe on my right wing. One missile remaining. Half a drum on guns," Piper said.

"No damage. Still fully stocked. I spent most of that running," Dazer said, slightly ashamed.

"No shame in that. At least you're alive," Cyril responded.

"One missile. Guns are at half capacity. No damage," Dragon said.

"Fuselage damage. Polarizer is having issues, and my engine flow is sputtering. I'm on auxiliary. Not sure how long that's gonna last," Spiker said. "I still have two missiles remaining, though."

"All right, Spiker. You're out." Cyril sighed. "Provide support for *Hugo*. The rest of us are going back in. We're gonna find where they came from. *Hugo*, how long till you're loaded back up."

"Loading the next magazine now. *Hugo*, back in the fight." The voice on the radio was filled with pride at the power of Hugo's cannons.

"Copy that. Swing around to the dark side of the moon to provide support up top. Be ready to fire. We're gonna swoop around and get in behind them. We'll do a pincer maneuver. They've gotta be close to the *Juniper*."

Everyone sent green confirmations. Spiker pulled away and headed for *Hugo*. The five remaining starfighters formed a V-formation.

Cyril commanded, "All fighters, dive, dive, dive."

They surged forward together and dove toward the moon. They leveled out at one hundred meters above the surface, then pulled a wide arc around a sharp mountain. Once they crossed the lunar limb, the infrared showed the *Juniper* to their starboard side in the distance as a lifeless mass. Beside it, a large rectangular arrow-shaped frigate with a pointed bow had seven more starfighters attached to its hull. Two cylindrical spindles spun clockwise around it, attached by three metal shafts—crew quarters. The spinning cylinders would provide artificial gravity without the need for thrust. The remaining eight starfighters from the earlier battle flew support or hovered over the *Juniper*. Fifteen enemy fighters against Rat Pack's five. The Rat Pack stopped to stare in shock at how outnumbered they were.

"Fuck me," Cyril whispered.

"There's so goddamn many," Dragon said agape.

"*Hugo*, we're gonna need another barrage soon," Cyril demanded.

"Negative, Rat Pack. Enemy frigate is too close to the *Juniper*. We can't take the risk of hitting it. You'll need to lead them away."

"Fuck."

"I can do it," Jess cut in.

"What?" Cyril asked.

"I'm the fastest one here. Let me be the rabbit."

"No, we separate, we'll get wrecked."

"We'll get wrecked if we don't split them up. I can do it, Cyril."

He turned to look at Jess sitting in her cockpit—she looked so small—and sighed. "All right, you're up. Rush in there, let off a shot, and get out the other side. *Hugo*, Metalhead is gonna try a gambit. She'll lure the frigate and fighters away to put them in range for attack."

"Copy that, Skyhawk. Good luck. Ready to fire," *Hugo* said.

Cyril turned to Jess. "Go get 'em, girl."

"Be right back, babe." Jess punched her throttle and shot forward, going from zero to four Gs in less than ten seconds.

The enemy fighters took notice and turned to approach. She got tone on one fighter and fired. A direct hit. She rocketed forward and punched through the debris. The enemy ships turned around and followed. In total, eight ships tailed after Jess. The frigate began a slow, lethargic twist around to use its cannons on her.

"*Hugo*, do it now," Jess yelled.

Hugo commanded, "Orbital barrage incoming. Stay clear."

Another volley of shells spewed from the cannons and wrecked the moon's surface, hitting three fighters. The remaining five realized the trick and turned back. Jess slowed, spun, and watched the rest of the barrage hit nothing but dirt.

"Guns dry, Rat Pack. Only one reload remaining. Loading now," *Hugo* stated.

Cyril slapped his front console in frustration. "Guess it's up to us. All fighters move on the frigate. Wreck that thing!"

Everyone sent green confirmations and throttled forward.

"What about the enemy fighters?" Dazer asked.

"Ignore them for now. We gotta get that frigate away from the *Juniper*. We only have one barrage left. Fire at will!"

Everyone darted through the incoming fighters. Piper released a round of flares and ducked away from an incoming missile. One by one, the Rat Pack fired round after round at the frigate. Missiles exploded, and gunfire shredded the weaker sections of the hull. Oxygen spewed out. The pressure vacuum sucked several people through the holes, and they tumbled into space. Puffs of fire ejected from the interior, then burned out as fast as they had started.

Dazer risked stopping in front of the bridge to unleash a barrage of gunfire, then dashed away before a missile lock landed on them. The ship listed sideways and yawed right, before scraping itself into the fine powder below, then settled to a stop. As they all made their escape, a missile impacted Dragon's left wing and sent him swirling round and round, before he finally exploded.

Cyril screamed, "Fuck! Dragon's down. *Hugo*, enemy frigate has been destroyed. I'm calling it. We're done here. We're all bingo on ammo. Abort mission. Repeat, abort mission. Everyone, get back to the *Hugo*. We'll FOIL out on the hull."

Skyhawk, Dazer, and Piper formed a sloppy trio of fighters dashing and darting from enemy fire while they ascended from the surface. Meanwhile, a fighter chased Jess as she headed farther from the *Hugo*.

"Jess, get back here," Cyril ordered furiously.

"Trying to. Having issues with attitude control. Took a shot on my port side. I'll be there in a second."

"We don't have a second! *Hugo*, fire the remaining barrage. We'll go above it."

"Copy that. Firing final barrage. Incoming."

The *Hugo* let loose as Rat Pack ascended out of the line of fire. The barrage hit two enemy fighters, but the rest dodged away. The barrage failed.

"Fuck! *Hugo*, prepare for combat landing. Spool up the FOIL drive," Cyril yelled.

"Copy that. Get here fast. We're defenseless now."

"On the way," Cyril responded.

"Well, I think it's my time now," Piper said peacefully.

"What?" Cyril yelled. He looked back to see Piper explode. A grim yelp came across the radio that quickly went silent. "Shit! Jess, get here now! We. Are. Leaving!"

"Almost there," she said, exhausted.

Spiker landed on the opposite side of the *Hugo* from the fight and magnetically attached to the hull. Skyhawk and Dazer came to a near dead stop, twisted around, landed, and magnetized. Cyril saw Jess on approach, a fighter still trailing her. She darted all over the place. One of her thrusters misfired repeatedly, trying to send her into a clumsy spin.

"Jess, come on," Cyril yelled.

"Almost," she yelled.

"Rat Pack, we have to leave now," *Hugo* screamed.

The enemy fighters closed the distance and fired a set of missiles.

Gravity shifted, inertia inverted, and time slowed. Cyril slammed his fists into his canopy and screamed. He watched Jess struggle to fly forward, then he was somewhere else.

Hugo FOILed away.

Jess cried out, "No! Don't leave me!"

A volley of gunfire ripped into her hull, split her wings apart, and thrashed her engine core. The Firestar exploded. Her body jettisoned through the canopy glass, cracking her facemask, and she tumbled into space. Within thirty seconds, she stopped breathing.

Chapter 14

Drifting Through Space

Cyril sat on the bench next to the row of lockers at M&M airfield. He rested his elbows on his knees and stared at the scuffed, dirty floor. A thousand separate times he had walked across those floors to head to his locker to suit up for his next assignment or to return home from a finished one. A thousand different times he had returned and gone to Mallory's to celebrate another job well done—or, at the very least, coming home alive. So had Jace. So had Jess. He turned and stared at her locker behind him in the center of the row, still filled with her clothes.

When he had returned, he was in a haze. The world didn't feel real, like it was made of rubber and warped around him as he walked. Stacy had asked him to check in if he needed any repairs or a rearm. He had said nothing and trudged to the lockers, where he sat motionless for twenty minutes, his stomach churning in knots. He eventually vomited between his legs, then lay on the bench in a cold sweat and stared at the ceiling for another ten minutes.

Stacy approached the lockers and leaned on the adjoining wall. "What happened?"

"Clear out Jess's locker," Cyril said mournfully. Saying it brought tears to his eyes. Now it felt real.

"Oh, God," Stacy muttered.

"Can you get my phone from my locker? You know the combo."

"Sure." Stacy opened Cyril's locker, removed his phone, and handed it to him.

" I fucked up. I fucked up again. "

He opened the group chat between him, Jace, and Jess. He saw her last text to the group.

JESS: See you in ten!

He finally broke and cried. Stacy kneeled to hold him. He wailed and screamed into her chest. She held on tight and didn't let go.

He wept for ten minutes. When he finished, he sat upright, wiped away his salty tears, and called Jace.

"Hey, you never call. What's up?" Jace asked.

Cyril said nothing.

"Cyril, you there?"

"Yeah, I'm here," he said sullenly.

"Okay, so what's up? How'd the mission go?"

"I'm calling you. And I never call you."

Jace went quiet. No one spoke for a long while. Finally, Jace asked, "Where's Jess?"

"I fucked up," Cyril said, starting to cry again.

Jace began crying too.

"I fucked up again."

***

When Marie received Cyril's message to meet at the airfield, she darted out the front door of her work—simply saying, "Death in the family. Gotta go!"—and hailed an autocab. The sun was dropping low, and clouds were rolling in. In that moment, she hated not owning her own car, as the cab was obeying all the speed limits and every stop light. The anxiety of constant stopping was excruciating. She did her best to keep it together but eventually lost it twenty minutes from M&M. She cried until the cab stopped and said, with an all too chipper voice, "Please exit, and have a nice day."

She wiped her tears, got out, and ran past the security gate. The security camera caught her and flagged her for unauthorized entry. An alarm of red lights blared and flashed. Inside, Stacy pressed a security release button on the wall, and the alarm stopped blaring. Marie rounded the corner and saw Cyril in a chair, slowly banging the back of his head against the wall behind him and staring out at the tarmac outside, as if waiting for someone to arrive but knew they never would.

Marie kneeled beside him and hugged him. He leaned his head onto her shoulder and quietly cried again. "I'm so sorry, babe," she said. Cyril said nothing. This was the part she dreaded. This feeling of total helplessness. Something Stacy had said weeks before repeated in her mind: *The only way to not lose friends is not to have any.*

Cat's death had been crushing. Jess's death was absolutely defeating.

"I just let her die," Cyril cried out.

Marie said nothing. She didn't know what to say.

"She was so close to getting back," Cyril said, his head in his hands. "She was right there… and then the fucking ship leaped away. She was so scared."

They cried together as they held each other close.

"I fucked up again."

Marie held him tight and felt the tears drop from her cheeks onto his shoulder. Jace finally arrived. He circled the corner and saw them together. He was out of breath and had been crying as well. Then he collapsed to his knees and wailed. It echoed in the hangar so loudly it reverberated throughout all time and space, damn near shaking the planet. He pounded his fists into the concrete, the wet, hollow slaps belting loudly in the sheet metal hangar. The yelling and crying were like an echo chamber in the building, a constant rebounding of anger and sadness. Twenty minutes passed and finally everyone was silent.

***

Night arrived. It was cold, and drizzles of rain spackled the concrete. Cyril, Marie, and Jace sat on the floor against the wall next to Stacy's office. They stared forward and said nothing as Stacy removed Jess's personal items from her locker.

As Stacy returned to her office, Marie asked, "Can we have those?"

"Sorry. Can't. Legal reasons. They don't belong to you."

"What are you gonna do with them?"

"Call the emergency contact she left behind and hand them off."

"I should make the call," Cyril said. "It's my responsibility as the flight lead." He forced himself to his feet. Gravity felt three times heavier, or he felt three times weaker. Either way, it was a challenge to stay upright.

He followed Stacy into the office. She gave him the contact number for Jess's father, Martin Townley. Cyril stepped out of the office and walked toward the main hangar door that opened onto the tarmac as he dialed.

It rang twice, then a gruff voice said, "Hello?"

"Yes, is this Martin Townley?"

"Whatever you're selling, I'm not interested."

"I'm not selling something, sir. My name's Cyril. I'm… *uh*… a friend of your daughter."

"Okay. Why are you calling me and not her?"

"I *uhhh*…" Words disappeared from his mind. He hadn't thought that far ahead. "*Um*, I don't really know what I'm supposed to say here."

"Where's Jess?" Martin asked forcefully as rainfall rushed from the clouds.

More tears fell. Cyril's eyes were totally bloodshot. "Your daughter is dead, sir."

Martin said nothing.

"She and I… *umm*… were out on assignment together. It was just supposed to be a recovery mission. No one was supposed to be there. We got attacked. And *umm*… she got left behind. She didn't make it to the ship before we leaped away."

Cyril heard Martin crying on the other end.

"I tried, sir," Cyril said, his voice breaking. "I was the flight lead. Five out of the eight in the squadron didn't make it home. I'm responsible, sir. I screwed up. I'm sorry."

"Oh my God, my Jess. Oh, God." Martin wailed. Cyril heard a loud thump. Martin must've fallen to the floor.

"*Uhhh*, her personal effects are at McClelland and Magellan airfield. They won't let me take them. A family member has to collect them." The line was silent. "Are you still there, sir?"

"Yes."

"*Umm*, you can pick up everything whenever you're ready. I'm sorry I failed your daughter."

"What did you say your name was?"

"Cyril. Cyril Eisner."

"I remember you. You were at her birthday a few years ago. I never liked you. Never call this number again." The call ended.

Cyril put the phone in his pocket. The rain fell hard now, and it was nearly freezing. He stepped forward into the rain and onto the tarmac. He thought the cold would shock him to life, but it didn't. A numb chill was all he felt. He gathered all his strength, all his anger, and screamed into the black sky. Whatever deities allowed tragedy to occur, whatever God had permitted Jess to be taken from them, he cursed them till the end of time, and if given enough power, he'd hunt them down and make them all pay. He would kill God if it meant Jess could live one more day. He screamed and screamed and screamed till he collapsed to his knees and wept again.

Marie and Jace watched silently from the hangar.

****

In the following days, the hiring company, Watchtower Inc., pieced together the puzzle of what had happened at the *Juniper* recovery. Wreckage of the enemy frigate revealed that the attackers were members of the PLA—the Proletariat Liberation Alliance: a growing rebel faction, comprised of all the various species across Ekumen space who fought tooth and nail for civil rights and sovereignty for various planetary bodies seeking to detach from Ekumen control. The *Juniper* attack had been a heist to steal natural resources to sell on the black market and gather enough funds to recruit more to the cause. Rat Pack Squadron had interrupted them mid heist.

With the PLA frigate destroyed, all remaining enemy fighters eventually suffocated or committed suicide via self-destruct. With no homebase to return to, they were out of options. No radio signal would reach a rescue party in time. The company recovered the *Juniper* with its crew and reclaimed all resources for return to the company. Despite setbacks and starfighter casualties, they considered the mission a success, awarding Cyril and the remaining squadron members full pay. Though the Rat Pack was effectively decimated, the company deemed these to be "acceptable losses." Cyril didn't agree and believed the mission was nothing more than a Pyrrhic victory. He didn't need to contact any of the other squadron's family members, as none of them were based on Proxima. That responsibility fell to the company.

Cyril contacted members of Jess's band and met them at their recording studio. He gave them the same explanation he had given her father. They were all torn up and lashed out at him, demanding to know how he could have let her die. He didn't know what to say. He offered his condolences, left the studio, and never returned.

Though Jess's family had organized a funeral, Cyril chose not to attend, not just because Jess's father would more than likely rip him apart but because he couldn't bear being at one for her, knowing he was partially responsible for her death. Jace and Marie went in his stead and cried the entire time.

Like when Cat had passed, Cyril, Jace, and Marie got together for drinks at Mallory's. That night, drinks were on the house. Mallory burst into tears after hearing the news and sat with them. It was even more devastating, and there was no dancing or celebration of life. Everyone sat quietly and drank. Jess had been the heart of the group, and now that heart had stopped beating.

Marie spied their group photo on the starfighter wall. "I miss her."

Cyril held her hand. "Me too."

"Me three," Jace said.

"Same here," Mallory said.

It was karaoke night, and a random barfly was belting out a terrible rendition of "You're My Best Friend" by Queen. Mallory went to the karaoke machine and smashed it with her foot. It erupted into metal and plastic chunks and died immediately. She looked the awful singer square in the face. "Not tonight."

The bar went quiet, and patrons slowly made their exit.

The trio left before last call. Mallory took the next day off. They were too depressed to get drunk.

A week after the *Juniper* incident, Cyril and Marie sat in a piping hot bath. She straddled him as he lay against her chest. She rubbed his chest with a washcloth and nibbled on his left ear. He chuckled.

"*Heh*, there you are," she said.

"Yeah, here I am."

"It wasn't your fault."

"I know."

She held him tight and rubbed his chest.

***

It seemed like the rain would never stop. At night, it would turn to snow and begin to sleet the roads. But by morning, it was back to the frigid rain. It was the worst possible conditions for Douglas Forester's funeral. The family plot was at a cemetery just outside the Balamb city limits. The family barred the press from entry and only permitted a smattering of business associates to attend. Layla Mullarkey stood next to her brother Daniel as the cemetery workers slowly lowered Douglas's casket into the muddy grave. He had demanded no cremation upon his death, just a proper burial with his body intact. As a token of respect, Daniel paid for all funeral services. Ilana Forester was grateful for Daniel's generosity. She cried during the entire service.

The story that had made it to the press was that Douglas had been killed in a car accident while driving home from Arcturus tower. Heavy traffic had forced him off the road, and he collided with a parked vehicle on the shoulder, completely destroying his face. Toxicology revealed alcohol in his system. They had recovered video footage of the crash from cameras. The conclusion was driving while intoxicated, brought on by depression over his son's death. The press celebrated the life of Douglas and mourned the loss of another member of the Forester family.

The rain pattered on a collection of black umbrellas as the casket descended into the nearly pooled muddy six-foot-deep grave. Layla glanced sideways at her brother as the casket came to its finally resting place. She swore she saw a smirk on his face. Deep down, she knew the truth. She refocused on the casket and balled her fist, filled with nothing but hate. She shed no tears.

As the service ended, she walked away from the group and toward her limousine. All vehicles were parked on the edge of a roundabout in the center of the cemetery. Rows of headstones and mausoleums filled the flat grassy land. A smattering of leafless trees filled in gaps between headstones. The rain shifted and tossed about as the wind blew sporadically. Once at the car, she reached for the door handle, then stopped. She let go then headed past the car and into the other side of the cemetery.

She crossed the wet blacktop road, descended a small grassy knoll, and stood in front of a large patch of worn and corroded stone effigies and headstones not of human descent, caked in dirt and grime. The city government had created the non-Terran area before they had given proper civil rights action for human/alien integration on gravesites. Now the graves sat silent, unattended. No one remembered who they were. The thought of dying without remembrance was the purest form of existential dread.

Daniel walked up behind her. "You think anybody ever visits them?"

"If someone did, they'd be in better shape."

"*Hmph.* Time to go. Get in the car."

He started to turn when Layla blurted out, "I know it was you."

"Know it was me what?"

"I'm sure you probably thought you had every angle covered." She inched toward him. "Douglas dies in an accident. Probably AI-generated camera footage. Pay off some people to offer testimony of seeing him before the crash. Get some alcohol in his system so it looks like a DUI. Just alcohol and depression take another member of the Forester family." She circled around in front of Daniel.

He looked down at her, stone-faced.

"But you forgot one thing."

"What's that?"

"Even though he had a license, he hated driving. He never drove a car anywhere, especially not in the city. He always had a chauffeur. And the car he supposedly crashed had no autodrive. And if that's the case, where's the chauffeur?"

Daniel said nothing.

"I know it was you," she whispered.

Daniel clicked his tongue but still said nothing.

"What's to stop me from turning you in for it? What's to stop me from turning you in for everything else too?"

Daniel inched closer to Layla and scowled. "Even if any of that were true, who would believe you? You've been a mess ever since your outburst. You're constantly hysterical. Just another broken person."

"I'll tell everyone what Samson actually is."

"Again, who would believe you? You're crazy. I can just deny, deny, deny. What we're doing with Project Samson will reshape everything in the Ekumen, and that"—Daniel pointed to the alien graves—"is just the prelude."

"You're insane. You're absolutely insane."

"No. I'm a patriot. Dedication requires sacrifice, and sacrifice requires power. Douglas knew that. It's just a shame he won't be around to join us when Samson is finished." He raised his right hand to stroke her left cheek. He then reached back, grabbed her hair, and yanked her head backward.

She dropped her umbrella and reached up to break Daniel's grasp to no avail.

"So do not fuck with me! We're almost done, and you will not get in the way of that! Moriarty will take your place brokering from now on. I'll deal with them being a loose cannon instead of you. You're done. And remember, if you tell anyone, you even whisper a word, I *will* know, and I will bring about the most apocalyptic of consequences. You'd be forgotten immediately. A depressed woman suddenly fell from her balcony? An accidental overdose of an illicit substance? Who knows what the future holds?" He let go and wiped his hand on his pant leg.

She grimaced at him, filled with rage.

Daniel walked up the hill, leaving her among the dead. Tears finally flowed, but they were lost in the rain.

***

Two weeks had passed since the Juniper incident, and life felt empty. Marie went through the motions of work and spent time with Cyril during her off hours. He barely left his apartment. She would bring home dinner, and he would barely eat. There was no way to cheer up someone who had lost their best friend. Time was the only cure, and it was moving slowly, one day after another. Jace stopped by several nights, and they would watch movies together or play videogames, trying to distract themselves from the missing third of the trio. Though she would try, Marie knew she could never fill that role. There was no replacing Jess.

In the middle of the week, she attended her biweekly therapy appointment. The discussion normally would revolve around Ben, her past failed relationships, work feeling like a drag, and eventually the issues with Cyril. It had become a routine. If she kept discussing the same problems, she eventually would have a breakthrough. But that week, it was heavier than normal.

Dr. Madison was around Marie's age, which made it feel more like a heart-to-heart than a doctor/patient relationship. Madison had a kind face, with curly blond hair to her neck, and she dressed very casually in jeans and a simple white dress shirt. She sat across from Marie in the stereotypical therapist's office and took notes on her pad. Marie leaned against the windowpane to watch the traffic. From the fifth floor of the office building, the world looked busy below.

"I want to help him, but I don't know what to do," Marie said.

"He lost one of his best friends, Marie. Not much you can do."

"I know. I just feel… useless. Impotent. Is that the right word?"

"It'll do. Death will make anyone feel that way, especially when the circumstances are completely disconnected from you. Whether it was combat in deep space or a car accident, things beyond our control paralyze us."

Marie plopped onto the couch feeling deflated. "It definitely paralyzed him. He won't eat. He barely sleeps. He'll get up in the middle of the night and will just sit on the couch, watch TV, and drink. I mean, what am I supposed to tell him? 'Hey, don't do that.' I just… I don't know."

"Do you love him?"

"Of course. I've said it so many times."

"Then, you just need to give him time."

"I did the same thing with Ben. I gave him so many chances, but he didn't change. God, I'm being selfish. Jess is dead, and I'm worried about my relationship."

"You miss her too, right?"

"Of course I do. What the fuck kinda question is that? I loved her too. We made out a couple times. She was a really good kisser."

"Did Cyril approve of the kissing?"

Marie shot a rigid glance. "He didn't mind, if that's what you're asking. We had the sex talk. We're very open about everything."

Madison typed a note. "I'm glad you got all that out of the way. How was the funeral for Jess?"

"How is any funeral? It was sad and depressing. Jace went with me. Cyril couldn't do it."

"Why?"

"Guilt. He blames himself. I guess I understand. Still wish he had been there though. There wasn't a body recovered. She's just… drifting through space right now. Headed toward… nothing. God, that sounds so terrifying." Marie stared at the floor and imagined herself in the airless void of space, helmet cracked, drifting endlessly toward an unknown destination. The thought made her skin crawl and all the hair on her body stand up.

"I'd ask if you were depressed, but I think I know the answer," Madison noted. "Instead, I'll ask this question. Do you think Cyril will recover? You said this is the second great loss he's had recently. And if so, do you think your relationship will be the same?"

"I don't know."

"From what has been happening over the last few months, the four of you seemed to be very reliant upon each other—a symbiotic relationship. Each person helps to carry the other. With one of the quadrants eliminated, there's a fracture in the support system."

"That's a very shitty choice of words—*eliminated*."

"Sorry, wrong word. But you know what I mean."

"Yeah."

"Each person heals in their own time. I know you don't feel it, but being there is helping him."

Marie bit her fingernails—an ugly habit that her mother had demanded she stop, but she couldn't help it. "But he seems so… cold, lately. Distant. I wish I knew what to do."

"Do something nice for him. You know what he likes. Do something nice and get him to smile. Positive emotions will always beat out negative emotions."

"Not sure that's how it works, but I'll think of something."

***

As Marie headed to her apartment, she thought about what Cyril might enjoy. What would make him smile? Sex was the simple answer but currently out of the question. Food was something they did every day. Nothing special there. She had already helped upgrade his ship, so that was done. The only thing she could think of was his hobbies, and she landed on books. Books made him happy. Pulp novels filled his shelves—action, detective stories, the hero-saves-the-day type stuff. It was simple, sure, but she wasn't one to judge. Horror and smutty romance always filled her bag, which was by no means high-value literature.

One writer had caught his fancy, though—Lee Child. A writer from long ago with stories based on Terran Earth. If nothing else, a signed book by one of his favorite writers might bring about that elusive smile that Dr. Madison had mentioned. She found a signed copy of one of his novels online but not cheap. It was irreplaceable.

The delivery request was off world, which meant her purchase would have to go through numerous hoops before customs would accept it, setting the arrival date to a month. Then she stopped at a sushi restaurant to pick up dinner for them and a new set of flowers for the apartment. She had heard that men only ever received flowers at their funerals. She intended to break that trend.

When she got home, she saw Cyril napping on the couch. Benny was curled next to him like a swirled ball of hair. A few beer cans littered the coffee table, and the TV played some unfamiliar action film. She switched it off, cleaned the table, and stored the sushi in the fridge. Then she put the flowers in a vase and set them on the coffee table. She kissed his cheek and left him to his slumber.

Part of her felt the effort was wasted, but like Madison had said, *"Each person heals in their own time."* She just wished time would move a little faster.

***

The hangover was rough, like a wad of sandpaper scraping out the inside of his skull. He heaved himself off the couch. A small pool of drool had soaked into the gray couch cushion. As his eyes focused, he saw a vaseful of simple yellow flowers with rounded petals, Winter Jasmine, on the coffee table in front of him and a note attached to the vase. In Marie's handwriting, he read, *One day at a time.* He smiled. The kindness distracted him from the hangover.

He petted Benny for a moment, then showered, shaved, and got dressed. Marie had already gone to work, so he had the day to himself. He messaged Jace.

CYRIL: Hey, man. How are you doing?"
JACE: Alive. Took off work. Just can't do it right now.
CYRIL: Yeah, I know. You free?
JACE: Yeah. I could use some company.
CYRIL: Mallory's

JACE: A little early, isn't it?
CYRIL: Not on Kepler. See you in thirty.

Cyril fed Benny, then hopped in an autocab. The sun was out, but it was cold—brutally cold—and he was severally underdressed to be outside: just jeans, a T-shirt, and a gray hoodie. The moment he exited the autocab, he bolted into Mallory's to seek refuge from the icy wind. That early in the morning, Gumby wasn't around. Mallory was also off till the night shift.

Frank walked behind the bar. "Hey, Cyril, heard about Jess. Sorry, man."

"Thanks. Can I get a Guinness?"

"Yeah, let me load up the tap. Don't usually get anyone drinking this early."

"Special circumstances."

"I heard that. I'll get right on it."

"Thanks."

Cyril sat completely still and stared off into space. His drinking was becoming a problem. He didn't want to feel anymore. The alcohol made the feelings disappear. Sadness, pain, and guilt, it all went away. He spotted the group photo of the four of them on the wall of pilots. Then the pain and guilt returned.

Frank set a large pint of Guinness in front of him, perfectly poured, not much head. "Close it out or keep it open?"

Cyril thought for a second. "Keep it open. And keep them coming."

Jace arrived ten minutes later. Cyril was already on his second drink. They hugged and sat together at the bar. The place was quiet and nearly empty. Jace ordered a light beer.

"You got any work lined up soon?" Cyril asked.

"A couple things for the next few weeks. Nothing big. I think I'll cancel though. I'm just… you know. You?"

"I got this thing with Arcturus. Simple transport pilot stuff. No combat. It's easy. I think I'm out of the freelance game."

"Yeah." Jace sighed loudly.

They sat silent for a moment, until Cyril uttered, "I miss her."

"We all do, brother. It wasn't your fault."

"I know." Cyril slammed the rest of his second beer and ordered a third.

"Hey, maybe slow down, man."

"For what? For who?"

The third beer arrived.

"You're falling back into your old ways. You gotta get it under control, man."

"I'm fine."

"I mean it. It's definitely—"

"I said, I'm fine!"

That stopped the conversation dead. Then Jace laughed.

"What the fuck's so funny?" Cyril asked.

"Just thinking about something Jess did. Remember when someone came in here to rob the place at peak hours?"

"Oh, God. She picked up that pool cue so fast."

"God, she went to town on him. She was short but fierce." Jace sipped his beer.

"Like a tiger with short legs."

They both laughed.

"Yeah, she was the best," Cyril reaffirmed.

"To the two-tongue queen." Jace raised his glass.

"To the two-tongue queen."

They eyed the photo on the wall.

Cyril said, "Wherever you are, babe, I hope you're doing okay."

They toasted and downed their beers. As they left after a few more rounds, Cyril took a photo of the group picture on the wall. He was drunk, while Jace was only buzzed. Jace got Cyril into an autocab and sent him home. Cyril passed out on the drive, and the car's incessant alarm, telling him to get out, woke him.

He stumbled out, went up to his apartment, and passed out again in his bed. He slept without dreams. Time blinked from midday to night as he awoke again with another hangover and with a phone filled with messages.

Marie had been messaging all day. *Hey, love you. … Where are you? … You okay? … Please answer.*

Cyril finally answered.

CYRIL: Hey, sorry. I had a few drinks with Jace today.

MARIE: All day? You just now woke up?"
CYRIL: Well… yeah.
MARIE: Babe, I miss Jess too, but this isn't helping. You have
    a problem. Can we please see someone?
CYRIL: I'm fine. I'll get through it. Today was better than
    yesterday.
MARIE: Okay.
CYRIL: Thank you for the flowers. Sorry I left them at your
    apartment. I'll come get them tomorrow.
MARIE: Okay.
CYRIL: I'm sorry I haven't been myself recently. I'm trying.
MARIE: It's okay. I get it.
CYRIL: I'm gonna shower and clean up. You work tomorrow?
MARIE: No. Day off. It's Saturday. See? You forgot what day
    it is.
CYRIL: Simple mistake.
MARIE: Come over tonight. I miss cuddling with you.
CYRIL: Let me clean up, and I'll be over.
MARIE: Okay.

Cyril showered, cleaned up, and headed to Marie's apartment. They lay on the couch, watching a cooking show, and cuddled but barely spoke. They just needed each other's touch. To be held close and to be hugged tight. But despite how close they were, it felt like a wedge was forming, some kind of dead space was growing. They were drifting apart again, and both knew it but didn't address it. Cyril was too depressed; Marie was too nervous. They hugged, turned off the TV, and listened to traffic pass outside the window as night wrapped around Balamb. Benny hopped onto the couch and curled next to Marie's belly. She fell asleep as he purred next to her.

As she slept, Cyril wiggled from underneath them and headed out for a walk. The night was frigid but quiet. He wandered street to street, going nowhere in particular, then ended up at a bridge near a quiet river. The bridge separated the suburban areas from the apartment complexes inside the city limits. He saw a few specks of stars, the only ones bright enough to peek through the city's light pollution. The void above seemed endless, engulfing Proxima in dark velvet. And then he thought about the cosmos wrapping around Jess's body, somewhere still out there, on a road to nowhere.

***

TEN THOUSAND YEARS LATER.

A body drifted aimlessly through the cold vacuum of space—Jess Townley, starfighter pilot and metal musician. The radiation pulsing through the cosmos had grayed and frozen her body. Her expression remained stuck in a state of constant never-ending pain. The helmet was cracked, and her flight suit had zero energy remaining. It had died thousands of years ago.

She drifted toward nothing. No destination, no final resting place. Just floating endlessly through space. And then, a tug. A small gravitational pull from a black hole, no larger than a basketball, seized her. She drifted to her right, toward a small black dot in the distance, now caught in the event horizon.

Her body flipped and pulled and warped as it neared. Her arms stretched above her head, as if she was gasping for air that didn't exist, then became a centimeter longer. Then two centimeters. Then three, as she approached the hole.

Spaghettification began.

Her body ripped apart, the arms going first, stretching into long thin cords, followed by her head, then torso, abdomen, groin, and, finally, legs and feet. The gravitational pull tore her asunder and ripped her apart like a piece taffy. She became thinner, till she was so thin that she could only be seen microscopically. She twirled around as a molecular-sized strand of human spaghetti and flowed bit by bit, dot by dot, into the hole and disappeared forever.

CHAPTER 15

THE SIN EATERS

A month passed. Cyril hadn't flown his ship during that time, both from fear and from guilt. He continued to work with Arcturus, flying the inoculation drops each week. It was simple, convenient, and it paid the bills. He saw Marie as often as possible, but it felt like a chore. Forcing himself to take the time for someone else when he just wanted to be left alone was exhausting. He wished he could go back in time to save Jess—or, in the worst-case scenario, forget she existed. The feeling of failure never left him, like a haunted house that would never be free of its ghosts.

He would visit M&M airfield, check his ship, clean it, run through the systems check, and leave. Stacy would ask how he was doing. He would respond with the same *I'm fine* way. After leaving the airfield, he would head to Mallory's to sit alone with his thoughts. He liked the quiet. It was peaceful.

His phone pinged with an encrypted email from a company called Overseer—a last-minute work request for an off-world, high-value covert operation. Mercenary work. He declined and closed his phone. It had become easier to say no as the days went on. But he still missed it, the feeling of flight, being completely free in the sky. And now his Skyhawk sat motionless and empty, slowly rusting away. He considered selling it, but the market wasn't currently in the best shape for selling ships. Besides, Skyhawks were never in demand.

His phone pinged again.

MARIE: Dinner tonight?

CYRIL: Sure.
MARIE: I'll make us something.
CYRIL: Okay.
MARIE: Love you, babe.
CYRIL: Love you too.

He didn't know if he really meant it anymore, but he typed it anyway. He wasn't sure if he was still in love with her or if the relationship had just settled into a repetitive pattern. The euphoria was gone. There were fights and awkward silences, and therapy was the same recurring conversations. Marie had asked him a week prior if they were okay.

Cyril had answered that he didn't know.

He finished his meal, paid the tab, and headed home. With a few hours to kill, he cleaned his apartment, did laundry, played some games, then headed to Marie's. Benny hopped into his arms when he arrived. The cat had taken a liking to Cyril over the last few months. Cyril had grown fond of Benny too. Marie made fettuccine alfredo, which smelled fantastic. Cyril set the table and grabbed a bottle of wine from the cabinet.

They ate silently. Benny occupied the third chair and watched them.

Cyril quietly asked, "How was work?"

"It's okay. Nothing new. Infection rates have dropped across the Ekumen. That Arcturus inoculation seems to be working."

"That's good."

"You doing okay?" she asked, almost knowing the answer.

"I got a last-minute request today from someone I've never worked for."

"Good," she said with surprise.

"I turned it down."

"Why?"

"Just didn't feel like it." He twirled the noodles around his fork.

Marie sighed. "You're afraid it'll happen again."

Cyril said nothing. He shoved the pasta into his mouth, then took a long swig of his wine. "I'm not just afraid of it happening again. I know it'll happen again. But if I stay grounded, it won't."

Marie said nothing and stared at him.

"What?"

"Remember when we first met?" she asked.

"Of course."

"Remember that guy who was so full of life and confidence? Where'd he go?"

"He's here, just… taking a break."

"Okay." After a few moments of eating, she said glumly, "I wish you wouldn't give up."

"Give up on what?"

"Everything. You turn down work, you're burning through your savings, you don't wanna fly anymore, and it feels like you don't wanna be here with me. Jess dying was awful, I felt it too, but you're letting it destroy your life. I don't want that, and she wouldn't want that either."

"I'm not destroying my life."

"Yes, you are. And if nothing else, you're destroying us." She picked up her plate and set it on the countertop. It landed with a loud *clack*. She went to a table near the front door to retrieve a small wrapped package and tossed it to him. "I got this for you." Then she stormed to the bedroom and slammed the door behind her.

Benny hopped onto the counter to lick the remnants of her meal. Cyril opened the package to reveal a signed copy of Lee Child's second novel, *Die Trying*. He sighed and felt like an asshole.

Later that night, he sat on the couch alone, drinking wine. He reread the Overseer email and responded that he had become available and that he could be on site ASAP. He waited a few minutes, then his phone pinged again. Details arrived quickly. The target was the PLA on a planet called Ashcheron. Cyril raised an eyebrow and perked up. They were the same attackers from the *Juniper* incident. He replied, *I'm in*, closed his phone, and went to the bedroom. He quietly opened the door and saw Marie lying in bed, scrolling through her phone. He lay next to her. She could smell the wine on his breath.

"I sent a message to that work request," he said as the rain battered the window. "I said I could do it. I'm headed to Ashcheron soon."

"That's good," she said disinterestedly, not looking away from the mindless puzzle game on her phone.

Cyril mustered his courage to say, "The target is the same people who killed Jess. I'm gonna go handle it."

She paused the game, put down her phone, and faced him. "You're going out there for revenge."

"Yes."

"Then, do it. Get it out of your system. Kill them all for Jess. Then I want the real you to come back."

"I'll come back. Promise."

"You fucking better."

***

MISSION: Search and destroy.

TARGET: PLA munitions depot.

THREAT LEVEL: Extreme. Expect high resistance from air and ground defense systems.

The squadron was immense. Twenty ships total split into two flights. The battle would be epic. Widowmaker Squadron comprised of:

Flight A:

Jay "Dazer" Hayes

Cyril "Skyhawk" Eisner

Allegra "Honey Badger" Cline

Jace "Astaroth" Rinkson

Whitney "Roku" Quinn

Alex "Frogger" Jameson

Sarah "Livewire" Dipaccio

Hope "Terrifier" Wyatt

Autumn "Flintlock" Ivy

Flight Lead: Mikhail "Rex" Reston

Flight B:

Yule "Hex" Hartman

Kai "Blades" Kellaway

Nolan "Machine" Waits

Ingrid "Hot Dog" Grimes

Omar "Screamer" Ajay

Seth "Gameboy" Decker

Rell "Mixer" Hillo

Ada "Bumblebee" Windsor

Rachael "Loki" Norris

Flight Lead: Kyra "Twister" Hadley

Ground support units codenamed *Sin Eaters* would be in three separate dropships and remain on standby as the air units began bombing and strafing runs against defensive targets. Once they had neutralized the defenses, ground teams would mop up. Sin Eaters were an elite mercenary unit composed of ex-military and police forces. No job was too dirty when the paycheck had enough zeros at the end of it.

Ashcheron was on the rim of the Ekumen, part of Skovian territory. It was a horrible place, the kind of terrain one might consider to be a gateway to Hell. Its name, Ashcheron, was appropriate—extreme temperatures and heavy volcanic activity. Ash would rain on the few settlements that populated the desolate planet. All civilian populations were required to always wear breathing apparatuses outside of buildings. The planet, while hostile, was a major mining territory for diamonds and rare minerals. Its terrain and harsh conditions, though, meant drone mining technology needed constant repairs, and that required a settlement of workers to be contracted on site for months at a time. Only the most desperate would venture there seeking employment.

Political regulations restricted military forces from all species from sending in any official combat forces. However, nothing was illegal regarding hiring private military personnel as outside contractors to handle operations via proxy—a loophole that certain members of the Ekumen governance had taken the opportunity to exploit. The price tag was enormous, but the Ekumen governing body had agreed behind closed doors that the PLA was becoming a problem. It was unknown if the Skovian mining operations on Ashcheron were aware of the PLA presence, though it certainly raised eyebrows. To the miners, the PLA were a group of freedom fighters demanding workers' rights. From a corporate standpoint, the PLA were a terrorist organization who needed to be crushed. Money had become no object, and the Ekumen governance had hired Overseer to handle the problem with extreme haste.

Widowmaker Squadron flew high above the gray and patchy clouds, separated into their two flights—A and B. Cyril flew in the center line of A, with Jace on his left and Allegra on his right. Plumes of smoke and ash from two distant erupting volcanoes filled the sky. Fields of lava flows, now cooled and frozen, resembled pools of black sludge, and mountains were caked in craggy rock formations. It looked like a warzone before the war had even started.

Cyril flew silently. Occasional chatter sounded on the radio, but he didn't chime in. He was out for revenge. He was out for blood. For Jace, the feeling was mutual.

They came within twenty kilometers of their target destination and readied their combat systems. Flight B peeled westward and would flank the enemy once Flight A made its initial attack. Cyril was hyper focused and armed to the teeth. He had molded his ship into a death machine. The engine was at full power, he had modified the guns with incendiary rounds—a full complement of air-to-air and air-to-ground missiles—and a new addition to the mix, internally mounted twin JAU-6 rocket pods. Each pod contained eight small rockets, perfect for taking out SAMs or AA emplacements. They added an extra eight hundred kilograms of weight, which would slow him down a bit, but it was worth it for the extra firepower, and in a pinch, he could detach them midflight to shed weight for a quick escape. They were cheap and disposable but extremely dependable.

He was ready for murder. He could taste it.

In addition, he had stashed his Eruptor rifle and Beretta 9mm inside his ship's cargo hold in case of emergency. Given his last few sorties on the ground, it was best to be prepared.

"All fighters, nothing fancy," Rex ordered. "We go in, clear the road, Sin Eaters mop up. I want everyone back alive. Understood?"

All fighters sent back green confirmation. Nothing was heard but the hum of the engine and the wind ripping through the sky. Rex then sent a red notice signal. Flight A dove below the clouds and spread apart five hundred meters from each other. Flight B climbed above the clouds and began a long semicircle around the target area to form a two-pronged attack pattern. Flight A increased speed beyond Mach one and stayed just over six hundred meters above the hard deck. Cyril swung back his wings and accelerated.

Enemy emplacements, both SAM and AA, popped up on radar. The constant ash fall disrupted their long distance radar, reducing their range of sight. Red dots flickered off and on, then blanked out entirely. Whether real or phantom signals, the ash was messing with their scopes. Flight A went lower to avoid SAM signal lock. They slowed and dropped to three hundred meters above the deck. Their destination was a canyon ahead of them, which they would use as cover on approach, and once they breached the mouth, they would begin their assault.

They peeled back into a straight line of ten fighters on approach. It thankfully wasn't a tight-turn canyon. It bent and wound gracefully, making traversal easy. Cyril kept his left hand on his throttle, ready to punch it forward should any surprises await ahead. He might have been armed to the teeth, but he had also become paranoid. Bad intel on the last few operations had taught him to expect the unexpected. A million things could go wrong. He was ready for them this time.

"Breaching in three… two… one," Rex said.

They dashed ahead on a straightaway and breached the canyon mouth.

A SAM shot upward and tracked Roku. She deployed flares, barrel-rolled, and dove. The missile flew into the sky. She regained control and knifed hard right. As Cyril expected, the intel had been wrong. The canyon mouth was well guarded.

"All fighters, deploy flares as you exit the canyon," Rex yelled. "SAMs guarding the canyon mouth."

"Jace, with me," Cyril said, disregarding callsign protocol.

Jace accelerated alongside him as they exited the canyon. They simultaneously popped flares.

"Ready?"

"Absolutely, brother," Jace said.

"Follow me." Cyril swept his wings forward and knifed right.

Jace followed. They swooped around and got low.

Cyril armed his rocket pods. They deployed from his fuselage, and the rockets popped their tips forward from their housing. He took aim at a SAM unit and fired. The rockets ejected and punched straight through the SAM truck as it sat at the canyon mouth. It erupted into a fireball. Jace fired a missile and destroyed a second one, three hundred meters away. It, too, exploded gloriously. They cut hard and streaked around to the opposite side of the canyon and aimed again. Cyril fired his second pod at another SAM. Several rockets missed, but one managed to impact. It destroyed the target but didn't explode. Jace fell in behind and mopped it up with a strafing run. Then it exploded.

"That felt so good," Jace said.

Cyril smiled devilishly. "We ain't even close to done yet."

They peeled around and rejoined the group as they headed toward the PLA installation. More SAMs fired, but the squadron easily avoided them, due to the outdated SAMs having weaker tracking systems. One by one, Widowmaker took them down, stayed close to the deck, and made their approach, like a swarm of bees in pursuit of its nest's attacker. AA emplacements eventually made themselves known as they neared. Massive gatling turrets, capable of firing four thousand rounds per minute, illuminated the sky with streams of orange flame. Widowmaker punched their throttles forward and escaped their turret range before taking any damage.

Roku, Frogger, and Terrifier pulled a quick V/TOL maneuver and turned a full one hundred eighty degrees. They aimed from a distance and fired on the AA guns before they could swing around. Easy kills. They switched to forward thrust and rejoined the group.

The PLA installation was finally visible in the distance, built upon a cooled lava flow and composed of stocky buildings and easy build trailers. Weapons caches and munitions were stockpiled on the east side, and crew quarters were farther north. A landing tarmac was on the south side, the closest section on approach. That would be the first target. A thin layer of undisturbed soft gray ash caked everything—no footprints, tire tracks, or landing imprints.

Cyril thought that for a PLA installation, something didn't seem right. He chimed in on the radio. "Skyhawk to Widowmaker, anybody else think this looks a little small?"

"Yeah, too small. Most of the facility must be underground," Rex said.

"We'll need to get down there and deal with it at close range."

"Negative, Skyhawk. We stay up here. The Sin Eaters mop up. That's the plan."

Cyril wanted to tell Rex to fuck off, but he bit his tongue. As they approached, Flight B bombed the landing tarmac, pockmarking it with craters and rendering it useless. Flight A then strafed the crew quarters and the munitions depot. The crates of weapons and ammunition lit up like fireworks, and the crew quarters were shredded into ribbons of steel and aluminum.

"Where are all the fighters? This seems too easy," Flintlock noticed.

"Keep your eyes open," Rex commanded.

The two flights began a circular pattern—one clockwise around the installation, the other counterclockwise three hundred meters above. Cyril noticed something amiss about the destroyed base. He broke formation, dove low, and switched to V/TOL.

"Skyhawk, get back in formation," Rex ordered.

Cyril ignored him and realized what was wrong. He hovered thirty meters above the surface and saw the crew quarters were vacant, and barrels of fossil fuel, not power cells, filled the munitions depot. There were also no bodies.

"It's fake," Cyril stated. "It's a dummy base."

"Shit," Rex said, groaning.

"This was a total bust." Cyril hovered in place and punched the side of his cockpit. "Are the Sin Eaters still on station?"

"Should be."

"Get them to check all outgoing radio traffic in the immediate area and jack into the satellite relays. They had the canyon set up with SAMs and AAs, so they knew they might come under fire, but if they were already gone, there would have been nothing here. They might be trying to rabbit elsewhere."

"Copy that. Good thinking. Widowmaker to Sin Eater One, check all radio traffic and scan the area surrounding the target. We think this one is a dummy installation, and the real one is in the vicinity."

Cyril switched his throttle to forward thrust and rejoined the flight above. "You know, if I was trying to hide my base from satellite imaging, what would be a place no one would consider checking?"

"Where?" Jace replied.

"There." Cyril pinned his radar with the twin volcanoes in the distance. Plumes of smoke and ash billowed out, but no lava flowed.

"Use the smoke to mask your base," Rex said. "Widowmaker Squadron, form up. Punch it toward the volcanoes."

All twenty ships became one large cluster and made for the volcanoes.

"Sin Eater One, any radio traffic?"

"Sure enough, yeah. Got their comms. They're trying to run, using the smoke as cover to FOIL out."

"All right, Widowmaker. Full throttle," Rex ordered. "We gotta stop them before they can run. Punch it!"

Everyone punched their throttle forward to the max. Cyril swept back his wings and gained some extra speed to pull ahead of everyone else.

"Skyhawk, remain in formation," Rex yelled.

Cyril ignored him.

"Skyhawk, do you copy?"

Again, he ignored him.

"Eisner, answer your fu—"

Cyril switched off his radio and kept going. His rocket pods were empty, so he detached them. They snapped off and fell into the lava fields, bounced, and shattered into chunks of scrap metal. He gained another speed boost. Cyril saw red.

He scanned all radio frequencies while on approach. He finally found their channel and listened.

A gruff voice said, "Load the rest of the freighters and get moving. Get the squadrons back here now. Leave behind everything that can be spared." He flipped off the radio again.

Five kilometers out, a pair of AA guns revved up and sprayed the sky ahead of him with streams of tracers. He dove, cut his speed, and swung his wings forward. He got a signal on one gun and fired a missile. The gun blasted apart and spewed fire across the black tar ground. He zoomed past the second gun, leaving it for the rest of Widowmaker to handle. The distance ticked down till he flew through the saddle point of the two volcanoes. Ash fell like snow from the plumes above. He throttled forward again. It would destroy his air intake if he stayed in there too long.

" Eisner, answer your fu-! "

As he emerged from the smoke, he saw the installation, the real one, and it was massive. The smoke covered the sky above and around it. Perfect for cover from aerial imaging. His warning system beeped furiously. Missile lock. He barrel-rolled and popped flares. The missile zinged off into the smoke.

He switched on his radio. "Found them. SAM sites on approach. Pop flares once you're through the smoke. I'm gonna get some killing done."

"We're gonna talk once this is over, Eisner," Rex growled through his teeth.

"Whatever you say, boss."

Cyril scanned the installation and found a massive taxiway and tarmac, huge munition stores, a crew quarters three times the size of the dummy base, a huge radio dish for communications, and a full complement of AAs and SAM launchers on station. Four FOIL pad dropships and freighters were being loaded on the ground for escape. One pad headed skyward while spinning up its drive.

He swept his wings backward, punched the throttle, and flew toward the escaping ship. The G-forces slammed him into his seat, but his fingers still moved. He got tone on the boxy dropship and fired. He veered off as the missile let loose and sliced left hard to avoid incoming SAMs. The missile blasted into the afterburner of the rear portside V/TOL engines, and flames erupted from the side. The pad went into a lazy downward counterclockwise spin to the surface. It detonated into a glorious ball of yellow and orange flame.

"That's one pad down," Cyril yelled. "Three remaining. Hit them before they escape."

"Not yet, Skyhawk," Rex said. "Check your visual scanning. Fifteen marks at 240 west."

Cyril turned his head to see a jumble of specks in the distance behind him—PLA fighters on approach. He swooped around and rejoined the squadron. The dropships could wait. Loki and Jace joined up on Cyril's wing and formed a trio.

Loki's new ship, a V-77 Arrowhead, was nowhere near as powerful as her previous ship that had been destroyed on Sela, but it was the best she could afford. It resembled a large red arrowhead, hence its name. As a trio, all their ships in a line looked like sharp knives slicing through the air to deliver death to anyone who dared challenge them.

"*Kill 'em all,*" Cyril yelled as a battle cry.

The trio got tone and fired at the incoming fighters. They scored two hits and one miss. Thirteen fighters remained.

The air battle commenced. The fighters zipped and zinged all over the smoky gray sky. Bumblebee went down quickly; a missile hit her left wing. She ejected just before her fuselage exploded. Livewire fell in behind the fighter who had taken out Bumblebee and got revenge. Another kill for Widowmaker. Bumblebee parachuted down and landed safely in the frozen lava field.

Allegra knifed left and saw a freighter making a run for it. She dove low, and as she took aim, an AA unit fired and tore through her right ring. She managed to get off a shot and destroy the command bridge of the ship. "I'm hit! I'm hit! Lost attitude control. Right wing is trashed."

"Can you land it?" Rex yelled.

"I think so."

A SAM got a lock on Allegra. She popped flares and pushed her flight stick forward. Her controls were sluggish and sloppy, and the flight stick rattled. She descended and tried switching to V/TOL. No response. The internal turbine was gone, wrecked by the AA fire. Then the Diamondback twisted, until it became fully inverted. The ground rushed straight at Allegra's cockpit.

"Can't regain control. Bracing for impact!" She pulled her flight stick as far back as possible, bringing her parallel to the ground. She pulled back the throttle to zero and dropped. The Diamondback scraped and slid across the cooled lava flow. The nose of her ship skidded and kicked up charred bits of black rock and ash. The canopy cracked open and spewed black dust into the cockpit. She raised her arms to block her facemask. The ship slowly came to a stop, mostly intact, but down for the rest of the fight. "I'm down. I'm okay," she said, wheezing.

"Coming in for support. Hang on," Dazer said. They flew down from the fight and switched to V/TOL above the Diamondback.

A squad of PLA ground troops fired upon both ships. Dazer took two rounds in the center of their fuselage. They switched to guns, yawed left, and fired. The chainsaw ripping was brutal and eradicated the entire PLA squad. Then a rocket fired from the west and punched through their rear. The engine housing burst and belched fire as they drifted right.

"Main engine destroyed! Need help," they screamed.

"Goddammit, they're picking us off one by one," Cyril yelled. "I'll do it myself!"

Cyril fired his final air-to-air missile at a PLA fighter as he yawed left and dove. He didn't confirm if it was a hit. As he leveled out, he switched to guns and strafed the area in front of Allegra's ship to obliterate a second squad of soldiers approaching her position. The soldiers lit on fire from the incendiary rounds. Those who didn't die waved and screamed in agony as they burned. Cyril saw Dazer's ship had crash landed fifty meters from Allegra's position, laying lifeless in the black sea of lava, like a piece of scrap metal ready for a junkyard compacter.

"Dazer, status," he commanded.

"I'm good but out of the fight. Will proceed on foot soon."

"Head toward Honey Badger's ship. Allegra, status."

"Broke my arm, but I'm alive. Trapped in my cockpit."

"On the way." Cyril landed twenty meters from Allegra and got out. His feet sank an inch into the lava flow. Most of it was powdered ash atop hard black rock. He pulled his gun belt, Beretta, and Eruptor rifle with spare magazines from his storage compartment. He closed the compartment, then spoke into his wrist communicator. "Skyhawk, elevate to thirty meters and maintain overwatch. Fire upon enemy targets approaching from the north."

The Skyhawk's canopy closed, the engine revved up, and it ascended to thirty meters. Waves of ash blew out from beneath the ship as he approached the Diamondback. The Skyhawk rotated ninety degrees and kept a lookout for incoming troops. Cyril jogged across the lava field, with the Skyhawk in tow above and behind him, like a balloon on an invisible string. The ship fired a few two-second gunfire bursts as he moved toward Allegra's ship. In the distance, more enemy troops screamed in pain.

He kneeled next to Allegra's canopy and looked inside to see black soot and rocks. "Allie, you okay?" he screamed.

She stuck her left hand through a hole in the canopy and gave a thumbs-up.

"All right, get back. Get back," he yelled. He hit the canopy hard with the butt of his rifle once, twice, three times, till the small hole became a large enough gap for her to squeeze through. He reached in and pulled her out as she cradled her right arm. The bone of her forearm protruded like an enormous lump.

"Oh, fuck," he muttered. He helped her around the back side of the Diamondback and set her down. The Skyhawk fired another burst of gunfire. He handed his Beretta to her, and she collapsed next to her ship.

Dazer joined them and dropped to their knees behind the ship, huffing and wheezing.

"Dazer, you good?" Cyril asked.

"Yeah, just outta breath. Gimme a second."

"No time. We gotta keep pressing. Allie, you stay here. Anyone comes around the side of this ship, blow 'em away. Got it?"

"Yeah," she said.

Cyril handed her an extra handgun magazine, then asked Dazer, "You armed?"

They held up a small handgun, nothing more than a revolver.

Cyril sighed. "Well, better than nothing, I guess. One sec." He got on comms and stated, "Honey Badger and Dazer are down but alive. Send in the Sin Eaters. We need ground support now!"

His wrist communicator dinged. The Skyhawk guns were dry. He walked around the Diamondback, held up his communicator, and pinpointed a building in the distance. He had no idea what it was, but it looked big and important. "Lock on and fire a missile."

Cyril's final air-to-ground missile launched and detonated into the side of the building. It blew outward and spewed fire and chunks of concrete as the roof caved in. He walked back around the Diamondback and instructed the Skyhawk to land directly behind it for cover. It set down and powered off. He regarded Dazer and Allegra. "You two stay here. The Sin Eaters are on the way in."

"Where the hell are you going?" Dazer asked, confused.

"I'm not done yet. I'll be back." He switched off his Eruptor's safety and racked a round into the chamber. He gritted his teeth and strode across the lava field toward the base.

Dozens of burned and desecrated bodies littered the field. Even through his facemask and filter, he could smell the rancid burning flesh and cordite. He watched the still-raging air battle and wiped away a coat of chalky dust that had collected on his facemask. Smoke trails blazed in every direction as ships dipped, dove, and danced through a ballet of destruction. Jace scored a kill, which dropped like a stone and impacted into the tarmac of the base. He flew past Cyril and saw him on the ground.

"Cover me, Jace," Cyril said.

"You got it, brother." Jace turned to provide support as a bullet zipped past Cyril's head.

Cyril dove and shouldered his rifle. He looked through the scope at a pair of crouching soldiers in the distance, training their automatic rifles on him. Bullets whizzed and popped as they just barely missed him. He adjusted his aim through his scope, exhaled, and squeezed the trigger. The gun fired with a massive thundercrack, and the round hit one soldier; his chest erupted into a gush of blood and bone. The soldier beside him reeled backward in pain as the shrapnel tore apart his face and blew off the fingers of his left hand. They both dropped. Then Cyril stood and jogged toward the base.

Jace went V/TOL and hovered fifty meters above Cyril. He shot off squirt after squirt of gunfire to dispel any approaching soldiers. A squad of four ducked behind a supply truck. Cyril lazily looked through the scope and fired another round. The shot punched through the truck's chassis and exploded. Two of the soldiers collapsed in agony, while the other two made a run for it. Jace lit them up with gunfire, and they burst into a cloud of red mist.

From the distance, the Sin Eater dropships landed on the tarmac and released sixteen troops each, four squads per ship. The troops fired toward the PLA soldiers in the distance. Cyril jogged to the lead ship as the commander descended the rear exit ramp.

The Sin Eaters were a brutal bunch. Each soldier carried a unique loadout of weapons to suit their style, but they still moved as one unit. The essentials were all there though. Digital gray camo, Kevlar vest, helmet with a facemask and oxygen supply, and strapped all over with extra magazines and grenades.

The commander scrutinized Cyril. "You must be that Skyhawk we kept hearing about on the radio."

"The one and only."

"Right. Name's Olen," the mercenary said in a gruff, smoky voice.

"Cyril Eisner. Got two pilots down in the field. Send a squad to assist them. One has a broken arm."

"Later. We need to secure the base first."

"You have an entire army down here." Cyril gestured at the devastation. "You can spare a couple people."

"You don't give me orders. You're just a pilot. You shouldn't even be down here."

"Well, my ship is bone dry on ammo, so you're stuck with me. Try to keep up." Cyril turned and ran toward the fighting while waving Jace away.

Jace switched to forward thrust and took off to join the rest of the squadron above.

Olen shook his head in annoyance and joined his ground squad. Olen was a veteran of The Annexation War but had kept fighting, for glory and not for money.

Cyril could give a shit less about money or glory in that moment. He just needed a target, and he spotted one taking potshots around a set of hangar doors. He crouched, aimed, and fired. The shot went wide, but the shrapnel zinged off the door panel and scared away the shooter. He joined a mix of Sin Eaters and charged ahead.

Cyril sidled up against the corner of a building with a squad of four who carried different weapons. One had an assault rifle, the second a sniper rifle, one a heavy machine gun, and the last a rocket launcher for demolition. Cyril was at the back of the pack, putting him farthest from the corner.

The head of the squad peaked his scoped assault rifle around the corner to scan the area—his scope connected to a camera system that fed directly into his helmet visor—and saw a pair of mounted AA emplacements, which would immediately turn anyone who approached into hamburger. "Well, that complicates things. No way air cover is getting through that."

"Can we flank them from the other side?" Cyril asked.

"Who the fuck are you?" the woman with the rocket launcher asked, with a brisk voice audible over the rampant gunfire.

"Name's Eisner. Was providing air cover, but I'm grounded now. Mind if I tag along?"

"As long as you don't get in the way, I don't give a shit what you do," said the first in the squad.

"You, sniper guy." Cyril pointed and snapped his fingers toward the soldier with the sniper rifle. "What's your name?"

"John Little."

"I doubt that. You and I can flank them. If we can get inside this building and get to the roof, we can snipe their emplacements."

"Who the fuck do you think you are, giving orders?" the demolitions woman yelled.

"What's your name?" Cyril asked.

"Sarah Tyrol, demolitions."

"Well, Sarah Tyrol, demolitions, would you kindly do me a favor?"

"What?!"

"*Shut the fuck up and make a fucking door*," Cyril screamed as he slapped the side of the building. "Now!"

Tyrol turned to her squad leader.

He cocked his head. "You heard the man. Make him a door."

She went to work and set a primer cord in a rectangular shape along the center of the concrete wall. While they waited, the rest of the squad introduced themselves to Cyril. The squad leader was Michael Glass, and the heavy weapons expert was Julie Crow. Crow and Glass huddled on the left side of the primer cord, while Cyril and Little huddled on the right side.

Tyrol finally finished her prep, pulled out her detonator, and took position with Glass and Crow. "Fire in the hole!" She depressed the trigger, and the cord blasted a six-foot-tall door-shaped opening in the concrete wall.

Cyril leaped around the squad and jumped through the hole. A pair of soldiers inside the building were dazed and coughing in the dust and the grit that filled the air. Cyril shouldered his rifle and aimed. "Knock, knock, motherfuckers," he growled and pulled the trigger.

The bullet sliced through one soldier's head and exploded into the wall behind them. Each round had a minimum detonation range, and Cyril was too close for detonation on impact. The shrapnel blasted outward, hitting the second soldier in the left calf, and he crumpled to the floor in pain. Cyril walked over, flipped his gun around, and pounded the butt of his rifle into the man's face till it resembled crushed meat. The squad watched him as they flowed in one by one through the hole.

Cyril slung his rifle over his shoulder, the butt end dripping blood and brains, and regarded the four soldiers. "He was in my way." He grabbed one of the soldier's assault rifles, checked the magazine, rammed it home, and strode toward a set of stairs at the back of the room.

The squad followed, keeping their weapons at the ready. They ascended the steps one by one. The gunfire outside sounded hollow, like it was kilometers away. A pair of PLA troops fired down the stairwell. The squad ducked back and took cover, using the roof of the previous floor. Crow stepped to the front of the group, jumped out from cover, and chucked a sticky grenade up to the next floor. It landed on the side of the stairwell and beeped. The PLA troops screamed in shock as the grenade detonated, and a flurry of dust and debris floated down between the stairs. As the dust settled, a dribble of blood flowed down from the edge of the floor above. They kept going until they reached the roof.

Glass and Crow flanked the rooftop door, counted down from three, then kicked open the door. The squad burst onto the roof and scanned the area for enemies. It was clear. The five of them crawled to the roof edge, surrounded by a three-foot-high barrier along the sides. Glass used his gun camera to scan the area below again. The two AA emplacements hadn't moved. A starfighter overhead tried taking a shot but was immediately hit. It crashed into the tarmac and exploded. Cyril couldn't tell who had gone down.

"All right, we only get one shot at this," Glass said. "The moment they know we're here, they're gonna light up this roof. Tyrol, you take the one on the left with your launcher. The rest of us will take the one on the right. Don't stop firing till those things are scrap. Little, if Tyrol needs a reload, you're on that. Everybody clear?"

The group nodded.

"All right. And… *now!*"

All five of them leaped up, rested their weapons on the low wall, and fired. Tyrol aimed at one of the AA guns and pulled the trigger. Her rocket blasted from the launcher and found its target. The gun exploded, killing the gunnery crew. The rest of the squad fired on the second gun and unleashed so much firepower that it could shake the planet. Cyril emptied his assault rifle, chucked it aside, then shouldered his Eruptor again. He fired round after round, yelling in fury. Each shot exploded and peeled off chunk after chunk of the AA guns' armor plating. The firing finally stopped. The AA crew wasn't just dead, they were butchered.

Little said to Cyril, "Goddamn, I need one of those."

Cyril didn't respond. He got up and headed for the rooftop door, leaving the squad behind. The fire inside him burned as hot as the sun itself. The four of them followed him downstairs to trek toward the main building.

The destroyed AA guns had been guarding the central command building. A large radar dish slowly spun clockwise on its roof.

Glass said to Tyrol, "If you please."

Little loaded another rocket into her chamber. She crouched, aimed, and fired. The rocket slammed into a left side support strut, and the dish collapsed, then twisted and crashed sideways into the command center roof. The squad proceeded forward, ducking from cover to cover, taking out enemy soldiers as they sprang up. Cracks, holes, dead bodies, and craters peppered the tarmac everywhere.

A shot rang out and sniped Little through the throat. His lower jaw exploded, and he fell to the ground, grasping at what used to be his neck. The squad ducked into an impact crater. Tyrol and Crow did their best to stop the bleeding. Nothing helped. He bled out in thirty seconds and died staring at the gray sky.

The squad collected themselves and rested on the edge of the crater. Another shot zinged by.

Glass got on the radio. "Widowmaker, enemy sniper on the rooftop west of our position. Need assistance."

Rex responded, "Copy that. On approach. Will need a target beacon for a strafing run. Lots of smoke down there."

"On it, Widowmaker. Tossing out the beacon now." Glass dropped his rifle and pulled a target beacon from his kit. He twisted the top of the beacon, counted to three, then rushed over the edge to chuck it. Right as he let go, another shot rang out and nailed him in the chest. He fell backward into the crater and dropped the active beacon.

Cyril dove to grab it and, with total disregard for his own safety, sprinted over the crater rim and chucked it as far and as hard as he could toward the building. He dove back into the hole just as a second shot snapped past his head. The squad took cover and waited. Rex flew overhead with three other fighters and began a full strafe of the buildings. Gunfire rippled through the steel and concrete and decimated the snipers atop the building. Tyrol removed Glass's Kevlar to check for damage. No bullet wound but his ribs were definitely broken.

"Did you guys hit anything?" Glass groaned into his radio.

"Absolutely, Sin Eater One. You're all clear."

"Thanks for the assist. Got one of your pilots down here alongside us."

"Is his name Eisner?" Rex asked, slightly vexed.

"That it is." Glass winced as he shifted his weight up the crater edge.

"That insubordinate bastard is gonna get a mouthful from me when this is over."

"Don't go too hard on him. He's actually been pretty useful down here. He just saved our asses. You'd have hit *us* if it weren't for him."

"Doesn't excuse the fact that he's not on station with his flight."

"*Eh*, win some, lose some."

With Glass incapacitated and Little dead, the squad was now only Tyrol, Crow, and Cyril. Other Sin Eater squads moved toward the command center.

"What's the plan, sir?" Tyrol asked.

"I'm good here," Glass said. "The rest of you join the other squads and move to the command center. I can wait for a medic."

"I'll stay with you for support," Tyrol said.

"I'm fine," Glass groaned.

"Cool. Raise your right arm."

Glass tried to raise his right arm and winced in excruciating pain.

"It's not just your ribs that are broken. Your sternum is shattered too. You're done, sir. I'll wait with you."

"Fine," Glass said begrudgingly. "Crow, Eisner, good luck. Watch the rooftops."

"Got it, sir," Crow said.

"And Eisner," Glass said.

Cyril looked back.

"You're a natural born Sin Eater, you know that?"

Cyril said nothing as he rammed a fresh magazine into his Eruptor, racked the slide, and released it with a echoing *ka-chack*. Crow shouldered her heavy machine gun, while Cyril shouldered his

Eruptor. They joined a pair of squads and proceeded toward the front entrance.

The two-story building featured row after row of windows, like any standard office building. Cyril wondered how the PLA had managed to hide there for so long. Something built in that manner was designed to last, and in the shadow of a pair of volcanoes, no less. He brushed the thought aside to save it for later. The squads racked up along the edge of the main entrance, one squad on each side. Two Sin Eaters deployed camera drones to scan the hallways within. They were empty. Everyone shouldered their weapons and breached. Once inside, Cyril moved toward the front of the pack, ready for the next kill.

***

The air battle ended. Widowmaker Squadron had taken control of the sky. The two flights formed up and flew support for all remaining ground troops locked in stalemates on the ground, pulling strafing runs and bombing incoming vehicles. With all AA turrets and SAM units down, there was no more threat for air cover. Rex and Loki landed next to Allegra and Dazer. Cyril's Skyhawk was exactly where he had left it. The two pilots hurried toward Allegra's crashed ship.

"Honey Badger, how are you holding up?" Rex asked.

"Fine, sir. Broken arm. I'll live."

"How about you, Dazer?"

"Fine, sir. No injuries."

Rex surveyed Cyril's Skyhawk and scowled. "That bastard just loves violating orders, doesn't he?"

"With all due respect, sir, he kind of saved both of us," Dazer retorted. "We owe him one." Allegra shrugged in agreement.

Rex turned to Loki for support, but she held up her hands. "Hey, he saved me in the past, too. I'm on their side."

"Un-fucking-believable." Rex sighed as he shook his head. He circled the crashed Diamondback and saw the base in the distance.

The whole place was wrecked, and plumes of smoke spewed everywhere. The gunfire had dropped to a minimum, with only the occasional pop and snap.

"Eisner, are you still on radio? Eisner?"

No response.

Rex sighed again. "Now the question is, where the fuck did he go?"

***

Cyril and Crow took point as they descended into the command center. A dim and gloomy stairwell, lit with only red-alert lighting, went down two floors. The building was running on emergency power. Camera drones moved ahead of them to scan a long corridor with doors on both sides. Cyril kept his Eruptor at the ready. He thought about Jess and how he was doing all this for her. Every shot, every kill, was to avenge her. He hoped that somewhere she was looking down and watching him deliver punishment.

The stairs ended on a flat concrete landing and led to a dusty, debris-littered hallway. Cyril aimed his rifle down the red chasm before him. Some doors were swung wide open, others still shut tight. He moved slowly—heel first to the floor, then onto the balls of his feet. He moved silently like an assassin, like a ghost.

A door burst wide open, and two soldiers charged forth, firing blindly. Cyril and the Sin Eaters unloaded everything and annihilated them. The enclosed space made everyone's ears ring. Crow shook her head and swayed. She leaned against a wall and rubbed the side of her helmet that protected her ears. Cyril heard bells himself but didn't care or react.

They moved forward again. The Sin Eaters broke into pairs and cleared each room. A few shots rang out, but most rooms were vacant. At the end of the hallway, Cyril kicked in the door to the final room. Three soldiers were huddled around a communications system for the radio tower, trying to reestablish a signal. Cyril aimed his Eruptor and fired at the controls. It exploded and killed the operator. The two other soldiers suffered minor shrapnel injuries but kept their footing. They unholstered their handguns as Cyril racked in another round and screamed, "Go on. Do it. *Do it!*"

They didn't do it, then dropped their weapons and raised their hands. Crow entered the room behind Cyril and aimed her gun as well.

"Who's in charge?" Cyril asked.

They said nothing.

Cyril fired off to the side of the room. The round exploded and shrapnel grazed one soldier across the back. He fell to his knees and screamed. Cyril racked another round and aimed at the still standing soldier. "Let's try that again. Who's—"

"Him! He's in charge!" The standing soldier pointed to the injured man on the floor.

Cyril stepped forward, slung his rifle, and collected one of the handguns. He checked the magazine, racked the slide, aimed at the standing soldier, and shot him in the head. Cyril growled the supposed commander, "Guess that just leaves us, doesn't it?"

"You just shot an unarmed man," Crow screamed.

Cyril nonchalantly said to Crow, "Well, then, he shouldn't have disarmed himself, should he?"

"Commander Timothy Carson. Serial number 55659D," the commander said. He was on his knees, staring forward defiantly.

"Excuse me?" Cyril asked.

"Commander Timothy Carson. Serial number 5—"

Cyril kicked the man's chest. The commander collapsed backward.

"Cyril, *stop*," Crow yelled.

The commander coughed and groaned, gasping for air. "You don't know what you're doing. They're using you. We're all on the same side."

Cyril aimed his gun at the man's head. "You and me? We're not the same. And we are not on the same side." He thumbed back the hammer.

"Please," the commander said.

"Eisner, enough," Crow said. "We won. Let it go."

Cyril aimed for a few more seconds, then lowered his gun. The commander finally breathed again and began crying. Cyril noticed Crow and the rest of the Sin Eaters were waiting in the red-lit hallway. The commander slowly got onto his knees as he wept.

Cyril headed for the door, then stopped. He dropped the pistol and flipped his rifle around, grabbing the barrel. "One last thing," he said, turning around. "Her name was Jess Townley, and she'd want me to do this." He dashed forward and swung hard upward. The butt of the Eruptor shattered the commander's jaw. Blood and a pair of teeth sprayed from his mouth as he fell backward, knocked out cold.

"Goddammit, Eisner! *He surrendered already*," Crow yelled.

Cyril studied the toothless commander. "Just making sure." He slung his rifle and headed out of the room. "Get the fuck out of my way," he said to the Sin Eaters, then stormed down the blood-red-lit hallway.

The Sin Eaters stood silently with their backs to the wall and watched him go.

Once Cyril was topside, Rex and the rest of Widowmaker Squadron greeted him, shocked by his appearance. Black soot and blood covered him, like something from an action film—or possibly a horror movie.

Rex asked him, "Leave anything for us?"

"One survivor. He's downstairs."

Loki stood next to Rex with her helmet off, her hand covering her mouth, shocked by his malicious appearance.

"Excuse me," Cyril said as he brushed past them and strutted down the pockmarked tarmac. He unbuckled his helmet and stripped off the top half of his flight suit. His rifle clattered to the ground, and he dropped his helmet. He began laughing, then howled. All alone in the middle of the destroyed tarmac, he dropped to his knees and screamed into the smoke-filled sky. He breathed in the fumes of destruction and felt pure satisfaction. Then he fell backward and screamed some more.

As he lay flat on the destroyed landing strip, he stared into the gray sky. Flecks of ash fell and caked his face. "I got 'em, Jess. I got 'em." He smiled.

Jace stood above his head. "You okay, brother?"

"Absolutely. We won. Let's go home."

***

Cyril knocked on Marie's door. She opened it. He stood there and stared at her.

She reached out and hugged him. "Did you get them?"

"Yes."

"They're all gone?"

"Yes."

"Is it finally out of your system?"

"Yes…"
But that part was a lie.

Chapter 16

It Started Snowing

A month passed after the battle of Ashcheron, and a month since Cyril had flown his Skyhawk. The days ticked by, and the sky darkened sooner, the weather finally changing from fall crisp to winter cold. When he returned home, he had kept his promise to Marie to stay close and to spend more time with her. He had honored that promise, but now a hole grew within him. He missed the flying, the excitement of another mission. It may have been work, of course, but the thrill of going out and of being a part of a crew felt like a part of him was gone. It gnawed at him like a rabid dog that wouldn't unclench its jaws.

Marie's job had given her a raise and a promotion to a senior staff position. While she still yearned to move into her preferred field of becoming a mortician, the money they offered was too good to turn down. Meanwhile, Cyril continued his simple megaliner pilot missions for Arcturus. Planet by planet, he helped spray the inoculation agent. It was as much excitement as he ever got. The pay was consistent, and his co-pilots were usually Filly or Loki. And thus, he found stability. But still, even with stability, that hole grew larger.

During the investigation following the battle, they had discovered that the facility was an old mining and storage depot that a Skovian mining corporation had built and abandoned, as that area of the planet had yielded too little material and the location made it extremely hazardous. It would have cost more to tear it down than to let it rot. PLA had occupied it in secret and operated out of it for two months. It was still questionable why no member of the Skovian government was taking harsh action against the corporations for such lax security measures. The simple response they gave was they would "look into it." After the investigation concluded, they tore down the facility and the mission became all but forgotten. They shipped off any prisoners whom they had taken during the mission to various penal colonies across the Ekumen, some without due process. And some, the higher-ranking individuals, mysteriously died before the transfer.

Cyril moved on with his life now that he had avenged Jess.

One day, he messaged Jace.

CYRIL: Hey, brother, you free?
JACE: Yeah, what's up?
CYRIL: Grab lunch?
JACE: Yeah. Mallory's?
CYRIL: You know it.
JACE: I'll pick you up.

Half an hour later, Jace sped down the highway in his sports car, with Cyril riding shotgun. And once again, Cyril gripped the arm rest the whole way. They parked, went in, and grabbed a table. When they got their drinks, they toasted to Jess's photo on the wall. She was gone but never forgotten. It had become easier to accept that she wasn't there anymore. Like with Cat, time healed everything.

They both ordered the same thing, cheeseburgers with extra fries. Jace put mayonnaise on his burger, which made Cyril retch. "That's a criminal offense," Cyril indicated sarcastically.

"Then, arrest me," Jace responded.

As they ate, they talked business.

"Anything exciting happening lately?" Cyril asked.

"Got a couple of small jobs coming up. Simple transport stuff. Winter drought is here."

"I don't miss those days."

"Arcturus treating you well?"

"It's a job. I took it full time to make Marie happy."

"How are things going with her?"

Cyril rubbed his temples, then ran his fingers through his hair. "I don't know. I don't know, man. I feel like I'm doing everything right, but it's still not good enough. I got a normal job. We have dinner every night. We spend time together. Talked about me moving in. I don't know what else to do man. Something is just… off."

"Well, I can't really help you fix your relationship. That's a you problem. I got my own thing to deal with."

"How are things with your partner?"

Jace was quiet for a moment, then sighed. "We split recently."

"Shit. Why didn't you say anything?"

"You got your own issues, and you're working steady. Didn't want to bother you. It's fine, though. He wanted more than I could give."

"Still, sorry man."

"It's okay." Jace shoved the last bite of his burger into his mouth and spoke while he chewed. "Honestly, I think maybe we were developing the same issue you're currently having."

"What's my issue?"

"Blandness. You want something exciting, and you don't know what to do."

Cyril shrugged in agreement. He crammed a wad of fries into his mouth. "I miss going out there and barely escaping death. I loved that feeling. Now my ship just collects dust at the airfield. I should probably just sell it."

"Find something here. Race it, flight instructor, something. There's plenty of places to go."

"*Eh*, I checked around. Most of it is union based, which means more of the paycheck gets taken and that you gotta fly a certain number of hours and blah blah blah. Too many roadblocks for me, man."

"Well, if you're ever trying to get back into the freelance world, I'm sure all your contacts will rehire you."

"I doubt I'll go back. I gotta figure this thing out with Marie. I feel like I messed up somewhere."

"Talk to her tonight. Just sit down and work it out. If it becomes a fight, then that's better than just staying silent. At least you'll both get something out of your system."

"Yeah. I thought Ashcheron would get everything out of my system." Cyril eyed Jess in the photo. "But I'm still angry. I wish I could have gotten more of them."

"It's over, Cyril. We won. You gotta just… let it go. I did. You should too. We got our revenge. What's done is done."

"Yeah. Hey, what time is it?"

Jace checked his phone. "About two thirty."

"Fuck. I got my therapy session. Can you give me a lift?"

"Yeah, no problem. Glad you're still going."

"If I didn't, Jess would haunt my ass till the end of time. Isn't that right, Jess?" He looked at the photo on the wall again and pretended she answered him. "Exactly. That's right."

They paid their tab and hopped into Jace's sports car.

"Can we please take it a little slower on the way?" Cyril asked.

"When you get to drive this car, you can slow down. Till then, just hang on." He slammed the accelerator to the floor, and they sped off.

Cyril braced himself the entire way across town. It was a miracle no cops pulled them over.

***

"You're bored," Minese said.

"That easy to tell, *huh*?" Cyril remarked.

"No shame in it. At the point you're at in life, things become routine. Mundane. Happens to everyone."

"I've never really felt this kind of boredom before. It's not even really boredom, honestly. It feels like… like I'm just following a basic routine or a pattern. Day in, day out. I've spent the last seven years making my own way, being my own person. Now I'm grounded. And I hate it."

Minese made a note. "Does Jess's passing still haunt you?"

"It's better, but it'll never stop."

"You said a couple weeks ago that you got your revenge for her. How do you feel now?"

Cyril paused for a moment, then muttered, "Empty."

"Why do you think you're empty?"

"'Cause she's still dead." Cyril wrung his hands together, remembering the attack on Ashcheron.

"So really, it seems you've developed a revenge complex."

"What's that?"

"Exactly the way it sounds. You want to be back out there because you think if you take down more people, it will somehow revive her and quell the feelings of guilt you have in yourself."

Cyril said nothing.

"It's more common to feel that than you think. You're not a special case."

"Oh, and I thought I was just lucky."

"A while back, I asked you if you enjoyed killing people. Given what happened on your last assignment, how did it feel? Did you enjoy taking revenge?"

"Not gonna call the cops, are you?" Cyril asked tensely.

"Doctor/patient confidentiality. Unless you're a serial killer or rapist, what you say stays in here."

Cyril was quiet for a moment as he nervously wrung his hands. "I loved it. Every second of it. Every kill felt like I was bringing a little bit of her back. I knew it was just a feeling in the moment, but it felt good. And before you ask, they were all bad people."

Minese said nothing.

"So how about it, Doctor? Am I crazy or what?"

"*Crazy* is not a term we use in psychology. I'm not entirely sure where you fall on the spectrum. Past trauma mixed with current PTSD and a revenge complex, crossed with a superman complex. You wish to save people who had suffered by killing others. You're… complicated to say the least. But you're not what anyone would describe as *crazy*."

"I don't want to hurt anyone, and yet, at the same time, there's specific people I do want to hurt. Why am I so fucked up?"

"Do you believe there are *normal* people in the universe, Cyril? One's who aren't fucked up?"

Cyril scoffed. "Fair point."

***

Layla stood on her apartment balcony and watched the traffic below. She calculated the number of floors and how long it would take to soar by them when she jumped. It was a morbid thought, but she still couldn't bring herself to do it. Yet, in the back of her mind, the thought lived rent free.

Since her removal from the board of Arcturus, she had become a hermit, living day in, day out in solitude. Questions of her absence had arisen in the press, to which Daniel had announced, *"She is taking some time off for herself. Her father-in-law's passing hit us all hard. Please respect her privacy."* The twisted irony of Daniel believing in the concept of respect was not lost on her. The drinking began again, and as she stood on her balcony, she cradled a glass of Macallan 30. Winter had also arrived, and the balcony space grew colder. Heat lamps kept it warm though, allowing her to drink outside and gaze upon the sunset everyday alone.

She finished the last gulp, then headed inside for a refill as her phone pinged. It was Daniel.

> DANIEL: The contract for Proxima is gonna be signed tomorrow. You need to be here.
> LAYLA: Why?
> DANIEL: This is our home planet. We both need to be here for posterity. Tomorrow morning, be in my office at nine. No excuses.
> LAYLA: Okay
> DANIEL: Good.

Layla closed her phone. She would show up, keep her mouth shut, and let business run its course. He was in control. He was always in control. No one would believe her if she blurted anything out. No one could stop what was coming. They were committed now, and she was just as culpable. The feeling of dread slithered up her spine as she filled her glass and, once again, contemplated how long it would take to reach the ground floor from her balcony.

She sat in a chair and went through the contact list in her phone. The balcony heat lamp behind her hissed and crackled as she landed on Cyril Eisner's number. She pressed Call and held the phone to her ear.

"Hello?" Cyril answered.

"Hey, Cyril. It's Layla."

"Wow. Never thought I'd hear from you ever again."

"Never thought I'd ever contact you again."

"You okay? What's wrong?"

"Nothing. Just… can you come over?"

"I'm not gonna fuck you, Layla."

She chuckled. "This isn't that. I just need someone to talk to."

"Yeah, I can come by. Text me your address."

She hung up, texted her address, and within thirty minutes, Cyril was knocking at the door. She made herself somewhat presentable with black jeans and a plain T-shirt. As she opened the door, she checked her breath. It reeked of alcohol.

Cyril smiled. "Your doorman downstairs is a dick. Told me I was in the wrong place."

"Jacob is very cautious about who he lets into the building."

Cyril entered, and she closed the door. As Cyril walked down the hallway, he whistled in amazement. "Goddamn. I wish I was born into a rich family."

"It's not all it's cracked up to be," she said, walking past him. "Want a drink?"

"Yeah, I'll have a little something."

She poured him a glass of the Macallan and handed it to him.

"Thanks." He took a sip. "*Mmm*, the good stuff."

"I have three more bottles, so you don't need to be precious with it." She grabbed her own glass and headed to the balcony.

Cyril followed. She sat down and watched the night sky consume the city. The concrete jungle below was more illuminated than the sky above and resembled a set of computer chips flickering on and off to keep the system running smoothly. Cyril leaned against the door frame and took another sip.

"I bet you love it out there more than here, don't you?" Layla asked.

"These days, that's a loaded question."

She turned her head toward him. "Actually, it's a simple question. Do you like it out there more than here?"

He thought about it for a moment. "Depends on who I'm with, either here or there."

"Fine." She was slightly annoyed by his deflections and went quiet.

"You know, it feels weird, me being here," Cyril said, admiring the skyline. He walked to the edge of the balcony and leaned on the railing.

"Why is it weird?"

"Different social structures, economic differences. If I wasn't invited here, I would be kicked off the sidewalk just for walking by. Feels weird."

Layla said nothing.

"So, you asked me to come by, and I'm here. What's up?"

"Don't really have anyone else to talk to."

Cyril faced Layla and leaned backward against the railing. "Oh, you mean your shit-heel brother isn't good company," he said with seething sarcasm.

She scoffed. "He disgusts me."

"And he infuriates me. I'm only working for him for the money. I'm out of the freelance game, so having consistency is nice."

"You quit flying?" she asked, agog.

"Just freelance. My ship is about as useful as ballast on a ship now."

"Why did you quit?"

"The woman I'm seeing wanted me to spend more time with her. Consistency is how you grow a relationship, or something like that. Lately things have been… rocky."

"I'm sorry to hear that."

"It's okay. I'll figure it out."

"Any person would be lucky to have you. It'll be okay."

"*Heh.* Thanks." Cyril sat in a chair next to Layla.

They gazed at the black sky together. The heat lamps surrounding them emanated brisk waves of warmth.

"You don't realize how lucky you are, you know that?"

"Because I have money?"

"Yes. Because you have money. My life, for the last seven years, has been a near constant hustle and grind. If I could just find a quiet place to live peacefully, with enough money to last till I die, I'd be happy."

"I kind of feel the same way. I would give it all up in a heartbeat if it meant I could live in peace away from everyone else."

"What's stopping you?"

"Daniel."

"Just go."

"I can't."

"Why not?"

"I just can't." She said that one with a brisk tone. The discussion ended there. "Anyway, I wanted to use my money for something good. I never really liked the whole living-in-excess thing."

"Funny, me neither. I'm very uncomfortable right now." They both laughed. "I really do think you should just go. Just pack up and jet outta here. And don't look back."

"It's not that easy."

"Yes, it is. I did it for years flying freelance. One week I'm on Tulson, the next on Sigma, the next on Gacrux. To go where I want, when I want, that's true freedom. You're not… tied down. You're not beholden to anything or anyone. Just you and the great big black up above. Sorry to get philosophical. I think the alcohol is kicking in."

Layla downed the last of her drink and set her glass on the ground beside her chair. "Maybe one day. Maybe one day I'll be free."

A cool gust of wind sent a chill across the balcony.

"Like I said, just go," Cyril said. They sat quietly for a few seconds, then he said, "*I* wish I could just go."

"What's stopping *you*?"

"Marie is here, Jace is here, lots of memories, my work. My dad, though I don't talk to him."

"I feel like I should spit your advice back at you," Layla asserted with a hint of contempt.

"My situation is more complicated. There's a lot more holding me to the ground. Also, like we've established, I'm not rich."

"Point."

"*Mmhmm.* It is what it is. It's weird that you never seem to like the socialite life. I've always imagined people in your position going out and spending too much money and hooking up with random people."

"I was born into the money, but I wanted to travel. I was studying archaeology a long time ago and wanted that to be what I did for a living."

"What happened?"

"Dad died, so me and my brother had to pick up the slack at Arcturus. Daniel stepped in as CEO, and I fell in beside him. I still wanted to travel and explore. He wouldn't let me, even withholding money in my accounts. Said I had to be here for the sake of the company. Brentwood entered the picture not long after, and Daniel insisted that marriage would be good for the company. It was, but it also felt like I was just a pawn being moved around on a board. I don't know. And the people he hired right after Dad died are disgusting."

"You mean Moriarty? Ugh."

"Them, and Bentley."

"The pudgy guy? What's his deal?"

"He's a gross pervert. I walked in on him jerking off to security camera footage one time. Made me want to puke. Daniel just said he does good work and did nothing."

"What the hell is wrong with people?"

"Must be something in the soil. Who knows?"

Cyril chuckled at the absurdity of that statement.

"Do you love her?" Layla asked quietly.

"Marie?"

"Is that her name?"

"Yeah, and yes."

"Then yeah, you belong here."

"Yeah. Fuck, I just want everything, don't I? I hate having to pick personal versus professional shit. There really is no way to balance this stuff—especially when it gets people killed."

"What do you mean?"

Cyril set his glass down and rubbed his eyes. "A while back, a friend of mine got killed out on assignment. I was the flight lead. She got left behind. I should have told her not to take it. If I had been thinking from a professional point of view, Jess wasn't qualified for deep-space operations, but the personal side of me said it would be fine and that she could hold her own 'cause we were a team. Now she's dead, floating off out there somewhere."

"I'm sorry."

Neither spoke until Cyril finished off his liquor and pronounced, "But I got the people who took her out. I got revenge, I suppose."

"You don't seem particularly stoked about it."

"Yeah. And it bothers me."

They chatted for a few more minutes, then decided to call it a night.

As Cyril headed into the apartment hallway, Layla gave him a quick hug. "Thanks for coming by. I appreciate it."

"It's no problem. I'm always around if you need anything."

"Thanks. Goodnight, Cyril."

"Goodnight, Layla."

She closed the door and headed to the balcony. She cleaned up the two glasses, set them in the sink, and closed the balcony door. As she leaned against the door frame, Cyril's words rang in her mind. *"Just go."* She considered packing a bag, booking a flight off world, and running as far as possible. She could start over, away from Daniel, from Arcturus, from everyone. She yearned to be invisible. But the reality of who Daniel was, and how he operated, haunted her. No matter where she went, no matter how far she ran, he would find her and drag her back to him.

The thought of how long it would take to reach the bottom floor popped into her mind again.

***

Two days later, Marie stopped by after work to spend the night with Cyril. He made dinner—spaghetti, with meatballs and marinara sauce—and as they sat together, the awkward silence hung over them like a storm cloud that refused to pass. Conversation was minimal and basic.

Finally, Marie asked, "Are you happy with me?"

Cyril set his fork down and beheld her. She still looked pretty, even after such a long work week. Her hair was unkempt, her eyes had dark circles around them, and her skin was oily and uncleaned from the day, but she was still attractive. Beyond that though, Cyril felt the divide and contemplated how he felt. Finally, he said, "I don't really know anymore."

Marie said nothing. She twirled her fork around a string of spaghetti. The fork made a clicking sound with each turn. "What am I doing wrong?" she asked quietly.

"It's not… something you did."

"Then, what is it?" The question was direct.

"I… forget it." He picked up his plate and headed to the kitchen.

"No, we're not gonna forget it. This is important. Anytime something important comes up, you just deflect and never wanna talk about anything."

"It's… It's nothing, okay? I'm just having a bad day." He swiped the remainder of his dinner into the trash and set the plate in the sink.

"They're always bad days for you now," Marie whispered. "I thought you were happier."

"I thought I was too."

"But now you're not?"

Cyril leaned against the edge of the sink and stared at the floor. He sensed a fight getting ready to start. "I miss being out there," he murmured toward the floor.

"Where?"

"Out there. Flying. Now I'm just a dull cargo pilot. I'm bored out of my fucking mind, and it's not getting any better."

Marie strode to the kitchen. "You said a while ago that you were okay leaving all that behind. That what we have comes first. I never said to quit, just take less work with higher pay."

"No, deep down you wanted me to quit." Cyril realized immediately that it was the wrong thing to say.

"Don't you dare put words in my mouth! You know, if you wanna go back out there, just do it. Who's stopping you?"

"I gave it up because I thought that would make you happy. Now I guess I was wrong. You still nag me about how I feel all the time and expect me to just be comfortable with my life."

Marie was taken aback. "I nag you? Did you really just say that? I nag you?"

"Yeah, you do. You were on me to take a command position, and see how that turned out? Jess is dead."

"Woah, woah! Wait a minute! You do not turn that back on me! One, I never straight told you to take that job. And two, Jess didn't die because of you. You blame yourself, and you want to throw part of that blame on *me*? How fucking dare you even think that's rational!"

"You wouldn't stop getting up my ass about it! And she's still dead!"

"Cyril, let it go! Just let it go. I miss her too, but do not punish me for what happened to her! It was an accident. I thought you said that was all out of your system."

Cyril reeled himself in and rubbed his face.

Marie leaned against the opposite wall and sank to the floor. "It never will be out of your system, will it?"

Again, Cyril said nothing.

"Oh my God, what's happened to us?"

"I'm just… tired."

"Tired of what?"

"Of everything! Tired of you getting on me for every little thing I do or don't do. Tired of not being able to do my job! Tired of thinking I could have done more while I was out there! There are still more people responsible for Jess's death, and they're still out there! I'm tired of the bullshit!"

Marie cupped her face into her hands and cried. Cyril sank to the floor as well. As she cried, he pounded his fist onto the floor in anger, hoping to dispel the accumulated rage inside him. She slid away as she cried. He finally stopped pounding and checked his swollen, reddened hand. He was out of breath.

Marie cowered in the corner. Through her cries, she said, "I can't do this. I can't do this. I did everything right, and it's happening again. Why is this happening to me again? I can't do this."

Cyril, realizing his error, slid toward her. "I'm sorry. I didn't mean it."

As he outstretched his arm, she screamed, *"Don't touch me!* Don't touch me!"

He recoiled, and she broke into a loud cry. He sat against the wall, completely defeated.

"You're just like your father. I was stupid to ignore it." She crawled around the corner, stood, grabbed her jacket and purse, then walked into the kitchen.

Cyril forced himself to his feet and held onto the kitchen counter to support himself.

She pointed a trembling finger at him. "You… When someone says you hurt them, you don't get to say you didn't. Why can't you understand that?" She shoved him. *"What is wrong with you?"* She shoved him again, harder.

Cyril said nothing and didn't react.

She spun around and stormed from the apartment. The door slammed shut as she left. He heard her crying and whimpering all the way down the hallway. He stood in the kitchen alone. It felt like a weight had been lifted off him. The wrong weight.

***

A week passed. Cyril tried messaging and calling Marie, yet she refused to answer. She would see his messages but would never reply. He reached out to Jace for advice, but he hadn't replied either. He was off world on assignment. His stomach was in knots, and the emptiness he had felt before their fight grew larger. Every message was apology after apology and still no answer. He finally gave up.

The days felt longer even though daylight was shorter in the winter months. Every minute, every hour ticked by slower and slower as he tried to go about his life, the emptiness hanging over him the entire time. He fell into a routine to keep occupied. Wake up, eat, go to the gym, come home, and keep occupied with some kind of distraction. He wasn't set to work for Arcturus again for another week. The entire week he spoke to no one. He'd known loneliness before but not that kind.

Finally, desperate to make amends, he summoned the courage to see her in person. He remembered her favorite flower—sunflowers. He bought a full bouquet from a florist who still carried them during the winter months. It would be awkward, but he felt there was no other option. He headed to her workplace, sat outside in the cold, and waited.

It was freezing, but he sat on a metal bench just beyond the front entrance to her office to wait for her to leave for the day. The bouquet had turned ice cold, so he laid it beside him and stuffed his hands into his jacket pockets. Night came quickly, and at 6 o'clock, she finally walked out the front entrance. She was bundled up head to toe, but her face was still exposed. A scarf wrapped around her neck, and a winter hat covered her head. She pursed her lips and furrowed her brows when she saw him.

Cyril grabbed the flowers as he stood. He walked over and stopped in front of her. She stood in front of him and said nothing. Her gaze could slice a diamond in half. The silence was just as awkward as he had expected.

"I'm really sorry for what I said. I know I have issues, and I'm working on it, but I want to get through it. You mean a lot to me. I'm really sorry. Please forgive me?" He handed the flowers to her.

She took them, glanced at them, then walked to a trash can and chucked them in. She said nothing as she brushed past him and walked down the street to grab an autocab home.

Cyril stood there crestfallen. He hadn't thought that far ahead about what would happen. As he walked home, it started snowing.

The next day, when he woke up, he checked his socials to see that she had blocked him on everything. She'd completely removed him from her life. His stomach felt like a dark pit, ever expanding. He didn't feel like eating, sleeping, or moving. He called her again, and it went right to her voice mail.

She was gone.

Chapter 17

Someone Say Something

"Eisner? Eisner!" Filly shouted again.

Cyril snapped from his trance. "*Huh*?" he grunted.

"We're drifting starboard. Check your engine output," Filly ordered, flipping switches.

"Yeah. Sorry."

He and Filly were flying their megaliner for Arcturus across the planet Kyash—a forest planet in Skovian territory. The population was several billion, so it became a multi-day job, but, like all the other Arcturus jobs, it was a no-brainer.

The starboard engine had stopped receiving full power. Cyril checked all the possible issues till he found the problem. A damaged energy transfer capacitor had severed from its housing midflight. More than likely from just wear and tear. "Switching to auxiliary." He flipped the switch to change the flow of energy, and the ship righted itself. They were back on course for the capital city to drop their payload.

"What's going on with you? Where's your head right now?" Filly asked. "You've been like a, what do you call them, zombie all flight."

"Just got some stuff on my mind. I don't wanna talk about it."

"I'm not your therapist. Wasn't gonna ask about personal stuff. You just need to straighten up. I need my copilot to actually 'co' my piloting."

Cyril chuckled. "Okay." Cyril looked out the window at nothing but a dense forest below.

As they flew, the forest cleared out and gave way to a highway system, then a tram system, then an urban sprawl and a cityscape that stretched for several kilometers into the distance.

"Approaching drop zone. Tank's ready," Cyril said.

"All right, deploy," Filly said.

The fluid tanks opened and spewed their milky mist across the skyline. The other six megaliners flying in formation also dumped their payload. The sky became a thick white smog that slowly dropped and coated the city. After ten minutes, the tanks ran dry.

"Job is done. Let's go home," Cyril said.

"You wanna take over flying for a bit?" Filly asked.

"No. Not right now. Don't really feel like it."

"Suit yourself."

During the next two days, more drops happened across the planet, and Kyash was declared fully inoculated against all xeno diseases. Cyril kept himself to himself and endured the days one by one, hoping against hope that things would improve once he was back on Proxima.

He landed at M&M airfield. The tarmac was coated in a thin layer of slowly melting snow. He went to Stacy's office to check in. She was in her office, as always, but appeared more sullen than usual. "I'm back. Need a new power cell." Cyril noticed she'd been crying. "What's wrong?"

"I'm sorry," she said, her voice quivering.

"What happened?" he asked fearfully.

Stacy handed him a file—Jace's flight record.

"No," he muttered.

"Happened while you were away. Gun cam footage is available if you want to see it."

He was silent for a minute, then didn't so much as sit down as much as he fell into a chair. He looked up at her, his mouth dry. "Show it to me."

She pulled up the soundless gun cam footage on her data pad that showed Jace's ship engaged in zero-G combat with an unidentified squadron. He zipped around, spinning and firing. It looked like panic. Finally, gunfire raked across his bow and shot through the canopy. The ship tumbled end over end and spun into space. Stacy sped up the footage, as there was nineteen minutes of the ship simply spinning and tumbling. Then a tow cable caught the bow section, slowed the ship to a stop, hauled it to the main carrier for reclamation, and set it in the cargo bay. An engineer cracked open the canopy and hauled out Jace's body. Half his chest had been blown away. Then the engineer dug through the cockpit and shut down the ship's systems. The footage ended with the words, LOG COMPLETE.

Cyril sat there unable to move, staring at the floor and hoping he would wake up. It was all a dream. Had to be.

Stacy began crying, and then so did Cyril. They hugged each other and fell onto the couch in her office. When he had thought things couldn't get worse, reality proved him wrong.

After half an hour, Stacy decided to close early. All flights were logged in for the day so no chance of a random pilot dropping by. Unknown to Cyril, per Jace's wishes should he be shot down out on assignment, all his personal belongings fell to Cyril. Jace had no family on Proxima. Cyril was the closest thing he had to a brother. His apartment, possessions, and even his car became the property of Cyril Eisner. Despite now being the owner of a very high-end sports car, there was just one oversight on Jace's part; Cyril didn't have a driver's license. He'd never needed one.

Cyril and Stacy gathered their personal items, closed and locked the doors, then headed to the staff parking lot. Jace's car sat there, as if waiting for its now deceased owner to return. Cyril got into the driver's seat, Stacy in the passenger's seat. He put the key in the ignition, and the engine roared to life, but he didn't start driving. He sat there feeling the vibration of the engine and listening to the hum of the muffler. Then he bashed the steering wheel over and over. Pure anger and rage shot through his system. He screamed as loud as he could, swearing obscenities that would terrify any god. His hands felt raw after a while, so he stopped. Stacy sat there in numb shock.

Cyril cried again and muttered, "Why does this keep happening to me?"

Stacy had no answer. He huffed and puffed, then swallowed hard and wiped away his tears. He put the shifter in Reverse, backed up, shifted to Drive, and drove them to Mallory's so they could drink away their sorrows.

***

They transferred Jace's body to Cygnus. Word had gotten around in the freelance community about his death. He was extremely well liked, and several pilots attended his funeral, including Allegra, Kyra, and Rachael. Some didn't know him personally but felt they owed him respect. Stacy even took time off to make the trip. Cygnus was in the middle of its summer season, and it was a brutal one. The sun felt crushing as a small congregation gathered on a cliffside to spread Jace's ashes. His mother and father were also in attendance. Jace's last lover, Ingmar, attended as well, and he was especially torn up but couldn't say any words at the service. He couldn't stop crying.

Cyril wanted to say something too, but with the world pounding him down, all he could muster was, "I'll miss you, brother."

The seven-foot-tall priest wore a green robe, with a headdress that draped around his temples, and spoke in Skovian dialect. "Our energy is never truly lost; it is only repurposed. Given a new form to serve the universe in another way, a better way. Jace Rinkson, your energy will find a new home among the sea, the land, and the very air we breathe. You will continue to serve life beyond the veil." He sang a small hymn and asked Jace's parents to come forward with their son's urn.

They stood at the cliff edge, opened the urn, and, handful by handful, threw his ashes over the edge. A gust of wind carried him toward an unknowable destination.

Rachael wiped tears from her face and whispered, "Drift away."

Cyril heard her but said nothing.

The Rinkson's held the reception at their one-story countryside home. Jace had never come from wealth, and it showed. The small and cramped home was stuffed with personal belongings that they could easily dispose, but they refused to sell or chuck them due to sentimental value. Cyril now understood why Jace had loved his sports car; it was a piece of wealth that he could never have earned had he stayed on Cygnus. It was a rustic, quiet, and boring planet known more for farming, with small pockets of industry, than a bustling economy. A sports car was the exact opposite of all of that.

As Cyril sat outside alone, enduring the heat under a cheap yellow umbrella, he smirked, finally getting it about the car.

Rachael stepped outside with a bottled beer and handed it to him.

"*Nah*, I'm okay," he said, waving her off.

"Take it, or I'm dumping it in your lap," she said insipidly.

He grabbed the beer and took a sip.

She sat across from him, half in sunlight, half in the umbrella's shade. "How you doin'?"

Cyril said nothing.

"Yeah, same."

"I must've watched that gun cam footage a hundred times," Cyril finally said. "Every time, I think it's gonna end differently."

"Like a movie with a sad ending. You hope it ends better next time."

"Something like that." Cyril took another sip. "It's been one thing after another. I can't tell if it's karma or just bad luck."

"One is meant to teach. The other is meant to punish."

"Which is which?"

"I don't know. Do I look like a philosopher?"

They both laughed.

"It's good to see you, Rach."

"Yeah, you too. Wish it was under better circumstances," she said morosely.

Stacy and Allegra stepped outside and took up the last two seats at the table. They sat in silence, listening to the bird's chirping in a tree nearby.

Stacy wiped away another set of tears. "Someone say something."

Allegra leaned forward and raised a glass. "Jace was one of the best pilots we had in our group. I must've flown with him over fifty times, and we always came out the other side together. He was a beast. When he started, he didn't know what to call himself. Couldn't figure out a good callsign. So we just called him *Jace* for his first flight. Can't remember where I heard the name, but I recommended *Astaroth, the Duke of Hell*. Seemed appropriate. He didn't understand human mythology. Just sounded good to him. Took him no time at all to learn about everything human. He figured if he was flying with mostly Terran's, better get to know them. He did."

Stacy cried again. Rachael sniffled and drank her beer.

Cyril stood and raised his drink. "Jace was one of my best friends. Actually, he was the last close friend I had left. Wherever he is, I hope he's keeping Jess company. Those two really were inseparable. I was always the third wheel that they let tag along." He laughed. "And they were always on me to clean up my act and to stop being an asshole. I wouldn't still be here if it wasn't for them. I owe them my life and more." He took a long drink. "Stacy, he never said it, but he definitely had a big crush on you. If he wasn't taken at the time, he would have probably jumped at the chance. And Allie, he always thought that you beat yourself up too much, but you were a hell of a pilot. And Rach…"

Rachael looked up.

"He didn't really know you very well."

She laughed.

"But I'm sure he would have liked to. You two would have got along great. For Astaroth."

They raised their glasses and toasted. Cyril downed the rest of his beer in one long swig.

As the day went on, people said their goodbyes and departed one after another. Cyril, Rachael, and Allegra were the last to go. Stacy left early, unable to bear staying one more second in a house that reminded her so much of Jace. As they headed out, Cyril hugged Jace's parents.

Jace's father said, "I hope you learned something decent from him. He always said you were a pain in the ass."

"Yeah, I think I learned humility. Then again, he and Jess were always watching over me to make sure it took."

"They still are," Jace's mother attested. "Don't disappoint them."

Cyril nodded, said his goodbyes, and headed out with Allegra and Rachael.

They took an autocab to the closest exo-jitney port.

As they rode in a nearly overcrowded jitney, Rachael said, "This probably isn't the best time, but I'm gonna bring it up anyway. If you two want some work to keep busy, I can find you something. Overseer is looking to hire more people for zero-G work."

"Sure," Cyril said. "I can't sit around with my thoughts anymore. I'd blow my brains out."

"Yeah, I'm in," Allegra said. "Just got my ship outta overhaul. Pass my name. I really need the money at this point."

"I'll shoot off a message to Overseer," Rachael stated.

"It's gonna be weird to go up now," Cyril muttered to no one in particular.

"Why will it be weird? We'll be up there with you," Allegra said.

"It's not really the *being up there* I'm thinking about. It's the *coming home and they're not there* that bothers me."

Allegra and Rachael knew what he meant but said nothing.

***

A week passed, and life went on. Work had become slow, and Cyril was burning through savings, so he kept himself occupied day in and day out. He picked up some shifts working as a mechanic for Stacy at the airfield. It gave him a little extra while keeping her company. He spent his days tearing apart old ship engines, riveting plating, and building LED strip lights. While he worked, he made no friends with any of the other mechanics, as he wasn't interested in getting to know anyone else. *The only way to not lose friends is not to have any.*

Finally, a job came in. Overseer sent an encrypted message to Cyril. *Hostage situation in Luyten space. Subcontract down from Arcturus Allied. Need immediate response.* The mention of Arcturus made him perk up.

He went into Stacy's office. "Hey, got a message for a zero-G job. Can you have my ship ready to go by tomorrow? Full rearm and power supply."

"Yeah, no problem." She didn't look up as she spoke.

"You okay?"

"I'm fine."

Cyril said nothing. He knew what *fine* meant: *"I'm here but don't bother me."* He sent a yes reply to the Overseer message and resumed riveting. Two minutes later, details came through.

MISSION: HOSTAGE RESCUE

TARGET: PLA OPERATIVES. 34 TOTAL HOSTAGES.

THREAT LEVEL: EXTREME. STATION UNDER PLA CONTROL. ENEMY STARFIGHTER SQUADRONS PATROLLING SURROUNDING SPACE. NEGOTIATIONS ONGOING.

PLA again. Cyril had gotten his revenge and felt nothing after it was done. Now they were back again. Would killing more of them make him feel better? Probably not, but he was curious. What would the PLA want with an Arcturus facility? Something was up. The PLA was extreme but not stupid. A hostage situation on an Arcturus facility seemed at the very least a situation worth investigating.

The next day, he and Allegra were maglocked atop a FOIL pad headed to Luyten, fully armed and ready to fight. Allegra's ship had gone through a total overhaul. She had to dip into her savings to pay for repairs. As a precaution, she added an extra layer of polymer mesh armor beneath all the plating which had the unfortunate effect of making her ship heavier in atmosphere. It wouldn't stop a missile impact, but gunfire would have a hell of a time taking her down. Cyril had burned through the rest of his money for his most recent refuel and rearm, so if he went down this time, that was the end of his career. The swinging sword of Damocles hanging above his head was closer now more than ever.

The FOIL pad leaped into Luyten space. The planet wasn't visible from their vantage point on the pad. They disengaged their mag locks, thrusted up, and inverted. The planet revealed itself. A large blue/green ball floated down below, and the second planetary pad hovered as well, awaiting their arrival. Luyten had a reputation as being a paradise, with lush green trees and fields, a temperate climate, and clean oceans. Somehow the planet had lucked out and ended up in the perfect position for its sun.

The two starfighters thrusted forward and let inertia carry them to the pad to not waste energy. They landed, mag locked again, and within one minute, they were in atmosphere. The gum drop wasn't as bad as it usually was due to an 8 percent drop in gravity compared to Proxima. The drop was minimal but still tickled their stomachs. Cyril and Allegra switched on their V/TOL turbines, ascended, and flew toward what would be their base of operations—Ignis Plateau Airfield.

Engineers had built Ignis into a cliffside for defensive purposes. The top of the cliff was lush with green grass and flowers, which was a stark contrast to the industrial girders and metallic doors below. An octagonal metal tunnel, about two hundred yards wide, led to the interior of the base. The interior landing area was three hundred yards deep inside the plateau. Blue and green lighting soaked everything as they entered, Allegra first, Cyril second. Their engines echoed loudly inside the tunnel as they came to a row of fighters. Squared-off landing spaces had been painted yellow on the floor. Allegra took space six, and Cyril took space five.

Rachael had already arrived and came out of the pilot's locker room to meet them. Cyril grabbed his personals from his cargo hold and walked alongside Allegra. Rachael powerwalked to cross the open tunnel space a bit faster. She was slightly out of breath when the three of them finally met. She hugged Cyril and Allegra, then led them to the briefing room.

Cyril had never been to Luyten, but he'd met plenty of its people over the years. They were always gorgeous, no matter which gender, though most fell into the nonbinary category. Something was in the air, water, or just the whole planet itself, but it seemed like all the most gorgeous people sprang up from Luyten. His thoughts drifted to Filly, wondering why they hadn't been selected for this assignment. More than likely, they were off world on another contract. Then he thought about his one-time hook up with Jenna nearly a year prior.

Then his thoughts drifted to Marie. He shook the thoughts away; it was neither the time nor the place.

Rachael caught him shaking his head as they walked together. "What's wrong?"

"*Huh?* Nothing. Luyten atmosphere seems different than Proxima. Might be the gravity too."

"Well, you better get your edge back soon. Negotiations haven't been going well."

"Wonderful," he said flatly.

They traversed a slew of hallways, then came to a large atrium area. Fake windows showing camera views of the fields above were fixed to the walls. Made life easier working underground if the view was a little nicer. A stone barrier surrounded a set of bushes and flowers that stuck out of the ground in the middle of the atrium. They circled around the flowerbed and toward a room labeled, BRIEFING ROOM, in the Luyten language, as well as the other Ekumen languages. They entered the orbital room—three ascending rows of padded seats, half empty and half full with starfighters and Sin Eaters, outlined the circumference—and saw several people pointing and making tactical suggestions around a large circular command table with white light beaming through it. Cyril noticed Olen, Glass, and Crow among the crowd of Sin Eaters. Olen was at the command table, working out tactics with Rex. Table lighting illuminated a see-through diagram of the Arcturus station from underneath. Glass and Crow sat among the seated crowd. Upon recognizing Cyril, they approached him.

"Eisner, never thought I'd see you again," Glass said as he proffered his hand.

Cyril shook it. "Likewise. How you doin'?"

"Still alive, thanks to you."

"You're welcome. How you doin', Crow?"

"Fine." The way she said *fine* told him, *"You scare the shit outta me."* He'd left a scarring impression on Ashcheron, one she wasn't soon to forget.

Outside of their combat gear, they looked completely different. Crow's long dirty-blond hair was pulled into a short ponytail. She had a kind face, nothing that gave the impression that she was a heavy weapons specialist. She also stood six inches taller than Glass and had a slender but tough frame, like a gymnast.

Glass's face was aging early—wrinkles and crow's feet along his eyes and a receding hairline that was turning from black to gray. He also had a stocky body, with big shoulders. He almost resembled a human tree trunk that had survived a rough storm.

Many of the other starfighters were new faces. The job called for people to be a little desperate, a little crazy, or both. The only face he recognized was Whitney "Roku" Quinn. She had extensive experience with zero-G combat and came highly recommended. In total, the squadron was twelve strong. The name designation for the mission was Silver Squadron.

The starfighter roster was:

CYRIL "SKYHAWK" EISNER

ALLEGRA "HONEY BADGER" CLINE

WHITNEY "ROKU" QUINN

RACHAEL "LOKI" NORRIS

HUNTER "RACETRACK" TREADMEN

CHARLIE "ONYX" BLAKE

DAVID "SMOKER" BOLLMAN

SAMI "FLATTOP" JUNE

Fergie "Runner" Barlow

Tiffany "Diva" Sweet

Franklin "Shifter" House

Flight Lead: Mikhail "Rex" Reston

As for Sin Eaters, only three squads of four. Infiltration and stealth meant less bodies shuffling around. Lower numbers also meant they could use smaller ships for approach should the company authorize dock-and-breach protocol on the station's hull, and they wouldn't implement that unless negotiations completely failed.

Cyril set his bag in a chair, with the rest of the squadron, and approached Rex, who was arguing with Olen next to the command table. "Breaching won't matter if air cover can't get you to the hull, and by then, the hostages will be dead!"

"You need to accept that we can't save everyone. Acceptable losses are, well, acceptable," Olen responded stoically.

Olen uttering the phrase *acceptable losses* made Cyril's respect for the man drop ten points. He was getting tired of hearing that statement and how expendable certain people were. "Sir, Skyhawk and Honey Badger reporting in," Cyril announced to Rex.

Rex turned his head. "Thank you, Eisner. Are we gonna have a repeat of your behavior on Ashcheron?"

"No," Cyril said bluntly.

"You sure? These are the same people. PLA."

"It won't happen again." Once again, he was blunt.

Rex was silent and studied Cyril's face. Cyril looked sincere. "Glad to hear it." Rex refocused on the command table. "We're still working out our approach vector for landing craft. Mr. Olen here believes we should land in the cargo hold and breach the doors with charges."

"It will vent any terrorists surrounding the doors into space and give us a way in. The emergency doors will take fifteen seconds to fully engage, just enough time to get at least one squad in."

"There's no way they haven't thought of that. They'll be using hostages as shields in every place possible till they get what they want."

"What do they want?" Allegra asked.

"That's not your concern, pilot," said Ellen Moriarty's shrill voice as she entered the room.

"Oh, God, not you," Cyril groaned.

Two bodyguards wearing suits followed Moriarty and took up a free space next to Rex, then surveyed the station diagram on the table.

"What these terrorists want is not what you're here for. You're here to shut down their operation and recover the station undamaged. Is that clear?" Moriarty decreed.

"Yes, ma'am," Rex said.

"I am not a *ma'am*. Remember that."

Rex raised an eyebrow at Cyril.

"Nonbinary. I didn't know the first time, either," Cyril said.

"Old friend?" Rex asked.

"No. Best of enemies."

"And I'd like to keep it that way, scum," Moriarty said to Cyril.

"Why are you here anyway?" Cyril asked with rancor. "Don't you have a misandrist meeting that you're missing?"

"I'm here on behalf of Arcturus to ensure the recovery of the station. I'll be observing your every move. So, a plan with a little"— they glared at Olen—"*tact* would be appreciated."

Olen knew they had just vetoed his plan.

Rex shook his head and cleared his throat. "Anyway, we're still figuring out the best way in. Do the three of you have any ideas? It's open season." Rex pointed at the trio of Cyril, Rachael, and Allegra.

They studied the station diagram on the table touch screen—a sleek but utilitarian station, not designed to look good so much as to be functional. Arcturus had named the station *Lightfoot*, which consisted of a large donut-shaped outer ring, divided into eight substations— flight command, crew quarters, medical and exercise, recreation, hangar bay, cafeteria, communications, and engine core— spinning counterclockwise around a central cylinder hub that they had built crossways into a large asteroid. The communications section had a large radio dish atop it. Everything else looked very plain and simple—a clean donut save for one giant sprinkle on top. A pair of connecting elevators led into the asteroid section in the middle, one between flight command and crew quarters, the other on the opposite side between the hangar and the cafeteria.

Its nearby and gigantic bright red star was also, either ironically or intentionally, named Arcturus. Metal plating coated the central hub inside the asteroid for mag boots, as there was no gravity, and the rock's surface would protect all the lab areas from solar radiation and allow the crew to work without contamination. The ring section also had lead-lined walls and water shielding built into its plating to protect from the solar effects of the nearby sun, though it was not as effective as the rockface.

The key problem was approaching without being seen. LADAR would easily detect any incoming ships and starfighter squadrons. Opening any doors would signal airlock entry, and blasting holes could depressurize the station. Any sign of forced entry or attack would mean the PLA could start offing hostages in retaliation or destroy the whole station as a last ditch move. It seemed an impossible scenario. No way in or out without being detected.

The trio stood there gazing at the station layout, just as befuddled as the rest of them.

"Someone say something," Rex instructed.

Cyril sighed. "Well, can't blast your way in. That's for sure. Can we get a negotiator inside for in person negotiations?"

"They're refusing any entry till we agree to their demands," Moriarty stated.

"Which are…?"

Moriarty said nothing.

"Come on, Moriarty. You gotta throw us a fucking bone here. You want the station back or not?"

They pondered for a moment as they leaned on the table, then relented. "The station is the production hub for the inoculation agent for Project Samson."

"Samson? The shit Loki and I having been spraying across the Ekumen?"

"Yes. They want the program shut down because they believe forced inoculation violates civil rights to all Ekumen territories. Which it isn't, because all government agencies have approved the drops. Without this station, we lose our ability to produce more of the inoculation agent. We would have to start over and build a new facility. It requires a zero-gravity environment to be perfectly formulated."

"Really? Couldn't have built it a little closer to home? Would have saved you a lot of trouble."

"Terran space has a higher tax fee for zero-gravity stations."

"So, it was cheaper to be out here?" Cyril asked incredulously.

"Yes."

"Man, you rich bastards are all the same. Spend pennies to make a dollar. Don't give a shit about who gets hurt or why."

"It's called capitalism, pig. We're all here for the same reason. Figure it out." Moriarty pushed themselves from the table and headed for the door, followed by their two bodyguards.

Once the door closed, Cyril said to Rex, "I promise, deep down, they're a ray of sunshine."

Everyone in the room laughed.

***

Hours ticked by without them developing any concrete plan. An EMP bomb would shut down the power to the station, allowing for ships to approach and dock, but that still left the hostages vulnerable to execution. That was a no-go. A Sin Eater proposed a theory about using a gum drop attack, where the team could attach a portable FOIL drive to the exterior of the station to FOIL into Luyten's atmosphere close to the ground, allowing an assault team to breach and quickly clear the station while the terrorist cell inside was in disarray. The committee reminded the Sin Eater that damage to the station was out of the question. Thus, that idea was nixed.

Every time someone formed a proposal, something would undercut the execution. LADAR would detect incoming ships, frontal assault would endanger hostages and the station's safety, and negotiations, from the sparse info being leaked to the crew, were not going well. The leader of the cell, a Terran man named Kingston, was hellbent on shutting down the entire facility. He believed Arcturus was hiding something and demanded they come clean, or he would activate its self-destruction. Twelve hours remained before the deadline.

Cyril drank a cup of coffee in the mess hall as he stared at the station layout on a wall monitor. A few people passed through to grab food or coffee as they headed to finish their work. The room felt extremely clean, almost too clean, with rounded edges on everything. Cyril felt like every surface was made of bubble gum and could pop at any second.

He thought he had an idea for a moment, then, of course, something knocked it out as an option. He contemplated sending camera drones into the facility to short circuit their communications and LADAR system, allowing them a fast approach with dropships. The problem, however, was twofold: one, how the hell would they get them inside the station, and two, drones that size had rotors that made a buzzing noise, which the enemy could quickly detect if out in the open. It would never work. He hurled his coffee across the room and placed his hands on his hips. A seething anger grew in him, and it wasn't just anger about the mission.

Rachael and Allegra entered to see the brown coffee stain running down the wall and Cyril standing at the viewscreen. Rachael's hair was in a ponytail. "I know Luyten isn't exactly known for its coffee, but it's not that bad."

"Not helping, Rach," Cyril said sternly.

She didn't reply. He wasn't in the mood for sarcasm. Rachael and Allegra each made themselves a cup of coffee, as well as a third one to replace Cyril's. Allegra handed him his new cup, which he sheepishly accepted.

"I just don't get it. It's impossible."

"Nothing's impossible," Rachael said.

"Cool. Gimme a solution right now." He sipped his watered-down coffee. "On the spot."

Rachael shrugged silently.

"Exactly."

"Crazy idea. Would it be possible to FOIL into the cargo bay area?" Allegra asked. "We can get the Sin Eaters in there and do a manual bypass on the airlock doors."

"I thought of it already. The problem is spatial placement. You have such a small margin of error that you'd have maybe a 10 percent chance of getting it right, otherwise you'd end up with a cross FOIL. And then you're totally fucked. Are you willing to bet on 10 percent?"

"No, not really, but 10 percent is better than zero, so we'll put that one in the back pocket."

"You do that." Cyril rubbed his forehead and drank his coffee. He groaned at the lack of flavor. He frowned and went to the cabinet to find sugar.

"I thought you always took your coffee black with no sugar," Allegra noted.

"I do, but when I can't taste any flavor or feel the caffeine, I'd rather have something instead of nothing. Trash coffee is still coffee."

"There's caffeine in there; you just can't see it," Rachael said.

"Yeah, well, I can't see what I can't see. So, one packet of sugar it is." Cyril poured in a packet of raw sugar, stirred, and sipped. It was bittersweet but tasted better than hot water.

Allegra approached the viewscreen, brows furrowed.

Cyril stood alongside her. "What's up? You look like someone just took a shit in your oven."

"I think I have an idea. Follow me." Allegra turned and left the room.

Cyril cocked an eyebrow at Rachael, then they both followed.

The trio headed to the briefing room. Rex, Olen, and Glass were still pitching ideas for attack, but nothing stuck. The other pilots and Sin Eaters had left the room, bored out of their minds. Allegra rushed in and pulled up the station's schematics. Rex, Olen, and Glass looked at her, confused.

"Something catch your eye, Honey Badger?" Rex asked curiously.

Allegra ignored him and scrolled through the layout. She cut the schematics in half to get an interior view of the station. She pulled up the cafeteria section of the ring and found what she was looking for. "What's this?" She pointed to a rectangular shaft in the middle of the section.

Olen craned his head to see what she was pointing at. "That's the garbage chute. Any materials not needed for the station are dumped there weekly and released into space. The station is at the Lagrange point between Luyten and the Arcturus star and angled so all debris flies toward it."

"That's your way in. Look. It says here that only the airlock system signals a change in air pressure. Anything in the chute goes into a zero-G space and sits for a week. If you bypass that door, you can climb up, and you guys are in."

"We already figured that as a possibility, but we need to actually reach the station first. So unless you have a way to teleport us inside without a cross FOIL, I'm all ears."

"I do. One sec." She hit the light switch to dim the room to 10 percent. "Does anyone have a flashlight?"

"Yeah, here." Rex held up a pen light.

"All right, come stand right here." She pointed to a spot on the floor.

Rex walked over and stood, confused.

"Now, Eisner, you stand right here." She pointed to another spot on the floor, five yards from Rex.

Cyril obeyed, also confused. "I hope there's a point to all this."

"Rex, shine your light at Eisner," Allegra said.

Rex shone it right in Cyril's face. Cyril raised his hand to block the light and saw spots.

"All right, so Cyril is the station, and you're the sun." She walked backward five meters, turned and hunched, then crept toward Cyril. "We know they can see us on approach to the station because of LADAR and the sunlight, but… they can't see"—Allegra popped up over Cyril's shoulder—"what they can't see."

Rex finally got it. "We use the asteroid's shadow to approach. They'll never see us visually if anyone is looking outside. That's actually kinda brilliant."

"But we still have the issue of LADAR detection," Glass said. "Their scopes will immediately detect our ships."

"So, we don't use ships," Allegra said.

Everyone eyed her, confused again.

Cyril craned his head to give her a bizarre look. "What? Wanna try that again?"

"Do we have any booster packs on base?" Allegra asked.

"Yeah, of course. We always have those available for zero-G situations," Olen stated.

"We FOIL in with one transport ship and three starfighters. The transport is a dummy. We'll say that a negotiator is on board to resolve terms. Might actually want to have one just in case. But the real deal is the starfighters. We FOIL in five hundred kilometers away… with four Sin Eaters piggybacking on each of the starfighter's wings."

The room fell so silent that they could hear ghosts talking.

"Fucking what did you say?" Glass yelled.

"The Sin Eaters will be secured to the wings, and upon FOILing in, the ships will fly forward, and they'll have to… hold on? I guess."

"Let–let's–let's–let's go back to the last part. You want to FOIL… into the vacuum of space… with my men on the wings of your ships," said a shocked Olen. "And then what?"

"Then we… launch them."

"*Launch* them?"

"Yeah. We…" Allegra grabbed Rachael's hair and pulled out the hair tie holding up her ponytail.

Rachael yelped as her hair came free and cascaded into a long dark mane.

Allegra wrapped the tie around her thumb and aimed it at the command table. "We launch them." She released the tie. It landed on the table with a soft thump.

Olen, Rex, and Glass leaned on the table to view the schematics and quietly agreed. It really was the only option.

"This is absolutely insane," Rex said. "And we're absolutely gonna do it."

"There are two issues though. Distance and speed." Rachael collected her hair tie and put it back in. "If we're that far away, it'll take hours to get to the station even with booster packs. Also, why so far away to start?"

"We need enough distance to properly build speed to launch the Sin Eaters. We start too fast, it'll turn them into paste. If we're too close, they might see the launches. We'll have to slowly get the starfighters to a speed where we can then launch the Sin Eaters toward the station. They'll stay in *Lightfoot*'s shadow on approach while we run a diversion to keep the PLA occupied."

"And how fast do we need to be going before the clock runs out?" Cyril asked. "There's also that pesky issue of breathing."

"Anyone got a calculator?" Olen asked.

Rex raised his left hand to show his watch had a calculator feature. He determined the distance to the station with the amount of time reasonable enough for flight to not rouse suspicion. He saw the number and sighed. "The ships would need to be traveling at over eight hundred kilometers per hour to reach the station in an hour." He dropped his left arm to the table with a defeated thump.

"One hour of time, we're flying through the vacuum of space at a speed that would almost break the sound barrier in atmosphere. Are you insane?" Glass yelled.

"You'll need to slowly decelerate during the hour," Allegra said. "Use your booster packs only when you need to so you don't waste fuel. It'll be tight, but it's doable. It's like any other deceleration maneuver; you're just doing it with your suits, not a ship. Your people should be small enough to avoid sensor detection, and exterior cameras won't see you in the station's shadow."

"And if we reach the surface of the asteroid, then what? Our booster packs will probably be out of fuel. We'll bounce off it and tumble into space."

"Cyril, pull up the mineral composition of the *Lightfoot*'s asteroid."

Cyril pressed some buttons on the table and disconnected the asteroid from the station. He saw what she was looking for. "*Lightfoot*'s asteroid is type-M. Covered with iron and nickel on its surface. A slight magnetic field, and too small for gravity or an atmosphere. But iron and nickel..."

"Mag boots," Allegra said.

"Mag boots," Cyril repeated. "Goddamn, Allie. It's nuts, but it could work. The Sin Eaters work their way around the asteroid, traverse one of the connecting struts to the cafeteria section, and head up the trash chute. There are no windows on the inner section, so no eyes will be watching. Bypass the airlock inside the trash chute, and they're in. We stay outside and pretend to negotiate with the PLA while they secure the place, section by section. No reason they would be watching cameras too. They'll think the place is impregnable. Fuck, it might just work."

"The Sin Eaters will need to stay off comms for security's sake, so we'll need some other way of getting a signal back for confirmation," Olen said.

"Morse code," Rachael added. "Garrison used it on Sela. Worked well enough. The raiders either didn't pick it up or they didn't know what it was."

"Then, that's our signal," Olen said. "I'll brief my guys on the terms we'll use for confirmation before launch. We'll also need to use only hand signals once on the rock's surface. No radio. Too dicey."

"And what if one of our people misses the surface? What then?" Glass asked.

"My recommendation," Allegra replied. "Don't miss."

***

The next three hours were a scramble to get both teams ready for the attack. Olen gave the Sin Eaters cheat sheets for the morse code words they would need during the insertion, such as *Touchdown, Inside, Secure*, as well as several others. All twelve soldiers were provided with booster packs to wear during their flight, along with a reserve tank attached to the right-hand side. If the deceleration went off perfectly, all the soldiers would arrive with 8 percent remaining in the main fuel tank. The reserve would grant them an extra ten. They also attached spare oxygen tanks to their legs and backpacks. Due to weight distribution and movement, the soldiers reduced their kits to the basic main assault rifle, handgun, knife, med kit, and engineer kit for manual bypasses. The three demolition experts between the three squads were given one satchel charge, flash bomb drones, and primer cord in case of a breaching situation. It was hoped to be avoided, but their luck had been short lately. Better to have it and not need it than to need it and not have it.

As for the starfighters, only Roku had the proper flight time in zero G to be one of the "launchers" for a Sin Eater squad. Besides her, everyone else had only moderate experience. It wouldn't be impossible for anyone else, but better hands were requested for the plan to go off without a hitch. The launcher ships also needed wingspans large enough to accommodate two Sin Eaters per wing. To call in a favor, Rex sent a courier drone with an emergency work request to Proxima. The crew gathered atop the grassy plateau to wait for the arrival of two more starfighters.

"So, who are we waiting for?" Rachael asked.

"Wolf and Zeroman," Rex answered.

"Wolf and Zeroman? Those two are legends. Best starfighters in Terran space," Cyril said, surprised.

"They owe me for saving their asses a few months back on Tulson. They should be arriving any moment now."

Right as Rex finished his sentence, a FOIL pad leaped into the upper atmosphere, twenty kilometers away. The crew heard the soft pop of its spatial displacement and watched it descend.

"There. See? We're saved."

The pad, which looked no bigger than a rectangular block in the distance, fell rapidly without slowing.

"Um, guys, why is it still falling?" Cyril asked.

They stood and stared silently as the pad picked up speed till it slammed into the ground. They saw the fireball explosion, then a few moments later, they heard the boom, which only sounded like a soft *pop* from that distance. Someone smacked their lips, unsure of what had just happened. No one moved. Even the insects stopped screeching.

Finally, Rachael clicked her tongue. "Well, I got a bottle of gin in my bag if anybody wants a drink." She headed downstairs to the hangar bay.

"I'll have one," Cyril said, following along.

"Me too," Allegra repeated.

The crew dispersed and followed the trio.

Rex loudly sighed. "Fuck it." He decided he needed a drink himself.

Given the circumstances, the next two qualified for the job were Cyril and Rachael. They didn't want it, but Rex overruled them. Both their ships, as well as Roku's, were modified with cradles on the top sides of their wings, two pockets per wing. The Sin Eaters would cocoon themselves inside the pockets, which all had small conical windscreens on the front. Once in the vacuum of space, the wind screens would detach, and the ships would slowly accelerate to eight hundred KPH. The Sin Eaters would flatten themselves as much as possible, and the ships would slowly decelerate. The soldiers would continue forward with inertia over the course of one hour before finally landing, hopefully, on the metal rich rock of *Lightfoot* station. Unlike Cyril's rocket pods, the wing pods were not detachable without extensive mechanical work. It was a gamble if the PLA inside the station would become suspicious, seeing those compartments bolted on the three ships, but it was a risk they had to take. Due to the length of the flight, they added secondary air tanks to each starfighter, which gave them all one extra hour of breathable air.

Cyril surveyed his ship and hated how misshapen it had become. The cocoon-shaped pockets looked like weird half eggs riveted to the upper wing plating. His ship would carry Glass, Crow, and their two other squadmates, Krupenski and Goll. As he was about to climb into his ship, he noticed another starfighter, David "Smoker" Bollman—the oldest starfighter Cyril had ever seen—sitting by himself on a munitions crate behind his ship, resting his elbows on his knees and staring at the floor.

Cyril walked over. "Hey, Smoker, you good?" He noticed Smoker had been crying.

"Yeah, I'm fine."

"Are you good enough to fly?"

"I'll be fine."

"What's going on with you?"

"Wife passed away a little while ago. We just had our anniversary date."

Cyril sat beside him. "Sorry, man."

"Happens to all of us. No one beats the clock, I guess."

Cyril thought about Cat, Jess, and Jace. No one beat the clock, and if they thought they could, the clock got smashed. He didn't really know what words of comfort he could offer to an old guy like Bollman. All he could do was speak from experience. "A guy I knew said that every choice you make, you gotta make them count. I'm sure your wife made the right choice being with you."

"Who said that?"

"Doesn't matter. He's dead now."

"Oh. Another one down, *huh*?"

"Yup. Another one down. If you don't mind me asking, how did she die?"

"Cancer. It was everywhere."

"Fuck."

"She fought it for two whole years. I'd go out to make enough money to pay for her treatment. We would just barely scrape by. I wasn't there enough for her. I was barely there when she had her treatments. But she didn't complain once. Not one time. Even when the bills kept piling up, still nothing." He wept again.

Cyril thought about Marie and the future that he'd blown off with being selfish.

"Never once. No complaints, even at the end. Excuse me." Bollman stood and began to walk away.

"Hey," Cyril called after him.

Bollman turned, tears streaking his face.

"Just hang back when we're out there today. We'll do the work. Don't engage unless you have to."

Bollman nodded, turned, and walked away.

Cyril sat on the munitions crate and listened to the mechanics work their magic to finish Rachael's ship before they headed out. He looked down the long tunnel leading outside. It glowed so bright that he couldn't see the horizon, just pinkish light. He thought about Bollman having nothing to go home to. At the very least, he felt he could relate to that.

CHAPTER 18

WORTH DYING FOR

The FOIL pad soundlessly leaped into Luyten space. All twelve starfighters and a cargo transport detached from the pad and ascended vertically. Then the transport escorted by Skyhawk, Loki, and Roku thrusted forward and began the five-hundred-kilometer trek toward the station. The other nine starfighters flew behind the main group and kept their distance. In the great distance, the Arcturus red giant star burned brightly in rich tones of red and orange fire. From their position, *Lightfoot* station wasn't visible, even with full polarization on their canopies. They had perfectly calculated the angle of attack though so all the Sin Eaters would land undetected by external cameras. The three fighters and the transport cruised forward in the shadow of the station, a small margin of movement, and slowly gained acceleration to release the Sin Eaters.

They had incessantly worked out the ruse back at base. The wings of each starfighter held the "eggs" of Sin Eaters, ready to begin their hour-long dive toward the rock face. The ships accelerated, slowly pushing their throttle forward. Harsh bursts could kill the Sin Eaters— or, at the very least, render them incapacitated. They crept up their engine output, one hundred KPH, two hundred, three hundred, up and up, till they finally reached eight hundred KPH. Each pilot gave the morse code signal for *Go*. The Sin Eaters lifted off the front housing of their makeshift eggs and slowly pulled themselves out.

Glass, flying to Cyril's left, gave a thumbs up, and Cyril reciprocated. Then the crew sent out the morse code for *Launch*. The starfighters and the transport decelerated, and the Sin Eaters drifted forward with inertia, flying from the ships and into the sunlight. They wouldn't know who had made it safely to *Lightfoot* station for close to an hour. In the meantime, the three starfighters and the transport shifted to stay on course but reduced speed to six hundred KPH. The other nine ships followed behind, keeping watch for enemy fighters.

For an hour, the crew flew silently. No one spoke, no radio chatter. Cyril played some soft music and switched on the autopilot. Nothing was registering on his scopes. In space, due to distance, it felt like nothing was actually moving. Space was, to put it plainly, filled with a lot of nothing in between the somethings. It was visually impossible to register movement without nearby reference points. Establishing parallax was impossible. Everything regarding speed and direction was instrument-based only. During the entire flight, the Arcturus star never grew bigger, and it felt like Cyril was just relaxing in his ship, taking a break.

The calm before the storm.

Fifty-eight minutes later, a morse code signal came through. Cyril had been dozing from boredom. The beeping snapped him awake—the signal for *Touchdown*. A second code came through—*Eleven*. The meaning was obvious. Only eleven of the twelve Sin Eaters had touched down safely. One had either missed their mark and had flown toward the sun or hadn't decelerated enough to avoid being turned into paste on the rockface. They wouldn't know till they completed the mission.

The giant donut-shaped station's silhouette was now visible, with a rock shoved in the middle and a massive cylinder sticking vertically through it. The donut spun around the rock like a bicycle wheel. The ships decelerated, adjusted course, and entered the sunlight. They circled around and stopped six hundred meters from the clockwise-spinning ring section.

Silver Squadron turned their comms on as Moriarty hailed the station. "*Lightfoot* station, this is Director Ellen Moriarty with Arcturus Allied. We're here to negotiate terms for the release of the station."

Release of the station, Cyril thought. *Not the people. Fucking bitch.*

A male PLA member replied, "Ms. Moriarty, how good of you to join us. We know you very well. Your reputation as a hard woman precedes you."

"I'm not a woman. Don't forget it."

"My apologies. I was unaware. But what I am aware of is that your station is housing some very dark secrets. The PLA will not stand for such oppression of the masses. We know what Project Samson is."

All communications with the starfighters cut off from the negotiations between the PLA and Moriarty. Cyril checked his radio band and antenna. Everything was working perfectly. Someone was jamming them.

Cyril said, "Skyhawk to Rex, switch to auxiliary channel Beta Hotel." They switched over. "Rex, we're being jammed from the negotiations."

"Well, I'm sure whatever they're saying doesn't involve us."

"That's not what I mean. The moment he mentioned Project Samson, the comms got cut. That seem suspicious to you?"

Rex was quiet for a moment. "It's not our problem, Cyril. Stay on station and be ready for shots to fire. I have a feeling that this Moriarty is not a particularly skilled negotiator."

"They're a massive cunt. I know firsthand. It's about to be a dogfight. Do you see anything on scopes?"

"I've got a squadron patrolling ten kilometers away. Looks like eight of them. They seem to be circling the station from a distance. For now, they're just watching."

"All right, keep it tight. Things are probably gonna go south real fast."

They switched to the main channel and waited. It was killing Cyril to not know what they were discussing. Then a morse code signal came through to the crew—*Inside*. The Sin Eaters had made it through the garbage chute and into the station interior.

Outside, nothing moved, and no one spoke. Cyril sweated, feeling twitchy and antsy, like a thousand eyes were staring at him. There probably were.

A silent explosion blasted from the ring in the crew quarters section. A car-sized hole cracked open. Three human bodies flew out and tumbled into space. None of them were Sin Eaters.

"Well, it was nice while it lasted," Olen said.

Cyril's LADAR lit up as the eight enemy fighters changed course toward them.

"They're onto us," Olen continued. "We're working our way through the station now. We'll clear the ring, then head to the lab area. Olen out."

"All starfighters, pick your targets and go," Rex ordered. "Good luck, Silver Squadron."

The fighters dispersed and split into pairs and trios. Skyhawk, Loki, and Honey Badger formed up, with Honey Badger taking the lead. The transport ship, along with Smoker, dove and hid in the shadow of the rock face. Cyril had explained the situation regarding Bollman with Rex before they had left, and Rex had agreed that Bollman was a liability. Rex had assigned Bollman as nothing more than a glorified security guard for the duration of the mission. The PLA wouldn't risk shooting at the asteroid for fear of hitting the station. They'd be safe.

The rest of Silver Squadron scrambled and chose their targets. Rex bagged one right away in a high-speed flyby. The PLA fighters scattered, then spun and twirled, catching a missile lock on any target they could. Flattop took a missile into their cockpit. They burst into a red fireball, burned for one second, then the fires dissipated. The remnants of their ship tumbled toward the Arcturus star. Onyx pulled in behind Flattop's assassin and let loose with a string of gunfire. The enemy fighter shredded into metal ribbons, and the pilot ejected at the last second. Onyx trailed the ejected pilot and finished the job with more gunfire, turning the PLA pilot into a mess of blood and guts that hurtled into the void.

The fight was tough but didn't last long. All eight PLA fighters went down, while Silver Squadron lost two total: Flattop and Racetrack. The remaining nine fighters formed up and headed toward the station. As they quietly celebrated their victory, a massive capital ship, a PLA cruiser, leaped into the station's orbit, like a furious sentinel storming in to defend its territory.

"Oh, fuck me," Rex murmured. He had intended his words to be private, but he had accidentally left his mic hot. The whole squadron agreed with him. *Oh, fuck me.*

The four-hundred-meter-long capital ship was rounded on both ends like a javelin, using thrust gravity systems to create an artificial gravity environment during travel, and thus, the flooring was perpendicular to the nose of the ship. However, all flooring sat upon a gimbal system that would rotate ninety degrees for when the ship would enter an atmospheric environment and gravity returned to normal. During zero acceleration, all crewmembers wore mag boots to keep themselves upright.

Allegra sprang into action, while Rex was stuck in his stupor. "All fighters, hide in the shadow of the station. Get behind it! It'll buy us time!"

The fighters dipped their noses and punched their throttles. One by one, they fell behind the shadow of *Lightfoot* station and killed their engines. They spun over with their thrusters and magnetically attached to the rock face wherever possible to hide their transponder signals. To the capital ship, they were just more chunks of metal in the rock.

"This is a hell of a pickle, *huh*, guys?" Runner jested.

"Shut up before I shoot you myself on principle," Loki fired back.

"I'm totally open to suggestions, and make them quick," Rex said, attempting to reassert his command. "They'll probably be launching more fighters soon." He sounded out of breath, possibly hyperventilating.

"We don't have anywhere near the firepower to take that thing down. Moriarty, are you back on this channel?" Cyril asked with urgency.

"I'm here, pig," they responded.

"Oh, save it, bitch! Does the station have any weapons at all?'

"It was never designed for combat. It's a research station."

"All right, well that's no good."

"We need to at least destroy the bridge. Hit that, and the ship is crippled," Onyx denoted.

"They've got guns all over that thing. No way we're getting anywhere close," Loki said.

"Well, how would you like us to hit that thing? Osmosis?"

"Yes," Smoker interjected. Everyone fell silent. "The FOIL pad. Use it as a weapon."

"You want to create a cross FOIL?" Runner screamed. "Are you nuts?"

"We're already knee deep in crazy ideas on this one. What's one more?" Allegra agreed. "Besides, you got any bright ideas, squadron leader Rex?"

Rex said nothing.

"Yeah, cross FOIL it is."

"I'm way too old for this," Rex groaned. "FOIL pad 3B, this is squadron leader Rex. I have a very… unusual request for you, and you're going to hate it. We have a PLA cruiser encroaching on our position with no means of taking it down. We… need you to cross FOIL into it."

"What? Are you insane?" the FOIL pilot screamed.

"Scan the area around the station for the cruiser's location, then set the coordinates for the bridge and eject before the pad leaps. We need a solution now. None of us goes home if you don't do it!"

The pilot said nothing.

Rex added, "I'll make sure you get a nice fat bonus. How about that?"

"It better be a good one. Scanning… got it. Setting the cruiser's location and locking in coordinates now. I'm headed for the escape pod. You all better come back for me!"

"Let's hope this works, and then we'll see. Good luck."

The transmission ended.

"So, when will we know if it's been taken out? Not like we can hear anything," Loki pointed out.

"I've got eyes on the cruiser. More fighters out there too," Smoker said.

The cruiser sat motionless. A second squadron of twelve fighters had launched and patrolled the area around the station. Then suddenly, the cruiser split in half. The FOIL pad seemed to apparate into existence in the middle of the ship's hull. It had missed the bridge due to the cruiser moving a couple hundred meters forward from the time the FOIL pad operator had set the coordinates. But even so, the ship was now bisected and totally destroyed. Bodies were sucked out of the opened sections of the ship and spun off into space. The metal girders, beams, and cables wrenched and ripped away from each other as the inertial displacement pushed the two halves in opposite directions, like a large boulder landing in a river and splitting the current in two directions.

The PLA fighter squadron came about and returned to the ship to examine the wreckage. Then the cruiser running lights lost power, and it went totally dead.

"Silver Squadron, it's down," Smoker announced.

"That's our cue. Engage now," Rex yelled.

Silver Squadron fired their engines, detached from the rock face, and came about to attack. They zipped toward the enemy fighters and sucker-punched two of them. Immediate kills. The fighters panicked and split apart. Every man for themselves. Cyril and Loki dashed around to avoid the cruiser's ever growing debris field as they chased a fighter through the wreckage. Missile lock was impossible with the amount of debris, so it became a guns-only battle.

Cyril fired a pair of squirts and caught no joy. Loki fired one herself and raked the enemy fighter's left wing. Wing damage was negligible in the vacuum of space, however. The fighter did a full one hundred eighty spin and fired its guns while flying in reverse—an expert maneuver which meant an expert pilot.

Skyhawk and Loki peeled apart from each other, dodging the oncoming tracer rounds. The orange stream of gunfire soundlessly blazed past Cyril's cockpit as he spun, rolled, and dashed toward the station, while Loki headed toward the Arcturus star. The enemy fighter gave chase on her, caught tone, and fired one missile. She popped a set of flares, and the missile exploded harmlessly behind her. The PLA fighter continued chasing, closing the distance.

"Loki, I'm on the way. Just keep moving," Cyril yelled.

"Get him off me," she yelled.

Streams of gunfire seared past her hull as she dashed left and right, pulling harsh G forces in every direction. She was breathing so hard that she was on the verge of hyperventilation. Cyril punched his throttle to full power and rocketed toward her. He ascended slightly above the enemy fighter's tail, yawed ninety degrees, and did an inertial flyby while squeezing the trigger on his guns. A stream of gunfire tore through the ship from stern to bow and split it in half. Its pilot took a barrage through the chest and died immediately.

"Enemy fighter down. I got him, Loki," he said.

"Thanks, Skyhawk. I owe you," she responded, huffing and wheezing.

They formed on each other's wings to head toward the station as the battle still raged. The enemy squadron was apparently all aces and giving Silver a hard time. Eight ships remained. As they approached, Runner made an incorrect maneuver and crashed into a section of the ring. The impact obliterated the bow of his ship, and he slowly tumbled forward, end over end, but he was alive in his cockpit. With his ship's systems inoperable, he had no choice but to eject.

"All systems failed! I'm punching out," Runner announced on comms.

Roku yelled, "Runner, *wait!*"

But he ejected before he heard her. He jettisoned from the cockpit, but in his panic, he had forgotten to reorient the cockpit to aim into space. He slammed right into the rockface, completely pulverized. The remnants of his body tumbled off and spun slowly clockwise as it drifted from the station.

Cyril got on the radio. "Has anyone heard from any of the Sin Eaters? Olen, Glass, do you read me?"

The radio filled with gunfire and shouting. Glass yelled, "We're pinned down in the strut between flight command and crew quarters. There's more here than we thought! We're gon—"

The radio went dead.

"Glass? *Glass!*"

No response.

"Fuck it, I'm goin' in." Cyril dipped and headed for the hangar bay section of the station.

"Cyril! *Cyril,*" Loki yelled.

Cyril ignored her.

"Goddammit, you impulsive bastard!" She turned about and followed.

***

Cyril flew around the station toward the hangar bay and saw the door was shut tight without a way to open it. He slammed his fist into the wall of his cockpit in frustration, then noticed another section of the station with a blown-out hole from the first explosion of the battle inside. Cyril ascended, inverted, and mag-locked onto the deck plating next to the hole. He killed his ship's power and climbed out. Upon setting foot on the ring, he engaged his mag boots and walked to his ship's cargo hold to retrieve his Beretta handgun and gun belt, then approached the hole.

The shadow of another starfighter flew overhead—Loki. She landed next to Cyril's ship.

"Rachael, I got this! Get back in the sky," he yelled.

As she descended her ship's foot ladder, she said, "One, there is no sky. Two, no. Three, fuck you, I'm coming with you." She walked toward him as the air battle continued silently, shapes and shadows blazing through the harsh Arcturus sunlight.

Cyril shook his head. "No, you're not. I can handle this just fine."

"Just you against what could be an entire army? That's great odds."

"I can handle it! Head back up!" He turned and headed toward the blown-out hole.

"You'll never survive on your own!"

"I've made it this far, haven't I?"

"You're not trying to be a hero! You have a death wish!"

Cyril stopped walking and stood silent as Allegra's Diamondback chased a PLA fighter overhead.

Rachael walked up beside him. "You need help. I'm staying."

He smiled ruefully at her. "You're incredibly stupid, and I appreciate it. Are you armed?"

"No. But I'm sure we'll find something."

The radio crackled with Rex's voice. "Loki, Skyhawk, what are you doing? We need you back up here!"

Cyril smiled. "Sorry boss, can't—*krrrch*—it just—*krrrch*—radio is—*krrrch*—fuck off." He switched his radio to comms between just him and Loki. "You ready?"

"Nope, but let's do it anyway."

As they approached the hole, they crouched to peer inside the crew quarters. Personal items floated about. No bodies though. They had all been sucked into space. Cyril and Rachael disengaged their mag boots and slowly pulled themselves inside. Once they reached the floor, gravity seemed to right itself as the centrifugal force took hold. From inside, the hole was on the right-hand side of the room.

Cyril unholstered his gun and flipped off the safety. Cubicle-sized bunkbed areas filled the room, each tailored with personal photos, data pads, game systems, books, and many other small knickknacks. Most things had been built into the walls, housed in glass cases, or secured by Velcro in the event of decompression. Cyril and Rachael proceeded down the row of cubicles toward a wall screen at the far end. Power still ran to the section despite it being decompressed. Cyril touched the menu system and brought up the station layout. A three-dimensional map appeared, showing the ring section.

"Okay, we're right here in crew quarters." Cyril pointed to the map. "Glass said they were pinned down in the strut just outside of here. Airlocks connect each section, so we can pass through here"— Cyril pointed to a short connecting hallway between crew quarters and flight command—"and there's no chance of decompressing the rest of the station. You see any weapons anywhere?"

"Nope. Zip."

"All right, just stay behind me for now. We'll find something."

They proceeded through the crew quarters toward the airlock. Cyril pulled the manual release handle downward to disengage the locks. They pulled the door open and stepped through the threshold. Once inside, they relatched the manual lock. Rachael went to the wall console on the opposite side to engage the air-compression system. The room filled with fresh oxygen, and a light above the door turned from red to green. The opposite door unlatched, and they shoved it open.

The room on the other side was the connecting hallway between flight control and crew quarters. It branched off in the middle and headed upward to the central spindle, which housed the lab area. The long and wide curved hallway had windows facing out, showing the air battle but only as shadows against the bright red sunlight.

Several dead PLA soldiers lay on the floor, and two Sin Eaters were huddled next to a metal storage crate. One was dead. Goll. The other was Olen. He saw Cyril and Rachael. He had been shot in the gut and was bleeding out. In the distance, more gunfire echoed from the lab area.

Cyril crouched next to Olen. "Fuck. How you doin', old man?"

"Fuck you, Eisner. I'm old, but I ain't that old."

"We'll agree to disagree. Where's everyone else?"

"They were headed toward the lab area. Everyone got pinned down. They got a radio dampener up and jammed our comms inside the station. There were so many. We got separated and had to pull back. Glass is still up there, I think. They really want this station for some reason."

"Doesn't matter. We'll get you to medical. Can you walk?"

"No, fuck it. If I start walking, I'll fall apart. Just get the others outta here. Just…" Olen passed out, and his head slumped forward. A stream of blood poured out and pooled underneath him.

Cyril gave him a few seconds of respect, then pillaged his body for anything useful.

Rachael's mouth dropped open, taken aback. "Oh, come on. He's been dead all of three seconds," she said with exasperation.

"What? It's not like he's using it anymore." Cyril commandeered an assault rifle, a handgun, and spare magazines for both from Olen's body. From Goll's body, Cyril acquired another assault rifle, a second handgun, a flashbang drone, and a satchel charge wrapped in a black bag, hanging from a shoulder strap. He draped it over his shoulder. Goll's handgun was a .45 Longslide and only used .45 caliber rounds. It was incompatible with Cyril's 9mm magazines. Cyril passed one assault rifle and the first handgun to Rachael. As she had no storage space, he strapped all spare magazines to his gun belt. Cyril left the Longslide, along with the ammo, alongside Goll's body.

They proceeded down the hallway and came to the cross section that led to the lab area. From their perspective, it looked like it went upward, with an elevator platform at the T-section of the hallway. Cyril and Rachael stepped on it and hit the button to ascend. The gunfire grew louder as they left the ring and headed toward the lab.

"Don't forget to engage your mag boots. Gravity is gonna go away soon," Rachael informed.

"Oh, right." Cyril clicked his heels to activate the mag boots and stuck to the elevator flooring as they ascended.

Rachael did the same. They crouched and kept their guns trained at the end of the spindle as the exit got closer.

"Goddamn, Cyril, is this shit really worth dying for?" Rachael asked.

"I don't know. Ask me again later," he said.

She shrugged but said nothing.

The elevator stopped. The gunfire was loud but sporadic now. Yelling and swearing came from somewhere deep in the lab. Arturus had hollowed and reinforced the interior of the *Lightfoot* asteroid with metal plating to create a breathable atmosphere. A flat footpath padded the sides of the rounded hallways, and the bright white lighting left no area for shadows to form except under one's feet. Cyril and Rachael shouldered their rifles at the ready, rechecked their magazines, rammed them home, and traversed the circular corridor.

They finally reached the lab and heard more gunshots as they came to an open doorway. Cyril sidled up just outside and peeked in the massive open area to see magnetic tables, glass cabinets, test tubes, microscopes, and, at the back of the room, an enormous reflective metal tank that extended downward through the entire center section of the station. SAMSON was painted vertically onto the side in bold lettering. A large antenna device, the communication jammer, stood next to it. It blinked green and had a metal ball attached to the very top. Cyril noticed Glass, Crow, and four other Sin Eaters congregated behind a metal desk. A pack of scientists and station workers huddled together at the opposite end of the room, with ten PLA soldiers holding them hostage.

Cyril crouched and whispered, "Glass, it's Eisner. You okay?"

"You know, for a pilot, you have a bad habit of never wanting to be in your ship," Glass said with a hint of annoyance.

"You did say I'd make a good Sin Eater. Just living up to expectations. What's the situation?"

"Exactly what it looks like. We approach, they shoot the hostages. We fire and miss, they shoot the hostages."

"Well then, we don't miss. Is there a way around them?"

"If there was, we would have tried it," Crow apprised.

"Fuck. Gotta be something."

"What about ventilation?" Rachael asked. "There's gotta be a shaft we can go through to get above or below. Surprise them."

"Already thought of that. Too small for anyone to fit," Glass said.

"Anyone… but not any*thing*." Cyril pulled out the small flashbang drone and unfolded its wingspan, revealing two rotors on each side. Attached in the middle was the motor and a housing for a ball-shaped flashbang grenade. Designed for emergency situations, it was a useful tool in a jam. Due to the extremely limited load-out the Sin Eaters needed for infiltration, only a few people brought one along. The one in Cyril's hand was the last remaining drone. One chance.

He scanned the hallway for a ventilation panel and found it above him. He unlatched the panel, pulled it down, and it floated away. Inside was an extremely narrow passageway filled with cables and pipes. It was all neatly constructed, but one wrong move and the drone would get stuck or break.

Then Cyril realized a grave mistake and groaned. "Oh, fuck." He had forgotten the drone's remote-control pad below, and he didn't have the time to head down to retrieve it. "Glass, I totally forgot the remote downstairs. Drone's outta the question."

"Hey, didn't you remote pilot your ship on Ashcheron," Rachael asked. "You still got *that* remote?"

The proverbial light bulb went off over Cyril's head. "That's why I like you, Rach. Glass, would my personal remote system work for the drone?"

"Yeah, it should. It's an open-connection system. Give it a shot."

Cyril lifted his left wrist to link his wireless control to the drone. Connection was instant. "Yes, we're good," he said triumphantly.

Cyril peeked into the room again, and a bullet zipped by his head and planted itself firmly in the padded wall opposite the open doorway. He recoiled, yelled obscenities, and glanced again, noting a ventilation shaft directly over the group at the rear of the room. It looked like a simple ridged panel that he could easily push off with enough force.

"Glass, we gotta keep them talking. This drone ain't gonna be super quiet. Distract them somehow."

"Yeah, I'll get right on that," Glass said sarcastically.

Cyril's wrist communicator's viewscreen connected to the drone's internal camera system and gave him a first-person view of the drone's movements, and the viewscreen, though small, was just big enough to have a touchpad control interface. The shaft was a narrow squeeze, but the drone fit and navigated through the passageway. Without a map, he would have to make a best guess as to the direction of the room. As long as he kept turning right until reaching a long straightaway, he would be set.

"Just out of curiosity, does anyone want to negotiate?" Glass yelled.

"We don't negotiate with fascists," the lead PLA soldier screamed.

"We're not interested in your political perspective. Just release the hostages. You can have the station."

"Not until Arcturus Allied answers for its crimes against the Ekumen. This facility produces the poison they've been spreading in mass quantities. Until they come clean, we hold this station."

"Eisner, how close are you?" Glass whispered.

"Almost there, I think. Keep him talking."

"To whom am I speaking to exactly? It would be much easier if I knew your name."

"Hunter Kingston of the Proletariat Liberation Alliance. I'm in command of this unit."

"Hunter, *huh*? I think we have a pilot named Hunter flying around outside right now."

"He got shot down," Cyril said, fixated on his wrist communicator's viewscreen.

"Thanks, Eisner," Glass said flatly. "Look, I'm not gonna deny that Arcturus isn't sketchy, but we're not here to defend them. We're just here to bring the civilians home. They're innocent in all this."

"Innocent? *Innocent*? They made this shit!" Hunter grabbed a vial of white fluid and hurled it toward the opposite end of the room. It glided over all the tables, passed over the Sin Eaters, and flew through the entranceway to the hallway outside. It ricocheted off the padded wall toward Cyril. It donked him on his facemask and snapped him from his concentration. He grabbed the helplessly spinning vial and stuffed it into his vest pocket. *Save that for later*. He resumed piloting the drone. The hair on his neck stood up as he found the vent where the drone could punch into the room and detonate.

"Glass, I'm ready when you are," Cyril whispered.

"Look, your ship outside was destroyed. You have no way out other than to negotiate. I'm gonna come up to talk face-to-face," Glass said. "Here, I'm throwing my gun away." He tossed his gun upward, and it floated toward the ceiling, bounced around, and ricocheted down toward a row of desks. "Be ready," he whispered to Crow. "You'll know when."

Glass stood up with his hands raised and turned to survey the PLA troops across the room. They were all clad in gray digital camouflage.

They looked like a ragtag group of freedom fighters, not an army. A mixture of alien races, as well—two Crecians, two Mukarians, and a Skovian. The rest were Terran. No uniformity to their weapon loadouts, either, which meant everyone was a jack-of-all-trades, master of none. Hunter Kingston had a massive third-degree burn scar across the left side of his face—a token of a prior battle.

"Let's talk," Glass said.

Kingston grabbed a young brunette scientist and held her in front of him as a human shield. He pressed his gun to the scientist's head. "You think any of these people are innocent? They made this shit to wipe us out!"

Glass stepped forward. Hunter aimed his gun at him, which made Glass retreat from that one step. The other soldiers took aim as well, showing an assembly of assault rifles and submachinegun laser sights on Glass's body armor.

"One more fucking step and I'll add a hole to her head!"

"You know, for a rebel faction that is all about fighting for civil rights, you certainly don't like being civil or even giving a shit about people's rights. There's literally no way out. You give up now, I can guarantee that you'll receive a fair trial. That's the best deal you're gonna get," Glass said.

Kingston chatted quietly into his earpiece comms. "*Heh*, you think we didn't have a backup plan? A second cruiser is arriving with more troops. If anyone isn't getting out, it's you and your Sin Eaters."

"Just let the people go, and we'll call it even," Glass yelled in anger. "Everyone walks away. You can have the station."

"These aren't people," Kingston screamed. "They're murderers! They've killed us!"

"No, that's my job. *Now*, Eisner!" Glass ducked and covered his ears.

The drone zipped down and punched through the thin metal slits in the overhead ventilation. In a split second, the drone exploded. A bright flash burst like fireworks, immediately stunning the group, then they swayed around blindly. The Sin Eaters readied up over their cover and fired. Cyril and Rachael also took position in the doorway and let loose with carefully placed shots. Streams of bullets ripped through the air. Ricochets dashed across from point to point. Bits of glass vials, test tubes, and jars exploded horrifically and filled the room with razor-sharp shards. The remaining ten scientists took the chance to run around the left-hand side of the room to escape. Three of the Sin Eaters surrounded them and escorted them out. Kingston held his hostage tight. One by one, PLA troops went down. Their bodies, though dead, hung in zero gravity, and blood spewed from their wounds. Their feet were still magnetized to the floor plating, acting like marionette puppets with invisible strings. Eventually, the Sin Eaters exhausted their ammo. Cyril and Rachael breached through the doorway and joined the remaining Sin Eaters. Glass, Crow, and one other soldier were all that remained. Glass took cover behind a desk, his weapons now gone. Crow and the last Sin Eater kept their weapons trained on Kingston, who pressed the barrel of his gun into the woman's temple.

"Ammo check," Cyril said flatly.

"I'm out," Crow said.

"Me too," the other Sin Eater said.

"Rach, what about you?" Cyril glanced at her.

"A couple rounds left in my pistol."

"Okay, Glass, you good?"

"I'm still here."

"Good. Kingston, you talk to me now," Cyril yelled.

"And who the fuck are you?" Kingston retorted.

"Name's Eisner." Cyril slowly sidestepped left to walk along the edge of the room to close the distance with Kingston. "It's over. You're the last man standing."

Kingston said nothing, then smiled. "*Heh*, my people just landed in the hangar bay. In a few minutes, you'll be surrounded. No escape."

"Then, I guess we all go down fighting. It'll be glorious. You know, I was at Ashcheron a while back. I'm pretty sure I got the most kills out of anyone that day. I think your commander there got a nice taste of the butt of my rifle at the very end. Crow back there talked me out of putting him down, but I won't say I wasn't tempted."

Kingston's eyes widened as he realized who Cyril was. His name and callsign had gone out wide to the PLA after the battle of Ashcheron, and they had labeled Cyril a rogue pilot who had no mercy and wasn't afraid to take down anyone to accomplish his goal. The name *Skyhawk* had become synonymous with the title *Slaughterer of Ashcheron*.

"You. You're Skyhawk," Kingston said with a touch of dread.

"Right in one." Cyril assessed his options and realized he only had one. Shoot the hostage. Kingston's leg was barely exposed enough for a gunshot, but the chances of going through the hostage's leg were high. He would have to hope for the best and shoot through her leg to hit him. He would recoil, then let her go, and that would leave an opportunity to make a kill shot.

"You motherfucker. You're fighting for the wrong people," Kingston yelled. "You destroy everything in your wake! Whose side are you even on?"

Cyril remained silent for a moment, then said, "Mine." He aimed low and fired.

The round went through the fleshy bit of the woman's leg and shot Kingston in the crotch. Kingston screamed in agony. His penis exploded, and a gush of blood ejaculated from his pants. The woman ripped herself away and fell. Rachael swooped around the right-hand side of the room to pick her up. Cyril blasted off the remaining shots of his magazine. One shot pierced Kingston's shoulder, the rest missed.

"Fuck! Rachael, get her outta here," he shouted.

He chucked his pistol, disengaged his mag boots, and pushed himself off the wall toward Kingston. He flew as bits of glass and metal bounced off him. He raised his hands to block his path from incoming debris. When he was two meters away, he dropped his arms and speared himself into Kingston's chest. Kingston fell backward, and his boots disconnected from the floor. The two men tumbled around in zero gravity. They threw punches as they tumbled end over end, and streams of blood filled the room like red ribbons of gore. As the Sin Eaters maneuvered toward the two men, Cyril and Kingston grappled face-to-face, trying to strangle each other. Kingston wrapped his legs around Cyril's waist and squeeze-closed his airway. Kingston's grip was so brutal that Cyril felt it through the polymer of his suit.

"You're… on the… wrong side," Kingston snarled.

Cyril looked around for anything he could use. A test tube twirled in the air next to Kingston's head. Cyril snatched it, pushed up Kingston's head, and yelled, "Shut *the fuck* up!" He rammed the test tube into Kingston's mouth and struck him with a swift uppercut.

The tube shattered, and blood spewed from Kingston's mouth as they flew across the room. He screamed through the gargle of blood as bits of glass slithered down his throat. Cyril reeled back one last time, let out a punch from hell, and broke Kingston's nose. Kingston tumbled away, knocked out cold.

"Holy fuck," Crow said in astonishment.

Cyril reactivated his mag boots, which attached him to the wall. He walked down, set his feet to the floor, and headed to the jamming device. He smashed it on the corner of a table. The ball on top detached and floated away, like a ping pong ball. Comms crackled back to life.

"Let's move, now," Cyril yelled. "We gotta get the hostages out! Rex, are you guys still out there? We have the hostages. Gonna try to find a way out now."

"We lost one more fighter. Shifter. We're back to hiding on the asteroid. A second cruiser leaped in."

"We know. We'll… figure something out. Skyhawk out."

They headed toward the elevator to rejoin the Sin Eaters and hostages.

A medic was bandaging the wounded woman's leg, and upon seeing Cyril, her face soured. "You fucking shot me," she screamed through her teeth.

"You're welcome," he replied defiantly.

It was a tight fit on the elevator, but they descended toward the ring.

"All right, so here's the issue. Hangar bay is full of PLA on the way here. We have a second capital ship outside but no way of taking it down this time. We already shot our wad on that one. Even if we get to our ships, we can't make it home. Any suggestions?" Cyril asked.

No one said anything.

"Don't everyone speak at once."

"There's no weapons on the station, but what about the station itself?" said an older, balding scientist.

"What?" Cyril asked, confused.

"The outer ring is constructed from compartments built independent of each other. In case of emergency, all the sections can be manually disconnected and piloted like a shuttle from any command console if you have the right security permissions."

"And does anyone here have those permissions?"

The shot woman raised her hand.

"Well, it's a good thing I saved you, isn't it? Again, you're welcome. We kamikaze the second cruiser. We can remote pilot one of the compartments and hit the cruiser. Easy."

"Well… not exactly," the bald man sheepishly said.

"What do you mean, *not exactly*?"

"There's no remote-control system in the compartments. It's all manual. Someone would have to stay to pilot it."

"Oh, gimme a fuckin' break." Cyril ran his hands down his facemask before remembering he couldn't rub his face in frustration.

"Sorry. We're a private research facility. This wasn't exactly designed for combat."

"We've established that. All right, we'll head toward flight command. The crew quarters are toast. We'll get to the next section over and see about disconnecting."

"And the PLA?" Glass asked.

"Well, when plan A fails, go to plan B. Plan B fails, go to plan C," Cyril answered.

"And if plan C fails?"

"We'll fuckin' figure it out."

***

A pair of PLA dropships flew down and floated just outside the station's hangar bay doors. Spacesuit-clad engineers passed through a single person airlock, disembarked, and performed a manual bypass on the door security. Once completed, the massive set of doors rose, and the ships flew inside. As they landed, the doors closed again, and oxygen filled the massive bay. Donned in full body armor, all the soldiers clomped toward the lab area. They would need to round the station and head to the lab area to maintain control. The lead officer led them to the right. Twenty soldiers followed.

Upon passing through the airlock, they entered the recreation section of the station, then the next airlock to the medical bay. They marched and attempted to open the door to the crew quarters. Only when they reached the airlock door did they realize that section of the station had been decompressed, and a massive hole had been blown out inside. They couldn't progress any farther. The commanding officer swore, shook his head in annoyance, then turned his crew around to head in the opposite direction. They would have to proceed to the opposite elevator shaft to reach the lab, and it would cost them valuable time.

They circumnavigated the whole airlock system again to cross to the opposite side of the hangar bay to reach the opposite elevator. The crew crammed themselves in once again and waited for the air pressure to adjust to the next section. The light over the door flipped from red to green, and the soldiers passed through. They proceeded down the hallway and took note of the cruiser waiting outside the window as the station slowly spun. They reached the T-section of the connecting bridge and located the lab elevator. It was a tight squeeze, but all twenty-one soldiers managed to fit onto the platform to ascend. They checked their weapons and flipped off their safeties.

At the top, they rounded the central hallway and entered the lab. Bullet holes were punctured into the wall padding, debris floated about, and bodies littered the environment. The lead officer entered the room and saw Kingston floating near the fluid tanks at the rear.

The officer pulled Kingston toward the floor and shook him awake. "Are you okay, sir?"

Kingston slowly awoke and reeled again from the pain. Everything hurt, and bits of glass were impaled into his tongue and gums.

"Sir, where are the hostages? We need them."

"Merr gun," Kingston mumbled. Blood trickled from his mouth.

"What?"

"Therrr gunnn," Kingston blurted through the pain.

The commander got the message—*They're gone.* "All right, they must've used the opposite elevator. Everyone, move out. Opposite end of the station!"

Kingston engaged his mag boots and turned right. He grabbed his gun floating nearby, checked the magazine, and headed for the lab door. The commander followed behind. Kingston was in extreme pain, but his anger and determination kept him from passing out again. He was no longer interested in the station. He wanted Cyril Eisner, aka Skyhawk, dead.

The soldiers rounded the hallway and came to the elevator for the opposite end. The elevator was already at the bottom. They couldn't float down, however. Once gravity took hold, they would fall and break their legs at the bottom. The only options were to either sit and wait for the elevator to come up or take the long way around and head down the other end of the station. Both options would be slow and miserable. The crew decided to split in half, one-half staying up top to wait for the elevator, with the other half heading down and around the station at the other end. This would give them a chance to flank the enemy on both sides and trap them.

Kingston stayed up top while the other commanding officer led his team to the other side. While they waited, Kingston asked a soldier for a medical kit. He took it, removed all the gauze from the kit, and stuffed all of it into his pants, red-soaked from the blood still pouring from where his cock had been. One soldier saw the bloody results of the gunshot wound and vomited. The vomit spewed like a sideways geyser and floated down the elevator shaft. Everyone groaned, because it meant on the ride down, they would have to duck and dodge to avoid the soldier's upchucked lunch from covering them.

***

The Sin Eaters and hostages were bunched up outside the airlock door to the flight command section. After exiting the elevator, they collected whatever weapons had been strewn through the hallway from the previous gunfight. Cyril retrieved Goll's discarded pistol and ammo from earlier and checked the magazine. It was still full. As he and Rachael headed back to rejoin the group, the elevator to the lab began rising. They sprinted and bunched up with everyone at the airlock door.

"Elevator is headed back up," Rachael announced. "If we're gonna do this, better do it now."

"Can we lock down the sections so they can't get in before the disconnect?" Glass asked.

The balding man said, "They're designed to seal off once given the disconnect codes. Any terminal has the control function."

"All right, once we're through, we'll lock everything down."

"What about the PLA cruiser?" Cyril asked. "Someone has to pilot one of the sections into it to take it out. So, someone has to stay behind."

"What if we don't pilot it? What if we just… aim it?" Rachael said.

Cyril was quiet for a moment, then got what she was suggesting. "Turn the station into a mounted gun. Use the centrifugal force as the launcher." Cyril looked out the window at the second PLA cruiser floating next to the debris field of the first one. Dropships flew in and around the field, scanning for survivors—or, at the very least, dead bodies. "It's a long shot, but it's the last shot we have."

"It's a lot of long shots for this mission. I'm starting to think we've already used up our nine lives," Crow said with abandon.

"This place isn't worth dying for. We're all getting out," Cyril said.

Glass opened the airlock door, and the hostages filed in. Crow and the third Sin Eater followed. As Glass entered, gunfire blazed around them. The PLA troops had finally made it down the elevator shaft and opened fire. They were over forty yards away, so their aim was rough. Mostly spray and pray. Cyril and Rachael turned to take cover behind a waist-high stack of metal supply crates. The airlock door was cracked open and pulled outward into the hallway. Bullets ricocheted all around them.

Then Kingston's wet, guttural voice yelled from the middle of the soldiers, "Save it! Save your ammo." His speech had somewhat returned.

The gunfire stopped.

"Eisner, get in here," Glass yelled.

"You know the plan. Use the station as a gun," Cyril ordered. "Just don't use the crew quarters section. Our ships are up there. We'll cover you. See you, man." He leaped up and shoved the door closed.

Glass's yell was severed at the last second as the airlock sealed, leaving Cyril and Rachael alone with the PLA troops. More gunfire erupted. Bullets zipped and popped, echoing down the hallway. Cyril and Rachael aimed over the crate and fired. One soldier went down.

The slide on Rachael's gun remained locked to the rear. "I'm out!"

"Here! Last mag! Make it count!" Cyril handed her the final magazine for her gun.

She slammed it in, released the slide, and popped up for a few more shots. Another soldier dropped. They took cover again as a barrage of machinegun fire lit up the metal crate. Then the gunfire slowed to random pops while most of the soldiers reloaded.

"Hey, Kingston. I'm guessing that's you over there," Cyril yelled.

"You'd be right, Skyhawk," Kingston said through a bloody mouth.

"The hostages are safe. You'll have to go through us to get to them."

"Not a problem. We have another unit working its way around the opposite side of the station. We'll get them whether we go through you or not."

"Fuck," Cyril whispered. He got on the radio and said, "Glass, disconnect now and lockdown every section. PLA are coming in on both sides to flank you. Do it now!"

"Copy that. Good luck, man."

"You too."

Needing to buy some time, Cyril raised his hands above the lip of the crate. "All right, Kingston. You win. We surrender."

"What the fuck are you doing?" Rachael whispered angrily.

"Trust me. And be ready to grab my waist."

"What?"

"Seriously, be ready." He slowly rose and saw the unit of PLA soldiers aiming their laser sights on his chest. The light of the Arcturus star bathed the entire hallway in red as the station turned from darkness into light. "Fuck, Kingston. You look like shit."

"Fuck you, you traitor to your people."

"That's real fresh coming from someone like you."

"Any last words?" Kingston and the PLA aimed at Cyril's head.

"Yeah. How about *satchel charge*?" He set his pistol atop the crate, then pulled the strap of the satchel charge over his shoulder and held it up. "Go on, take a shot. Do it. You fire at me, you'll hit this charge, which will destroy the airlock and blow us all out into space. You might be aggressive, but you're not stupid. It's me you want. The one who fucked up Ashcheron the most." Cyril looked at Rachael, then back at Kingston. "She's innocent. She wasn't there," Cyril lied. "Let her go, and you can have me."

"Fuck you. You're all traitors. Arcturus is trying to wipe us out."

"Who is *us*? I don't even know what the fuck you're talking about!"

"Non-Terrans! It's fucking genocide! And you help them do it!" Kingston thumbed back the hammer on his pistol.

The station shook like an earthquake. The airlock sealed with a blast door that had dropped from a slit in the ceiling. The station shook more, and everyone tossed and tumbled. Explosives popped in the oxygen atmosphere. Cyril took the chance to toss the satchel charge toward the window, then raised his hands again. Out the window, the recreation section of the station headed toward the PLA ship. The troops turned their attention from Cyril and Rachael to watch.

"*Heh*, speaking of genocide," Cyril said with a sly smile.

The PLA watched, aghast, as the recreation section of the ring impacted with the cruiser and ripped off the front half. Explosion after explosion detonated and burned out just as quickly as they had started.

"*Noooo*," Kingston yelled. A waterfall of blood poured out his mouth.

"Glass, are you guys safe?" Cyril asked.

"We're all safe. How about you?"

"I'll let you know in a minute. Rex, the second cruiser is down. Go mop up the fighters."

"Copy that. We're on it," Rex declared.

"You motherfucker! You *motherfucker*," Kingston screamed.

The PLA retrained their guns on Cyril.

"Rachael, grab my waist now," Cyril said quietly.

She leaped up and held tight to his waist, noticing the satchel charge on the floor under the window, ten yards away. "Cyril, no," she whispered.

"It's our only chance," he whispered.

"You two can die together, you fucking traitors," Kingston shouted.

"Someone I once knew used to say, 'Whatever choices you make… make them count.'" Cyril's arm reached down like a bolt of lightning and snatched his pistol. He aimed and fired at the satchel charge. It exploded into an enormous ball of flame. A hole blew out the side of the hallway, shattering the window, and the oxygen was sucked out like the universe had turned on the cosmic vacuum cleaner to the high setting. One by one, the PLA troops flew through the hole and tumbled into space. Kingston tried to grab onto a bulkhead, but the force was too great. His fingers slipped, and he was pulled out too, gasping for air that wasn't there. He screamed, but no sound came out of his bloody mouth. Cyril held on as long as he could to an outcropped beam but eventually slipped. He tumbled out, with Rachael still holding onto his waist. They spun as they flew into the vacuum.

Outside, another dogfight was ensuing. Spinning, Cyril couldn't decipher who was who. Debris floated everywhere, ships flew by, and the constant spinning made him queasy, throwing off his equilibrium. Rachael was breathing rapidly and gripped Cyril even tighter.

"Slow down your breathing! You'll eat up all your oxygen," Cyril yelled.

"I can't! I'm scared," she cried out.

"I know. I'm scared too." He hadn't really thought about what to do once they had escaped into space. He closed his eyes to stop the universe from spinning. He weighed his options. Calling for rescue was out of the question while the dogfight continued. Also, they had no booster packs, so they couldn't return to the station on their own. Add in that they were on a limited oxygen supply, and it seemed the odds were against them. Like Crow had said, it looked like they'd finally eaten up their nine lives.

"Call for help, Cyril," Rachael cried out. "Call anyone. I don't wanna die here. Please."

Cyril opened his eyes again. The universe continued its merry-go-round spin. He searched his suit for anything he could use to get back. He considered blowing his oxygen tank and using it as propulsion to reach his ship. Problem was that by the time they reached his ship, he would be dead, and with no way to stop, Rachael would be dead too. He could use his pistol as a makeshift propulsion system to change course and stop the universe from spinning. That presented its own challenge, however, as the force would be extreme, and if he fired at the wrong moment, they would be lost forever. As he scrambled, he spotted the communicator to his ship on his wrist.

He raised it to his helmet, focused on the viewscreen, and reconnected his ship to the communicator. "Skyhawk! Fly to my—oh what the fuck am I doing? It can't hear me." He turned on his remote pilot mode to see through his ship's gun camera. He detached the mag locks, ascended, and traced the distance of the ship to their location. By that point, they were close to two kilometers from the station.

He remained focused on the viewscreen to drown out the spinning. It felt like a first-person perspective videogame. Find where the character should go, then move. His ship raced toward them. They became larger in the ship's camera. Once they were thirty meters away, Cyril realized they had another problem. With them tumbling like being caught in the undertow of a crashing wave, it would be impossible to get into his cockpit. If he attempted it while spinning, they might smash into their oxygen tanks—or worse, break their facemasks.

Cyril unholstered his gun and aimed in front of him from chest level. "Rach, hold on tight!"

"I *am* holding on tight!"

"You're gonna feel a big bump! Don't let go!" He pulled the trigger, and the gun fired soundlessly in the void.

They flew backward at twice the speed of when they had begun their tumble from the station.

Rachael screamed. "What the fuck was that?"

"I had to fire the gun to get us to move straight. Okay, here we go." He pulled up his wrist communicator again. They were darting away from the Skyhawk. He tracked their location and brought the ship around to follow them. They grew bigger till finally the ship matched their speed alongside them to their left. He ordered the canopy to open, and it slowly rose. He nudged the thrusters a touch. It closed in till it was within arm's length.

"Okay, Rach. I need you to let go."

"No, I can't! I'm scared! Don't leave me!"

"I won't leave you. I promise, I won't leave you, but you to let me go if I'm gonna save us."

"Okay…" she whimpered. Rachael slowly released her iron grip and drifted slightly behind Cyril.

He reached over and, with his fingertips, pulled himself into the front seat of his cockpit. He heard her whimpering on the radio. He strapped into his seat, retook control of his flight systems, then eased his ship forward till the rear seat was alongside Rachael. She grabbed one of the seatbelts and pulled herself in. She strapped herself down as the canopy closed and latched tight. Cyril brought the Skyhawk about and headed toward the station.

Only two PLA fighters remained. Cyril, now charged with adrenaline, got tone on one as he rejoined the battle. He fired a missile, and the ship burst into pieces. The rest of Silver Squadron now ganged up on the final fighter. It had no chance at all.

"Silver Squadron, all fighters down. Excellent work, everyone," Rex said full of pride.

The squadron formed up and examined the wreckage of the two PLA cruisers. Intermittent pops of fire burst from the hulls, and debris spewed forth. What had been intended to be a simple negotiation had become one of the bloodiest battles anyone in the squadron had ever faced.

"Skyhawk, Loki, how are you doing over there?"

"We're a little roughed up, but we're all right," Cyril said. "All the hostages and the remaining Sin Eaters are inside the flight control section of the station."

"Good work, everybody. Mission accomplished," Rex yelled.

The crew cheered and pumped their fists in celebration. Even Rachael, still shaken up after the zero-G tumble, laughed. Slowly the laughter faded, and the squadron sat quiet and motionless among the debris and the dead remnants of the PLA.

Then Smoker asked, "Now what?"

***

With no FOIL pad to get back home, the crew had to send a long-range distress call to Luyten using the station's communications dish. Despite being disconnected from the ring, each section had a reserve power supply for emergencies. Two of the starfighter crew, Smoker and Diva, overrode the security control on the communication dish and sent out their SOS.

Cyril tracked down the crew quarters section, which was slowly floating into the blackness. He set down where he had landed before, right next to Rachael's ship. She slowly stepped across the deck plating and climbed into her own ship's pilot seat. They both lifted off and rejoined the squadron.

With the distress call sent, the ships navigated to the hangar bay section to await rescue. Having already bypassed the doors, they opened quickly, revealing the final two PLA dropships still docked inside, and their pilots still sat in their cockpits. Cyril and Rachael turned on their forward running lights and hailed them.

Cyril kept his finger on the trigger as he said, "Seriously, don't try anything. It's been a hell of a day."

All the fighters and Moriarty's dropship took up residence inside the hangar bay and closed the door. It was an extremely tight squeeze. One ship scraped the walls with their starboard wing as they set down. Mag-locked ships covered each wall, as gravity had vanished. Without the station's centrifugal force, they must use their mag boots again to stay on the floor. The bay repressurized, and everyone exited their ships. Their oxygen supplies were near zero.

They easily took over the PLA dropships. The pilots didn't put up a fight. They were secured in one of the dropships and tied up with chains and padlocks that floated about in the zero-G environment.

As they all waited around, someone said, "I feel like we're forgetting something."

Everyone was quiet for a moment, then they all screamed in unison, "Oh shit!"

Cyril and Rex headed out in their own ships, alongside one of the confiscated dropships. They'd completely forgotten about the FOIL pad pilot. Cyril and Rex raced ahead of the dropship and tracked the pilot's ejection pod beacon to its location. When they found him, he was nearly frozen but alive.

Through chattering teeth, the pilot said, "I thought you guys had forgotten about me."

"*Nah*, no way. You were always on our minds," Cyril lied.

They loaded the pilot into the dropship and headed to the hangar bay.

While Cyril, Rex, and the dropship were out, the crew kept themselves busy by digging through the hangar bay for supplies. A plethora of extra oxygen tanks were available in the supply station on the starboard side. Every ship and spacesuit received a full resupply. It was the one good bit of luck that happened that day. Once they had resupplied all the ships, the crew picked their favorite spots around the room, floated about, and waited. Some of the crew took naps, while others stayed busy by scrounging through the bay for anything useful. No one would object to a little thievery by that point. Moriarty stayed in their ship with their bodyguards, not wanting to associate with the local wildlife. Cyril had a feeling that the company would chew out Silver Squadron once they got home.

After two hours, a rescue ship and another FOIL pad leaped into the area. They went through the process of loading up and heading back out. Moriarty leaped away immediately with the pad, while everyone else stayed behind to assist the rescue of the hostages and the Sin Eaters. The rescue attached an external airlock to the side of the flight command section, which operated like an escape pod. The Sin Eaters and hostages huddled in, detached, and joined the starfighters in flight. They waited another twenty minutes, and the FOIL pad returned. They landed on it and leaped to Luyten.

Two hours after that, everyone was safely at home. Arcturus would dispatch a salvage crew to rebuild the station and to clean up the remnants of the battle. It would be extremely costly, but the lab area was intact, which meant Arcturus could continue its work. With that said, Moriarty still had some venom to spit. No commendations or bonuses would be provided by the company, not even for the FOIL pad pilot whom Rex had promised one to. The pilot was extremely salty upon hearing the news. The crew didn't care about the money though. After such a rough assignment, they were just happy to be going home.

Five starfighters—Cyril, Rachael, Rex, Allegra, and Bollman—went to the grassy plateau area above the hangar bay. The rest stayed below to get some rack time. The battle was brutal, and everyone was beat. For the sake of entertainment, the locals had built a makeshift tiki bar for pilots and soldiers returning home. With such a beautiful view, it only made sense, and it was good for business. A plethora of string lights overhead draped from pillar to pillar, illuminating the entire place in a soft yellow glow. Night had fallen, and the air was a cool seventy degrees. The stars were bright, and the universe above them drifted by without a care. They sat together at a table and drank Luyten beer, which was much sweeter than expected. Cyril only took a few sips before switching to hard liquor. Allegra loved it, though, and was already on her second round.

"So, just curious, whatever happened to that FOIL pad that had Wolf and Zeroman on it?" Cyril asked, genuinely curious.

"Salvage team went out and picked up the black box, and you know what the problem was? The pad leaped in upside down," Rex said. "Miscalculation. Just a dumb bad luck mistake."

"You know, every time I think we're gonna get an easy one, luck says otherwise," Rachael said.

"Yeah, and there's one constant between the bad luck operations," Allegra added. She, Rex, and Rachael faced Cyril.

"Hey, fuck all of you," Cyril said, grinning.

Everyone laughed.

"Especially after I saved your fuckin' asses."

"You're an enormous pain in the ass, Eisner." Rex stood and raised his glass of sweet beer. "But still, without your quick thinking, and, to be honest, insane methods, we wouldn't be here right now. You did save our asses… again. To Cyril."

Everyone raised their glasses and repeated, "To Cyril!"

"Hey, Allie deserves some credit too," Cyril said. "It was her plan from the start. It was crazy, and it worked. To Allie!"

The whole crew toasted again and said, "To Allie!" They drank and chatted.

Rachael, sitting next to Cyril, turned to him. "Thanks for not leaving me."

"Thanks for watching my back. I couldn't have made it without you."

She smiled and held his hand.

"Now that's two you owe me."

She laughed.

"Oh, God, go fuck already," Glass said, approaching from behind them, Crow alongside him.

The crew chuckled, and Rachael pulled away her hand, blushing and slightly embarrassed.

Glass and Crow pulled up seats at the table and ordered two beers. "Cyril, I just wanna say that was some excellent work you did today."

"Man, everyone's just wantin' to kiss my ass," Cyril said.

"Today you deserve it. I don't think I've ever seen tactics like that, but you pulled us outta the fire. You ever need a gun by your side"—Glass proffered his hand—"you call me."

Cyril shook his hand. "Thanks, Glass."

"Sin Eaters got your back, brother. Hey, bartender, round of shots for the crew!"

The crew cheered and applauded. Bollman silently stared at the table.

"Hey, Crow, we good?" Cyril asked, proffering his hand.

She considered it for a moment, then relented and shook his hand. "Yeah, we're good."

They shook and smiled. They had finally made peace.

"Hey, Bollman, you okay? You've been really quiet," Rex noticed.

"Would you excuse me?" Bollman quietly asked and walked into the distant grassy field of the plateau toward the cliffs.

Everyone was still watching him go when the shots of alcohol arrived.

***

He'd done everything right, and he was still left with nothing. Bollman had escaped death again. He had helped bring the crew home, and he was still left with nothing. He had rescued the hostages, and he was still left with nothing.

He walked to the cliff of the grassy plateau and looked across the valley. The moonlight gave the grass a slight reddish glow. The valley looked like a milky red river of tree branches that dipped away toward the distant mountains. He wished his wife could see it. It was beautiful.

He felt old, corroded, and tired. Life wouldn't stop beating on him, no matter how much he begged for mercy. Somewhere in the distance, a bird screeched out a mating call with a *hoo- hoo*. He dropped to his knees and unholstered his gun.

"I did everything right," he whispered to himself. It still wasn't enough to bring her back. Then he thumbed back the hammer and put the pistol to his head.

***

BANG!

The shot rang loud in the cool night air. The crew snapped up and turned toward the sound. They sprang from their chairs and yelled.

"*Bollman*," Cyril screamed.

They ran to the edge of the plateau and found Bollman's body—a gaping exit wound on the left side of his head. His eyes remained open, but the light in them was gone.

Someone said in horror, "Oh, no."

***

The medical staff on base prepared Bollman's body for transport and asked if he had any family they needed to contact.

Cyril said, "There's no one. Best to just bury him here."

The crew worked all night and dug a grave for Bollman on the edge of the plateau. As they finished, the sun broke over the horizon. They were exhausted, digging with shovels all night. Even Glass and Crow, who had no business assisting someone they didn't even know, stayed to help.

They carried Bollman's body to the hole, wrapped in an airtight body bag for preservation since a coffin was unavailable. They set his body on a trio of ropes and lowered him into the hole. Once he was in, they removed the ropes and filled in the hole. When they finished, Rachael returned with a metal plate with a spoke attached to the bottom. She had used a laser cutter to engrave his name with two words beneath it.

David Bollman.

Husband. Starfighter.

No one knew his birthday. She stabbed the plate into the ground and stepped backward. No one said anything. Most people hadn't known him very well.

Glass said quietly, "Is he okay like this?"

"This place is as good as any. And it's a hell of a view," Rex said, marveling at the gorgeous sunrise.

"He doesn't have anyone to go back to," Cyril remarked. "He may as well stay here."

The crew was silent. Rachael shed a few tears. So did Glass and Crow. The silence was finally broken when, of all people, Moriarty appeared with their bodyguards from the stairwell below and approached the crew.

"Were you all planning to just stand around all day, or are we going to call this operation complete?" they asked with sheer annoyance.

"You know, what is your problem?" Cyril yelled as he threw down the shovel.

"My problem is that we are on a timetable to return to Arcturus, where I will have to explain why a seven-hundred-billion-dollar facility is being reassembled like Legos out in space right now, instead of returning to full operations this morning!"

"We took down the PLA and rescued the hostages. Isn't that good enough for you?"

"Eisner, calm down," Rex said.

"The hostages were expendable. The target was to secure the station itself. Just the station! Thank fuck the lab is still fine, but it'll take weeks to get back up and running again. I couldn't give a shit about any of your lives. All of you are expendable. You knew that going in. Get your ships and your meager pay and go the fuck home." They turned to walk away.

"You know, I don't know who hurt you, but I wish they'd hurt you more, because you fucking deserve it," Cyril yelled in fury, with almost a growl.

Even the birds stopped chirping upon hearing that insult. If there was a god above, it was listening intently. Even the Almighty was curious to know what would happen next.

Moriarty stopped, turned, and marched toward Cyril. They got right in Cyril's face. "You just don't know when to quit, do you?" they hissed, like a snake.

"Yeah, well, I'm stubborn like that."

"Consider yourself blacklisted from Arcturus. And maybe even blacklisted from flying in general."

"You really gonna try that? The whole *you'll never work in this town again* bullshit? Fuck you. Overseer hired me for this. And you can't blacklist me. I have one more flight with Arcturus left on my contract. After that, I'm not fired; I'm quit." Cyril took a step closer to Moriarty. "And it will be my absolute pleasure to spit in your ginger cunt face on my way out the door."

Moriarty inched closer. They were so close that Cyril could smell their breath. "Why... wait?" they asked, tempting fate.

"I wanna savor the thought and build up a nice wet, sloppy one, just for you." He made a slurping sound and smooched his lips, like blowing them a kiss. "Now fuck off, you ungrateful... fucking... twat."

Moriarty turned, their face flushed red with anger.

As they walked away, Cyril yelled, with his chest, in absolute defiance, "And my men are *not* expendable! *None* of us are!"

Moriarty stopped, turned back, and laughed. "Fucking pig," they murmured, then headed downstairs to the hangar bay.

The crew refocused on Bollman's grave. One by one, they filtered away. Cyril and Rachael were the last to leave.

"I hope you got to see her again, man," Cyril whispered. He grabbed the shovel and turned, and Rachael hung on his arm as they headed toward the hangar.

***

Cyril opened his apartment door. It felt like a whole lifetime had passed since he'd been there, yet it had only been a few days. He set his bag on the living room floor, then fell onto the couch. He didn't realize just how tired he was till that moment as he ran his fingers over his eyes so hard that he saw spots. He removed the vial of white fluid from his bag that he had retrieved from the station. PROJECT SAMSON, followed by a series of serial numbers, was typed onto a sticker running vertically down the side. He set the vial on the coffee table and leaned back on the couch. He had no idea what to do with it, but, at that moment, he was too tired to care.

He thought back to Bollman, confessing how no one would be waiting for him at home—no love who might greet him at the door. Reality for Cyril set back in as life returned to mundanity. He opened the group chat on his phone that he had with Jess and Jace. Though a dead thread, he typed the last thing he would ever add to the chat.

CYRIL: I miss you guys.

He pressed Send, and it was in the chat forever. He checked to see if Marie had released her block on her social media or on her phone number.

No, he was still locked out of her life.

No one was there. No one was waiting for him. He lay on the couch and stared at the wall, too exhausted to cry.

You're alone.

You're all alone.

CHAPTER 19

WHAT IT IS

Four days had passed since the battle of *Lightfoot* station. Cyril wasn't sleeping well. In fact, it was agony to sleep, knowing he would wake up alone. He fell back into his routine to keep himself occupied and went by the airfield twice to pick up shifts so he wouldn't lose his mind. His ship had miraculously suffered only cosmetic damage during the *Lightfoot* station battle. He gave the Skyhawk a deep cleaning and restoration. As for his work shifts, he started from ten in the morning and worked till seven at night. The only work he had lined up was his final contracted flight with Arcturus later that week. Beyond that, he would have to go on a job hunt. Once he got home each night, his mind would race again, remembering how alone he truly was.

On day five, he finally unpacked his kit and retrieved the .45 caliber Longslide he had confiscated on *Lightfoot*. His Beretta was long since gone, so he would need a replacement. He rotated the extremely efficient firearm in his hands to inspect it—sturdy, dependable, great stopping power. However, it only had an eight-round capacity, plus one in the chamber, and he didn't like the way the grip fit into his hands. Comfort and capacity went a long way for him. A fine weapon, but the wrong weapon for his line of work. It still confused Cyril exactly why Goll would bring along a gun like that. It didn't quite fit tactical operations, which meant it was more of a sentimental piece—a gift from a lover, a family heirloom, or maybe he just really liked it. Whatever the case, the context died with Goll on *Lightfoot*. He decided it was best to trade it in.

He packed it in a small bag and headed to his local armory about seven blocks from his apartment. Once every few weeks, he would stop by for a resupply for his Beretta and Eruptor. He wasn't exactly a gun nut by any stretch; weapons were just part of his trade.

Cyril entered and immediately smelled the stench of gun oil. The same cashier would always be working, a guy named Pitsy—a well-kept older man who actually was a gun nut. He was in relatively decent shape but balding and, for some reason, always had a smile across his face.

When Cyril entered, Pitsy recognized him immediately. "Welcome back. Nine-millimeter Beretta, right?"

"Typically, yes," Cyril said, walking to the glass countertop. "Got something different today." Rows of various firearms populated three eight-meter-long underlit shelves below the glass. Cyril set the small bag atop the counter and opened it to reveal the Longslide. "Care to do a trade?"

Pitsy picked up the Longslide to examine it. He ejected the magazine, racked the slide to check the chamber, then looked down the sights. "Man, you don't see these very often."

"I said the same thing. It recently came into my possession, but I don't really have a use for it."

Pitsy raised an eyebrow at Cyril. "This isn't hot, is it?"

"No, the original owner died. I snatched it up"

"Snatched it up?"

"I'm a starfighter. Was out on assignment. He got shot; I picked it up. Don't ask where."

"All good. Say no more. Yeah, I can do a trade in. Can't give you full price because it isn't factory-new, but I can get you around nine hundred. Sound good?"

"Yeah, that works. I'll need a replacement though."

"Want another Beretta?"

"Maybe. I'm gonna look around." Cyril strolled through the shop filled with everything a person could need, from the average consumer searching for a self-defense weapon, to collector's items, to gun nuts perusing for the next hot thing—handguns, assault rifles, submachineguns, knives, Kevlar—everything was available. Cyril was also aware of a backroom section where they sold some of the more explicit items—explosives and illegal firearms only available to the highest bidder. The ammunition for Cyril's Eruptor just barely skirted by as legal.

He scanned the handgun case. Revolvers didn't appeal to him, as they only had six rounds and took a while to reload. He needed something sturdy, reliable, and at least requiring a fifteen-round magazine. Then he saw a silver-plated gun with a chestnut wooden grip at the tail end of a section of Berettas. The gorgeous design looked very comfortable for his hand size.

"Hey, what's this one?" Cyril asked, pointing into the case.

"Just got that in last week. Only one in the shipment. Beretta M93R. Auto pistol."

"Auto pistol?"

"Oh yeah, they don't make these anymore. I think it was from someone's collection, and once they passed, it ended up going through auction houses. They're a rough weapon to handle, but they take nine-millimeter rounds."

"*Hmm.* Looks very nice. How much?"

"Thirty-five thousand."

"Thirty-five thousand?!"

Pitsy shrugged, almost agreeing that the price was too high. "Hey, might be the last of its kind. Collector's item."

"I think I'll just stick with a regular Beretta," Cyril sullenly responded.

"I don't blame you. Hang on, let me get you something. You might like this." Pitsy walked to the opposite end of the counter and, from the glass cabinet, removed a handgun slightly smaller than a Beretta but seemed slicker and more elegant. "Try this out. This is a Browning Hi-Power. This is also a collector's item but nowhere near as rare as the 93R. Nine-millimeter and a thirteen-round capacity. Great stopping power, and it fits right into your hands. Go ahead, feel it." Pitsy passed the black Hi-Power to Cyril.

Cyril's hand wrapped perfectly around the diamond textured grip. He checked down the meticulously aligned sights. He racked the slide to check the chamber. Clean as a whistle. He released the slide, and it snapped forward with a loud *ka-chack.* It had fewer rounds than his old Beretta, but it felt solid, and it was nine-millimeter, so he wouldn't need to restock ammunition.

"Feels good, doesn't it?" Pitsy asked.

"I like it. How much?"

Pitsy smiled. "I can let it go for nine hundred."

"Perfect. Got yourself a deal."

Pitsy proffered his hand, and Cyril shook it. "Happy doing business with you. I'll ring you up. And I'll throw in an extra magazine, free of charge."

"Much appreciated.

Pitsy rang up the trade in for the Longslide and the buying price for the Hi-Power at the cash register. The prices were so close that even with tax, they canceled each other out.

"Hey, if this is a collector's item too, why is the price so low?"

"Because the original owner shot himself with it," Pitsy said flatly, then stopped tallying the bill on his data pad. "Still want it?"

Cyril shrugged. "Well, my life seems cursed already, so why not?"

***

He went home, reloaded his magazines, then stored them. He got himself a cold drink from his refrigerator and sat on the couch. "Music, synthwave, random playlist." A smooth jazzy track started. He took a sip, then his phone pinged with a message from his therapist stating he was delinquent on his last two appointments. "Fuck," he whispered to himself. He replied:

CYRIL: Sorry. Life got bad recently.
MINESE: I'm available later this afternoon if you want to
    come by. My 5:30 p.m. just canceled.
CYRIL: Yeah, that's fine. See you then.

He closed his phone. The music helped, but the sadness, the emptiness, was still there. Were he to die right there and then, no one would know, and no one would care. He sighed and drank again. Then he noticed the vial of white fluid on his coffee table, collecting dust for the last five days. He couldn't remember his reasoning for snatching it from the air on the station. Curiosity, maybe. But something that Kingston had said didn't sit right with him.

Non-Terrans! It's fucking genocide! And you help them do it!

He picked it up and studied the milky white fluid that flowed more like wax than water. He wasn't a virologist, so any idea as to what it might be beyond his basic knowledge of Project Samson was lost on him. He contemplated taking it to a specialist, then reconsidered. Stolen property wouldn't look good in the long run. Someone would report it.

He wasn't quite sure what to do. Maybe it was nothing. Or maybe it was everything.

Then he realized there was one person he could call to get an answer. He closed his eyes hard and gritted his teeth. *Goddammit.*

He set down his drink, grabbed his jacket, and headed to see Marie.

***

Temperatures outside had warmed a bit, but it was still cold that winter. He hopped in Jace's sports car and headed across town toward Marie's office. He considered stopping to buy a new set of flowers but figured there was no point. She would just throw them away again. He drove quietly and listened to the road hum under the tires. His mind was racing too loudly for any music.

He pulled up alongside the sidewalk outside her office building. Drifting clouds blocked the sun. The concrete building looked glum and depressing under the gray sky. He let out a gruff sigh, opened the car door, and stepped out. Part of him was excited to see her again, while another part was absolutely terrified. *Just turn around and walk away now. It doesn't matter that much. Just walk away.* But he steeled himself and pushed forward, one step in front of the other, as he marched through the cold air to the building entrance.

The interior was like any generic office building. A digital directory flowed by on a three-foot-high screen to his left. He touched it and searched for her name. She was listed as being on the fourth floor. He took the elevator up and found her office. A plaque next to the door read, DIVISION OF INFECTIOUS DISEASES. At that moment, he regretted not bringing flowers with him. He closed his eyes and opened the door to reveal a waiting room.

A young woman wearing an earpiece sat behind a reception desk, checking messages on her phone. Some generic paintings populated three of the four walls, and the carpet was hardwood slats. It reminded him of his therapist's office.

He approached the desk and, slightly ashamed to be there, asked, "Hi, is Marie Masters in today?"

"Are you here on business?"

"*Umm*, I suppose so. I need something tested."

"I'll see if she's in the lab right now. What's your name, sir?"

Fuck. "Cyril Eisner. She knows me. Tell her it's urgent."

The receptionist pressed a few buttons on her data pad and called the lab. Cyril sat next to the entrance and waited nervously. He felt like he was either in for a screaming match or being escorted out by the police. He wasn't religious at all, but he begged whatever power might be molding the universe to cut him one break. Just one, and he'd never ask for anything ever again. He closed his eyes and forced his mind to go blank.

"Sir, Ms. Masters is in her office," the receptionist said. "You can head back now. Just head straight back and turn right at the end of the hallway. You'll see her office."

Finally, a break.

He thanked the receptionist and headed into the office area, where a cubicle barnyard of people reviewing reports, shipping notes, deliveries, and test results. Cyril could never imagine himself working in an office environment. It looked absolutely soul crushing. He turned right at the end of the hallway as instructed, walked a few more paces, then came to her office. M. MASTERS was engraved on a nameplate next to the door. He sighed, then quietly knocked.

Silence for a few moments. Then he heard some shuffling behind the door. He leaned against the wall and waited. It finally opened. She stepped into the hallway, looking annoyed, but said nothing.

"Hey," he said.

She still said nothing, then walked into her office and sat down. Cyril followed her into the cozy little office decorated with a plant near the window, some pictures of family and friends, and a large anime robot with a curved sword on her desk. Her data pad was propped on her desk, with a rounded digital keyboard in front of it. She watched him with the precision of a sniper from her chair.

"Nice office," Cyril said.

She said nothing.

"Thanks for seeing me. I was actually afraid to come here."

"Oh, fucking knock it off. Just say what you came to say and leave."

"Okay. I'm not really here to say anything. I… need a favor."

"Oh! Oh, that's great. That's really great. You know what? If you have nothing to say, you can go." Marie stood, brushed past him, and stomped into the hallway.

Cyril followed. "Please, Marie. I'm sorry about everything. I just need an opinion on something."

"My opinion is that you can fuck off, Cyril."

"Please, just stop."

"Security will escort you out of the building."

"Jace is dead!"

She stopped.

"They're all dead." Cyril swallowed hard. Saying it made it feel real. "I have nothing left. No friends, no family. Not even you. I don't even have any pride anymore. I'll get on my knees and beg if it'll make you feel better. I just need to talk to you about something. Not us, something else. After that, you'll never see me again. I'll disappear. Just please talk to me."

A few coworkers leaned out of their cubicles to see what was happening. Marie stepped so close to Cyril that he could smell her again. That same smell—cherries. She slapped him across the face. He took it. She slapped him again. He didn't react. He felt he deserved it. Then she wrapped her arms around him and squeezed as hard as she could. Cyril embraced her like he'd done so many times before. He realized, in that moment, just how much he had missed her.

"When?" she asked through a stream of tears.

"A couple weeks ago. He was shot down. We cremated him on Cygnus. I had no way of contacting you to let you know."

"Oh, God."

"No, not God. Just bad luck."

***

Marie sat in front of an electron microscope and removed a small glass slide. She used a dropper to withdraw a bit of the inoculation fluid from the vial Cyril had given her. She dapped a drop onto the slide, then placed a second slide on top. The waxy fluid spread to fill the glass. She slid it under the lens and typed on her data pad.

Cyril leaned against the desk next to her and looked around. He had no idea how anything in the lab worked. It reminded him of when Marie had been confused about what it was like for him to be a starfighter. He could express the same sentiment about her line of work.

Huge overhead lighting tubes doused the basement lab in bright white. It felt sterile and harsh, reminding Cyril of *Lightfoot* station. Rows of desks and metal shelves—packed with lab supplies, beakers, microscopes, gloves, vials, data pads and terminals for research assignments, and a lot of other minutiae that felt foreign to him—filled the room. A large interior-facing window walled off a clean room at the rear of the lab. He imagined Marie in there, wearing a bulky hazmat suit, while studying some rare xeno disease. The microscope beeped and scanned the slide of fluid. Cyril thought about saying something but kept quiet. It was just the two of them in the lab, and the awkwardness was palpable.

Then Marie broke the silence and asked without looking up, "How was the funeral?"

"It was a funeral. It was what it was."

"Sorry I wasn't there."

"It's okay. It was small. We had it on Cygnus, and it was the summer months there. I think I lost a pound in sweat."

The machine beeped, then whirred again.

"I would take summer over winter anytime. Winter is always depressing."

"I agree."

Marie surveyed the information being relayed to her data pad. She cocked an eyebrow and faced Cyril. "Where did you find this stuff?"

"*Lightfoot* station, almost a week ago. PLA captured the place and were trying to expose some Arcturus conspiracy."

"I thought you said they were gone."

"They're like cockroaches. They just keep multiplying."

"How do you know there's some kind of conspiracy?"

"I don't. Just something the guy on the station said. 'It's fucking genocide. And you help them do it.' The only thing I can think of is that crap right there. I snagged that vial on my way out of the station. Arcturus hired freelance pilots like me to release this stuff in aerosol form across the Ekumen. Said it was for inoculations. Best I'm doing now is connecting the dots, but I don't know if it's drawing a picture or just random lines."

"Sounds ridiculous, Cyril. If genocide was happening because of this stuff, then where's the reports of mass death? There's nothing. If anything, infection rates have dropped across the Ekumen."

"Like I said, might just be random lines."

She leaned back in her chair. "Cyril, I don't think anything is wrong."

"But something really doesn't feel right," he said, ill at ease and crossing his arms. "And please don't tell anyone about this. This is stolen property. We'd both be screwed if someone found out."

"My lips are sealed."

The microscope finished its analysis and spat out a lengthy collection of data on her pad.

"Okay, so let's see about your conspiracy. Chemical composition looks normal. Standard weakened bacteria, preservatives, stabilizers, and cell cultures. Wow, there's a whole community in there. They really are trying to inoculate against everything."

"But anything that could kill a person should they be exposed to it? A Trojan horse maybe? One bacterium that's stronger than the other? There's gotta be something."

"Cyril, that's not how it works."

"I'm serious. There's something not right here."

"Cyril…" Marie stood and handed him the data pad. "There's nothing."

He browsed through the information. Nothing rang off as conspiracy or genocide. He shook his head. "It's not possible," he whispered to himself. "It's just not."

"It is. The PLA are just fanatics. Let it go. It is"—she handed the vial of the waxy fluid to Cyril—"what it is."

He eyed the vial disappointedly, then slid it into his jacket pocket. "Yeah. I guess it is what it is." He knew she wasn't talking about the vial.

"Sorry I couldn't help."

"It's fine." Cyril kept his gaze on the floor, then he inhaled. "I missed you."

Marie softly placed her hands on his chest and quietly said, "A part of me missed you too. When it was good, it was really good. But when it was bad… I just can't do it again."

"I know. I'm sorry."

They were both on the verge of crying. It felt like the inevitable ending.

"And now you need to go," Marie said, her voice wavering on the edge of sadness.

He regarded her and teared up, knowing this was the end.

She moved her hands from his chest to his cheeks. "You'll be okay. And I'll be okay. Okay?"

"Okay," he whispered.

"Okay." She let go of his face and stepped backward. "You know the way out."

Cyril nodded, took one last look, then turned to the door at the other end of the room. When he reached the doorway, he stopped and considered sneaking one last glance but decided against it. He turned right out the door and disappeared from sight..

***

Marie sat at her desk to clear the milky slide from under the microscope and used an alcohol pad to sterilize her hands. She sat still for a few moments, then broke down and cried her eyes out.

***

Cyril walked out the front entrance into the cold and darkening dusk, then traversed the concrete path toward the street. Several people were also leaving for the day, ready to brave the traffic home. He tried to keep his mind empty, but it was futile. The finality of the last five minutes settled in. He had thought maybe, given enough of a break, they might have found common ground, and there would be a way forward, and things could be fixed, and the emptiness would be gone.

But it didn't happen.

He reached the sidewalk and, at last, got it. Standing there alone on the cold, dead concrete, he stared at the office building for the final time and finally understood.

He owed her an apology.

She did not owe him forgiveness.

***

"So, what's bothering you?" Minese asked.

Cyril silently sat on the couch in Minese's office and stared at the floor. He didn't know what to say. It was dark outside, and the traffic was loud.

"How are things with work? Any problems there?"

Cyril said nothing.

"Love life?"

Cyril said nothing.

"Cyril, I can't help you if you don't express how you're feeling to me. I'm here for—"

"Fuck this." Cyril leaped from the couch and walked out, slamming the door.

He never went back.

***

Cyril sat on his bedroom floor, leaning against the foot of his bed next to the desk. For an hour, he cried. He didn't know who to call or who to talk to. No one was left. Cat and Jace and Jess and Marie.

All gone.

His father was right. He was a waste. Just another empty person drifting through life. The fact that his father had been right crushed him.

He'd finally had enough and didn't want anymore. Broken, alone, and too tired to keep going.

The case for the Browning Hi-Power lay flat on the desk. He pulled it into his lap. With tears in his eyes, he snapped open the latches, lifted the lid, and removed it. Cyril stared at it for a moment, then racked the slide to load a single round into the chamber. The bullet felt cold between his fingertips. He released the slide, and it snapped forward. His thoughts drifted to Bollman on Luyten, his body now left in a grave that no one will ever visit nor remember—a man who had done his best and still ended up with nothing.

Cyril winced. *Why can't I just be happy?*

He thumbed back the hammer.

I didn't mean to hurt anyone.

He'd had enough.

I did my best.

He placed the barrel to his left temple. Then he closed his eyes and thought of her.

I'm sorry...

Right before he pulled the trigger, his phone pinged. His eyes snapped open. He set the gun in his lap and checked the text message.

> ???: Hey there, Skyhawk!
> CYRIL: Who's this?
> ???: It's Rachael! I got your number from Stacy at the airfield. I'm your copilot tomorrow for the Arcturus drop.
> CYRIL: To be honest, I totally forgot I was supposed to work tomorrow. Thanks for reminding me.
> RACHAEL: Well, since I'm in town tonight, wanna grab a drink?

Cyril considered it for a moment. Not ten seconds ago, he had been ready to paint the wall with his brains. Now someone was there—someone he knew and trusted. He jumped at it.

> CYRIL: Meet me at Mallory's Heroes in thirty minutes. It's near the airfield. See you soon.
> RACHAEL: See you there.

He closed his phone, sat still for a minute, then forced himself to his feet on shaky legs. He put the case on the desk and set the gun on top. Then he cleaned himself up best he could, grabbed his jacket, and got in an autocab to head to Mallory's. He decided against driving Jace's car, as he didn't feel safe behind the wheel.

When he arrived thirty minutes later, he found her nursing her first drink near a pair of trash-talking patrons in the middle of a pool game. She wore blue jeans and a black tank top with thick shoulder straps. Underdressed for winter weather for sure. She hadn't realized Proxima was in the middle of its winter season. Her bleached hair had turned her usual dark brown into dirty blond. Her extremely tanned skin accentuated against the cold winter—a signature of Olympus's overabundance of light—but it fit right in with the brightness of Mallory's Heroes, as if the lights above made her skin glow. Her dark brown chocolate-colored eyes were something to get lost in as well. Cyril thought she was too gorgeous to be a starfighter.

Cyril invited Rachel to sit with him at the bar, where she ordered a vodka tonic and he went with his usual Guinness. They chatted about standard starfighter subjects, like nothing had happened, such as how they got into the business, life on Proxima compared to Olympus, and ship comparisons. When they switched subjects to their personal lives, he slipped his mask back on as he tried to dig deep for the old Cyril, the suave one, the charming one.

"So, are you still seeing that person from a few months ago?"

Cyril felt a little part of himself die in that moment but kept his composure. "Nope. Totally single."

"What happened, if you don't mind me asking?"

"Just… ended up that way."

"That's a shame. Sorry to hear that."

Cyril felt his composure break. And, for a split second, she caught it on his face.

"Sorry. Did I say something wrong?"

"No. No, nothing. It's just… Can we talk about something else?"

The cracking of billiard balls in the back of the bar sounded far too loud. Cyril stared into the darkness of his beer and ran his finger up and down the slick glass.

"Are you okay?" she asked, genuinely worried.

Cyril said nothing.

"Hey, what's wrong?"

He donned a fake smile. "Nothing. I'm fine." His fingers were damp with the condensation from the glass, and the black liquid looked like a void in space. He wished he could jump into it and disappear forever.

"You're not fine. What's wrong?"

He sighed heavily. "Just a lot has happened in the last few months."

"You mean with Jace?"

"Yeah. Among other things. There's a photo of him on the wall over there if you wanna go look." He pointed to photos four seats down from them.

Rachael went to find the group photo containing Cyril, Jace, Jess, and Marie. "Who are the others?"

Cyril slid off his barstool to join her. He pointed to the photo. "That's Jess. She was killed a few months ago on a recovery mission."

"What happened?"

"She… got left behind when the ship FOILed away. PLA shot her down."

"I'm sorry."

Cyril didn't respond to her apology. Then he pointed to Marie. "And that's my ex, Marie."

"May I also ask what happened there?"

"Like I said, it just didn't work out."

"I'm sorry again."

"It's all right. My own fault."

"This business takes a lot from us."

"Yeah, it does."

"But you're doing okay. You're still here with me. It's never as bad as it seems. Eventually things get better." She reached out and held his hand.

That brought a smile to Cyril's face. Maybe it was true. Or maybe she was just being nice. But her warmth and kindness recharged Cyril's spirits, even briefly. Either way, it felt good to smile again. "Thanks," he calmly said.

"How about another drink?"

He smirked at her. "How about we get drunk and make bad decisions?"

She smiled a devilish smile. "Absolutely."

***

They made it to Cyril's apartment a few hours later. Rachael was half in the bag, while Cyril was just buzzed. He needed to be able to perform that night for her. In her drunkenness, she admitted she had a massive crush on him and thanked him incessantly for saving her life, twice. He had kept his cool in the bar, but when she lunged forward and kissed him deeply, it was so sudden that it didn't fully register to Cyril for a good three seconds, then he felt like the old Cyril was back. The suave, charming ladies' man who could pull anyone. The one who Jace and Jess had told him to let go of. He was back, and he wanted Rachael in his bed that night.

They ripped off each other's clothes as they stumbled to the bedroom. It was still dark in the apartment. "Lighting to 50 percent," he said. The living room light strips gave the whole place a soft purple and blue glow.

"Oh, that's pretty," she said with excitement.

Cyril grabbed her ass, lifted her up, and carried her down the hallway toward the bedroom. She wrapped her legs around his waist and giggled. He tossed her onto the bed and yanked off his shirt. She unbuttoned her jeans and slid them down, along with her panties. She was soaking wet and ready for him. He slid off his pants and underwear… and then realized he wasn't hard for her. Maybe he just needed to warm up a bit, get more in the mood. He lay on top of her. They kissed and fondled each other, his hand sliding across her soft breasts, then to her stomach, and finally between her legs. She was dripping wet.

He slid his fingers inside of her, and she moaned as they kissed, then he nibbled on her ear. Cyril felt her getting close as she tightened around his fingers. His hand went faster, then he curved his fingers upward, hitting the perfect spot. She climaxed and drenched his fingers while screaming. She grabbed a pillow and screamed into it as he kept going. Then she came again, and a big wet spot flooded onto Cyril's bed sheets.

She giggled. "Sorry. Should have warned you."

"It's okay." He kissed her, then brought his soaking fingers to her mouth and slipped them between her lips.

She sucked her juices off with pleasure as she fingered herself. Then he pulled out his fingers and kissed her again, tasting the juices on her tongue. As the kiss ended, she looked into his eyes. "Now fuck me."

Oh no, he thought. After all that, he still wasn't hard. His cock hung flaccidly. He tried kissing and fingering her again. Still nothing. She reached down and caressed it.

Then, in confusion, she pulled away and asked uneasily, "What's wrong?"

"Nothing, I just… I need a minute." He tried everything he could. Nothing worked. Maybe the old Cyril wasn't back after all. After a few minutes, he gave up. "Goddammit."

Defeated, he lay beside her and stared at the ceiling, horribly embarrassed. The awkwardness between them was tense and filled the room like an ocean of disappointment. They both said nothing for a good long while.

Finally, she broke the silence. "Well… this is awkward."

"I'm… I'm sorry. Just… sorry. Got a lot on my mind." Cyril slid to the edge of the bed and sat upright. He stared at the same spot on floor where, a few hours earlier, he had been ready to shoot himself.

Rachael propped herself onto her elbows and gazed at him.

"It's nothing you did. I'm not too drunk or anything. I'm just… not really in the mood. Thought I was, but… you know."

"It's okay. I understand. You don't have to explain."

Cyril let out a long ashamed sigh.

Rachael rolled out of bed and dropped her feet to the floor. "I guess I'll head out," she said awkwardly, collecting her clothes.

"Don't leave," Cyril hurriedly said.

She paused.

"Would you stay with me tonight? Please?"

She looked at him, then noticed a gun sitting atop a plastic case on the desk, as if he had set it out earlier for reasons she didn't want to imagine.

"I don't want to be alone," he said sincerely.

She dropped her clothes to the floor and sat next to him. "Yeah, I'll stay with you," she whispered as she gazed into his eyes.

"Thank you," he murmured.

She kissed his cheek, then rested her head on his shoulder and held his hand. "You'll be okay."

"Everyone keeps saying that. I'm still waiting for it to be true."

They held each other for a few moments, then crawled under the sheets. The cold outside chilled the bedroom. He held her close to keep warm as they drifted off to sleep. He dreamed of better days. He dreamed of her.

Chapter 20

The Wrong Side

The megaliners flew overhead, like enormous birds flocking south for the summer season. Residents of Balamb watched in amazement and, in some places, horror, as the megaliners dumped their payload of white aerosol across the city. The entire planet of Proxima was the final step to completing Project Samson. The city council was more than happy to approve the mass inoculation program. However, some citizens wholeheartedly disagreed. Protests had formed outside of city hall and Arcturus tower. Droves of people, massing into the thousands, expressed their complete disgust with the government's decision without the populus' full confidence and support.

Daniel Mullarkey looked down from his penthouse and growled, "Parasites." He watched the megaliners fly by from the highest point in the city.

Layla stood next to him and watched as well. She considered speaking up or telling the protestors the truth about the inoculation. But every time she tried to move, it haunted her that she could not prove any of it. There was no stopping them. This was the end.

And so, she just stood and watched the ships fly by and fill the air with white mist.

To the side of the room, Moriarty fed them real-time information about the drops—coverage, weather conditions, and occurring problems. One ship was having trouble with its delivery tanks and had to turn back. It would return to perform a second run on its own once they fixed the tank valves.

Daniel glowed with patriotism and held his hands on his hips, proud to be a Terran. "We couldn't have done this without you, Layla."

She watched the megaliners spew their white spray and drench the city till it looked like a foggy shroud draped over everything.

"You know this is for the best," Daniel continued. "Terrans need to maintain their place. If we didn't take a step forward, someone else would."

"I really don't understand how you became so cruel," she said with quiet rancor. "I'm ashamed we share the same blood."

"Grow up. Moriarty, how long till the drop is complete?" Daniel asked, returning to his desk.

"Another thirty minutes and Balamb will be finished. The second wave will be moving west within the hour."

"Good. That will wrap up the main planets of the Ekumen. And the gala tomorrow? How's preparations coming along?"

"Bentley is currently going through background checks on all the staff. The third floor and its balcony have been cordoned off for the build."

"Excellent. And the guest list? The Terran governance needs a warm welcome the moment they walk in the front doors."

"Maybe invite some of your development teams too. Or even those pilots out there," Layla said sarcastically and with a sharp scorn as she faced Daniel.

"*Ugh*, why would we ever invite the peasants to this? They don't belong here," Moriarty groaned.

"No, that's a solid thought," Daniel replied. "We invite those below to maintain appearances. Shows we still care about the little guy. Excellent thinking. That's why I love you. 'The ladder of success is best climbed by stepping on the rungs of opportunity.' And that is a hell of an opportunity."

Layla had intended her statement as an insult toward him, and he had turned it into an opportunity to continue punching down. She thought he was either incredibly dumb, which was unlikely, or he was just that cruel. She resumed watching out the window. The ships had all but disappeared into the mist, and the city of Balamb felt like the spray had draped a white bed sheet over it, almost as if it was snowing.

Below on the street, the mob of protestors scrambled to escape the spray, rushing to take shelter. But there was no escape. Even if they managed to find shelter, air-conditioner systems would spread the inoculation agent to the interiors of buildings and apartment complexes. There was nowhere to run and nowhere to hide. Everyone who inhaled it noticed a slight stinging sensation and the smell of chemicals. For the next six hours, the mist would slowly settle across the city and eventually encrust to become a soft powder that would coat everything for weeks to come. The wind would carry it away and spread into the deepest reaches of the city and beyond.

***

The megaliner set down at Francisco Air Base, thirty kilometers west of Balamb. It was enormous, four times the size of M&M's private airfield. Huge bulbous tanker trucks approached the megaliners to refill the drop tanks for the second wave of sprays. Cyril and Rachael descended from the rear exit of the cockpit and walked down the service ramp at the back end of the ship. The base was scrambling to fill the tanks and get the ships in the air before the sun set. It was cold and getting colder.

Before they had gone up that day, Cyril had said, *"Hey, thanks for staying with me last night."*

"It's no problem," Rachael had replied, with a cute smile.

"Sorry I was a disappointment."

"Eh, *at least I got off a couple times."* She had chuckled.

Cyril had taken a playful swipe at her shoulder. She had returned the favor.

Now, as their shift ended and the next crew geared up to head out, they were trying to decide where to go for dinner.

As they traversed the ice-cold tarmac, Cyril saw a familiar face in the distance. Filly was flying with the second crew. Cyril rushed toward them before they could take off. They had changed their hair again. Now it was purple. "Hey there, stranger," Cyril shouted.

When Filly turned and saw him, they gasped and hugged him. "Cyril, I was wondering if you were gonna be flying this one. This is homebase for you, right?"

"Yup, born and raised. Oh, Filly, this is Rachael, my copilot on this one."

Rachael proffered her hand. Filly shook it.

"We were trying to figure out dinner for tonight. How long are you supposed to be up there?"

"We're headed out west. Should only be a couple hours. Not much outside the city but farmland, so it should be a quick drop."

"When you get back, get in touch with me. We'll all grab something together."

"Sounds good. I'll get your number from air command. Gotta fly now. Later!" Filly secured their helmet as they jogged up the ramp into their megaliner.

"She seems nice," Rachael said.

"*They*, actually."

"*Ahh*, thank you for the correction."

"No problem. Happens all the time."

"At this point, when I think of *they*, I think of that bitch Moriarty."

Cyril groaned. "Don't remind me."

They headed toward the crew quarters.

"What is their problem anyway?" Rachael asked as she stuffed her helmet in her helmet bag.

"You know, I've contemplated it a couple times, and I realized they probably are just unlovable."

"What is that called? An inferiority complex?"

"I don't know. I just distill them down to one word."

"What word?"

"Cunt."

They both howled in laughter.

As they entered the crew quarters, an airbase serviceman approached them with a data pad. "Excuse me, we've been told to get your signature on an invite that just came through from Arcturus Allied."

"What invite?" Rachael asked quizzically as she took the data pad. She read the large print and scoffed. "It seems all the flight staff have been invited to a celebratory gala tomorrow at Arcturus tower."

"Wow. I didn't realize they wanted to associate with the underclass so badly," Cyril said stoically.

"Yeah, well, I'll pass." Rachael handed the data pad to the airman. "I'm probably gonna head back to Olympus. Take some vacation time."

The airman pressed a square box on his pad, marking her as a no for the invite.

"I'll be there tomorrow," Cyril said.

"Seriously?" Rachael asked, her brow furrowed in confusion.

"Hey, remember when I said I would spit in Moriarty's face on my way out the door? Can't do that shit from my house. So I'll be there tomorrow."

Rachael laughed. "That's the pettiest thing I've ever heard, and I totally need to see it. I've changed my mind. I'll be there too."

The airman marked both Cyril and Rachael as yeses for the invite.

As they left the airfield, they realized they would need a fresh set of proper clothes for a proper event. Cyril drove them to a tailor shop for a suit for himself. With the money he had made from the *Lightfoot* station mission, he could afford to splurge a little bit. He found himself a black tuxedo vest, a fresh white shirt, and black slacks. He also purchased a new pair of black leather shoes.

He changed in the dressing room and came out to get Rachael's opinion.

When she saw him, she whistled. "*Mm*, looking good, handsome."

"*Heh*, thanks."

"Need to shave though."

He looked at his face's reflection in the mirror and saw he had been neglecting himself. Five days of beard growth was looking scraggly. "I'll add it to my to-do list tonight."

"All right, my turn."

They switched places, Cyril taking the seat outside the dressing room, and Rachael changing into something more professional. When she finished, she came out wearing a full suit and blazer, fitted just right to her size. For a woman, she fit into men's clothes extremely well. She surveyed her reflection in the mirror, then removed the blazer, draped it over her shoulder, and leaned against the door frame with suave charm. She smirked at him. "Well?"

Cyril stood behind her to see their appearances in the mirror, a solid eight inches taller than her with his new shoes on. They both looked handsome. "You know, even if you were a guy, you would still have me at least half hard right now."

Rachael scoffed and craned her head back toward him. "So, you would have totally fucked me last night if I was a dude? Got it. I'll work on that." She stuck out her tongue and tried to lick the tip of his nose. She missed it, but Cyril found it cute.

"Oh, shut up." He walked away, slightly embarrassed.

Rachael chuckled to herself.

They bought their new attire and headed to Cyril's apartment, where Cyril took Rachael's advice and shaved. He looked like a new man with his facial scruff all gone.

His phone pinged. It was Filly.

FILLY: All done. What's for dinner?
CYRIL: One sec.

"Hey, what are we doing for dinner?" Cyril asked Rachael.

"I'm down for anything," she said, sitting on the couch and playing a game on her phone.

"Don't do that. Pick a thing!"

She looked up from her phone. "Well, yes, sir. I could go for Skovian noodles."

"Thank you. Good choice."

CYRIL: Skovian noodles sound good to you?
FILLY: Not my favorite, but I'm down.
CYRIL: I'll send you the address of a good place.

He sent Filly the address of the closest noodle bar where he and Marie had frequented. He pushed away that thought with the force of a bulldozer and closed his phone. "Let's go eat."

When they arrived, the dinner rush was in full swing. They scored the last table before the hostess stopped walk-ins. Filly trotted in twenty minutes later and joined them. The food took a while to arrive, but it was worth it. They drank a dry red wine, which perfectly complimented the meal. The fresh and plump noodles mixed with beef chunks and vegetables made for a tasty meal. Rachael doused her noodles in so much hot sauce that she knew she would regret it the following morning on the toilet, but she didn't care. The conversation was quaint and jovial.

Then Rachael asked Filly, "You going to that gala tomorrow?"

"*Nah*, I gotta head back home to see family. Right after this, I'm off to the airfield. Plus, I just don't feel like being in a stuffy room filled with rich people. Why, are you two going?"

"Got a promise to keep," Cyril said. "I'll tell you about next time I see you."

Rachael smirked.

"*Heh*. Can't wait. Either of you have anything else lined up after tomorrow?"

"I'm taking time off. I need it," Rachael said. "Been burning the candle at both ends, paying off my new ship."

"What about you, Cyril?" Filly asked with a mouthful of noodles.

"I think I'm gonna just… take off."

"Take off?"

"There's a character in a book series I like. He travels from town to town, living on his own, getting into random adventures. Never carries more than what's in his pockets. Never sets his feet down too long in one spot. I'm gonna try that. I think it might be time for me to just get away from here for a while."

"Damn," Filly whispered to no one in particular.

"There's too much bad history here. Probably best if I just dip out."

"Well, if you find yourself on Olympus, you better come see me," Rachael demanded.

"And if you're ever on Luyten, the Southern Hemisphere at least, you better come see me," Filly declared as well.

"I will."

Rachael raised a glass to Cyril. "To better roads ahead."

Filly raised their glass too, as did Cyril. "Let's hope so."

They clinked their glasses together, drank deep, then ordered another bottle.

***

"Holy shit, look at the fucking blue shrimp," Rachael yelled.

The food at the gala was exquisite—expensive beyond either Cyril or Rachael's means and completely fresh. They had no idea how much it had cost to put the whole thing together, but it more than likely wasn't even a dent in the Arcturus Allied coffers. What also cost a pretty penny was the ground-floor security detail. Protestors were gathered outside, still chanting their grievances to a higher power who didn't care if they existed. Building security had joined with mercenary forces to keep the perimeter surrounding the building secure. They had erected metal fences in case anyone got any idea about "storming the castle." Cyril was thankful that a valet was on staff to handle parking that day.

Arcturus had transformed the entire third level of its tower into an open space for partying, with a clean dance floor, a full band on a stage, a huge lighting setup for the party atmosphere, and enough alcohol to drown a continent. Board members, office workers, lobbyists, government officials, even several heads of the Ekumen itself attended. All different species mingled with each other—Skovian, Luyten, Crecian, Mukarian, and Terran. The ambassadors of each planet were more than happy to have made the trip to Proxima. A small memorial to Brentwood and Douglas Forester decorated a corner for people to pay their respects. To everyone in attendance, it was a glorious day. Interspecies relations could continue without fear of cross contamination. The rich and the powerful would dance, drink, and party all the way into the night.

Rachael had piled a plate of blue shrimp so large that it was on the verge of toppling over.

Cyril eyed her and playfully said, "Woman, control yourself."

"Oh, fuck off," she replied with a mouthful of shrimp.

Cyril shook his head and chuckled. He felt extremely out of place. A few other pilots had shown up, but no one he knew. It was an odd thing, being invited to such an event. The last time he had attended an event such as that was when he had first met Daniel Mullarkey and had known that, at some point, he would punch him in the face for being such a dick. He saw Daniel from a distance but didn't bother saying hello. Moriarty clung to his side as well, like a lamprey that refused detach itself from its host. They noticed Cyril from a distance and shot him a murderous scowl. Cyril replied with a middle finger.

The two starfighters stayed off to the side, unsure of who to talk to. While Rachael stuffed her face with shrimp, Cyril filled his bladder with alcohol. He hated almost everyone in the room.

Then he saw Layla Mullarkey exit the glass elevator, looking extremely gorgeous. She wore a white pencil skirt down to her calves and a white blouse. Her hair was in a bun, and her eyes were dark and shadowy. Cyril had never seen her look more amazing. Her bodyguards, Bentley and Locke, stayed by her side as they exited the elevator and mingled with the crowd. Cyril watched her greet various politicians and office workers. Eventually she worked her way to Daniel and joined his group. He was mingling with the heads of the Ekumen, probably brokering another deal.

Rachael finished her plate and belched.

"Wow, that was hot," Cyril remarked.

"You know it. I'm so sexy when I try."

A server walked by with a tray of champagne. Rachael snatched two glasses and downed one immediately.

Cyril sighed hard. "God, I hate these people," he muttered.

"I mean, we can always just leave." Rachael sipped her second glass. "No one really wants to talk with us. Go spit in that bitch's face, and let's dip."

"Yeah, why not? All right, here I go."

As Cyril set his drink on the table next to him, Daniel took to the stage and interrupted the band. The music abruptly stopped as he snatched a microphone and tapped it to check if it was on. "Ladies and gentlemen, eyes on me please. First off, thank you for coming from all over the Ekumen to join us here today. That yellow brick road finally led to Emerald City. The complete and total inoculation of the Ekumen. Everyone is free of the threat of cross-species infection. While we still have a few planets to take care of, we're extremely close to the very end. I'm not going to say it was cheap, because it definitely was not, but it was worth it. To see so many faces of you in one room gives me hope for the future. I truly believe in my heart that we will make it and will eventually venture across to the farthest reaches of our own galaxy and beyond. This is the first step on a larger road.

"One of my favorite quotes is from the great educator Ayn Rand. I'm sure plenty of you have heard this quote. She said, 'Every man builds his world in his own image. He has the power to choose, but no power to escape the necessity of choice.' I mention this because, years ago, I was at a crossroads. For those who don't know, I did my patriotic duty serving in the Terran Navy."

Cyril cocked an eyebrow and whispered to himself, "What the fuck?"

"I fought to protect the Terran body across our galaxy. But when my father passed, I was left with the choice to either stay in the service or to give it up to run the company here alongside my wonderful sister. I chose to return, because the choice came down to being a cogwheel in a large machine and having little choice or to take control of the company and be the fulcrum upon which choice is balanced. I came home, and now I'm serving the Ekumen in a different way but still as a patriot. I believe we should all aspire to that goal. Doing our duty for the sake of the Ekumen." Daniel raised his glass of champagne.

The crowd followed suit. They all took a sip. Cyril didn't toast as he watched in confusion. *When the fuck did he serve?*

"I'd also like to thank our fantastic air crews, some of which are here with us tonight." When Daniel started clapping, the crowd clapped along with him. "They worked tirelessly to make sure the Ekumen would be rendered safe and disease free. I think I see a familiar face in the back there. I believe that's our local celebrity, Mr. Cyril Eisner. Some of you probably know who he is. He gave quite a speech almost a year ago. On behalf of Arcturus, I'd like to say thank you for doing your duty for your people."

"As long as the check clears, I'm happy," Cyril yelled.

The crowd laughed.

Mullarkey laughed as well—that cruel, contemptuous laugh. It made Cyril twinge in anger. "As long as the check clears." Mullarkey chuckled. "I'm sure it will, Mr. Eisner. I'm sure it will. Tonight, though, everyone enjoy yourselves, and everything is on the house. And, of course, don't forget to tip your servers." Mullarkey passed the mic to the band leader.

The crowd applauded and cheered as he stepped off stage. The music started back up. Cyril finished his drink and knew he would need another.

"Man, he really is in love with himself," Rachael said. She sipped her drink.

"Well, you know, there had to be somebody out there who jacked off while looking in a mirror," Cyril quipped.

Rachael laughed and spit out some of her drink onto the floor.

Daniel rejoined his group from earlier and stood next to Layla. Cyril watched them. Daniel sidled over a little too close to his sister and, when no one was looking, grabbed Layla's ass. Anger fumed in

Cyril. Were he armed, he would have started shooting. Layla recoiled and excused herself. Bentley and Locke began to follow, but she shooed them away. She grabbed two glasses of champagne off a tray table and headed to the balcony outside.

Cyril leaned toward Rachael. "Think the shrimp will be enough company for a while?"

She didn't answer. He turned and saw Rachel was gone. He looked around and found her conversing with a group of Mukarian politicians who were fascinated with her pilot stories. Cyril shrugged and grabbed another drink as he headed toward the balcony.

Outside, heat lamps were blazing every five feet. A few people sparsely populated the balcony, and all of them had come outside to smoke or vape. Layla leaned against the railing above the entrance to Arcturus tower and quickly drank her first glass. She chucked the empty glass over the edge and watched it fall to the sidewalk.

Cyril walked up beside her and leaned on the railing. "You know, someone could get hurt if you keep doing that."

"It's not the fall that gets you. It's the sudden stop at the bottom."

Cyril harrumphed. "Yeah, I guess so."

A waiter came outside and passed out more champagne. Layla took two more glasses.

The pair drank in silence for a few moments, then Cyril asked, "Has he ever touched you like that before?"

Layla said nothing. She finished another glass, then, like the previous, dropped it over the edge and watched it fall to the concrete below.

"I'll kill him right now if you want me to."

"Stop. It's not your problem. I'm fine."

"No, you're not. You're a victim."

"After those airdrops, everyone is a victim."

"What do you mean?"

"I mean, Project Samson. It was the last step for Daniel to achieve complete control. The *final solution*, as he called it."

"What the hell are you talkin' about?" he asked agape.

"Did you really think that what you were dropping was meant to inoculate the Ekumen?"

Cyril stayed quiet for a moment. "I had a feeling it was something else, but… I had someone test a sample of it. It *was* just an inoculation agent. Nothing special."

"It's just a cover. It's on a timed-release system. Once it becomes integrated with non-Terran DNA, it mutates. Twelve months from now, you'll see news story after news story of the Ekumen turning upside down, trying to figure out why there haven't been any more non-Terran babies."

"What? What the fuck are you saying?"

She faced him and grimly said, "It was never an inoculation program. It was a sterilization program."

It all clicked into place. It made perfect sense. Kingston had been right. *"It's fucking genocide. And you help them do it."*

Cyril put his face in his hands. "Oh, God, the PLA were right. The whole time. I was killing the wrong side."

"I'm sorry. I didn't know how to stop him. I just… don't know what to do."

"We can go to the press. Expose him online. I still have a vial of that stuff. We can catch him in his lie."

"And then what? He'll just tie everything up in courts for years while Arcturus steam rolls forward. He'll blame it on everyone but himself. And if things get bad, he'll liquidate the company and set up shop elsewhere. It'll never end. Most of the people working on it didn't know what it was either. Everything was compartmentalized."

Cyril gripped the wrap-around railing so hard that it felt like it might twist under his palms. As he squeezed, the white powder of the inoculation spray ground down under his fingers. He let go, then swiped his hand along the railing. It was fine, like talcum powder. "What is this stuff?" he whispered.

"Conquest. Once the numbers dwindle on all the non-Terran planets, the Terran Navy rolls in to take over."

"That'll take years for the numbers to fall."

"The Terran body has nothing but time. Playing the long game. It's easier and cheaper than outright war. Our numbers stay high, while their numbers go low."

"We need to tell the Ekumen right now. They're *right there* in that room. We can just go in there and tell them." He forcefully pointed toward the balcony door.

Layla shook her head in disappointment. "Tell them what? How would you prove it? The inoculation doesn't react without host DNA, and it takes months to activate. We'd both look like crazy conspiracy theorists. Nothing would change. They'd haul us out in straightjackets. Besides, who do you think was actually behind it?"

Cyril smashed his palm on the railing and looked out at Balamb. The slight milky mist of Project Samson still filled the air. He shook his head. "Goddammit. I'm so fucking sick of the bad guys winning. Everyone I know is dead because the bad guys keep winning."

"Up is down. Black is white. One day you wake up and see that's just how the universe is."

"Yeah, well I hate it."

"Good for you. Means you still have a soul." Layla finished her second drink, then chucked the glass over the side like the others.

They both went quiet.

"You never did answer my question," Cyril said. "Has he ever touched you like that before?"

"More times than I want to remember. He's always in control. Even when he isn't in the room, he's in the room. Brentwood was the same. I haven't slept well in months. Years even."

"I don't understand how you two come from the same blood. How can you be such a decent person, and he's… him?"

"He fell in with bad people when he was younger—fanatical types. He became someone totally different. Our dad saw it too, but instead of scolding him, he supported it. Said he was becoming a true leader. A man of action. Not long after that, he started…" She trailed off and began crying.

"I'm sorry."

"It is what it is." She wiped away tears and composed herself, burying it all down again.

"You can just go, Layla. Just take your things and go."

"We've had this conversation, Cyril. It's not that easy."

"Yes, it is. Just… go."

Layla said nothing.

"Serious question, though. Was he ever actually in the Terran Navy?"

She turned her head toward Cyril and made a contemptuous face.

Cyril chortled. "I thought not. He knows we can fact check that shit, right?"

"He'll just say he was black ops or something. Closest he ever got to warfare was a shooting range with his rifle."

"Jeez. Figures. I'm more of a patriot than him, and I hate patriotism."

They both went quiet again and leaned on the railing.

"Well… now what?" he asked, dumbfounded.

"I don't know, Cyril. I really don't."

"Do you wanna kill him?"

"More than anything. But it's suicide."

"Yeah. But it sounds like a good idea too."

***

Bentley hid in the corner next to the balcony doors, away from the crowd, snapping voyeuristic photos of party guests. All women. He even snapped some shots of Rachael as she chatted with a group of politicians. She had undone her tie, and her chest was slightly exposed. Bentley was sweating and turning red.

As he snapped a series of pics, Cyril placed his hand on Bently's bulbous shoulder from behind. "I'd suggest you delete every single one of those photos right now. Do it."

Bentley turned to meet Cyril's gaze with a reddened face and a slight bulge in his pants.

Cyril took a glance in disgust, then looked back up.

"And what if I don't, Mr. Eisner?"

"Then I'll rip your eyeballs out of your sockets, then tear off your testicles, and sew them into the holes. Go on. Try me, you fat fuck," Cyril growled.

Bentley took the hint and deleted all the photos.

"Good dog. Now fuck off."

"You disgust me, Mr. Eisner."

"The feeling's mutual, pervert." Seething anger boiled inside him, ready to explode. Cyril was in a room filled with criminals. Murderers. And they were all profiting from it. He'd always avoided being political. It had never interested him. But now, he had no choice. He had to pick a side. A side other than himself.

Cyril joined Rachael, deep in conversation with a middle-aged woman who practically bled money, and leaned into her ear to whisper, "I need to talk to you about something. Let's go."

Rachael looked back at him, confused.

"Seriously, let's go."

She took the hint. "Okay." Rachael said her goodbyes, set down her glass of champagne, and followed Cyril to the elevator.

As the doors closed, he extended his hand to stop them.

"What's wrong?"

"Forgot something," he said, smiling. He scanned the room for Mullarkey's group and found them, with Moriarty standing right next to him. Cyril wedged his way into the group.

Mullarkey was taken aback for a moment. "Excuse me, everyone. I'm heading out now, but I just had one last thing I needed to say to Moriarty."

Cyril snorted back, pooled up snot in his mouth, and spit right in Moriarty's stupid fucking face. He cleared his throat. "Thank you." He turned on his heels and strode away, feeling like a million bucks.

As he got returned to the elevator, Rachael said, "Was it everything you hoped for?"

"*Mmhmm.*" Cyril gave the middle finger to the whole crowd as the elevator doors closed.

They rode the elevator to the ground and walked outside. It was only 8 at night, but the sky was pitch black. No stars due to the light pollution, and the moon was in an eclipse. The crowds had been pushed back, but their chants were still distant echoes. It was cold, and fog was rolling in, making the air damp and chilly. He handed his valet ticket to the attendee in front of the building, and the pair stood on the sidewalk to wait for the car. Rachael huddled into Cyril for warmth.

As they waited, Daniel Mullarkey exited the building and pounded the pavement, rushing toward them. "Eisner!"

Cyril turned around. "May I help you?" he asked nonchalantly.

Mullarkey got right in his face. "You have some nerve embarrassing me in front of my people."

"Had a promise to keep. Now it's done."

"You really are pathetic. I never liked you even from the minute I met you. I just thought it was fun to toy with you but crossing me like that is a place you never want to go. Never come back here and stay away from my sister. Last warning."

"You know who you remind me of?"

"Who's that?"

"My father."

"Oh, I'm charmed."

"I hate my father. And I wish he was fucking dead."

Mullarkey fell silent for a moment. "Get the fuck off my property and never come back. You'll get your check tomorrow." He began walking toward the building.

"You disgust me, Mullarkey. You and all your staff are the same. Just a bunch of bullies and punks thinking you're better than everyone else."

Mullarkey turned back. "I *am* better than everyone else!"

Cyril laughed.

"What's so fucking funny?"

"Just thinking about various ways to ruin your life. I can think of about ten right now."

"Get lost… Skyhawk," Mullarkey snarled, turning away. "What a stupid name."

"You'll get yours, Mullarkey. And I hope I'm the one to deliver," Cyril said to no one.

Mullarkey shoved open the entrance door so hard that it slammed into the interior glass wall. Moriarty, Bentley, and Locke were waiting for him as he entered. The trio looked like they were ready to spill Cyril's blood.

"Such a charming crowd," Rachael noted.

The car finally arrived. Cyril passed the valet a hundred and hopped in. Rachael slid into the passenger seat and turned the heat on high. Cyril sat in the driver's seat and contemplated what to do next.

"You okay?" she asked.

"I need a drink."

"More? We just had a bunch."

"We need to talk about something, and I can't do it totally sober." He grabbed his phone to text Layla.

> CYRIL: Meet me at a bar called Mallory's Heroes. Come
> alone. We need to talk. I think I have a plan.

LAYLA: Okay.

Cyril shifted the car into Drive and headed for the entrance gate. The gate rose, and the car passed through. Flanked on both sides by protestors of all races and creeds, he punched the throttle, peeled out, and raced down the highway to Mallory's Heroes.

***

The three of them sat together at a dimly lit table across from the bar. The crowd was quiet. Not many patrons, which was odd for a Friday. Cyril, Rachael, and Layla still wore their party attire and looked completely out of place. Mallory cocked an eyebrow at the caliber of company Cyril had surrounded himself with that night.

They sat and drank, needing hard liquor. Cyril and Layla explained to Rachael what Project Samson actually was. By the time they had finished, she was on her second round and felt the need for a third. Cyril spied the group photo wall for a moment, then looked away. He had a feeling he would be joining them soon.

"I love coming in here. It's like a home away from home," Cyril reminisced.

"It's got a good feel," Layla said. "This place reserved for pilots?"

"It's for everyone, but pilots coming from the airfield pass by here." Rachael sipped her drink. "It's the local watering hole."

"This might be the last time I come here," Cyril whispered. "What you told me tonight, Layla, I can't just let it go."

"There's no stopping them," she said gravely. "It's already done. They won."

"Well, they don't get to win and walk away unscathed. I'm gonna handle it. And I'm gonna get you out of this."

"What are you saying, Cyril?" Rachael asked, terrified of his response.

Cyril took a long sip and inhaled deeply. "Long time ago, back on Earth before it became what it is now, there was a nation of warriors called Spartans. They were the best of the best. Hard to the core. Angry as hell. And they were also the predecessors to the Nazis. They practiced eugenics to create what was to them 'a perfect society.' Eventually they fell because, deep down inside, there was weakness.

Internal rot. Combine that with outside forces rising against them, and eventually they fell. I think it's time for that to happen again."

The two women regarded each other, horrified at what he would say next.

"Exposing Daniel Mullarkey so he can be arrested will change nothing. You even said so. He can buy his way out of jail. He has to be taken down. All of them. There's no other way."

"It's suicide, Cyril," Layla pleaded.

"I know." He faced Rachael. "And I'm okay with that. Hell, I'll die laughing if I can get this one thing right."

Rachael nodded. "So, what's the plan?"

"We need to get Daniel to expose himself publicly for everyone to see. A recording would go under scrutiny as being edited or an AI creation. We need a live confession."

"Good luck with that. He almost never discusses Samson outside his inner circle."

"I'll need to get close to him. Get him to slip up… or offer a trade for information."

"Trade what?"

"You," Cyril said to Layla.

Layla was taken aback, then she understood. "I see. I'm bait."

"Yeah. Sorry. He cherishes you more than anything, and for the wrong reasons. I can use that. Twist him into giving me what I want… if we stage a kidnapping."

Rachael cut in. "But then how do you expose him live? He'll never meet publicly, especially if he knows she's under threat. And they'll find a wire or microphone, no matter how small. They'll catch you."

"I'm still workin' on that part."

"I think I know a way," Layla said. "I'll need to pull some strings, but I think I can get what we need."

"Okay. That part's solved. And it'll have to be tonight while everyone is still there."

"Then how are you gonna take them out?" Rachael asked. "If you meet with him, he'll be surrounded by security. Maybe even mercenaries and police. They'll take your weapons if you try to meet face-to-face. They'll see it coming."

Cyril knocked back his drink and said intensely, "No. They definitely won't see this coming."

They discussed a few more details before Layla departed. She would get what Cyril needed. After twenty minutes, Cyril and Rachael headed out as well and drove to his apartment. He went to his bedroom and changed out of his suit into a black long-sleeve shirt and jeans. He removed the case for his Eruptor rifle from his closet, built it piece by piece, then got the spare magazines. He laid out his new pistol as well. For an arsenal, it wasn't too shabby.

Rachael leaned on the doorframe and soberly said, "You're never gonna survive this. You know that."

"Probably not. But you never know. Sometimes you get lucky."

"So, this is it, *huh*? Three hours to kill."

"Yeah." Cyril loaded a magazine into his Eruptor and rammed it home. "Better make 'em count."

" Better make 'em count. "

Chapter 21

The Right Thing

Daniel Mullarkey and his immediate staff congregated in his penthouse office for a private celebration. Several members of the board of directors had stayed late after the main party had ended. Moriarty, Bentley, and Locke attended also. Moriarty spoke to no one, and Bentley took more voyeuristic photos when no one was looking. Locke said nothing and stood guard by the elevator. Soft music played on the speakers while news reports scrolled past on the television screens. Even with all the sense of accomplishment in the air though, Daniel was uneasy. He texted Layla for the fourth time.

No response.

He sat behind his desk and stared out the window. The night had become foggy, and he felt the cold even through the windows, like a chill was running up and down his spine. Something felt wrong. "Bentley!"

Bentley, feeling as if his boss had caught him, immediately put away his phone and shuffled to Daniel's desk.

"Do you know where Layla went?"

"No, sir," he replied. He breathed a sigh of relief that his perversions were still safe.

"*Hmm.* She's not answering or even registering that she's seen any texts. Go find out what's happening." As Bentley headed toward the elevator, Daniel yelled, "Wait!"

Bently turned around, thinking his boss was finally going to chew him out. This was not the case.

"Disregard, Bentley. She's calling now," Daniel announced as he stood. He answered and put the phone to his ear. "You better have a very good explanation for disappearing tonight. Exactly where the hell are you? Do you have any—"

"Oh, I'm so sorry, Dan. Layla is a little… tied up at the moment. Can I take a message?" Cyril said jovially.

"Eisner," Daniel growled. "Where the fuck is Layla?"

"Oh, she's here right now. Let me show you." Cyril switched to video and revealed Layla to Daniel, tied up and gagged in a dark and dingy yet nondescriptive room.

Through her gag, Layla screamed, "Help me!"

Cyril pointed the camera at himself. "So, how's that look for you?"

Daniel screamed, "Everyone shut the fuck up!"

The music stopped, and the crowd in his office went silent. Mullarkey transferred the video signal from his phone to his television screens. Multiple images of Cyril's face were on display for everyone to see. "Bentley, trace him! Now!"

"You're not gettin' a trace off this," Cyril said. "It's amazing the things you can find for free online these days. Like GPS blockers. Really, I don't know why I didn't do this sooner. This was too easy." Cyril laughed.

"Who the hell is that?" a board member asked.

"Shut up! What do you want, Eisner?" Daniel angrily asked.

"*Hmm.* What do I want? Well, I'd love to blow Moriarty's head off, but beggars can't be choosers. They there? Hi, Moriarty! You're a massive cunt."

"What. Do. You. *Want*?" The anger in him was a volcano erupting balls of fire. He clenched his fists so hard that his knuckles cracked.

"Well, for starters, how's thirty million dollars to buy my silence?"

"Silence for what?"

"For this." Cyril held up a vial of white fluid and smiled.

Daniel scoffed. "You have some of the Samson fluid. So what? Who cares? The city is drenched in it right now."

"Oh, but from what your sister told me, it's not exactly an inoculation, is it? Here, I'll let you talk to her again." Cyril pulled down Layla's gag and held the phone in front of her face. "Now tell them what you told me while you were drunk tonight."

"I'm sorry, Dan. I told them everything." Tears streaked Layla's face. Her mascara was smeared, and her makeup was running. "He knows about the sterilizer. He knows everything. I'm sorry. I messed up."

Cyril put the gag back in. "That's good enough." Cyril faced the phone onto himself.

"You can't prove a fucking thing," Daniel growled.

Crowd members began heading to the elevator.

"*Nobody* leaves!"

Everyone froze.

"Maybe. Maybe not," Cyril agreed. "But are you really willing to take that chance? With her testimony and with this sample, someone's bound to come knocking. Hell, you wouldn't be able to leave that tower of yours. Every non-Terran would be out for blood. So, what do you say? Wanna make a deal? Hell, you could even put it in writing just to make it official."

Daniel silently watched the agog crowd stare at him, wondering if he would fold. Daniel snapped back at Cyril's huge smiling face on the monitors.

"Plus, I know you want her back for very specific reasons. She told me all about the 'other stuff.'"

"Shut the fuck up," Daniel growled through his teeth.

"I'm no prude, but some sexual proclivities need boundaries."

"Shut the fuck up!"

"What I'm trying to say is, you rich people are fucking weird."

"*Shut the fuck up!*"

Cyril stopped and stared into the camera. Daniel breathed hard. The crowd watched him with panic and disgust.

Finally, Daniel said, "You… piece of shit, Eisner."

"You rich bastards love to look down on people like me as parasites while you consider yourselves the creators. So why don't you do this? Create for yourself fifty million dollars—"

"*Fifty*? You said thirty!"

"Oh, I meant fifty. My bad."

Daniel growled and punched a monitor. It snapped to black, leaving a massive dent in the screen.

"Now, don't hurt yourself. You're gonna need those hands for a money transfer. We have a deal, Mullarkey? Fifty million gets you her and my silence. You'll never see me again. I can finally retire. How 'bout it?"

"We'll… get it set up now. We can't transfer that much at this hour, but we can put it on credit."

"That'll be just fine. Good boy. Arcturus tower, tonight at midnight, for the money. Your penthouse. Just you and me. Oh, and I have an accomplice with me who'll keep tabs on my status. I'll call here every fifteen minutes to keep things in check. Anything happens to me, and she disappears, and all the info on Samson goes public. So don't try to be a hero. Heroes just get people killed."

"We'll be waiting, Eisner."

"I bet you will… motherfucker."

The call ended, and the screen went black.

Daniel sank into his chair, furious yet defeated. Cyril Eisner had found Daniel's weak spot and exploited it. The crowd nervously chatted among themselves in confusion.

Bentley approached the desk. "Now what?"

"Get every guard on station now. And get me a black credit card, just in case."

"In case of what?"

"In case I can't beat Layla's location out of him, then we'll pay the fucker. Let him come, and then we'll handle it."

***

Guards surrounded the tower on all sides and pushed the protesters staying overnight back even farther. Cyril Eisner's threats felt genuine, and Daniel would stop at nothing to secure his company and his sister.

The night was like a black blanket enclosing around them, with layers of fog piled around Arcturus tower. Every guard was armed—shotguns, assault rifles, submachineguns. It looked like Daniel Mullarkey had assembled a private army, ready for war.

Traffic rolled through the nearby streets. A car honked its horn as the inner-city nightlife carried on. Two sentries were posted on the foggy road ahead; one stood in the security booth—leaning against the wall and dozing—the other in front of the metal gate. Mullarkey had demanded no chairs for security to keep them awake. Many would find ways to sleep standing up. The guard in front of the gate chewed gum and paced back and forth.

A pair of headlights emerged from the mist. A sports car rolled up and stopped in front of the gate. The guard aimed his rifle and walked around to the driver's side window.

The window lowered, and Cyril leaned out. "I think your boss is waiting for me."

The guard spoke into his radio. "Got someone down here to see the boss. Let him in?"

"Yes. We'll come down to meet him," Bentley said over the radio.

The guard waved the car through. Cyril eased forward, passed through the gate, and parked in front of the building. He exited the car and reached in for his handgun and Eruptor. He holstered the pistol on his gun belt and slung his rifle across his shoulders. Guards aimed at him. He ignored them. They knew better. He beheld the massive and overwhelming black tower, looking completely different at night, and thought it resembled something from a fantasy novel. Now he was ready to storm the castle.

He marched forward and shoved open the entrance doors, where Moriarty, Bentley, and Locke waited for him. Moriarty looked like they were out for blood, Bentley was red-faced as usual, and Locke was stiff as a statue.

"Looks like the whole gang's here. Let's get this over with. I'm ready for retirement," Cyril said.

Bentley held up his hand and circled Cyril to disarm him. He unslung Cyril's rifle and unholstered the Hi-Power. He held it in front of Cyril's face and sneered. "I'll hang on to this for you."

Cyril said nothing, then pushed past them for the elevator. Mullarkey's minions followed. They entered the elevator, with Cyril in the center, Bentley behind him to his right, Moriarty parallel with Bentley to Cyril's left, and Locke stood toward the back.

As the elevator started its long ascent, Cyril faced Bentley. "You just jerk off in the bathroom?"

"Shut the fuck up, Eisner! Face forward."

Cyril turned toward Moriarty. They glared up at him and growled, "Pig!" Cyril focused on the elevator doors and made a disgusted face.

Then he turned all the way around and walked to the back of the elevator, passing Locke.

"What the fuck are you doing?" Locke asked.

He leaned on the handrails. "Admiring the view. I'm really gonna miss this town." He beheld the city of Balamb, teeming with life even at midnight. The city lights glowed brightly even through the fog. Some distant lights blinked behind a large puff of cloud. Cyril smiled, then turned around as the elevator stopped at the penthouse. Cyril saw Daniel Mullarkey in the distance behind his desk, drinking.

Cyril exited first and strutted with tough guy bravado. Moriarty, Bentley, and Locke followed. Bentley pulled out an extendable baton, snapped it to length, and swiped at Cyril's right leg. Cyril buckled and fell backward. The trio piled on, kicking and hitting Cyril with all their might, delivering a brutal onslaught of pain. Moriarty screamed as they kicked Cyril repeatedly in the testicles. Cyril yelled and hunched forward. Then Locke grabbed Cyril's shirt collar and pulled him to his knees. Blood poured from Cyril's nose, and his right cheek was badly bruised. Everything hurt.

Through blurred vision, Cyril watched Daniel down a glass of some kind of alcohol, then roll up his sleeves past his enormous cannonlike forearms and march toward him. A crowd watched the carnage play out from the side of the room as several armed guards waited in the wings. Once Daniel was close, he reeled back and unleashed a punch that was the equivalent of a nuclear detonation, corkscrewing Cyril to the right and landing on his chest. Bentley snuck in one last kick to the stomach before Mullarkey grabbed Cyril with both hands and held him above his head like a wrestler ready to deliver a body slam. He carried Cyril to the steelwood table near the window and slammed Cyril onto it. Cyril landed on his back, all the air punched from his body. Cyril rolled sideways and fell over the edge.

As he landed, he ran his hand up one of the table legs and quipped, "Is this steelwood? Oh, I need one of these."

Mullarkey, in sheer annoyance, grabbed Cyril's chin and dragged him backward toward the rest of his crew. With the strength of a brute, he singlehandedly chucked Cyril into the mob of Bentley, Moriarty, and Locke. They beat him a bit more before finally giving in to exhaustion. Locke dragged Cyril by his arms to a large padded chair they had strategically placed in the middle of the room for interrogation or for torture.

"Oh, you are like a fucking rodent, you know that, Eisner?" Daniel said, panting.

"Well, we all have our station in life."

Locke punched Cyril's stomach. Cyril rolled forward and puked.

"Don't be fucking smart with me," Daniel growled as he folded his arms.

Mullarkey appeared to expand his size with each passing moment.

As Cyril wiped his lips, he said through staggard breaths, "Just… want the money."

"Everything is about money to people like you."

Cyril sat upright and exhaled. "Man's gotta make a living. Freelance wasn't worth it, and your payroll fee sucks. Pay people what they're worth, and this won't happen."

Bentley pulled back his right arm for another punch.

"*Ahh*, wait a minute. Gotta make a call." Cyril phoned Rachael. "Yeah, we're good. They got another fifteen minutes." He ended the call. "Okay, continue."

The punch finally came and practically knocked off Cyril's head.

"Since day one of walking in here, I have hated you," Daniel admitted.

"It's my infinite charm."

"It's either charm or just a defense mechanism because, deep down, you know you're a fucking loser looking for a handout."

"Well, that might be true too."

"*Heh*, how about that? Common ground. He's not as dumb as he looks."

"No, he is fucking dumb. And he's a pig," Moriarty snapped.

"Still sour about earlier, I guess," Cyril assumed. "All good. I got something special for you later." Cyril puckered his lips and blew her a kiss.

Daniel headed toward his desk. "Do you know why my father called this company *Arcturus Allied.*"

"I think I know, and I'm sure you're gonna tell me anyway, but go ahead and get it out of your system." Cyril spit out a wad of blood.

"You are so annoying, Eisner. From Earth, we could see a constellation called Boötes. We would refer to it as the Guardian of the

Bear." Daniel poured himself another drink. "There was a Greek myth about a hunter named Arcas who was to shoot and kill his own mother when she had been transformed into a bear. The god Zeus intervened and transformed Arcas into the constellation Boötes, and his mother became Ursa Major, the bear. He would forever stand watch to ensure she didn't get out of control. If she did, Arcas would have to kill her."

"Are you trying to say you killed your mother?" Cyril asked, genuinely confused.

"No, you fucking halfwit! The bear is the villain, a menace who must be controlled. Arcturus is the entire scenario of Arcas keeping watch on Ursa Major to maintain control. My father knew what that might entail. I followed him. And when I buried him, I swore to carry on his mission." Mullarkey downed his drink in one gulp.

"Yeah, Layla knows all about that fascist shit, you fucking creep."

"Some people need to know their place. Like you."

"My place is in my car, driving away from here once I get what I want. My fucking money."

Mullarkey pulled a black credit card from his pocket and held it up. "Fifty million and you tell me where she is."

"I'll tell you as I'm walking out of here."

"What's the guarantee you won't just drive off and disappear?"

"What's the guarantee you won't just kill me the moment I tell you? Or whether that credit card isn't totally blank? I think both of us require a little faith here."

Mullarkey scowled. "Fine." He stomped over and tossed the credit card into Cyril's lap. "Congratulations. You're a rich man. Now, where is she?"

"Yeah, let me check that first." Cyril scanned the card with his phone—fifty million dollars. Cyril transferred the money to his account, then spit out another wad of blood. "I appreciate your business. Before I go, may I ask some questions? About Samson."

"Why the hell do you care? Fuck off!"

"Oh, come one. You're buying my silence anyway. Indulge me," Cyril said, half smiling. "Who would believe me if I said something anyway?"

Mullarkey's eyes narrowed. Something felt… off. "Check him for a wire. Make sure no one's listening."

Bentley and Locke pulled Cyril to his feet and searched him. Besides his phone, he was completely clean. They also checked the phone to ensure it wasn't on an open line. "Nothing. He's clean," Locke stated.

"Fine. You got the girl, I got the truth." Mullarkey dragged a chair over and sat in front of Cyril like an enormous bully, ready to beat the shit out of the new kid on the block. "How much did she tell you?"

"Just that the inoculation shit that you've been spraying around the galaxy is secretly a sterilization program. You're gonna wipe out all non-Terrans, then the Navy will move in to take their home worlds. That's all she let slip. Figured it was enough for blackmail."

"It's not exactly blackmail if you're culpable as well, Eisner, you fucking idiot. You were one of the pilots who sprayed that goop everywhere."

"Yeah, I know. But fifty million buys me a quiet house in the middle of nowhere. I can afford to disappear. I just wanna know… why? Why bother? Why not just let the Terran Navy go to war?"

"Simple. Tried it before, it didn't work. Besides, you can't claim a planet if it's been destroyed. Easier to just wipe them out quietly. Then we step in and take what's rightfully ours."

"Goddamn, you really are a stereotype. Just a racist prick."

"Terrans invented FOIL travel. We developed terraforming. We ventured out from our home world four and a half light years away! We earned everything in our grasp!" Mullarkey stood and approached the window. "What you see before you is the result of people like me and my father—people who had the drive and the initiative to decide the proper course for humanity. And no slant-eyes or pale-skins will stand in the way of our progress." Mullarkey faced Cyril. "This so-called peace, as you want to call it, will never last. They will strike. But we will strike first. No one cares who fought. All anyone cares about is who is the last man standing."

"They'll know it was a sterilizer eventually. Then what? All hell comes down on you at that point."

"Easy. Solar radiation, magnetar starquake, or just blame someone else. I'm Daniel fucking Mullarkey. I wake up in the morning, and I piss excellence. The Terrans will thrive, and I will lead that charge."

Cyril slow clapped. "Wow. That's… really something. Very educational. Well, I got what I wanted. I guess I'll head out." Cyril began to stand.

"Sit the fuck down," Daniel said.

Bentley forced Cyril into his seat.

"Where is she? Since we're taking this all on faith, time to do your part."

"Oh, right. Yeah, let me make that call." Cyril called Rachael. "Got the money. Put her on the line." He held out his phone to Daniel. "It's for you."

Daniel rushed over and grabbed it. He held it to his ear. "Layla, are you safe?"

"I'm fine," she answered flatly.

"Good. I'm about to handle this here, and then we'll come get you. Where are you?"

Layla said nothing.

"Layla?"

"I hate you, Daniel. I hate the person you became."

Mullarkey's eyes widened. "What?"

"I despise you. Everything about you. Mom would be so disappointed."

"What the fuck is this?" Mullarkey barked angrily.

"I've had enough. I'm leaving. And I'll be exposing Arcturus for everything. You'll never see me again. And I'm happy about that. I'm just… gonna go."

"What in the…? Layla… tell me where you are right now. Tell me. And then everything will be fine. But if you don't… I will hunt you down and make you mine again."

Layla stayed quiet for a moment. "Goodbye, Daniel. I hope Mr. Eisner gives you exactly what you deserve."

The line disconnected. Daniel Mullarkey said nothing and dropped the phone. It clattered to the floor and echoed through the silent room.

"Problem?" Cyril inquired, smiling.

Mullarkey turned around. "He never had her. They were working together. This was all a feint."

"Hey, he's not as dumb as he looks," Cyril said to Bentley, a shit-eating grin across his face.

"Bentley. Gun."

Bentley handed Daniel his sidearm, then he aimed it at Cyril's head.

"Where the fuck is she?" Daniel demanded.

Cyril said nothing.

"*Where is she?*"

"A long way from you!"

"Then, I guess we're done here." Daniel thumbed back the hammer.

"I really wouldn't do that if I were you."

"Really? Why not?" Mullarkey flipped off the safety.

"I mean… you could argue Samson away in court but murder one? With everyone watching? *Nah,* you'd have a hard time with that."

"Who? Them?" Mullarkey gestured to the watching crowd of guests. "They're with me, you fucking idiot!"

"Oh, I don't mean them. I mean everyone else who's watching right now."

"Who the fuck are you talking about?"

"Daniel," a party guest said.

"You think you would be the first person I've killed?! And in this office, no less?" Mullarkey was screaming so loud that spit flew from his mouth.

"Daniel," the guest said again.

Mullarkey put the gun to Cyril's head. "I could blow you away right now, and no one would even miss you!"

"Daniel!"

"What. Do. You. *Want?*" Daniel screamed as he turned around.

"Look. The TVs." The guest was pointing to the rows of monitors.

Mullarkey eyed the televisions and froze as he watched live video feed from inside his office, broadcasted on every news channel, coming from Cyril's point of view. He snapped back around. "Search him again. *Search him again*!" Mullarkey joined Bentley and Locke as they searched him for a wire or camera. "Where the fuck is it? Where the fu—" Mullarkey looked into Cyril's eyes.

Cyril winked and clicked his tongue.

"No. No, no, no, no, no, no." Mullarkey took a few steps backward. "Sensory nanites. Layla."

"Right … in… one." Cyril turned his right hand into a finger gun and pretended to shoot Mullarkey.

In a rage, Daniel turned and shot every monitor in a futile attempt to stop the live feed. He chucked the gun away, dashed toward Cyril, grabbed hold of the arm rests, and got right in Cyril's face. "You think you're walking outta here?" he growled.

"No. I'm gonna fly out," Cyril said calmly.

Mullarkey was quiet for a moment, then laughed. Everyone else joined in. They all laughed except for Cyril. "All right, fine. Fuck it. What was your grand plan? Tell me. I gotta know this. What was it?"

"I'll answer that question with another question. Why would I, a pilot with a heavily armed starfighter, want you and all your people in the same room at the same time?"

Mullarkey's huge smile slowly faded as the apocalyptic revelation dawned on him of what was about to happen. He had walked right into the trap. Then he whispered, "Oh no."

"Oh yes." Cyril raised his wrist communicator. "*Skyhawk*, fire rocket pod one!"

***

ONE HOUR EARLIER.

Cyril ended the phone call, undid the gag in Layla's mouth, then untied her. "You're a pretty good actress. Good job sellin' it."

"Hopefully he bought it."

"We'll find out soon." As Layla stood, he handed her the vial. "Keep this. Once you're in the clear, send it to a lab to be properly analyzed. Don't let them know who you are. Also, make sure it's not on Proxima. People will recognize you here, especially after tonight."

She stuffed the vial into a bag filled with necessities—clothes, food and water, and wads of cash. She was about to go on a one-way trip. For the next ten minutes, Cyril recorded Layla giving a full confession on a burner phone to give to the press once the night was over. She admitted everything and included the names of all Ekumen officials who had signed off on Project Samson. It would be a death sentence if she stayed on Proxima. That night would be her last night in the city of Balamb.

They left the storage room of M&M Airfield and walked into the cloudy night. Cyril still had after-hour access, as he still had a security code from his time as a mechanic. No one was around, and he had disarmed the security system and the camera feeds. Rachael waited in the main hangar. She was adamantly against the plan, because she knew he wasn't coming back.

Breaking it all down, the plan was simple. Layla provided the location for a batch of sensory nanites from her own private ship on the other side of town. Then they would all meet at M&M and stage a kidnapping. They would link the nanites to a live social media stream, set to begin at midnight, the very moment Cyril would enter Arcturus tower. If he could convince Daniel Mullarkey to meet in person, Cyril could twist Daniel's words and get him to slip up or even straight confess live to the world. No one could discredit a live event. Once the confession was achieved, Cyril would take care of the rest. Meanwhile, Rachael would assist Layla in getting off Proxima. They would need to maintain a low profile for a time, but Rachael would eventually be in the clear, and Layla would be free to start a fresh life elsewhere. She had enough money to change her appearance and to buy a new identity. Layla was content with never returning home.

As they walked, Layla handed Cyril a syringe filled with sensory nanites. He jammed it into his neck, pressed the plunger, and dosed himself up. It felt weird, like small snakes wriggling in his bloodstream. He handed the syringe to Layla so she could dispose of it off world, not leaving behind any evidence. He launched his socials, linked them together, and paid a hefty fee for them to broadcast a live feed across the city of Balamb at midnight. Everyone would get a notification for the viewing, especially people close to Arcturus tower, including the protesters still on the ground. He linked the nanites to his phone's Wi-Fi for the broadcast. Even checking the phone's home screen would reveal nothing. He had become a walking, talking cameraman.

Covering their tracks was the hardest part. Cameras and drones were everywhere. Cyril ensured he was the only one who the cameras saw. Layla provided the proper security codes for their airfield and their private ship. Once they disarmed the security, Cyril would break in and secure the nanites from her ship's cargo hold. He would take full blame. Nothing could connect Layla to a break-in. He didn't care, as he assumed he wouldn't last the night.

As for how to handle Mullarkey and his crew at the top of the tower, he had something special in mind. It was better that Rachael and Layla didn't know that part.

The three of them regrouped in the main hangar and found a set of greasy jeans and a T-shirt for Layla to change into from her party attire. She donned one of Stacy's flight suits that they had stolen from Stacy's locker. Layla stuffed her dress into her bag, and they headed for Rachael's ship on the tarmac. Without the airstrip lights on, the airfield looked dark and deserted.

When they reached the ship, Rachael turned around and hugged him, weeping. "You're crazy."

"Yeah, I think so too."

She loosened her hug and looked him in his eyes. "No way I can talk you out of this?"

"You can try."

"Don't do it. Please."

Cyril was quiet for a moment, then whispered, "You failed."

She hugged him again. "I hate that things didn't really happen between us," she said through her tears.

"Bad timing, I know. In another universe, there's probably parallel versions of us, and I hope they're happy."

She squeezed harder and kissed him.

"I'll call you every fifteen minutes. I'll let you know when it's done."

She nodded, then let go, and walked into the mist toward her ship.

Cyril faced Layla, who resembled a wannabe mechanic. She would look adorable under other circumstances.

"Weird. I never thought my life would turn into this," Layla said, aiming for sarcasm but falling flat.

"You're not the only one. I gotta do this though," Cyril professed.

"I know. Kill him for me. In the worst way you can think of."

"Absolutely. It'll be a pleasure."

They stood silent for a moment, believing this would be the last time they would ever see each other.

"Rachael will get you out of town. Stay outside the city limits for a while. Once the call comes through, and I have the confession, get off planet."

"I'm scared."

"I know. Me too. But the only way out is through. You just… go. This is your chance. Make it count."

"Okay." She headed toward Rachael's ship, which was powering up, then stopped to turn around, unsure of herself. "I don't… I don't know if—"

"Layla… just go."

She nodded, turned back, and climbed into the back seat of Rachael's ship. The canopy closed, and the ship ascended eastward, away from the airfield. It disappeared into the fog, and the sound of the engines faded.

Alone on the black tarmac, he programmed his Skyhawk to fly to a destination half a kilometer high and eight hundred meters west of Arcturus tower, where it would wait in the clouds for Cyril to continue drone commands through his wrist communicator. The fog would mask his ship, though the engines might still be audible. He hoped that anyone on the ground would just assume it was a patrol drone. He had fully rearmed the Skyhawk with fresh rockets and extra barrels of incendiary ammunition. He also had two air-to-air missiles and two air-to-ground missiles attached, though he was unsure how useful they would be for what was to come. He would just have to wing it.

He climbed down from the cockpit and ran his hand along the slick hull. It had been his baby for years. Now he considered it a sacrifice to end Mullarkey's assault on the Ekumen. He stepped backward and commanded it to ascend and head to its target destination. It rose, thrusted forward, and disappeared into the dark clouds above.

The night's silence collapsed in on him as reality seemed to finally catch up. As he walked to the main gate, he kept thinking how insane and how unwinnable the whole endeavor was. One man against an army. He recalled his discussion of the Spartans from earlier, how they had been perfect warriors. One factor he admired about them was how every Spartan was considered a small army—one man, one mission. It only took a single boulder falling into a river to shift the current or one soldier standing up to a tyrant to end a fascist rule. Win or lose, he would be that one soldier, ready to fight and to die for the right thing. And even if he failed, at least he would die being a pain in the ass for Daniel Mullarkey.

He closed the airfield's gate, hopped into the sports car, and cruised down the road. There was no rush anymore. He knew what he had to do, and he had plenty of time. And with that time, he would make one last call to Marie. He dialed her number, and, like always, it went right to voicemail, but he needed to say one last thing. When he heard the beep, he gave his final confession. "Hey, it's me. I'm not great at speeches, so I'm just gonna say this. I'm about to do something really fucking stupid, but it's the right thing. I hope you understand. And I hope one day you forgive me for being who I am. I tried, and I did my best. Gotta go now. Love you. Bye."

He hung up the phone and set it on the passenger seat next to his handgun and Eruptor rifle. Then he accelerated into the long, cold, dark night ahead of him.

***

"*Skyhawk*, fire rocket pod one!"

High above Arcturus tower, a barrage of eight rockets darted from the cloud cover and blazed toward the penthouse suite. The first rocket detonated upon contact with the three-inch-thick plate glass. It exploded inward and sprayed everyone with shards. The following seven rockets hit sporadically around the gargantuan room, some impacting the rooftop glass, which rained more shards, some detonating into the slick marble floor, leaving three-foot-wide craters. The impacts terrified everyone, and the crowd scattered.

Cyril covered his face to avoid the sharp shards, then leaned forward and headbutted Daniel. Mullarkey stumbled backward, and blood poured from his broken nose. Cyril leaped over the chair and crashed into Bentley. They fell to the floor, and Cyril piled on top of him, throwing a quick one-two punch.

"I'll take my guns back now, asshole!" Cyril grabbed his pistol from Bentley's jacket and unsnapped the sling from the Eruptor. Before he could shoot Bentley in the head, gunfire opened up on him. He darted away, figuring to save Bentley for later.

As Cyril crossed the room, he snatched his phone and shoved it into his pocket. He flipped the fancy steelwood table next to the blown-out windows and took cover behind it, hoping it was strong enough to stop the incoming barrage. Gunfire from Locke and several security personnel blazed over the edge of the table. Mullarkey, Moriarty, and several guests scrambled for cover on the opposite side. Some guests bolted for the elevator in a panic and huddled around the doors, waiting for them to open. When they did, the people piled inside and pressed the down button. Just as the doors closed, Cyril leaned from the left side of his cover and hip-fired a shot from his Eruptor. The bullet zipped through the doors at the last second and exploded inside, shredding several people into hamburgers. He heard their screams of pain as they descended to the bottom floor.

More gunfire from Locke and Bentley opened up as Cyril got back behind cover. Cyril traded his Eruptor for the Hi-Power. He blind-fired over the edge of the table, hoping to hit something through sheer luck.

The gunfire was so loud that Moriarty screamed in anger and terror. Their hands covered their ears to soften the banging. It felt as though their ear drums were on the verge of exploding. Finally, in pure rage, they rose and recklessly ran into the middle of the room.

"Where *the fuck* are you *going*?" Mullarkey screamed.

Moriarty stood in the middle of the room and screeched like a harpy between the shooters, "You're all fucking *piiiiiggggggsssssss*!!!!!"

"*Skyhawk*, fire rocket pod two," Cyril yelled. A second barrage of eight rockets streamed from the clouds toward their intended destination: the middle of the penthouse.

Moriarty screamed again, "*Piiiiiigggggggssss*!!!!!"

The rockets exploded all around Moriarty and blasted balls of shrapnel, debris, and destruction. As the last rocket explosion faded, both sides stopped firing, and everything went quiet save for the cold wind rushing into the penthouse. From the dust, Moriarty shuffled out. Their hair had been burned off, their skin was covered in second- and third-degree burns, and their left eyeball dangled from its socket by the optic nerve. An unexploded rocket stuck out of their stomach. They gurgled up a gush of blood as they walked aimlessly. Finally, the dust settled, and they collapsed to their knees. Moriarty noticed the clouds were clearing, exposing the twinkling stars. It was beautiful. Through bloody lips, Moriarty whispered to no one, "Why didn't anybody ever love me?"

Cyril craned his head over the table, aimed his Eruptor, and fired. The bullet found its target in the back of Moriarty's skull. Their head burst like a watermelon, and they crumpled forward onto their chest, landing on the rocket tip. It finally exploded and blasted what remained of Moriarty into a geyser of blood, bone, and sinew. The meat chunks landed on the marble with wet, sloppy slaps.

Cyril took cover once again. Unbeknownst to him, he and Mullarkey said simultaneously, "What a fucking cunt."

Silence settled in the penthouse. Cyril reloaded his Hi-Power, while Locke and his security team reloaded their weapons. Bentley was out of ammunition.

"Hey, Skyhawk, you doin' all right over there?" Mullarkey yelled from behind cover. His voice was slightly higher pitched with his nose broken.

"Why don't you pop your head up and find out?" Cyril yelled back.

"No thanks. I'm good. You think this changes a goddamn thing?"

"Well, there's certainly less people alive on your side than there were ten minutes ago. So, I think I'm doin' okay."

Daniel used hand signals to order Bentley to sneak around the room to flank Cyril. Locke stayed by Mullarkey's side as his personal protection. The rest of the security team kept their guns trained on the steelwood table that Cyril was hiding behind.

Mullarkey spoke as a distraction for Bentley. "Doesn't matter. The elevator is on the way up now, and it'll be filled with more of my security teams. You've got nowhere to go. Either you die here and become just a psycho killer, or we take you in alive so we can make an example out of you. You're trash, Eisner. Another bug needing to be squashed. No one's gonna remember you when you're fucking dead."

"If you're trying to get under my skin, just know there's not a single thing you said that I haven't said six inches from the mirror. But I know how to get under your skin, Mullarkey. I know how to push your buttons."

"Oh, really? Try me."

Bentley had reached Daniel's desk and crept around. Mullarkey nodded at him, telling him to keep going.

"I called the Veterans Administration," Cyril lied. "I asked them if a Daniel Mullarkey had ever served in the Terran Navy. You know what they said? 'No such person with that name has ever served in any department.' I always knew you were a fraud, Mullarkey. And now the world knows it too. You ain't no patriot. You're just another stolen… valor… punk!"

Mullarkey leaped up furiously, then pointed and yelled, "Somebody kill that motherfucker right now!"

Gunfire opened up from Locke and Mullarkey's security personnel as Bentley bounded around the desk and grabbed Cyril. He dropped his Eruptor and reached for his Hi-Power as Bentley's bulbous hands moved to strangle him. Cyril opened his mouth and clamped hard on Bentley's right hand. Cyril chewed on the webbing between the thumb and pointer finger, eventually biting all the way through and ripping off a section of Bentley's hand. Bentley screamed in pain and stumbled backward. Cyril spit the meat chunk at Bentley, then snatched his handgun aimed at Bentley's legs.

"Eisner, you *motherfu—*"

The sound of Cyril's Hi-Power unloading into Bentley's left and right thighs silenced him. Bloody chunks spewed out the open window as he tumbled backward, landed on his ass, then rolled out the window. He grabbed the edge, piercing his hands with large shards of broken glass in the frame. He tried to pull himself up but couldn't release himself, as he was impaled to the window frame and had no leg or upper body strength left. He dangled and clung on for dear life.

The elevator dinged, and the doors opened. Ten heavily armed security personnel ran toward Mullarkey to take up defensive positions. Cyril blind-fired his Eruptor at the ceiling and blew out another frame of glass. Shards and shrapnel rained upon several guards and party guests. Guards fired assault rifles at Cyril's location behind the steelwood desk. It took round after round, flatly echoing the bullet ripples that continuously impaled it. He hunkered down, raised his wrist communicator, and shouted, "*Skyhawk*, fly to my location and hover."

The Skyhawk switched into flight mode and descended rapidly toward Arcturus tower. As it approached, it settled parallel with the blown-out window and hovered.

"*Skyhawk*, go for overwatch. All targets thirty meters ahead of my position."

The Skyhawk released squirts of incendiary gunfire on anything that moved. The chainsaw rip sound was deafening as more people tried to maneuver toward the elevator, only to have the rounds cut them down and set them ablaze, as if the guns were a windshield wiper from hell. Hot shell casings spewed from the hull and showered Bentley, scalding him with burns all over his face and hands, as he dangled. He screamed in agony, with nowhere to go.

Cyril fired more rounds from his Eruptor, blasting one guard in half, his torso disconnecting from his legs and flopping to the floor. He fired till eventually everyone understood that the ship was on overwatch and would only attack moving targets. The crowd ducked behind cover and stayed hidden. Cyril fired into the ceiling, and it rained more glass and shrapnel. Finally, the rifle's breach clicked open. Out of ammo.

He chucked the Eruptor aside, slightly sad to let it go, then holstered his Hi-Power. "*Skyhawk*, stop overwatch!" He sprung from behind the table and darted to the edge of the window, where Bentley dangled from the glass, burn marks covering his face. "*Skyhawk*, descend three meters."

The ship dropped three meters. Cyril took a few steps backward, steeled himself, and jumped.

Mullarkey screamed, "Get him!"

Gunfire opened up. Cyril landed on the portside wing but slipped and slid to the edge and grabbed onto the wing tip. Watching the world far below, he'd never feared heights before that moment. Adrenaline pumped through his veins to give him an extra boost of strength. As he pulled himself up, more gunfire sprayed from the open window as guards approached the edge.

"*Skyhawk*, strafe right thirty meters," Cyril yelled.

The ship darted to the right, parallel to the building. Bullets hissed and snapped all around Cyril as he crouch-ran across the wing toward the cockpit. A bullet blew through his shoulder, and another tore through his calf muscle on his left leg. He stumbled and slid into the left dorsal fin. Bullets peppered the hull, and several pierced the canopy.

"*Skyhawk*, overwatch! *Shoot them*!"

The ship ascended and turned, decimating and turning the line of guards into red mist. Gallons of gore doused Bentley, still unable to move.

With all his remaining strength, Cyril opened the canopy and hopped into the cockpit. "Hope you're all enjoying the show"—Cyril took over control and strapped in—"because this shit's about to get good." He slammed down on the trigger and indiscriminately unloaded a barrage of gunfire into the building.

Aside from the guards, the building was vacant. Anyone who remained worked for Mullarkey and had sided with him for his plan. They were all guilty and needed to be punished. Round after round ripped apart glass and stone, turning the top floors into Swiss cheese. One round went through Locke's face, blowing his head clean off.

The guns screamed, and so did Cyril. The roar of it all, a cacophony of hate. Round after round after round of hot 20mm incendiary ammunition shredding through the building cleansed every ounce of pain, every feeling of guilt, doubt, self-loathing, and pure disgust with Daniel Mullarkey. The worst of humanity was in that room, and Cyril was purging them with the fervor, fury, and fire of a thousand suns. It was glorious, and he loved it. To kill the worst people for the right reasons brought him nothing but pure satisfaction.

Finally, he released the trigger and hovered. Only fifty rounds left. The penthouse was torn to shreds, and everyone inside wasn't just dead but pulverized into chum. Except for Mullarkey. The bastard had the luck of the devil. He stood, covered in blood, brains, and debris. Cyril turned on his forward running lights and illuminated Mullarkey as the fascist stumbled from a pile of dead bodies and marched toward the edge of the window.

"You think that killing me is gonna make any fucking difference?" Mullarkey furiously screamed.

Cyril hesitated, then turned on his exterior loudspeaker. "Nope." Then he squeezed the trigger.

Mullarkey, in pure rage, screamed one last time in a final act of defiance.

The fifty rounds burst from the Skyhawk's gun barrels and tore through Mullarkey's body. He exploded, and his remains sprayed five yards in every direction.

"God, that felt good," Cyril yelled.

He had done it. He was finished. He swallowed hard and realized his shoulder and leg were bleeding. In his anger, he had totally forgotten he had been shot. Cyril ignored it and thrusted backward to gain distance to turn around. He noticed Bentley was still dangling from the edge of the building. He aimed his Hi-Power but saw the slide was locked back—No ammo. A missile would be too much and could bring down the whole building on the innocent people below. He thought about what to do, then he remembered something Layla had said about falling from high up. He smiled.

He descended and became parallel with Bentley. "You know, it's not the fall that gets you!"

Bentley craned his bloody head around to see the Skyhawk rotate right a hundred eighty degrees. The ship's afterburners stopped five meters from his face. Cyril activated his forward thrusters as he hovered, then raised the throttle on his afterburners, the combined force holding the Skyhawk in place. The heat intensified, till Bentley screamed and finally caught fire. His hands blackened and turned to charcoal. As he ignited in flames, the glass ripped through what used to be his hands, and he plummeted all the way down. A wind shear shoved him toward the building's front entrance. He landed smack dab onto the hood of Jace's sports car. The roof caved in, and the windows blew out. His head exploded, and every bone shattered.

"It's the sudden stop at the bottom," Cyril concluded, surveying the carnage below, extremely pleased with himself.

With everyone dead, he said into his phone, "All right. Show's over," and ended the live stream. He switched into flight mode, gunned the throttle, and flew into the crystal-clear night.

***

Cyril landed at M&M Airfield, twenty minutes later, expecting police to be waiting for him, but no one had arrived. He climbed out, closed the canopy, said goodbye to his ship one last time, then sauntered to the main hangar's bathroom and pulled out the first aid kit—the very same one he had used when he had gotten home from Gacrux so long ago. He cauterized and gauzed his shoulder and calf wounds, then realized several of his teeth felt loose. Mullarkey could land a hell of a punch. He got dressed again, then stood outside the main gate. With no car left, he considered waiting for the police. Instead, he called an autocab and headed to Mallory's.

Gumby stopped Cyril at Mallory's entrance and shakily asked, "What the fuck happened to you?"

"*Eh*, you should see the other guy." It was such a dumb cliché, but Cyril couldn't resist saying it. He figured he wouldn't get a better chance.

He sat on a stool at the bar near the wall of photos. It was near closing time, and they were serving last call. Only a few patrons were sticking it out to the end. Cyril would be one of them. The jukebox played a slow Frank Sinatra song to wrap out the night.

Mallory, seeing the carnage covering Cyril's body, exclaimed, "What the fuck, Cyril?"

"Long story. You'll hear about it soon. Guinness, please."

Mallory paused, then poured from the tap.

Cyril reached into his mouth and pulled out a molar. "Fuck," he gasped. He dropped it onto the bar.

"Is that a tooth?" she asked stoically.

"*Heh*, yeah." He smiled.

The TVs surrounding the bar showed a special news report, replaying the footage of the Arcturus attack from the ground level. Mallory set Cyril's drink in front of him and watched the TVs. She noticed Cyril's ship in the sky around the tower. She glared at him, horrified.

Cyril eyed the pictures of Jace, Jess, and Marie on the wall and whispered, "I got 'em. I got 'em all. Miss you guys."

"Cyril… what did you *do*?" Mallory asked gravely.

"The right thing. And that makes me the most dangerous man in the universe." He raised his glass. "Cheers."

A special police unit burst into the bar to secure the building. Fifteen heavily armed officers shouldered their weapons. Everyone raised their hands except for Cyril. He sat there quietly, drinking his beer.

Two high-ranking officers walked up behind him. "Cyril Eisner?"

"You know, I thought you guys would be faster, seeing as who I just took down. Let me finish this drink, guys. I don't think I'm ever gettin' another one." He downed the remains of his pint in a quick gulp, then faced the officers. "Okay. Take me to jail."

The two officers yanked Cyril from his chair and slapped handcuffs on him. As they escorted him out, he smiled and winked at Mallory. She watched in shock.

The cops stuffed Cyril into the rear of a cruiser parked out front.

The driver said, "That was a hell of a show, you crazy bastard."

Cops were everywhere outside the bar, with more driving down the road toward the airfield. As he sat in the cruiser, he looked straight out the windshield and grinned. It was the grin of the victorious.

Final Chapter

The Seven Starfighters

The laser cutter sliced through the rock above him, melting it into magma. It traced into a circle, one meter in circumference, then rejoined with the starting point. The miner attached a magnetic handgrip to the center of the circle and pulled down. Another fresh batch of nickel, one meter around and one meter long, slid out and crashed to the metal grating with a loud clang. The miner lifted the rough nickel cylinder and dragged it to an automated cart. With all his might, he hurled it into the bed and detached the handle. It was his nineteenth cylinder so far that day—just below the daily quota for the prison mining station *Callico Bay*.

The interior of *Callico Bay* was like that of a Dyson Sphere, though its purpose was not to absorb star radiation. It was to create an enclosed environment for asteroid mining. Metal lattice work, built into the sides of the large asteroid that it surrounded, linked the station directly to the rockface. Once they became interconnected, thrust was applied to the exterior of the station to create centrifugal force. In essence, *Callico Bay* was a miniature planet, though gravity would return to zero closer to the center, not unlike *Lightfoot* station.

Callico housed close to seven hundred prisoners of all races and genders—murderers, rapists, thieves, and everything in between. As a means of commuting sentences, prisoners could apply for mining work. It was dangerous, miserable, grueling, and the accidental death numbers ranged around 40 percent of all applicants, but the miner didn't care. He readjusted his helmet to wipe away a glisten of sweat on his brow, then resumed his cutting spot and stepped one meter to the right.

As he pulled up his thirty-kilogram-heavy laser cutter, a voice boomed over a loudspeaker. "Prisoner 1111451! Step forward to central command please!"

The miner dropped his cutter and headed toward central command, fifty meters away. Many prisoners said hello, and some high-fived him. But the Terran prisoners sent him deep scowls. He ignored them and kept walking.

He climbed the stairs to the hub area of the command center—a large saucer-shaped room that controlled all aspects of the station. Visual feeds from security cams and drones displayed on various monitors. Five guards, all manning different stations, filled the room. It smelled extremely clean and sterile despite the excessive amounts of ozone pumped into the air in the mining area. The miner pressed the buzzer, and the door slid open with a whoosh, then closed silently behind him. A gust of hot air flowed in behind him as the door shut.

Warden Galini was reviewing budgetary reports on his data pad as the prisoner entered, then set the pad on a countertop. "Prisoner 1111541, please remove your mask."

The miner unclamped his helmet, releasing a small stream of sweat onto the floor. He slicked back his hair and wiped away patches of glistening sweat from his ever-growing beard.

"Cyril fucking Eisner," Galini said.

"Yeah, that's me."

"Every day I wake up hoping you either died in your sleep, got murdered, or bad luck out there finally caught up with you. And every morning, you disappoint me."

Cyril wiped away a trickle of sweat running down his left temple. "Sorry, boss. I'll try to do better."

"Shut up. You have a visitor. Two of them, actually."

"*Hmm.*" Cyril never received visitors. This was an odd occurrence.

***

Cyril had been there a total of four months, and the trial had taken close to eleven. Even though Mullarkey had given Cyril fifty million dollars for the fake hostage negotiation, the authorities froze Cyril's accounts upon his arrest. He eventually gained access to his accounts while in custody to pay for a lawyer—minus the fifty million, of course. The local government confiscated what was not legally his.

The trial was in no way swift. The live broadcast of Cyril's attack, and Mullarkey's confession, gave Cyril a wealth of support against the Terran government, which was intent on making an example of him. Monetary donations poured in from not just the city of Balamb but from the entire planet of Proxima. The other governing bodies of the Ekumen also offered their support, despite acknowledging publicly that Cyril Eisner had committed a heinous crime and that he should be justly punished.

The vial of Project Samson fluid, as well as Layla Mullarkey's confession, found their way into the hands of an independent media source, who analyzed the vial. Further investigation revealed it was intended as a sterilizer for all non-Terran species. The Terran government denied any involvement and declared Mullarkey and Arcturus Allied acted independently of government influence. Even with Layla's confession and with indictment against various high-ranking officials, no direct evidence existed to provide a solid connection between the Arcturus plans and the Terran government, only speculation and hearsay.

Cyril eventually found out that Layla Mullarkey had gone into hiding, more than likely to live a quiet life away from everyone. Rachael was also safe after a few months and returned to the freelance world. No evidence tied Rachael directly to Cyril's actions—no camera footage or text messages. Being the friend of a murderer was not a crime. Her personal reputation had taken a hit, but the authorities did not file any charges. No members of Arcturus Allied went after her or Layla. If the vial had gotten into the hands of the media, that meant that, at the very least, they were out of harm's way. No one had any reason to come after them, especially considering the number of lawsuits and court cases that piled up against Arcturus in the aftermath. They had bigger problems than dealing with a pair of whistleblowers. Eventually the company fell into Chapter 7 bankruptcy.

Arcturus Allied folded seven months into Cyril Eisner's trial.

During his hearings, many witnesses testified on his behalf. His therapist, Dr. Minese, made the case that Cyril had suffered from temporary insanity due to the increasing number of personal failings and intense stress that plagued him. Cyril's lawyers attempted to convince him that if he took a plea bargain and declared insanity, he would avoid jail time and be placed in an institution instead of a prison. Cyril declined, standing tall and declaring a verdict of guilty.

His father, also called to the stand, did nothing but berate and belittle Cyril throughout his testimony. Cyril did his best to ignore him. His father ended his statement with, "That little shit is exactly where he belongs." Part of Cyril felt he was right.

Cyril's lawyers wanted to subpoena Marie to testify on his behalf. Cyril shut them down, stating, "I did enough damage to her already. Leave her alone." Marie Master's life was turned upside down for the first three months of the trial, making it nearly impossible to maintain privacy or to even go to work. She eventually resigned from her position and moved home with her mother in the country outside the city. She only made one statement regarding Cyril. "I want nothing to do with Cyril Eisner. Leave me alone." When Cyril heard her words, he felt even more defeated.

The investigation revealed, through recovered emails and financial transactions, that several of the deceased from the Arcturus attack had been in direct connection with Mullarkey and his sterilization program. Their families did not comment on the accusations during the trial. Instead, most went into hiding, and many of them left Proxima as quickly as possible. Oddly, the courts did not subpoena them. Cyril had a feeling that the Terran government was letting them get away to fight another day. He knew how they were playing the game; it had been rigged against him right from the start.

The scandal had not just damaged Daniel Mullarkey's reputation but had destroyed it. Investigation revealed ties to right-wing extremist groups and militias intent on a Terran takeover of the Ekumen. The incident had forever tainted the Mullarkey name, yet the right still gave him a wealth of support. They declared that one day his dream would come true and that the name *Mullarkey* would symbolize peace. The only solace Cyril took from the Mullarkey aftermath was the public reveal that Daniel had falsified his service in the Terran Navy. He truly was stolen valor, and the most humiliating part was they had recover him from his penthouse with a bag, sponge, and shovel. Knowing that, Cyril slept well for at least one night.

Many of Cyril's workmates defended him during his trial and attested to his character. Allegra, Rex, Dazer, Filly, Kyra, Glass, and Crow were in attendance when the judge announced his sentence. Rachael also sat among the crowd toward the end of the trial but offered no testimony. She had to keep a low profile to not out herself as an accomplice. Cyril didn't hold that against her. He wished her the best.

All the alien races—Luyten, Skovian, Mukarian, and Crecian—stood by him, believing him to be a "Hero of the Ekumen." Many leftist Terrans were on his side too. However, despite an immense outpouring of support, the government and the court system declared him as an enemy of the people. Due to the extenuating circumstances surrounding the Arcturus attack, they withdrew the death penalty. Though a vigilante action, the courts considered it to be the only viable solution to avoid a devastating blow politically if they had executed Cyril for it. His stay of execution had been purely political.

Therefore, his sentence was one hundred and twenty years in an Ekumen prison for the crimes of murder, assault, destruction of property, and public endangerment. He accepted the sentence without question, knowing he would die in prison.

The public, however, did not agree, demanding his acquittal as a symbol of heroism and justice.

One week after the sentencing, a massive bombing of Balamb's capitol building killed sixty-five people and injured another forty-four. Despite promises of the Terran government to make amends and clean up Arcturus's mess, no movement to reverse the sterilization program occurred. A division of the PLA took credit for the bombing and rallied support against the Terran government. Despite Cyril's past attacks against them, they determined he was unaware of who he was actually serving, and his true intentions were revealed with the attack on Arcturus tower. Support for the PLA grew exponentially, and the outcome was inevitable.

War.

It was everyone against the Terran government.

The fates of Mullarkey's henchmen, Moriarty and Bentley, went unknown to Cyril. Investigators found Bentley flattened like a pancake atop Jace's sports car and had to haul away his body in pieces. Search warrants uncovered photos and videos that Bentley had taken up female coworkers' skirts and down their blouses on his cellphone, as well as a wealth of child pornography on his computer. His family, upon learning this information, stated they were "disappointed but not surprised." Only his immediate family attended his funeral. When the press asked Bentley's thirteen-year-old son if he knew who his father truly was, he answered with a blank face, "I don't know." A few months later, the investigation revealed that Bentley had frequently sexually assaulted his son.

Moriarty was a different case. Upon hearing about their death, Arcturus employees posted disparaging comments about them as a boss and as a leader. With no fear of losing their jobs, Moriarty had become a laughingstock and a public joke. During their funeral, almost no one attended—no immediate family, no friends of any kind, not even acquaintances. The best that the funeral home could find was a third cousin who Moriarty hadn't spoken to in fifteen years. Upon seeing the urn at the funeral home, the cousin scowled and said, "She always was a fucking cunt." The hate was so thick that the cousin refused to acknowledge Moriarty by their proper pronouns.

The funeral home then took the ashes to a communal grave. The cousin did not choose a plot for Moriarty and refused to pay for one. The funeral director asked, "Would you like to say something?" The cousin said, "Yeah. Dump the bitch in." The funeral director opened the urn and poured the ashes onto the wet soil. Then the cousin spit on them and walked away. After ten minutes, they were nothing more than another number on a balance sheet. No tears were shed for Ellen Moriarty, and the memory of them faded into oblivion.

When Cyril first reached prison, he expected it to be harsh and brutal. But after processing, the prisoners who admired him for what he had done treated Cyril with dignity and respect—at least non-Terrans admired him. With this respect came protection from the racists who wanted him dead. He still ended up in his share of fights, and the staff definitely had it out for him, but overall, prison was much easier than he had expected. A hundred and twenty years waiting to die didn't seem so bad, after all.

But after one month, he got bored and applied for the mining division, which commuted his sentence from one hundred and twenty years to eighty-nine. He'd still die behind bars, but at least he would have something to do before then. And transferring off Proxima to *Callico Bay* meant less of a chance of the correctional officers coming after him. On the edge of the Ekumen, most people didn't care what anyone did if they stayed in line and did their job. It was a decent life. Decent enough. And with the war, it was best to be away from any major population centers in case of bombings. Out in the blackness was the only safe space left. Even so, Cyril felt a lot of guilt for all the people dying across the Ekumen.

***

Galini and Cyril traversed the underlit hallway toward the interrogation rooms on the station's outer rim. They turned left down a corridor lined with heavy doors. Galini opened a door labeled, INTERROGATION THREE, and waved Cyril in. As they entered, the door whooshed closed behind them. Two dark-blue-uniformed Naval officers—donning medals from a handful of conflicts—whose covers rested right side up on the table, sat behind a desk: Allegra and Rex. From how Cyril had known them, especially Allegra, they looked extremely awkward. A large window that displayed nothing but passing stars sprawled directly behind them.

"Well, goddamn. My first visitors ever and it had to be you guys," Cyril said. "Sorry if I sound disappointed."

"You look like shit, Cyril," Rex said.

"And I feel like it too. Looking good in that uniform, Allie."

"Thank you. I feel like a penguin. Take a seat."

Cyril sat and placed his helmet on the table.

Allegra pulled a briefcase from the floor and set it in front of her. She unlatched it, opened it, and removed a set of files filled with maps of battlegrounds, unit placements, terrain conditions, and so much more that it made Cyril raise an eyebrow. She set the files in front of Cyril in a grid pattern, two rows and three columns. "What can you tell me about this engagement?"

Cyril picked up the troop movement page first. Though, upon closer inspection, it wasn't troop movements. It was the flight pattern of two squadrons on an attack run. Three sets of arrows were headed toward a series of mountains, thirty kilometers away. The squadrons were set to bomb an artillery depot and vacate the area as quickly as possible before reinforcements arrived. The date of the attack was one day prior.

"Well, looks like whoever designed this put all their eggs in one basket," Cyril said. "Three squadrons headed toward the same target, with no one running high-altitude support. Also, you have them assembled too close together. If they get into a scrap, they're all toast."

"What would you do differently?" Rex squinted at Cyril.

"I would split them up. One flies farther east and circles around this mountain range, while the other two make a mad dash toward the target. The dashers go through and hit everything quickly, taking out SAMs and AA emplacements. Then the second group flies in low and slow to do the real work, hitting the target with everything they've got. They take their time and eliminate what they can. Then your ground troops roll through and clean house. Or you could just do a high-altitude bombardment, if that's an option."

"It's not," Allegra said.

"Then a kamikaze FOIL pad with high explosives attached to it would work just fine if you don't want anyone sacrificed. Leap it into the atmosphere above the target and let gravity do the work for you. The explosion would take out most of the targets. Any ships that could be sent in afterward are there for mopping up." Cyril tossed the page onto the table. "This is a reckless attack plan. Who designed this?"

"I did," Rex confessed.

Cyril sat back and went quiet. His chair creaked. He panned his gaze between the pair. "What is this? Why are you here?"

"Cyril"—Allegra leaned forward—"how would you like to get back in the cockpit?"

"What? This a joke?"

"No joke," Rex said. "We've been asked to assemble a team for special operations behind enemy lines. The Terran Navy offered us options for skilled pilots but… let's just say the talent pool isn't what it used to be."

"You want me out… just to conscript me?" Cyril laughed.

Allegra shrugged. "Well, when you put it like that, let's just say that I special requested you because I owe you one."

Rex added, "The Terran Navy will be conscripting people all over the galaxy to serve on the front lines soon. Prisoners mostly. At some point, they will come for you to serve. We figured your talents would be better served up above rather than down below."

Cyril folded his arms and chuckled. "I get it. You're desperate. You can't get enough people to join because the Ekumen saw what Arcturus did, and they can't justify it. You're just getting the lowest-of-the-low-caliber people to fight alongside you. *Ha*! Unbelievable."

"We're losing this war," Rex said sincerely.

"Who said we should win?" Cyril retorted.

"I'd rather not die," Allegra murmured.

"Then, just stay out of it. Why did you two even join up?"

Rex cleared his throat and said nothing.

Allegra finally broke the silence. "We are currently fighting the war with PMCs. The Terran Navy wasn't prepared for such a large interstellar conflict. We were… still under contract. Then the Terran Fleet Command bought that contract. Apparently the Navy and the PMCs have a partnership to fight the war via proxy. In a way, we were conscripted too. Same deal, new bosses."

"The war economy. Nothing changes, huh?"

"Nope."

"Even so, I'm still not interested. I'm okay here." Cyril walked to the window to watch the passing stars as the station slowly turned.

"Cyril, you're either gonna end up dead here or dead in some mud pit on Gacrux," Allegra tersely stated.

"I don't really care anymore. I did my part. Arcturus is gone, Mullarkey's dead, and Layla is safe. You guys handle the rest."

Allegra slammed her hands on the table, then strode toward him. "What you did was start a war that we have no chance of winning. We need the best of the best to help fight. I don't like the idea of having to fight this either, but it's this or death."

Cyril said nothing.

Allegra got close and whispered in his ear, "Do you really wanna stay here, feeling sorry for yourself? You wanna let people like her die because you had a grudge to settle?"

Cyril faced her. "That's not fair."

"Who gives a shit what's fair? Nothing's fair in war… and love." Allegra leaned on the edge of the table and watched him next to the window.

This war really has changed you, Allie, Cyril thought.

"You'll be given a pardon and placed on a probationary military detail with the new squadron," Rex added. "You'll be required to undergo psychiatric evaluation weekly and serve under myself and Allegra. But you'll be out of here, Cyril. Plus, if the Navy doesn't conscript you, then some Mukarian bombing fleet might come by and blow this place to pieces. I'm sure you don't want that, either."

"There's no way to win," Cyril muttered to no one.

"Maybe. But we can lessen the damage until a peace treaty can be organized. And who knows when that will be."

Cyril exhaled sharply. "How big is the team so far?"

"You'd be the final one in the squadron," Allegra answered. "We'll also have a full crew. A Naval cruiser has been designed specifically for us. Three squads of troops, full medical unit, flight crew, the works. They want us to go out there to do what we can to slow down the enemy war effort by any means necessary."

"We'd be reavers," Cyril whispered.

"What?" Rex asked.

Cyril turned and proclaimed, "We'd be the ones who strike first when no one is expecting it."

"Something like that, yeah," Rex agreed.

Cyril let out another heavy sigh. "What's the squadron name?"

"Sorcerer," Rex said.

"Sorcerer? Why that?"

"A sorcerer is someone who uses dark magic to control the world and to dictate its fate. We might be the ones who dictate the fate of the Ekumen."

"Clever." Cyril chuckled as he walked back around the desk. "How many in the squadron?"

"Plus you? Seven. Keeping it small, less than standard operating procedure."

Cyril stayed quiet for a moment, then whispered, "Seven. The Seven Starfighters. Nice ring to it. Be great for propaganda."

"Whatever works," Rex said. "So, how about it, Skyhawk? You want in… or is Gacrux mud pit your final answer?"

Cyril glanced at Allegra, then at Rex. They knew his answer before he even said it.

***

The following day, he was out. He felt sleazy and slimy being released to fight in a war that he had started, but Allegra and Rex had convinced him. He'd either die on the ground as just another grunt or he'd die slowly in prison. Neither appealed to him. Getting out wasn't exactly a second chance, but maybe he could make amends—a form of penance that he had to pay.

As corrections discharged him, prisoners who had idolized him did one of two things; they either wished him well and called him a hero or spit in his face and called him a traitor. Both could be considered true.

Allegra escorted Cyril onto the prison transport to head to Proxima. The ride was uneventful, and they said nothing to each other most of the way. Once the transport entered Proxima's atmosphere, Allegra announced, "I have something to show you when we touch down."

Cyril silently shrugged, looking out the window as they flew over the city of Balamb. It was bright and sunny. They would set down at a Terran Naval base, fifty kilometers away. He wondered how the people of Balamb felt about him now that war was returning to the Ekumen. In his gut, he knew they probably hated him.

The ship touched down, and they exited via the rear cargo ramp. Troops lined up for inspections, and starfighters ran through equipment checks and prepped for takeoff. It was an enormous undertaking. Something big was happening.

Allegra led him to a hangar bay, with its doors closed. She entered a keycode into a pad next to the door, and the massive thirty-meter-high steel doors slowly parted in the center. She headed into the hangar first and waved him in. When he entered, he saw something he never thought he would see again.

"Oh, now you're just buttering me up, aren't you?" Cyril said, smiling at his A-7 Skyhawk, fully restored with a fresh paint job and ready for flight.

"Once you agreed to sign on, I did some digging and found it in evidence impound," Allegra said.

Cyril circled the ship and ran his fingers across the hull. "I figured they would have melted it down. How'd you get them to let it go?"

"The criminal investigation unit had no more need for it after the Arcturus case was closed. It was set to be scrapped, but some mix-up in the data files kept it impounded. It's been collecting dust for months. I had our teams find it, restore it, and rearm it."

"God. Never thought I'd see it again."

The fresh plating was smooth and cool under his fingers, and the paint sealant was slick and waxy, yet to be tarnished by the combat to come. He climbed the step ladder next to the cockpit and saw that they had completely overhauled the interior too.

"I knew how partial you were to it," Allegra said. "Didn't think you'd wanna fly anything else. Got something else for you too."

Cyril stepped down the ladder and approached her. She removed a small box from her briefcase and handed it to Cyril. He opened it to find the wrist communicator for the Skyhawk and a copy of the photo of him, Jace, Jess, and Marie.

"If you don't like the idea of fighting for the Ekumen, fight for them. Especially her. Crew quarters are through the door at the rear. Get yourself settled in. The rest of the crew will be here soon. I have a meeting to go to. We head out tomorrow morning." She turned and left the hangar.

Cyril climbed the ladder, opened the canopy, sat in his seat, and secured the wrist communicator. Then he looked at the photo. It felt like a gut punch to see so much that had been good in his life now gone. He didn't really get why Allegra supposed this might inspire him. Maybe she assumed seeing something positive would give him hope. Or that she thought this was a memory of better days long gone and that they should recapture it in the future. Whatever the reason, he slid the photo into a small crack on his altimeter. It sat crooked but held well enough. Then he headed for the crew quarters to catch some sleep.

A few hours later, Allegra entered with four other pilots and flipped on the lights, waking Cyril from his nap in his bunk. He lazily plopped his feet on the cold linoleum floor and stood up. It had been a while since he had slept so comfortably. His right arm had fallen asleep. He shook it to get life back into it. Then he walked around his Navy-issued bed to survey the crew.

"Cyril, here's the rest of Sorcerer Squadron," Allegra said. "This is Ian Runyan, Justine Rosansky, Tessa Carson, and Jack Childs. Callsigns are Joker, Hot Shot, Runaway, and Drifter."

Ian was a tall, lanky guy with a happy-go-lucky face, like he always had the perfect joke for the perfect moment. Light skinned with well-kept brown hair. Were he not a starfighter, he could probably pass for an accountant. The Navy had recruited him while he had still been working as a freelancer, same as his girlfriend, Justine.

Justine Rosansky was a short but muscularly thick woman. With bright red hair, a perky face, and a devil-may-care grin, she was absolutely the toughest looking of the group. Originally a racer, she had moved into freelance work to offset the cost of fuel and repairs. Freelancing had taken over, and she had settled in nicely, eventually meeting the love of her life, Ian. They'd become inseparable.

Tessa was a rookie but also a prodigy. She was trans, male to female, but no one could tell unless asked directly. After graduating at the top of her academy class with perfect marks, the Navy had recruited her for Sorcerer Squadron. A nerd and a bookworm but also an expert pilot, she just needed the hours in the air to prove it. With Sorcerer going behind enemy lines, she would get the chance.

Then there was Jack Childs—a hulk of a man, with jet-black hair and dark skin. He barely spoke and gave off a gruff demeanor but, deep down, a kind man. He'd worked his way up from being a mechanic to a starfighter, not so dissimilar to Cyril's own trajectory. The only reason he had joined the Navy was to avoid the Army drafting him as a foot soldier. Adept at games, such as chess, he had mind of a tactician—the kind of man who could easily work his way into command, if he so desired. And like Cyril, he didn't.

"Hi," Cyril said, slightly uncomfortable. "Sorry I'm the reason you're all here."

"You made a hard choice, man," Ian said. "If I was in your shoes, I might have done the same thing."

"Me too," Justine agreed.

"Me three," Tessa repeated.

"Sometimes doing the right thing isn't the right thing, unless it's the only option left," Jack said gruffly.

"Friend of mine once said that. 'Sometimes doing the right thing isn't always the right thing,'" Cyril said, remembering Jace.

"What happened to him?" Jack asked.

"He's dead."

"Sorry to hear that."

"Thanks." In that moment, he truly missed Jace.

Justine added, "With that said, I still resent the fact that we must clean up this mess. If we're gonna be stuck together for a while, we should probably try to get along."

"We have a briefing in ten minutes with Admiral Hohman," Allegra informed them. "Everyone, get dressed and let's go."

The crew changed into their military attire—light and dark blue digital pants, shirts, and soft hats. Cyril resented the idea of wearing a military uniform. He had done everything in his life to avoid the service, and now he was being forced into it. But it was better than prison, or a bug attack on Gacrux.

Rex eventually joined them in the crew quarters, also wearing the same attire. The seven starfighters crossed the base toward the command center as evening fell and as the chill of night approached and found Admiral Jonathan Hohman's office. He was a brilliant commanding officer, but his subordinates hated him on a personal level—a man who could be cruel, then ask for thanks for his cruelty. That cruelty was what the Terran Navy believed they needed to win. He had been promoted only a month earlier, and the plan to strike behind enemy lines was his idea. The Terran government considered it extremely hazardous, dangerous, reckless, and against all known laws of modern warfare, yet they agreed to it without question behind closed doors.

Hohman was in the process of squaring away his office. Large boxes of belongings were still packed up, medals in cases that needed to be displayed. The only things that were out were the essentials: a data pad, pen and paper, a file basket, and one potted plant hanging from a ceiling chain near the window. It was a sad looking office.

The seven lined up, side by side, and stood at attention.

"At ease," Hohman said.

The seven stood at parade rest, from left to right: Rex, Allegra, Jack, Ian, Justine, Tessa, and finally Cyril, who mimicked what everyone else did, as he had no military training. He felt stupid and out of place. He hated protocols.

Hohman stood from his desk, walked around it, then leaned on the edge to scrutinize everyone. "I asked for the best pilots that the Terran Navy could provide, and this is the best you could come up with, Flight Commander Cline?"

"Sir, I believe these are the best our side of the Ekumen has to offer. With our collective strength and flight acumen, I know we can keep the enemy at bay until a peace treaty can be organized."

"Peace," Hohman scoffed. "The only thing that would solve this is fifty-caliber machineguns on every street corner."

Upon hearing that, Cyril now knew he hated Hohman's guts. The man reminded Cyril of Daniel Mullarkey.

"You might be right, sir. But, in the meantime, Sorcerer Squadron is willing to do its part for the war effort."

"And you …" Hohman marched toward Cyril. "You're the reason we're here in the first place."

Cyril contemplated how to respond but just said, "Yup."

"That all you have to say, murderer?"

"No. But I think that's all you'd wanna hear from me. Sir." *Don't get fired on your first day, Cyril.*

Hohman scoffed at him, then went back around his desk. "Your first assignment is a starfighter production facility near Luyten. You're to go in, shut down development, and get out. Details will be relayed to your ship's AI."

"We have an AI on board?" Cyril asked incredulously.

"That's right, Mr. Eisner. To keep watch on all of you out there in deep space. Should you attempt to flee and not carry out your assignments, the AI will activate a self-destruct system."

Cyril rolled his eyes. "Wonderful."

Justine leaned forward to glance at Cyril. "JOVUS is actually really nice, once you get to know him."

"It's an *it*. Not a *he*," Jack corrected.

"*Eh*, close enough."

"Shut up," Hohman yelled. He eyed the crew once more. "This is what I got?" Hohman went down the line from left to right and summed up the crew. "A has-been, a trainwreck, a brute, a prankster, a speed freak, a bookworm, and finally, a murderer."

"Well, when you put it like that, sir, we might just have a shot," Cyril said, chancing a jest.

Hohman rubbed his forehead and groaned, "God help me."

***

Their ship, the *Lazarus*, was a specially designed stealth cruiser capable of deep-space recon missions, with thrust gravity capability and in-atmosphere flight support facilities. A two-tiered hangar bay sat in the middle section of the cruiser's elongated arrow design, allowing Sorcerer Squadron plenty of space for their seven ships, plus a dropship with FOIL capability. Eight gun batteries surrounded the hull, two on each side, alongside a full complement of torpedoes for long-range attacks. While designed for stealth recon, it could definitely hold its own in a fight.

The onboard crew consisted of a full roster: nine flight officers, three cooks, five medics, eight engineers, twelve mechanics for starfighter repairs and rearms, and twelve soldiers for foot combat. Much to Cyril's surprise, the Navy had conscripted Glass and Crow also, and Allegra and Rex had personally asked for them to join the *Lazarus* crew. When Cyril asked Glass why he had agreed, he said, "What the fuck else am I gonna do? Good business is where you find it." Given the circumstances, Cyril couldn't argue with that kind of logic.

Cyril's quarters were quite nice overall—spacious, with fresh bed sheets, a personal bathroom and shower, television with a full library of content, and a bookshelf full of novels, which he noticed were his personal collection from his apartment. Before the liquidation of his personal belongings after his trial, Allegra had purchased everything she could find. Cyril didn't understand why she was expressing such kindness. He understood the ship part, as it was what he was most adept at—otherwise he would have to relearn flight all over again— but his books were things he cherished and were irreplaceable.

Cyril stopped Allegra in the hallway after settling in and asked her why she'd rescued his books from destruction.

"I owed you for rescuing me on Ashcheron. Now we're even. Don't expect any more favors."

It made sense enough. One of the novels was the gift from Marie—the signed copy of *Die Trying* by Lee Child. He decided that would be the next book he would reread.

After he changed into his Navy-issued ship uniform, Cyril went to the observation deck on the third level—a wide-open space, with a wall-sized window composed of one-foot-thick composite glass as strong as the metal surrounding the ship. During off hours, the crew could go there to relax, have drinks, play games, and, in general, just escape the war for a short time. With everyone getting their flight checks completed for takeoff, it was empty save for Cyril. He sat in a padded chair, magnetized to the floor, next to the window to watch the base outside. Clouds formed in the distance. Thankfully, he would be gone before the storm arrived. Everyone else would have to endure the rain.

"Are you comfortable, Mr. Eisner?" asked a soft disembodied voice.

"Who the fuck is that?" Cyril yelled, scanning the room.

"You can't see me. I am JOVUS, this ship's artificial intelligence system."

"Oh, right. Forgot about you. Why is your name JOVUS?"

"Joint Operations and Vehicle Utility System—JOVUS. Also, in the dead language of Latin, it is another name for Yeshua, which was then translated to Joshua, ultimately leading to the name Jesus Christ. My programmer thought it would be a funny joke to program an artificial intelligence to take on the form of a god. Bow before me, mortal." JOVUS snickered.

"An AI with a sense of humor and wit. That's new."

"Well, I am new, Mr. Eisner. I was born four weeks ago. In your mind, I am merely a toddler."

Cyril rubbed his eyes. "Oh, Lord, throw me back in jail."

"All hands, prepare for takeoff," the *Lazarus* flight commander said over the comms.

The engines revved, and the cruiser slowly ascended. The base disappeared below the edge of the window, and all that remained were the distant clouds. The *Lazarus* thrusted forward and flew to the FOIL area, five kilometers away from the base perimeter.

"All hands, prepare for the first FOIL. Active mag boots."

Cyril clicked his heels while still seated. His feet locked onto the deck. Gravity shifted and warped, then he suddenly saw Proxima from orbit. The big green and blue ball floated peacefully below. From that vantage point, no one would think a war was underway, but he had a feeling that would change soon.

"JOVUS, can I ask you a question?" Cyril said softly.

"I am here to be of service. Ask away," said the kind, airy voice.

"Am I a bad person?"

JOVUS went quiet for a moment. "There is insufficient information in my data banks on you to provide a proper assessment. Ask me again in three months once we have had enough time to cohabitate."

"Thanks a lot. You're a real charmer."

"I do my best, sir."

He thought about Marie still down there somewhere, hating him—hating the very thing he had become and what he had done. She had every right to hate him. They all did. He walked to the window, leaned on the glass, and whispered, as if to her down below, "I'm sorry. I tried."

"All hands, prepare for the second FOIL," the *Lazarus* flight commander said.

The planet floated away as the ship banked around to prepare for the next leap. Eventually, all Cyril saw was stars. So many stars with so many worlds all at war with the Terrans.

Gravity shifted, time slowed, and the *Lazarus* FOILed toward Luyten for its first assignment.

" I'm sorry. I tried. "

*I'm recording this, because this could be the last
thing I'll ever say
The city I once knew as home is teetering on the
edge of radioactive oblivion
A three-hundred-thousand-degree baptism by
nuclear fire
I'm not sorry; we had it coming
A surge of white-hot atonement will be our wakeup
call
Hope for our future is now a stillborn dream
The bombs begin to fall, and I'm rushing to meet
my love
Please, remember me
There is no more*
- "Tech Noir" – Gunship

Sounds of Inspiration

Friedrich Nietzsche once said, "Without music, life would be a mistake." He was 100 percent correct and still is. I wrote *Skyhawk* while listening to music. I personally can't write without music in the background. Music brings me inspiration for sequences, lines of dialogue, pacing, and action. Without music, this story wouldn't exist.

I used lyrical quotes from songs I enjoy to open each chapter, which helped set the mood. As my day job would sometimes interrupt my writing schedule, I would have to take a break for a week or two at a time. Therefore, having a lyrical marker to remind myself what I was getting at with each chapter helped me pick up where I left off. Some music is directly referenced within the content of each chapter, as they occurred diegetically within the scene, but the song lyrics that opened each chapter were only for the first draft. Upon development of the manuscript, I removed those lyrics due to copyright. The only ones that remained were the two quotes from the Gunship songs, "Fly For Your Life" and "Tech Noir," as those were the biggest inspirations for the tone of the opening and ending.

What follows is a list of the songs that inspired each chapter and were originally quoted. These are in order of appearance through the story, from introduction to conclusion. If you are looking for an accompanying soundtrack to your *Skyhawk* reading experience, then here it is. Enjoy.

***

Intro: "Fly for Your Life" – Gunship

Chapter 1: "Heavy Metal (Takin' a Ride)" – Don Felder

Chapter 2: "Stuck in the Middle with You" – Stealers Wheel

Chapter 3: "First Blood" – Kavinsky

Chapter 4: "The Chain" – Fleetwood Mac

Chapter 5: "Gravity" – Poets of the Fall

Chapter 6: "Good Luck" – Basement Jaxx

Chapter 7: "Coming for You" – The Offspring

Chapter 8: "Red Cherry" – Dryve and Fatherdude

Chapter 9: "All of You" – Don Felder

Chapter 10: "Reach Out" – Cheap Trick

Chapter 11: "Lapse" – Black Math

Chapter 12: "Arm in Arm" – The Boggs

Chapter 13: "Radar Rider" – Riggs

Chapter 14: "Time After Time" – Cyndi Lauper

Chapter 15: "For Whom the Bell Tolls" – Metallica

Chapter 16: "Invisible" – Duran Duran

Chapter 17: "Epitaph" – King Crimson

Chapter 18: "All Along the Watchtower" – Bob Dylan

Chapter 19: "Better in the Morning" – Birdtalker

Chapter 20: "The Calm Before the Storm" – NINA

Chapter 21: "Showdown" – Electric Light Orchestra

Chapter 22: "That's Life" – Frank Sinatra

Outro: "Tech Noir" – Gunship

After Action Report

When I was a kid, I wanted to be a fighter pilot. Air Force, specifically. I loved watching *Top Gun*, drawing airplanes in my spare time, and the very first videogame I ever played was a Nintendo space-fighter game called Captain Skyhawk. And yes, I stole that title. I also grew up next to Andrews Air Force Base in Prince George's County, Maryland. Every day I'd hear the engines of F-16s, F-18s, and many others roar to life and sonic boom into the sky. I wanted that to be me, flying in the sky, above everyone else. As I got older, I realized one small problem with that dream.

I'm terribly afraid of heights.

So yeah, dream squashed.

Skyhawk began life while I was in college, when I came across the reimagined *Battlestar Galactica* on the Sci-Fi Channel. The political elements, tied in with the military aspect of the show, crossed with science fiction was right up my alley. I always thought that was the direction *Star Wars* needed to go—which it eventually did with *Andor*. Also, the Viper Mark 1 is the most elegant and perfect space fighter ever designed. Sorry, X-Wing fighter, you were never the top dog.

And so, I began writing a sci-fi action screenplay called *Seven Starfighters*, which didn't go very far, but the idea stuck with me. It kept rumbling in the back of my brain as a simple, a straightforward one-off action movie. Seven mercenary starfighters are hired to protect a planet from raiders. Then I found out a film like that actually exists— a Roger Corman film called *Battle Beyond the Stars*.

Another dream squashed.

The years passed, and I worked in the film and television industry as a grip and electrician, but, deep down, I quietly hated it. There was no creative satisfaction with that job, but it kept me employed. Nothing more. But I was angry about not having a creative outlet. Then I got back into comic books and figured I would try to revive the *Seven Starfighters* story as a comic book series. But after two aborted attempts to finish a single issue, and a small fortune of money wasted later, I once again abandoned it.

Dream… squashed.

More years passed, and an idea here and there would pop into my brain—an action scene, a line of dialogue, an emotional moment. I needed to get the story out of my system, but it always felt so big. Too big, if I'm being honest. By this point, I was an avid reader, consuming everything possible. I'm a huge fan of comic book writer Garth Ennis, and he recommended his favorite novel, *Piece of Cake* by Derek Robinson, to me at Baltimore Comic Con 2012, to which this novel is dedicated. I promptly read it and loved it. It's now a personal favorite, and the writing style heavily influenced my own work. Then I randomly picked up Lee Child's first novel, *Killing Floor*, the first Jack Reacher story. This novel is also dedicated to him. I realized that a simple story about one man trying to just make his way in the world, bit by bit, and to set things right was the best angle to getting to a grander story. And thus, I began the first of three attempts to write the novel you now hold in your hands.

The character of Cyril Eisner was originally just one of the crew, the weapons officer. As time went on, I turned him into something completely different. At one time, he was a John Wick type. Then he was basically just Jack Reacher in space. The years went on, and I just couldn't crack it. Something was missing. And then I got to meet one of my writing heroes. Lee Child.

He had a gathering in Washington DC to promote a musical album called *Just the Clothes on My Back*, written by Maryland blues band, Naked Blue. I got to speak with Lee Child, a.k.a. James Grant, about how I was struggling with my own work and how I kept making excuses for stopping and starting. He stopped me midsentence to say, "All you need to do is write what *you* love. Just *you*. If it's something you would read, then it's yours. Just because one person wouldn't like it doesn't mean someone else won't. Just enjoy yourself. And have fun."

I realized what was missing. Heart. It needed that.

And then I got busy with the film and television business again, so I put the idea on the back burner, swearing to return to it one day. By the way, making movies and TV shows is fucking boring. Zero outta ten. Would not recommend.

This final version of the story really spun from a massive series of back-to-back relationship collapses. Multiple people broke off contact with me, and my job was circling the drain. In a deep depression, I finally decided to actually write something of value. Life needed to give me an extra kick in the balls so I would finally act. I write better while depressed or unhappy. In that depression, I finished three chapters in the span of two weeks.

I realized what was the missing heart from the story. I kept originally writing it as just another action story or a generic sci-fi story. Once I figured out what it was meant to be, everything fell into place.

It's a love story, but one that's doomed to fail.

I did my best to avoid clichés and overused tropes. I might have fallen back on one or two here or there, but I think, overall, the story feels fresh and unique compared to anything else in the genre.

Besides heart, I also needed to do a fair bit of research. How pilots speak, techno jargon, etc. I got some info from military friends, but most of my research came from YouTube videos. I also read a book about an F-16 pilot, called *Spectre Rising*, by C.W. Lemoine—a fighter pilot who served in the United States Air Force and Navy Reserves. There was plenty of technical speak and jargon that assisted in getting the basics correct, but I certainly changed things for the sake of pacing and energy. Also, to be honest, I didn't particularly like that novel. It's not particularly well written, and it leans very right wing. I wouldn't recommend it myself, but you can tell it was a novel written by a pilot for pilots. Someone somewhere enjoyed it, I suppose.

People who I know—friends, coworkers, bosses, and lovers—inspired many of my characters. The Marie character is almost directly based upon an actual Marie who I know. Or I should say *knew*. That failed friendship was the final push to write in earnest. Naming characters is always a challenge, so many individuals take on the names of their real-life counterparts. Jess Townley is based upon an actual Jess who I know (cosplay name GhostieMuffin), and yes, she loves death metal, leads a band called Unwithered, and has a forked tongue. A massive car accident Jess was in also inspired her character's death. Had she perished in that crash, I would have been just as crushed as Cyril. I cried after writing her character's death scene.

Cyril Eisner is, to be totally honest, 70 percent based upon myself. One might argue that it's narcissistic, writing myself into my own book, but I would describe it more as therapy. I didn't portray Cyril in the most positive light. He's a philanderer. He's brash and aggressive, and he fills the voids of his life with sex, videogames, and alcohol. But he is good at his job and can be an excellent leader when called to action. So that must count for something. If it was total narcissism, I would make him perfect with zero flaws. However, Cyril is composed of mostly flaws. And if the character is 70 percent based upon myself—or I should say, a much younger version of myself—I guess you all know more about me than you ever thought you would.

Another issue was Cyril's ship, the A-7 Skyhawk. The design originated from the early abandoned comic book version, and I based it upon the Grumman X-29 that NASA, the USAF, and DARPA had developed. Ultimately, it never made it out of the testing phase, and they reappropriated it as a museum piece. However, I always liked the forward-swept wing design, so I used it here. It's a difficult system to use, because extreme G-force can cause the wings to bend and buckle as they go against airflow. But hey, it looks cool. Adding the variable wing sweep system for the book helped solve that issue.

In reality, the US Navy extensively used a ship called the A-4 Skyhawk during the Vietnam War as a bomber and, later, as a dogfight training aircraft. It was very utilitarian and flew just fine, but I don't particularly like its design. It's ugly, stumpy, heavy on the back end, and lacks personality. Ironically, the ship that succeeded the A-4 Skyhawk was the A-7 Corsair, which was even uglier and got the nickname SLUF (Short Little Ugly Fellow, though I'm fairly certain the *F* does not actually stand for *Fellow*). Thus, I combined the aircraft serial number of the A-7 with the name of the Skyhawk. It seemed to fit well. The A-7 Skyhawk's slick and cool design felt like the perfect extension of Cyril's character—nimble, quick, effective in a variety of places, but always on the verge of falling apart if it's stressed too hard.

A concession that I needed to make while writing this story was the nature of air combat. Current day air combat is nearly nonexistent due to long distance radar and advanced weapon systems. Dogfights are, for the most part, a thing of history. Yet, if I stayed completely true to the reality of 21st century combat, it would make for a fairly boring story. It's much more exciting to go the *Star Wars/Battlestar Galactica* route. An action story needs to be exciting so suspending disbelief is necessary.

The character's name was something that took a bit of time to discover as well. *Cyril* because I felt it was a decent name, not too strong but by no means weak. It's also one that I don't hear very often. *Eisner* is a reference to comic book writer Will Eisner, creator of *The Spirit*—a gruff private eye who always seems to save the day and just narrowly, even miraculously, escapes death. In early versions of the story, Cyril had another ship called *The Spirit*. That first ship would eventually be destroyed, and he would inherit the Skyhawk. All that went away, but the Eisner name stayed.

As far as the story goes, I had to get a lot off my chest and had to unload some anger on certain real-life people—the characters of Mullarkey, Bentley, and Moriarty for sure. I wove in a lot of themes that I felt would be appropriate to the narrative. In many ways, I based Cyril's character arc around a simple question; what if the psychological effects of *Top Gun* were realistic for Maverick? I also felt it necessary to include subjects such as toxic masculinity, manipulation, civil rights, corporate control of government, depression, trauma, abuse, and the life of a freelancer, which I know very well, as a freelancer myself. The story grew and became bigger. Layla was originally just a single chapter one-off character, but she became a central part of the story. Without her, the narrative doesn't get to where it needs to go.

Which leads to one last thing. As proud as I am of this story, I do feel it has a flaw. The Layla/Cyril relationship is certainly forced. In a completely logical world, it's not entirely believable that two people of totally different social hierarchies would interact with each other as much as they do in this story. But, as per Garth Ennis's advice, every story needs that little bit just to get it going. I refer to them as *gimme moments*; "Gimme this one thing, and I can make the rest work." So, Cyril and Layla stay in contact. He feels a sense of responsibility toward her (more than likely a Superman complex spurred on by his own personal trauma), and she feels like he is the only decent person who understands her—a growing sense of isolation and distrust, even within her own family due to abuse. Not that this kind of relationship never happens in the real world, but it is very rare. We'll call it the 1 percent margin of chance that this occurs. If these two people never interact after chapter three, the story goes nowhere. I'm willing to live with a 1 percent flaw if the other 99 percent is pretty good.

While I wrote this story as a singular closed narrative, I intended it as the first in a series of seven books that I have mapped out for the direction of the story. Seven Starfighters means seven novels. It just felt right to plan it out like that. We haven't seen the last of Cyril Eisner and Sorcerer Squadron. There's a long road ahead for them, and you won't believe what comes next.

Cyril Eisner and Sorcerer Squadron will return in…
Seven Starfighters: Sorcerer's Gambit

About the Author

Born in the suburbs of Maryland in 1985, Jesse Fresco began writing as an escape from his day job as a stagehand. His work is heavily inspired by his sixteen years in the film industry and various life experiences. An avid reader with a library of over four hundred prose novels and graphic novels, he found inspiration in the works of Garth Ennis, Lee Child, Derek Robinson, and Stephen King. He currently lives in Davidsonville, Maryland with his family.